The Unforgiven

The Unforgiven

A. Katie Rose

SF
Rose

For Bruce, deartháir mór
Because we, all of us, need to be forgiven
tá mé chomh mór sin i ngrá leat.

Acknowledgments

A writer, no matter how talented, he or she is, can create a great book without the aid of outside influences. From cover artists to editors to proofreaders to those folks who read and can assist an author in the smallest, and most important, of ways.

I must offer a very special thanks to Cheyenne Khoury for her insightful and incredibly helpful suggestions when I felt at a loss for words as well as inspiration. One day, Cheyenne, you'll never fear to have someone read your work.

Of course, an editor knows best. Thank you, Brenda Blanchard, for your amazing editorial advice. I hope you'll be there for all my future projects. And you, too, Shawnee Bilbrey, for reviewing my novel and aiding in its construction. I can thank you a thousand times and it will never be enough. Both of you are my good friends as well as my editors. I hope you both will be there, for me, in these capacities, always. God bless you, my dear friends.

Without a great cover, a book is lost. In an incredible stroke of luck, I commissioned Nadine Ewing, aka Lady Akyashaa, to produce the cover art for *The Unforgiven*. Her amazing talent is a rare opportunity for me, and I am both grateful and proud she agreed to craft it.

And I must add a special thanks to all my friends and associates who offer me nothing except encouragement in all my writing efforts. You make all of this work so worthwhile.

Contents

The Unforgiven

From the north the red will rise,
Under her wings grace shall fall.
Seek ye the child of innocence,
The holy defender, the chosen of the light,
Of purity born, of blood she seeks.
By north and by south,
Brothers not of blood, but of bond, bear the flame,
Under the dark and the light, the shadow will rise.
Three cycles shall pass
From the dark side of the moon.
By fire and steel, magic falters,
Kissed by fate, by fate answered
When the moon and the sun
Are joined as one,
From tears of strife, from the bitter ashes,
From sorrow and from rage
That what was once parted
Shall again be one.

CHAPTER 1

Irrefutable Charges

Cursing, the two brainless hulks dragged me from the tavern.

"Don't ever come back!" the innkeeper, Tamil, shouted from its dark, inner depths.

His high-pitched, annoying, nasal voice failed to succumb to the noises of the early morning traffic and the thump of my own boots dragging across the cobbles. Not even the heavy, labored breathing of the hulks drowned out his obnoxious tirade, even when the doors closed behind us.

You think I'll ever want to? I half-thought. My brainwaves malfunctioned, shorted out, and created a vacuous state of euphoria combined with an impressive hangover. I saw little save blinding early morning sunlight. The strong ale and mead I drank the night before churned in my belly, and my head ached like a log recently split by an axe. The nasty sickness in my gut quite effectively incapacitated my instinctive urge to fight back.

With the ease they might toss a bag of garbage, Tamil's bouncers flung me headlong from the tavern's front porch and into the street. I rolled three times, skinning my arms, chest and nose before fetching up against the rear wheel of a passing wagon.

The wheel's spokes smacked the back of my head in quick succession at the same time the driver's curse spilled into my ears. He spat, and his nasty tobacco, along with his spittle, struck my shoulder. "Get oudda way, bleeding wanker."

The wagon passed on. Without its questionable support, I fell flat into something cold and wet. Opening my eyes didn't help much. I witnessed little save whirling stars and flashing lights. The pain from my injuries hadn't yet bypassed the liquor. As I'd passed out cold in the tavern's corner amid the half-gnawed bones, nasty straw and the tavern hound's shit sometime around midnight, I knew the alcohol's grip on me would pass shortly.

Not much past dawn, I guessed, half-rising, peering about. I squinted into the piercing rays, and shut my eyes against the awful glare. The stars still spun, and my head with them, but the flashing colors had wandered away. Things improved, such as they were. I sat up carefully, stiffly, running my tongue over my teeth. All accounted for and wearing their usual fuzzy sweaters. *Did I sleep with my jaws open?* My mouth tasted as though Tamil's fat tabby used it for a litter box. I sighed, and thought, *that's scarcely new.*

I ran my hands down my shirt, wiping them dry of the piss wetting them. I wiped my fingers and streaked the cold, aromatic urine of some delightful creature down my shirt, then hesitated.

I glanced down. My shirt wasn't there. I gazed down at my own bare and dirty chest, pronounced ribcage, and the new streaks of malodorous piss and filth my fingers traced downward.

Dammit. Who stole my shirt?

I cast about, half-thinking to find it there in the horse or cow or camel piss I sat in, but no go. *No shirt. Who in the name of hell would steal my only shirt? I know I wore it when I passed out, er, fell asleep. Maybe Tamil's bum stole it. He forever eyed me with envy and a sort of covetous greed. But–my shirt? Please!*

I tossed my stringy black hair from my eyes with my dripping and reeking right hand. I peered about, bleary-eyed, before glancing downward. At least I wore my britches. Safe, at least, from too many outraged stares and scornful sniffs. Encompassed in frayed

[2]

brown homespun stained with too much drink and not enough food, at least some parts of me remained decently covered. I still owned my boots, though they prayed for a resoling. Had I tried, I could count my every rib.

Dirty, my pale skin exactly matched the color of a fish's belly. My chest appeared almost piebald, white with patches of black grime. I sighed, my head spinning like a wicked imp. I seriously needed a bath and a tan, in that order. Wishing heartily for the bath, I leaned on my right hand, my left rising to assist my equilibrium onto a new path of self-discovery.

As I floundered, trying to rise with little balance and zero ability, I fell backward on my ass on the cobbles. My already stained breeches soaked up some critter's pit stop with rapid enjoyment. My nose wrinkled, offended, as the early morning sun suddenly vanished. I grimaced. *Oh, great.* Whoever stole my shirt now stole the sun. My morning started out just dandy: tossed from my comfortable bed with no shirt and now no sunshine–gods help us all.

I squinted, trying to see past the crap in my eyes. I swiped half-heartedly at my blood seeping into the right one with my balancing left hand. The urine's salt stung something chronic, but my gesture helped. In a manner of speaking, that was. My sight stilled blurred, but if I looked downward, I saw grey cobbles, red stains and my boots. *Feet, must stand on. Get them flat, get them under you and stand, you alcoholic nimrod. Hop it.*

Attempting to rise, I turned first my shoulder, then my neck, and froze. A very peculiar object stood on the brown cobbles, slightly in front and to my right. Large, dark, black, and hauntingly familiar. *Wait, give me a second, I know what that is.*

A black hoof.

Glossy, immaculate, attached to a black pastern. Hooves travelled in pairs. Where one found one, one might find two. I slewed around, my damp black hair falling across my eyes. Aha! Just where I expected it, another black hoof stood on the cobbles to my left.

Craning my neck, I lifted my face, my reeking hair obligingly sliding from my questionable vision. I blinked rapidly, swiped my hand across my eyes again. This time, I cleared some haze and blood from my eyes. Yet, the great, abominable shape remained indistinct. Backlit by the sun, it peered down at me, surrounded by a bright halo of light. Long hair framed a dark face with hooded, shadowed eyes. Like a great shaggy demon from the depths of hell, it stared at me as though plotting how best to steal my soul. A blast from the past spoke up, its voice deep and humorous –

"Hello, Van."

I wilted, flopping like a wet sack onto my back as though I no longer had a backbone. My useless hands fell limp to my hips and I shut my eyes. My spine's qualifications never entered the equation, but that was beside the point. I thought not to hear that deep voice ever again. I ran from it, hid from it; I survived in the shadows and rejoiced in its absence.

However, despite my best efforts, that melodic yet quirky lilt haunted my restless sleep over the last two years. No night but passed with that same voice overriding the alcohol in my blood. It never asked anything save the same question, over and over . . . .

"Are you ready?"

Never, I tried to answer.

Yet, my blood leaped forward and saluted. *Yes. Yes, I am.*

Are you effing kidding me? How in the name of all the gods did he find me here, in the kingdom's arsehole? I know I covered my tracks, for who in the name of hell would search for me in the city's nastiest pisspot? *Surely all my dues have been paid?* I wanted to scream.

I shut my eyes, but he shifted his feet slightly and permitted the sun's entire light to blaze in all its glory into my face. I winced at its piercing agony, the spears lancing my eyes and my head, my belly roiling in protest. I scrubbed my hands over my face, feeling the growth of at least three days on my jaws.

"Still trying to drown your sorrows, I see."

I lowered my hands enough to squint up. "Can't," I replied around my thick tongue. "Little bleeders know how to swim."

"Imagine that."

[4]

Though I tried not to slur my words, I knew they sounded as though I newly woke from a heavy binge. "What're you doing here? Please don't say you're just in the neighborhood. I know better."

"Get him up."

Hooves clopped on brick cobbles behind me, striking sparks in my sensitive hearing. Strong hands lifted me, raising my once inert body, standing me, within reason, on my feet. Had their hands not kept me upright, I'd no doubt collapse back into the dirt and piss. Which was worse? Lying in the gutter or facing one's best and oldest friend?

I shook off their hands and, had I a shirt, might've straightened it. As it was, I squared my shoulders and flung my hair from my face. Dignity scattered to the four winds, I could at least appear as though I faced him on even ground. Sticking my thumbs in my belt, I drew a deep, steadying breath and locked eyes with him.

"How'd you find me?"

Malik'an'lakna'ra, Lord Captain Commander of the King's Weksan'Atan Forces, folded his arms across his massive chest. A tiny smile rose to his deep eyes and no further. "I've kept tabs on you."

Sobriety took a firm hold on my runaway wits at last. *1 ll need every damn one of them right now,* I thought, while summoning the shards of my dignity. Though I stank of shit, piss and last night's sorrow, I straightened my spine. Dirty, bleeding, I summoned all my willpower to remain upright and sober. *I am of the Einion nalad Clan. My blood is as good, as pure, as any here. I wear the black scars on my cheeks, the marks of the Clan. I am worthy.*

At least, once, not so long ago, I was.

I glanced up into my once-upon-a-time friend's face and set my hands on my hips. "I ask again: what do you want?"

Malik's lip curled. "His Majesty commands you."

"I don't work for him anymore."

"You're an officer in his Atan."

"Oh, right. His Majesty's Secret Police. But if it's a secret, why does everyone know about it?"

"Blabbermouths."

"I never said a word."

"Never said you did." Malik tried for a smile but failed. His stern façade wasn't conducive for humor or smiling. Too military, too disciplined, for the common proclivities of life. "You're an Atan. You'd know better."

"I'm retired, remember?"

"Once an Atan, always an Atan."

"Don't quote scripture to me, bro," I snapped.

His heavy brow lifted. "Bro, is it? So you remember your old ties, after all."

From his polished black hooves to the top of his head, Malik stood taller than an average man by several hands. A Centaur of the highest order, Malik descended from the Old Blood, the *Malana akana*. From his hips up, Malik appeared fully human. Broad chest, flat belly, his biceps bulged under their arm bands of beaten silver. The black headband across his brow not only held back his wealth of shoulder-length black hair, but the multi-rayed star badge on the silk proclaimed his high rank in His Majesty's service. Battle harness crisscrossed his huge chest, as his sword hung in its leather sheath across his back and dangled over his equine withers. Silver steel cuffs protected his wrists from his bowstring; his quiver of bristling arrows hung from his belt over his massive horse shoulders. The hilt of a slim dagger hung in its sheath in his harness, ready to hand. As black as his hooves, his stallion's jet coat gleamed under the new sun's rays; his thick black tail swept across his hocks, voicing the annoyance his expression carefully hid.

A collar of beaten gold around his bull-neck proclaimed him royal. As a Malana'akana, Malik claimed kinship with the gods themselves. Still, he bent his great knee, bowed his royal head, to the human King. As did most everyone else in Bryn'Cairdha.

Except me.

I sighed in my turn. "Tell your boys to back off."

Malik tossed his head. Instantly, the Centaurs under Malik's command retreated, abandoned me, and stalked into line with their brothers. There, behind Malik in classic military formation, they stood at parade rest. Arms behind their backs, eyes blank and facing forward, their front hooves stood shoulder width apart. Swords hung at precise angles, leather harness polished to a sheen, long hair under their brow-bands curled onto their bared human shoulders. Military discipline at its finest. I tried to forget how I once stood as they did.

Beyond them, Malik's troop of cavalry disrupted the new morning's commerce by standing silent in the street, thereby forcing wagons, carriages, foot and horse traffic, mule-skinners, traders, and the local whores and vagabonds to move around their silent horses. The King's banner floated on the early summer breeze, tickling its silk and set it to dancing like a Faery-child. Heads swiveled in my direction. Horse, mule and ox traffic slowed as the onlookers gaped. The King's own royal Atani forces arrested a common drunk. I didn't need to hear their whispers: *He must have murdered someone. Surely he ll hang. Let s attend the execution, wot? I ll bring the ale, you bring your sister.*

"You still haven't answered my question."

"I need you," Malik replied simply. "You were, and always will be, the best."

"Please," I said, my tone bitter. "No one's missed me for two years. Why am I so popular now?"

"Princess Iyumi has been kidnapped."

"Good riddance."

Malik sighed, his dark face darkening further in annoyance. However, his military bearing, calm façade and unflappable nature kept his tone and expression even. "She's the High Priestess and our future Queen."

I snorted, crossing my arms over my bare, mottled chest. "You don't like her any more than I do. She's insufferable."

"Whether I like her or not doesn't make a difference. I'm putting together a team to fetch her back, and I want you on it."

I stared at him, stunned and uncomprehending. "Are you daft? No!"

Malik had the gall to smile comfortingly...yes, comfortingly down at me. "Here's your opportunity to find redemption."

"What makes you think I'm searching for...that, what did you call it? Redemption?"

[7]

His eyes wandered the street, the piss and shit-laden cobblestones toward the less-than busy activity of the folk who lived in this section of town. A few low-class merchants worked here, yes, men who sought to cheat more than they hoped to sell. Out of work mercenaries wandered in search of any master, the honest as well as the desperate. Thieves watched the unsuspecting from shadowed doorways. Those few women about at this hour were the whores whose johns left their one-room hovels last night.

His deep brown eyes roved over the sign behind me, the emblem of the white rear-end of a laughing horse. The Horse's Ass. A tavern so seedy even the whores and cutthroats found little to attract them there.

"You like living in the gutter?" Malik asked.

"It's home, be it ever so humble."

"His Majesty has commanded you restored to your former rank and all its privileges. Reluctantly, however. He doesn't like you much."

"Tell him I respectfully ask him to kiss my arse."

"Dammit, Van, I need you."

"No, you don't." I crossed my thin arms over my scrawny, filthy chest. "Order Cian to this detail."

Malik lifted his broad shoulders and glared down his hooked nose. "I did. He and ten others of your Clan are ready and waiting for you to lead them. My team consists of a wing of Griffins, a troop of Minotaurs, three units of cavalry and an untold number of creeping spies."

I shook my head, grinning faintly. "You really don't need me."

"I do, indeed."

Malik's fist clenched as he half-raised it, his expression tight. "You're the best of them, Van. No other Shifter has your precise detail. None have your nerve, your wit, nor your cunning. You take on what others fear to. Unless you're part of it, my mission will fail utterly."

"Nice speech." I hooked my thumbs in my belt again. "Pity you bet on the wrong Shifter."

[8]

Malik's fist dropped to his side and opened. He relaxed. Not a welcome sign, in my book. His expression shut down, frozen into that hard as granite Malik face. "You'll make me force you?"

"You don't have to force anything on anyone." I shrugged. "It's your choice, brother. Make it and go. And leave me be."

A thinning of his lips created something akin to a smile at the same time his eyes hardened. Malik's hard-bitten Atani face wasn't designed for emotions like humor. A shiver of dread wriggled like a grave-worm down my spine. I'd seen that look before his powerful hooves knocked a man's head clean from his shoulders. My hand tried to creep to my neck, but I quashed its cowardice with firm resolve.

"No can do," Malik replied, feigned sorrow shadowing his tone. "I'm under orders to take you back."

I loved the guy, yet I always hated that aspect of his personality. Malik adored mockery, and sarcasm was an art he practiced often. He never failed to poke sardonic humor at those beneath his royal nose. The egotistical, self-centered bastard that he was.

"You'll come with me either of your own free will or in chains," Malik promised, his hands resting on his horse shoulders, akimbo. "Either way, you come with me. Your choice, of course, my dear Van."

"Spare me."

Laughing, I reverted to my favorite form, the falcon. Leaping into the morning sunlight, I soared upward, its welcoming rays lingering on my feathers. Rising on the light breeze, I caught a thermal and rose yet higher within an instant. Far below, Malik stood amid his soldiers, gaping upward like a landed fish. "Catch me now, meathead," I called.

Below me, Malik and his cronies fell away quickly. I pushed my wings into working hard, seeking the sun. Climbing high and fast, I left the stench of the street, the Ass, and the piss I fell into far behind. I always loved flying. When I flew, I imagined the world far away, where I was no one and nothing. I had no past and no future. There was no present, no cares, no sensations save the whisper of the wind beneath my wings, the cool breeze tickling my beak.

[9]

In my falcon body, I rose high, swift, my wings taking me away from the grief, from Malik, his patrol, and his crisis. I saw them with my keen raptor vision, far below, shading their eyes to see me better. *Ah, Malik, my brother, you forgot who I am. You called me the best. And so I am. Go away and leave me alone.*

I reckon I forgot who he was.

Just then, twin manacles of dark pewter fastened upon my wing joints. Like malicious tentacles, they bit deep and no amount of fighting on my part would or could shake them loose. *Damn you, Malik. You can kill me with these bloody things.*

Only one magic in the known, and unknown, world prevented a Shifter from changing forms: those dark pewter manacles. The power of the Old Ones, the magic the Centaurs, the Minotaurs, the Griffins, the Faeries all called their own, rested within them. No one knew exactly how they worked, not even the scholars. Save for those gifted few.

The dark manacles' secrets, the inhibitors of any and all magic held a dire, dark spell woven into the fabric of magic and stilled it completely. A Shifter's magic permitted the change from one's own form into any shape within the known universe. Yet, the pewter's power rendered a Shifter incapable of utilizing his gods-given powers.

The Minotaur's magics hushed when chained with those strange objects. The Griffins learned to fear it, and the Centaurs hated the very sight of that dark gleam. Only the Faeries laughed at its ancient magic, but they laughed at everything. Even humans with the awesome powers at their disposal were rendered as helpless as infants when the manacles were employed.

Obviously, Malik learned, or was taught, the secrets of the dark metal. And he never told me, the cad.

Frozen, my wings refused to work properly. My helpless flapping prevented a death drop to the very hard ground below me, but the remaining airborne option departed swiftly. I beat hard, desperate, my body spiraling rapidly out of control. My raptor's sharp vision caught glimpses of the town beneath spinning like a top, and forced one simple conclusion from me.

1 m in trouble.

Dizzy, last night's mead threatening to reverse itself with a vengeance, the world spun around and around and around. *I'm gonna die. My Lady Goddess, as you love me, let me hurl on Malik's impeccable shoulder before you take me to your bosom.*

My swift wings failed to save my life, therefore I must rely on others if I wished to breathe a while longer. However, that prospect sucked rocks. Down, down, I spiraled, my small body rotating as it dropped. The ground below rose faster than I liked, and I'd hit terra extremely firma within moments. Without help, I'd smash into little bits of feather and falcon on the dirty brown cobbles. Though I wished myself dead many times over the last couple years, I wasn't so sure I wanted to meet my Maker just yet.

Malik, if you want me alive, you'd better do something.

I always suspected a sadistic streak ran down his spine, the kind that enjoyed watching a worm wriggle in the mud at his feet. An even-tempered beast under normal circumstances, I supposed I pushed his good nature to its limits. He wanted me to think I'd die, just so he could save me, and preen under my gratitude. While I wanted to spit on his polished hooves, I wished he'd rush in to save me, post-haste.

Uh, Malik? Hello? Anytime now.

Malicious, Malik waited until the very last instant to catch me within the folds of his power. Like a cold blanket, his magic seized me in its grip. I felt my body slow its rapid descent, seconds too late. I'd hit the ground hard, but I'd survive.

I fell with a wretched, ignominious thud to the cobblestones at his feet, losing precious feathers and waking a headache that rivaled my best hangover. Dazed, I gasped for breath, my beak wide, my form locked into that of my falcon. I breathed in piss and coughed out mead. Choking, gasping, I floundered, unable to get my talons under me so I might yet stand.

The sun vanished again as Malik bent down. He picked me up.

Not by my small body, the falcon that could fit nicely into his sword-calloused palm. Hell, no. Malik had a vicious side to his calm and affable nature. He plucked me up by my feet and held me before his eyes as though evaluating his next meal.

[11]

Viewing the world, dangling toes up and beak down from the hand of a Centaur gave me much needed perspective, I'll admit. The Horse's Ass wasn't the home I thought it was. I liked The Signal Seller, an inn across town kept by a woman who loved books and often quoted chapter and verse. She also adored cats. If I turned myself into a long-haired, striped tabby, she'd allow me into her lap and would read to me. Maybe I'll saunter on down to the Signal and be her cat for the next year or ten.

A scroll appeared in Malik's left hand. "Vanyar ap Llewellyn ap Hydarr," he announced in a deep rolling tone. I swear the vagrants in the streets halted long enough to listen to his captivating voice. "I've a list of charges against you."

I sighed and the world steadied a bit. At least my stomach calmed. "Tut," I commented. "Your desperation is showing. Terribly unsuitable for one of your calling, you know."

The manacles on my wings didn't allow for furling them across my back. Forced, however hateful this action was, I spread them wide. Much easier on the wings, less so on my raptor's immediate dignity.

"His Royal Majesty has charged this miscreant with public drunkenness and intoxication," Malik intoned, pretending to read from his scroll.

"Um," I answered, slow, careful. "It's legal, and expected, on this side of town."

"– lewd and lascivious behavior –"

"She said she was eighteen."

" – indecent exposure –"

"Uh, from where I sit you'd be accused of the same. Your whatsis hangs as large as –"

"Part of my culture. What's your excuse?"

"Someone stole my shirt."

"Are you sticking to that pathetic story?"

"I don't have a chance, do I?"

"A snowball's in hell. Maybe. If you're lucky."

"Gods forbid–"

"Conduct unbecoming an officer and an Atan." Malik's voice rose.

[12]

"I left the Atan years ago. That doesn't qualify."

"–disrespect to His Royal Majesty–"

"I've disrespected him for years, too, however that's mostly private. How'd you know about it, anyway?"

"I know everything."

My eyes chanced upon his glassy, shined and polished, hind hooves. "We're friends, aren't we, Malik?"

My question halted his feigned gaze on his magic-inspired scroll. He frowned, half-turning toward me, his brows lowered. I interrupted his train of thought, yet he'd forgive me. This time. "Yes, Van."

"Friends can ask one another personal questions, isn't that true?"

"Of course, my dear chap."

"Inquiring minds must know."

He sighed, his hand raising me up to eye level. "Is there a question in your future?"

I jerked my beak toward his rear. "How do you polish your back ones? I know you hate servants and such noble pleasantries."

"Can we stay on topic, please?"

"I ask," I went on slowly, "because I suspect it'd be very difficult for one of your, er, stature, to polish your own hooves. Do you, like, bend under?"

"His Majesty also charges–"

"If you're that bendable, dear boy, please suck your own–"

He shook me vigorously. The ale and mead I drank last night threatened an immediate and chronic upheaval. "Don't," I choked. "I'm gonna hurl."

Malik extended his arm, and me, well away from his military and pristine self. "Knock yourself out."

I managed not to barf, but my belly roiled alarmingly. "Quit shaking me, will you?"

He did so again, just out of sheer cussedness. My belly heaved, but I managed to lock my throat in the nick of time. "This is a side of you I've never encountered before," I gasped, viewing the Horse's Ass and its customers from an odd vantage point. Tamil's poxy face looked just like the painted Ass, from its' rear-view appearance. How extraordinary.

"His Majesty also charges you with high treason and murder."

"Fine," I replied, willing my revolted belly into submission. The world spun for a few more awkward moments, then quieted. I met his dark eyes and grim expression with jovial mockery.

"Take me to jail," I said, shrugging my feathers. "I need a vacation, anyway. I can sleep, eat three squares a day, no worries."

Malik lifted me higher, his deep eyes on level with mine. His aristocratic lips smiled in a way that sent a shiver down my falcon spine.

"Oh, no, Van," he replied, waving me gently back and forth. "No cushy cell for you. A high treason sentence, for an ex-Atan, means you go straight to Braigh'Mhar."

A sudden, icy chill ruffled my every feather. *Gods, no.*

The royal courts sent the worst of the worse to Braigh'Mhar upon their conviction. Raithin Mawrn terrorists, murderers, rapists, robbers, killers, soldiers convicted of treason–all save the petty crimes of theft or burglary, prostitution or debt–eventually found their way to the frozen north. The locals, and cursing inmates, named it the hell beneath hell.

Bound on all sides by glaciers and bald mountains, any who escaped Braigh'Mhar died from exposure within moments of leaving its high, protected walls. None might survive but within the comparative safety of the prison's protections. Native, six-limbed trolls guarded the twenty-five rod high icebound prison walls. Mindless, trolls ate anything that moved, or didn't move. That menu included road kill, the occasional rat and freedom-seeking prisoners. To date, no fool bypassed their alert senses, nor their voracious appetites, to escape into the sweet freedom the mountains offered.

Long accustomed to this brutal landscape, the trolls inherited inches thick layers of fat beneath their tough, reptilian hides. A diet of high fat and protein, fed raw and bloody by the prison officials, prevented the deepest cold from killing their species in infancy. Their natural protection and constant hunger kept them alert, cautious, and prowling for inmate-meat. The monsters' efficient

[14]

night vision and breath of flame caught many unsuspecting escapees before the brutal cold could. Only by remaining inside might one escape certain death from either the blasting cold or the trolls. Braigh'Mhar effectively shut the world out, and its enemies in.

The mountains also hungered for blood.

Had a fortunate inmate succeeded where others failed, ducking the alert guards and starving trolls, and survived the perilous trek into the sharp-toothed mountains, he'd face a worst death than what he'd fled from. Ice, starvation and a lengthy, agonized death awaited him with open legs. Running to her for comfort, he'd perish under her lethal, icy kiss. Blinded by white, his blood turning to ice in his veins, his body slowly froze as he believed he lay warm and safe under layers of warm quilts. The bald, ice-enslaved rocky peaks held more traps than a willing whore. Men tried. Men died.

Those prisoners who opted to remain within the prison walls found savage means of survival. Savvy jailbirds created gangs for protection, and killed off the weakest prisoners. Wars between gangs flared often, and kept the prison's funeral services (the trolls) busy. Prison guards left the inmates to their own devices, unless they rioted. If that occurred, the wardens simply turned the hungry trolls loose to run amongst the rebelling prisoners and shut the heavy steel doors behind them.

Criminals not immediately executed were sentenced to Braigh'Mhar either for a later death sentence or for a life inside its heinous walls. No parole was offered or expected. If the gangs didn't gut you, insanity surely would.

"I can't go there." My tongue felt numb.

"The manacles you wear now will accompany you," Malik went on, implacable. "Your hands will be bound behind you, twenty-four seven. There's no chance you'll change your form into that of a mouse and wriggle free, or escape. There you will remain till the end of your, er, single, tortured week."

My tongue all but refused to work. "You wouldn't."

Malik half-smiled with a shrug, indolent. "I don't pass sentence. His Majesty will."

[15]

"I gave His Majesty many years of loyal and dedicated service," I said, my voice wild.

Malik frowned at his scroll. "Oh, there it is. I almost overlooked it. Absent without leave. Almost two years to the day. Wow. What a coincidence."

"I had to run, dammit."

"Oh, yes." Malik smiled thinly. "From your Atani brothers."

My soul cringed. "I didn't mean for it to happen," I whispered. "I–"

"Your own arrogance and callous stupidity caused many Atani deaths. No punishment is good enough."

"Then execute me. Cut my head off."

Malik drew me close to his face, eye to eye, his expression wide, cunning and cruel. "Oh, Van," he replied softly. "That's much too easy for one such as you."

"Gods–"

"You deserve nothing less than incarceration for what little remains of your life."

"Send me anywhere but Braigh'Mhar. Please."

"Why? You sent ninety-nine point nine percent of the Braigh'Mhar inmates there yourself? Right?"

I raised a scoff. "Ninety five point eight, bro," I snapped, my voice hoarse. "You did your share."

He shook me again. My feathers rattled from stem to stern. "I never committed treason."

"Nor did I–"

"You did. Disobeying a direct command from the King or his first-in-command...that would be me...is treason at its highest level."

"What order did I disobey?" I demanded.

Malik bared his teeth in a pseudo smile. "I ordered you to see me in my quarters after Dalziel, to explain what happened. Instead, you bolted like a rabbit."

"I had to, dammit!" I shouted, my wings wide. "They were going to kill me."

"Of course they wanted you dead. You got their brothers blown to kingdom come."

[16]

"I sent them in to save lives, rescue hostages. My intel was sound, they were hot to go in. I didn't know...there was only one, I was told, only one...you weren't there. Nor was His Majesty. I did what I had to do."

"You broke protocol," Malik sneered. "And it cost the lives of your unit. You live though they died."

I groaned, shutting my eyes. "I'd trade places with them all in a heartbeat, given the chance. But that matters as much as a flea in a sandstorm. Don't it?"

"You're pathetic, Van."

"And then some. How long?"

"Oh, the boys are wagering you survive anywhere from two days to a month," Malik remarked agreeably, his smile bright and more predatory than a shark's. "Among the general population."

"I demand a single cell. And protection."

Malik's face fell. "Oh, gee, sorry. This just bites rocks, bro. Treasonous ex-Atani aren't allowed special privileges. Treat them like the criminals they are, the King says."

"Shit."

"How's by those souvenirs? A piece of your hide will fund an inmate's bad habits for a month."

I groaned.

"Those bad boys'll take weeks to kill you." Malik's soft voice held more malice than a bared sword. "Choose that, or–"

"Or?" I hated myself for it, but I leaped toward the temptation he offered. "Or what?"

"Reclaim your place and your soul by joining with me," he said. "Help me bring the princess home."

Bitterness rose like the bad mead in my belly. "Oh, sure," I tried to scoff. "Trade one sentence of death for the other. You know damn well what'll happen to me."

Malik's brows drew down as though he pondered the implications. "Oh. All your brothers who remember Dalziel."

"Bastard," I hissed. "You know they'll kill me."

"You'll be under my protection."

"No offense, Malik. But that's as effective as a linen cloth against a sword's strike."

His dark eyes met mine. "Take it or leave it."

"Malik, where'd that cruel streak spring from? I've never seen it's like before."

"Choose, or I'll choose for you."

I sighed, swinging from his fingers like a bat at roost. I wrapped my wings about me as best I could, stilling my shivers. "If I'm to die, better I die at the hatred of my own kind than the torments of my enemies. I was yours before. I am yours after. I'm still yours, for whatever life remains to me."

"Now that's what I like to hear. Positive and encouraging. You're a true Atan, Vanyar. Perhaps you'll redeem your honor on this mission."

"Honor is a walk on slippery river rocks," I replied, my tone as cold as I could make it. "Too treacherous for words."

Casually, he flicked his fist. His motion tossed me up to land, talons-first, on his bare shoulder. His manacles vanished, leaving me free to fly, change forms or do as I pleased. Instead, I furled my sore wings, a tiny falcon perched beside his face, gripping his skin with my sharp talons without cutting him. "You're a bastard, Malik."

His deep-set eye met mine the instant he quirked his upper lip. "And then some."

Striking a gallop, with me stuck to his shoulder with wings half-spread for balance, Malik's hooves sparked lights from the cobbles. Behind his flowing tail galloped his Centaur unit, two by two, the sound of their hooves like thunder in the almost silent streets. What few folk roamed at this early hour scuttled hastily out of his path, their curses swallowed. Wagons drawn by horses, mules and a few laden oxen trundled aside, their drivers yanking on long reins. Attendant mercs on rearing horses spurred their mounts out of the way, gloved hands kept well-away from sword hilts.

I glanced behind. The mounted cavalry parted in twain and flanked the galloping Centaurs, the King's banner snapping in the wind. Behind it flew the Atani flag: the grinning Death's Head skull. Charging across the quarter's wide industrious center, Malik plowed through matrons and shopkeepers alike. Shouted curses hadn't time

[18]

to fill his ears as his hard hooves forced peasants, workers, thieves, whores, or convenient aristocrats aside or risk being trampled by an annoyed Centaur commander and his Atans.

His wild hair cloaked me, enveloping me like a burial shroud. I didn't try to toss it aside, nor did Malik, though the comparison gave me the heebie-jeebies. Had I the guts, I'd force Malik to send me to Braigh'Mhar, find peace within a sort-of honorable death. Like the coward I was, I sat on his shoulder as he took me into a future I didn't want. I longed to fly free, flee, as I ran away before. But my past would ever follow like a hungry pup, always there, never satisfied.

Face your enemies.

Sure, I thought. *Easier said than done.*

CHAPTER 2

By the King's Command

"Your Highness."

With an effort, I dragged my eyes from the scantily clad women dancing in the smoky tavern's great room. Wearing little save silken scarves over their lower faces, their lengths of heavy hair cascaded over their slender shoulders and covered their naked breasts. Gold chains slung about their tiny waists jingled in time to the music from the bells in their hands and the sultry music from the invisible lute player in a dark corner. Silver links around bared, slender hips held up a single strip of silk covering their loins, their bucking hips and asses bared to the room's scrutiny or lust.

Seductive and tempting, a dancer's dark eyes held mine and spoke to me across the tables of sweating, swearing men. She danced for me alone, her hips and arms swaying to the music, her naked bosom half-hidden from me. Ah, but her dark eyes. Those huge sloe eyes spoke of such sweet promise that I knew the sweat trickling down my cheek had nothing to do with the heat from within the room. Within the hour, she'd be mine. I had gold enough for the entire–

"Prince Flynn."

Sergei's nasal voice intruded upon my fantasy. I broke from it, breathing hard, my chest on fire. Gods, but the air was stifling in this dank, smelly inn. My dancer pouted, seeing my attention shift from her, and danced for the hulking mercenary at a table to my left. He pounded his fist on the wood, sending ale, food, plates and utensils flying. For a moment, I saw myself lunging from my chair, my sword stabbing deep into the gorilla's thick, hairy neck. His blood fountained high, coating me, the dancer and his fellows in thick red spatters. Then my girl would turn her smile on me, her hips swaying in time to the music, her fingers beckoning, her eyes—

I gripped my sword hilt hard enough to hurt, and scowled at my father's errand boy. "What?"

Sergei bowed low. "Forgive me, my prince, but your father has commanded your presence."

Beyond the heads of my fellow inn-folk, I glanced at the dark windows. "It's past bloody midnight."

"I know, Your Highness." Sergei groveled in such a cringing manner I wanted to kick him. "Your father—"

"Go on, Flynn," mocked Jarvik, one of my inn cronies. "Daddy calls."

Snickers abounded. I glared at them, but they ignored me and cat-called one another, shoving one another's shoulders, laughing. Amid the male horse-play and rough-housing, I heard 'daddy's boy', 'prince pussy', and 'the royal sissy' as I rose from my table. My hand itched to put an end to the torment, but I was but one among many who could outdraw and outfight me, even on their worst day.

My father called them my friends, but they hardly qualified. When sober, Jarvik, Tann, Evsham and Ivard were pleasant enough companions. But when drunk, like a pack of feral dogs, their vicious natures emerged, banding together to attack the hand that fed. 'Twas my hand that fed them and lavishly.

"Go on." I shoved Sergei in front of me, marching him toward the tavern doors.

The bouncer, a huge man with a bald head and frightful scars on his neck and face, bowed me though with the only respect I ever got in that wretched place. I slapped his meaty shoulder in passing, and flipped him a gold crown. "Thank ye, Highness," he muttered to my back.

Sergei waited with barely stifled impatience at my horse's head in the lamplight outside the noisy tavern. Bayonne greeted me with a nicker and extended muzzle, ignoring Sergei's hands on his reins. I took a moment to caress his grey head and stroke his ears, my affection for the dappled stallion overriding my anger. One of the few who loved me, Bayonne accepted me at face value. My first and only horse, I picked the dark grey colt out of my father's milling herd of royal mares and their offspring. My illustrious sire scoffed at my choice, but fell silent later when Bayonne grew into a stunning stallion who won every race I ever rode him in. Calm, sensible, highly intelligent, Bayonne obeyed my every command with courage and alacrity.

I vaulted into my saddle under Sergei's withering glare and turned Bayonne about. Leaving Sergei to scramble for his own mount, I loped Bayonne through the darkened streets. Most folks had gone to bed, their hearths banked, shutters closed. Only thieves, vagabonds and whores wandered the hot summer night. I heard the Night Watch chase a miscreant down an alley while passing under countless street lamps lit to ward off the evil in the darkness.

If I received scant respect at the tavern, the palace, Castle Salagh, wasn't much better. I handed Bayonne to a stable lad to care for, just as Sergei clattered into the courtyard on his skinny bay. The boy took my reins from me without a glance, a bow or even a yawn. The castle guards in their stiff military tunics and high leather boots nodded as I passed. Their hands gripped halberds. With scornful eyes, they watched my back with hate and derision.

My father, King Finian, the Fair as he was often called, ruled the kingdom of Raithin Mawr with an iron fist. He killed with wanton bloodlust, executed his people for the most minor of crimes. He hanged or beheaded any man, woman, child or farm animal that spoke against his rule, taxes or policies. Yet, his people loved him. I still hadn't figured that one out. The high and the simple folks beat one another for a glimpse of him, or my mother, Queen Enya. They crowded the streets, shouting their names, crying their adoration. Quick to weep at the slightest recognition, they hailed my royal parents as saviors, just beneath the gods themselves.

On the other hand, they scorned me, the King's heir apparent.

They hated me on sight. All things being equal, I hated them back with the same malevolence.

[23]

I don't even know what'd I'd done or how I'd earned their animosity. I hadn't won any battles, but there hadn't been any wars to fight. I spoke to the nobles and barons with fairness, and ever their eyes watched me with derision and laughter. Learning from the best masters money purchased, I wielded a sword, shot a bow, rode a horse... still, I wasn't good enough. I stood at my father's right hand, yet to him they looked for leadership. My mother loved me, but her people didn't.

I was, and always had been, the kingdom's whipping boy.

Panting, Sergei led me through the twining corridors, past drowsing guards, dashing servants, and a few late courtiers returning from unsuitable liaisons with the opposite gender. I trod past portraits of kings and queens of Raithin Mawr glaring down at me, their disapproval skipping across my very thick skin. I didn't care what my ancestors thought. I didn't much care what my father thought. Hell, I didn't care much what anyone thought save—perhaps one. All right, two.

Sergei led me to the upper chambers of the palace, the high towers, where only the royal family and their closest relatives were housed. I followed, yet I knew every inch of those dank stone walls. I'd lived there since birth, fled from my sire's anger down their hollow corridors, hid within their shadows when he or his henchmen tried to catch me. Within their granite grasp, I learned that princes didn't always get the best of everything.

In the west tower, I climbed the steep staircase. The light cast by Sergei's torch sent huge silhouettes across the dank, stone walls. Down the slick hallways, past the closed doorways guarded by family retainers, I strode rapidly, following Sergei's quick shadow. My hand ever hovered over my sword, for I never knew who or what may pop out of nowhere to swing a fist at my face.

"Flynn?"

Her voice, soft and fluid, the dulcimer chimes of an angel, called to me from the darkness of a doorway. I halted at the sound, pausing mid-step and turned toward her like a puppet dangling on his master's strings. To hear that voice, to see her face, to hold her hand for even a moment...I'd surrender my rotten life.

[24]

Her tiny frame hugged the shadows as if borne from them, her magnificent blue eyes uptilted toward mine as she stepped forward to intercept me. I'd no need to say her name, yet I spoke it, for it resounded in my own ears like sweet music.

"Fainche."

My jangled nerves calmed instantly, as though a soothing balm flowed through and over them, and brought with it a sweet peace I seldom felt. She held a strange power, my sister did, to bring forth a side of me no one knew existed. I reached out my hand. A tiny slip of warm skin rested in it as I drew it toward me. Twelve-year-old Fainche emerged from the darkness like the devil's nymph, her eyes oddly shining in the torch's light. For her I withstood my father's beatings, the nobles' scorn, and the commons' spit. I'd endure it all at the gates of hell if she offered me that one single, loving glance.

Only two people in the entire kingdom kept me sane in this demented world. Without them, I'd long have succumbed to insanity and fled into the wilds to live life as a hermit in a cave. Only they kept me rooted, enduring, hopeful. For them alone I endured the naked hate and scorn on every face. Because of them, I felt hopeful that one day I might live a life as a normal man.

My sweet sister and my beautiful mother.

Her wild mane of hair, blonde like mine, trailed down her shoulders. Her fetching azure gown trimmed with gold and mink matched her eyes, the same exact shade of blue as my own. She stepped toward me, her hand quivering within my fingers. Tugging from my grip, Fainche smiled and snuggled close; her arms wrapped tightly around my waist.

"What are you doing up so late?" I asked, bowing over her small shoulder to hold her within my arms. I worked it so her ear rested against my heartbeat.

"I wanted to see you."

I found a grin and a semblance of real humor. "Lurking in the shadows will do that."

Fainche giggled. "I heard Father call for you. So I waited. I knew you'd come."

"And to think I might ignore such a beautiful maiden."

[25]

"Flynn!" Her shocked laughter brought a grin and a lightening to my heart. "You scoundrel."

I brushed my lips over her sweet-scented hair. "What does that old boor want?"

My lack of respect sparked yet another surprised giggle from her. "Father will beat you."

"And if he dares, I'll dream of you tending my injuries."

She snickered. "Drama queen."

I laughed, taking her by the arms and holding her away from me. "Come on, tell me. I know you're always lurking in corners, hearing things you shouldn't."

Sergei sighed and waited just out of earshot with ill-concealed impatience. I waved my hand at him, yet without my previous animosity. Sergei pouted and folded his arms across his meager chest.

I held my sister at arm's length, grinning. "Come on, sis. Out with it."

Trying to scowl, Fainche's sweet face dissolved into a grin. She never could feign anger with any success. Her sweet and passive nature prevented it. She seized my bristled cheeks within her small hands. "Father has a mission for you."

"A what?"

"You know. A special errand. You're to fetch someone for him."

My humor dropped by several notches, instantly and coldly. Dread dropped its icy load into my belly and spread its fingers into my blood. "Who am I to fetch, exactly?"

"I can't remember her name." Fainche's brow furrowed as she tried hard to think.

Many palace folk called her thick-witted and slow. Certainly our parents shielded her from the public view, and overly protected her from the coarseness of the world at large. I'd heard the gossip: her Royal Highness Princess Fainche was cute, but an idiot, entirely without any substance upstairs. No, Fainche wasn't stupid exactly, nor had she inherited the family gifts of high intelligence. Fainche was . . . special.

What she lacked in brains, she more than made up for in sheer sweetness and purity. I knew the gods dropped her on this earth as

[26]

a gift, as we humans lacked for angels in our midst. Evil touch her? If it tried—well, evil best be ready for the wrath of Flynn should it ever dare eye her.

"The Bryn'Cairdha princess, you know? Princess I...um, Iyum, maybe? Iyumi!"

Fainche danced in place, her pale, wheaten locks bouncing, and her blue eyes eager. "Did I get it right? Oh, please tell me."

"Yes, dear heart." I stroked her pale silky tresses. "You got it right."

"Oh, good."

Her small arms crept around my waist again, like cold and homeless kittens. Only she loved me unconditionally. Only she coaxed from me the warmth, the kindness, the *I-never-want-to-be nasty-to-anyone-ever-again* attitude. In her presence, I felt I might one day accomplish something good. I reached for the Flynn that someone might actually like. My soul cried aloud for that rare individual in this crazy world who liked me for me.

Once I left her side, reality descended with the thunk of a hammer to the skull. *Like Prince Flynn? Are you nuts? He's a rabid mongrel with a title.* The day a stranger cared for me would arrive when hell vomited up its vile inmates and the world collapsed in upon itself.

I felt her triumph against my chest, her smile under the hollow of my throat. Fainche's blonde mane spilled across my arms, its rich scent tickling my nose and threatening a sneeze. Sniffling, regaining control of my wayward sinuses, I gently pushed her away and negligently swiped her hair from her tiny face.

Sergei scowled and gestured imperiously as if to say, *Get on with it and let's go.*

"Do shut up," I muttered, cross.

"What did you say?" Fainche brushed her hair back, glanced from Sergei to me and back again. She peered up at me, concerned. "Don't be angry, Flynn. He but does his job."

I sighed as I gazed on her sweet innocence. Fainche's naturally sunny disposition made meadowlarks appear grouchy. She lived within the earthly bounds of the angel's purity of spirit, seeing naught save the world's goodness. I'd give up everything if it meant I could dwell in such a place, free from cares and men's evil, happily caught within them in a long span of years. I'd count myself free and blessed.

Her face nestled into my chest at the same instant she sighed. Her arms tightened about me; those small slender and delicate limbs anchored themselves to my body as tightly as a steel cable. With her pale face tilted up to me, she dug her chin into my breastbone.

"You'll succeed in your task," she murmured. "I know it. I saw it in the fire."

Gods, she didn t own magic–did she?

"In the fire?"

Resting her cheek against my chest, Fainche sighed. "I see things, sometimes. I saw you riding in under the light of the moon with a silver-haired princess. She's holding something–a baby, maybe. It cries and wriggles."

Gods. She has the Sight. They ll kill her if they knew.

Over her shoulder, I glowered, trying to appear the ruthless, ill-begotten bastard I was. I didn't want to risk Sergei overhearing her sacrilegious words. Magic was forbidden in our land. Not even the King's daughter was immune to the harsh punishments given if found guilty of practicing magic. Her words were lost under the horrible vision of her dangling from the city gate by a rope. My gut clenched. Sweat sprang from my brow.

Sergei rolled his eyes and folded his arms, hardly impressed with the danger I presented. Under my father's hand, he certainly knew I dared not touch him. *One day, Sergei,* I thought. *One day 1 ll see you regret this.*

Fainche felt my tension and glanced up into my face. A rapid–there and gone–frown creased her sweet face before collapsing into her usual light, happy expression. Nothing fazed Fainche for long.

"They're waiting for you, brother."

Fainche drew away from me, her angel's cheeks rounded in all the right places, smiling. Mine, in contrast, bore all rigid angles and granite planes, as hard as oak and twice as thick. I knew folk named me dumber than a brick wall, as sensitive as a randy goat and more

[28]

pathetic than any loser in the gutter. I heard their voices time and again, read it in their contemptuous eyes, felt their scorn on my skin.

As long as their slurs didn't touch this daughter of heaven, I didn't care.

"They?"

Her fingers entwined mine. Those delightful dimples at the corners of her mouth dug in deep. Her blue eyes sparkled. "Mother waits for you, too. Will you say good-night for me?"

I bent at the waist and kissed her knuckles. "For you, my love, I'll do anything you ask."

Fainche giggled as though I were a true courtier and withdrew into the shadows. Her hand snagged mine, trapping it until she vanished utterly, the shadows swallowing her whole. My soul wept at her departure.

Stiffening, I snapped my fingers at a nearby guard. Half-asleep at his post, he eyed me with no little distaste as he straightened from his indolent lean against the wall.

That bloody bastard took his sweet time to approach via my summons, his thumbs hooked in his swordbelt with that exact mercenary touch of arrogance. *My father s men...Ill-trained, haughty, full of their own testosterone, they jumped when my sire spoke. Yet, with me they discovered the merits of questioning authority.*

Despising his arrogant sauntering answer to my command, I hoped his incompetency didn't include getting Fainche hurt. Eyeing him from head to toe, I knew a slouch when it irritated me. I may not be my father, but I sure as shit kept records. One day, this obnoxious ass will wish he'd been a fraction more respectful.

"D'var, escort my sister to her rooms."

The palace folk adored Fainche as they revered my mother. She was my direct opposite, and everything I wasn't: lovely, sweet, caring, good–the adjectives go on. I knew they hoped and prayed I'd die young, childless, and leave the throne to her.

D'var brightened at his new duty, and deftly retrieved her from the shadows. Ushering her before him like a dog with his sheep, his bulk didn't quite hide her face peering over her shoulder. In the near dark, Fainche's teeth gleamed. My stony heart softened as it always did when she used that special *I-love-you-Flynn* smile.

Together, soldier and sister vanished into the shadows beyond the torchlight. The darkness returned with a sharp thump. I swallowed my bitterness and stifled my curses. Her absence, even for a short while, left a gaping hole in my soul.

"Your Highness, please."

Sergei's voice, nasal and annoying, raised new hackles on my neck. I eyed him with open hatred. I prayed for the guts to finally cut his obnoxious throat as he gestured impatiently, pointing down the half-lit corridor. Sighing, I gestured for him to lead on, absently wishing for–I don't know–anything. Of the four huge towers rising high over Castle Salagh, the western one was home to the royal family. The south and the east housed whomever my father favored at the moment–family members, nobles, or the myriad military officers. As long as I could remember, the north tower remained empty. My own lavish chambers lay around the far side of the tower from my parents', while Fainche's quarters stood opposite mine.

Banners bearing the Raithin Mawrn crest, the unicorn and spotted cat rearing toward one another as though dancing on a field of lush green, lined the corridor leading to my parents' chambers. At the far end of the long marble passageway, a twin set of huge doors stood silent and closed. Palace guard in their purple, white and gold uniforms stood stiff. My ancestors' and now my father's emblem, the royal eagle flying above crossed swords, brooded in embroidered silk on their breasts. Black cloaks lined with scarlet silk hung from throats to heels, their deadly pikes in their right fists. With strict military discipline, they looked neither left nor right nor at me as I walked past them.

Even so, I felt their curiosity, and their hatred, on my back.

Sergei departed after delivering me to the very gates of hell and vanished like a phantom at dawn. The door-wards, all but identical in their blue and silver palace tabards, swung wide the huge oak and teak doors. Laced with silver chasings and heavy chains, the monstrous doors, so wide three horses could walk abreast, creaked like coffin hinges. I passed the elderly wardens and into my parents' private bedchamber as though walking on deadly spikes. At least those old men bowed, even if they faked their obeisance.

"Boy," my father called as the heavy doors swung shut behind me with a resounding slam and the rattle of chains. "Come here, lad, come here."

Like a fat and stupid hare ambling into the wolves' den, I obeyed him.

I likened walking into my parents' personal rooms with that of a stroll in a museum. Huge and expansive, walled with dark oak beams and its vaulted ceiling high and buttressed, I wended my way among standing suits of antique armor. Sightless knights glared down at me, swords clasped within gauntlets of steel. Dead horses reared and screamed silently, jaws agape. Glass-topped tables held notable weapons, aged manuscripts and scrolls, and tapestries so old a breath could crumble them to dust. Paintings of warriors, knights, great men and women hung on the walls, their miniscule eyes watching my every move.

Dead critters hung as trophies on teak mantles, their coats dusty with age. A stag with an incredible spread of antlers gazed outward in sorrow. A huge black bear snarled down at me from my left. A grey and tan wolf's head stared in rapt fascination across the room at a wild hog with tusks larger than its head. An incredible spread of horns from an immense feral bull one of my ancestors slew hung over the great fireplace, a fire large enough to roast an ox in blazing inside. Despite the summer heat outside, the chill of the dank walls demanded a blazing hearth.

Their bed, the size of a small room and hung with blood- red curtains, stood off to my right, covered in quilts and furs. *1 d draw those drapes every night,* I thought. Having all those dead people and animals watching me make love might cow me into abstinence. Should I one day inherit this room, I suspected I'd never sire offspring.

Seated in huge armchairs beside the roaring fire, my parents watched me enter. As ever, I glanced first to Enya, my mother, to gauge her mood. If my father raged, she wore a tight-lipped smile that warned me to tread softly and watch his hands. Tonight her lips widened in a soft welcome, her incredible blue eyes luminous in the firelight, informing me my sire lounged in a genial, if not happy, frame of mind. I relaxed a fraction.

Both Fainche and I inherited her wealth of blonde hair, blue eyes and pale complexion. I easily tanned under the summer sun, but, as neither Mother nor Fainche left the palace often, their skin remained as pure as spun silk. My wild, uncut mane fell to my shoulders while theirs cascaded to their hips. One of my father's hounds peered up at me from under Enya's heavy wealth, all but buried in gold silk.

Mother smiled as I approached, and her beauty stunned me as it never failed to do. Clad in a simple pale yellow robe, her hair loose and falling to the carpet and hides covering the floor, she appeared to me as regal as any goddess. Tranquility seeped across my screaming nerves, her presence acting as a soothing balm, and I relaxed for the first time since Sergei's summons.

As usual when they were alone, in private, my father's hand rested on hers. Finian, oddly enough named the Fair, was as dark and swarthy as a pirate. His thick mane, the color of a raven's wing, curled to his shoulders. My sire liked beards, and kept a full one on hand. They made him seem wise and just, he often joked. Finian, stocky and broad across the shoulders, wasn't a big man. Most men, including me, towered over him. But he owned a commanding presence. No eye could or ever did pass him by. One loved him totally, or hated him to his bones.

I fell into the category of the latter.

Dutiful son that I am, ever their obedient subject, I crossed the distance toward their chairs with lowered brow and neutral expression. Two rods from their chairs, I knelt, my hands behind my back.

"Father," I said stiffly, formally. "Mother."

"My son."

Like my sister, Enya's voice might challenge an angel's for purity and sweet resonance. No wonder the people loved her so. Her skin glowed like alabaster marble, and, despite bearing two children, her waistline remained as slim as a maid's. Full rounded breasts bulged in all the right places, and her smile brought every man to his knees

[32]

in homage. She descended from a long line of kings, ruling before the Mage Wars, who claimed kinship with the gods themselves. When I regarded her, I firmly believed she was a goddess in truth.

Even my corrupt and crude sire worshipped the ground she walked on. He adored her with the same reverence as he might offer the official Raithin Mawrn goddess. Peasants, merchants, yeomen, nobles, foreigners...all of them fell prey to her beauty. She had but to smile and the earth fell to her delicate fingertips.

"Boy, you reek like a whore's den."

I winced.

"Are you a prince or a damn hound seeking his bitch in the gutter?"

As did everyone save my mother and my sister, my father found little in me to enjoy and much to condemn. If he found delight in his eldest born when I was small, I never heard tell of it. My earliest memories were of his beatings when I missed the target with my arrow, fell off my bucking horse, or lost my wrestling match. His laughter and coarse jests at my expense followed me at court. Naturally, his favorites laughed along with him, and their lackeys sang the same tune. Nothing I did was ever good enough. In his eyes, and in the eyes of his people, I fell far short of the royal family standards. I never measured up to the expectations the King had for his only son, no matter how hard I tried.

Only my mother dared turn his hand from me, beg him with soft eyes and a tear or three to be kind, to offer me some affection. Her methods worked, for he'd never gainsay her in anything until she walked out of sight. At her disappearance, the torments began again. And again. And again.

"Hush, Father," Enya said, her musical voice soothing his annoyance, her fingers entwined with his. Instantly, his demeanor changed from angry to adoring as he glanced toward her. "He's exploring his adulthood. Don't make me remind you of your own search for independence."

Finian chuckled. "Of course, Mother. Let's not give the boy any bad ideas."

He lifted his hand, and hers with it, to his thick lips to kiss. I glanced aside, wishing I had the guts to kill him for daring to lay his filthy slobber on her flesh. Her tinkling laughter stilled his displeasure and my fury, easing both at the same time.

Finian's dark eyes descended on me and his free hand beckoned me from my knee. "I've an errand for you, boy."

I tried to recall the last time he called me by name, and couldn't. I was never 'Flynn' to him. To him, I was, ever and always, 'boy'. Perhaps I should officially change my name to 'Prince Boy'.

Stifling my irritation, I obeyed him, striding the few steps closer to their chairs. Maintaining a discreet distance should his anger rise enough to lash out, I'd room enough to dodge. Quicker with his fists than a whore with her G-string, Finian's speed left a cobra gasping. Had I a gold crown for every time he hit me before I knew he was annoyed, I could arm the royal cavalry.

Warily watching his hands, I half-smiled the expected *I'm-listening-with-avid-attention* curving of my lips. I truly hated the farce, but had I not played into his fatherly fantasies, he'd not just beat me but murder anyone associated with me. For Fainche's sake, and that of my mother, I dared not defy him in expression, word or deed. I feared him, but kept that much to myself.

Much to my relief, he nodded and smiled at me as if happy to be in my company. On those occasions, though rare, I could pretend he loved me. Outside of his lack of naming me, I could imagine us as father and son, united in a common bond of blood and caring for one another. As usual, he saw only what he wanted to see, and didn't notice my lack of enthusiasm this particular evening. His excitement spilled over and quashed his prior aggravation.

"My spies have captured her," he said, forgetting I was allegedly ignorant of what the errand was.

Though he worshipped Fainche with the same adoration he reserved for Enya, I didn't want him to know she heard rumors and passed them on to me. He might not care, and then again he might care enough to chastise her.

My mind shied from the memory of Fainche imparting her secret. I dared not think such thoughts, half-fearing he'd pluck them from my head and punish Fainche in my stead. Though I knew he'd never read my mind, my gut feared he might.

I willed such thoughts away and dipped my brow. I faked a bland *l-don t-know-anything-at-all* expression and its neighborly half-smile. "Pray tell, my father."

"We caught that infernal bitch princess whatshername."

I exchanged a confused, lightning swift glance with Mother. "Who, sire?"

He glanced my way and waved his hand, dismissive. "Oh, right. I didn't tell you."

Like you ever tell me anything, I thought, damping down my resentment.

"I commanded my spies keep watch on Princess, er, Iyuma? Ayumas?" he said, half-laughing at his own memory loss.

Enya chuckled under her breath and leaned her bosom toward him, her wealth of blonde hair sliding across her face as she ducked her head onto his broad shoulder. "Iyumi, Father. Princess Iyumi."

"Of course. How silly of me."

He bussed her porcelain cheek, then bent to spill more filth from his mouth onto my mother's pale fingers. "Now I remember, thank you, my love. Beautiful girl. A fit queen for you, boy."

I bristled, fear nudging my spine. A queen? I, er, already had –

Enya lifted her gently smiling lips to murmur in his ear. Though I closely watched and strained my hearing to its highest level, I caught only 'boy', 'Blaez', and 'princess'.

"Thank you, mother."

Finian beamed, his cheeks rosy with triumph and red wine. His rough fingers caressed her knuckles as Enya lifted her lovely face to offer me a ghostly wink and a quick nod. Dread wormed its way down my spine and a voracious rodent gnawed my guts. When Finian smiled at me, trouble followed on fleet feet.

"Gods be praised, she rode out without an escort and they caught her," Finian continued, nodding, still grinning like a dark, leering monkey. "My spies, those loyal and dedicated men, seized her venomous person. They're on their way here, right now, boy.

Praise the gods, we captured the Bryn'Cairdha prophetess and princess."

My jaw sagged a fraction. "Prophetess?"

Finian smiled wide and rubbed both hands together in unashamed delight. He rose from his chair to pace behind my mother's and stroked his blunt fingers down her smooth, pale cheek. She leaned into them, smiling, Fainche's dimples curving into deep hollows to either side of her full, rosy lips. Why she loved him, why she *could* love him, fell far beyond my ken. *She loves you, too,* a small voice inside of me mentioned with casual indifference. Perhaps there was no accounting for taste.

"Indeed, boy, indeed. She knows the child's been born and where it lies."

Child? Prophecy? What the hell was he–

Somewhere inside my head, a memory flashed. My father speaking of the sacred prophecy, eons old, of the fabled child who would eradicate magic from the lands forever. That in its birth, the two lands of Raithin Mawr and Bryn'Cairdha would find peace and plenty as one land. Countries conjoined, one people, one destiny, as they'd been in the beginning.

The people and rulers of Raithin Mawr prayed for that time to come, fearing the evil shape-shifters, the bizarre creatures, and the hold magic had upon their neighbors to their south. They were cursed, the folk of Bryn'Cairdha. Men who could take on any shape they desired were nothing less than demons. They surely worshipped the cursed ones, for how else could the melding of man and horse, eagle and lion, bull and man occur? Strange spirits kept them company, weird lights with wings flying hither and yon, dropping deadly secrets into their ears. What evil was this?

The cursed folk of Bryn'Cairdha were nothing less than malevolent and the abhorrence of those upright and strong under the gods' light. *Kill them,* spoke the Raithin Mawrn mantra. *Kill them, scourge their evil and take their lands.* I grew up under the priests screaming invectives against the Bryn'Cairdha people, largely ignored them as the rantings of lunatics, and seriously considered crossing the border in search of sanctuary.

[36]

Bryn'Cairdha and Raithin Mawr had never been neighborly, despite the close quarters. Minor wars broke out over the centuries, here and there, never serious. They minded their business, we minded ours–with the exception of the fanatics. Those extremists sent in their suicide-crazies to plant bombs and blow up, not just themselves, but our folk they took hostage. Crazier than a fox in a trap, they thought to single-handedly wipe out magic every time they killed themselves. *Bezerkers.* I never suspected my own father counted as one of them.

"She's our key," he went on, pacing, excited. Back and forth on the priceless carpet he strode, waving his hands, as Enya eyed him sidelong. She caught me watching her and dipped her face, a *we-know-better,* milk-mild mien crossing her expression before vanishing an instant later.

"This is our chance to take from them what is ours."

"And what is ours?" I asked.

"What? Our rights, of course. With the child in our hands, we'll scourge that black land to our south, kill the demon King and his family, and take what was once ours."

I caught a sympathetic glance from my mother as her slender fingers hid a smile. *Humor him,* those blue depths suggested. Her prior attitude shifted into the realm of *do-as-he-says* despite the non-verbal alliance of moments ago. I frowned slightly before Finian's bulk passed between us.

"Uh." I coughed diffidently. "When was Bryn'Cairdha once ours? Sire."

Finian waved a restless hand, still pacing before the fire, stomping the fleas from the carpet. "Centuries ago, boy, centuries ago. But we will prevail, I swear it. Bryn'Cairdha will merge with Raithin Mawr and her two people shall become one. Without their evil magic or their loosed demons."

I bit my tongue as he swung hard toward me, raising his hand. Though I stood too far away for him to strike me, I flinched anyway, out of instinct. My hand crept toward my sword and dropped away without touching the hilt. He didn't notice my protective stance.

[37]

"Escort her here, boy," he said, his tone commanding, yet eager. "You're royal, a prince, my only son. She deserves the highest honor, my son and heir extending his hand in friendship. She'll give us the child, of course."

"Uh, give, sire?"

He waved his hand, impatient. "She'll see the truth, boy, count on it. She'll find the errors in her ways and find the right path."

"And if she doesn't?"

Finian folded his hands behind his back and rocked back on his heels. Enya watched him for a long moment, then, with the fire behind her, watched me. Within her deep eyes I read nothing at all. I waited, patient, knowing he liked the sound of his own voice too much to not continue.

"She *will* give us the child," Finian said at last, his tone low and thoughtful.

This was getting too weird. Between her eyes and his calm, I suspected I was out of my element and swimming the wrong way. I didn't want to hear more. I took his tone as my dismissal. I dropped to my knee in quick obeisance and backed the required three steps, head bowed, before turning. Inside my mind, I planned a rapid and evasive route among the dead knights and stuffed horses, hoping to disappear as quickly as a rat down its hole. I didn't much like the comparison, but it certainly suited the situation.

"You'll leave at dawn."

I halted with my right foot raised to take that crucial fourth step in escape. I spun about, my throat tight as I gulped. I hoped he hadn't heard the dry click. I bowed low. "Your will, sire."

His next words froze me before I might straighten the thing I called a spine. "You'll marry her, boy, in due time."

My head rose involuntarily as my gut stiffened. My fists clenched, though I forced them to open and hang at my sides before he noticed and beat me for defiance.

"Sire?"

Finian waved his hand again, expansive, permissive. "Princess Iyumi. She'll be your wife. The marriage will ease the transition and unite our two nations as one."

[38]

"Um," I began, my mouth dry as cotton and twice as sticking. "I'm already married."

Finian's brows lowered and he ceased his happy pacing. His dreadful eyes settled on me and his right hand clenched into the familiar fist I dreaded. "You married Sofia against my will and better judgment. I allowed it as the match made your mother happy. But I will annul it, posthaste, and you'll set her aside. Do I make myself clear?"

"Father, please—"

The King stepped closer to me, looming, hiding my mother behind his bulk. "Set her aside. Or I'll execute her," he said, his tone low, for my ears alone. "Is that what you want, boy? Shall I kill her, so you'll be free to marry Iyumi?"

"No, sire."

I dropped to my knee, lowering my head for the blow, my hands clasped behind my back. "Please don't."

"Then find your excuse to set her aside. I don't care what it is."

Still on my knee, I bowed low. "Immediately, sire."

"Go on then. See Commander Blaez at dawn. You have your orders."

I did indeed. I danced to them, marched to them, obeyed them when my blood sang a sad song of unrequited freedom. I dared raise my eyes from the carpet when his fist failed to knock me flat onto it. Finian returned to his heavy, scarlet-cushioned chair, smiling at my mother as he took her hand, kissing it, gazing deeply into her cornflower blue eyes. Just as though he hadn't threatened to murder my wife under the laws he created. He'd kill me just as quickly should I fail him.

You can escape him, that inner voice muttered. *You can be free of him, and go where you will.*

Right. Sure.

Bowing low, walking backward the expected steps, I retreated from my parents' private chambers. Walking faster than I had on arrival, I dodged the suits and mounts without raising my eyes from the azure slate floor. Like magic, the huge oak and teak opened wide as though the wardens knew the instant I came close, although they stood on the far side.

I crossed the threshold, sweating, my tunic sticking to my back, my shoulders. I didn't turn around, yet heard the solemn creak of centuries-old hinges. The door-wards shut the great teak and silver doors with the same hollow boom and rattle of chains as I stumbled into the corridor, all but blind. I straightened at last, shaking, unmindful of their pitiless stares. I dragged deeply of the cool, moist castle air, my lungs relishing the change of atmosphere. My sigh of relief caught on a sob, snagged my throat. I walked away, feeling as though I'd just escaped the executioner's axe.

Sofia.

Under the torchlight and the guards' blank-eyed enmity, I ducked into the shadows where I belonged. Anonymous. A well-bred nobody. I grinned bitterly, with no humor. *I do what I do to survive,* I told myself. I'll tell Sofia to go home. Find another man, one better than I, and bear his children. After she scratches out my eyes, she'll do as I bade her. In due time, I'll marry Iyumi, as commanded.

Protect Sofia, gods of old, I thought, praying without conviction. *For I love her.*

CHAPTER 3

A Broken Code

"Are you ready?"

I nodded, trying to forget how his voice echoed in my dreams with that very question. I straightened my uniform, and eyed Malik sidelong as he held my sword out for me to accept. His unfathomable, deep-set dark eyes studied me as I hesitated, wiping my damp palms on my tunic.

"It's yours," he rumbled softly. "Cleaned and oiled once a week, sharpened monthly. Go on."

I took its heavy weight onto my palms, and curled my fingers about its plain leather sheath. "Malik–"

"Can it, plebe," he snapped, wheeling away from the gratitude he saw in my eyes, heard in my voice. His hooves resonated off the slate tile flooring as his broad hands crossed his immense chest. His shaggy black hair, held from his face by his rayed star headband, cascaded down his bare shoulders. "Put that bloody thing on, and be ready," he said to the twin doors that led into his command center.

I obeyed him, sliding my sword's sheath onto my belt and rebuckling it about my hips. Its heavy weight, both familiar and comforting, granted me much needed courage. *Are you ready?* I bloody hoped so, for all our sakes.

Clean, shaven, and sober for the first time in months, I stood at his right shoulder, taking up my former position as his second-in-command. Three hours in Malik's private chambers and attended by his mute Centaur servant, Innes, gave me the appearance of the man, the soldier, I once was. Inwardly, however, I quaked. Three hours of sobriety left me nauseous, shaky and craving drink as I never had before.

"I dare not give you more time to recover," Malik said as his magic dumped me in a hot bath upon our arrival. "Every minute wasted meant another hour on the chase. Sober up but fast."

While I soaked in hot water and suds to my chin, Malik's hand on my brow purged much of the ale and wine from my blood as though I'd gone a week without a drink, not a few hours. Now clean from my alcohol consumption and my years as a bar-fly, the horrid queasiness and my shaking hands informed me that was not–*quite*–enough.

Cleaned, sober, wearing my Atani uniform with its insignia of rank on my shoulders, I felt the creeping weakness of the unhealthy lifestyle I'd been living. Sweat dewed my brow and my tunic beneath its leather harness crossing my chest grew damp. I'd lost much weight and muscle tone over the last two years for the black Atan uniform I wore hung loose. Knee-high black boots still fit me and gold spurs jingled when I walked, but my fitness to ride a horse was at best laughable and at worst dangerous.

"You're an Atan," Malik murmured, raising his head as Innes strode sedately into view, ready to open the doors at Malik's signal. "The King's chosen."

I nodded sharply, and sucked in my breath. I stiffened my spine. "My Lord Captain Commander."

Yes, I am an Atan. I am First Captain Vanyar, and Malik s right hand. Outside Malik's authority, I answered only to the King himself. I've fought the enemy, shed my blood, witnessed enough death and horror to last a lifetime. I earned my place at Malik's right hand, and I'd kill to maintain it.

I breathed in a slow shuddering breath to quell my belly, staring straight ahead at the gilded double oak doors, waiting for them to open upon my destiny. Waiting, patient, I pondered Malik's private chambers I stood in, and knew so well. I knew this place upside down and backwards. How many days did Malik and I spend in here, receiving reports, conferring with patrol leaders and ferreting out Raithin Mawrn terrorists? How many nights did we share company: drinking ale or wine, talking shop, sharing gossip and secrets? How many times did we seriously discuss those ever mysterious and elusive creatures known as . . . *girls?*

We spent endless nights brooding or chuckling into our mugs: brothers, companions, the best of friends.

Beyond the massive double doors of heavy teak and inlaid with silver and gold waited his Atani sub-commanders in the huge conference room slash conference center adjacent to his private suite. Called by Malik to organize the hunt for our missing Princess, they waited with reports, intel, idle gossip, speculations and questions that held no answer.

Ready or not, sober or not, the moment arrived. By standing with him, I silently accepted his mission: retrieve our royal Princess whatever the cost. I'll finish this task or die trying. I will, I *must,* conquer the effects of the last two years of indulgence. Or slink back to the gutter and slit my throat, forever shamed. This one chance at redemption knocked only once before ambling on down the road.

Innes stood by, patiently awaiting Malik's request to open them. Innes, his silent, aging and only Centaur servant, kept his private chambers neat and organized. I'd known him for years, yet never inquired as to his history, or conferred with him directly. Rumor had it that Innes was a not-so distant relation whose tongue had been cut out by Raithin Mawrn mercenaries. True or not, Innes never spoke. Nor did he ever smile.

Malik glanced down at me, his dark expression soft, and, oddly, mildly affectionate. He toyed with the solid ruby signet on his left forefinger, a sure sign Malik fretted. The many hard angles and planes of his face didn't smile easily, yet he found a small one somewhere. "For what it's worth," he said, "I'm glad you're back."

"I wish I could answer I'm glad to *be* back," I said, my tone low. Lifting my face, I met his eyes squarely. "Bringing me here might be a costly mistake, Malik."

He tilted his face slightly, considering. "I think not," he replied slowly. "What do you fear, Atan?"

[43]

I stiffened. "I fear to fail in my duty, my Lord Captain Commander."

"You fear . . . what?"

"I fear to die without honor, my Lord Captain Commander."

"And?"

"I fear to live without honor, my Lord Captain Commander."

"You need a haircut, First Captain Vanyar," Malik said, his heavy lips lifting slightly. "But, as ever, your King and I both need you. Come. It's time."

Waiting for his signal with the patience of a saint, Innes placed his hands on the gold handles. His dark, hooded eyes never left his master. Innes' strong capable hands readied, awaiting his lord's command to open the heavy doors. As Malik's personal servant, he'd not cross the boundary into the vast conference room. He left the military life behind him, in another age.

Malik dropped his chin, once, in a nod.

Innes swung wide the doors. Side by side, we strode forward in marching step, into the vast vaulted and buttressed conference chamber. With my head high, and my hand gripping my hilt, I gazed strictly forward, my eyes carefully blank, seeing yet not. My spine ramrod straight, none watching might find fault in my precise military bearing. *I was an Atan.* I was . . . I *am* First Captain Vanyar of the Weksan'Atan and the Lord Captain Commander's second.

Like a spirit, Innes bowed us through the solid oak before silently shutting their expanse behind us. With a hollow boom, the comforts of a simple life closed hard behind me. For me, I could no longer turn back. Why did my throat suddenly dry up? Damn, but I needed a drink.

In the Old Tongue, Atan meant 'loyal'. Only the best of the best were invited to join the King's royal Weksan'Atan, his private army. Humans, Clan, Centaurs, Minotaurs, and Griffins competed every year to be among those tested. Only those individuals, the rare few with the deadly skills, the high intelligence and the proven loyalty made the cut into His Majesty's Weksan'Atan.

The King's Royal Secret Police.

The royal army protected the realm, the royal navy her shores. Liveried guards shielded the city and the palace at the same time

[44]

the City Watch protected the city from thieves, miscreants, common murderers, rapists, and dishonest innkeepers. Highwaymen roamed the nation's road system and protected the vulnerable travelers, merchants, pilgrims, peasant class and the occasional foreigner. Local aristocrats governed their own territories with their soldiers and knights, maintaining the King's peace on their estates in his name.

However, the Weksan'Atan protected His Majesty, his family and sniffed out the machinations of our enemy to the north, the Raithin Mawrn. Some likened us to the realm's Home Defense Ministry. We did indeed defend King and home with our blood and our lives. We acted as the King's sword, his justice, and his mercy. Although we often neglected that last portion, we fiercely considered ourselves his devoted right hand. As obligated to one another as we were toward our liege lord and King, our blood oaths included protecting and serving our own. No other military arm claimed that privilege. Our savage loyalty to each other bordered on the fanatic.

We'd kill–or die–for one another.

Like a jealous step-brother, the Raithin Mawrn connived unceasingly to overthrow or undermine our nation's roots. They raided across our common border stealing horses, cattle, women and a pig or ten. Their suicidal raids constantly blew up villages, roadways, civilians, or the passing patrol.

Patriots, they called themselves. Terrorists, we called them. We Atani ferreted them out, killed or executed them, and comforted the victims of their plots. Until now, no member of the royal family ever came in contact with these rats. Our spilled blood ensured it.

As I stalked forward at Malik's right shoulder, I stiffened my spine into severe military precision, and pondered what it meant to be Atani. Loyal to none save the King and the order. Willing to kill or be killed for the same. Finding no mate fit enough to withstand the rigors of life with an Atan. Never regretting the offspring we'd never see.

As a child, I ever challenged my Shifting talents, and grew high in my Clan's estimation. I practiced my art, studying the anatomy of all creatures, and used my imagination when I had no other recourse. Most Shifters needed time to focus on the object or creature they wished to change into, and the change emerged over a period of several seconds. Unlike my Clan, I changed forms in an instant and constantly learned how to mold my body into anything at all. Many tried to imitate me, and their attempts never failed to make me laugh.

At the ripe old age of ten, I killed my first Raithin Mawrn. A wild fanatic with a hand-held bomb threatened to blow up the five children he'd roped to himself. He'd lit the fuse and it grew shorter by the second. The parents of the children screamed in panic as army soldiers and Atani sought to convince him that his demands would be met should he merely pinch the tiny flame.

I don't recall his ultimatum, only his leering, fish-belly white face and drooling, gaping mouth. I changed myself into a black adder and slithered, unseen, behind him. My fangs in his foot surprised him into dropping his bomb. It fell from his fingers amid the legs of the crying, frightened children.

Before it struck the ground and exploded, I changed, instantaneously, into a falcon. Catching the bomb on the fly, I lifted it, winging hard, wheeling, over the heads of the soldiers and watching crowd, the spark hissing balefully as the flame burned the fuse. I had perhaps ten, maybe twelve seconds. If I was lucky.

Fortunately, I knew the vicinity. I beat hard for a nearby lake, banking over it just as the flame sputtered toward the explosives inside the box. Flinging it as hard as I could toward the water, I folded my wings. Dropping like a stone, I banked hard left and swooped into a nearby thicket of oak trees. With a stout trunk between me and the shattering explosion and cascade of lake water climbing high, I weathered the bomb with only ringing ears and a ruffling of my feathers.

The Raithin Mawrn died under my venom, his skin turning blacker than his soul before his final convulsions killed him. He collapsed in his ropes with the furious parents kicking his corpse and the soldiers cutting free the frightened children. The King, hale and healthy then, rewarded me with a pouch of gold and a pat on the head. The children grew up and remain, to this day, my friends.

At the elderly age of fifteen, I passed all the tests and won my right to wear the Death's Head ring, the Atani symbol. All Atani wore them on their left hands: the toothily grinning human skull with its huge empty eye sockets. The Death's Head signified both death for our enemies and life for those we loved.

Even in exile, mine never left my finger.

The years passed as they tended to do. I rose high under Malik's new command and killed or imprisoned the enemy. I proved my worth and stepped up in rank and his friendship. Worthy of both, the King himself praised my skills.

Ever the exception to the rule, I rose swifter than most and fell harder than anyone. No one in the Atan ever screwed up. Such incompetency was forbidden. In my turn, I cost a dozen Atani their lives through sheer stupidity and my own arrogance. I killed the soldiers under my command and succeeded in turning every Atani brother against me in one swift act. *One day 1 ll be memorialized in a statue somewhere,* I thought. The inscription should read: *Do as you are told and absolutely do not do as he did.*

My thoughts jangled to a halt as Malik stalked toward the head of the table. As though roped like that long ago fanatic to the children, I strode at his shoulder in perfect lock-step. The inhabitants of his command center instantly snapped to attention. Faces front as though they stared straight ahead, yet I felt their eyes slide sideways toward me. I heard their thoughts, their surprise, and their condemnation: *What the bloody hell is he doing here?*

At the head of Malik's huge conference table, Padraig'al'amar'dar bowed his head over his clenched fist thumped against his bare chest. Malik's First Lieutenant, and my replacement as second-in-command, Padraig saluted his Lord Captain Commander. A Centaur of Malik's high bloodline, Padraig's equine body was the color of rich mahogany, his legs, tail and shaggy hair as black as midnight. Four perfect white stockings rose halfway to his knees. He stepped into my boots the instant I departed with my Atan brother's enmity like hot breath on my neck. Of all, Padraig stood the most to lose upon my return. He'd dare not kill me, not openly at least. His dark eyes followed me as he withdrew from the reports he'd been perusing.

"My Lord Captain," he said, his hooves echoing hollowly against the tile despite the crowded room. His fingers flicked parchment toward Malik. "These reports gather the latest intel from our watchers. Something's happened."

Malik arrived at the head of the table, with me still held tight to him by that invisible rope. He frowned down at the reports Padraig indicated. "Indeed," he murmured.

He picked up a parchment and read, his dark eyes flicking back and forth. He chose to read for himself the latest news rather than be informed by his subordinates. He dropped that particular report, only to pick up another. The skin over his tight cheeks darkened, telling me the news was anything but good. Malik kept his emotions in check, yet I read his face as easily as he read the reports. Malik wasn't happy. And when Malik wasn't happy, ain't nobody happy.

I waited, patient, my arms behind my back, at ease, waiting for him to finish. I surveyed the room without appearing to, my eyes slightly lowered. Most present watched me rather than their supreme commander, lips tightened. Those with beaks rather than lips parted them as watchful eyes regarded me with curiosity or resentment or a weird combination of both. I felt no welcome, no gratitude, yet I also felt little hostility.

I concentrated. Expanding what little magic talent I owned, I touched the room's occupants. Most regarded me with a neutral curiosity, much as one might expect from visitors viewing a zoo exhibit. Many soldiers present I didn't know, nor did they know me. They'd only heard of my exploits. And regarded me much as they might that selfsame zoo critter. I felt much condemnation from those who did know me . . . yet no open animosity, no desire to flay me alive.

Before I could probe further, Padraig eyed me sidelong and scowled, as though he knew I tested the room. Before I could lift my lip in a sneer, informing him of what I thought of his knowledge, Malik stirred. He sighed, and looked up, his dark face bland and devoid of expression.

"How inappropriate," he murmured. I knew he didn't speak of the reports.

Padraig stiffened and looked anywhere but at me. I breathed deep and released my magic. I resumed my military bearing and pretended Padraig and his animosity didn't exist. I glanced around the chamber, finding little had changed in the past two years.

Malik's command center was just that. Half the size of Caer Bannog's parade grounds, his oblong-shaped, high-walled audience chamber could easily fit twenty-plus Centaurs. High-pillared perches provided room for almost thirty Griffins, and yet could also comfortably accommodate a troop of Minotaurs and humans. A special chair at the head of the grand conference table allowed the King to attend these meetings in comfort.

Two Minotaur guards flanked the huge doors onto the great central garden where serving girls laughed and filled their pitchers from the fundamental fountain. Hemmed in by high walls and guarded by all the kingdom's myriad species on its ramparts, the courtyard's jungle garden hosted lush and towering plant-life, singing birds, and an escaped monkey or three. These defenses provided plenty of privacy for the commander who wished for the spying eavesdropper's hearing and the lip-reader's eyes to fail utterly.

Flanking the table stood a trio of Centaur sergeants, two commanders of human cavalry, and three Griffin flight leaders. Clan Chieftain of the mighty Minotaur nation, Ba'al'amawer, in his purple and white tunic, tan breeches, and twin swords belted to his broad hips stood at Padraig's right hand. His emblem of the Eastern Sun rising in splendor marked each shoulder as cloak clasps, his dark scarlet mantle falling to his booted heels. He too, saluted formally as did the Minotaur guards at the huge teak doors inlaid with gold that led to the garden beyond.

I caught the eye of Lieutenant Cian, a member of my own Einion'nalad Clan, and offered a quick nod of greeting. We both stood close in blood to our own Clan Chief, and played together as children. A tall Shifter with reddish-blonde hair that fell well past his shoulders; his pale skin contrasted sharply with his dark brown eyes. Slender, almost to the point of emaciation, he owned strong, broad shoulders. Wearing a black tunic with the Death's Head symbol on each shoulder, and black breeches; his dark gold cloak fell to his spurs. He stood behind Ba'al'amawer and his Minotaur guard with a neutral expression, and eyes dark and hooded. Alarm bells rang inside my head when he didn't return my acknowledgment. His face in shadow, I felt those eyes on me and the weight of his stare. Standing at military ease with his hands clasped behind his back, Cian all but vanished into the gloom. Only the clasp at his cloak, the Tiger's Eye emblem of the Clan, gleamed under the light.

Malik's attention shifted to a folded message, doubled upon itself as though held within a tight claw. Unrolling it, he read quickly, his shadowed eyes flicking back and forth. Malik's frown turned into a dangerous scowl. He glanced up and gazed down the long table.

"They've stopped? Why?"

Padraig flipped yet another parchment though his fingers. "We believe, my Lord Captain, that our Princess Iyumi has fallen ill."

Malik's eyes narrowed. "Ill?"

"This is what our spies in place tell us," Ba'al'amawer replied with the famous calm the Minotaurs possessed. Despite their close relationship to bulls, Minotaurs seldom acted out of anger, passion or sheer joy. Slow to anger, slow to laugh, and also slow to act with haste or without thought, the Minotaur presence in the Atan prevented many impulsive acts against the Raithin scum. Had they not preached, and enforced, peace and logic, we Atani might well have killed ourselves numerous times in our haste to slaughter the hated beserkers.

"The Raithin Mawrn idiots dare not move for fear of harming her. She lies in a faint within caverns as they sought refuge within, and they've sent desperate messages home."

"Home? How?"

"Birds, my Lord Captain. Messenger pigeons."

"I see."

"I have begged the services of Queen X'an'ada, asking that her Faeries to kill these birds before they reach their destination."

[50]

"Good luck with that," Malik replied. "You know the Faeries hate killing things."

"They also hold She Who Hears in high regard," Ba'al'amawer said. "They wish her home as much as we do."

"Uh, huh." Malik's gaze dropped to the table. He flicked through the parchments, one after the other; his hands and eyes never still.

"Why was she abducted in the first place?"

My question dropped among them like an Raithin Mawrn bomb. Silence descended with a thud as all eyes swiveled toward me. Shock reverberated throughout, as though I'd blasphemed rather than asked a question.

Malik raised his right hand. "I haven't taken the time to explain to First Captain Vanyar the circumstances regarding the princess's abduction. He hasn't yet been briefed."

Under the guarded silence, Malik picked up a quill and fiddled with it for a long moment. He made a notation on the parchment with a frown, and glanced up. "Lieutenant Padraig, I trust you've briefed the rest of the staff?"

"Indeed, my Lord Captain. All stand ready."

"Good." Malik made another notation on his report.

"What haven't you told me?" I demanded.

"The child's been born," Malik said, returning his gaze to the table, his fingers fiddling with his quill. He made a brief notation, and the scritch of the pen shrieked across my nerve endings.

"I see," I replied, my tone neutral. Inwardly, I sagged. *Oh, gods.*

I saw indeed. The child prophesied centuries ago, and awaited with both fierce eagerness and terrible dread by both countries. The child blessed by the gods to bring together the split countries, Bryn'Cairdhans and Raithin Mawr, as one nation again. Magic, non-magic, human, non-human—all bonded under one flag, one brotherhood, one king. I remembered the prophecy, having often read it in ancient manuscripts during my school days.

> *From the north the red will rise,*
> *Under her wings grace shall fall.*
> *Seek ye the child of innocence,*

The holy defender, the chosen of the light,
Of purity born, of blood she seeks.
By north and by south,
Brothers not of blood, but of bond, bear the flame,
Under the dark and the light, the shadow will rise.
Three cycles shall pass
From the dark side of the moon.
By fire and steel, magic falters,
Kissed by fate, by fate answered
When the moon and the sun
Are joined as one,
From tears of strife, from the bitter ashes,
From sorrow and from rage
That what was once parted
Shall again be one.

The Raithin Mawrn feared, and hated, our powers of magic. Those of us who walked like men but shifted shape into anything at all both confused and terrified them. In a land of humans only, parents told their children tales of bloodshed and murder in the night by Minotaurs. Their belief that Griffins flew in search of unborn babes to devour, ripping them from their mothers' wombs, answered all their superstitious questions. Our Centaurs and Shape-Shifters, and even the laughing Faeries, were evil, vomited from hell to plague their nation.

As a land that fostered magic and encouraged its growth, we accepted the half-bred as brothers. The Centaurs, the Minotaurs, and the Griffins lived and worked with humans as equals–intelligent beings with talents and magic powers much like our own. The Raithin Mawrn envisioned our destruction. We hoped and prayed for peace. They saw the prophetic child as the sign the end of Bryn'Cairdha drew nigh. We saw the child as our salvation and our truth.

Stirring from my reverie, I glanced up. "That's why they took her. She knows where the child is."

Malik straightened slowly. His hooded eyes met mine as he nodded, his right hand still marking a spot on his map. "Of course,

Princess Iyumi will refuse to divulge the child's location. The Raithin Mawrn will do anything to get their hands upon it."

"Do we even know what species the child is?"

As the Atani council waited, a smile rose to Malik's eyes and no further. "Her Highness knows, certainly."

"But she didn't tell anyone."

Malik grimaced. "Unfortunately, Her Royal Highness rode out with only a pair of guards for protection."

"Why?"

"She, um–"

"Malik."

He straightened and took his hand from his map. "She thought to find the child through secrecy and stealth, bring it back here before anyone knew of its birth."

"What happened?"

"Somehow, the Raithin Mawrn knew and sent a secret patrol of their own. They set their trap and she bumbled into it. They took her."

"How in the name of all the gods could that happen?" I asked, my fury rising. "We're supposed to protect her. We dropped the ball on our most sacred duty?"

"You'd know more about that than any of us."

The anonymous voice filled the silence my words left behind. I clenched my fists, searching for the owner of the voice. Buttresses high and wide held up a vast ceiling, and encouraged a hall that echoed. Sounds bounced off clay tiles and discouraged eavesdroppers. Thus voices tended to resonate from everywhere and anywhere. As crowded as the room was, I couldn't discern who spoke. I only determined its source was human. Griffin voices had a singular pitch and nothing could imitate a Minotaur's deep rumble. I knew a human voice when I heard it; however, many humans crowded Malik's command center.

"Chill, bro," Malik muttered, his eyes still lowered as though he perused report after report, his hands never still. "It's all good."

"It's hardly–"

"Our enemies have magic."

Ba'al'amawer's deep voice rose like a small earthquake. His muzzle and great horns lifted as his deep-set eyed swiveled around the great chamber. None dared meet them, but dropped in deference to the huge Minotaur with the crossed swords on his breasts and the twin hilts beneath his enormous man-like hands. They might be slow to anger, but a Minotaur enraged might be equated with a high-mountain avalanche: steep, cold and as implacable. Once hit, one died under its rolling, impervious menace.

Malik and me, and even Padraig, turned toward him, aghast.

"What?" I snapped.

Ba'al'amawer's enormous bull shoulders rose and fell in a calm Minotaur shrug. "They fear what we have, the magic powers we call our own. Despite this, some control it, use it, and yes, hide it. Through it, they saw the princess depart into what she thought was hidden. Thus they sent the crude spies to track her down. And seize her royal person."

"They have magic?" First Lieutenant Grey Mist's voice rose amid the muttered babble that rumbled from a hundred throats. A huge, grizzled Griffin with more experience than any save Malik and I for fighting the Raithin Mawrn spoke, his voice rising on a sharp crescendo. "Those bloody hypocrites. They slay our folk while believing magic evil, yet they–"

"Thus they took her," Padraig said into the malicious silence, his tone icy. "They hurt her."

"She's faking it," I said quickly, before the room might erupt into outrage. "She's delaying them."

Malik nodded at the same time Ba'al'amawer rumbled, "Our princess was unharmed when they abducted her."

"She's too smart to fight them," I said. "She's forcing them to slow down. By delaying them, we can catch up and rescue her."

Ba'al'amawer's bull brown eyes watched me with quiet assurance, his curving horns rising from his head all but touching one another at the tips. His bovine ears twitched occasionally, and his muzzle failed to smile. Minotaurs could smile if they wanted to; but it just never looked quite right. To those unfamiliar with Minotaurs, or their facial expressions, it appeared much like the baring of broad teeth.

[54]

His adjutants, Raga and Muljier, flanked him, wearing the same twin swords, long cloaks and Eastern Sun clasps. They ignored me as though I was but a serf and beneath their notice. In better times, I raised more than one tankard of ale with them, sharing laughs and lewd jokes about our superiors. Once friends, now enemies, they remembered Dalziel as though it happened yesterday.

"Our until-recently absent brother may be quite correct," the Chief rumbled. "Our adored princess is as conniving as a cat at a mouse hole. Our eyes in the sky report more Raithin Mawrn have crossed our borders and ride hard toward the heart of our land."

Malik raised his eyes from his reports. "Whose eyes?"

"I ordered a Griffin patrol to seek out the Shifters," Ba'al'amawer continued, his tone mild. "Those in closest contact with the enemy. They sent a messenger." His huge head swiveled over his massive shoulder at the same moment his ears twitched. "She should be here–ah! She arrives."

Malik's human door wardens opened the huge double doors onto the broad stone and tile patio lined with a low stone wall. A huge pillar perch stood atop the wall where a winged messenger might await the Lord Captain Commander's pleasure.

At Malik's gesture, the slender light brown Griffin with her ever pristine mane of white feathers dropped to the floor and furled her huge wings over her shoulders. She saluted. Her clenched taloned fist rested over her breast as her beak dropped, granting obeisance to her superior. A light chain hung around her wide lion shoulders with the emblem of her rank resting against her feathered chest.

She s a First Lieutenant now, I observed, by its lion's head emblem. She advanced in rank since I saw her last.

"Report, Lieutenant Sky Dancer."

Sky Dancer saluted again. "My Lord Captain Commander. The Raithin Mawrn have halted. They've Her Highness in custody, yet they've stopped a hundred leagues from the border. They've taken shelter within caves, fearing we may fall upon their rear. Reports indicate Her Highness has fallen ill."

"As I've just heard," Malik snapped. "What else?"

"By the conversations our Clan spies overhear, my Lord Captain," Sky Dancer continued smartly, "they speculate that Princess Iyumi has created this illness as a delaying tactic. Yet, they dare not continue should they be proven wrong. She lies in a faint, and they haven't the strength to force her to move. They are but a small number of simple humans, four at most. They need help."

"Someone is coming to meet them," I said, forcing Sky Dancer to glance my way. "Right?"

When I spoke, Sky Dancer recognized my voice. Her face swiveled, her eagle's beak slackening in disbelief. Taking in my Atani uniform, my unnatural good health and standing at Malik's right hand, her amber eagle's eyes widened in un-military fashion. Like all Atani, she hated me on sight, though no Griffin died at Dalziel. Atan brothers died, and I yet lived and breathed. That was condemnation enough in her keen raptor's vision.

"Who?" Malik asked.

With swift precision, Sky Dancer pretended I didn't exist and faced Malik as though I hadn't spoken. "The Raithin Mawrn wait for their heir apparent. He's on his way to take command and escort Her Highness with royal pomp into Raithin Mawr."

"Prince Flynn himself?"

"Indeed, my Lord Captain. Our spies inform us he intends to wed her and bind our two nations under one."

"That's half the prophecy," Malik muttered, scowling and staring at his maps. "Where, Sky Dancer?"

Half-flying, half-leaping toward the table, Sky Dancer bent her huge head toward the strewn maps and papers, her wicked beak parted. Furling her angel's wings, her lion tail lashing from side to side, her right talon rose, hovered, and then lit upon a point midway between our position and the border of Raithin Mawr. "There, my Lord Captain."

"He's not even close to succeeding," Malik muttered, peering down. "Does he even realize we can drop on him before he can take a shit?"

"No, my Lord Captain." Sky Dancer raised her beak, her fierce eyes wild with enthusiasm. My presence failed to deter that or her confidence. "They think themselves secret and undiscovered. My

[56]

unit remains high, among the clouds or hiding in the sun. They've no clue they've been detected and followed. Sir."

"Of course they hide themselves," I said, earning myself a raptor glare. "They know we've eyes in the sky. What are their exact coordinates?"

Sky Dancer replied to Malik, not me. "My Lord Captain, they've taken shelter within the caves along the Khai River. Those beneath the towers, sir."

Malik turned away, seeking the caves Sky Dancer spoke of on his maps. His fingers traced as his brow furrowed, his full lips thinning in concentration. Ba'al'amawer politely and respectfully, his bull head nodding his regard, pushed me aside to add his opinion as several officers, Padraig included, leaned forward to see better.

With those around the table intent upon the map, only I caught the sign.

The instant Malik's back turned, Sky Dancer's hardened eagle's eyes met mine. Her raptor's beak slammed shut. Black-tipped ears canted backwards as her lion's tail lashed behind her in a short, rapid back-and-forth manner. 'Twas clearly Griffin body-speech for: *I m pissed but royally.'*

Ah, so the predator sought her prey. I stilled my eyes from rolling. How dramatic.

Behind Malik and out of his direct sight, Sky Dancer's predator eyes promised swift retribution. Her right fist rose as her naked talons crisscrossed in a rapid-fire sequence. I recognized that ancient sign–vengeance. A dire warning, a singular promise. I'd die the instant Princess Iyumi returned home and this mission closed.

Her flat, raptor's gaze never left mine, nor my challenging response left hers. Forget that I saved her from an Raithin Mawrn trap not so many years ago. Forget the time I changed into a Griffin and flew wingtip to wingtip with her in a dance of wind and sun and clouds. Forget how I shed my blood alongside hers for our King and sovereign nation. Forget how she flirted with me...pleaded I remain a Griffin for life to be her mate.

I straightened my spine, answering Sky Dancer glare for glare. She wasn't at Dalziel. I was. She heard the rumors. I knew the truth.

Atani soldiers died while hostages survived. She cared little for the lives I saved that day and mourned my soldiers who sacrificed themselves willingly.

Sky Dancer stiffened suddenly, and her wicked talons dropped as Malik spun on his heels. His hooves clicked sharply on the slate tiles as his tail whipped sideways in the wind of his rapid movement. I always suspected Malik had a third eye that watched all behind his very back. Perhaps his magical powers informed him of the malicious activity his eyes failed to see. I know my own magic wasn't that puissant. Mine was geared more for tricks and sleight of hand than Malik's subtlety.

His hooded gaze caught Sky Dancer within their dark depths as though reading her mind and her animosity. Her beak rose, and her eagle's eyes lost their savagery. Resuming their military, under-inspection blankness, her amber raptor's eyes narrowed to stare straight ahead. Her right foot hit the mosaic tile at the same moment her angry tail ceased its lash.

I knew Malik too well to be taken by his innocent *1-don t-know-what s-beneath-my-nose* façade. He knew immediately Sky Dancer threatened me, and she knew full well he knew. Still she faced him, unrepentant, fearless, uncompromising. She had a backbone, all right.

Beneath his scrutiny, Sky Dancer stood at attention, her eyes front, talons on the tile, and her lion's tail stilled. "My Lord Captain Commander."

"Do we have a problem here, Lieutenant?" Malik asked.

"No, my Lord Captain."

"What do you want, Lieutenant?"

"My next orders, my Lord Captain."

"Good," he replied, his tone icy.

He turned back to his conference table and officers, his hands clasped behind him. Sky Dancer stood as though under inspection, silent and well-disciplined. I turned my back on her to squeeze my way between officers to have a look at the map myself–and drew up sharply.

Cian watched me with the same predatory intensity that marked Sky Dancer's vengeful eyes.

[58]

My blood grew as cold as Malik's voice.

"If Prince Flynn runs his horses into the ground," Malik continued, his attitude frosty, "he could easily arrive at the caves by sunset. We must have our people and plans in place before then. That gives us only six hours."

One of the Griffin flight leaders stirred, his feathers ruffling. "My Lord Captain," said Commander Lightning Fork. "Permission to speak."

"Of course, Commander."

"A Shifter brought word of a storm rolling toward the Khai River Valley."

"That may slow Flynn down," Padraig observed, running his hand through his dark locks.

Malik brightened slightly. "It may be enough to give us the edge. We must conduct this mission with utmost quiet and secrecy, people. We dare not alarm her kidnappers, for they may kill her out of hand. Should they get wind of our approach, they may seek to hide behind her, cowards, knowing we'd never risk her life."

Malik again studied the map on the table before him, took up his quill and scritched yet another notation.

"We must have absolute surprise," he said, raising his head. "Our numbers are strong; our Shifters must hide in various guises and report on every word, every movement and every fart. The Griffins' unit will mark Flynn's progress toward the river. Communication is essential. We *must* know where he is at all times."

He nodded at the Griffin flight leaders: Commanders Storm Cloud, Lightning Fork and Swift Wing. "We need eyes from above watching their every move. Order your Griffins to maintain contact with the Clan on the ground. We need their eyes and their speed as messengers."

The hairs on the back of my neck stood at attention. Cian hadn't ceased his hypnotic stare. *What is that boy up to?*

"I have Lieutenant Gaear and a dozen Shifters in various guises nearby, listening and watching," Chief Ba'al'amawer rumbled. "Their current reports are right there, my Lord Captain. The four spies haven't stuck their noses from the cave since they went in, though whether they suspect they've been compromised isn't yet known. Five units of cavalry ride with my Minotaur infantry, marching hard toward the Khai River."

Malik nodded. "Now tell me something I don't know."

"We have but ten days to the dawn when the sun and moon rise together, my Lord Captain," Ba'al'amawer replied. "According to His Majesty's esteemed scholars, the dark side of the moon occurred three months ago – three cycles. The tenth day from today marks the end of the third cycle."

Malik nodded. "You're absolutely correct, my friend. Dawn must rise on that evil day with the child and Princess Iyumi in our hands."

"My Lord Captain," said Lieutenant Wind Warrior, a Griffin with an unusual black mane that ran under his belly. "Perhaps our Griffins should attack, hard, now, drive Prince Flynn away–"

Malik's shaking his heavy head forced the dark, grizzled veteran to slowly shut his beak.

"I wish to humiliate Flynn," Malik said slowly, grimly. "I plan to gaze into his pitiful, cowardly eyes and name him craven. I'll send him home to his despicable sire with his tail between his legs and a message: 'Keep your filthy hands off our Princess, our King, and our land or I'll personally cut both your throats.'"

In the tense silence, Malik jerked his head at me.

I stepped forward smartly as Chieftain Ba'al'amawer retreated aside with his massive head bowed. All jumped swiftly when Malik was irritated.

"Van, I want you–

A scream rose, deafening across the chamber. "Die as she died!"

As the officers around the table slewed about in surprise, taken off-guard, I shoved Malik hard with my shoulder and my limited magic. Like the others, he first gaped in confusion, his eyes seeking the threat, his mouth open. Despite Malik's size and four legs, he staggered under my charge, his hooves unable to catch on the slick, slate tiles. With arms flailing, he slid several feet, well away from me and the impending attack.

Flames burst over the conference table, forcing the Atani officers into recoiling and burning Malik's precious reports. Padraig shouted something I couldn't hear as the Griffin flight leaders screamed, leaping backward, wings flaring, and smoke curling from their feathered manes. Ba'al'amawer's guards bellowed and rushed Cian, catching him low across his waist and forcing him down as the ball of fire raced across the huge chamber.

The flames passed over the heads and horns of the Minotaurs, dismissed Padraig out of hand, and rushed upon me with the speed of a striking snake. It streaked toward my chest and homed in, leaving behind blackened wood, ash and an outraged, yelling Atani council,

Before an eye might blink, I dropped to my belly. Having worn the shape of an angry serpent a hundred times, my skill in dodging that very creature outstripped the ball by several, important seconds. The fireball passed harmlessly over my head.

I felt its heat crisp my neck, my back, and its flames licking my breeches and warming my boots. Its crackling evil snicked into my ears, its hungry mouths seeking nourishment from the air, and, having missed its target, sought new prey. It passed beyond me in an eye-blink and into empty space, harmless.

Cian, you stupia—

A rising scream of agony rose high, overwhelming the shouts loud in the chaotic chamber. I scrambled halfway to my knees, confused. What did the fire find? Who stood behind me? *Gods, no—*

Still at disciplined attention Sky Dancer waited, obviously unable to see the danger streaking toward her through the tangle of Minotaur and Centaur bodies. Cian's deadly magic, his hatred and lust for vengeance missed me and honed in on the next viable body. An innocent whose only crime was to be in that chamber at that moment.

I whirled around, sitting up, cursing, my mouth dry. The fireball struck her dead on, setting her feathered mane alight and spreading to her face, her lion body—her tawny, trim frame. Within a fraction of a second, she lit up like a holiday bonfire.

[61]

Before the flames caught a firm hold, or bit too deeply into her lion fur, I altered. *Water.* Only water might swamp those wicked flames and cool her burns. Two or three large buckets might suffice, but I never did anything by halves.

My body, shaped into of a wall of water, cascaded over Sky Dancer and drenched her from her beak to her tail. I swept away and drowned the flames, engulfing her body and prevented new fires to birth from loose embers. I hoped my cool and soothing currents prevented Cian's attack from seizing a firm hold. The fire blackened her body, scorched away her feathered mane. Raw patches of flesh gleamed reddish and angry across her neck, chest and back. The flames scorched up her wings, charring her feathers halfway to their furthest tips. What remained smoked lazily as she weakly waved her wings, trying to remain upright and on her charred, taloned feet.

Was I in time? Did Cian's vengeance take out one I loved? For, despite her hatred of me, I did indeed love her. I didn't exactly have eyes to see with, but I felt her heart racing beneath my touch, heard her sharp intake of breath. I felt her struggles to breathe beneath my weight as her pulse beat a frantic rhythm. She drew in ragged gasps, agony widening her eagle's eyes and beak. Thank all the gods there are . . . She was alive. *Alive.*

The fireball Cian cast was out, anyway, as I gathered myself back into my own body. I retook the water into myself, feeling slightly woozy, and exhausted. Very seldom did a Shifter change into inanimate objects. While not exactly forbidden by the Clan, it wasn't exactly condoned, either. Too many Shifters lost their lives by not understanding what made up the object they changed into. A granite boulder, for instance, didn't have a heart to beat or to send life-giving blood through the body that still needed it. Thus, a foolish Shifter died from suffocation or lack of proper circulation by staying too long within that shape. Biological, living creatures worked best.

One of the most dangerous objects for a Shifter to change into was water. Liquid tended to evaporate, get lost between cracks to vanish. The Shifter might not get them back. Instant death for me should my brain, or my heart, or my liver not return when I reverted

[62]

to myself. Though I retained the shape for only mere seconds, not long enough for my heart or lungs to wither, I knew I stood too close to that great black barrier: death.

As I breathed deep, gasping, my head spinning, I discovered I'd survive. With a rapid check of my arms, legs and face, I surmised what remained of me in Sky Dancer's feathers and fur wasn't life threatening. I still owned everything I was born with, including my shaggy hair, but I lost necessary energy.

Sky Dancer collapsed.

I caught her heavy head in my arms at the same instant Malik screamed. "Take him! Take him down!"

I heard the thrashing of bodies as Minotaur, Griffin and human officers threw themselves at Cian. He went under, hardly struggling, buried under a mass of furious Atans with Padraig shouting for ropes. Bellowing with rage, Ba'al'amawer led his troops into the fray, wading in and forcing Cian facedown into the mosaic tiled floor with his tremendous fists and weight. I caught a swift glimpse of Cian's bloodied face before a Minotaur smacked him upside his head with one very hard bovine fist.

Cian thus attended to, his powers neutralized, I collapsed on my butt beside Sky Dancer. I pulled her beak into my chest, trying to hold her still with my arms around her undamaged head. She gasped and choked, her tawny eyes wild, and glazed with shock. Consumed by raw panic, she swept her talons toward me. I avoided them deftly, my arms tightening about her yet unburned and pristine feathered cheeks.

All magic had healing powers within it. Many magicians earned their living as healers. Those, like Malik, whose power surpassed most, might bring one back from the brink of death. My own magic wasn't puissant, but I knew enough to stem a flow of blood, and keep a victim alive long enough for the medics to arrive. I also knew how to ease pain.

As though willing my body to change forms, I dropped my mind into a trance. I zeroed in on the agony she felt. Her pain was mine. Her panic mine own. "Sky Dancer!" I yelled, both verbally and within her mind. "Baby girl, you're gonna be all right. I promise, you're gonna be fine. Calm down, baby, I've got you. You're all right, just calm; and be still. Shhh, baby. Just hush, you're all right."

My left hand holding her head still, my right crept around her beak to rest between Sky Dancer's wild, panicked raptor eyes. I sent in my power, watching closely as her beak slowly closed. Her talon relaxed and opened, no longer trying to snag my intestines. Limited though my healing magic may be, it was enough. I shunted her agony away, aside, and effectively killed her suffering. With soothing magic, I halted the burns from creating further damage and quieted her outraged nerve endings.

She calmed under my words and my hands, yet her raptor's eyes rolled in their sockets. Sky Dancer hissed, her survival instincts informing her the danger hadn't yet passed. She'd fight until death claimed her. I felt her body tense, knew she coiled her muscles in preparation to rise. I held on, tightening my grip as she scrambled, her claws raking the slate tiles. No longer in pain she may be, but if she moved too much she'd increased the damage done by the flames by a hundred-fold.

She tried to rise, regain her feet, and her black-tipped tail struck the floor time and again. She thrashed, yowling like a cat in heat, her front talons raking furrows in the slate beneath her. Only my tight grip on her head kept her down. In her desperate struggle to survive, she may yet gut me with those deadly talons. I did like my intestines where they were, however, though they constantly complained about the food. Her Death's Head ring, shaped to fit a talon, flashed in my eyes and made me blink.

Help! Why isn't anyone helping me?

I jerked my head at Commander Storm Cloud, silently demanding his strength and assistance. Wings flaring wide, he leaped over the blackened table, calling over his broad shoulder for Lieutenant Wind Warrior. His stronger talons held Sky Dancer down with grips to her unharmed front legs and shoulder as the black-maned Lieutenant lay his larger, heavy body across hers, his tremendous wings wide and shading us all. He deftly avoided her raking claws, pressed his powerful front talons onto her unburned lion hips and ribcage, and stilled her efforts to rise. Her tufted tail lashed across his beak, but he accepted the punishment with equanimity.

I knew the Atan enough to exchange salutes and the occasional "Nice day, what?", and accepted the respectful dip of his beak in lieu of a more formal gesture. Wind Warrior, also bearing the lion's head emblem, eyed me sidelong without animosity and some humor as he held Sky Dancer down. "Good job, sir," he muttered, from the side of his beak. "Incredible instincts you have."

I raised a faint grin. "I got lucky."

"Say what?" Storm Cloud asked, his attention diverted. Although his talons still pressed Sky Dancer into the solid slate tiles, his face and focus turned toward the ruckus surrounding Cian, Malik, Padraig and an uncounted army of Atani officers and enlisted cavalry soldiers.

"Is that a luck Faery on your shoulder?" Wind Warrior asked. "I need one, if you have one to spare, that is. Sir."

I offered Wind Warrior a lopsided grin before Sky Dancer all but heaved me onto my back, freeing herself from my grip. I kept my breath for her, and didn't answer him.

"Dancer, honey," I muttered into her ear, leaving the stronger Griffins to hold her down. My hands delved deep into the soft feathers of her cheeks and forced her glazed eyes to look into mine. "It's all good. Help is on the way."

"Enemies!" she screamed, struggling. "Protect him!"

"No, baby, the enemies are taken. Calm now, my love, calm and be still. There's my girl. You're safe."

My powers, waning quickly, did the trick at the last. She relaxed a fraction, her front talons lowering slowly. Her tawny eyes opened, rolled up at me. She recognized me, remembered our infatuation, and forgot how she hated me. They fastened upon mine as her beak widened in a weak raptor grin. I found a genuine smile for her and stroked my left hand over her black-tufted ears.

"Hey, kid," I murmured, my fingers delving deep into the soft feathers of her cheek. "How's by you?"

"Van?" she asked, her eyes rolling like a pole-axed horse. "I saw . . . I think . . . did you come see me?"

[65]

"Why, yes, I did, girl. Don't you remember?"

"No. Where's my feet? I can't feel my feet!"

She struggled again, weaker, trying to thrash and regain her footing. Her tail smacked once again Wind Warrior upside his head, and he sighed. His weight never flagged, his razor-tipped talons deftly avoiding her torn and bloody body with a skill not even Storm Cloud owned. He'd already scratched her several times without noticing the damage he'd caused.

Panic gripped my soul. I knew that look, that final stage-four incomprehensive panic as one stepped closer to the barrier between life and death. She drew closer to that dreadful and unseen barricade between the living and the dead, and nothing I did could halt her going. Sky Dancer died, by inches, within the shelter of my arms.

"Medic!" I yelled. "I need a medic here!"

"Van, it's too late. Where are my feet? I know...It's too late."

"It's never too late, girl."

I stroked my hand across her face, her neck, her eye sockets, her long, tufted ears. I willed her amber, raptor eyes to gaze nowhere but at my face. I forced my mental words into her mind, into her soul. *"Look at me, baby. Look at me and you'll be all right, I promise. Look only at me and I'll save you. I swear I will."*

She tried to obey me. Her stricken amber eyes hung onto mine, desperate, frightened, yet strong in will and in courage. *"I see you, Van. Help me, please! It hurts so bad."*

My grip tightened. *"See me, baby, my lovely lady. Focus, baby, focus on me. I won't let you go. I need you, my precious girl; I want to keep you, I'm lost without you. Shunt the pain away, I know you can. Focus. Concentrate. The pain is nothing. Your heart is everything. The pain is nothing."*

"Van!"

"I know it hurts, but be calm," I said, aloud. "Stay calm, ignore the hurts, ignore the agony. It's hard, I know, but always remember I'm here. I'm always here, for you. Pain can't kill you, ignore it and rise up, soldier. You're an Atan. You suffer, yet you live. Remember, First Lieutenant, lay still and hear me. See me. I'll not let you go–"

[66]

"I'm an Atan."

Her weakened yet strong voice rose high and rolled over my idiotic nonsense. She listened to only what she wanted to hear. She was a soldier. She lived for nothing and died for everything. *Gods, please, have mercy don t let her think like that.*

Sky Dancer relaxed.

My gut roiled. Oh, this isn't right she's gonna–

In one sudden, swift movement, Sky Dancer lunged upward and forward. Storm Cloud lost his grip as Wind Warrior cursed. Her huge head broke from my arms, her blackened wings wide, at the same instant I clamped what was left of my magic upon her vulnerable consciousness.

Like changing one's form into an inanimate object, the Clan frowned upon mind-meddling, throwing one's self into the mind, the will, of another. I meddled in Sky Dancer's mind anyway. I forced my will upon her. Using all the strength of my power and limited magic, I thrust my way into her consciousness. By dominating her will, I forced her into obedience. "*Behave yourself, Dancer, and trust me. Lay quiet. Be calm. Be still.*"

Unwilling and unwittingly, she obeyed my command. My will forced her to lay still, but her emotions ran rampant, unfettered. Her beak widened in a cry of panic and defiance. Storm Cloud cast me a glance of frightened confusion, his wings rising. He knew how to prevent the enemy from approaching the castle walls. He knew how to keep his soldiers alive in battle. Kill an enemy from three hundred rods away and he's in his element. Comfort one in the throes of complete hysteria? Gods have mercy.

"You're useless there, Storm," I snapped. "Go help Malik."

"You sure?"

I jerked my head.

The once organized conference room vanished. A scene of chaos, shouted orders, louder questions and wild speculations emerged as Malik fought to regain control and command his officers to see sense. Padraig flanked him, sword drawn, bellowing orders at the group of Minotaurs and humans squashing Cian into jelly. Storm Cloud left me and leaped into the fray, his wings wide, bellowing orders to his soldiers to stand aside and guard the conference room windows. In case Cian had allies, I surmised.

"Cian," Sky Dancer muttered, her ears pinned. "Cian. It's him. I know, it's him."

"I know, Dancer," I murmured, my hands and will busy, keeping her calm and still. "Hush now. He can't hurt you."

"Van . . . forgive me."

Cian, all but buried under the heavy combined weight of humans and Minotaurs, bloody and defiant, twisted his neck to find me. I forgot Sky Dancer's panicked words as I met his calm, implacable gaze. I caught my breath, frozen, my hands on Sky Dancer's body feeling nothing but ice running through my veins.

He marked me.

I met his dead glance, and suppressed a shiver. My skin crawled as though it discovered a life of its own and deserted for warmer climes. I've seen that look before, that righteous expression foretelling my doom. Raithin Mawrn mercenaries and religious fanatics seeking the myriad of heavens often offered it before their deaths. Never before had I witnessed it from my own kind, my own kin.

Cian relaxed under their weight and combined Atani ministries, blood tricking from his nose, broken teeth and crushed eye socket. *That ll leave a scar,* I half-thought, my thoughts jangling. *Focus, dammit, focus. Cian s helpless. He s no longer a threat.*

Yet, he didn't change forms and escape.

A clever Shifter could revert into any form and escape the strong arms and combined weight of Malik's council. I know I could. Cian, while good, could never hope to best me. But duck out from under the physical restraints of a handful of Minotaurs and Griffins? Dead easy. Even a Shifter of Cian's limited talents could escape. Why hadn't he?

This can t be good.

Given no time to think or evaluate, Malik's voice rolled over my thoughts and pushed them under. "Get him up, dammit. Ropes won't help now, Commander. Stand him on his feet."

Cian rose under the grip of three Minotaurs with Padraig's sword at his throat and Commanders Swift Wing and Storm Cloud standing to either side, talons out and ready to cut Cian to ribbons. Malik snapped the pewter manacles over Cian's wrists, binding them in front of him. As they had me, their power prevented him from changing shape or escaping.

"Medic!" I yelled again, disconcerted that Cian yet smiled beneath the weight of Minotaurs, Griffins and Malik's magic. A mild, 'Oh, this is just lovely' expression lay across his face. He glanced my way, and his bloody, gap-toothed grin broadened.

"Shit," I muttered just as the doors to Malik's conference chamber burst inward.

The King's royal bodyguard entered at a brisk pace, fanning about the huge chamber. While within the safety of his own palace, the King normally didn't travel with more than a handful of guards. As more than a dozen Centaur and human soldiers advanced in, the trouble Cian caused had no doubt been heard by keen equine ears. In no time at all, royal escort swung into formation before we even knew the King had arrived for a visit.

His Majesty's Centaur guard preceded him, swords out and leveled. They stomped inside, ringing us round, heavy tails sweeping sideways, dark hollow eyes unrepentant and unforgiving. Like statues, they lined the chamber walls, silent, still, awaiting orders for something to kill. Human guards in their white and silver tunics, black breeches and gold shoulder chains trotted in. With hands on nocked and ready bows, they filled the spaces between the Centaurs and waited, spines stiff and eyes alert.

In his litter, borne by four identical gold Centaurs with sweeping white manes and tails, His Royal Majesty King Roidan ap Cailean ap Fiachra entered the now crowded conference hall. His expression tense and his fine lips thin to the point of emaciation, our ruling monarch glared slowly around the frozen tableau before him. His pale blue eyes wandered from Cian, in shackles and guarded by no less than five monstrous Minotaurs, and two Griffin Commanders to a saluting Chief Ba'al'amawer.

Malik straightened from his threatening position over Cian and sidestepped to face his King. Gracefully, he bent his foreleg, and bowed over his knee, his fist hard against his chest. "Your Majesty."

Padraig led the others in the same salute, the Griffins dropping their beaks over their fisted talons and what Minotaurs not involved in keeping Cian secure also bowed. As much as I hated greeting my King from the awkward position of holding Sky Dancer still, I managed a half-salute as Roidan's glance found mine.

"The King," Sky Dancer gasped. "Let me up."

She raised her eagle's head in a gallant effort to rise, but I locked my arms around her huge head, hugging her tight to me.

"Van, damn your eyes!"

"Be still, Lieutenant."

Despite her first coherent words since Cian's attack, I didn't budge. I may have blocked her brain from feeling her injuries, those injuries could be made worse by her thrashing around and saluting. I exerted my soon-to-be-exhausted will over hers once more, demanding she lay quiet, unmoving. She relaxed, calm, quiescent, but her eyes roved the council chambers, never still. Roidan seldom stood on ceremony and two Atani soldiers who couldn't greet him properly fazed him about as much as a buzzing fly.

"Llyr." Roidan's sudden voice broke the tense silence.

The thusly addressed human guard broke from his spot on the wall near the door, marched forward, and saluted smartly.

"If Healer Ilirri isn't attending Sky Dancer within five minutes," Roidan said, never taking his eyes from me, "I'm docking you a month's pay."

Llyr didn't take time to salute again. He dashed out the door, his sword slapping against his thigh. Though he did take his arrow from his bowstring in order to run faster.

Sky Dancer was but one of several hundred Griffins in the Royal Weksan'Atan. That the King knew the names of the people who served him, despite their species, gave him a certain edge. That he was our liege lord and master, we offered him our loyalty and lives. That he knew *us*, we offered him our fanatical devotion.

"Boys," he said, his tone genial. "Put me down, please."

His golden bearers lowered his sedan chair to the floor, then stepped smartly aside, facing him. As their sheer equine bulk prohibited them from assisting him, his royal attendant strode forward. Daragh, a hugely muscled man dressed in peasant homespun, served primarily as the King's legs. Bending, he picked up the King as gently as he would a child, and set him on his cushioned chair at the head of the huge table. Though not in the military, Daragh then stalked behind Roidan's chair to stand behind him at parade rest.

Roidan sighed and scratched his nose. "Care to explain this fracas, Malik?"

Long of red hair and drooping mustache, King Roidan's pale blue eyes missed little. They swept over us in less than a heartbeat and knew more of what on in the undertones than we did. Roidan's family line held more power, more subtlety, and far more intelligence than our wisest mages. His eyes knew what we but suspected, seeing clearer than a Griffin's predatory gaze. His wisdom surpassed that of the professors teaching at university. His power, and that of his ancestors, kept Bryn'Cairdha safe for generations uncounted. He commanded. We obeyed.

"I'm to blame," I burst out as Malik's jaw dropped to speak.

Roidan's eyes widened in mild surprise.

"Your Majesty," I amended, ducking my brow while still holding a struggling Sky Dancer still. Through my inattention, my will conquering hers slackened. She reclaimed her own and coiled like a striking cobra. Despite her injuries, that girl was far stronger than I. I growled under my breath at Wind Warrior, and he increased his weight on her shoulder and thrashing lion quarters. Sky Dancer hissed malevolently and tried to throw me off.

Roidan leaned back in his chair and folded his hands across his stomach. He wore as he usually did, a simple robe of light brown silk, belted with bright yellow satin, and brown slippers on his wasted feet. No crown graced his head, nor did he need one. A simple rope of twisted gold graced his thin neck, yet he carried his royalty as a cavalry soldier carries his nation's banner. He needed no crown or rich brocade to declare him King and fit to rule.

Crippled from the waist down from an Raithin Mawrn attack many years before, King Roidan still commanded the loyalty and respect of his people, vassals and military arms. Despite his infirmity, the King led his country through wars and famine, drought and pestilence, plenty and riches. He took power at the ripe age of fourteen, led soldiers into battle and kept them alive. None in the Atani order sought a leader more worthy to follow.

"Why is that miscreant here and annoying me, Malik?" Roidan asked, his brows lowering. "I thought you killed him long ago."

"My apologies, sire," Malik replied, once more bending his great knee. "I didn't know where he was until recently."

"He's a traitor and a murderer," Roidan snapped, scowling. "How dare you bring him here. Why is he wearing my uniform? My uniform!"

"Sire." Malik stepped forward and blocked the King's view of me with his heavy body. "The error is mine, as is your punishment."

He bowed his dark head, his dark hair swinging low, covering his face. "But I brought him because I need him. He's the best there is, and you need the best if we're to rescue your daughter. Your Majesty."

"I don't like it," the King snapped. "I don't like him. He's a disgrace to all you stand for. All you *should* stand for."

"Your Majesty is, of course, correct," Malik replied, his voice, soft, mild, respectful. "Right now, I'll hire the demons vomited from hell if it means bringing the princess home safe."

"I think you bloody well did."

Malik merely lowered his noble brow and said nothing.

From the floor, I watched as King Roidan's hot stare flicked from me to Malik and back again.

"Damn it, Commander," Roidan groused, his anger plain. "Don't you dare manipulate me. You're manipulating me again, aren't you?"

"Yes, Your Majesty."

"Captain Vanyar." Roidan barked, struggling to his feet.

Daragh stepped forward to assist him with his hand under the King's left arm. Only then could Roidan stand. His royal right finger pointed down, at me, marking, condemning. His angry stare behind it chilled the blood in my veins. "I haven't forgotten your stupidity, boy," he growled. "You killed my soldiers."

"I did, Your Majesty."

I bowed my head, still pinning Sky Dancer's beak to the slate floor, wishing either Malik wasn't so desperate nor Iyumi so stupid.

[72]

Without them, I'd be safe in my tavern, forgotten and alive. The King's voice promised a very long, excruciating, execution. Why did I leave my flask behind in Malik's private chamber? I craved a drink. I didn't just crave it, I bloody *needed* it.

"When this is over–"

He didn't need to finish. His eyes said it all. *You're one dead Shifter.*

"I'm yours, Your Majesty," I replied, my voice thick. Lying on my back, my arms around Sky Dancer's head, I no doubt appeared as idiotic as my words. Her cheek against my chest, her deadly beak widened and snapped perilously close to my nose. I grimaced with the effort, as she tried to raise her head enough to throw me off. "Execute me, please. I deserve it."

He sighed, still annoyed, but his finger dropped. "Not until my daughter is returned. Should you prove your loyalty in this endeavor, I'll see to it personally you die an honorable death."

"All I can ask for, Majesty."

The conversation rattled me enough that trying to force calm into Sky Dancer's agitated brain proved useless. I had none of my own to offer her. Only by utilizing both rapidly weakening magic and Wind Warrior's strength did I keep her flat on her side, her head on my chest. I snorted tiny feathers, and fought for my own breath. Her head was bloody heavy. Her tail struck the floor, and Wind Warrior's beak, time and again, lashing, as she growled low in her throat. I ducked my head and evaded a deadly slash from those wicked front talons.

"Kill him now," growled a voice from the back. That same voice I heard before but couldn't identify.

Malik half-turned, his heavy tail swinging against his hocks as he, too, sought to put a name, a face to the voice. He scowled, his hand on his sword, as Padraig also turned and searched.

"Interesting suggestion," Roidan said, his fingers stroking his chin as he frowned, deep in thought. His fingers twisted the end of his mustache. "Shall I?"

"Please don't, sire," I replied, gasping with effort and breathlessness. "Malik needs me, to get your daughter back. I'll surrender, after we have her home."

"Malik? Do you truly need this egotistical, murdering scoundrel to bring Iyumi home?"

Malik nodded slowly. "Sire, I did fetch him from the gutter specifically for this mission. Otherwise, I'd let him rot in the hell he chose for himself. Only he has the skills I need to bring Her Highness back. I know he's a, pardon the pun, royal pain–"

"I should have locked him away years ago. For his own safety, of course."

"I know, sire. He's certainly not worthy to breathe the same air as Your Majesty. However, his skills are legendary and I do need him. The Princess Iyumi is in grave danger."

"But . . . him?" Roidan sighed, resting his chin on his fist. "Come on, Malik. An officer as competent as you surely can find someone, er, less criminal."

Malik bowed over his arm across his chest. "Not in the short time we have, Your Majesty. I swear I'll keep him under control. His murdering self shall never trouble you."

Into this heated mix, the tiny Griffin Healer, Ilirri, darted into the room from behind His Majesty's royal escort of Centaurs and human soldiers. Her swift eyes fastened on Sky Dancer, and she spread her wings. Half the size of most Griffins, she flew across the blackened table in a graceful leap, ignoring King and Atani commanders alike. Every eye, including Cian's, watched her with awe. Only one so dedicated to her patients might fail to acknowledge her liege lord and master. Or the heavy armaments of the Atani.

Dropping lightly to all fours, her lion tail lashing, Ilirri furled her wings. Her beak bent down and her bright amber eyes focused on Sky Dancer, assessing her injuries with the swift skill that prevented many deaths among my Atani brothers and sisters. Without fuss or drama, her talons closed over Sky Dancer's broad brow.

"Has it been five minutes, Malik?" King Roidan asked.

[74]

"No, sire," Malik replied as Llyr returned to his spot against the wall, gasping for breath. His arrow returned to its bow-string as his spine stiffened. His blank eyes stared straight ahead of him, although triumph seeped from his pores.

"Crap," Roidan muttered, sour. "I might have saved myself a few pennies."

"Let her go, Vanyar," Ilirri snapped, raising her beak. "You're no good there. You, too, Wind Warrior. You're hurting her."

"But . . ." I said, "she'll, er–"

On the receiving end of her fierce raptor glare, I obeyed. Releasing Sky's Dancer's head, I rolled out from under as Dancer flipped her beak upward, in triumph. Sky Dancer tried once to rise and fight. Ilirri muttered under her breath and Sky Dancer collapsed in a heap, her blackened wings falling like limp sails. Her beak rested atop her talons as her tufted lion tail ceased its lash.

I staggered upright, feeling slightly woozy from the terrible drain on my powers and energy. In addition to changing my body into a liquid, I hadn't used my magic much in the last two years and I was out of practice. Between the two, I'll have one hell of a headache come tomorrow.

"Give me room, boys," Ilirri barked at us, her lion tail lashing with annoyance. Her neck feathers ruffled as she once more concentrated on her unconscious patient. "Begone with you."

"But–"

"Wind Warrior, I'm not telling you again."

"But–" Wind Warrior repeated. With my hand on his feathered forearm, he halted further protest.

"Leave go," I muttered, leading him away. "Trust me, you're well out of it."

The big Griffin's beak shut tight as he permitted me to guide him from Sky Dancer's side. Although we both hesitated, and glanced back with concern, Ilirri had her patient well in hand. "She's a bitch when she's healing," I muttered.

"Vanyar."

Though Ilirri's voice held nothing save quiet assurance, I recognized a threat when I heard it. Those who pissed off Ilirri often issued swift and genuine apologies before certain important bits vanished without a trace. One Centaur I refuse to name was still missing his elemental genitalia as he never acknowledged he wronged her. His parents named him Radu, the Atani ranked him First Sergeant, and malicious folks called him 'Entire' although he certainly wasn't.

"Ilirri." I bowed low even as I dragged Wind Warrior with me, staggering under the weight of a Griffin several times larger than a draft horse. He shut his beak, I noticed with pleasure, as he caught the nasty flash from her predatory gaze. He gulped and swept his tail protectively over his precious bits.

"Sir, is she really . . ." Wind Warrior began, casting a quick glance over his massive shoulder.

"That bad?"

"Um . . ."

"No, son," I replied, tugging on his arm. "She's far worse."

Sky Dancer slept, free of pain, ignorant of the drama enfolding; her mind and body open for Ilirri's healing magic. Her huge and blackened wings drooped, half-hiding the smaller Griffin behind them, collapsing like limp sails. Sky Dancer's eagle eyes slid shut, just as my tentative probe into her mind fell far short.

"Beat it, Vanyar."

"Yes, ma'am."

At the same moment we boys retreated, Ilirri's clever talons worked loose the buckle on the leather satchel she carried across her neck and shoulder. Ointments and powders spilled out as she selected what she wanted. As Sky Dancer's burns were extensive, Ilirri emptied her vials in a hurry.

Under our fascinated gaze, the King's included, Ilirri shut her tawny eyes and her breathing evened. Under her power, Sky Dancer slept, oblivious, no longer in pain and her healing just beginning. As Ilirri's talents healed me more times than I cared to count, I knew Sky Dancer lay in the nation's best talons. No one, inside or outside the royal court, could heal as well as Ilirri. In that, Malik stood second best in the lives saved.

"I'll fix her," Ilirri muttered as her healing magic poured into Sky Dancer. Her small beak lifted as she gazed over her tawny shoulder. "I know a spell, an old one, that speeds the regrowth of feathers."

She swiftly dipped her beak, finally acknowledging her King. "Majesty, she'll be flying again in a few days, you can count on it."

"Good," Roidan replied. "I've a feeling I'm going to need her."

His pale eyes rested once more upon me. Freed from constraint, I stood and offered a much improved salute, my arm across my chest and my chin lowered. I half-thought he'd speak to me, yet he didn't. I didn't know whether to be relieved or worried.

"Now then," Roidan snapped, garnering our immediate attention. "What happened here?"

"Your Majesty–" Malik began.

At the same time, I burst out, "Cian's hated me since–"

"Captain Vanyar," Roidan barked. "When I want your opinion, I'll send a memo. When I want your advice, I'll give it to you. Until then, shut thy mouth."

I obeyed, with a snap.

"Lord Captain Malik."

"Sire."

"What in the name of creation happened here?"

In true Centaur form, Malik glanced from me, to Cian and finally to his liege lord. "Cian is a traitor," he replied simply, his hand loose at his sides.

Roidan scowled. "I should name that idiot Vanyar as head of my Atani," he muttered. "I know that much, Commander. Don't push my good nature. I'm rather irritated these days."

"Very well."

Malik straightened his spine and his heavy tail lashed. "Cian mounted an unprovoked attack against First Captain Vanyar, and grievously injured Lieutenant Sky Dancer instead. Though his treachery was not aimed at Your Majesty, his actions are deemed vile, venomous and unworthy of an Atan, nor a Bryn'Cairdhan citizen. I recommend he be hanged forthwith."

"That's the Malik I hired," Roidan muttered, smiling. "You're ever bloodthirsty, conniving, and simply too loyal for words. I always knew you'd side with the just, the pure. And, um, me."

"He hasn't been tried yet," I gasped, stumbling forward, breathless and falling to my knees. "Not yet guilty and all that."

Freed from Sky Dancer responsibility, Wind Warrior followed, his huge wings wide and sheltering me. His oddly protective stance brought forth feelings of both gratitude and horror from within me. I almost got Sky Dancer a fiery funeral and this old boy *likes* me?

"Cian deserves death," Wind Warrior grumbled, his talon on my shoulder. "Why do you protect him, Van? Captain, I mean."

I rose to my feet, angrily brushing his talons away. "He has the right," I growled, unable to control my tone even in Roidan's presence. "As do we all."

Malik eyed me up and down, dispassionate before turning to address the King. "He does have a point, Majesty."

"And a valid one, damn it all." Roidan sighed deeply and scratched his thin chest. "I want to execute him, feed my bloodthirsty nature. I haven't presided over an execution in months."

Resting his chin on his fist, his elbow on the mahogany planked table, his light blue eyes roamed, measured, sized up. They roamed over the council chamber, assessing, reading each face, each stance, his powers picking stray thoughts from those present: who hated whom, who felt fanatic loyalty, who felt jealousy, anger, love, lust or just plain old ordinary greed. No set of eyes that met his failed to drop instantly, avoiding his judgment. Cian paled, his skin ghostly under his bruises and blood, as the King's royal eye marked him.

That acute blue gaze rested on me at the last. His glance shifted from my face to the sword at my hip and back again. His right brow lifted. My hand instinctively dropped to its hilt.

Ba'al'amawer bowed low, from his waist. "We all bend the knee to your despotic and bloodthirsty rulership, Your Majesty. But pray tell, have mercy. Throw this traitor into the dungeon until he can be tried and convicted. He has served you well in the past."

"Oh, bother." King Roidan eyed Cian with distaste before jerking his chin toward the Minotaur Chieftain. "Imprisoning him means I have to feed him and I'm much too miserly for that."

My fingers roved over the ornate hilt belted to my hip, lingered over the falcon's parted beak. Its wide-spread wings formed the crosspiece and twin sapphires rested where a falcon's raptor gaze might see. I frowned. As Roidan leaned upon Daragh's strong arm and sat once more on the cushions of his sedan chair with a sigh, I remembered with a sharp jolt upon whose hands I received it.

From Roidan himself. On the very day I swore my oaths as an Atan.

At the same instant, as though reading my mind, Roidan glanced from my face, down to the gold inlaid hilt under my palm and back again. That's twice now. Is he trying to tell me something? He tossed me a lightning fast wink, so quick I doubted I'd seen it. Yet, his face remained mildly reproving, as before.

I pondered the wink and the sword. He wanted me to think about it. No one else received such a gift on the occasion they joined the military. I had. *Why?* I never stopped wondering why I, among them all, earned the King's favor and with such a weapon. My thoughts wandered away from the current debacle to that day when I donned the Atani uniform and the Death's Head ring.

Caught between boy and man, I knelt before King Roidan, my bare head lowered. Even in his chair, he looked down on me, as befitted the ruling monarch. Throngs packed his throne room: many relatives, no few nobles, and a quarter of his military forces. Griffins perched on tall pillars built for them. Minotaurs, heads above all others, ringed the great hall. Centaurs mingled with humans, joking, laughing, teasing the soon-to-be Atani recruits. Malik, a Captain then, stood at my shoulder as my sponsor.

"I've instilled it with much power," Roidan told me on that long ago day in a ceremony most had forgotten, his breath tickling my ear. "Use it. Cut your arm with it, now. Bathe it in your blood so it may know you."

Fifteen years old, I obeyed him. Its razor edge sliced my inner arm, my hot blood coating its blue-tinged length. I felt little pain and no alarm as the tempered steel, folded thousands upon thousands of times, absorbed, no, sucked in, my essence. I never forgot how it glowed blue, as though with an inner light, upon receiving my sacrifice.

No one had ever asked me why I cut myself and bathed my new sword with my blood. Perhaps they thought I swore a personal blood oath of loyalty to King Roidan–such was common enough. Malik, near enough to witness everything, never spoke of it, despite our close friendship. Nor did I.

Many years and a thousand experiences later, I abandoned the King's gift. I left my horse in the courtyard and ran into my chambers, minutes ahead of the blood-hungry mob wanting my head decorating a pike, horrified at what had just happened to my unit. My sword, far too noticeable for my health, I left lying on my bed. I changed quickly from my half-burnt uniform into nondescript clothing, grabbed a few essentials and vanished into the streets.

I forced my attention off my blade and my past with an effort. My guilt, never assuaged, rolled about in my gut like a wayward boulder. The weight of Cian's stare finally forced me to glance into his eyes. Ignoring Roidan and the possibility of his own execution, he watched me with an implacable patience. As though listening to the insignificant whine of a mosquito in his ear, Cian continued his stony regard, sending me his silent message: *I missed killing you once. I won t miss again.*

I rolled my eyes slightly. *Bite me.*

His red smile widened a fraction and his eyed danced.

Malik noticed finally that Cian ignored his King all this time and stomped forward, his hand up. As quick as he moved, Storm Cloud advanced first, his wings furled over his back and his lion tail up and lashing with suppressed rage. He swung his fist. But it was his bared talon that ripped Cian's face from eye to chin.

Cian stumbled back into the arms of his guards, crying out in agony and terror. Blood poured from his lacerated cheek, spilled onto his chest and shoulder, his uniform soaking up some of the mess. Red blots pattered to the pristine slate floor, droplets that smeared as Storm Cloud stepped on them as he lowered his huge and deadly beak to stare into Cian's suddenly alert and panicked eyes.

"His Majesty may not mind the obvious disrespect," Storm Cloud rumbled, his neck feathers at stiff attention. "For he's a rather forgiving fellow, and he tends to overlook faults."

Storm Cloud raised his bloody talon and slowly tapped Cian on the nose with it. "But I certainly do. You will face His Majesty, on your knees, with all the courtesy his royal person deserves. Now."

Storm Cloud's right fist lowered across his body and slashed swiftly from left to right. He effectively struck Cian across his shins, effectively knocking his legs out from under him. Cian cried out as he crashed onto his knees, his ripped cheek waving like a red flag. A heavy Minotaur hand twisted Cian's head on his neck until his faced his King properly.

"Why, Commander Storm Cloud," Roidan gushed, his tone light and teasing, "how kind of you."

Storm Cloud slowly straightened into tight military attention, his black-tipped tail coiling about his feet. Its furry tip swept languidly back and forth. He saluted, formally and ritually, his talon across his white chest and his beak bowed low. "Always, my King."

I glanced over my shoulder, eying Ilirri and Sky Dancer on the blue slate tiles. The latter lay limp and all but lifeless, as the former still held her talons to Sky Dancer's brow, pouring her magic into her patient. If Sky Dancer had died, Ilirri would have stirred and said so. I'm sure of it. That Sky Dancer lived and Ilirri still healed was a good sign.

A sensitive soul and quite prolific in reading vibes of all kinds, Ilirri felt my worry and lifted her beak. Like Minotaurs, Griffins can smile in a limited way, and Ilirri offered that and a swift wink. "*No worries,*" she said, her voice silent, echoing within my mind. "*You did good, soldier. 1 ll keep you posted.*"

I tried to reply with a nod, but she already turned away.

Despite her offered comfort, I worried anyway. My guilty conscience reared its nasty beak and spit. Another someone I cared about got hurt because of me. *Malik, you shouldn t have brought me here. I bring pain and death wherever I go.* Damn, but my throat and gut craved a good strong drink right now.

"First Captain Vanyar."

The King's voice jolted me from my thoughts. I straightened. "Er, yes, sire?"

I squared my shoulders, altered my face into a respectful, attentive mien and wished Cian's fireball had done its work properly.

Roidan leaned forward, his eyes intent, as though reading my thoughts. "Malik brought you here against my express command. However, I'm not without a few intelligent moments. You're the only hope my daughter has. Will you bring her home?"

I dropped to my knee and bowed my head over my clenched fist. "Or die trying, Your Majesty."

"Good."

Roidan eyed Cian with distaste. He waved his hand, dismissive. "Take this creature to the dungeons and imprison him there. He'll have his trial, once my daughter is returned and peace is restored. He's to remain in his manacles. I'll not have him turn himself into the worm he is and escape through the cracks in the walls."

The Minotaurs bowed as best they could with Cian in their grip. Dragging his limp and bleeding body, they stomped toward the door. Malik's door wardens opened them, their dark, bovine eyes hard and uncompromising. I couldn't help but wonder: was their anger for the attack on me, or the injury done to Sky Dancer?

Dragged out of the chamber, leaving a slimy blood trail, Cian stumbled repeatedly as the implacable Minotaurs politely escorted him out. The huge doors shut hard behind them, guards ramming home the bolts in case Cian had friends.

While I wanted to glance again behind me, I dared not take my eyes from my King. Sky Dancer will live–won't she? Ilirri winked. She wouldn't have is she thought–

Roidan's snapping fingers brought me around. Daragh stepped forward to His Majesty's side and picked him lightly up. As though he handled a priceless treasure, Daragh settled Roidan comfortably in his sedan chair and arranged a light blanket around his useless legs. As his golden Centaur bearers stepped into harness and lifted his sedan, Roidan beckoned Malik.

"My friend," Roidan murmured, smiling into Malik's dark eyes. "You'll fetch her back. Won't you? My daughter? I know she's a handful and, damn it, she can be a real bitch sometimes, but . . . ."

The King's smile trembled a fraction as he gazed upward. "She's my kid. And I love her. You know?"

Malik's heavy lips twitched. He, among us all, alone bore the right to touch our monarch with familiarity. He gripped Roidan's arm almost tight enough to hurt. Roidan never flinched, but gazed into Malik's face with affection and hope reflected in his eyes.

"I'll have her back and bitching in no time, my King."

"Now that's what I wanted to hear."

Roidan settled back into his cushions as his Centaur and human guards formed about him in readiness to march. Daragh paced beside him as his golden bearers shouldered their royal burden and turned toward the guarded doorway.

Malik stepped away, out from under, his salute unseen. Yet, Roidan's face and shoulders appeared with the chair's lace curtains spilling over his head and half-concealing his face. The Minotaurs swept wide the mahogany and teak doors, saluting.

"Don't forget," he called as his escort bore him away. "I want Vanyar hale and healthy until I can dispose of him myself."

CHAPTER 4

Princess Yummy

Under me, Bayonne galloped hard, leaping dead fall and rocks, dodging twisted trees, his heavy legs crashing through dense thickets. Up hills and down short valleys, we splashed across an untold number of streams, frightened herds of deer, elk, wild birds, a few foxes and a bear. My company galloped behind, on my heels, following like a curse.

Inside my head, I sang the same damn refrain around and around: *Why have those idiots stopped? Why did they hold up in a bloody cave to wait for me when they needed to ride hard toward the border?* My father's messenger, via a pigeon, informed me that the princess had fallen ill. The men were desperate for instructions. *What do we do? We cannot move her.*

The hell they couldn't. I needed no set of eyes in that cave to know she faked it. The longer she delayed them, us, the closer the Bryn'Cairdhans were to rescuing her. If the King's Atans dropped around our necks–gods help us all. I cursed under my breath. Those stupid, stupid fools. We're in enemy territory, dammit. Any wild creature might be a Shifter in disguise.

I glanced up at the faint scream of a hunting eagle. I caught a brief glimpse before it vanished over the tree-lined mountain top. A dreaded Shifter? Or perhaps was it in truth a Griffin, that abominable lion-eagle creature sent to spy on us? A shiver crept down my spine. We'd crossed the border three days past, riding around the eastern end of the deadly Shin'Eah Mountains and into the heart of Bryn'Cairdha. We rode deep into enemy territory with no protection and a zero back-up plan. In my curses, I didn't fail to mention my father's name rather frequently.

Commander Blaez spurred his jet black stallion to gallop hard just behind and to the right of Bayonne's silver shoulder, spur-blood flecking his flanks. As my father commanded . . . take Blaez. I'd no choice. I despised the man and rightfully so. Folk disliked me, but Blaez they hated and feared. He loved to kill and savored it. He adored pain and forced much of it on his victims. A fire-worshipper of the worst order, he created the many bombs my father's fanatics took into Bryn'Cairdha. He's blown up soldiers and commoners alike, his victims innocent and guilty (although I, forced to admit it, knew most were in the former class), and one day hoped to murder the Bryn'Cairdhan royal family in a riot of blood and fire. He sacrificed puppies and prayed to his demon gods that he, single-handedly, might break the magical powers of Bryn'Cairdha.

That we rode to take into custody one member of that self-same family, the one more powerful than all the others, never seemed to enter his ugly head. That my father, the King, commanded I marry this latest scion of the royal Bryn'Cairdhan family branch jolted him not one jot. That she was the only one who knew the location of the secret child, he cared less. If he could, he'd set her afire with one of his naphtha creations and, under her agonized and dying screams, roast weenies.

Gods above, protect us all from that flaming idiot.

The gods never answered my prayers before. Why would they now?

The hills rose and dropped as we thundered on into the late morning, leagues upon leagues from safety. The terrain slowly altered the further from home we rode. The thick forests of Raithin Mawr slowly changed to rolling green hills, tall grass, thickets of oak, juniper, pine, fir and evergreen dotting a landscape as open as a whore's legs. Any fool might see us, riding hard, our dark cloaks flapping in our wake. High above, tall barren cliffs offered the unlimited sight of us as we galloped across highland tundra, dodging heavy boulders and light deer, exposed and vulnerable.

So far, no army soldiers, Atan or otherwise, descended upon us with wild yells and waving swords. While that, in and of itself, was no comfort, I at least tried to remain hopeful. In a desperate attempt at optimism, I half convinced myself that we'd caught a lucky break. A gift from the gods. The Secret Police, the Weksan'Atan, had no idea where their High Priestess and princess slept. If they didn't know about *her*, they didn't know about *us*.

You re not an idiot, the voice in my head said, sounding eerily similar to my father's bellow. *Don t believe that, not for a moment.* As depressing as it was correct, I knew my hopes held no concrete value. They, those clever, magical beasties, knew very well we'd invaded their borders, and knew exactly where their royal heir lay, feigning a deep coma.

I'd braced myself time and again for the Bryn'Cairdhan troops to fall. I almost hoped for a confrontation–an attack, any attack, that told me my enemies didn't just watch from afar. A straight-forward fight reassured. This weird silence crept under my skin like brazen fleas. Though not exactly cold, I shivered and tightened my cloak around my neck as I gazed up at the frowning cliffs.

Though I heard no voice of complaint, no vocal worry, no muttered curse from the men riding hard behind me, I understood their silence. Like me, they feared this oppressive calm far more than any spooky Shape-Shifter, or man-horse. Though too well-paid to cut and run, I realized these mercenaries weighed their skins against my gold. Was it worth it?

Our enemies watched us, and I knew they watched us. If that was an advantage, I doubted it'd help much. They bided their time, drawing the enemy in, cutting off our escape before pouncing. They but had to wait for me to make a mistake. If I didn't make one . . . .

I knew the gods laughed their celestial asses off over that.

"Gor, mate," Blaez grumbled. "Where are they?"

"Not a town, nor a village," commented Blaez's man, his favorite guard dog. I knew him as an out-of-favor knight named Sim, who long-since should've lost his title along with his lands for his heinous and bloody crimes. As Blaez's best friend, my father overlooked the rapes, the murders, and the molestation of young peasant children. If Sim aided and abetted in the kidnap of the very powerful High Priestess, his sins were forgiven. "Not even a cotter's patch. Where the devil are they?"

"We're inside their lines by a hundred leagues," said a mercenary knight who went by the unlikely name of Buck-Eye. "They can't just let us ride straight in and grab their heir? Right?"

Blaez and Sim spent every waking moment together, fast friends and co-conspirators. Had my royal sire cared about the raped, murdered and plundered peasants unlucky enough to cross paths with this pair, he might have strung them up by their ankles over a *mau la ti* ant mound. One bite of the inch-long, carnivorous insect brought forth a nasty blister on a man's skin. A hive? The longest any prisoner lasted was twelve agonizing hours. Perhaps he didn't taste good.

"Suck it up," I snapped over my shoulder. "They watch us. Deal with it."

"Prince Pussy," Blaez muttered at my back.

We climbed higher yet through the late afternoon of our fourth day in Bryn'Cairdha, the lowering sun blinding our eyes. Our mounts' hooves dug into broken rocks and dodged the occasional pale tree corpse and thickets of thorny, tough-looking green-grey bushes. Discovering a twisting game trail, I followed it up and up, my horse thrusting himself higher and higher. I leaned forward over the pommel, my left hand on his reins, my right tangled in his mane to prevent an embarrassing slide over his dappled rump.

An elk trotted away from Bayonne's sudden invasion of his territory, pausing just out of bowshot to stare at us over his shaggy grey shoulder. Flipping his tail over his butt, he ambled out of my sight, ducking under the scrawny, high-altitude trees. Was that a true elk or an Atani Shape-Shifter? Sweat tricked down my back.

[88]

The sheer, steep angle of the trail slowed us to a careful walk, our mouths all but tasting our mounts' manes. I spit out charcoal horse-hairs and glanced back, down. In single file, stepping exactly in Bayonne's hoof-prints, they watched where their horse placed their feet and not at their surroundings. *Bloody fools.* Should an Atani patrol rip into their flanks, they'd sit their saddles and gape. I almost wished they would, just to witness the looks of surprise on their idiot faces.

While, no obliging Atani force arrived to entertain me, a nasty looking storm rolled in from the west. Black and oily clouds loomed on the horizon, lightning flashing with their murky depths. The humidity level rose as electricity danced across my skin. Thunder growled in the distance, long after the lightning flashes ceased. *An hour away, no more,* I guessed, listening to the rising wind.

Since birth, I've the knack of not just predicting storms, but also foreseeing its individual severity. I often informed those listeners, who cared about such things, of its intensity and its power. My father not just heeded me, but often bragged about his talented and bright son to his friends. I suspected that was his only source of pride for me, his eldest born. In all else, I rated a close third, or perhaps fourth, in the race for his affections.

I sniffed the chilly breeze as the temperature dropped several notches. At this high, alpine altitude, cold rain easily turned into sheets of slick ice. I cursed my, or my father's, lack of sense and foresight. For bad weather, only our thick wool cloaks offered scant protection. I knew this bloody tempest meant business, and we were ill-equipped to handle it. Could that evil Atani magic create early winter storms? One part of me doubted their power; the other part screamed in dire panic.

My clothes and hair clung to me in a sticky mess, and I sweated heavily. Bayonne gasped for every breath, white foam slicking his neck and chest. Behind me, my crew of Blaez and his three cronies, as well as the five soldiers loyal to me, cursed as their mounts slowed to traverse the treacherous terrain in relative safety. I heard mutters of 'shelter', 'this is madness', 'think it's got hail in?' outside the clip-clop of Bayonne's hooves and the rising wind.

[89]

Twisting in my saddle, I waved my arm, impatient. "Idiots. Kick those beasts. Keep up."

The ominous storm and the terrain made them nervous. *Did I know what I was doing?* I didn't need to hear their mutters to know they wondered if I wasn't as mad as the Bryn'Cairdhans. Madder than the proverbial march hare I may be, but they still owed me their allegiance. I planned to make full use of that.

"Damn your eyes," I yelled. "Move your asses. We stop for nothing."

My father, while hoarding his love, gave generously of his gold. My monthly allowance might easily support a high lord's estate and arm a dozen knights. I used it to purchase the loyalty of hard-bitten soldiers, and preserved the rest. My own men didn't like me any more than anyone else, and gossiped about me behind my back. Even so, they guarded it faithfully. Dead princes didn't pay well. Live ones had their uses, and I rewarded them handsomely.

The storm rolled inexorably toward us as I urged Bayonne to a never asked for pace. His hooves tripped and slid over the sharp rocks as he took the steep climb at a lunging trot. *We must reach the river before the King s Atan,* I thought, sweating. *We must. Or we ll never see home again.*

I grew up on tales of the Atani viciousness, their cruelty, their lust for the blood of my folk, the Raithin Mawrn. While I wasn't stupid enough to believe them all, considering how much grief my father's fanatics brought upon them, I knew this much: we kidnapped their heir and they'll stop at nothing to get her back. If they catch us, I seriously doubt they'll send me home with a smack on the wrist.

Amongst the tales of the impressive Atani, I'd heard stories of their Braigh'Mhar. The terrible cold, the ice, the high walls and the guarding trolls. Word spread long ago of the prison gangs who killed the weak, and preyed upon one another. Catch Prince Flynn in the act of stealing their High Priestess and throne's heir? If they didn't execute me first, I'd face a very short life sentence inside their wretched prison. In Braigh'Mhar, I'd be jail bait within a day.

As the landscape grew increasingly treacherous, I, cursing under my breath, reined Bayonne in to slow his headlong pace. The ground rose steadily, pocked with stunted trees and rocky ground, eclipsed by huge boulders that forced a horse to go around at a careful walk. The sky and the storm vanished behind tall hills strewn with heavy, jagged stones, scrub oak and thickets of pine, fir, dogwood, and twisted, stunted trees I could put no name to. Wild roses with thorns as long as my finger grew amid the harsh rocks, and tiny purple flowers with a sickeningly sweet scent forced me to sneeze time and again.

"I don't like this," Blaez muttered, his black puffing just behind Bayonne's tail. "We're too exposed, too vulnerable."

I rubbed the stinging itch from my nose. "This is your fault."

"Mine? How?"

I slewed in my saddle, leaving Bayonne to mind his footing. "These are your lads, Blaez. And not a one has the ability to find his own ass with both hands and a map. You sent in stupid spies."

"They're all I was given," Blaez muttered, a sharp whine raising his tone.

"Spare me," I gritted, facing front once more.

Stumbling over jagged stones, Bayonne kept his feet as easily as he kept his head. I let him pick his way down the far side of the tall hillock, casting an uneasy eye on the approaching storm. Lightning flickered with its inky depths, thunder growling in the distance. Darkness filled the entire sky, dropping bright daylight into gloomy nightfall. The sun vanished, the threatening clouds shrouding me in a misty half-light. Fine droplets of rain kissed my face, dampened my hair and Bayonne's tossing grey mane.

"Who has the bloody map?" I yelled over my shoulder. "Where's the bleeding Khai River?"

"Two leagues," Boden's voice from the rear shouted. "That way."

That way indicated a steep climb up into the sheer, dark sky. Lightning flickered deep within the bank of angry, roiling clouds. *Of course.* A river cut deep channels between mountains, and the tall cliffs around us trapped the Khai within their stony embrace. Should we ride to the top, follow the cliff-face, we'd soon descend into the long cut in the hills to the great river. Dead easy.

Nudging my horse with my heels, my weight tilted forward to allow him his balance, Bayonne bucked and heaved his way up the perilous incline. My left hand tangled in Bayonne's thick mane, I shot a swift glance over my shoulder. Blaez cursed fluidly, and struck his black with his whip to increase impetus. I hid a grin when his actions merely served to panic his horse. Fearing the whip more than the perilous rocks, the black bounded up and away from the whip's lash–only to trip, hard, over the uneven terrain.

Blaez fell off, tossed over his stallion's shoulder, shouting invectives. He hit the merciless rocks on his back and shoulders, his whip falling from his nerveless fingers.

Too well-trained to bolt, the black stallion stopped and sweated, knowing he'd earned a sound beating. His head rose as his nostrils flared, and he cast a white-ringed eye at his master. Fear-sweat bloomed on his neck and flanks.

Prepared to deliver righteous justice, Blaez roared himself to his feet and advanced on his luckless mount. He caught his whip up and raised his hand–

I reined Bayonne around and ripped my sword from its sheath. I swung at the same instant Blaez's whip-hand swung downward.

My razor-honed blade parted the lash from the whip's stem. The descending whip, without its punishing lash, hit nothing save air and earth. Blaez faltered, stumbling, knocked his shin on a sharp rocks. Blaez yelled, incoherent with fury, trying to stumble forward while rubbing his leg. His horse backed away with white-ringed eyes, seeking shelter amid the horses behind. I pushed Bayonne between the two.

"Leave off," I ordered.

"How dare you . . . ." he sputtered, staggering to his feet, snatching at his own sword. "You should learn some manners, princeling."

I whistled sharply.

At my prearranged signal, two soldiers wearing my sigil, hand-picked and chosen for their skills at arms and their mercenary hearts, spurred their mounts through and past Blaez's cronies. Bows creaked above the sound of the rising wind as they drew arrows to their ears. Blaez stared up, gaping and stunned, as my henchmen pointed razor-tipped arrows at his face and chest.

In a similar move, my other three drew down on Blaez's pals, effectively halting them when they sought to ride to his aid. His three friends carefully sat their saddles and raised hands from sword hilts, their throats bobbing as they gulped. The sweat trickling from their ghostly pallors wasn't from the sheer drop a mere rod away nor from the howling wind that threatened to toss them over its edge.

No one ever accused the Commander of cowardice. He fought well and hard, and the men he led lived to drink his health. Blaez glared around at the hard eyes and deadly armament surrounding him and his followers. His lip curled.

"You don't have the guts, Prince," Blaez scoffed, sheathing his sword, then brushing dirt and rock dust from his hands and breeches. "Your sire sent me along to keep you in line, boyo. Don't you forget that. I'm in charge here."

I leaned my arms over my pommel and grinned down into Blaez's smarmy, sneering face. "Care to wager on that–boyo?"

I straightened, and, leaving my reins on Bayonne's heavy neck, nocked an arrow to my own bowstring. "You, dear Blaez, must be taught a lesson on respecting one's betters."

As his jaw tightened and his muddy eyes narrowed, I knew he expected me to point my arrow at him. My smile widened.

"Care to pick or shall I?"

As his thick lips tightened, his eyes bulging in their sockets, Blaez stared toward the direction my eyes travelled: into his own sworn men, his bodyguard and constant companion. I all but felt his denial along my skin: *Flynn won t do it. He s a coward and no mistake. He s never killed a human being and to do so now, with cold blood, he ll rip his soul to shreds.*

Will it? Perhaps. Did I care? Not one jot. My father always said a prince should never shirk from his duty, no matter how dirty the task. Leaders must often be executioners, and to gain the respect, the fear, of these men, I'd have to dirty my hands. Unless Blaez, his men, and even my own henchmen feared me, they'll always threaten my life.

The big dog rules here, I thought. *And 1 m the big dog.*

I lowered my bow, squinting down my arrow's sight. My tip sharpened on Blaez's leading pal, his friend since boyhood and sworn liegeman. That bad boy raised both hands in surrender, sweating worse than his horse and his eyes pleading for mercy. "No, my lord," Sim whispered, fear-sweat sliding down his cheek. "I beg you. Please."

"Do you also beg, Commander?" I asked softly, my arrow trained on the pudgy face blubbering within my sights. "Implore me not to. Plead for my mercy, and perhaps your chum will live."

"You haven't the balls."

I relaxed my fingers.

The best arms masters my father paid trained me, beat me bloody, but gave to me the best instruction in the world. Those beatings taught me how to aim a bow, loose an arrow, and kill my target. My reputation spread as a poor swordsman, but no rumors spoke as to my talents as an archer. No one cared enough to listen to those that praised my skills.

My arrow took Blaez's best friend between his panicked eyes and knocked him over the rump of his roan stallion.

He fell to the rocky, unforgiving earth, stricken, his limbs still dancing as his heart thought he yet lived. He jigged and jagged on the stony soil before his heart failed to communicate with his already dead brain. Thus he died, a trickle of red seeping from my arrow down his heavy, hooked nose. Lying still at last, his spirit fled to the folk who kept count.

My victim's mates cringed away, shrinking, as Sim's horse danced sideways, tail lashing and dark eyes panicked. My own lads eyed me sidelong, still pointing their arrows, and nervously wet their lips. They hadn't believed I'd do it, either.

"Is this what you mean by balls?" I inquired politely, nocking another arrow.

Blaez stared at his fallen friend, his ruddy skin drained of all color. "You—oh, gods—"

"Tsk, Blaez," I commented dryly. "Your sentimentality is showing."

Commander Blaez mumbled incoherently, stumbling toward his dead friend. Dropping to his knees, he lifted the corpse into his arms. His voice, thick with tears, spoke not much above a mutter. "Gods...Sim, gods, no...Sim..." were the only words I clearly heard. His shaking hand closed the dead man's glazed, staring eyes.

At his obvious grief, my conscience reared up and stabbed me in the ribs. *"You killed in cold blood."*

"Who cares?"

"You didn t have to kill him."

"Yes, I did," I replied fiercely.

"You ve done murder."

"So? It s done every day. He needed to die."

"No, he didn t. You could have wounded him and still make your point."

"Wounded he d have slowed me down."

"You murdered a defenseless man," Blaez muttered, staggering sideways as he groped his way to his feet, staring, pale, at the corpse. Grief etched long lines into his already creased, leathern face, his brow dotted with sweat. Hiding behind his hands, a short coughing bark of lament emerged to tickle my conscience.

"What have you done?"

"Only what I had to do to stay alive."

Blaez's shocked, dull brown eyes and lank, oily hair showed over his thick, bulbous knuckles. Did I know how much he cared for Sim, a scoundrel who liked to rape young girls and boast about his courageous feats in the taprooms? Did I care that that I killed a man my father would have hanged from the turrets had he been anyone save Blaez's best friend?

The answer to both questions was no.

"Truthfully," I answered, nocking another arrow. "I murdered your defenseless man. Shall I murder another?"

I pointed my deadly tip at Blaez's second favorite, Buck-Eye. I knew this wretch as a mercenary soldier no regular army officer wanted under his command. The type of man only Blaez could attract. While his crimes should surely see him strung up by his ankles and his throat cut, the King granted him pardon. For Blaez's sake.

He blanched and raised empty hands. A weak grin crawled across his blunt face and terror filled his pale blue eyes. "Please, Your Highness," he begged. "Please, don't."

"'Please' is it?" I replied lightly. "I like this new respect. How 'bout you, Commander Blaez? Care to share with the class? What have you learned here today?"

Blaez dropped his hands from his ugly face. Sweat, and tears, slid like tiny rivers down his flat cheeks. He stood as tall as he could, lightning illuminating his eyes, the icy wind whipping his damp hair across his mouth. "You're in charge, Your Highness."

"Um," I muttered, my eyes rolling sideways and up. "You sure? I thought I heard you claim the big dog position here."

"My mistake," Blaez answered, lowering himself to lie flat on his belly. His huge nose and brow struck the damp, stony earth. "You're the big dog, Your Highness."

"Ah," I replied casually, lowering my bow and returning my arrow to its quiver. "Is this a true conversion? Or are you saying what you think I want to hear?"

"No, Your Highness." Dust blew out from under his face. "I mean, yes, Your Highness."

"Well, that's certainly clarifying. What of you chaps?"

Buck-Eye and his pal, Kalan, slid down from their horses. Keeping hands clear of their weapons, they each dropped to their right knee, their hands behind their backs. In unison, they bowed their heads. "You're the big dog, Your Highness," Buck-Eye choked.

"Your will, Highness," Kalan muttered.

"So glad you agree. Now then, you boys will, very carefully now, draw your swords. With your hands on the hilts, you swear your undying loyalty to your new boss."

"You can't–" Blaez inhaled the dust beneath his nose and coughed.

"Oh, but of course I can."

I grinned down onto Blaez's squirming body and trampled on no doubt a dozen royal laws as to fealty and obligation. "I can and they will."

The pair exchanged wild glances. "My lord, we've already sworn–"

"Oh, very well, then," I snapped, impatient. "First they'll disavow their loyalty to you, Blaez. Then they're clear to re-swear to me. Come on, let's get this done."

Rade, the oldest and most experienced of my henchmen, lowered his bow and returned his arrow to its quiver. Nudging his horse in behind Buck-Eye and Kalan, he urged them to their feet. Unless they wanted stallion hooves imprinted on their backs, they'd best get up and walk. Into their new future.

As they stumbled forward, Blaez lifted his face enough to watch, half-horror, half-disbelief warring across his broad, flat face. Buck-Eye and Kalan walked a few steps toward me, yet never once looked to their former liege lord. As one, they nodded.

"I disavow of my oath of loyalty and fealty to my lord Commander Blaez," Buck-Eye said, his tone low. "I do so swear to honor and obey His Royal Highness Prince Flynn of Raithin Mawr. The gods strike me dead should I prove false."

"I accept your oath and your service. I'm curious, however, Buck-Eye. How'd you get that handle anyhow? Buck-Eye?"

"M'lord, I once shot a buck through his eye at three hundred paces. M'lord."

"Well done. I'm certain to have a very good use for you and your marksmanship. Kalan, are you ready?"

His comrade nodded, dull eyes on the rocky ground. "I, Kalan of Alamara, disavow of my allegiance to Lord Commander Blaez and forthwith shall owe my sword and my life to His Royal Highness Prince Flynn. Gods strike me dead if I prove untrue."

"Welcome," I said, my tone light and expansive. "I accept both your oaths as binding and lasting. As your liege lord and master, I command you in all things."

"You do, sire." Buck-Eye bowed his head.

"Yes, Your Highness." Kalan said. "I'm your man from now on."

"Good. Commander Blaez."

At the sound of his name, Blaez scrambled to his feet, staggering, dark rock dust coating his damp face. "Eh?"

"Will you also swear your undying loyalty to me?"

As though struck by a poleaxe, his brown eyes cleared. A scowl crept across his thick lips and heavy brow. He wiped dust and grit from his dark face with his filthy hands. Balancing himself at last, on his feet where he belonged, Commander Blaez straightened his spine. He must have remembered to whom my father offered his devotion. My royal father loved him. However, he hated me. Blaez's fingers tickled his sword's hilt, safe within the warm, defensive blanket of my sire's fickle affections.

"Never."

I half-shrugged. "So be it. With or without an oath, you'll do as you're told."

"Bastard," he hissed, his pronounced lips thinned to the point of emaciation.

"You wish." I rolled my eyes. "Unfortunately, my parents were wed within a temple in front of hundreds of witnesses. Royal weddings and all that. I popped into existence a mere two years later." I snickered. "Did it take that long for Pop to finally approach her? And she's so beautiful, too."

"You've no right."

"The one who bears the might is *always* right." I sniffed, feigning mild annoyance. "Doesn't that just suck rocks?"

Blaez found his courage and a nasty grin from somewhere amid his personal possessions. "It does indeed, prince of nothing."

I laughed. "Oh, how you make me smile, Commander. You're the life of the party, what?"

"Of course, Prince. I bring smiles wherever I go."

"No doubt," I murmured. "Shall we ride, gentlemen? My bride awaits me in those barbaric caves yonder."

My new henchmen, Buck-Eye and Kalan of Alamara, swiftly mounted their horses, while Blaez obeyed more slowly. I jerked my chin at the dead man's horse, nibbling on weeds with his reins tangled in his mane. "Take him behind you," I said to Rade. "That's a nice roan. I think I'll keep him."

[98]

Blaez shot me a glare filled with hatred as he settled himself in his saddle. "You'd best watch your back, Prince."

I chuckled. "I have seven good men right here who watch it for me," I replied easily. "Meanwhile, you lead the way, Commander. I think I'll keep yours in sight for a while."

Muttering curses, Blaez kicked his black into a lunging trot up the hill, and cast one last lingering look over his shoulder. Not at me, but at the dead man we left behind. I squashed the inner voice when it wanted to berate me again, gritting my teeth. *I had to do it.*

"No, you didn t."

"Shut up."

I nudged Bayonne into line behind him while Rade, leading the blue roan stallion, and Buck-Eye paired themselves at my back. The others followed in single file as my man Boden, my clever navigator with the map, hollered instructions from the rear.

Princess Yummy, I thought. *Here I come.*

The storm delivered all its menacing promise.

We rode along the top of the rocky cliffs, the massive Khai River thundering below with another league yet to ride before we reached the cave and the princess. The footing, treacherous without the added howling winds, slashing rain and lightning cracking right over our heads, grew a starkly evil attitude. Blaez's black horse stumbled and tripped his way downward, half blinded by icy sleet. The rocks, large, rounded and in the best conditions tricky, were now slicked with clinging ice. Sure-footed Bayonne slipped and slid down the narrow trail with me clinging desperately to his mane.

I hugged my cloak more tightly around my neck, my hood up for added protection. I was soaked, and shivered uncontrollably. Peering through the half-light and rain, squinting against the stabbing lightning, I watched for every potential step before Bayonne put his hoof there. His quarters slung low, fighting against gravity and the screaming winds, Bayonne remained calm, and used every good sense in his quiet head.

"This is madness!" Blaez shouted above the wind and barking thunder. "We'll ride right over the edge!"

"My prince!" Rade called. "We must stop! We should wait this out, it's too dangerous!"

I reined Bayonne in long enough to swivel in my saddle. "We keep going," I snarled, taking my hand from my cloak long enough to point upward.

A black raven swooped, blowing past, its wings wide as it permitted the wind to carry it along. Buck-Eye and Rade followed my gesture, tracking the bird until it vanished into the heavy trees above the cliff.

"Those devil-spawned Shifters are watching us," I bellowed, my throat sore from yelling. "We must get to the caves before the Atan. Or none of us will see home again."

Rade nodded and turned to wave the others forward. As I nudged Bayonne into his careful walk down the slippery, treacherous slope, Blaez called over his shoulder again. "We'll go over the bloody edge, you stupid fool."

"When I see you go over," I called back. "I'll know not to go that way."

Had Blaez actually fallen into the dark depths of the Khai as he feared, I might have cheered. He didn't, the lucky bastard. I rode several rods behind his black, guiding Bayonne to follow in his exact hoof prints. The storm pounded away at us, making me curse and shiver, my saddle as wet and slippery as the rocks. Time and again, the bright lightning lit the sky with a light that rivaled high noon, revealing the terrain ahead for brief seconds. I saw no more evidence our enemies watched us, but I felt no comfort. Those hell-cat Griffins might watch us even now, stalking us from above.

A nerve-wracking hour later, the nasty weather blew past and into the east. It left behind a cold wind and sullen sky, but at least the rain no longer blinded us. Thunder growled in the dim distance, and I gauged the time as mid-afternoon. Wet and cold, the wind still cut through to my very bones. Had anyone suggested a stop for a fire and hot wine, I'd be the first to jump from my saddle. No one did. I cursed my luck, and stuck to Blaez's back like a burr.

The terrain eased as well, the high cliff slowly vanishing behind as the slope gentled. The churning river, swelled with rainwater, rushed swiftly past a mere rod or so below. Marshy earth, dotted with pockets of twisted oak and pine trees offered decent footing. Bayonne tried to nibble the tall grass as we trotted amid thickets of bramble and wild flowers.

"We *are* on the correct side of the river?" Blaez asked, half turning in his saddle. "Right?"

"If we're not," I replied, eyeing the swift, deep Khai, "we're screwed. There's no swimming that bugger."

"Yes, my prince," replied Boden. I'd given him the map and the messenger's report to compare, as he was not just bright and able, but owned an uncanny sixth sense for direction and terrain I'd swear only the gods owned.

He urged his horse into a rolling canter up beside Bayonne, pointing. The youngest of my band, he was also one I wished I could trust. Close to my own age, his open, pleasant expression, curly brown hair and smiling grey eyes made me wonder if he could ever be a friend. I reined Bayonne in as Rade, Buck-Eye and the others gathered around us.

"See those tall rocks, there?"

I followed his finger, nodding. "Yes."

"If the message is accurate, the caves are just below them."

"Well away from the water," Blaez added, walking his stallion toward us, "yet sheltered from the weather."

"Did the message say what the terrain around the caves was like?" I asked.

"No, my prince. It only gave instructions to follow the river from the cliffs until we saw columns of tall rock towers."

Blaez, no fool, frowned. "We could walk into a trap and never see it."

"Exactly."

I glanced around, uneasy.

From several rods away a doe stepped daintily from the twisted knot of trees toward the river, her white tail flipping back and forth. Broad ears twitching, she found an eddying pool and dropped her head to drink. Blaez, Boden, and Rade all followed my stare.

"You don't think–" Buck-Eye began.

Though she clearly heard his voice, knew we stood there watching, the doe finished her drink and lifted her head. Her huge liquid eyes regarded us solemnly, before she, tripping lightly, ambled back into the forest. A deer, unafraid of our presence, in daylight–how could there be any doubt? A bleeding Shifter.

"They want us to know they're watching," I gritted, my fear rising.

Above, a hawk screamed from on high, its *chirk-chirk-chirk* call rising over the rushing of the huge river. I glanced up, only to see it vanish over the rock towers. Another one circled lazily over the river, soaring on the cold breeze, before drifting away until the trees behind us blotted it out.

"What do we do?" Blaez asked, his voice tight. His hand gripped his sword hilt, yet his muddy eyes ever watched the river, the trees, the sky, waiting for the attack to come.

"We've no choice," I said, nocking an arrow to my bowstring. "We have to go in and get her."

"But–"

"There are nine of us," I said, making my tone as confident as possible. "Plus the spies in the cave. The Atan haven't had time to get here. A few Shifters, and we can eliminate them if we have to."

"Of course we can," Rade said, following my lead and readying his own bow. "Grab her and get out. Right, Your Highness?"

Glancing around at their faces, I observed little of the contempt I was used to seeing and instead recognized an eagerness to ride at my side. Might I actually trust these men to fight for me and truly guard my back? Could Sims's death have not been in vain, in truth?

"Time to find out, I reckon."

Nudging Bayonne into a swift trot and trying not to watch every way at once, I estimated the distance to the rock formation. Though thickets of bramble and knots of trees stood in the way, I guessed the caves were a hundred rods from us. The closer we rode, the more open the country became. The grass grew thicker, yet the dense pockets of pine, birch, oak and bramble thinned out. I breathed easier when I sighted the caves, for the lack of cover and no bristling Atani troops waiting to take my head meant we'd gotten there before them.

I raised my fist, calling a swift halt. "Blaez, you, Buck-Eye and Torass, flank right. Rade, Boden and Lyall, flank left. Stay on your horses and watch. Yell if you see or hear anything. Kalan, Todaro, and you, Kadal, come with me."

As Blaez and Rade led their men to the left and right, I nudged Bayonne forward at a quick trot. Kadal and Todaro flanked Bayonne while Kalan placed his mount directly behind Bayonne's tail. As Rade had handed over the reins to the blue roan to Kadal, I had an extra horse. *A mount fit for the princess,* I half-thought, my instincts on high alert. Rather than unsheathe my sword, I kept my arrow nocked and guided Bayonne with my knees.

I tried looking everywhere at once, suspecting a trap. *This was too easy. No way we should get this far without a fight.* Yet, I found nothing out of the ordinary. No bizarre deer drinking water, no raptors screaming from on high. I tried to relax, but my shoulders refused to unwind and my fingers incessantly drew down on every moving shadow.

All seemed peaceful and tranquil, outside the rushing river, that was. The breeze blew dank and chilly, but the sun rolled out from behind the grey clouds. I heard muted voices coming from inside the cave, the tones of casual conversation. Not panic or alarm. If the kidnappers had horses, I saw none in evidence. How did they get her this far without horses?

Approaching within ten rods of the cave, I stopped. Blaez, Rade and their men halted to either side of the towers, bunched together like sheep before a storm. Though armed and mounted, they kept their backs to the forest. I didn't like that. Their stances, their postures screamed like an irate fishwife: *We're scared and we're idiots.*

There was nothing I could do about it, however. I had to get Princess Iyumi out, on a horse and galloping as hard as I could for the border with no time for stops. If the Shifters watched, they'd soon report my presence and the direction we travelled. The ruthless Atan would dog my heels every mile.

"Ho, in the cave!" I yelled. "This is Prince Flynn. Come out with the princess."

Exclamations and curses abounded, and I listened to the mad scrambling as men got to their feet. The caverns echoed, resounding and drifting out and upward on the light wind. I cursed under my breath. What were they doing in there? Playing dice around a fire and drinking ale? Why didn't they have a guard posted?

A dirty man in leather breeches, faded green tunic and a floppy hat emerged from the cave's mouth, a sword in his hand. Several days growth of beard covered his face, and his eyes swept the area, trying to see every which way at once. Instantly, I knew he felt out of his element, that this errand to fetch a girl brought him to the brink of his limited ability. This time, I cursed my father for sending an idiot to do a competent's job.

Those orbs fastened upon me, and his tired face lit like the rising sun. "Your Highness," he gasped. "Thank all the gods you're here. She's inside. We can't move her, she–"

"Shut up, you moron," I snapped. "Bring her out. Now."

He stuttered and stammered, his pallor beneath the dirt paling to the color of old wax. "We can't, Your Highness. She's out cold. If we move her, we might–"

I waved my hand and he shut his teeth on his rapid tongue. *Hell and damnation,* I thought, swinging down from Bayonne. My men dismounted with me, leaving their reins on the ground. Well-trained, our horses remained where they were as I led my crew of three toward the moron with the sword and floppy hat.

"Put that thing up," I snapped, striding forward, pointing my nocked arrow at the ground.

I glanced around, seeking trouble before it landed on me with both feet as the stupid spy hastily sheathed his blade in my presence. As I stood fairly tall and he didn't, I loomed over him, witnessing, with no small satisfaction, him blanche. His skin paled into the same shade as a dirty sheepskin. His fear only made me angrier.

"Where is she?"

"In h–here, Your Hi–Highness," he stammered. "N–next to the f–fire."

I jerked my head at Kalan, ordering him to mind the floppy hatted spy. I certainly didn't need him to create mischief while my back was turned. Who knew where his true loyalties lay?

Hesitating a rod or so from the cave's mouth, I glanced around, my bow and arrow at the ready. Some small bird fluttered in the trees to my left and I swung sharply around and raised my bow, expecting an immediate attack. When none came, I took a firm grip on my runaway fears and stalked forward, one slow step at a time.

The cavern was huge, many rods tall and twice as many deep. Sand covered the floor, and the bones of some predator's victims poked through here and there. Sparrow and barn swallow nests erupted like crusty pimples across the pillars of salted rock formations. A fire burned merrily amid a rock ring, collected firewood piled against the cave wall. I entered cautiously, glancing around. Three spies stood up as I, and my escort entered. They dropped to their knees as they recognized me, shivering with panic. I paid them no mind.

She lay on a pallet of pine branches and blankets near the blazing fire, on her side, her back to me. Her Royal Highness, Princess Iyumi of Bryn'Cairdha. My future wife. I paused, taking in the sight of her. For a moment, my heart hesitated, paused in its rhythmic beat. It began again, pounding in my chest in long, heavy strokes. My lungs ached, for I hadn't drawn breath since entering the cavern. *Have mercy*, I thought, my brain short-circuiting.

I'd imagined her hair blonde like mine, but the long tresses that burst over the woolen blanket owned a silvery sheen that set my blood afire. Never before had I seen it's like. Damn, but it appeared, in the firelight, the same color as the chasings on Bayonne's bridle. Molten silver poured across the dark blanket in a river, glimmering with a light of its own.

Pale, alabaster cheeks met my inspection, but as her eyes were closed, I guessed they matched the blue of a summer sky. Under the blanket, her small, trim body lay outlined and forced me to guess that while standing her head might reach my chest. A full, rounded breast slowly rose and fell with her deep, even breathing. I almost forgot my business, and the Atani threat, as I gazed at this exquisite creature. Next to her, Sofia's regal beauty paled as the full moon eclipsed the stars.

"She fainted, Your Highness," the floppy hat spy whined, wringing his hands. "She's sick, I tell you. Something's wrong. She hasn't moved since we put her there."

"The only thing wrong is your presence," I murmured, stepping lightly on the balls of my feet. "Get lost."

I glanced behind, out of habit, and found my men urging the other wretched spies to their feet and shooing them out the cave mouth. Like chickens seeking shelter to roost in, they fled, scrambling to escape. Even my floppy friend vanished, leaving me alone with the legendary She Who Hears. My boys hovered near the entrance, watching both inside and outside the cave, never relaxing for a moment.

"Hail and well met, Princess. My name is Flynn, but you already knew that."

She didn't move nor did her breathing change. I tipped my head sideways, considering. Did I see her eyelids flicker or was it the firelight? "Get up now, honey, it's time to go home."

Iyumi didn't move. Though I knew in my head she faked it, my heart wondered. How could one person have such strict control? Perhaps she was as sick as the spies thought.

"Up you go," I said, seizing her by the arm and dragging her upright. The blanket slid to the sandy cave floor, exposing a slender waist and lovely legs beneath a short blue tunic, skin-hugging black leather breeches and a dark grey cloak lined with scarlet. Her body limp, hung from my left hand.

My quick perception captured the flash of steel illuminated red by the firelight.

My right hand rose from instinct and a sharp need for self-preservation. Many years of arms-masters beating competence into me gave me a reflexive speed similar to that of a striking snake. I seized her wrist and twisted sharply.

[106]

She cried out once, a brief exclamation of pain as the deadly knife dropped to the sand, killing its light. Still she fought on, raising her left hand to smack, hard, against my cheek. Her blow rattled my teeth and burned my skin, but hadn't enough weight to actually force me to let go. I didn't, and raised my left fist. Her tiny, frail body hung from my hand as though dead, gutted and ready for butchering. She weighed as much as newborn fawn, and dangled from my grip with her toes barely touching the sand. I held her there, mildly amused as she cursed invectives, dancing on tip-toe, and swiped at me again with a new knife in her hand.

"Princess Yummy."

She yowled like a feral cat at the name, and lunged toward me. Only my grip on her right arm kept her both in place and my guts inside my belly. The second dagger followed the first, and I half-wondered how many she kept hidden in so few hiding places. Regaining my sense of humor, I half shook her, gazing up and down her luscious length.

"Are you through?" I asked mildly. "Cuz, you know, I can do this all day."

"Animal," she grated, twisting and struggling, trying to break my hold. "Put me down, you're hurting me."

"If I do, will you behave?"

For answer, she shot a rapid foot toward my crotch. Like the knife, I saw the blow's arrival and reacted, instantly. Her toes caught my thigh and hurt her more than it did me. I tsked in annoyance.

"Oh, cease with the drama already," I snapped. "You're caught and I'm an evil bastard, so let's just move on shall we?"

"Pig." Her spittle struck my cheek below my right eye and oozed south.

Now that was uncalled for. Reddish haze crossed my vision as my rage grew out of proportion, rising high and fast. *Oh, you stupid bitch.*

I answered her insult with a swift backhanded slap. My right blow exploded across her right cheekbone, my heavy signet ring cutting deep. Her head snapped to the side, droplets of blood slinging wide and far. Iyumi half-screamed in pain and anger, her silver-gilt hair cloaking her, half-hiding her face. Her hands reached for my tunic and fell away. Limp and boneless for a moment, she almost blacked out, yet her clenched hands still sought to strike at my face, my throat. Never did she instinctively cover her injury to protect it.

A fighter, I thought, *a warrior bred and true.* "Calm down," I said, my tone low. "I don't want to hurt you."

I knew she had sky-blue eyes. Those beautiful orbs narrowed with hate and rage as she sniffed back her tears of pain. Her free hand wiped blood from her lacerated cheek. "Oh, but I want to hurt you."

A third knife stabbed toward my gut. Knowing she didn't have many weapons, but plenty of magic, I sucked in my belly as the dagger kissed my tunic.

"Bad girl," I growled, my tunic shredded. I seized her left wrist and twisted hard. The third blade joined the first pair as she cried out.

Ignoring her curses, her obvious pain, I twisted both her hands behind her back. My foot kicked her ankles shoulder-width apart. That kept her effectively off balance as I wrestled her into some semblance of quiescence. "Rope," I gasped, tossing my sweaty hair from my eyes. "Quick."

My newest henchman, Kadal, ran forward with not a rope but a belt. *Good enough.* I wrapped the tough leather around her wrists, behind her back, and cinched it tight. She may use magic against me, but she'd do it without her hands. When I let go, she staggered away and screamed foul invectives.

"I'll kill you slow, you Raithin pig," Iyumi snarled, blue eyes sparking fire. "No one touches me and lives."

Her creative vocabulary startled me. *Princesses shouldn't speak like longshoremen.* She added interesting words my experience in rough taverns never encountered. *I could use that one,* I thought, as she compared my manhood with that of a pygmy monkey.

"Is this how the girls of your land greet their intended grooms?" I asked mildly, turning her around.

I snapped my head sideways, just in time. Her aim, while accurate, missed me and shot past my shoulder. "Cease this nonsense or I'll have you gagged."

"Raithin Mawrn shit," she hissed.

I sighed. "So be it."

At my gesture, Buck-Eye rushed into my territorial bubble with a length of cotton sacking in his hand. Dropping it, he dashed out again before I might shoot him for his lack of good manners.

"Open wide," I gushed, forcing the gag into her mouth, past her wicked teeth and tied it within the lengths of that incredible hair behind her neck. *Keep her rebellious spirit,* I thought, praying. *Give me that body and that hair. All I ask, oh ye Lords of Grace. That s all l ll ever ask of you.*

Bound, gagged, Princess Iyumi glared as if by looks alone she might slay me where I stood. Having weathered such looks since the ripe age of four, I shrugged it off. Years of hatred and contempt thickened my skin to the potency of an elephant's, and Iyumi's hatred bored me silly.

"I know you can do better than that," I sighed. "But, it'll have to wait. Commander Blaez."

"What?"

His obnoxious voice from outside the cave mouth annoyed me further. "Gather the men. We're leaving."

"About bloody time."

Dragging the resisting princess with me, I pushed her past Buck-Eye, Rade, Boden, Torass and Blaez. The useless spies watched me from several rods away, sweating more than the mild afternoon required. With no horses and no weapons, I knew they hoped I'd take them with me. They were my father's faithful servants, after all. I'd an obligation to save them.

They seemed to forget one tiny matter: me and that silly whore named 'obligation' parted company a long time ago. If my father wanted them saved, let him come get them. I'd neither the time, the manpower, nor the horses to help them get home.

"Run," I advised them, dragging Iyumi across the sand toward Bayonne and the roan's empty saddle. "Before the Atani come."

"But, Your Highness–"

I ignored Floppy Hat's plea, and pushed past Bayonne to lift Iyumi into the roan's saddle. Struggling, trying to scream past the gag in her mouth, Iyumi whipped her head around, trying her best to smack me in the face. Yet, all she accomplished was to blind herself with her own hair. On she struggled, whipping about like a viper in my hand, always trying to bite. I deftly avoided her fangs, and set her aboard the blue stallion.

Blaez, Rade and others trotted their mounts into a circular ring about Iyumi and I, forming a protective ring as Kadal and his mates swung into their saddles. *About bloody time,* I thought, approving of their alert, military stance. Rade, Buck-Eye, and Boden raised bows with nocked arrows aimed high, while Blaez, Kalan, Torass and Lyall bared their swords as their horses sidling sideways, nervous. Todaro edged his champing, sweating mount closer to me, acting as my immediate bodyguard. The horses–the men– they sensed something–

Too impatient to heed their warning, I grabbed Bayonne's slack reins and growled to Buck-Eye. "Keep her there."

He nodded, his dark eyes wide, and his lips thinned as his own fears showed. He gripped Iyumi's shoulder, holding her in firm place when she would have thrown herself to the ground. The roan tossed his fine head; his huge eyes ringed white. He snorted, and his charcoal tail lashed from side to side. I half-hoped he wasn't planning to buck his passenger off.

Seizing my pommel, I vaulted into Bayonne's saddle. Taking my reins, I groped for my stirrups as I opened my mouth to–

Bayonne's head dropped between his knees as his hindquarters thrust skyward, kicking high. I had time for a *What the–'* before his third wild buck catapulted me from his back. I landed, hard on my back and hips; my lungs swooshing out my air supply. I had difficulty getting it back. My head smacked something hard that splintered upon impact. Stunned, wrenched, breathless, I blinked dirt from my eyes as Bayonne stepped between the sky and me. His dark mane fell over his cheek as he lowered his muzzle. Huge equine eyes danced with mischief.

[110]

"Hail, Your Highness," Bayonne said, his reins spilling to the ground beside me. "Sorry about that, I know it was rude. Hope I didn't hurt you."

Before I could make my mouth form a word of reply, all hell broke loose.

Wildly, I stared past Bayonne's huge shoulder to the trees and sky beyond. Screaming Griffins in full flight mode, wingtip to wingtip, blasted past, low overhead. The wind of their passage blew Bayonne's mane across his eyes and my hair across mine. The effect they had on the horses was nothing less than catastrophic.

Bayonne planted himself in a position of protection as the horses belonging to Blaez and the men exploded in all directions. Like me, Blaez came off almost immediately, as did Kadal and Rade. Their horses bolted into the forest. I lost sight of the others and had no idea if they managed to remain aboard as their horses fled, or if they were tossed to the ground out of my sight.

Princess Iyumi.

The wild thought of her, bound and gagged on board a panicked horse, flitted across my mind. *What have I done?*

In the midst of horses careening in all directions, massive Centaurs galloped across the grass and river sand, raising bows ready with nocked arrows. Pale grit, kicked up by their slashing hooves, drifted amid the long tossing grass as at least a dozen of them scattered wide. Never before had I seen the legendary half-man, half-horse creatures. Terror sang from my every nerve ending, and had I the ability to run in that moment, I'd have run screaming like a girl from that sandy clearing.

Kadal, with more courage than I'd credited him, yanked his sword from his sheath and bellowed. A challenge, no less. Despite the chaos, he heard Bayonne's words and knew him for a Shifter. Running, raising his blade, he lunged toward the silver creature pinning me to the ground. Though he'd been my henchman for almost a year, he took his bodyguard responsibilities more seriously than I did.

A great black Centaur, his massive chest crisscrossed with leather and his wild mane of hair bound by a headband arrayed with a star, galloped from amid the rearing, shouting Centaurs, his bow nocked and aimed. Kadal never stood a chance. That bastard shot Kadal through the throat as he lunged toward me with sword raised. Kadal stumbled and fell, gurgling, his fingers trying to yank the feathered shaft from his gushing neck. He fell on his face, bleeding out like a slaughtered lamb.

I groaned, wanting to shut my eyes from the sight of Kadal, a man who offered his life up for mine, dying like a hunted buck. I didn't, and watched him gasp his last breath out on a stream of red. Despite my need to protect myself from my enemies, and those who hated me, I never truly thought anyone might actually die in my defense. While I hadn't an opportunity to pause and reflect on my worthiness of his sacrifice, I did swallow hard and offer a quick prayer of thanks that he didn't suffer.

Amid the organized chaos of Centaurs and Griffins securing the area and the perimeters, the Minotaurs arrived. Slower moving, I guessed they'd been held back as the reserve, ringing the area. Just in case any of us slipped past the Centaurs and Griffins, we'd never pass the alert and deadly Minotaurs.

Troops of royal cavalry galloped in from behind the rock towers and circled the area, ringing the outer limits. As the last of them arrived and rode into position, the uniformed cavalry faced inward and their entire unit stood at parade rest. At least fifty of them, I guessed. With swords in hand, the humans aboard their snorting mounts waited for their next orders.

How in the name of hell did they hide all these man-horses, two-legged bulls and flying lions? *Magic,* my mind whispered. Evil magic hid them, waited until I blundered into their trap. They used the princess as bait, and like a supreme idiot I blundered straight into it. *Braigh Mhar, here I come.*

Buck-Eye, in terror, fell to his face, screaming in horror. Two Minotaurs and a Centaur glanced at one another in confusion. After watching this spectacle for several moments, the Centaur reached down and gently raised Buck-Eye to his feet. Buck-Eye slowly calmed as the huge chestnut rested his hand on Buck-Eye's shoulder and spoke quietly for several moments. My man nodded slowly, half-smiled, and unbuckled his sword belt. The Centaur accepted it with respect and grace.

Blaez, of course, fought on. He screamed and thrashed, trying to fight with nothing but his hands and his terrors. A Minotaur, annoyed, kicked his feet out from under him. A huge bay and white Centaur with a lion's head emblem on his chest scowled in irritation and flipped him over onto his face with one lazy hoof. Within seconds, my father's pride and good friend lay on his face with his hands tied behind his back. He breathed in dust and coughed out his curses.

Beyond the huge body of the Griffin and Bayonne's heavy form, I caught a swift glimpse of a huge Griffin loom over Rade. With a nearly black mane that crept down his chest to his belly, he reached out a deadly talon, aiding Rade to stand. Thrown from his horse, coughing, bleeding from his nose and mouth, Rade accepted the assist. A grey-coated Centaur offered a white cloth for him to clean himself up, and even tilted Rade's chin back to more closely examine his injuries. I suspected he offered light, clinical advice, and saw Rade half-laugh in answer.

Rounded up like cattle, Lyall, Kalan, and Boden surrendered, raising their hands high as the Centaurs herded them into a tight group, arrows trained. Torass was pushed into their midst by a huge Minotaur with a broadsword nearly twice the size of mine. Todaro, keeping his whimpers of panic behind his tightly clenched teeth, stumbled into their company with a Centaur's heavy hand on his shoulder. His weapons lay in the huge bay and white Centaur's hand, seized from him at his surrender.

Between the half bulls and half horses, and the cavalry units that sat their mounts with bows in hand and arrows at the ready, we hadn't a hope in hell of escaping. That didn't preclude the spies from trying, however. Floppy Hat and a fellow spy, creeping like mice to the side, suddenly fled, and broke for the forest and freedom. Twin Centaur arrows caught them in the back. The third man watched his brothers fall, and screamed in utter terror. He bolted in the opposite direction. A Griffin the size of a barn dropped on his back like a hawk on a mouse, and snapped it in two.

He died, his eyes bulging from their sockets. A shrill high-pitched *eee-eee-eee* sound emerged from behind his bloody lips.

The other spies fell into the heavy grass, twitching, screaming in agony and terror. Not yet dead, but dying too slowly. A single Centaur, similar in color as Bayonne with grey hair falling to his broad, bare shoulders, advanced slowly. He pulled his dagger from his belt. Leaning down, he cut first Floppy Hat's throat, then the other spy's. His heavy mouth frowning, as though he touched something nasty, he cleaned his blade on Floppy Hat's shirt, sheathed it, and stalked away. He left them to bleed to death, choking, gasping for life. Their life's blood soaked into the sand, turning it black.

I fought to get up, find my breath, help them.

Bayonne planted a heavy hoof on my chest. "Sorry, old son," he said regretfully. "Your pals are toast."

He raised his grey head, watching as the Centaurs rounded up the skittish horses, herding them back across the sandy clearing. Several enormous Griffins landed to all fours, furling angel's wings across their eagle shoulders. My horse paid me no mind, as his attention seemed riveted upon the organized chaos that was once a silent clearing beside the mighty Khai. My hand crept toward my sword hilt. Perhaps I could stab him before he realized–

"Don't, boy," my horse warned.

The pressure on my chest increased, shutting off all hope of breathing and listened as my ribs creaked. Bayonne's head swiveled down, his ears cocked, and his formerly mild brown eyes now hard and menacing.

"Think you can draw that before I burst your heart like an overripe plum?"

Gasping for air, my chest slowly sinking under the weight of what I thought was my horse, I raised my hands in surrender.

"Good lad."

The pressure withdrew, although Bayonne kept his hoof squarely planted, should I get stupid again. I breathed in deep, ragged pants, the pain slowly receding. My ribs ached fiercely, but I knew none were broken. I'd had every rib busted in the past, so I knew what it felt like. Bayonne knew just how to apply enough pressure to get the job done without lasting damage.

More Griffins joined the flock already present, bellowing questions and orders to one another and the Centaurs. Several others back-winged to join their mates on the ground, their long lion tails lashing. Three circled low overhead, while others flew higher, over the towers and the trees. *Keeping watch.* In case I had more soldiers hidden and ready to ride to my rescue.

Another troop of Minotaurs, marching in step with massive broadswords in their hands, stomped in from the north and entered the bristling ring of cavalry. Like their brothers-in-arms, they carried banners of a grinning skull on a field of azure. I recognized it, a shiver crawling down my spine. The symbol of the King's dreaded Weksan'Atan. The Bryn'Cairdha Secret Police.

"Where's the princess?" the black Centaur with the star headband shouted. He half-reared, his front hooves boxing the air as he raised his bow in his right fist. "Your Highness! Princess Iyumi!" He dropped all four hooves to the ground. "Find her! Search everywhere! I want every orifice within a league from here turned inside out. Go!"

They might appear disorganized and frenzied in my opinion, but those beasts under his command obeyed instantly. The Minotaurs split into smaller clusters and bolted to the four points of the compass. The cavalry, up till now silent and watchful, also sprang into action, and formed smaller units that galloped into the woods and followed each direction of the surging river.

"Boy," Bayonne commented, his tone low and thoughtful. He raised his silver head and glanced around, up and down, seeking their lost heir. His black-tipped ears canted backward at the same time his nostrils flared red. "You better pray she's all right."

"She was," I wheezed, choking. "Until you showed up."

"If she's dead," my horse said, his tone dark. "So, my friend, are you."

"Princess!"

"Princess Iyumi!"

A cadre of Griffins launched themselves into the air, calling Iyumi's name as they split into a wide aerial circle. Those Centaurs and Minotaurs not guarding Blaez and my henchmen widened their search, probing into the forest, the river, endlessly calling. Was she dead? Did she fall off her terrorized horse and break her neck? I'll never live with my conscience if I killed her by putting her on that horse.

"There she is!" screamed a huge Griffin, owning a collar of gold and an emblem of a stars glowing over a half-moon dressed in silver around his pristine, white-feathered mane. He crouched, his massive wings wide, lion haunches coiling beneath him. He launched himself skyward, his white and brown wings taking him higher and higher with every downward stroke.

I'd no idea Griffins appeared as barbaric and beautiful as pagan gods of lore. I watched, entranced, by the sheer grace and raw elegance of these beasts as they flew or prowled like hunting cats around the caves and the river. On the ground, they furled those incredible wings across their shoulders, mantling them in tan and white feathers. Long feline tails lashed with unrepressed emotions. Large, tufted ears flattened or rose according to their anger, curiosity, or personality.

The impressive beast I admired suddenly dove like a frightened trout and flew no more than three feet off the ground, the tall grass kissing his feather-fur belly. Wings wide, his front talons taut under his wide shoulders, his lion rear trailed far behind him. Graceful, awesomely beautiful, he rose, his colossal wings wide to capture the wind. He blew past Bayonne's silver head, offering me a swift, grim glance from those yellow raptor eyes.

"Your Highness!" he called, back-winging to slow his forward speed. The black Centaur galloped past, sending stinging sand into my eyes, as two more Griffins, a second grey Centaur and a huge Minotaur with immense curving horns and a rayed star on his breast ran past. I turned my head to see, but between the grit, my hair and the many hoofed legs, I saw nothing.

"You can get up now, Your Highness," Bayonne said, taking his hoof from my chest. "Try anything stupid and I'll knock your head off."

[116]

"I won't," I said, staggering to my feet. I cast a quick glance up, under my brows. "I promise."

My ribs still ached and my head swam, but I could stand. Courteously, Bayonne offered his shoulder for support, and feeling oddly grateful, I accepted it. "Who are you?" I asked, but my horse didn't answer. I followed his high head and bright piercing glance.

In an amazing feat of horsemanship, Princess Iyumi trotted the blue roan out from under the trees and into the milling midst of shouting Centaurs, flying Griffins and bellowing Minotaurs. Still gagged, her hands belted behind her back, she urged the reluctant horse forward. While the roan tried to shy from the massive, unfamiliar and dangerous beasts, her knees guided him expertly and firmly.

"She may be a royal bitch," Bayonne said, his tone admiring. "But she sure can ride a horse."

"I reckon so," I said, awed.

No doubt the roan bolted with her still aboard, yet she not only kept her seat, but turned the horse around to return to the frightening place amid her rescuers. Never in a million, ten million years, could I have accomplished the same. The black Centaur took her down from the sweating roan, and, with gentle fingers, removed the gag. She raised her lovely face to speak to him, yet I heard not what she said.

His already gloomy face darkened further as he examined the swelling and cut left by my ring. My guilt returned. I hit a helpless woman. Why in the hell did I hit her? So she spat, so what? Our countries are enemies after all, and I was there to kidnap her, for gods' sake. I lost my temper–the long and short of it. I deserved whatever punishment they gave me.

As I watched the huge Minotaur wearing the purple cloak untie her hands, the huge Griffin with the black mane landed to all four feet beside Bayonne. His heavy collar amid his neck feathers gleamed under the sullen, shadowy sunlight. I jolted and swung around, fearing an attack.

I reckoned seeing my entrails hanging from his talon wasn't his first priority. He merely eyed me up and down, his expression cold.

I never thought an eagle's face could offer such a wide variety of facial emotions. In less than two minutes, I'd seen more Griffins smile, scowl, grimace, laugh, frown, and light with hope than a barroom of tavern crawlers.

Raised on tales of the monsters who lived south of our beloved Raithin Mawr, I couldn't help but feel death's cold finger on my neck. Evil magic that slew in the night; the mix-breed horrors who flew across the dark skies–winged lions who murdered in cold blood all who crossed their paths. Minotaurs fed their greedy, thirsty calves on the corpses of small human children. The worst were the Centaurs: the accursed blend of man and horse. The devil's spawn, neither horse nor man. All Raithin Mawrn knew they sucked their victims dry and nursed demons on their breast milk.

What I witnessed for myself, first-hand, dropped my jaw.

Unprepared for the raw, elegant beauty of the beasts, I caught my breath as they flew, wingtip to wingtip, over the tops of the low forest branches. None on the ground seemed interested in eating my men; in fact, two Griffins spoke firmly yet kindly to Boden and Torass when asking for their surrender and arms. My lads obeyed them, smiling hesitantly up into the savage beaks that pointed downward. A Minotaur with the same muscles as an aged bull lifted Torass's face with his finger under his jaw and smeared a cut on his cheek with a salve.

I returned my focus on the huge tawny and black Griffin in front of me. He furled his wings and raised his talons to push at my shoulder. I gave ground, realizing those razor-tipped talons might gut me in a blink. A contemptuous snort erupted from his nostrils and his black-tipped tail lashed.

"You got him under control, Van?" the Griffin asked, scrutinizing me up and down.

"No worries, Windy," my horse said, turning his great head to eye sidelong the savage Griffin who stood more than thrice his size and outweighed him by tons.

Instantly, Bayonne vanished. I gaped, my mouth working soundlessly, as a young man with coal-black hair and striking green eyes stood in his place. He stood as tall as I, and bore the slender, athletic body of a dancer. Two slender scars crossed each high

[118]

cheekbone. I guessed him about my own age, our only similarity. His expression was open and his mouth smiled, an endearing boyish grin that I'd never replicate in a hundred years. I seldom smiled and he owned a face that couldn't help but. People despised me at first look. This young man was both charismatic and confident, and I liked him on sight. No doubt all who met him did.

He wore a simple tunic of grey with black leather trousers, a wide belt that held his sword and dagger around his hips. A cloak of deep blue, clasped at his throat with the pewter emblem of a lightning strike surrounded by glittering stars, lay back from his shoulders. He raised his hand and rested it on the Griffin's shoulder. "Wind Warrior," he said, his voice as deep as the river behind him. "Meet His Royal Highness, Prince Flynn of Raithin Mawr. Say hello, Windy."

Wind Warrior snorted, his tone contemptuous. "He's a snake, Van. You should tie him up before he escapes."

Van chuckled. "Oh, I think he's a model prisoner. Don't you?"

"You should at least disarm him."

Van merely laughed. "Your Highness," he said. "Forgive my friend. He's a boor, and very suspicious. And my apologies for not introducing myself properly when you asked earlier."

He rested his fingers on his chest and bowed slightly, his even white teeth gleaming amid the scruffy half-beard on his cheeks and jaws. "I'm First Captain Vanyar of His Majesty's Royal Atani Forces. This is Lieutenant Wind Warrior. He doesn't look it when he's being so stiff and unfriendly, but he's a good fellow, truly, and a fine comrade to drink with."

"Don't lie to the boy," Wind Warrior hissed, glaring. "We haven't drank together."

"We haven't? Gotta fix that, Windy."

"Uh," I began, sizing Wind Warrior up and trying to imagine him drinking in a tavern. "Drink with?"

"Sure," Van replied easily, his white grin flashing. "He does like his white wine."

"Shut up, Van," Wind Warrior grumbled. "And how the hell do you know I like wine? Here now, if you don't disarm him and tie his hands, the Captain will have you scrubbing floors. Again."

"Wouldn't want that," First Captain Vanyar replied cheerfully, holding out his hand. "Makes my knees ache something chronic. Sorry, Your Highness. Your sword, please."

Under the tense scrutiny of Wind Warrior, his talon raised to strike, Captain Vanyar's pleasant but firm resolve, and the three huge Minotaurs with heavy blades drawn and ready crowding my back, I half-shrugged. Only surrender might keep me alive.

"I'm for Braigh'Mhar, I expect," I said, trying for lightness as I unbuckled my swordbelt. "Or the executioner's block. Either way, I'm dead."

"Above my pay grade," Vanyar said, accepting my sheathed sword. "Turn around, Your Highness. If you don't mind."

I obeyed, facing the bristling Minotaurs who stood high over my head, staring down at me with hard bovine eyes. They fingered their weapons as though wishing to try them against my neck. I put my hands behind my back as Vanyar bound them together with fire-hardened leather thongs. I noticed he didn't bind them too tightly, whereby my hands might die via a strong circulation lack, nor did he tie them so loose I might escape them. Comfortable enough as a prisoner, I met the calm gazes of these creatures I'd been taught to fear since childhood.

Nursery tales spoke of the blood-thirsty Minotaurs who slaughtered children in their beds and ate them raw. As I gazed up into their savage, shaggy bull faces, human hands clasping bared steel, I found a small shred of courage. "What do you gentlemen prefer for supper?"

The huge creature on my right blinked in surprise. "A good, steamed cabbage with carrots and onions," he replied, his deep voice mellow with an odd quirky lilt. "Lettuce and alfalfa work just well, though I do love cabbage."

"Cabbage!" the huge bull to his left grumbled, nudging his mate with a sour expression. "Give me lentils, peas, turnips and lots and lots of green beans. Though I must agree on the alfalfa part. Mwwaa!" The Minotaur kissed his fingers. "Gotta love leafy alfalfa."

"Don't forget the turnip tops. Mixed with timothy, clover, and sweet, sweet bean sprouts," the third massive bull-soldier commented. "And mushrooms. And buttermilk. Mustn't forget hot, fresh bread covered in honey."

As the other two condemned their mate for his love of mushrooms, Vanyar's breath tickled my ear. "Minotaurs are vegetarians," he murmured. "Forget the buttermilk part, though. Not a one of them would refuse a tall mug of warm ale. All that wheat and barley, you know."

"You knew what I was thinking?"

"I guessed. Raised on nursery tales, were we?"

"Er, yes, rather."

Vanyar turned me around to face him, his once smiling face now earnest and sincere. "Listen, Flynn," he said, his voice pitched low. Although I knew Wind Warrior and the Minotaurs heard our conversation clearly, 'twas as though only he and I existed. Alone, the two of us. The chaotic, dust-raising Atani capture of us and the rescue of their princess might never have happened. We might be friends sharing a laugh and stories over ale in a rustic tavern.

"My time as your horse," Van began, his hand on my shoulder, "told me much about you. You're not a bad fellow, really. Let go your hate. Find your own soul, not your father's. Be your own person."

I choked, never imagining I'd hear such advice from another human being. Floundering in unchartered waters, I grasped at the only question that made sense. "How long?"

Van grinned. "Since your mid-morning break. You saddled and bridled me, not him."

"Where's Bayonne?"

"On his way home. He's safe, no worries."

I nodded, more afraid than when Van bucked me off and the Griffins screamed in. I feared more for the safety of my soul than my own life.

"Listen, Flynn," Vanyar said, glancing toward the group of Blaez, Buck-Eye, Rade and the others who stood amid their Griffins and Minotaur captors, hands tied behind their backs and their weapons seized. "They planned to kill you." He smiled as he caught my eye. "Men speak freely in front of their horses. Blaez and Sim plotted your death on this enterprise."

My breath caught in my throat. My blood chilled in my veins. "What?"

"Your own men wouldn't avenge you, had they seen you with your throat open. They'd cut and run, the bloody cowards."

"My father—"

"Sanctioned it. I'm sorry."

My fear dropped and my guilt fell away. My father connived with Blaez to kill me. That nasty, scheming bastard paid Blaez to assassinate me. Murder his own son and heir. Cold leeched into my bones. *Why?*

As though reading my thoughts, Van murmured. "You're a threat to him. Why, I don't know and neither did they. They spoke of hints and vague rumors, no absolute truths."

I met Van's sincere emerald gaze with my own. "Thank you."

"Had you not killed Sim when you had," Vanyar said softly. "You'd be dead now."

"It doesn't absolve me," I murmured, shrugging my shoulders, trying to make sense of it. "I murdered him."

Vanyar ducked his head. "So you did. You'll have to live with that."

"Smarten up," Wind Warrior hissed. "The Lord Captain comes. And he looks righteously pissed off."

Van straightened and retrieved his hand. His shoulders squared in tight military discipline, yet he shot a swift glance and a quick word my way. "Courage."

The massive black Centaur with the star on his brow-band stalked toward me, Princess Iyumi straddling his massive equine back. Her silver-gilt hair streamed down her body to the Captain's sleek, equine shoulder, her porcelain cheeks bloodless and pale. Her incredible blue eyes hardened when they latched upon me, and a dirk appeared in her right hand without her drawing one.

Flanking the black commander were no less than five Minotaurs, the one with the rayed star on his mantle marching at his right hand. Another Centaur stalked at his left, long black hair streaming over his bare shoulders. Three Griffins circled low overhead as two Griffin pairs, wings furled over their lion backs, flanked the group and towered heads tall over their brothers.

l m in serious trouble now, I thought.

The black Centaur, obviously the Lord Captain of whom Wind Warrior spoke, halted before me, his stern visage a mask of restrained rage. The slender princess on his back rested her free hand on his massive left bicep. The colorful bruise I gave her, plus the nasty cut, showed clear on her pale cheekbone. Dried blood oozed dark down to her chin, as she never wiped it off.

"You craven coward," the black said, yanking his dagger from his belt. "You gutless wonder. You *hit* her."

"Malik, don't," Vanyar began, stepping between us.

The huge Centaur jerked his head, once. Instantly, two Minotaurs pounced on Vanyar and dragged him back, out of the way. He yelled and cursed, but the bulls paid him as much heed as they might a yowling cat. Wind Warrior stood behind me, stiff and unrelenting, and prevented me from backing away from that bared steel and those hate-filled dark eyes.

Have mercy, I thought. *Kill me quickly.*

CHAPTER 5

She Who Hears

The sun glinted off Malik's steel.

His strike didn't sever Prince Flynn's throat as I expected. Instead, his blade's edge slashed Flynn's cheek from his left eye to his mouth. Bright blood poured from the wound as the prince staggered, helpless, against Windy. Shock and terror convulsed his face as he opened his mouth in a silent scream of agony.

Chief Ba'al'amawer and his aide-de-camp, Muljier, seized his arms and pulled him upright. Under their superior strength, Flynn sagged; his tanned skin paling to ash as his eyes rolled back in his head. He came near to passing out, blood soaking his sky-blue tunic and the royal emblem: the eagle and crossed swords.

As I cursed, fighting the hands that held me, in vain, Princess Iyumi leaned forward over Malik's black withers. "Commander, cease. This instant."

"I'm just getting warmed up," Malik snapped, raising his knife again.

"Commander, I forbid you. Cease and desist."

"Malik!" I yelled.

Coming to himself, shaking off both the obvious shock and the tearing pain, Prince Flynn shrugged off his burly guards. They relaxed, leaving him to stand alone with his bound hands behind him. Flynn raise his gory, ripped face, his dark blue eyes clear. On his own two booted feet, Flynn bent his head to swipe tickling blood from his chin and smeared it onto his once pristine sky-blue mantle. He faced Malik squarely, a faint smile coaxing his red-stained lips. His blonde mane wet with rain and oily sweat plastered to his brow and cheeks.

"Please," he said, his voice hoarse. "Put me out of my misery. I'll be ever so grateful."

"Meet your maker, boy."

Malik raised his hand, lifting it across his left shoulder. I knew his next cut would sever Prince Flynn's carotid. I squirmed from the Minotaur's custody and ran forward. At the same moment, Princess Iyumi slid from Malik's sleek back and lunged to place her small body between Malik's knife and Prince Flynn's vulnerable neck. Her shoulder struck my ribcage. I glanced down at the same instant she tilted her face upward toward mine.

I winked. I wasn't quite certain of what I wanted to communicate in that swift gesture. Perhaps a 'you and me against the world' camaraderie. Or a 'together we can win this' bonding moment. Mostly, I think, it was a moment in which I looked on a pretty girl and liked what I saw.

Whatever my motives for winking, Iyumi hesitated. Her lips parted as though to speak. Instead, she ducked her head and rounded on Malik with fury.

"Commander Malik," Iyumi barked. "I forbid you to kill him."

Malik hesitated, lowering his hand slightly. His narrowed eyes widened, lessened in their murderous intent. His tight jaw loosened a fraction, yet anguished fury hoarsened his voice. "He dared lay his filthy hands–"

"I'll seek my own vengeance, Commander," Iyumi declared with hands on her hips and flaunting both her femininity and royal authority. "In my own time and in my own fashion."

"But–"

Malik stared down at her, baffled, confused, his righteous anger warring with his need to obey a royal command. He dared not refuse her, yet how could he not avenge her? "Your Highness, no–"

"Step aside, please."

"Do it, Malik," I advised. "She's the boss."

"And you're my bitch, Vanyar. Shut thy trap."

Flynn waited through this drama, towering two heads over Iyumi. Bleeding, his face in shreds, in no doubt screaming agony, yet his calm eyes watched her with respect, and, is it possible–wry humor? His glance caught mine as I backed off, and he winked. He shot a lightning fast quirk from his uninjured cheek, a quick gesture of light and laughter.

I stifled a chuckle, wishing this Raithin Mawrn prince wasn't the despised enemy. Deep down, I knew his royal sire created the beast he was, without his consent. Without that in the equation, I could even think of him as a friend.

She may see clearly from one eye while the other remained at half mast, but they screamed the alpha role. Backed by not just her purple blood but a huge amount of natural courage, she squarely faced a pissed-off Centaur Commander easily capable of breaking her spine with one hand. Never blinking, Iyumi stared at Malik until he glanced aside, and dipped his brow.

"Your will, Highness," he murmured, his voice tense.

"It certainly is," she snapped, her tone biting.

"Don't think you're off the hook, boy," Malik snarled, over her head, pointing his finger at Flynn's nose. "You'll pay for what you've done."

Flynn lifted his shoulders in a sparse shrug, his eyes narrowed. His bloody lip curled in disdain. I knew a deliberate provocation when I saw one, and Flynn stroked his finger down Malik's last nerve. "I've a few coins in my pocket," he drawled. "That enough?"

When Malik tried to throw himself at Flynn, Ba'al'amawer hip-shot Princess Iyumi out of the fight line, and caught Malik's descending fist. With his massive frame between them, the Clan Chief effortlessly halted Malik's attack. Muljier seized Flynn's arm and dragged him backward so hard the young prince fought to keep his footing.

"I honor you, my Lord Commander," Ba'al'amawer rumbled, his hand locked around Malik's wrist and its stained dagger. "You are my good friend. But She Who Hears has spoken. I pray you, turn your wrath aside this day."

Malik stared into Ba'al'amawer's brown eyes, his throat bobbing as he swallowed. For a moment I thought Malik might rear back and strike out with his deadly front hooves, and thus take the Minotaur Chieftain out of the equation. A Centaur of Malik's high caliber was more than equal to a Minotaur when it came to a fight.

Drawing in a deep breath, Malik nodded, lowering his hand with the deadly blade. Ba'al'amawer let him go, but put his huge hand on Malik's shoulder. He tossed his chin over his shoulder, and smiled. Heavy lips pulled back from broad teeth; it appeared more a grimace than a smile, but there was much warmth in it.

"He's not worth it, my friend," he said. "Never kill a helpless creature, you have told me time and again, unless 'tis from mercy and kindness. Remember? Pray don't stain your soul over one such as he."

Malik drew a ragged breath and managed a smile. Placing his own strong hand on Ba'al'amawer's burly shoulder, he nodded. "Thank you."

Ba'al'amawer dipped his huge horns in respect.

"Are you through now?" Iyumi asked, her tone dripping acid.

The two dropped their arms and stiffened their spines. In unison, they offered her quick chin dips, and saluted with fists pressed against their chests. Her angry eyes flashed across me, as though daring me to speak. I grinned impudently in return as she slowly turned to face her would-be kidnapper. She stepped toward him, into his personal airspace, gazing up into his eyes. Flynn's defiant expression softened with pain, yet his back remained as proudly erect as ever. Iyumi's lips parted as though to speak to him. I'd no idea what she might say–'you bloody bugger' or 'kiss my royal ass' were both at the top of my list.

She said nothing. She stared only into his dark blue eyes, intent, her expression tightly closed, shut. I swear she gazed deep into his soul, but perhaps that was only my fanciful notion. Both Flynn and I suspected she meant to speak, for she drew in breath, words ready. But he turned his lacerated cheek toward her. *Don t.* His eyes dropped. *Please.*

My regard for him rose a notch. He stood firm, bound and bleeding, surrounded by his enemies, yet he showed no weakness, nor any fear. At that same time, he offered Iyumi her opportunity for vengeance and calmly accepted her sentence, whatever punishment that may be. Though he may never admit such, I knew Flynn knew he'd done her wrong.

Iyumi nodded. Blood drying to black on her right cheek, Iyumi turned toward the crowd of Atani soldiers and royal prisoners. Her upward glance took in the Griffins circling low overhead and she set her hands on her black, leather-bound hips. Her scarlet-lined grey cloak fell from her shoulders to her boots. That incredible wealth of silver-gilt hair covered her from head to knees, a waving shroud. As though chiseled from marble, her cold face and haughty expression brought none to their knees in adoration. Instead all, including Malik, Ba'al'amawer, Flynn and me, listened with awe. We listened to She Who Hears, our Bryn'Cairdhan High Priestess and the gods' voice.

"Hear me," she said, speaking well below a shout.

The outer cavalry soldiers melted inward, unwilling to miss a word. Minotaurs, Shifters, Centaurs and those Griffins watching the forest and the river, crept closer. Shifters crept in on hooves, bellies, spindly legs or whatever means they used to convey their bodies into the inner circle. Several Faeries, unseen and unheard till then, buzzed over the heads of the watching crowd of savage Atani warriors. Her voice magnified via magic; it reached all and halted every activity.

"Flynn and his idiots will be escorted to the border," Iyumi said, turning about, her arms crossed over her chest. "Immediately. No further harm shall come to them."

Malik glowered. "They are terrorists and prisoners. After trial, they'll be sent to Braigh'Mhar."

"Kill him," shrieked a swift-winged Faery, hovering over my shoulder. She peered down at Flynn with a very un-Faery like mien of anger. Her buzzing set of eight wings permitted her to hover like a kestrel, before darting like a hummingbird to another spot. In turn, Flynn's bloody jaw dropped as she dove toward his eyes. Witnessing a brightly colored nymph with an elfin face and tiny pointed ears the size of your large butterfly tended to make one think one's mind had come adrift.

"Are you for real?" Flynn asked, under his breath.

For answer, the Faery, whose name I didn't know as she never paused to introduce herself, smacked Flynn across his nose for his impudence. He blinked.

"Chill now, dear," I murmured, raising my knuckles in invitation.

Faeries liked to sit on one's fingers or hands, alighting like tiny angels to sing, giggle, and make a jest at one's expense before fluttering away amidst high-voiced laughter. The most non-violent folk upon the world, our Faery sisters lived for love, took nothing serious, and sent forth a plague of sweet innocence upon the cruel, cold world. I personally swore that had not the Faeries lived and loved, our life in our dreadful lands might easily turn black. Anger a Faery? One had to work very hard to accomplish it.

"Chill now, dear," the Faery piped, imitating my voice. Laughing in high C, the Faery buzzed my nose before joining three of her sisters in an aerial dance over Iyumi's silver head.

The object of their adoration glanced up at them, once, before returning her icy gaze upon her would-be kidnapper. "Ze'ana'ta," she murmured. "Be a love and find me a nice flower. I need one for my hair. Take the others with you, please."

"Flower," Ze'ana'ta repeated. "I like purple."

She flicked across Iyumi's whitish skin to plant a swift kiss upon her cheek before flying away, a tiny bright spark against the sullen grey sky. Her sisters chased her, screaming laughter. Those among us, long-used to their flighty and spastic behavior, ignored them. Only those unfamiliar with their skittish habits watched until she vanished, gaping like fishes. Flynn's expression changed from panic to awe within a heartbeat.

[130]

Iyumi turned, ever so slowly to face Malik. Her dark brows lowered, and her fair lips thinned in severe annoyance. No wonder few dared cross her. Angry, fearless, with enough clout to behead each and every one of us, Princess Iyumi paced forward until she stood nose to nose with Malik. She had to tilt her head back to accomplish it, however. He dropped his chin to his chest in order to see her at all.

"If Flynn dies," Iyumi grated through tightly clenched teeth. Her finger poked him just north of his sword belt and south of his navel. "His devil sire has the right to declare war. And war, my brainless, testosterone-laden Commander, is the last thing our country needs."

"He wouldn't–"

"He would."

Iyumi's voice lowered at the same moment it rose. "Pick your brains out of your muscles, boys and girls," she growled, turning round to face us all. "This isn't the fight we want. We must find that child, or not a one of us shall be spared. Put your big boy pants on, send these maggots home, and help me find her. In that order."

"You heard our Princess," Chief Ba'al'amawer bellowed, shaking his broadsword. "Put them on their horses. I want five Griffins, five Minotaurs, five Centaurs and ten cavalry to escort His Royal Highness back to the cesspit they swam from. Commander Lightning Fork."

"My lord."

"You're in charge. Escort His Highness to his border."

"My lord."

Wind Warrior turned Flynn around, breaking the interested stare he flashed Iyumi, and, with two Minotaurs, escorted him toward the milling Atani, terrorists, horses, hissing Griffins and assorted Minotaurs. I jogged to catch up. As Ba'al'amawer sorted out each unit, Malik shouted for those not attending the prisoners to form up. A horn sounded, echoing through the caves and the river.

From the forest into the massing Atani bounded a swift doe. I recognized her immediately: Aderyn, my father's brother's daughter. I hadn't seen her since before Dalziel, and had no idea how she felt about me now. Close as children, we both joined the Weksan'Atan at a young age, and shared our experiences, laughter and kinship. My breath caught as she changed into her raven-haired, pale-complexioned beautiful form.

She didn't see me. She strode into the mix surrounding the prisoners, asking questions, offering suggestions, her hand on her sword's hilt. Her cloak of hunter's green covered her from throat to heel, her black hair falling to her waist in a thick, heavy braid.

Another Shifter, Valcan, flew in on swift raven's wings and changed forms before he hit the ground. Tall, flaxen-haired with a scattering of freckles across his nose and cheeks, he joined Muljier in settling Flynn's cohorts aboard their skittish horses. With their hands still bound behind them, mounting on their own might be a dubious affair.

When Windy, a Minotaur named Raga, and I sought to lift Flynn to the roan stallion, Iyumi called out, her voice ringing across the tumult. "The blue is mine. I claim him."

"She does have taste," Flynn murmured. He glanced at me, his eyes amused. "That's an awfully nice horse."

I itched to do something for him. I waved my hand at Windy and Raga to wait. They backed off, granting me both privilege and respect due to my rank and authority. "Flynn."

"Van?"

I called on my pedestrian magic. Running my hand down his cheek, I urged healing into the gaping slash. Under my limited power, the wound's lips joined, ran together, smoothed out. Blood vessels rejoined and nerve endings melded, flesh knitted. While not exactly a healer, my powers could only start the healing process, not heal Flynn fully. *At least,* I thought, *he wasn t in such pain.*

Taken aback, Flynn jerked away from me. He stumbled backwards and only Raga's firm stance kept him from a humiliating tumble to his butt. "What have you done?" he whispered, his voice hoarse. For the first time, I saw real fear in his eyes.

"All magic has healing elements," I replied. "I'm not an adept, but I can heal a scratch now and then. Malik now," I jerked my head over my shoulder, smiling. "He'll bring you back from the

[132]

grave. You'll still ache a bit, boyo, but within a few days you'll be as good as new."

I grinned into his stunned expression. "Can't do much about the scar, though. Don't the ladies love scarred warriors?"

Flynn offered me a wry grin. He straightened his back and tossed his damp hair from his eyes. Despite the blood on his face, his bound hands, he reminded me of a hero from the ancient tales. A warrior who refused both the mercy and clemency offered by his enemies. A man who feared not death, but life.

"I wouldn't know, First Captain Vanyar. When you get yours, be sure to let me know?"

I laughed. "I never kiss and tell."

"Kill joy."

Windy and Raga boosted him up onto the dead Raithin Mawrn's mount. As a cavalry lieutenant took the reins of the horse and pulled it behind his own, Flynn cast his chin over his shoulder. "Look after yourself, all right? And wish me luck."

"I will, brother," I answered. "Go in peace. Live at peace."

"I will if I can." His lopsided grin widened. "Not so sure I'm permitted."

Before I answered, the lieutenant kicked his horse into the milling group of cavalry and mounted prisoners, each led by an Atani officer. Ba'al'amawer's Minotaurs strode beside each Raithin Mawrn, as two Griffins circled low overhead and Commander Lightning Fork rose high on swift wings and shouted down orders. The remaining trio rose higher, above the trees and the rushing river, spotting trouble before it arrived. Those mounted Atani flanked the group as they trotted upstream and vanished under the trees.

"No, no, and finally, NO!"

Princess Iyumi glared at Malik, bristling with anger, her irate heel striking the ground with finality. "There is no highway option, here, Commander. It's my way or get out of my way."

"Your father instructed me to bring you home."

Iyumi's voice rose to emulate a furious fishwife. "My father isn't here, you bone-headed donkey! I am! And I'm telling you, I'm going after that child."

Malik crossed his arms over his chest. "Not while I'm in charge here, Princess."

I stifled a grin as Iyumi puffed up and grew three inches in height. "You are not in command, dumb-ass. I am."

Malik raised his fist in a futile gesture. He half-turned away, scowling, his elbow raised to hide his mouth as he feigned a neck scratch. "I'm really not liking her," he muttered to me.

"A liege doesn't require her subjects to like her," Iyumi replied tartly. "Only demands his obedience."

"She heard that," I said, under my breath.

"You think?" Malik snapped, under his.

"Grow up, boys. Like now."

Iyumi's hands on her tiny hips made her look like a child in a tantrum, rather than a princess in a snit. Yet, her eyes sparked blue fire, and her witch's hair cascaded down her back and across her thighs, molten silver. She looked like a goddess of old, made of fire and steel, bearing a thunderbolt poised to strike one dead. Mortal men fell at her feet as the Old Ones worshipped at her altar.

I almost loved her in that instant.

"I lead," she snapped, turning around to include us all in her glare at. "You brainless twits follow. Is this clear or must I pound it into your thick skulls with a pole-axe?"

"Bitch."

The word floated on the light breeze, coming from the distant rear. A cavalry soldier possibly, or a Shifter. Not likely spoken from a Griffin's beak, nor from a Minotaur, as their voices were unmistakable. There were several Centaurs back there, and none smiled as they gazed at her. If I heard the hated title, no doubt Iyumi did as well. Malik scowled as his dark eyes scanned the crowd of Atani soldiers. If he found out who spoke, that soldier's punishment wouldn't be light.

Iyumi nodded. "Such you call me. And worse, I know. I've heard them all."

[134]

She turned in a circle, fury radiating off her like heat baking off a bonfire. Her right hand rose, palm up. "I'm a bitch, and you all despise me. I don't much care. I was born speaking the languages of the gods. All thirty of them."

Say what? I exchanged a swift glance with Malik. As surprised as I by this comment, he shrugged slightly. As She Who Hears, the speaker of the gods, Princess Iyumi interpreted the gods' will. But–born to this position, the gods' mouthpiece listening to what the gods had to say while still diddling her diapers?

"I've been the High Priestess since I was four years old. My will isn't my own. Nor is my voice. If any of you want this responsibility, please step forward." Her hand dropped to slap her thigh, her scowl dangerous. "If you think you can do a better job, then knock yourself out. I'll head home, put on a nice dress and drink wine in the garden. You, back there, who just called me that vile title, by all means, put on the mantle, speak for the gods as their will slams into your soul. I'm quite certain your shoulders are broader than mine."

Only the small crowd of giggling Faeries moved, fluttering over the heads of the crowd. If the silence thickened any more, I swear it might shatter like a dry twig. In the massed Atani force, no one spoke, coughed nor scratched a nose. But many eyes glanced toward their neighbors, or studied the ground at their feet. The shame I felt I glimpsed on many a face whether it had a nose, a muzzle or a beak. If I were in Iyumi's boots, my shoulders would crumble under the weight of all that responsibility.

Iyumi nodded, pacing in her circle. "I didn't think so. Only a merciless bitch can save this child of prophecy and keep our beloved nation safe from her enemies."

"Your Highness–"

"Don't 'Your Highness' me, Commander. Your own tongue has betrayed you."

Beautiful and cold sapphires glowed within her pale features, her slender brows all but met over her nose. Her right fore-finger rose to shoulder level and pointed to his face.

"I know how often you and Van drank ale in your rooms and cursed my name. How you jested at my expense."

That same finger drifted across me, Ba'al'amawer, Padraig, Raga, Windy, Muljier, Swift Wing, Aderyn, Valcan and every other soldier massed in the loose circle around her. I know my gut lurched when that menacing finger and chilly gaze marked me as guilty as sin. Indeed, yes, not a one of us stood innocent of the slanderous charge we lay at her door. Many armpits sprang in a sudden flush of heat as her eyes condemned us. Griffins flared wings and dropped their beaks as Minotaur horns dipped low. Human soldiers and mounted cavalry rapidly saluted, as though that alone might assuage her anger. Heads might literally roll should she demand revenge or justice in return for our insults.

Malik lowered his brow in both respect and homage, as his arm crossed his chest. "My liege."

Iyumi turned back to him. A slight smile crossed her face. Her granite gaze lightened a fraction as she eyed him sidelong. A swift hand-gesture tossed a heavy lock of silver hair across her shoulder. "I daresay I don't blame you."

I blinked. And in that infinitesimal span of time, everything changed. Her fair lips lifted as she turned in a circle to include us all. "Had I been in your position, I'd have called me a bitch, too. I'm not nice, hardly polite and respect for others isn't in my vocabulary. I earned your titles and scorn. However."

In that single word, she forced all breathing lungs to halt. Even the wind soughing through the pines ceased its whisper. The thunder of the river receded into the dim distance, like a dream half-remembered upon waking. Horses and Centaurs ceased swishing tails against persistent flies, and Griffin feathers lay flat as they tucked their wings tight to their shoulders. Minotaurs stood silent, jaws parted in bovine astonishment. Surely she utilized her powerful magic over the clearing, for what else could create such an effective stillness?

"However."

Iyumi's tone softened at the same time her right fist rose above her dainty head. "I'll not hear one more slanderous title from any of you, but I'll make you a deal. You call me either 'Princess' or 'Your Highness' from this moment on."

[136]

Her mouth softened into a fetching smile. "And I swear I'll be less bitchy. Agreed?"

"Agreed!"

The word tossed from mouth to mouth in rumbling approval, though several brandished swords high and hollered, "Yeah, Princess!" No few yipped the Atani battle cry, a high pitched, *ki-yi-yi-yi* as they cupped hands or talons about their mouths to increase the decibels.

In a rare show of affection, and a display no one present had ever witnessed, Iyumi took Malik's hand within both of hers. I waved for the tumult and chaos to shut down, willing them to quiet, be still and listen. The river's voice returned as a musical backdrop, and an eagle screamed from on high. A wolf howled far away, perhaps calling its mate, from the mountain's dense forests across the great river.

"You watched over my cradle, Malik," Iyumi said, her voice both low and light. "Don't think for a moment I've forgotten your loyalty, devotion or your love. I know I may own the first two. I promise I'll earn the third."

"My queen." Malik bent his foreleg, his fist thumping his chest as he dipped his chin low.

"The prophesized child has been born, my lads and my lassies." Iyumi said, her tone stern, as she glanced around at the ring of eyes, all soldiers, all of different species. Her wise blue vision took us all in, weighed, judged, and, hopefully, found none wanting. "But her birth mother is dying. Within days, no more than a week, she'll leave this earth. The child the gods predicted long ago will perish for want of nurturing . . . unless we find her in time."

"That's why you left."

My voice whipped her head around; her wild mane of spun silver flowing over her shoulders and rippling down her back to her hips. Those keen blue eyes, sharper than forged steel and tempered by the gods' own flames locked on mine. Iyumi's taut expression told me far more than her cryptic words.

"Indeed, Van," she replied, controlling her temper with an obvious effort. "Secrecy was the key."

Malik stepped forward at the same moment I cocked my head, catching the nuance.

"Was?" I asked sharply. "You said 'was'?"

Iyumi nodded, folding her arms across her small bosom, as though feeling a sudden chill. "The gods spoke to me in my dreams, showed me a world where evil ruled. A witch, wise in the ancient practices of black magic, has made heinous sacrifices and grows powerful."

Iyumi gazed around the silent clearing, the river's muted roar. Superstitious mutterings ran through the crowd of fierce, fearless Atani soldiers. Fingers and talons made the sign against evil enchantment as eyes flicked to one another uneasily. The magic we possessed and took for granted was as nothing compared to the dark powers one obtained through the worship of demons and blood sacrifice. Throughout the ages, our kind hunted down and executed these necromancers, stamping out demon worship. For over a hundred years, no witch dared practice this craft.

"Do you know who this witch is?" Malik asked, his voice tight.

Iyumi shook her head. "I know only the name she calls herself: the Red Duchess."

"A Raithin Mawrn noble?" I asked.

"She may be from Raithin Mawr," Iyumi answered slowly, considering. "She might also be from Bryn'Cairdha. Or she may be from another land entirely. One gently born, certainly, and one born to magic. A few libraries around the world still contain many ancient manuscripts that carry the understanding of demon worship and the dark arts. They are kept secret and under guard, but someone with connections and power could read them and gain their arcane knowledge."

"What does this Red Duchess want with the child?" Malik asked, his brow furrowed. "If she told the Raithin Mawrn, she must want them to conquer us. Yes?"

Iyumi shook her head, smiling with a heavy sadness I'd never seen on her before. "I doubt very much she cares about our fight with them," she said, her tone low. "She, too, seeks the child, the messenger. At the time of the prophecy, when the sun and the

[138]

moon rise together in the east, she will sacrifice the child on her demon's altar. If that happens–"

Silence descended over the clearing as Iyumi paced out from beneath our shadows and glanced up at the blue sky peeping from between tree branches. Sunlight draped her from head to toe. Shutting her eyes, she tilted her face upward as though reveling in the warmth and light. The mark from Flynn's hand stood out stark against her pale complexion. "Imagine this, my friends," she said, her eyes still closed. "A queen with all the power of evil at her fingertips ruling both our countries. With the demons she worships at her back, we'd have no chance against her. After grinding us into dogmeat, she'd rule us, and Raithin Mawr, and merge our two lands into one."

Malik and I exchanged a horrified glance. "But," I began, my throat as dry as dust, "that's the prophecy."

"Indeed it is."

"Impossible," Malik gasped. "That can't be right."

Iyumi lowered her face and opened her eyes. Turning back toward us, she swiped her silver hair from her face. "It is right, Commander," she answered him, her voice grave. "But then again, our prophecy is also right."

"But–"

"We walk a knife's edge, kids." Her voice rose so all near her could hear. "Should we wander off our given course . . . even for a moment, the chance we're given, the choice we took, is gone forever. None of us dare falter in our task."

"And if we do?"

Iyumi searched the crowd for the owner of the skepticism. Her confidence never wavered, nor did her pointing finger. The cavalry wretch at the back visibly wilted. His brothers cursed him, smacked him upside his head and pushed him forward. Knuckling his brow in homage, he quickly saluted formally, his face redder than an annoyed rooster.

"There are two sides to every prophecy. One side represents good and the other evil. Our version ends with peace and hope for

us all. Yet, should she win that child and murder it on her evil alter–
"

Iyumi smiled sadly. "Well, let's just say nothing will ever be the same again."

"Darkness will rule," I said softly. "Nor will it end here."

"You're more perceptive than I gave you credit for, Captain Vanyar," Iyumi replied. "Indeed, the Red Duchess will move to conquer other lands, destroying anything that's good or happy or peaceful in this world of ours."

For the first time I found admiration for this slender silver girl. With unquestionable courage and unswerving devotion, she set off alone to save us all. I finally understood her and the need that drove her. I also knew I'd never call her a bitch again.

Yanking my sword from its sheath, I dropped to my knee. Resting it on the palms of my hands, I raised it, gazing up into her sapphire eyes. "Your father gave me this sword," I said, my voice hoarse. "On the day I joined the Atan brotherhood. I now pledge it to you, my queen, for it is yours, as I am."

Her right hand rose to her chest as though suddenly unsure of herself. When it reached out to touch the blade, her fingers trembled. "I–" she began, and choked off. "I accept both, First Captain Vanyar."

"I should've been first to do that," Malik muttered as I rose and sheathed my sword. "I despise following in your steps, Van."

I grinned as Iyumi chuckled. "No worries, Commander," she said. "I know you thought of it first."

"I think we all have pledged ourselves to you, Princess," Ba'al'amawer, rumbled, gesturing around the clearing. "We're with you, to the end. Command us."

She didn't. Instead, Iyumi walked away, her head down, her silver-gilt hair hiding her face. The cavalry, the Minotaur soldiers, Centaurs and the Griffins, all parted for her like sea waves over rock. Beaks, muzzles and chins dropped as fists and talons crossed chests in salute. She halted at the river's edge beside an eddying pool of clear water. Dipping into a graceful squat, she filled her cupped hands and drank deeply. However, she didn't rise immediately after dashing excess water from her fingers. Her cloak piled behind her boots and her lengths of hair spilled over the loose soil, dead leaves and twigs. She appeared to study her reflection.

"Finian's thugs killed them," she said, speaking to the river. "The soldiers who accompanied me. They cut their throats in the night. I was powerless to save them."

"What do you mean?" I asked.

Malik's hand on my shoulder prevented me from going to her. "You have more power than any of us," I went on. I scraped his hand away, but stood still. "I know you faked illness to give us time to rescue you, but why didn't you free yourself?"

"Van," Malik said, his tone low, warning.

"It's a fair question, Commander."

Iyumi stood and turned slowly around. Bits of leaves and a twig or two clung to her tresses, but she didn't seem to notice. Her hands clasped in front of her, she appeared to be no older than twelve and as helpless as a newborn fawn. Naked fear twisted her lips and grew in her eyes. "I've no more magic than your average hedge wizard."

"What?" I snapped. "You're Roidan's daughter."

Iyumi smiled sadly. "That may be, Van, but the gods gave me their voice, not their power."

Extending her palm, a knife appeared in it. With a casual flick of her wrist, she sent it blade-first into the dirt between my ankles. "I can create simple things from nothing," Iyumi continued, as a single pink rosebud grew upon her palm. She tucked it into her hair over her ear, before smiling into my eyes. "Permit me to stop your heart, Vanyar."

That palm reached for me and planted itself squarely over my chest. Iyumi's face twisted in concentration, her eyes narrowed, her brows furrowed. *I should be frightened,* I thought, *she could kill me.* I felt her reach for magic, take hold of the power instilled in all of us—and listened as it slipped from her grasp. Like sand, it spilled onto the ground, useless. She tried once more to seize hold of the arcane within us all, only to have it melt away and drift like a summer breeze across the trees.

I took her cold hand within mine, and massaged her knuckles. She gazed up at me, tears filling those huge blue depths. "See?" she asked, her voice cracking. "As much as I'd like to, I can't kill you, Vanyar."

I raised her tiny fist to my lips and kissed it. "Offer me your smile," I murmured. "And I'll drop dead at your feet."

A blush warmed her face as she yanked her hand from mine. She spun away, her face returning to its former scowl. Quickly, she drew a deep breath and her voice, when she spoke, had hardened. "I haven't the power most of you have," she said. "I have the reputation, but nothing with which to back it up."

"Not true, Princess," I said, stepping into her personal space. "You have a kingdom at your beck and call."

"So you thought to delay them," Malik ventured.

"Exactly. Only my feigning illness convinced them to stop."

"Well, it worked," I said brightly, into the tense silence. "They stopped, we got you back, and it's all good. Right?"

She studied the ground at her boots. "Two have died on this expedition," she murmured. "More will die. Unless I go alone."

"You little fool," I snapped, protocol forgotten. "I'll tie you hand and foot to that damn roan if I must. You will *sooo* not go alone."

Malik, who never long tolerated disrespect to rank, stood shoulder to shoulder with me. "I'm with him, girl," he gritted, raising his hand. The sun glinted off his wrist cuff. "Try to escape me, and I'll do more than just tie you."

The dark pewter manacles suddenly appeared in his fist. No magical power of this world could resist that of the dreaded metal. No few stepped back, myself and Windy included, fearing the touch that parted us from our gods-given magic. Not even Roidan's daughter was immune to them, for she, too, eyed them with trepidation, her lips thinned.

Chief Ba'al'amawer stalked forward as Iyumi opened her mouth to protest. "Set aside these terrible ideas, Princess," he rumbled, his broad hand on the rayed sun over his breast. "For we are loyal, and would fain die as have you leave us behind. Where you go, we go."

[142]

Windy, his black-tufted ears canted backward, stalked on silent feet to stand at her back. No doubt, he expected her to bolt, run for the nearest horse and gallop away. Aderyn, her face set and cold, ducked out from behind Windy's massive form to stand at Iyumi's right hand. Startled, Iyumi eyed her up and down for a long moment, her tongue wetting her lips.

The other Atani soldiers, grumbling, their expressions intent, ringed us around. Cavalry soldiers kicked their horses to ride in a circle at the outer edges of the clearing, ducking under low tree limbs. Swift Wing and Grey Mist crouched, wings out and lion tails lashing, ready to hit the sky should the gods permit Iyumi to grow wings and fly her out from under us.

"We're with you," I murmured. "Like it or not, you're stuck with us."

Iyumi glanced aside, her hair hiding her face. "I can't watch you die," she whispered. "I can't . . . I can*not* . . . lead you to your deaths. For death is all I see on this path."

"Death isn't to be feared, Princess," I said. While my genes forbade my enfolding her in my arms, I could, and did, brush silver lengths from her face.

She glanced up, her lips thin, but from fear this time, not anger. "But–"

"It is but another journey," I went on, my voice low. "One we all must make, in our time. We Atani embrace death, we'll never run from it. Should any of us die protecting you, and this child you seek, then it's a good day to die. It won't be from any fault of yours."

"You can't be so sure," Iyumi whispered, cringing from my hand.

"You don't see all ends," Malik growled, folding his arms across his bare chest. "I have vision and power. I see death for some, yes, but not as many as you'd think. I also see hope, a hope for life, and for our Bryn'Cairdha."

"See?" I bantered lightly, my fingers teasing her cheek. "Malik has spoken. He's like a bloody oracle, but try his speech after he's had a few shots of that bitter homebrew of his. Grow hair on your chest it will, but he'll spout enough platitudes you'd think you staggered into a mayoral race."

"Vanyar, I swear I'll have you scrubbing–"

Iyumi tried, in vain, to stifle a giggle and leaned into my hand. Not enough to suggest she liked me, but enough to acknowledge she received my comfort and appreciated it. Stepping lightly away from me, Iyumi squared her shoulders and drank deep of the crisp mountain air. Tossing her heavy hair back, across her shoulders, she faced us with her hands on her black leather hips.

Her smile bloomed like a tundra flower, rare, and stunningly beautiful while it lasted. "Sometimes the gods let others speak for them. I reckon I'm not permitted to go alone– "

"Of course you can't," I began.

"–although I think that's the wiser course."

"Princess," I said, leaning toward her and grinning. "We don't always get what we want."

Iyumi half-smiled as she flipped me a sign seldom seen in Roidan's courts. "Bite me, Vanyar."

I saluted. "Your will, my liege."

"Cavalry, form ranks," Malik bellowed. "Clan Chief, you command the vanguard, Commander Swift Wing–"

Iyumi waved her hand. Possibly she used her limited magic. Or perhaps the gods favored her request, should she pray for silence. Either way, Malik suddenly cut off, his mouth working. He tried to form words, his hand at his throat, his dark eyes wide with effort. No command escaped his irate and blustering, though silent, lips.

"Have you forgotten so soon, my Lord Commander?" she asked, her tone like honey. "I'm in charge here. I may not go alone, but I *will* pick who accompanies me."

"Now wait–" I began and suddenly cut off. The same magic that gagged Malik now shut me up. I breathed, moved my tongue, but no words pushed past my tonsils. I settled for glaring at her as she scowled, dangerous and hard to handle–again.

"This band," she said, her hand gesturing around the massed Atani, "is too many. To hunt the royal stag, one must have a few smart hounds and an adept archer. We hunt a wise and clever witch. Less is more, this day."

[144]

"Princess," Chief Ba'al'amawer protested, his huge horns lowered as his dark eyes glowered. "You can't go alone. You just can't."

Iyumi smiled, though irritation clearly flowed beneath the bright facade. "Let me finish, Clan Chief. I was about to say that a handful of you loyal beasties will stay with me. The rest–go home."

No few grumbles and hot protests marked her announcement. 'Take me along,' ' I'll not fear any bloody witch,', 'I can ride better than you, bird-brain' 'me, please, pick me'.

Iyumi smiled, a rapid there-and-gone affair. "Secrecy is still necessary, and the Red Duchess will certainly be watching for me, us. She'll set spies to follow, if she hasn't already. We travel light and fast."

Her grim, blue eyes fastened upon Clan Chief Ba'al'amawer. "As dearly as you've earned your privileges, Chief of the great Clan, your Minotaurs must return home."

"Princess!" Ba'al'amawer's shocked bellow rolled across the clearing, echoed off the rock towers and drowned the rushing river. "Of course we come with you."

Iyumi walked to him, and took his great hands within her tiny ones. Tilting her head back to look up into his bull face and dark brown eyes, she smiled. Before this adventure, I thought Iyumi hadn't known what a smile was.

"I'm sorry, Clan Chief," she said softly, her blue eyes kind.

Kind? That was new.

She reached up, very far up, to clasp his furry cheek. "Minotaurs are the bravest, strongest and most loyal of my father's people. You're steadfast and never weary. But you're also the slowest. Forgive me, my noble Ba'al'amawer, but your folk cannot keep up with horses, Griffins or Centaurs. I require all speed on this mission–speed and secrecy."

"Princess–" he protested, but her hand stopped him cold.

"I have spoken, Clan Chief," she said.

He bowed low, his curved horns brushing past her shoulders. "I hear and obey, my Princess."

[145]

"I would charge you to protect my father," Iyumi said, earnestly looking deep into his face. "The Red Duchess may attack me through him. All of you," she added, turning her face about to include all the Atani soldiers within hearing, "all who do not accompany me now, never consider this a slight to your honor, your loyalty, nor your courage. You've all that and more. The King needs you more than I. And I beg you, keep him safe."

Real tears welled in those huge blue depths, but didn't fall. "He's frail these days. With your help, I can devote all my attention to the task the gods assigned me without fear of harm coming to my beloved sire and King. Not with all of you, fierce soldiers and warriors, protecting him."

"She's a bloody genius," Malik muttered in my ear.

"Tell me about it," I hissed in return. "With that speech, she'll have them dancing a jig and thinking it's a battle formation."

While they didn't exactly dance, I observed many chests puffed with pride, heads held high as fingers fondled weapons. Several Griffins expanded their great wings as if for flight, preening grandly, and cavalry soldiers drew swords and offered one another mock battle. Chief Ba'al'amawer nodded his huge bull head and sent Muljier off to organize his Minotaurs into marching order.

I noticed several officers who failed to succumb to Iyumi's charm. Windy watched her with narrowed eagle's eyes as Moon Whisperer and Grey Mist flanked him, silent and waiting. Padraig fondled his sword's hilt, his dark eyes watching me. Another Shifter, my kinsman Lieutenant Gaear, stood side by side with Valcan, their heads bent together, whispering. Two young cavalry soldiers, Edryd and Alain, also watched her through slitted eyes as they bent heads together, murmuring words I couldn't hear. Lieutenant Dusan stared at his horse's charcoal mane at Edryd's left flank, idly flipping his reins back and forth.

"Someone bring me my horse," Iyumi commanded, her fists on her hips.

Aderyn jumped first, trotting through the ranks to the blue roan Prince Flynn claimed from the man he'd killed. She led the docile beast past enormous Griffins and massive Centaurs before dropping to her knee at Iyumi's feet. "Your Highness," she said, her eyes on the ground.

"Sweet Aderyn," Iyumi murmured, touching her briefly on the shoulder. "Thank you. You'll accompany me, should you desire it."

"I do, Highness."

Taking the roan's reins from her, I tossed them over the stallion's blue-grey neck and offered my cupped hands for Iyumi's foot. "My liege."

"Of course, I hadn't forgotten your talents, my dear Captain Vanyar." Iyumi placed her left boot in my hands.

I tossed her lightly up to land in the roan's saddle and adjusted the stirrups to fit her as she gathered her reins. Settled in her seat, Iyumi lifted her pale yet lovely face. Still, her blue eyes bored like drills. "Lord Commander Malik, front and center."

Spine stiff, Malik advanced at a stilted walk, his head high and his black hair brushing his bare shoulders. The many-rayed star over his brow gleamed under the muted sunlight, as his left hand rested upon his sword's hilt. Precise, military and above reproach, Lord Captain Commander Malik saluted Princess Iyumi with his arm across his broad bare chest and his chin lowered.

"Command me, my Princess."

"You and First Lieutenant Padraig will escort me. As will First Captain Vanyar, Lieutenants Wind Warrior, Moon Whisperer, Grey Mist, and Gaear. I want Sergeants Aderyn, Valcan, Lieutenants Dusan and Alain, and Corporals Edara and Edryd. I also require the services of Second Lieutenant Kasi. Step forward, if you please."

In my two days back from exile, I listened closely to the chatter and picked up interesting tidbits. Thus, I stifled my surprise at Kasi's appointment. A Griffin new to the Atan brotherhood, her record, while decent, hadn't earned her any special marks. I'd no idea how well she'd react under violent pressure and thought perhaps this wasn't the mission to test it. Edryd, perhaps nineteen, with a shock of red hair and freckles over a pale complexion could shoot a fly at fifty rods from the back of a galloping horse. He joined his cavalry unit a mere month ago. His mettle–well, it just wasn't there.

"The rest of you," Iyumi said, her voice ringing. "Protect my father. I'll need my sleep in the days ahead."

Her quip created some laughter, some snickers and lots of 'pick up the pace, nimrod, I'm next' remarks.

"Those I just named," Iyumi declared, standing in her stirrups. "Come along. Ba'al'amawer, you're in charge of the Atani forces and will remain thus until our witch is defeated. I'll send word whenever possible."

The Clan Chief bowed again. "Your Highness."

He walked away to organize the trip home, and Malik ordered Padraig and Corporal Edara, a beautiful Centaur maiden with wild red-brown hair and a glossy chestnut coat, to the vanguard. The two cavalry officers, Dusan and Alain, were commanded to ride a hundred rods behind them. He ordered Windy and Misty to fly high and watch for any approaching enemies. Kasi would remain airborne above us as a swift messenger. He commanded Edryd to ride behind Iyumi as her immediate bodyguard, and Gaear loped alongside her stirrup as a wolf. Aderyn and Valcan reverted into bird form and flew away to watch our back-trail. Malik and I stood at her side, guarding and heeding her directions.

"Which way, Princess?" Malik asked.

As I whistled sharply, Iyumi turned in her saddle. Her attention on the departing troops, my sudden noise distracted her. "What are you whistling for?" she asked.

"My ride."

"Your–"

Kiera, my dark beauty, loped out from behind the tall rock towers. Her coat of jet black reflected the sun's bright rays, shimmering like lightning. Her silky mane fell past her massive shoulders and her tail brushed the sandy earth behind her. The white star between her dark eyes gleamed under the muted sunlight as her four glossy white stockings rose and fell, kicking the sand up behind her striking hooves.

Before flying away to replace Flynn's mount, I set her to following the Atani troops. She remained in hiding, after the attack

[148]

on Flynn and his idiots, patiently awaiting my signal. I swear Malik's breath shut off as he watched her lope across the clearing in obedience to my summons. He cared for her in my absence, loved her almost as much as I did.

"I thought you'd, er–" Iyumi began, watching with wide eyes my love slowed to a trot, then a walk before dipping her muzzle into my hands.

My heart ached every day I spent away from her, yet I couldn't take her into exile with me. How could I care for her properly as a tavern bum? Inn stables weren't good enough for the likes of her. No, Kiera fared well under Malik's devoted care, and I suspected she'd be better off without me. I never thought I'd see her again that day I disappeared into the streets.

"What, Princess?" I half-laughed, laying my cheek against Kiera's as she nuzzled my neck. "Fly?"

"Er, well," Iyumi said slowly. "Yes."

"And leave you to the entertainments Malik might devise?" I laughed, rubbing my hand between Kiera's dark, sloe eyes and over her tiny black ears. I caressed her silken neck under her heavy mane with my left hand as I tickled her lips with my right. "He'll have you weeping with boredom within hours."

Malik's eyes rolled. "Van, please."

Iyumi's knowing eye swept over Kiera. "She makes this roan look like a donkey by comparison. I've seen her in the royal stables, of course, but had no idea you owned her."

I kissed Kiera's muzzle. "She owns me, rather."

"No saddle?" Iyumi's brows rose. "No bridle?"

I chuckled as I grasped two handfuls of Kiera's heavy mane. Vaulting aboard her smooth, bare back, I settled my legs behind her shoulders and shrugged, still grinning. "She's never worn either."

"Van's horsemanship can fill volumes, Princess," Malik commented dryly. "He has your father's best cavalry masters scratching their heads."

Iyumi reined her new blue roan up alongside Kiera, and smiled. Damn, but didn't she have cute dimples. "I think Captain Vanyar can teach me a thing or two about riding."

"Anytime, my lovely liege." I bowed low, matching her grin.

She suddenly blushed bright pink, quickly glanced aside and all but stumbled over her tongue.

"Uh, north, Commander. We ride north."

CHAPTER 6

Tangled Webs of Deception

"*O*ne."

The whip cracked across my back and I jumped, my clenched teeth unable to halt the sharp hiss of pain. *Don t let him see fear,* I half-thought, shutting my jaws tight. *He ll see pain. He ll see agony. But he wants fear. He wants terror. He wants me begging for mercy, crying at his feet.*

Don t give him that.

"Two."

The royal executioner and dispenser of the King's justice called out the count. The huge, hairless hulk in a leather kirtle and knee-high boots cocked his arm back, his cat'o'nine tails swishing across the cobbles. I braced myself, but the sharp cut of leather and iron opened yet nine more bleeding welts. I choked on my cry of pain, biting my arm to prevent its eruption.

Don t give him what he wants. He feeds on your fear.

At least my father granted me a semi-private punishment. Only his court nobles, cronies, servants and hangers-on, not the general populace, witnessed his swift and just chastisement for my failure.

[151]

Inside the stone walls of the keep, Finian's soldiers lashed me to a hastily erected wooden barrier and stripped me of tunic and weapons. The half-healed wound from Malik's dagger itched incessantly, but under the cat's full effect I forgot its existence.

King Roidan's elite forces outwitted and outfought me. Commander Malik's troops deposited me at the border and turned toward their country. Free to go where I will and riding the real Bayonne, I returned to Castle Salagh, my father's palace, three days later. Blaez, Buck-Eye and the others followed behind me. Upon reaching the town, Finian's soldiers arrested me on the spot. My father sought to make an example of me.

Failure had its costs.

Commander Blaez stood at my sire's right hand, untouched, accepted, forgiven. As the third stroke forced my bare chest into the sharp splinters of the heavy wood post, I felt his eyes, his contempt, tingle along my skin. *Just one moment...I beg you, great gods. One moment in an empty room with him. I ll accept whatever punishment you decree, but give me that moment alone.*

Bracing myself for the next stroke, sweat streaming in rivers down my face and stinging my eyes, I squinted through the salt. Three figures huddled near the postern door that led into the great castle. My throat convulsed. My belly clenched. I scarcely felt the fourth slash of the wretched cat.

Queen Enya held my sobbing sister close, her huge beautiful eyes damp with unshed tears. Her free hand extended toward me, her mouth pleaded words I couldn't hear, but read on her fair lips. *My son. I love you, be strong.*

Garbed in a silken white dress chased with silver and sewn with seed pearls, I'd never seen my mother so beautiful. Like a goddess of old, her perfect features made the most powerful of men drop to her feet, her slaves. Her cloak of silver lined in scarlet fell to the cobbled stone behind her. Her wheaten hair, loose, spilled like spun gold down her shoulders and full bosom, shrouding her to her hips.

Fainche's small face, wracked with her screams of my name, turned bright red with the force of her panic and tears. Her small arms clasped my mother's waist, her blonde hair disheveled and matted, her gown of deep blue darkened with damp under her chin.

[152]

Fainche, I tried to say, but the fifth cut halted my breath and jolted my chest against the post.

The third woman neither wept nor called to me. She stood, poised and proud, dry-eyed as a royal princess should. She'd braided her red-gold hair into a tight coil at the back of her slender, pale neck. A rich gown of fetching russet and gold matched her hair exactly, and she wore a black cloak that fell to her black boots. Hazel eyes watched me with apparent calm, almost detachment. Despite this tranquil demeanor, her hands twisted themselves into knots at her waist. I recognized the look in those narrowed eyes. Panic. The eyes of a doe caught in the hunter's snare.

Sofia. My wife.

Cold rage grew in my soul. Like a viper birthed from a black egg, my hate replaced my fear. *You bastard,* I half-thought. *You brought them here, the only ones in this despicable world who loved me, to watch this farce.*

Your father tried to kill you, Van told me.

I didn't want to believe him. I told myself time and again–*he s the enemy, of course he ll lie and sow dissension.* Keep me and my father at each other's throats, and all of Raithin Mawrn will fall under the boots and wings of his devil creatures. They plan an invasion, I reasoned. They let me go for the sole purpose that I'd murder my sire in retaliation, and die in the attempt.

As often as I pondered Van and Iyumi's reasons for shielding me, I remembered his body protecting me from the black Centaur's blade, and his kindness in healing my cheek. I asked myself: *why would he?* He'd no need to lie to me. I lay under his hoof, at his mercy, and he spoke to me with kindness. Could pure evil lie behind those laughing green eyes and infectious grin? My gut told me quite firmly: *no.*

Under the sixth, the seventh, the eighth lash, I no longer tried to banish my pain, nor hide it. I winced, cringed, and shrank away from that awful whip, my pride in tatters. My brow and face cut, I sweated red blood and pissed my trousers. Still the executioner counted 'nine, ten, eleven' and on and on and on.

I pushed my half-healed scar into the wooden mesh holding me upright, my arms tied out to either side. When the agony of my father's torture sought to overwhelm me, swamp me, I remembered Van's kindness. He touched me with respect, with friendliness. He didn't have to heal me, but he did anyway. He saw in me something no one else ever had: a Flynn that somebody liked.

Despite my body's betrayal, my new icy friend didn't desert me. While I wanted to pass out, escape the savage, ripping agony, another part of me relished every cut of the whip. Every stroke meant one more stab of my sword in my father's lying, despicable gut. *I will kill you,* I vowed, blinded by sweat and my own tears. *If it means selling my soul to accomplish it, I will see you bloody and dead at my feet.*

Did he say twenty lashes or thirty? I didn't remember. An eternity passed since the soldiers lashed me to the post. The roaring in my ears not quite blocked the sounds of my own moans. My sire's royal murderer called out number twenty and fell silent. I braced myself for yet another, number twenty one, yet the bald fellow dropped the heavy cat, its leather stained with my blood. He walked away. Resting my head against the wood frame, I shut my eyes and breathed. I focused on simple breathing, my head spinning, scenting my own blood, sweat and piss. My ripped torso on fire, screaming in agony, I didn't hear him approach.

Finian yanked my head back, exposing my throat.

I opened my eyes a fraction, and gazed into his angry, hate-filled dark eyes. His shaggy black hair blotted out the sun, a blessing of sorts, and spittle coated his beard. He grimaced rather than smiled as he leaned to speak in my ear.

"Don't fail me again, boy," he hissed, his breath ranker than the odor in my trousers. "You'll bring that bitch to me, in chains. You hear me?"

"Get her yourself," I whispered.

Snarling, he slammed my head into the heavy post. A pity that didn't knock me unconscious. He yanked my head back again, blood trickling from my brow, between my eyes and down my nose. Queasiness filled my gut and I half-hoped I'd puke on his royal black mantle. "Bring that bitch to me, or I'll kill her."

[154]

I almost passed out until his fist shook my head rapidly back and forth. "Who?" I managed, confused.

His hot breath tickled my ear. "Fainche," he murmured, his dark eyes alight with malice. "I'll cut your sister's throat while you watch."

Fainche? His own *daughter?* He'd kill the one offspring he loved just to intimidate me? I tried to gaze past his shoulder. Enya and Fainche had vanished, yet Sofia still stood where she was, watching me. Her cloak trembled visibly, though no fear expressed itself on her pale features.

Finian grinned, his mouth close enough to kiss my cheek. "I'll tell her it's your fault, boy. She'll strangle on her curses, knowing you're to blame. Your wife and mother, too. If you'd see them live, you'll bring that royal whore to me. Understand?"

I could only nod, defeated. My voice deserted me, as did my defiance. Only my rage survived. Courage, a stranger to me, crept into my hand like a friend I never knew I had. *I will beat you,* I thought. Somehow. I watched him through a reddish haze as Finian jerked his head once, acknowledging my surrender.

Finian cut the ropes that bound me to the wood frame, and shoved his dagger into his belt. I lowered my arms to my sides, and forced myself to stand upright. The blood returning to my wrists tingled, yet the harsh sunlight on my ripped back burned my flesh anew. I let none of that show on my face, however, as I stood toe to toe with him.

"I'm going to kill you," I said.

He guffawed. "You haven't the guts, boy."

His fist in my face slammed me into the dust and cobbles. "Crawl, worm," he snarled, kicking me onto my face. "Crawl, you filth."

His boot struck my ass and slammed me face-first into the cobble stones. Distantly, as though from far away, I heard the derisive laughter of Finian's cronies and hangers-on, of Blaez, of my father's soldiers. Even Sergei's nasal titter reached through the roaring in my ears. I tried to rise, but his heel between my shoulders slammed me back down. "Crawl to your beloved."

So I crawled. On my elbows, my knees, my chin and cheeks raw and bloody, I crept across the keep. Like the worm he named me, I wriggled my way over the rounded, dusty stones until her boots wavered in my half-sight. Only when her strong hand slid under my shoulder could I rise. Her slender form caught my weight as I collapsed. Her soothing voice and words of encouragement helped me to regain my balance, my feet, and the shattered remains of my dignity.

With her aid, I staggered through the postern door, and shut the evil away.

"Flynn," Sofia said, her voice in my ear. "Wake up."

Groggy, resentful, I covered my head with my arm, trying to shut her out. When I closed off her insistent voice, I also shut out the pain, the memories, the rage. I drifted on a cloud of nothing, seeking its empty solace, its lack of grief and its comforting desolation. *Death must be like this,* I half-thought. No life, no emotion, no gut-wrenching grief, no life or death choices. Just coasting along a tide of soothing emptiness.

Until her hand dropped to my shoulder, gently shaking.

I reared up, hissing in agony, my jaw clenched to prevent a scream from erupting. "Gods, woman," I gasped, dropping my face into the warm pillow. "Don't touch me."

"Oh, Flynn." Sofia's voice choked with tears. "I'm so sorry. I thought–"

"Thought what?"

Easing myself onto my side, I blinked rapidly until the three Sofia's I saw merged into one. My head spun sickeningly, and my belly threatened to heave absolutely nothing onto her pristine lap. Though the ointments she soothed into the raw cuts on my back the night before cooled them enough to permit me to sleep, they hadn't yet healed me. I felt the dried herb concoction break apart at my movement and with them any semblance of scabs over my wounds.

"That–you know, it helped–"

Her hazel-green eyes feigned a tear or two, but I knew fakery when it dripped onto my neck. She loved my rank more than she did me, but at least her aid the day before was sincere enough. A living, breathing prince husband brought her more status than a royal widow. If Fainche inherited my father's title, Sofia's standing fell to that of a distant cousin, thrice removed. Sofia needed me alive and healthy if her social ranking were to survive. Only as my queen could she find true satisfaction and security.

"I'm sorry, it did," I admitted, raising myself onto my elbow. "My thanks, last night– "

"Flynn." She frowned slightly, her lips trembling, as she stroked her fingers lightly down my skinned cheeks and jaw. "What he did . . . it was wrong. I hated him for . . . for . . . that." She dropped her eyes to her hands, clasped in her dressing gown, a red-brown affair that matched the color of her braid. "He shouldn't have done that. You're his son."

I never told once her I loved her. I knew she'd use my emotions against me, beat me with them for every day of my life. In her selfish need, she'd blackmail me for her own gain. Yet, in that moment, I loved her more than ever. And those little words, 'I love you' trembled on my lips–

I held them back.

"It doesn't matter," I said instead, my heart slack in my chest. "Nothing does."

I rested my head on my elbow and wished fervently that Malik's knife slit my throat rather than my cheek. To me, death was far preferable to this living hell the gods sentenced me to. *Hey, let s make this guy suffer every known pain imaginable,* I heard them snigger. *Let s break him to pieces and see what happens.*

1 m in pieces, I wanted to snap. *Happy now?*

"He says I have to marry her," I said, my voice dull, my eyes shut.

"Marry?"

Sofia's voice rose in volume and sharpness. "Marry whom?"

"Princess Yummy, er, Iyumi."

"You wouldn't dare."

I paid little heed to the threat in her tone, and caught only her fear and grief. "I don't want to," I said slowly. "I have to. Or he'll kill Fainche."

"You'd set me aside? Me? Your *wife?*"

I heard the danger now, recognized the menace in her voice, felt its peril along my nerve endings. Opening my eyes, I fully expected a knife at my throat. But the only danger lay in her fury, her glance, her tight jaw. The full bore of feminine jealousy and hurt attacked me not physically, but emotionally. My words wounded her to the core, and there was no healing them. Not with words, not with ointments, not with magic.

"I'm sorry, Sofia," I murmured, lifting my hand to her delicate brow. "It's not what I want."

She slapped my hand aside. "You bastard," she hissed, her eyes gleaming with rage. "You planned this...planned it from the start–"

"No, I– "

"You and your conniving father and your bitch mother–"

I slapped her then. Not a quick, light reprimand, but a hard, bare-knuckled back-hand to her left cheek. Her face flew sideways, my signet ring cutting her cheekbone, as her spittle spun off into the air. Her right hand rose to swiftly protect her wounded cheek. I heard a choked-off sob, as Sofia reined in her pain and her fears as I never could.

My guilt rose to condemn me. Did I do anything useful save hit women? Did my sainted mother raise a serf or a prince? Did I have the guts to apologize, be a man, and acknowledge I acted in the wrong? I did, but did I have the balls to admit it?

"Sofia," I said, my hand cupping hers. "I'm sorry. I didn't mean–"

"Set me aside, you bastard," her voice hissed from behind her sheltering hand, "and I'll inform your father you have magic."

Icy cold dropped into my gut like a ton of lead. She knew. All this time she bloody *knew.*

Since birth I protected this most dire secret. My folk feared and hated magic in all its forms. Laws condemned those who practiced it, executed them with fire, with steel and with rope. Our race sought the eradication of the Bryn'Cairdhan people and the magical stain they represented. Magic was, and always shall be, banned and anathema. Those who wielded it should be burned as demons and witches.

Such was the teachings shoved down my throat since I arrived in this wretched world.

On that day when I innocently changed a hated barn cat into a rooting, snorting piglet, I knew I was different. I did things no other man or woman could. If I misliked the clothes my nurse put me in, I simply changed them with a thought. I tamed the wildest, meanest stallion in the stable with a mere touch. I called an eagle from the blue sky and watched it land on my wrist without cutting me with its deadly talons. I felt different, apart, and unique.

Until that day when a young, green-eyed Shape-Shifter healed a deep slash on my cheek with his finger.

Only then did I feel real fear, real panic.

For I was no longer alone.

That the King's only son and the heir apparent to his throne should possess that unlawful and cursed power – his fearful folk would tear me apart and feed my remains to the dogs. I protected my secret, stilled my abilities, and feigned a hatred for our neighbors to the south they hadn't earned.

Magic wasn't evil. Only people earned that title.

"Turn me in," I growled, my hand at her throat, "and I'll kill you. Remember this, my love."

I bent my face close to hers. Close enough to kiss, should I want to. My hand traced its way down her throat to the parting of her breasts, bulging from her simple gold and lace robe. My fingers returned to her chin, and forced her to gaze deep into my eyes. "Your heart is in my fist. When I die, so shall you."

Panic filled those twin pools. Her hands clasped mine, cold to the touch. Too much like her soul for my comfort. "You'd kill our child?" she gasped. "Our son?"

I jerked my hand away, the chill of her hands reaching my heart. "You lie."

"Do I?" She half-laughed, taunting me, rising from the bed to walk toward the door. "My woman's bleeding hasn't come for three months. I'm pregnant with your child."

If she'd stabbed me with a blade, Sofia couldn't have wounded me more. My child? My son, whom I'd raise with the joy and love my father never gave me. I'd teach him to hunt, to ride, to laugh, to sing–to simply love. My only chance to make something of myself that wasn't twisted or cruel or bitter. Not even my father could take that from me.

"Are you sure?" I asked.

Sofia half-shrugged, her expression neutral. The mark of my hand darkened her cheek already. "Time will tell, I expect," she replied coldly, setting her hand to the door. "The messenger arrived while you were sleeping. Your father expects you at the stables within the hour."

An hour? I wasn't fit to walk much less ride the lands in search of a prophetess. I slumped back into my pillow and covered my face with my arm. Hell's teeth. I am *sooo* dead.

"Flynn."

Something in Sofia's voice made me drop my arm and glance askance at her. She stood in the open doorway, clad in her usual colors of russet and gold. Instead of a coil, her red braid dangled from behind her right ear to drape over her full, ripe bosom to her waist. With the morning sun behind her, she looked lovely and beautiful and as deadly as a viper.

"You've a power he doesn't," she said, her tone low. "You can kill him and save your sister, save me. You've the ability to change things–forever."

She started out the door, then froze, considering. Her pale face turned over her shoulder. "You can finally be the man you want to be."

Gods above.

She shut the door behind her, leaving me alone with my pain and the wild ideas she intentionally planted. Me? Kill my father with forbidden magic and seize his throne? How long before the righteous indignation of the general, magic-fearing populace tore me limb from limb?

[160]

What was it Van said? 'All magic has healing elements.' Did that include my own? I'd no idea how to heal, much less heal myself. How do I tap into the forbidden pool of power deep within me? Folks like Van, Malik and Iyumi no doubt practiced every day.

Practice.

The echo of a whisper seemed to float down from the vaulted ceiling to drift, like a feather on a warm breeze, into my ear. *Watch and learn. Set free the wellspring of power you were born with.*

I inherited this, I reminded myself. How can magic be evil if the one who wielded it wasn't? It made no sense to believe, now, that fundamental magic contained malevolence. If it can heal, well—wasn't that a good thing? I can't let him win, let *them* win. If I'm to save not just myself, but Fainche and Sofia and my blessed mother, I must heal myself.

What did Van do?

He ran his finger down my cheek and my wound healed. Though I couldn't very well run my fingers down my back, I touched the cuts and abrasions on my face and chest. Hmmm.

Stiffly, cursing, the flesh over my back ripping like rotten linen, I slipped from the bed and staggered to my feet. Nausea, mixed with the hot, flaring agony, threatened to spill me onto the richly carpeted floor. The room spun, and noxious sweat dripped into my eyes. I almost raised my voice to call Sofia back, insist she help me. But that new stone in my heart, rage, kept my tongue behind my teeth.

Its potent fury sent new will into my legs, stiffened my spine, and lent me the aid I needed to walk stiffly to Sofia's dressing table. The rooms we shared since our marriage were simply and tastefully decorated. Abhorring my parents' private chambers, I insisted on pale cream carpeting over the cold stone slabs of the floor. Colorful tapestries depicting successful hunters bringing home fearsome boars, gallant stags, and hawks returning to leather-wrapped wrists hung from stout hooks. Scenes from ancient battles, warriors riding snorting, violently rearing stallions and men standing tall and bloody over the defeated enemy covered the boring stone of the castle's grey inner walls.

I permitted one armored knight to stand in a corner, his visor down over his featureless face, his sword angled high. The armor belonged to a distant relative of Sofia's line, and her connection to her noble lineage. It stood beside the great hearth, and a huge white fur covered the broad flagstones at its' feet. The fireplace itself could roast not one, not two, but three whole oxen if we were hungry enough to utilize it in such a fashion. A small fire was enough to keep us warm on the coldest of winter nights.

My apartments rested within the curve of the great west tower of the Castle. Opposite my rooms, my parents called their museum home. Fainche's chambers, smaller and with no outer balcony, lay on the far side of the curve, between my rooms and those of the King and Queen. The other chambers belonged to guests of the royal family–of which there were few and far between–lay mostly empty. I suspected many an ardent guard or army officer brought their willing liaisons to those rooms for privacy and illicit hanky panky. I suspected Sofia knew of these, but I never bothered to ask her.

Sofia departed through the two heavy oaken doors that swung onto the inner corridors. Another door, lighter and smaller, opened onto the massive, walled balcony. I often liked to stand there and watch the sun set, gaze over the town that surrounded Castle Salagh and dream of riding free over the distant hills. In times of strife, guards stood their watch on both entrances. Per my order, no guard lounged around my chambers for ten or more years. I never did like their spying eyes nor their unctuous smiles.

I liked warm, dark wood, and all our furniture captured that essence. The huge bed I just rolled from held four tall posters, with dark red hangings made from heavy satin. A servant's pallet lay at the foot, though I hadn't permitted a servant to sleep there since I moved in. Any attendants who looked after us resided in the outer chamber with a stout, barred door between us. Sofia's personal maid saw to her needs once I left the rooms.

I had no manservant. I dressed myself every morning and undressed myself every evening. I could brush my own hair, and tie my own boot laces, thank you. Never able to tolerate the fussiness of servants, I routinely sent them away as often as my mother assigned them to me.

With a sigh, I sat in Sofia's chair amid her scents, hair brushes, face, foot and tooth powders. Various jars and vials of ointments, creams, and medicines, topped with wax seals lay in an organized clutter. I half-wondered if within one of those vials lay a prevention of pregnancies. We'd been married more than three years. I lay with her almost nightly. The timing of this conception seemed almost too good to be true.

If it's too good to be true, then it generally wasn't.

Using her polished mirror, I examined my face. Swollen, red abrasions raked down my left cheek. A huge, purple-black goose-egg rose over my right eye, and my nose looked like the naked ass of a bottom-of-the-rung chicken. Scrapes and dark bruises all over my face gave me a hellish appearance. The scar left behind by Malik's blade and Van's mercy only intensified the evil monster I'd become.

For your own good, don t heal what s visible. Heal what isn t.

"*I have to experiment first,*" I replied.

Picking a small cut on the left side of my jaw, I ran my finger over it.

Nothing happened.

It remained red and raw and oozing.

Try it again, but this time flex your will.

Concentrate. Again, nothing. I pondered how I called the eagle to my wrist. I didn't use words. I merely looked up at him–and called. I don't recall willing him to come, but I suppose I had. Thus, if willpower is needed, perhaps I should focus my mind on thoughts of healing and *will* my cut to heal.

Feeling rather foolish, I stared hard into the mirror. My reflection glared back. Did my eyes always look that haunted? As I never used a mirror, not even to shave with, I didn't know. My yellow hair hung as wild as a horse's mane past my shoulders, and my cheeks appeared as hollow as a starved crone's. No regal, princely appearance for me, I reckoned.

Turning my face slightly, I concentrated on a narrow gash along my left jaw. A cut from the whip, no doubt. Lifting my right forefinger, I traced lightly along its length.

I *willed* it to heal.

My skin tingled as though hundreds of tiny fireflies danced along it. Heat grew and spread, burning, yet not with a fierce, savage heat. Rather the warmth felt akin to a cat's paw after waking from a nap: soft heat with a mild, tender pressure. Under my finger the wound knitted, melded, closed and vanished. In the mirror, I witnessed it fold in upon itself, turn into a faint red line before disappearing altogether. No trace of it remained.

However, whatever magic I called up continued, its warmth spreading, seeking other injuries, turning a wicked abrasion into a simple reddish scrape before it, too, popped out of existence.

"Whoa, Nellie," I murmured.

With an effort, I pulled the power back within me, shut down my will and took a deep breath. Like the cat returning to its nap, I felt it coil back, draw away and return to slumbering deep within me. Yet, it left behind an odd sensation. I cocked my head, trying to puzzle it out. The Flynn in the mirror frowned and his eyes narrowed. I hadn't changed, but I didn't feel the same. I was still Flynn, still looked like a wild mountain man, still burned with horrible pain from the whip and my father, and yet I felt–

–joy.

Yes, I felt joy. I felt exhilarated. I wanted to laugh and dance and love. A giggle actually popped from my lips before I knew it approached. I examined myself closer. The haunted look in my eyes wasn't there anymore. Could the handling of magic actually bring a person true happiness? Van certainly seemed a happy enough fellow, even if Malik appeared as sour as month-old milk. Maybe it didn't work the same on Centaurs.

If I, and those I loved, were to survive, not only must I hide my new-found powers, I must heal myself of the worst of my injuries. If using magic made me happy, then I, above all, must remain the old, nasty Flynn whom no one liked. Even if I liked myself better, I must hide that, too.

I peered once more in the mirror, and forced a dark scowl, narrowing my eyes. *Ah, there you are, you rascal. Prince Flynn, the Despisea.*

"Here, kitty, kitty, kitty," I muttered, focusing my will on my back injuries. "Time to play."

I slumped before a roaring bonfire, poking a stick into its deep red coals. I feigned exhaustion, yet felt exhilaration. Through the twelve long hours in the saddle, slumping as I did now, I pretended an agony I didn't feel. Oh, my back itched incessantly and the knot on my forehead kept a thumping headache locked within, yet those were mere annoyances compared to what I'd truly feel had I not healed the worst of my own father-inflicted injuries.

My heart, lighter than the sparrow flitting across the treetops, was more difficult to conceal as I practiced my rediscovered powers. Through slitted eyes, groaning now and again, I rode Bayonne, the real one, and lifted stones with my mind. Passing across a flat hilltop, I informed a winging falcon where I'd seen a careless rodent. She stooped, wings flattened to cut wind resistance and dropped, unseen from above, onto her unlucky prey. Upon entering a thick grove of heavy pines, tall oak, and thickets of brambles, I parted branches from Bayonne's face without lifting a hand. Behind me, Blaez muttered imprecations under his breath as those selfsame branches whipped across his face.

Pretend pain exhausted me more than real agony. My slump created a crick in my lower back that I yearned to straighten and stretch. I grew bored playing with rocks and breaking dead tree limbs. I challenged myself by calling up the wind. A sharp mountain breeze swept across the mountaintop, scenting of clean pine and high meadow grass as I inhaled in delight. With every magical feat I mastered, I grew more and more adept. I utilized less and less effort to accomplish a task, and soon a mere thought brought the result I wanted. Under the very noses of those who swore to slay all magic and its creatures, I rapidly learned how to wield my own.

[165]

Finian ordered me to accept that idiot Blaez. He and two others from my father's royal cavalry soldiers, Galdan and Hogan, accompanied me on my quest to kidnap, yet again, Princess Yummy. For my own protection, I ordered five of my own questionably loyal henchmen to also tag along: my newly fletched men, Buck-Eye and Kalan, and my other well-paid men-at-arms: Rade, Boden, and Torass, watched my back most carefully. Kadal, who died to protect me, offered them new incentives to keep me alive.

When two from the previous expedition, Lyall and Todaro, begged to accompany me, who was I to refuse them? I hiked their pay and their brows, in the hopes it also increased their loyalty to me several-fold. Dead princes tended to not pay their debts. Live ones–well, Prince Flynn was reputed to be filthy rich. Naturally, I fostered those interesting rumors.

"Why are they going north?" Blaez muttered.

I flicked a glance across the blazing fire. He sat on a large rock, much as I did, pouring an odd granular mixture into large, hollowed out bamboo reeds. Picking small rocks from the earth at his feet, he dropped them into the current hollow tube. He added small sharp nails from his saddlebags, and splinters of bone from the deer Lyall shot with his bow and we ate for our supper. Blaez peered down inside, shutting his left eye, and nodded sharply to himself.

He cut a length of waxed string, and stuffed one end in the open mouth. Permitting a length to dangle down the side of the bamboo, he sealed the mouth with hot wax. Setting it carefully aside, he began another.

"What're those?" I asked.

Blaez answered by scrubbing a new tube with sand, added his dark mixture, scouted for more rocks, funneled a handful of nails down inside and sealed the result with more wax. He carefully set it on the growing pile beside his rock chair and began another.

"Those things won't go off?" I asked. "By accident? Will they?"

"Not unless I want them to." Blaez flicked me a swift glance before returning to his task.

That bad boy has magic, I thought, gleeful. He's trying to hide it as much as I was.

[166]

I pretended not to notice and returned my attention to the fire.

Behind me, the men tossed dice to determine camp duties. A flick of my mind set the tossed dice spinning until Buck-Eye and Torass's chosen numbers lay face up, winning them the right to clear away the remains of dinner. With identical sighs, they set about washing up as Boden erected my tent and Lyall curried Bayonne and his own chestnut mount. Rade and Hogan hauled water, fetched wood for the fire, and sought the comfort of their own horses and Commander Blaez's black stallion.

How powerful was Blaez? He obviously knew a great deal more about magic than I did and no doubt practiced his craft without alerting anyone. Could I beat him if it came down to a fight? My father still wanted my head on a pike, and Finian owned Blaez body and soul.

Camp duties finished, the men sat around the huge fire, cross-legged on blankets and pallets, and drew weapons. They sharpened swords, checked arrows for bad fletching, tested bowstrings, set hidden throwing knives securely under arms, along steel-covered wrists, inside tall boot-tops. Muttered voices, discrete as to not disturb me, spoke of who might catch the third, the least desired watch, that night; whose horse out-travelled whose and a ribald jest or three. I tuned them out.

"North," Blaez muttered, not looking up. "I don't like it."

I didn't either. A direct route north would take Yummy and her friends deeper into the Shin'Eah Mountains. In following, we'd ride across tall, treacherous peaks where a sudden ice storm might lock us down until we starved. We didn't need the Atani Shifters to kill us, the ugly mountains would do their dirty work for them. Then Finian would kill Fainche and Sofia.

"We go north until told otherwise," I said, my voice as weak as I could possibly make it.

"Huh," Blaez snorted without looking up.

"Father's information must be correct," I murmured, not quite certain just how my illustrious sire got his intel that Iyumi and her pals rode hard for the north. I wasn't sure I wanted to know, either. "He has good spies."

The half-moon rode high, burning bright in the eastern black velvet of the night sky. Forest tops obscured its lower half, yet it drowned the stars nearest it. With soft chuckles and a tossed jest, my men settled into blankets on pallets, hoping they weren't picked for first watch. Although the first was easiest, the men were broke-backed weary and craved sleep as they never craved a woman's pleasure.

Soft, I muttered to myself. *As soft as bean curds.* How they managed the hard life of mercenary soldiers was beyond my immediate comprehension.

"I'll never sleep," I muttered. "I'll take first watch."

Blaez flicked me a glance then returned to his life's work–bomb making. Buck-Eye nodded and offered me a half-salute. My murder of Sim and obvious strength to bear up under the pressure of extensive wounds offered me a rare respect they didn't want to admit. Throughout the day, Blaez never once questioned a decision of mine, followed my lead and obeyed my every order. Where I led, they tagged along like obedient little hounds and shit when I told them to.

Though I wanted very much to crawl into my fur-lined pallet under my covering tent and sleep for two weeks, a sudden urge to be alone struck me. I wanted away from that camp and those treacherous, conniving knaves like yesterday.

I staggered to my feet. No sham this time. My legs below my knees fell asleep as I poked the fire with a stick. None present knew my hand never touched the stick to begin with. I groaned aloud as fresh blood tingled into my lower legs, ankles and feet. Balance escaped me as I tottered away into the darkness outside the fire.

"Get your rest," I said, my tone commanding, yet still weak. "Blaez, that means you."

Muttering and cursing, Blaez tucked his deadly toys into a canvas sack and lay down on his pallet of pine boughs and wool blankets. After tossing and turning, drawing his blanket up to his chin despite the night's mild temperatures, getting himself comfortable, he finally lay silent and still. His snores might wake the dead, but I hardly complained.

Something out in the woods, alive in the darkness, called to me. I cocked my head, listening. In my ears, I heard nothing save the soft sough of the breeze ruffling through the trees, the hoot of a hunting owl a short distance away, the live crackling of the fire and exploding pine knots. Very far away, a wolf howled, its soulful cry wavering on the night air. Another wolf answered the first, and I found myself dreadfully fascinated by the sounds.

Yet, when I listened with my other, more sensitive, hearing, I heard my name called. *Flynn.* The two sounds, the howling wolf and the night wind carrying my name on its breast gave me the sudden shivers. *What the hell?* I rubbed my upper arms, chilled, despite the warmth of the mid-summer evening.

"Buck-Eye," I said, my voice deliberately quavering. "You're second watch, Galdan, you're third."

I didn't wait around to listen to the grumbles of those chosen, or the happy chuckles of those who'd sleep sound all night. As though in great pain, I staggered into the darkness outside the firelight. I glanced back. Per my orders, the men curled into their pallets near the blazing fire, tossing a few crude jests back and forth as they snuggled beneath blankets, heads pillowed on saddles.

Once out of the firelight, I dropped the weakling sham and straightened my back. Raising my arms above my head in a long, soulful stretch, my spine popped audibly. I sighed deeply. Damn but it felt good to stand upright and walk firmly again. My back still itched abominably, and I paused long enough to scratch it against an oak tree. My skin too soft and newly healed for more than a quick up and down and sideways rub on the tree. As it was, the fiery burn flared higher, making me wish I'd left the bloody thing alone.

Following my gut, I turned abruptly right. My eyes adjusted quickly to the darkness, and with the rising moon behind me I saw easily. Dodging rocks and scrub oak thickets, I wended my way through the forest, ducking my head to avoid bumping my goose-egg on low overhanging branches. Even in the dense forest, my vision adjusted accordingly. Enough to not bark my shins, walk into a low-lying limb, or trip over a rock, anyway. The light wind brushed through the tree tops and whispered my name, though the wolves had long since quieted.

Within a few hundred rods, I stumbled upon what appeared to be an old path. Not a game trail, I was certain, for it led away from water and grazing, and climbed high toward the hill a mile or so away. It appeared to be a beaten path–leading to what?

My gut and the voice on the wind ushering me on, I traipsed along it, following its relative smoothness uphill. The trail steepened, winding its way around heavy boulders and tall trees. The vegetation fell away slowly the higher I climbed, and its sharp angle gave my lungs and legs a much needed workout. Did I call my men soft? Where was my horse when I needed him? Right now, I'd be happy to ride Van.

I huffed and puffed my way up, the trail folding back upon itself several times to avoid clumps of pine and elm, or clusters of fallen rock. Though the moon shown down only half-full, its light, and that of the bright stars, gave me plenty to see by. I avoided deadfall, worm-etched signatures burrowed into the bone-white skeletons of long-expired tree trunks. The light wind brushed pine boughs against my face or shoulders, as though caressing me in passing. *Flynn,* it called, whispering in my ears. The wolf howled, its cry resounding much closer. I drew my cloak closer about my neck, glancing around uneasily. I loosened my sword in its scabbard. Why didn't I make a torch to carry? Fire made a very handy weapon against fanged, furry things.

I worked my way higher, the moon-lit hilltop beckoning. Just a little further. Happy my back no longer ached, for I needed both it and my relatively strong legs. My lungs requested a leave of absence, but I denied them and forced them into subservience. If I survive this, I swear I'll give up drinking, gambling and chasing women.

Er, perhaps I'll give up drinking and gambling.

"Flynn."

I heard the voice again. Did I hallucinate, hear things that weren't truly there? I cocked my head, listening hard. It wasn't the wind, nor was it the wolf howling, near or far away. It was a woman's voice and spoke from beyond that rocky ridge.

My sword in my hand, I slowed my pace. I climbed but cautiously, following the beaten trail around the crown of the hill. I approached the ridgeline, keeping my body low and not exposing myself against the moonlight. Creeping like a flea along a hairline, I slunk from one shadow into another, peering over the low stone wall with only my eyes showing. I hid my sword in the shadows, praying its starlit gleam hadn't been seen by the occupant in the clearing.

Two forms stood by the light of a dancing fire at the crown of the hill. I peered around, seeking more human shapes, more potential enemies. The hilltop itself was ringed by a low stone wall, half crumbled by time and weather. Beyond the fire lay the ruins of an ancient building, fallen timbers drying to dust amid the broken stone walls of the collapsed structure. Only what appeared to be a stone altar remained intact on the far side of the blazing fire.

"Flynn."

The taller of the two shadowed forms spoke, without turning. I knew that voice. I knew that slender frame silhouetted against the fire's dancing light. I recognized that thick fall of blonde hair that fell to her hips, mantling her in gold. As regal as any goddess, and as beautiful as a spring dawn, Queen Enya watched the moon rise higher as I breathed her name, a sigh as much as a word.

"Mother."

She turned. With the fire and moonlight behind her, I saw only a dark silhouette of her exquisite, chiseled features. Her white teeth gleamed as she smiled. "My son."

Sheathing my sword, I stumbled out from behind the wall's inadequate protection. What the hell is she doing here? "Mother?"

Lifting her right hand toward me, she invited me to take it. Once I cleared the wall and advanced across the stone-less, treeless clearing, I clasped her fingers. Tripping over the small child at her feet, I glanced down once in confusion before her melodious voice cancelled all brain activity within my head.

"You've accepted your gift, Flynn," she said, smiling, her hand warm within mine. "I'm pleased."

"What are you doing here? What gift?" I asked, stumbling over my tongue, glancing from the child to her and back again. "Who's this–?"

Her pale slender finger over my lips silenced me as effectively as a gag.

"In due time, my son," she said, her voice calm, solemn and sure. "I'll reveal all, and answer your questions. But for now, accept what is and be silent."

Though a dozen, more, questions rose as far as my mouth, I shut them off, shunted them aside and waited. *It'll come, if you have patience enough.* Few can sit still on dire secrets for long. I was no exception, loth as I was to admit it.

As Enya shut her eyes and tilted her head back as though communing with the stars, I studied the small boy at her feet. With his left fist gripping a fold of her gown, his right thumb corked securely in his mouth, he studied me in turn. *Two years old, maybe.* I offered him a sly wink. A grin blossomed around the thumb and his solemn eyes crinkled at the corners. He's a cute little bugger, whoever he was.

A sturdy lad, his shock of brown hair curled thickly over his ears and neck, and his huge dark eyes watched me with calm trust. He wore a light green tunic made from good cotton and small black breeches. The light breeze lifted his tiny cloak, and ruffled the hair from his eyes. Those eyes. I frowned slightly. They reminded me of someone–

Enya stirred, and took a deep breath as though calming her shattered nerves. Turning, she smiled, and reached up a trembling hand to the knot on my brow. Tenderly, tears leaking from her lovely eyes, she brushed my hair aside and cupped my cheek. "Forgive me, Flynn," she said, her tone low and so soft I strained to hear her words.

"Forgive you?" I asked, my voice sounding harsh and chill in the wake of her dulcimer angel's voice. "For what?"

She ducked her face, hiding behind a veil of her hair. I leaned toward, over her, in order to hear her at all. "I failed to protect you, my son, my Flynn," she murmured. "A mother must protect her children and I've failed. I am so sorry. So very, very sorry."

A sob escaped the curtain and I straightened. Icy rage tingled down my nerve endings. I gripped the hilt of my sword, hard, to prevent a string of vile curses from spewing from my mouth. Not for what Finian the Fair did to me. That was unjust and cruel in itself. But 'twas as nothing as compared to the suffering he brought his timid and loving wife, the mother of his children. *I ll kill him,* I thought, not for the first, second or even the third time. I *will* kill him, for what he's doing to *her.*

I choked back my rage. I swallowed it down like bad medicine and forced calm into my voice and manner. I delved my hand through the blonde rain of her hair and touched her warm neck. "Mother," I said, my voice hoarse. "Mother. Look at me."

Enya obeyed, tears spilling from those blue-blue depths. Her lips trembled as she tried hard to smile, as she dipped her damp cheek to brush against my hand. Bending, I touched my brow against hers, looking deep into those blessed eyes she gave me. "It's all good, my lady," I whispered. "I love you."

Her fingers gripped mine in a fierce hold. "Oh, Flynn," she cried, swiping tears from her cheeks with her free hand. Her skin reddened slightly from weeping, yet I never found her more beautiful. "That's why I came. I had to find you. I couldn't protect you before. I must. I *must.* Your fa–"

She choked off, turning her face away once more. "Finian–he's sworn to kill you."

"I know. He's tried."

She swung back to me, clinging with desperate panic. "He's threatened to kill Fainche, also. He'll kill me, too, but I don't care as long as you both survive."

"He told me. If I don't bring Iyumi to him, he'll kill both of you. And Sofia."

"He sees you as a threat," my mother cried, gripping my arms, her nails digging deep. "He knows you're stronger than he is. I've tried so hard . . . so hard, to convince him you offer him only obeisance and obedience. You're a good son, after all. But he rants about you. Raves, like a lunatic! I'm not strong like you, Flynn. I'm–"

[173]

Ever so gently, I swiped her hair from her brow. "Hush, Mother."

"It's his mistress," Enya wailed, turning her face away, as though shamed. "She whispers in his ear, tells him things. He listens to her–he's unfaithful, but I love him so!"

I forgot the little boy as my mother wept in my arms. I smoothed her hair over her shoulders, murmuring nonsense words that always comforted the bereaved. Her tears dampened my shirt, and I counted backward from one hundred to cool my rage. That *bastaro*. I cared little for how he thought about me. That he dared spurn the love this delicate flower offered, this loving and sweet woman who adored the villain who sired her children. He dared to threatened her–*her!* The one who loved me beyond all reason, all ken, all life.

"Flynn," she said, drawing away from me, swiping once more at her wet cheeks, brushing her hair back. I reached for her hand, but she stepped away, rejecting my comfort as though painfully embarrassed. "It's good, really. I'm all right."

She took the boy's hand, bravely smiling through her damp eyes. Dragging in a deep, cleansing breath, she tipped her chin sideways, her smile begging my indulgence. Asking my royal pardon as though she were but a serf and I a king. "You've acknowledged your gift. At last, at long last, praise the gods."

"My–"

She nodded, her face lighting with fierce joy. "Yes, my son. Your powers. The magic I myself gave you. Through our shared blood, you are powerful and unconquerable. A true king indeed."

I jerked away, hissing, sucking air through my teeth. I never gave thought to where my power, my gift, came from. All along, I suspected I was unique, alone, a black sheep amid the flocks of white. Finian and his people certainly treated me as such. Now I discovered this gift travelled across lines of blood. From parent to offspring. I descended from a long line of magicians. If magic was evil, then by the gods of old, so was I.

I turned from her to better contemplate my heritage, my eyes staring sightless into the dark. I was born with it. Magic was in my blood. Not from Finian, by all the gods, but from Enya–my mother.

Power had to come from somewhere, I suddenly realized. Power. Blood. *Enya.*

Like a knife from the dark, I remembered.

I didn't want to get beaten. I wasn't supposed to be there. Hiding in the curtains of my mother's solar, I tried not to breathe and give myself away as I watched, horrified. My mother's afternoon tea splashed across the pristine carpet. An accident. Enya's tiny serving maid, I couldn't recall her name, had stumbled. Yet, I clearly remembered her petrified expression, and her huge eyes rounded with fear.

I remembered her screams of pain as a wide leather strap swung time and again across her buttocks and shoulders. My mother watched with calm detachment from her seat by the window, her sewing in her lap as still as the expression on her face. The maid, unable to move a muscle save those on her face, couldn't escape the grip that held her. Only she and my mother were the room's occupants. Nothing held the girl fast. No one held the strap's end.

"Please, Flynn," Enya begged, seizing my arm.

I blinked, drawn out of the memory and brought into the present as though someone dashed a bucket of water over my head.

"I'm not as strong as you. It took all I had within me, all my powers, to find you and bring you here, to this place."

"Why, Mother?" I asked, suspicion grasping its stone-cold fingers around my heart. "Why did you come?"

"To bring you this child."

Surprise into silence, I glanced down at the small boy, still sucking his thumb, his left hand dwarfed in my mother's pale grip. The diamonds on her wrist and fingers winked under the light of the half-moon. Oddly, the wolf howled again, sounding as though it sat at the base of the hill. A shiver crawled up my spine and took up icy residence at the back of my skull.

"Don't you see? Flynn, don't you understand?"

Enya's eagerness, her wild hope, her frantic desperation caught at my heart. "No, Mother," I admitted, my eyes on the boy gazing trustfully up at me. "I don't."

Unfortunately, I feared I did.

"You can have great power, son," she said, smiling widely, her hair a tangled mess. Her teeth gleamed under the moonlight, her lips smears of red. Blue eyes appeared dark garnet, as though a fox stood in the henhouse with its feathered meal in its jaws, caught by the light of the farmer's torch.

For an instant, a fraction of a thought, I loathed her. I hated her damp hand on my sleeve, her clinging body smothering me, her vile voice. I lifted my hand to slap her away–

Flynn.

My conscience called to me, its voice loud, strident and unforgettable. *This is your mother, for gods' sake. She s here to help you, you flaming idiot. Grow up, will you?*

Shame swamped me. I raised my hand, to caress her damp cheek. This wonderful, helpless creature gave birth to me amid blood and agony. And I'd repay her sacrifice with hatred and violence? Should I ever lift my hand against her in hatred, may the gods strike me dead.

"You must save Fainche," Enya said, through her tears. "My own life isn't important, but she, and you, are. I can give you the power you need to defeat him, my son. And defeat him you must, if you are to save your sister, your wife. Will you trust me?"

"Of course I will, Mother."

"This child is the key."

For the first time, she glanced down at him. Her fingers brushed through his dark curls; her face filled with love and light.

Suspicion tried to rear its ugly face again, but I kicked it in the groin and it subsided. My mother was–is–as innocent as this boy. She thought only of me, her son, a spoiled wretch ungrateful of her sacrifice. The unnamed lad lifted his chin toward her, before ducking his face, shyly, into the folds of her skirts.

"His mother is dead," Enya murmured, her voice hollow. "She died of an agonizing disease. One that he inherited, unfortunately."

I glanced down at what appeared to me to be a ridiculously healthy and strapping two-year old boy. "What disease?"

Enya turned her face away, as though the information distressed her. "It has no name," she whispered. "There is no cure. She died, screaming in agony. Within the month, this child will die the same

[176]

way. In horrible anguish and pain, his skin boiling from his bones, he'll suffer an unspeakable, torturous death."

Horrified, I drew away from the kid, half-hoping this disease wasn't contagious. "So why is he here?"

"He'll die anyway." Enya's eager voice, half-whispered, drifted to my ears. Her face still turned away from me.

I stared at the back of her blonde head, willing her to look at me. She refused that request and left me gaping foolishly at her wealth of hair.

"And?"

"The gods require a sacrifice."

Cold ice filled my veins. I stared down at this boy, this child of sheer innocence and trust. Sacrifice him? To save myself? Are you effing kidding me?

"You must do it, Flynn." She sobbed into her hands, her hair spilling about her. Her shoulders shook with intense grief. "He's going to die. Unless you do this, his death will be in vain. Your hand, your knife, will be of mercy. You'll do him kindness, not evil. Save him from that, and the gods will grant you the power to halt your father's evil."

"Mother–"

She cannoned into me, sobbing, helpless. Her arms tight around my waist, she wept into my shirt. Helpless, scared, I held her close. *This is wrong. It s wrong, it s so bloody wrong–*

"It *is* wrong, Flynn," my mother cried, her shoulders under my hands heaving. "But don't you see? It *must* be done. His death will spare him unbelievable suffering and grant you sublime power. You must do this. If you want to protect your sister, and Sofia. To protect me."

Fainche. Small, twelve years old and ignorant of the world and its evil. She'd known only kindness and grace until Finian forced her to watch my humiliation and punishment. Did she truly understand what she'd witnessed? Of course not. She'd stare evil in the face and laugh, thinking it a joke. I never, ever, want her to see true evil, in any form.

"I'll do it," I muttered. "Whatever it takes."

"Are you sure?"

Am I?

Enya lifted her hand, frail hope lightening her delicate features. "If only I were stronger, I'd take this burden from you, my precious son. But I cannot, for I am weak where you are strong."

Don t do this.

"I must."

My heart beat in thick, heavy strokes. "What must I do?"

"Place him on the altar."

As the little boy gazed at me, absolute trust in his eyes, I lifted him. He weighed no more than a pack, and his small hands crept about my neck. I ignored the small warmth they brought and avoided his dark eyes. "Lie down, little one," I murmured, laying him on his back. "Time for sleep."

The altar stone, despite the warmth of the night, oozed cold: bitter, chilling cold. I almost lifted him away from that icy lock, but Fainche's smiling face intervened. *You must do this, my son,* my mother's voice whispered, within my head. Keeping Fainche's face in front of my eyes, I smoothed the curls from the boy's brow and tried to smile down at him. "Go to sleep, little one."

Though my voice tried for lightness, I knew it failed. Such was his trust, however, for his eyes slid shut. I caressed him for a long moment, listening to the small, still voice in my heart. *This is wrong; this is evil; don t do it; don t you dare do it—*

"I have to, or they ll all die."

"What is his name?"

"His name?"

I shut my eyes to still the angry, defensive bark. "Yes, Mother. What is his name?"

"Finias, I believe."

"Finias," I whispered. "Dear one, sleep now. Angels open their arms for you. Go to them, and peace be with you."

The blazing fire at my back failed to warm me. The innocence in front of my face failed to bring me to mercy. Only the fear of what Finian would do to Fainche, to Enya, to Sofia, lifted my hand for the knife. *Power.* I needed power if I was to defeat him and save them. That's all that mattered. Their lives against this little, unnamed boy who'd die anyway, in agonizing pain? The choice should be easy.

It wasn't.

My mother placed the knife in my hand.

"His throat first," she whispered. "Then his heart."

I shut my eyes. I turned my face away.

I slashed.

Warm blood flowed over my hands as the body beneath me on the cold, hard stone thrashed, fighting for breath, fighting for life. My left hand pressed against his chest, I opened my eyes in slight shock. Finias struggled as though through willpower alone he might close the gaping wound in his neck. His hands tried to cover his throat, fight against the pain, the terror. His dark eyes met mine, panicked.

"Now his heart."

Without thought, I drove the blade deep into his breastbone, splitting it apart with a sharp twist. As purple blood, heart's blood, streamed over my hands, I cut his still beating, living heart from his chest. Dropping the bloody knife to the ground with a steely clang, I held it within my hands. It throbbed and beat still, hot blood oozing from my fists as the child on the hard, cold slab diminished, fell in upon itself as his spirit fled into the night. The wolf howled, its song lonely, alone, stricken with grief.

"Lay it on the fire."

Before its life followed on the heels of its master, I tossed the living heart upon the red-orange flames. It exploded into shards of light and sparks, smoke billowing and rising high into the night. The cloud obscured the stars and the bright moon, its bitterness drawing tears into my eyes.

Another howl rose, a deep note of grief and inarticulate longing. Not the wolf, this time. This cry brought the moon to tears and forced mountains to bow low. The earth herself trembled with the horror of what I'd just done. I heard this not with my ears, but with my heart. I knew then, instantly, the gods themselves wept at my sin.

My soul closed over the evil I'd just done, like a salve over an open wound. Healing never came. Never would come again. There was no atonement for me now. For a sharp instant, piercing regret swamped me, filled my heart with such an agony I feared it might burst. I wished fervently it would.

What have you done, you fool?

I don't know where the words came from, but they rose inside my head like an unwelcome ghost.

"What I had to do."

No earthly power is worth your own soul.

"If it keeps my mother and sister safe–"

But who will save them from you?

"Open your mind, my son," my mother whispered, her breath on my neck. "Receive your gift."

In ignoring the voices, I obeyed hers.

My bloody hands wide, palms up, I shut my eyes. I opened my mind, my body, my soul to whatever, whomever, might invade. I lifted my arms to the night, lifting them to the moon and the stars. *"Come to me,"* I called. *"Grant me your power. I offer you this life. In blood and sacrifice, on your holy altar, I gave it. I am yours, now and forever."*

Instantly, like a thunderbolt, power struck me. Flames erupted all around my body, yet I remained cold, as icy as the bitter winter wind. My blood boiled, raw, filled with fire and ice, rushed though me, chilled my soul. My eyes, blinded, saw visions of war, of peace, of great evil and greater sacrifice. Fathers offered their lives for their children, soldiers died for their king. Women lay raped and dead under reviling enemies, as their children rose under great oppression and avenged them. Peace treaties written as their signers plotted war. Great wolves howled under the moonlit stars as men fought one another for small gains. Red blood fed the orchards, the fields, the rivers. Men died as they always died, consumed in hate and evil and took everything with them to the grave. Ravens quarreled over their corpses as they stank unto the heavens.

I fell to my knees.

I wept as heat coursed through me. My blood burned, boiled, consumed what good might be left within me. My vision of Fainche withered and died under the onslaught. My tears evaporated the instant they hit my cheeks until I wept no longer.

I am changed, I thought. *I am a thing of evil. I sacrificed an innocent. I shall never again find solace in life, or in death. No sunlight shall warm me, nor any darkness shield me. Under the brightest noon my shadow will not fall. Never will I find peace– neither in life nor in death.*

Enya sidled close, her hands reaching for me. I flinched from her, the corpse of the boy dwindling on the stone table behind her. His small form shrank into that of a small husk, a fraction of what he'd been in life. His blood stained the dark stone. "What have you done?"

"Only what I must. What you must."

Her exhausted voice failed to bring me to her. The evil I'd committed must never taint her. The guilt was mine alone. I turned my face away. "You should go."

"My son–"

"Go."

"First, take this."

She held out her hand, palm down. A thin filigree chain swung lightly from between her fingers, catching the faint light of the moon. I stared at her pale hand, my senses dull, uncaring. The gem swinging back and forth caught my curiosity, and my interest, despite my inner woes. "What is it?"

"A scrying crystal." Her voice sounded as dead as the little boy. "Use it. Hold it within your hand and think of the one you wish to see. It'll help you find the princess and the child."

I permitted her to lay the object on my bloody palm. I closed my fingers over it without looking at it and tucked it away in my belt pouch. It might be of some use. Maybe. I didn't thank her.

She walked a few paces away before her small face appeared over her shoulder. Her eyes glittered under the moonlight–tears? Or something else entirely? "Remember how much I love you, Flynn."

Where once her voice might pierce me, I felt only a desperate ache instead. I nodded.

"You have the power to defeat her," she said, walking away, her voice hushed under the whispering wind. Only her silhouette showed dark against the trees, her face a pale blob amid the shadows. "His bloody mistress. Kill her you must, or all you love are dead and lost."

"I will kill him," I whispered as her lustrous gown shimmered in the night, vanishing on a breeze. "I will kill them both. Mother?"

Under the light of the moon, the wolves howled.

After wiping the boy's blood away, I stared down at my empty hands. Sim's blood upon my flesh dulled them to a pale pink. The boy's innocence, however, turned my skin a dark, deadly shade of purple-red. Heart's blood. No amount of cleansing will ever make them clean again.

I should bury him, I thought dully. His blackened blood dripped from the altar to the stony ground beneath, his corpse a small shrunken husk. His lively brown eyes now filmed in death, his face a frozen mask of disbelief, terror and rage. Rage? Of course, he'd feel rage. He trusted me and I–

I dug a deep grave beneath a tall pine tree. Using rocks and my hands, I hollowed out a well from the soft earth. Lifting his small body from the cold stone, I embraced him. My face against his still-warm cheek, my tears dripped onto his slack lips. Laying him in his resting place, I crossed his small hands over his waist and closed his eyes.

"Rest ye well, my brother," I murmured, kissing his cooling brow. "May we meet again, in hope and glory. Perhaps one day you may forgive me. Should I ever dare ask you for it."

I marked his grave with a large stick, crudely carved with his name. As the eastern sky turned pink with the coming dawn, I stood at the cairn I built over him and stared down. Where once I felt love and hate, grief and fear, hope and joy, terror and despair– now I felt nothing at all. Power thrummed through my veins. Yet, without emotions I was no better than the corpse at my feet.

Is there absolution for me? I asked the pale stars above. *Can I one day pay for this sin? Might I find absolution if I search hard enough?*

I heard no answer, not even the soft sough of the mountain breeze. The wolves had long since shut up. Even deep within me I heard no echo within me where once I discovered joy.

I must pay . . . somehow.

CHAPTER 7

All the Fires of Hell

Sitting before a roaring bonfire, I watched the leaping orange and yellow flames, mesmerized. Heat crisped my face as sparks flew skyward, melding with the summer stars high overhead. A pleasant enough activity, if not for the current subject under discussion from my brother and sister Atans.

They had no clue I hid among them, disguised, and within listening range, or they'd move their treacherous exchange elsewhere or halt it entirely.

"Just what did he do?" asked Second Lieutenant Kasi, the Griffin newly appointed to the Atani and Iyumi's official escort on this hare-brained mission.

Kasi sat, wings furled across her massive shoulders, her tail coiled delicately around her lion haunches and eagle talons. Catlike, the black-tufted tip swung back and forth, telling all she felt calm and relaxed despite the conversation's topic.

Murder.

Padraig sipped from the silver flask before passing it to Edara. She took a small drink, winced, her mouth screwed into a tight, fine line, and her green eyes squeezed shut. She passed it along to Gaear, hastily. He also drank, licked his lips, his action slow, melancholy. He drank again, his eyes on the blazing fire. He held onto the flask as though intending to drink it dry. No few eyes watched him with speculation.

"Uh, gonna keep that, Lieutenant?" Edryd asked, reaching across Windy's front legs to nip the flask from Gaear's fingers. Gaear's jaw dropped in silent protest, but Edryd already tipped his head back to sip.

"He listened to his ego," Padraig said heavily, poking the fire with a long stick. "He refused to listen to the courier issuing his orders."

Like most Centaurs, Padraig stood on his equine legs, a hind hoof cocked, resting. When not aggravating the fire, his arms hung at his sides, brushing his massive shoulders occasionally, as he all but drowsed before the warmth and light. Unfortunately, his bright eyes and lowered brows informed me his intent wasn't pre-sleep, but pre-meditation.

Beside him, Edara folded her arms across her bosom, as if cold, and kept all four hooves solidly on the ground. Her heavy red tail swept across her hocks now and again, restless. Her dark auburn hair hung in tangles to her shoulders, yet her pale emerald eyes roved the camp, circling from one to another, unsure.

"And?" Kasi prompted when Padraig fell silent.

Padraig roused enough to eye her sidelong, in annoyance. "Egos and orders never mix, young missy. Never forget that."

"Hello? I've never disobeyed an–"

"My father died at Dalziel."

Edryd's voice, quiet and solemn, hushed the voices and swung every eye toward him. He never raised his dreamy gaze from the blazing fire, yet raised the silver flask to his mouth. He drank deep, and, with droplets clinging to his full lips, he passed the flask to Windy. "He burned."

"Sorry, like," Windy muttered, and tossed half the flask's contents past his parted beak. He swallowed not once, but thrice before at last lowering it. With but a few drops left, he shook the nearly empty vessel in confusion, and passed it back to Gaear. Padraig scowled, half raising his hand as if to stop the swift action.

"Vanyar is a traitor and a murderer," Gaear intoned heavily, his fingers toying with the flask. "He should be hanged as one. I for one will tie the knot in his rope."

"Rather harsh, yes?" Windy said, eyeing Gaear sidelong, dislike clear in his narrowed raptor eyes. "He hasn't been tried for a crime much less found guilty."

"Only because the King–"

Gaear broke off, muttering behind the flask as he drained it quickly, and, after wiping his mouth, tossed it to Padraig.

"Got more of that?" Aderyn asked brightly. "I didn't get any."

"Bloody hope so," Padraig muttered. He rummaged through his packs for long moments before emerging with a fresh one. "Don't give it to Windy," he groused. "Whatever you do."

"Excuse me? Edryd and Gaear drank it all."

As the fresh flask passed from hand to hand, Padraig folded his arms across his broad, bare chest. The firelight danced across his heavy features, lit upon his dark hair and set his eyes to glittering. "Vanyar was the best," he finally admitted. "He could change into anything, anytime, anywhere. Nothing daunted him. He feared nothing, and laughed at everything. He rose high within the ranks...too high, some say. Too fast. The youngest First Captain on Atani records. And the first to fall."

"I still don't know what he did that was so wrong," Edara commented stiffly, her tail sweeping across her red flanks. "He's likeable, handsome, agreeable, talented, and the Captain loves him. As does Her Highness and the King."

Iyumi loves someone outside herself? That was new.

"The Captain is blind," Padraig replied, his tone stiff. "Don't get me wrong, for I'd follow the Captain into hell and not feel the fires. But he refuses to see. Get it? He likes Vanyar too much to blame him for the deaths."

"So what happened?" Aderyn asked, sitting cross-legged between Windy and Kasi.

I thought she knew, but by her quizzical posture and earnest expression, I suspected the rumors slipped past her. She always did keep her eyes and attention on what was, literally, in front of her nose and naught else.

Padraig lifted his face and filled his chest in indignation. "He ignored a direct command from headquarters," he snapped. "He was told not to engage the enemy, but to hold until reinforcements arrived."

"How can—"

"In his ego," Padraig continued cutting off Windy's question, his tone icy, "First Captain Vanyar disregarded current dispatches that two terrorists lived, inside. The hostages escaped, yes, but Vanyar knew better than to send in the troops. He believed the Raithin Mawrn mercenary wished to surrender, despite our spotters' reports he still pressed his thumb on the trigger. Should we kill him, his bomb takes out all within a hundred rod radius."

"But—" Windy began, his right fist raised with the flask enclosed within his talons.

"No buts," Padraig replied, his tone low and savage. "Vanyar knew the Raithin Mawrn intended suicide. Like all Raithin Mawrn spies, he's willing to take as many of us with him as he could. Vanyar sent soldiers in anyway, knowing they risked their lives for little gain. All save one hostage lived. Twelve Atani died as a result. He escaped the fires, but he should never escape justice."

My throat shut down. I seized the flask from Windy and tossed back a huge mouthful. The burning liquid took its sweet time to trickle into my belly, and I suppressed the sharp urge to cough. The blood on my hands. I can never wash the stain from my soul.

Windy eyed me curiously before retrieving the flask and taking his own drink. "That can happen to any of us. War is what we do."

"Vanyar's ego and stupidity caused the needless deaths of many," Padraig snapped, glaring at Windy. "Like a coward, he fled before I could arrest him."

"For what?" Edara asked. "Stupidity isn't a crime."

"It should be," Padraig growled. "When it costs Atani lives."

"If the Royal Tribunal couldn't have convicted him for any wrongdoing," Windy said, handing the flask to Edryd, "you haven't the right to bitch."

"I'll bitch about Vanyar alive and unpunished anytime I please, you black-feathered ass."

"Hey," Aderyn protested, half-reaching for the flask. "It's my turn."

As Edryd swallowed a large gulp, Padraig put his fists on his equine shoulders. "That's my mead after all."

"Ours now, Lieutenant," Edara said as she took the next turn drinking from the silver flask.

"Bloody ingrates," Padraig grumbled sourly, tossing more wood on the fire at the same time Edryd asked, "What do we do, then, Lieutenant?"

Sucking in a slow, deep breath to calm the craving for more mead, I pushed my self-castigation to the back of my mind. *This is a fact-finding mission,* I told myself, quelling my inner tremors. The urgent need to drink more from the flask sent my gut into flopping about like a fish in a net. Where was that mead? Only the hot, burning alcohol sliding down my throat could subdue the guilt, the horror, at what I'd done. Only its soothing ache silenced the ghosts within my soul.

Padraig threw several chunks on the already blazing fire, his high cheekbones shadowed by the rising flames. "Only thing we can do," Padraig answered heavily. "He deserves our justice."

"What's that supposed to mean?" Windy asked, rising to his feet and stretching wide his wings. "It's getting late, boys and girls. I know some of us have second and third watches."

Padraig shrugged his bare shoulders. "Since the King is reluctant to execute him, it's up to us."

Shocked silence fell over the Atan soldiers loosely grouped around the fire. I glanced over my shoulder toward the second blaze several rods away where Malik and Iyumi sat, nibbling the remains of their meal and talking in low tones. I half-wondered if his keen hearing or instincts for trouble alerted him to the current conversation. He never failed to know when problems brewed in his units. This time, however, Malik never glanced our way.

"You can't mean it," Windy said, his voice low, his tufted ears back.

Even Edryd froze in place, his jaw slack. "That's murder."

"It's justice," Padraig snapped.

"I'm with you, Lieutenant," Gaear said, glaring at Windy. "A chance to hang that bastard from his toes–just give me a chance."

"If the Captain gets wind of this– " Windy said. "We're all for Braigh'Mhar."

"He won't," Padraig replied. "We keep it among just us, and the others."

"And when Van's body is found?" Edara said, rubbing her arms as if cold. Her archers' steel wrist cuffs clanked on her armbands, illuminated under the light of the half-moon. "The Captain will know we killed him."

"That's why we make it appear an accident." Padraig glanced around, his eyes shadowed. "Like shit, they happen. If Van falls victim to one, then who's the wiser?"

"This isn't right," Windy muttered. "He saved Sky Dancer's life!"

"One good deed is never enough to wash the blood from his hands."

"I won't be a party to this." Windy's tail lashed back and forth, his black neck feathers erect and bristling. He flared his wings and glared at Padraig. "I don't think you'll kill him anyway. He's too smart for you."

"I'll kill him," Padraig snarled, his tone low enough to not reach beyond the fire. "Are you a snitch, Windy?"

"You know better than that."

"You know what happens to snitches, Windy, my lad."

I heard the low threat in Padraig's voice, as did Windy and everyone else. Aderyn cringed, refusing the flask for the first time. Edryd hung on every word Padraig said, while Edara shook her red mane and shivered, her bare arms pimpled in goose flesh. Gaear nodded fiercely, his heavy fall of black hair bouncing across his pale eyes.

Windy shook his head, his tufted ears flattened. "I won't listen to more of this. It's treason. You're too stupid to know this is dead wrong, Padraig. I for one won't mourn your death."

His black-tipped lion tail swinging back and forth, Windy stalked away from the fire. Padraig watched him closely, just in case he walked toward Malik and Iyumi. Instead, Windy vanished into the darkness beyond the light of either fire. He may not agree, yet he won't betray his brothers, either.

"I'm with you, Lieutenant," Edryd said. "He killed my father."

As Padraig nodded sharply, a new voice spoke up. "I'm not."

Padraig and his new cronies shifted in surprise. Obviously, they hadn't expected her to reply much less defy them. I came near to grinning openly as they gawped at the flame-haired Centaur. Despite her courage in battle and keen abilities with a bow, Edara seldom spoke up or ventured her opinions. She hugged the shadows, obeying every order given her.

Edara frowned, her delicate features crinkling into half-defiance, half-terror. She combed her fingers through her red locks as they flowed over and past her waist. "The Captain, he'll kill you," she said, her voice rising in fear. "I won't die, not yet nor for so little. He'll hang you all, for this stupidity. Or the King will."

"Edara– "

She shook her wild mane. "Count me out. Dumbass."

"I'm in," Gaear said. "Of course."

"And we all know you're as thick as river granite," Edara snapped, stabbing her finger downward toward Gaear's startled face. "Grow up, boy."

With an agitated flick of her tail, Edara followed on Windy's heels, perhaps to talk with him. She broke into a trot as the night swallowed her. The clop of her hooves over stone and tundra vanished into the darkness. All stared after her, jaws slack. I shut my eyes tight to halt the grin that tried valiantly to spread and reveal me to the others.

"Who'd have thunk," Padraig muttered, puzzlement crossing his dark features as he watched Edara vanish into the night. "She has sand, after all."

[191]

"He's my cousin, Lieutenant," Aderyn broke in, her voice apologetic. "I won't turn you in, but I can't kill him. I just can't. Sorry and all that, but count me out, too."

"Blood doesn't count that much– "

"Let her be, Padraig," I said, speaking for the first time.

Padraig glared at me. "Are you with me, Moon? You among them all should help us. You were there, you saw what he did. He must pay for his crimes. Right?"

"I dunno," I replied, scratching beneath my right eye with my talon. "Seems to me you're not truly avenging Dalziel. Perhaps you want Van dead because he's the Captain's favorite? A very sore point with you, yes?"

"Bah!" Padraig snorted and waved his hand at me. "You don't know what you're talking about."

"Right," I said, my tone sarcastic. "Go on, pretend no one knows of your pathetic rivalry. Van's always been better than you and you can't handle it."

"You're an ass, Moon."

"Commit treason," I scoffed, slanting my ears back, annoyed. "Once those fools find their guts, the game's off. And don't think they won't turn you in to save their own hides."

"We'll succeed."

"Just you, this fool boy and Gaear the Inept? Good luck with that."

"Hey." Gaear scowled at me.

I made as though to cut Gaear's throat with my naked talon, watching him flinch back, afraid. Though I just made Moon Whisperer a new enemy, I didn't fret over it much. Gaear was no match for the huge, battle-scarred and experienced Griffin.

"I've recruited the others, bucket-brain," Padraig snapped, furious. "Alain, Dusan, and Grey Mist have already agreed. And I know Kasi and Valcan will join us, right, Kasi?"

"Then she'll be executed alongside you, Padraig."

Kasi's beak dropped. "I don't think–"

"Get out of here, Moon."

Flipping him the sign inviting him to perform a certain impossible act upon himself, I turned my back on him. Crouching

[192]

low, I spread my wings and launched myself skyward. Winging toward the stars, I let the cool night breeze caress my feathers, my talons tucked beneath my lion shoulders. Scooping air into my beak, I filled my lungs and sought to release the dull rage Padraig's plot rose within me.

I knew he'd dare. I knew damn well he'd recruit the youngsters, the kids with the grievances, the younger members from the Academy. I knew full well he'd brain-wash them, make them believe I murdered my own soldiers. The only question was why. Indeed, Padraig and I vied for the position at Malik's right hand. I knew I'd never set him up to fall, and I expected that his noble and honorable blood stayed his jealous and dishonorable inclinations.

I sighed. Despite myself, I enjoyed the cool night air, the stars, the thrill of flying. Coasting along on a colossal wingspan and warm thermals, I dove toward the earth, only to swoop upward again, my wings beating strong. Moonlight shone down on me, huge over the mountains, forcing the stars into subservience. Griffins were the ultimate predator, the being birthed from the gods' melding the lion with the eagle. They possessed the instincts and abilities of both animals, one of the most talented creatures ever created. *I could live life as a Griffin,* I thought, my rage subsiding and my humor rising. Pity Sky Dancer hated me now.

The ground dropped away from me as I winged higher and higher, striving for the moon. Its light rippled across my wings, the occasional cloud wisping past beneath my talons. The air's temperature dropped the higher I climbed, but my lion's fur scarcely felt the chill. Only when the air thinned so much my brain refused coherent thought and my lungs ached did I at last wheel to the right and bank steeply earthwards.

I soared over the black landscape. Skimming over low-lying hills, dodging the occasional tall tree, only the steady moonlight illuminated the startled deer who fled in blind panic from my passage. A bear roared at me from a thicket as I buzzed past her muzzle, her cubs tumbling in infant play at her paws. A wolf paused and lifted its face toward me as I blew toward it, flying faster than thought. I sensed its curiosity as I left it far behind, sniffing the taut breeze my wake created.

Far below me, the forest sloped into a broad field with the twinkling lights of a village resting near the river. I didn't know the name of the village, but I knew I'd flown further than I intended. *Time to go back,* I reckoned.

Moon Whisperer had winged out on a scouting mission, one of his own making, at sunset. He liked flying on his own, seeking potential threats to the mission. As he hadn't drawn any watches that night, he was free to do so. After my last insult, Padraig would bite off his own tongue before seeking him out. Moon might wonder why Padraig refused to include him on his little soirees, but as Moon never much liked Padraig anyway, I felt reasonably safe from either of them discovering I sat there and Moon didn't.

High overhead, I circled the camp. My eagle's vision informed me Padraig's party broke up hours earlier. The night watches stood at their posts, and Iyumi had lain down in her pallet with a light blanket drawn up to her chin. If she slept, I couldn't tell. Malik still stood by the fire, his arms crossed over his chest, his head tilted back. His dark eyes watched for me, expectant. *Best not make him wait,* I thought. He'll never sleep until I report.

Mid-flight, I changed forms.

From Griffin to tiny sparrow, I shifted birds.

Down I spiraled, winging over the treetops, avoiding the sharp eyes of the watch, who'd wonder at a sparrow flying by night. An owl-shape might serve me better, but I wanted to remain small and unobserved. Owls, though silent hunters, were too big to pass unnoticed by those standing watch. A bird no bigger than a human fist might evade their swift eyes and quick observation. Suspicious by nature and training, an adept Atan on watch made copious notes of anything that walked, trundled, crawled, trotted, flew, swam, slithered or otherwise strolled past their collective yet determined mind-set.

Nothing dared pass their stiff vigil, I heard Alain say to Valcan, as I flitted beneath their collective radar.

Their eyes missing me by yards, I ducked amid the heavy forest of pine. Cruising amid the tree branches, hidden from sight, I swung first left then right, dodging trees and their clinging branches and vines. No Atan born could keep me in his sight if I wanted to remain unseen.

Dropping at last to my pallet beside the fire, I changed into myself. As though I'd been there all along, I yawned and rubbed my face wearily. I half-glanced over my shoulder at the watch, satisfied with their alert stances and faces turned outward. They had no clue I just buzzed under their noses. Padraig nor his cronies never noticed I hadn't been there all along. I eyed them sidelong, only to find most slept and Padraig himself dozed on his feet, his left rear hoof cocked and resting.

"Learn anything useful?" Malik asked.

I half-shrugged, and yawned a genuine yawn. "I'm to have a convenient accident."

He stiffened in outrage, his mouth opening. His hand fondled his sword hilt as his heavy black tail lashed.

"Sshhht!" I hissed. "They know you know and I'm dead that much sooner. Calm down, dammit."

He obeyed me, relaxing both visibly and emotionally. "Padraig?"

"With Edryd, Gaear, and others."

"Not Windy and Moon?"

I smiled. "Nope. Nor Aderyn or Edara. Probably not Kasi, but she's young and easily persuaded. But all the rest–"

"I can't have my unit plotting the assassination of my second-in-command," Malik complained, running his hand through his thick locks. "There's too much at stake here."

"Gee, thanks."

"You know what I mean, dammit."

A wail suddenly drifted on the night breeze, a cry of such longing and grief, my heart quailed in my chest. Never before had I heard such; a terrible sound–as though the root of all nightmares walked the night. As if a vanquished soul flew upon the darkness, seeking solace and finding none. Tears started in my eyes before the cry wavered on the wind and drifted into nothingness.

Iyumi rolled from her pallet, a knife in her hand and tears glistening on her cheeks. "Gods," she cried. "Gods, no, please no..."

[195]

Malik also stiffened before the sound died away, his head up and his sword in his hand. "No. They didn't, please say they didn't, it's a mistake–"

Only I had no idea what that sound meant. The others in camp hadn't even heard it. Padraig still slept, the watch kept their alert stance, the sleepers never stirred. Only the three of us caught its dying cry, its lonely wail, and only two of us understood its significance.

"What the bloody hell was that?" I asked, my sword in my hand, on my feet, prepared to fight.

"The sacrifice," Iyumi half-sobbed, on her knees, holding her arms over her chest. Her knife dropped to her pallet as her chin slid downward, her silver hair draping her from head to blanket. "They murdered an innocent. Ah, gods! How can you permit this sin?"

She broke into full sobs, threatening to rouse the entire camp. By some gut instinct, I knew this must remain among the three of us.

Unable to withstand feminine tears for long, I went to her. I held her close and let her cry on my shoulder. "It's all good, lady," I murmured, sheltering her within my arms. "Easy, lass. I'm here. Malik is here; we'll keep you safe, I promise."

Though my words were nonsense, Iyumi seemed comforted, somehow. She clung to me like one drowning, nestling into my shoulder as though belonging there. Her arms wrapped about my waist and tightened until my ribs creaked in protest. Her incredible wealth of hair covered my face, its scent threatening me with a sneeze. Yet, I felt drawn to her, wanting nothing less than to hold her for the next year. Or three–whichever came first.

Only Malik's soft voice broke us apart. "Princess. What did you sense?"

Iyumi lifted her pale and wan face from my shoulder. "A child," she murmured, her skin waxy pale. "Sacrificed on the demon's altar. That someone, whoever he is, now has the full power of evil at his fingertips."

"The Red Duchess?" Malik asked.

She wiped her streaming eyes, and drew in a ragged breath. Half-nodding to me, she withdrew from my arms and stood up.

[196]

Cocking her head to her left, her tongue tickled her lips, she pondered Malik's question with a seriousness that puzzled me. How did such a nasty, obnoxious bitch suddenly become as beautiful as a spring rose? Why did I suddenly want to kiss those slender, moist lips? *Because you re an idiot,* I reasoned, clamping down on my impetuous urge. I always had a weakness for feminine tears. Brought me no end of trouble, too.

"Perhaps," she admitted slowly, her arms crossed. "But I can't be certain. The gods are . . . upset."

"If not the Duchess, then who?" Malik asked. "Who else is involved here?"

"No matter, Commander." Iyumi turned her face away. "It's over now."

Iyumi suddenly stiffened as she realized I yet stood within her personal airspace. Her eyes sparked as her fine lips thinned. She sniffed, a delicate frown creasing her pale brow. She was the Princess and I was the lout she so often called me. She didn't speak, but I recognized an order when I saw one. *Bugger off.*

Swinging my arms wide, I half-grinned and bowed low. "Princess."

"Captain."

After a swift scowl toward Malik, as though venting her fury that he'd dare bring me along, she turned her slender shoulders and walked slowly away. She lay down on her pallet beside the dying fire, and drew her blanket across her shoulder, her back to us. Within moments, her breathing deepened, slowed, her body lax and silent. As though she slept the sleep of the utterly weary.

That performance should earn her several top honors, I thought. I sighed, scratched the back of my neck and met Malik's amused dark glance. She didn't fool either of us–she lay as wakeful as we. Had she a sign on her back saying 'leave me alone', she couldn't have been more clear in her command. An order we both obeyed.

Malik shrugged, and stalked a short distance from the fire to stand, watching the stars. He didn't sleep much, either. He never did, when enemies prowled about. Half-mocking, half-sincere, I saluted Iyumi's back, fist to heart, my chin dropped. I left her alone. Where she wanted to be.

That didn't stop me from standing vigil over her, however. I didn't take a single drink.

Sky Dancer winged in with the dawn's pink early light on her white and tan feathers, carrying bad news.

"My Lord Captain," she said, saluting, her newly fletched wings furled over her neat lion shoulders. Her trim tail coiled about her feet, the emblem of her rank, the snarling lion's head of a First Lieutenant, worn on a chain about her neck. "I have word from the King."

"Have you passed your medical, Lieutenant?" Malik asked, his arms behind his back. He frowned at her, disapproval etched across his dark features. I fought back a yawn, as I hadn't slept a wink. Neither did Iyumi, although she concealed it better than I.

Aderyn acted as Iyumi's maid and assisted her to wash and dress, currently busy braiding Iyumi's thick silver fall. I stood at Malik's right hand, at parade rest. Interestingly enough, Padraig found occupation in saddling and bridling the blue roan stallion. He never glanced toward me once. Edryd laughed and joked with Alain as they tended their own mounts. Behind Malik and I, Windy preened his wings, grooming his feathers until I thought they'd surely fall out from overuse. Moon more carefully tended his own, all the while eyeing Windy sidelong. I suspected words had passed between the two.

Sky Dancer held out a folded parchment to her commanding officer. "Healer Irridi's own recommendation, my Lord Captain."

Malik took it, pretended to peruse it before tucking it into his belt. "What is His Majesty's message?"

"Lieutenant Cian has escaped custody, my Lord Captain."

My jaw snapped shut on another yawn, and I bit my tongue. But Malik failed to rein in his own. He fair blistered the air with his curses. His choice of language brought Iyumi running, her hair falling from the braid Aderyn half-started. "Commander?"

Sucking down his anger, Malik bowed his head. "Forgive me, Your Highness," he said. "We have a problem."

"So I gathered, Commander," she snapped, her hands on her leather-clad hips. "Care to share?"

Malik swallowed his ire and moderated his voice. "Lieutenant Cian has been arrested for attempted murder on First Captain Vanyar, and grievously endangering the life of Lieutenant Sky Dancer," he said. "He's now escaped."

Iyumi stared from me to Sky Dancer and back again. "He's going to try again," she bit out, her words stone cold. "He's coming here."

"There's no evidence–"

"Shut up, Commander."

As Malik shut his jaw tight, I caught a self-satisfied glance from Padraig. He continued his chore after that one lightning flash toward me. Edryd nodded sharply at the news. Circling high above, on watch, Grey Mist glared down at me, while Edara stalked to my back, her hand on her sword hilt. *A camp divided.* Fully half hated me and wanted me dead, skinned and roasted. The other half planned to defend me to their last drop of blood. Not good. Not when we just started this expedition. Iyumi and the child are the most important. My life mattered nothing compared to that.

Iyumi's voice rose several decibels. "Wasn't that idiot manacled? How did he escape?"

"Yes, Your Highness," Malik answered. "I arrested him myself."

"There's evidence he had outside aid, Your Highness," Sky Dancer said. "The King has ordered a full investigation and has troops on his trail. He will be captured, along with those who helped him, and soon."

"He'd better," Iyumi snapped. "I need everyone here alive if I'm to recover that child. Rampaging lunatics I can do without."

She stalked back to her rock seat, my cousin in her wake. She sat with a snort, her arms crossed over her chest. Aderyn resumed the difficult task of braiding that silver mass into a thick, serviceable braid. Though her back remained stiffly toward us, her crossed legs and folded arms informed me Iyumi, like a petulant child, planned to have it all her own way. I wondered if Cian got the message, too.

"Thank you, Lieutenant," Malik said, nodding his heavy head. "You're dismissed. Return to His Majesty." He turned away, half toward me, his mouth parted to speak.

"I wish to stay, my Lord Captain," she said in a half-choked voice. "His Majesty does not require my services and I've an obligation here. Sir."

Malik turned back, in surprise. No one, except me on occasion, ever questioned his orders or his authority.

"Sky Dancer stays, Commander." The Princess's stern voice, her back still turned, offered Malik no choice.

She Who Hears had spoken. Mess with her meant messing with the gods and goddesses she represented. That and her royal authority—well, let's just say no one who lived dared gainsay her. Malik and his collective genes stood at attention and saluted.

"Very well, Lieutenant," Malik said heavily, his hands on his broad equine shoulders. "On this mission, you'll serve directly under First Captain Vanyar. You'll remain at his side, acting as his right hand, his messenger and his bitch. That understood?"

Sky Dancer dipped her beak to her chest, her taloned fist clenched against her snarling lion. "Clearly, my Lord Captain."

I scratched my brow to conceal my amazement as Malik effectively ordered her my bodyguard. Under Padraig's hooked nose, he cut me off from the plots of Padraig and his fellow conspirators. They'd hardly harm one such as she in order to kill me. Honor might stretch enough to convict me with no evidence. Yet, kill Sky Dancer, too? Heavens forefend. They'd never condone the killing of a fellow Atani just to appease their blood vengeance against me. Their honor forbade the slaying of not just innocents, but of their brothers and sisters in arms. Where I go, Sky Dancer followed. Should I eat, she held my cup. When I shit, she saluted. And should Padraig's enmity follow me, her sharp talons and wicked beak stood between us.

[200]

I eyed Padraig's stiff back and lazily swishing tail, noting he and Edryd alone among the camp failed to express shock, offer opinions, raise questions or eye me sidelong with speculation at the news of Cian. Did they engineer Cian's escape before we departed on our errand to fetch Iyumi? How far-reaching was Padraig's arm? I pondered how long I'd live with Sky Dancer guarding my back. Twenty four hours? Less?

She never glanced my way. If she hated her direct orders, her calm raptor eyes and shut beak revealed nothing. Lion-like, she stalked with eagle's head up to stand behind my right shoulder, ready, able and prepared. Her black-tipped tail remained quiescent, and confused me further. She should hate this assignment as much as she hated me. Perhaps she plots her own vengeance.

I expected as much as I nodded toward her, accepting her service. Surprisingly, she saluted my rank with the same deference she paid Malik. Her attitude bullish and aggressive, she nudged Windy aside with pinned ears and bared talons. *Back off,* she warned, *this is my turf, get lost or be lost.*

Windy grimaced and gave ground, his long lion tail lashing back and forth. He sat down not far away, his grooming forgotten. Sending him a swift wink and quick smile, I hoped to assure him that I hadn't, nor ever will, forget his loyalty. With a rapid jerk of his beak, he told me without words, *Chill, I get it, girls are the pits, .*

"We must travel, Commander," Iyumi said. Her pale face appeared over her slender shoulder. "Will noon be too early?"

As the sun had barely cleared the horizon, noon lay hours off. Goaded, knowing perfectly well she gouged his ribs with her stick, he nodded. "Grey Mist and Valcan, you're sky watch. Padraig, Edara, you're the vanguard. Kasi, Moon Whisperer, you cover the rearguard. Edryd, Alain, Dusan, you three scout one mile out. Report every hour. The rest of you, form up."

Those assigned their posts obeyed instantly. Padraig handed the blue's reins to Gaear and saluted Malik. After a brief, yet respectful, nod toward Iyumi, he trotted across the shallow stream we camped beside, water splashing silver under the light of the new sun. His hooves rattled over river rock and pebbles, his long hair rising from his shoulders from the breeze he created. He never glanced back.

Edara's salute to both Malik and Iyumi contained considerable more deference as she hastily gathered her chestnut quarters under her. Adjusting her bow across her back, settling her quiver at her right equine shoulder, Edara loped to catch up. If they spoke, I never saw or heard any evidence of it. They vanished over the green hill, side by side.

"Captain." Iyumi's face appeared over her shoulder once more.

"Princess?"

"See to my horse. I wish you to ride beside me this day."

"Princess."

I saluted her stiff back, and strode toward the blue roan. My own Kiera watched me from the edge of camp where she grazed the thin, high altitude grass, her black tail swishing against annoying flies. Though I approached another, jealousy never entered her mind nor her dark eyes.

Gaear nodded crisply as he handed over the blue's reins, his pale blue eyes hard, just as Malik's voice rose. "Lieutenant Gaear, you will fly as scout and messenger this day."

Stiff, obviously angry, Gaear saluted his commanding officer with the barest respect. Knowing Malik as I did, I knew he recognized Gaear's defiance and filed the information away, for later use. He'd not act now, for he was a patient Centaur. He'd allow Gaear enough rope before tightening the noose.

"An eagle, if you will, Lieutenant," Malik said.

As the blue dipped his muzzle into my hands, whiffing my scent, I watched, sidelong as Gaear paced away, needing room to change his shape into the eagle Malik ordered. I half-wondered if Malik commanded this form just to aggravate Gaear. Birds of prey were never his strong suit. He never liked flying, and his favorite animal shapes were the fox and the wolf. If and when he flew, Gaear preferred less complicated creatures like seagulls or sparrows. Birds with strange feathers, sharp beaks and curved talons—not his style at all. Mice and voles caught his attention far too often, and he tended to forget his marching orders under the fierce rule of his stomach.

Forcing my eyes to remain carefully neutral and cease their exasperated roll, I watched as Gaear frowned ponderously and slowly, methodically, shifted. His first attempt made me laugh, though I kept the sound behind my tight jaw. It looked like the retarded offspring of an owl and a wren: too-short wings, a bulbous beak and an interesting assortment of feathers. Any self-respecting eagle would die of shame. Both Iyumi and Malik stared hard at me, however, as though reading my mind, and knew my laughter bubbled close to eruption.

His second attempt produced a few improved raptor elements (a longer wingspan, a sharply curved beak) before he gave it up. He stood quiet, thinking hard, as camp quickly fell apart around him. Pack horses sighed down their noses as Windy and Moon stuffed their panniers with supplies. Grey Mist rose on ponderous wings, circling higher and higher. Valcan, more talented than Gaear, chose to soar effortlessly in his wake in the body of a black raven. Together, they rose higher yet, small dots against a pale, sun-washed sky. One flew north, the other south.

Gaear cursed under his breath, knowing full well his Shifter skill wasn't up to Atani standards. He tried again, and this time almost made the grade. Had he lengthened his wingspan, and shortened his tail, his majestic eagle might mount the morning breeze with grace and beauty. Instead, his human form blushed with angry heat as no few chuckles flourished.

"While we're young, Lieutenant?" Iyumi questioned ironically.

Ignore him, I told myself firmly. *Mind your own affairs.* I turned my back on Gaear's efforts, biting my tongue, hard. Tears of pain squirted into my eyes but I blinked them away. I tended to my assigned task as one deeply involved with it, but listened, laughter curbed sharply, as Gaear found an eagle's shape one far above his skill level.

Padraig may be half horse, but he has no clue how to saddle one. The stallion's relieved snort wet my cheek and neck as I loosened the annoying girth and settled it more comfortably around his belly. Untangling his reins, I adjusted his bridle for a better fit, and shot a swift glance over my shoulder. Malik frowned as Iyumi tapped her cheek with her forefinger, obviously annoyed. Choked laughter and coughed splutters abounded although no creature actually watched Gaear closely. Not that I could say for certain, anyway. *Gods above,* I thought, cringing inwardly. *It s not radical biology, for heaven s sake. Any Shifter over age four could do it.*

Gaear finally discovered what an eagle could and should feel like. Under the chuckles and disdain, Gaear's reddened cheeks vanished under an eagle's parted, yellow beak. Screaming his rage against those who laughed, he leaped into the morning light. His broad wings beat hard, striving for altitude and peace from ridicule below. He found a warm thermal and circled higher and higher until he was but a dark spot against the blue.

"About bloody time," Iyumi muttered. "I hope he isn't your best, Commander."

Malik floundered under the royal criticism, at a loss for words. A faint flush of beet red crept from his brow-band and slid south. Like smiling, Malik seldom blushed, and I knew Iyumi's tongue wounded him in his very sensitive core. Only the King dared reprimand him, if merited, and only in private.

"The best is at your service, my liege." I bowed low over my hand on my breast, grinning.

She eyed me up and down, her brow raised. Too royal to actually scoff, she offered a small, choked sound as she tried hard to prevent an eye roll. "Of course, Captain," she muttered. "I'm in the best of, er, hands."

"Hands, claws, talons, hooves," I replied, my tone light, "they're at your service. As are we all."

"Fall out," Malik barked, not quite recovered from the royal slight. "Moon, Kasi, why are you still here?"

The said Griffins saluted smartly and leapt skyward. After circling for a better vantage point, Moon and Kasi winged southward, flying wingtip to wingtip in precise formation. They vanished over the forest's green, spiked tops, winging toward the snow-tipped mountains on the distant horizon.

I watched them go, envy tickling my soul. I loved flying point, craved every order that sent me into the sky, listening to the earth's thrum below, and feeling that life's sorrows could never touch me

[204]

again. In whatever form I chose: hawk, falcon, Griffin, owl, or simple sparrow, I felt as free as I never felt before. The wind whispered through my feathers, granting me lift and altitude. I'd soar beneath their brilliance and uncomplicated freedom, and forget I had a history. Let that idiot Gaear stay earthbound and stupid. *Command me to fly. Please.*

"Van, you still with me?"

Edryd, Dusan and Alain vaulted into their saddles. With the barest of salutes, they set spurs to silky hides and galloped, hard, away. I knew the drill. One rode north, one east, the last west. The scout, Gaear this time, flew from one to the other, gathering reports before returning to brief Malik.

"Captain Vanyar?"

Startled, I broke from my daydream. "Er, yes. Quite."

Iyumi shook her braid in exasperated humor. "Dolt," she muttered.

I swore I'd never call her a bitch again. "Ignorant ninny."

"Captain Vanyar," Malik barked. "You're on cleanup duty for a month. Show some bloody respect, will you?"

"Only if I must."

I flashed Iyumi an impudent grin. She responded with a rapid, there-and-gone, smile. I knew she masked her real feelings, and she knew I knew. The bitch stood as her cover. Inside, where it counted, Iyumi guarded her innermost self. The sweet girl beneath the bitch, hidden from all eyes, loved love in all its forms, and valued the most trivial of lives. A spider may wander across her path, and she blessed it. A dog dare bite her and she caressed its ears. A young idiot prince might strike her across the cheek and she dared anyone to kill him for the offense.

What a girl. *No, a princess borne of blood and power,* I thought, quickly reassessing, realizing her girlhood had departed a long time ago. *She's a queen worthy of swearing one's undying loyalty to.* Happily, I'd offer my life for hers and never regret the loss.

With a practiced hand, she nudged the blue beside Malik. Her blue eyes turned up to his, she captured and enslaved his very soul.

Her voice low and musical, anyone within hearing paused in his labor to listen and sigh. Sweet, angelic and utterly kind. "Commander," she said, her tone sweet, as she lay her tiny hand across his scarred and calloused fingers.

"Princess?"

"Keep Vanyar on a tight leash, will you?"

"Uh– "

"I don't much like him these days."

Kiera trotted beneath me, her gait as smooth as spun silk. I knew Iyumi watched her sidelong, while pretending not to. Yet, every few minutes Her Highness's blue eyes slid sideways, only to stare straight ahead between her blue's ears. Then the cycle began again. While I inwardly grinned, amused, I pretended not to notice. Long had I grown a thick skin toward others' envy. Along with his lands and titles, I inherited my father's prestigious horse herd when he died. Kiera's dam colicked and died soon after her birth, leaving me to bottle-feed the four-day old filly.

As she grew older, I often changed myself into a horse and ran side by side with her. Over the open fields and bright sunshine, we bucked, nipped, kicked, laughed and played. She nuzzled my neck as I nipped her muzzle, finding joy in one another's company. Later, as she grew old enough to carry me, I never trained her, per se. I merely explained what I wanted her to do, and she did it.

I constantly received, and turned down, offers to sell her. From the nobility down to the King's common soldiers, I rejected potential riches and wealthy estates. Cavalry officers promised me the earth for one foal from her. She wasn't ready for babies, however. When Kiera wanted motherhood, she'd let me know. No stallion was good enough for her, and we both knew it. Until then, she was my mount, my confidante and my best friend.

When I ran away, I listened to her lonely lament in my dreams. She cried for me, refused to eat, and might well have died if not for Malik's care. I dared not take her with me, for who knew what might happen to her in the wretched state in which I found myself. As often as I dared, I winged in to see her, and perched above her stall. Kiera whinnied at me, her tone accusing, as I chirped my apologies. Being the forgiving creature that she was, Kiera all but ran me down when Malik tossed me head first into the royal stables. The bruises left behind by her affection still ached.

I took moments to breathe in the scents of the clean lines of rolling hills, the heather, the green pockets of pine, scrub oak and evergreen trees, and felt refreshed. Northern Bryn'Cairdha was always the most beautiful of the lands. Although fertile and lush, the country's farmers and ranchers tended to gather further south, closer to the cities and markets. This far north, the climate offered a short growing season and discouraged farms or villages. A few hardy towns thrived here and there, yet our course toward the high, ragged Shin'Eah Mountains distanced us from human settlements.

Iyumi refused to divulge the child's exact location, saying only it lay deep within the ragged peaks of the Shin'Eah. Unfortunately, those mountains bordered our land from Raithin Mawr, offering its protections from those rampaging idiots. Raithin Mawr claimed parts of those rocky borderlands, and neither country wished to contest a few peaks and steep cliffs where only hardy tundra and nimble sheep thrived. However, it was too close to our enemy for anyone's comfort, mine included.

When Malik asked what species the child was, she replied tartly, "That's on a need to know basis, Commander. And you don't need to know."

I put my hand on his arm to still him when he bristled, preparing a sharp retort. I shook my head slightly, my eyes lowered, silently asking him to back off.

Peace prevailed throughout the rest of the day, although very few of us spoke at all. Malik stalked in front, his bow in his left hand, his tangled black locks hanging half down his bare shoulders. His black hide rippled under the bright sun; his quarters bunched under him as his hooves slid and skipped over the rocky terrain. I rode beside Iyumi, as ordered, my hands free of reins or weapons. Aderyn followed behind the blue's charcoal tail, tripping over the stones in her favorite form: a deer. Sky Dancer tried hard to maintain an even speed, but we travelled far too slowly for her tremendous wingspan. Forced to continually fly past and circle back to stay with us, she constantly flew low overhead, time and again.

Shading my eyes, I tilted my head back to view Grey Mist circling high overhead. There was no sign of Valcan, though he must be up there somewhere. A quiver of misgiving shivered down my gut. That pair flew way too high in case of trouble. I didn't like it.

Once again, Sky Dancer blew over our heads and swept my hair into my eyes. The wind of her passage sent Kiera's mane flying and Iyumi's silver locks into her mouth. Iyumi scowled, her fair lips parted in disgusted annoyance as she once more dragged her hair from her face. "I swear I'm–"

"Protected, Your Highness?" I asked. "Of course you are. The Lieutenant merely seeks to keep your royal skin safe in these wild lands."

Iyumi scowled. "Don't you dare put words in my mouth, Captain Vanyar."

"Why, Princess–"

"Bite it, Captain," Malik ordered without turning his head.

I sighed. "Yes, sir."

Mid-afternoon evolved into late afternoon. The breeze freshened and lowered the summer temperature by several notches. I smelled rain on its wings, as Iyumi shivered and tried to hide it. A storm approached, casting the tall peaks of the Shin'Eah in clouds of swirling mist. Grey crept downward over their shoulders as thunder rumbled in the dim distance. Over the past hour, the terrain slowly rose, cliffs of rocks rising high above and below us as we wended our way amid them. Pockets of birch, alder, evergreen and oak trees slowly vanished, leaving behind only twisted pines, gnarled scrub oak and the ever-present heather.

Gaear blew in, his eagle's wings wide as he circled low over Malik's head. Malik paused, gazing up, as Iyumi reined in her blue stallion and Kiera halted beside him. Behind us, Aderyn nibbled on the heather, her white tail flipping back and forth.

"Report, Lieutenant."

Gaear tried to salute with his right wing and almost fell from the sky. "All is well, my Captain," he said, his eagle's voice high-pitched. "But I can't find Lieutenant Dusan."

I froze. Sky Dancer landed to all four feet beside Kiera and hissed, her lion tail lashing. She furled her wings over her shoulders and stalked a few paces away, her beak parted, her raptor's eyes watching the hills above us.

"Pray explain 'can't find'," Malik said, his tone as cold as the blood in my veins.

"Corporals Edryd and Alain ride to the west and east, pacing you," Gaear said, back-winging to land on a nearby boulder, his yellow talons clinging to the rock. "Yet, I've seen nothing of Dusan or his horse. It's as though they've vanished."

"And the others?"

"Lieutenants Padraig and Edara are but a mile to the front, as Lieutenants Moon Whisperer and Kasi fly a mile or so south of this location."

I knew Grey Mist and Valcan flew high, too high, in case of trouble. The storm blew in quickly, yet they hadn't dropped below its lower levels as regulations demanded. Thus, they couldn't see us, nor the enemies whom I knew were somewhere close by. The stiffened hairs on my neck told me so, and they've never lied to me yet.

"Get them back," I said.

"What?"

"Get them back here, you fool," I snarled, Kiera prancing sideways. "Call them in—now!"

Gaear launched himself into the air with a scream, his eagle's wings scrambled for altitude. He didn't bother to circle, but clawed for every rod of height, his wings straining. In perhaps his only wisdom, Gaear flew north—toward Padraig and Edara—first.

"Van—" Malik began.

I ignored him. My sword in my hand, the saliva in my mouth dried to dust as I examined the terrain. Taking the easiest way up the steep incline, we chose a wide yet shallow ravine lined with heavy rock and thickets of scrub oak. Above us, on our left, yet another rocky hedgerow formation bristled like an old man's spiked eyebrow. Another one similar lay to our right and slightly ahead of us. A narrow line of twisted trees with stiff branches separated us from them. Swiveling on Kiera's rump, my heart all but stopped in my chest. We had just wended our way past yet another rocky wall, as innocent and blithe as moon-calved lovers on the third date.

I spun my sword into my fist, eyeing the rocky terrain and massive outcroppings. "What are you boys planning?" I muttered.

Malik turned about, nocking an arrow into his bowstring. "Not a full all-out attack," he said. "They dare not risk killing Her Highness."

"Yet, they want us to run." I nudged Kiera closer to Iyumi as Malik searched the rocks for something to shoot at. "Don't you, boys?"

"Fleeing only increases their odds of separating us from her," Malik agreed. "Hold our ground."

"What do the Raithin Mawrn love the most?"

Malik cursed. "Explosives."

Thunder cracked over our heads at the same instant an explosion erupted, almost under our tails. Like the fires of hell, flames boiled up into the darkening sky, darker smoke trailing upwards to vanish into the storm's mist. The blue stallion spooked, snorting wildly, his nostrils flared. Iyumi controlled him with an effort, her hands on his reins, riding him out. He tried to rear and bolt, but her firm grip kept him grounded, unable to escape what terrorized him.

"I hate it when you're right," I yelled, falling soil and smoke almost obscuring Malik though he stood but a few feet from me.

"Down, down," Malik yelled, his finger pointing to a tall, rocky outcropping. "Under there. Now!"

With our bodies protecting Iyumi as she kicked the roan into a swift gallop up the short hill, we loped hard behind. Sky Dancer winged low overhead, her great wings swirling smoke and dust in a cloud that concealed us from our attackers. The natural breastwork, while between us and the explosives, wasn't big enough for a Centaur, a Griffin, two horses and a deer. Another bomb exploded, sending dirt, rocks and shrapnel striking the rock and forcing us to duck.

"Dammit!" Malik shouted. "Don't they realize these things can take her out as well as us? They need her alive!"

"They aren't known for thinking things through," Iyumi added, fighting to keep her seat.

Vaulting off Kiera, I seized the blue's bridle. Crooning to him, I rubbed my hand between his panicked eyes, and sent calming magic into his terrorized brain. My will overrode his instincts, and he quieted instantly. Another explosion, this one several rods behind us, forced me to duck, yet the stallion merely flinched. My girl, more sensible than most, snorted her concern, yet held still.

"My Lord Captain," Sky Dancer said, peeking over the top of the wall. "Permit me to flush them out, sir."

"Negative, Lieutenant," Malik replied, instinctively ducking as another explosion rocked the earth and blew a shower of heather, stones and a wash of dust over us. "I need you here, protecting the Princess."

Aderyn altered swiftly into the body of a lithe, spotted panther. "How can we fight them, my Lord Captain?"

Not one to waste arrows shooting at an enemy he couldn't see, Malik turned about, his arrow pointed up. "Where the bloody hell are Grey Mist and Valcan?"

Another fiery explosion into the ground a mere rod to his right made him jump. But he grimly held his ground as he searched for an enemy to kill. "Van? Got any bright ideas?"

"I'm working on it."

He, like Sky Dancer, peered through the gloom and smoke, then aside at me. "Bro, what do you see?"

I narrowed my eyes as I scanned the hillside above us. I caught a hint of silver and a dark grey mane mingled with the grey rocks and brown trees. Bayonne. Of that, I had no doubt. I half-spotted another horse, a black, trying to run off. Blaez. "It's Flynn."

Malik cursed bitterly. A third fiery explosion rocked the half-light as yet more thunder crashed around us. Flynn coordinated his attack the moment we entered his ambush at the same time the summer storm fell about our ears. Damn, that boy was good.

"We never should've let him go."

"If not him, then they'd have sent someone equally bad."

Thunder, not Blaez's concoctions, blasted low over our heads. Light rain fell, putting out the small fires the explosions started, quenching them into smoking ash. Dirt rained down on us as more explosions rent the vicinity, blowing all within its immediate environs into oblivion.

Yet, Flynn hadn't even begun.

The bombs blew in rapid succession, one after the other. Like fire blossoms, they lit up the misty half-light, tossing dirt, boulders and trees into the air like a child's twinkle-toys. Not even our questionable shelter protected us. Lightning flashed, brighter than the noon sun, blinding me with its sheer brilliance. Aderyn screamed as metal shrapnel tore into her spotted fur. Sky Dancer launched her huge body into the air, her lion quarters bloody.

Iyumi cried aloud as bits of nails and steel tore into her legs. Not even my magic could halt the stallion's sideways jump and kick in self-defense. Kiera bravely danced aside as blood blossomed on her flanks, shoulders and quarters, her heavy tail lashing. I shut my jaw tight as my legs and waist were peppered with white-hot shanks of metal, only Atani discipline preventing my cry from eruption.

"Sergeant!" Malik bellowed, dancing sideways as his own legs and flanks were ripped and torn. "Find Edryd and Alain!"

Aderyn slipped into the smoke, her lithe panther snaking among the protective rocks until she found no more cover. Her sleek body low to the ground, she galloped away at top speed, dodging one, two, three explosions that rocked under her flying paws. Within the span of several heartbeats, she vanished over the hilltop to the west, toward Edryd.

"Malik!" I yelled. "Can you make a shield?"

"Sky Dancer!" Malik shouted, cupping his hands over his mouth as she wheeled low overhead. "Find Grey Mist and Valcan! Now! Get Padraig!"

Though she clearly wanted to stay and protect us, orders were orders. Her tremendous wings beat hard for the grey clouds

[212]

overhead as yet another blast blew a heavy shower of dirt and rocks into our faces. This one, at least, didn't have the shrapnel.

"Malik!"

Reflexively ducking as yet another explosion blew up in my face, I vaulted aboard Kiera. She fretted under me, wanting to run, begging permission to take us both far from this deadly place. Malik raised his hands high over his head, ignoring the almost continual detonations, the thunder, the lightning and the rain that sluiced down his face and dripped down from his hair to his chest. His eyes closed, his lips moved soundlessly in the spell. Blood mingled with the wet on his black, silky hide, yet his tail never lashed under his intense concentration.

"*A la mahira!*" he shouted, bringing his hands sharply down to his equine shoulders in a rounded gesture. "*Jas da!*"

Quiet reigned inside the opaque bubble that grew from the grass at our feet, rose high over our heads, met and closed. Calm descended as the bombs broke against the shield and fell apart. Dirt, rocks, nails and bits of steel slid down the outside, yet none penetrated. Rain beat, serene, against the shield as lightning flickered outside. Thunder reverberated as a distant thrumming as though from far away. Iyumi breathed deep as her stallion blew down his nose and shook his damp neck.

"Now what?" Iyumi asked tightly, clearly in pain. When I would have gone to her aid, she flicked a hand at me, halting my forward motion. "I'm all right."

"Once our air support arrives, we'll flush them from hiding."

Malik hadn't relaxed. "Flynn knows we have Griffins," he said, stalking about, face tilted up as he searched the sky above. His heavy black tail swept across his hocks, as he restlessly pawed the broken ground with his right front hoof. "He'll have planned for them."

"He can't get bombs into the sky?" I said, half-laughing.

His hand swept lank hair from his cheek, and he turned to gaze down at me. His lips stretched into a narrow smile.

My amusement slowly died as I caught the grimness in his dark eyes. "Oh, shit–" I wheeled Kiera about with my knees. "Let me out, Malik!"

"Van–"

"Stay here and protect her," I snapped. "I'll get rid of Flynn."

"Of course I'm coming with you."

I wheeled around, my hand up. "You have command, my Captain," I said quickly. "I honor you, but think a minute. Only you can keep her safe."

At my finger, pointing not at him, but at Iyumi, Malik halted scowling. "Dammit, Van–"

"You know I'm right. Only you can keep this shield in place. If you're killed out there, or even knocked unconscious, there's nothing between her and our enemies."

Iyumi glanced from me to Malik and back again, her fair brow frowning. "Listen, boys–"

"You stay out of it, Princess," I snapped, flicking her a quick glance. "Malik?"

He blew out a deep gust of breath, running his hands through his long black hair, fuming, unable to offer me argument. "Dammit, I'm in command here. I should lead our soldiers."

"The wise commander knows when to order his soldiers into battle and let them do their job."

He glared at me. "You just made that up."

"So I did. Open the damn shield and keep our girl safe."

"Don't do anything too stupid, Vanyar," he yelled, yet the outer wall of the shield opened onto hissing rain, blowing wind and Flynn's explosions. I waved my hand over my head as I urged Kiera through the doorway and into chaos. The shield slammed shut behind us, as we thundered into the rain and lightning.

How does he time these so perfectly? I thought, as Kiera reared high, avoiding an explosion that ripped the earth apart under her front hooves. She danced aside, snorting, shaking her head, obeying my knees. Magic, perhaps? Did the Raithin Mawrn idiots have the same power as we? If they did indeed spell their bombs into going off when we wandered into range, then our footfalls triggered them. *Only a powerful magic could do that,* I gritted.

Gaear flew past my face, his eagle's beak wide. A bomb blew apart behind Kiera's tail, forcing her to kick backwards in self-defense and tossing Gaear about like a kite in a maelstrom. I followed his line of flight–I squinted into the lashing rain and blinding lightning–ah, there they are. I urged Kiera into a gallop toward them.

Padraig and Edara galloped headlong down the hill, arrows nocked and bowstrings pulled taut. The rain clamped their wet hair over their faces, shoulders and back, and their hooves dug deep trenches in the mud. Yet, neither found an enemy to shoot. Instead, two more explosions burst from the ground three strides from their faces. Padraig leaped hard left as Edara jumped right. Padraig's hooves slipped over the uneven ground, almost tipping him into a jagged boulder. Edara's arrow jolted from her bow and flew away into the storm and bombs.

Edara saw me. Her rear quarters slung low as she dug red hooves into the stony soil and loped down the hill toward me. "Captain?"

Flynn had other ideas. Two more blasts deflected her off her course, cursing roundly, as steel shrapnel dug into her legs, shoulders and flanks. She jumped right, away, bleeding profusely, as Padraig joined her. He shouldered her aside, putting his massive bay and white body between the deadly blasts and her. His bow nocked and arrow aimed, he pointed it all around before finally aiming at my chest. When I half-thought he might loose the arrow and rid himself of me forever, his bow lifted, his arrow pointed at the sky. With a rapid flick over his shoulder, he checked Edara's condition before lifting his hoof to step toward me.

"Halt!" I yelled. "Don't move."

"Are you nuts?" Padraig snapped. "We–"

"These explosions are triggered by motion," I snapped. "Designed to take us out and capture Iyumi."

"We can't just stand here and wait for them to get tired and go away."

Jerking my head, I indicated the surrounding rock formations. "We can't get to them without being blown into bits," I said.

The bombs had grown silent, as we'd stopped moving. Though once we sought to attack, to find and kill them, they'd begin again. Yet, it also gave us precious moments with which to plan.

"The Princess?" Padraig asked tersely. "The Captain?"

I jerked my head over my shoulder toward the bubble under the rocks. "Safe."

I sat aboard Kiera's broad back and looked around, rain stinging my eyes. Thunder cracked overhead, though I saw no lightning. The daylight had dimmed as the sun crossed over the unseen horizon, and the wind itself died down. I knew Flynn waited on me, waiting for the attack to come. When I gave no order, he also sat tight, patient. At least I hoped he'd be patient.

"Flynn has us surrounded," I said, my voice low. "He has bombs, and I know he can shoot them into the air. He can take out the Griffins."

"Once the Griffins are gone," Padraig added, "he can take the princess."

"Easily."

Padraig shifted his hooves. His hand lay lax on his bowstring, and his eyes wandered the vicinity, pinpointing, measuring. "What's your idea?"

"I need you and Edara to distract them," I replied. "Make them think you're attacking them, seeking them out. Encourage them to throw their bombs at you, waste their resources, for I know they're limited. Keep their eyes on you, but stay alive, dammit."

Padraig's lips quirked into a tiny smile. "And you?"

"I, and the Griffins, will flush them from their bolt holes," I replied. "Feel free to shoot them as they run. I'll need Edryd and Alain, as well as their skills. Dusan, I fear, is dead."

"He is." Padraig's lips turned down. "Gaear found his body. He was a good lad."

I cursed under my breath. "Are we clear?"

"Crystal."

"How's your magic?"

Gaear flew low over my head, wings spread wide, drawing my attention upward. Beyond him, Sky Dancer, Grey Mist, and Valcan, still in raven form, dove out of the clouds. Dropping fast, their wings furled, they split apart, streaking toward the rock formation to the north of us. Winging in from the south, Kasi and Moon Whisperer plunged toward the enemy hiding at our rear.

Dark streaks shot upward from behind the rocks, from every direction. Trailing smoke, the explosive-laden arrows flew directly into the beaks and feathers of the attacking Griffins. Smaller than the bombs planted in the ground, they were no less deadly. One by one, the missiles exploded, flames and shrapnel blowing everywhere.

Screeching in pain and fury, Moon snap-rolled right as Sky Dancer folded her wings and dropped like a stone. An arrow fired at her exploded with a deafening bang, forcing her to cut sideways, away from her target. Kasi, winging hard, sought to sweep wide around the hilltop and attack from the rear. But Flynn anticipated that, too. Two more arrows with their bulbous heads struck the sky mere rods from her flanks. The resulting blasts stunned her, and she dropped earthward, her wings lax.

I sucked in my breath and held it.

"Come on," Padraig muttered. "Come on."

Grey Mist dove, his wings flattened and his talons out, extended. Falling faster than Kasi, he seized her by her bloody hind legs with his front talons. Incredible wings wide, he braced himself, beating hard, he strove to hold them both airborne. His efforts slowed her fall, but not even his great wings and greater courage could keep them both from hitting the ground.

Despite the blasts rocking the air around her, Sky Dancer blew in from nowhere I saw and seized Kasi's front legs. Her angel's wings working frantically, her raptor eyes slitted shut with effort, Sky Dancer's power slowed Kasi's death drop only a few rods from the hard ground. Working together, wings beating frantically, Grey Mist and Sky Dancer carried her toward the relative safety of the hills to the east.

Breathing again, I wheeled Kiera. "Smoke!" I yelled to Padraig. "Create a smokescreen. Hide the Griffins from attack."

As I kicked her into a run, the earth blew apart around us once more. Ignoring the blasts, I galloped past the shield and its precious occupants. I heard Malik shout an order, but I couldn't hear what it

[217]

was. Gaear paced me, his wings beating hard to remain level with my head. "Find Aderyn," I snapped up to him. "We need another Griffin."

He winged high and away, diving toward the spotted panther loping downhill toward me. The archers made her their next target, shooting two devices. Both struck the ground a mere rod in front of her, sparing her a direct hit but peppering her with nails and steel. She screamed and leaped aside as Gaear reached her and circled, delivering my orders.

More explosions rocked the shallow ravine, informing me Padraig and Edara were on the move. As was their magic. Thick oily smoke boiled upward into the rain and falling soil, doubling in strength and intensity, rising high. Dropping from the sky, Moon and Valcan dove into its concealment, and for a brief moment, the arrows ceased.

Kiera slid to a rearing halt as the ground rose in flames and showered us with loose dirt and smoke. A rock the size of an egg struck my left shoulder and almost knocked me from Kiera's back. Savage pain ripped across my shoulder and chest, but I grimly ignored it. I sheathed my sword, and took my bow from my back. Nocking an arrow, I squinted through the smoke as Aderyn rose into the air, screeching her fury. She ducked into the smoke cover as an arrow kissed her tail and exploded harmlessly behind her.

On the hill to the west, Edryd halted his horse. Seizing his bow, he, too, knocked his arrow and sighted down it. A swift glance over my damaged shoulder showed me Alain had also stopped and awaited orders.

"Van?" Sky Dancer's voice emerged from the heavy smoke not far over my head.

"Tell the others," I gasped, my arm growing numb. "Grab rocks. Big ones. They can't see you, but you can see them. Let's deliver some payback."

"You got it, Captain, sir," she answered, her tone colored with grim humor.

Nudging Kiera into a lope, I circled around, adding my own magic into the mix, forcing the smoke into thicker and thicker columns. Her hooves tripped another explosion, the last one, it appeared. We galloped over the churned and scorched earth and no others blew up in our faces. Above us, flames licked the dense cover and blasts echoed through the hills. Flynn's archers knew the Griffins were up there somewhere, but failed to see them. *Firing blind,* I thought, urging Kiera into the clear and partway up the side of a small hill. I had to see.

The smoke obscured the enemy positions from my eyes but not from the Griffins. I grinned with satisfaction as cries and yells of shock and fear erupted from behind the natural fortifications. Moon danced out of the smoke, wings wide, his front talons holding a rock the size of my head. Taking careful aim, he threw it down and out. Aderyn dropped lightly to earth long enough to gather several rocks into her talons. Winging skyward again, she tossed one to Sky Dancer. Flying hard to either side of the rocky ravine, both flung their stones into the hidden Raithin Mawrn nest. Grey Mist, not to be outdone by the younger Atans, merely blasted low over the rocky concealment and dropped rock after rock from his arms, letting gravity do his dirty work for him.

Flynn's men boiled out of their cover and ran for their horses, concealed within a thicket of trees. I waved my bow. Didn't I say Edryd could shoot a fly off a horse's rump at a hundred paces? His arrow took a man through his throat, knocking him to the ground. The others, three of them, ducked into the wood. I didn't see Flynn, however. Nor was Blaez one of the riders who sought shelter within the trees. I waved my arm–my signal to begin a second wave of rock-fire.

Arrows from Edryd, Padraig, Edara and Alain flew across the shallow valley. Though they found no mark, their arrows kept the Raithin Mawrn pinned, their heads down. Grey Mist and Moon Whisperer both rose into the air with several rocks, and pelted the enemy location with heavy stones endowed by magic adding to the forces behind the throws. Valcan rose sluggishly from the ground, a rock the size of a melon in his raven talons. He tossed it, mid-air, to Sky Dancer, who caught it deftly. Flying hard, she threw it behind the fortification where I suspected Flynn was. I wasn't wrong, nor her aim untrue.

[219]

Flynn, on his silver horse, galloped out of concealment with that madman, Blaez, on his tail. More of his men reached horses and mounted up, spurring hard. Reining in at the southern edge of the ravine, Flynn wheeled his horse. Though I couldn't hear his yells, his gestures to his men were obvious. *Come on. Come on.* Exploding from the sheltering trees, his men galloped hard, spurring white-eyed mounts as they fled the wrath of the royal Atani.

Sky Dancer, Moon and Grey Mist burst out of the slowly dissipating smoke cloud, their intentions clear. Flynn and his devil-friends weren't going to get very far. With the enemy flushed from hiding and in full retreat, they intended to drop on the fleeing Raithin Mawrn enemy like falcons on luckless mice. Flynn's blood burned in her eyes as Sky Dancer screamed her challenge.

As his men vanished down the far side, Flynn raised both hands high over his head. I smiled within. *Ah, so he plans to surrender and save his men. How noble.* My smug thoughts burst asunder when the flames shot from his hands.

The flames boiling from him climbed higher, building in strength as it feasted on air and magic. Red, yellow, orange, roaring like an inferno, the fires reached hungrily toward the attacking Griffins. As far away as I was, I felt its crisping heat. I opened my mouth to scream something, anything.

There was no speed like a Griffin's speed. Sky Dancer wheeled sharply right, a hairsbreadth from the licking fire. Moon dove straight down, and exchanged beak for tail, flying hard and fast the way he'd come. Smoke billowed from his wings, but he appeared unhurt. Grey Mist roared in pain as Flynn's blaze hungrily reached for him. He, too, turned tail at the last second, flying faster than thought, beating hard, away.

The fire died. The ground smoked beneath the stinging rain, the blackened earth a stark reminder of the conflagration that nearly killed three Griffins. What few flames remained soon died under the onslaught of the wet storm. Like Faeries dancing on the wind, the smoke drifted upward and dispersed. There was no sign of Flynn.

I sat on Kiera, numb with pain and shock. Flynn possessed magic. *Magic.*

[220]

Malik's voice bellowed, recalling his scattered troops, but I barely heard him. How in the name of hell could Flynn possess magic? Obviously, the explosives were spelled to ignite with the vibration of steps. *Why?* Why would the treacherous Raithin Mawrn condemn us for our possession of magic, yet wield it themselves? If Flynn practiced those same arts we did, why did he permit us to capture him so easily?

"Van?"

I glanced up, my thoughts shattered. Iyumi loped her blue stallion to my side and reined in. Her brow puckered in concern and relief; she put her hand on my arm. "Are you all right?"

I started to nod, but something caught my attention. Stiffly, awkward with my injured arm, I put the arrow I never fired back in my quiver. Hanging my bow over my shoulder I reached for the object. Whatever it was, it was tangled in Kiera's mane.

"Van?"

I barely heard Iyumi's voice as I plucked the arrow from Kiera's mane.

It was one of ours.

[221]

CHAPTER 8

By Magic and Damnation

"We ran like rabbits."

Blaez sat cross-legged on the ground beside our campfire, warming his ale and scowling. Had we succeeded in seizing Princess Yummy as planned, he'd still find something to grouse about. So accustomed to his complaints, I paid him scant attention, and poked the fire with a stick.

I used my hand this time, not my power. Since the death of the little boy, using my magic made me feel like vomiting. Gone was the joy I felt in practicing my new craft. In its place, nausea and guilt swamped my guts, coating my tongue with slime. None of them knew I saved them as we fled from the Griffins' wrath. They assumed the enemy beasts had been called off, like hounds to a whistle. Only I knew that had I not turned and channeled my flames at them, our corpses would litter the hills right now, picked apart by the ravens and vultures.

I cursed under my breath at Vanyar's cleverness. Just when I thought I owned his ass, he turned my sure victory into my ignominious defeat. Damn him. Damn him and his flying hellcats.

[223]

Those rocks flung from out of the smoke was, no doubt, a stroke from a military genius. Rather than hate him, I raised my own skin of ale to him in a private toast and drank deep.

"What do we do now, my prince?" Buck-Eye asked, tending to a badly injured Rade. Under the Griffins' attack with the rocks, Hogan died from an arrow strike and Rade suffered several broken bones. Torass came through with a busted arm.

"We lick our wounds and go home," Blaez commented sourly. "Nothing else we can do."

"Shut up, Blaez," I said, my voice soft. "The King might find dissatisfaction in your performance this time." I turned my head to meet his hot eyes. "You certainly aren't immune to his anger. Care to taste the whip?"

Muttering, Blaez drank his warmed-over ale, hunching his shoulders as though fearing someone might take it from him. "My man died today. Not yours. Not fair, not fair at all."

"If I wanted you dead," I replied, my tone cold. "You'd be dead. Got it?"

He subsided, grumbling under his breath, hitching his way from the fire to his pallet. Galdan stood guard, his face expressionless, and his hand on his sword hilt. I wasn't the only one who noticed sweat trickling down his cheek. Without Hogan as his back-up, I suspected he felt alone and friendless. I knew my men liked and respected him, and none would raise a blade unless at my order. Unless Blaez himself provoked it, I'd no plans to kill Galdan.

Gathering his explosive materials, Blaez set to making more of his beloved bombs. He'd depleted his entire supply on our failed attack on the Atani, yet had a full pack-mule of material with which to create more. He began filling both bamboo reeds and clay pipes with nails, powder, small rocks and then sealing them with wax and string. I knew, earlier in the day, his bombs went off at the right time because Blaez set his spells for motion. Anytime a foot or hoof came close–boom! I let him believe I believed they were built that way. I pretended to ignore the many arrow-devices that didn't have a lit fuse, but exploded in the faces of the flying Griffins anyway. Blaez hid his powers most cleverly.

"Make them bigger this time," I told him. "We'll need as many more of those arrow-bombs as you can concoct. If you need an assistant, grab one. Boden is clever and learns quickly."

He ignored me, but delved into yet another pack and pulled out large glass containers. By their size, I knew he had them specially crafted for his effective bombs. How he kept them from breaking as we travelled was anyone's guess. *More magic,* I suspected.

"How is he?" I asked Buck-Eye.

Rade hadn't ridden long with Buck-Eye, but the mercenary knight treated him with the same affection and regard as though they'd been friends since boyhood. I liked that aspect of Buck-Eye's nature. Once he attached his loyalty, there was no shaking him from it. I pried him from Blaez's side for a simple reason: Buck-Eye hated Blaez, despite his allegiance to the ugly Commander.

"In pain, m'lord," Buck-Eye answered. "He'll make it, if we can permit him the time. But he's hurt bad, m'lord."

I can heal him, I thought. I knew my powers included those of healing. I could lay my hand on Rade's brow and will his bones to knit, wash comfort over his pain, and grant him ease. Like Buck-Eye, Rade freely offered his loyalty into my hand and service. Though my cynicism and paranoia worried he'd one day sink his blade into my back, he never once turned that suspicion into proof. Part of me craved to lay my hand on his brow, and damn the consequences. Perhaps one day, I may find some redemption for the horror I've done, for the evil powers within me. I wanted nothing else than to help Rade, and wash the wounds of my soul by saving his life. I dared not.

I bit my inner cheek, inviting the swelling, the pain. If I did, they'd know immediately I owned magic. Would they remember their oaths of loyalty and obeisance? Would they forget the gold I paid them and rip me limb from limb from sheer panic? Or would they obey the kingdom's laws that none may possess magic and live? Was Rade's life worth my own? Of course it was. But was his life worth Fainche's? Worth Enya's?

Never.

Tears welled in my eyes, but didn't fall. *He ll die, and I must abandon him to die.* He can't travel, and come the dawn we must ride hard for the Shin'Eah. Van, Malik and Iyumi won't waste time over such thoughts of good or evil. They'll heal the hurts of their fellows and carry on, the weight of guilt not hampering them at all.

I envied them that freedom.

Evil was a very lonely existence.

Ease his suffering, nimrod, a voice said from deep within me. The voice sounded strangely like Van's. *You know how.*

I did know how. Under the cover of the darkness and flickering shadows, I conjured a pouch of white powder. I cradled it in my hands, staring down at it. Years before I watched a physician give the white powder to a wounded man and named it blackroot. Being a chatty fellow, he explained its primary use as a pain killer. First dug from the ground it was indeed black, but after drying and processing it turned white. Use it sparingly, I was told. Too much, the physician said, and the blackroot stopped the heart.

I pretended to rummage through my saddlebags and discover the leather pouch. I tossed it to Buck-Eye. "Give Rade some of that."

"How much, m'lord?"

"As much as he needs," I answered, drinking from my cup, my eyes on the fire. "Oh, and give a pinch to Torass. It'll help him, as well."

No one seemed to notice the conflicting instructions. Buck-Eye dosed Rade heavily with generous amounts of the blackroot, raising his head onto his knee and offering the laced water to Rade's dry lips. Todaro added a small pinch to a cup of ale, and handed to Torass to drink. Torass tossed the liquor past his throat, and swallowed hard. He fell back onto his pallet, panting, cradling his broken arm.

"Sleep well," I muttered, sipping my own ale. It tasted bitter, oh, so very bitter, on my tongue. "Come dawn, things will look better."

"Who's on watch, m'lord?"

I should command old Sourpuss to the third watch. Unfortunately, I needed his skills as a bomb-maker far more than I needed him drowsing at his post. Given his love of the bloody things, he'll contentedly create them until dawn broke, then doze in his saddle as we travelled.

"Me," I whispered. "I'll take the first, you the second and Galdan the third."

I turned my face briefly over my shoulder toward Buck-Eye, yet I couldn't look at Rade laying there, his head cradled in Buck-Eye's lap. Despite my averted eyes, my ears heard his labored breathing soften, my power sensing the gradual slowing of his heart. From my peripheral vision, I saw him sink deeper into slumber, his pain gone.

"Get your rest," I told Buck-Eye. "He'll sleep sound this night."

"M'lord."

Buck-Eye tenderly lay Rade's head down, pillowed on his cloak. After tossing a bit on the cold, hard soil, Buck-Eye dozed. His hand pulled his blanket up to his neck as though chilled. I knew the instant he dropped into real sleep. I studied him a moment, wishing I hadn't the responsibility I had. I envied him his freedom to sleep, free from worries and the *dia-l-do-the-right-thing* questions. His wasn't the sleep of the dead, as Rade drifted toward, but the natural slumber of the bone-weary.

Around me the camp quieted, the snores of the men rising like a cacophony of disharmonic music. Blaez still worked on his explosives, his eyes down, as the pile of devices beside him grew. I knew he'd keep at it until weariness forced him to sleep. As he seemed to require little of that, he'd work and create the devices we must plant to kill the Atani, seize the princess and find this wayward child everyone blathered about.

The waxing moon shone down on me as I walked away from the camp, the men and the blazing fire. My power informed me only two owls, the many numerous buzzing insects annoying my ears and an early fox noticed me walk into the darkness beyond the fire. Just as I wanted it.

I knew my men were safe. Both my gut and my power told me so.

Thorny vines tried to trip me up as I paced slowly from the firelight and into sheer darkness. My eyes, needing a fraction of light to see by, saw nothing but shadows and trees. I listened to the soft sough of the wind through the pines, its cool fingers stroking my neck and cheeks. My sweat dried under its velvet strokes; my heart trip-hammering in my chest.

I don t belong here, I thought. *This place is holy and I am not. Forgive me, please.*

Out of sight and ear-shot of the camp, I sat down on a nearby oak stump, rounded by weather. Its rotting trunk lay half-buried in thorny brambles, and a small rodent squeaked within its crumbling core. *A good spot to post my watch.* Here the forest thinned and the ground gradually rose toward a shallow hill. Above me, the stars glittered like diamonds in a bed of black velvet, the moon but a speck upon the eastern sky. A shooting star flashed across the distant horizon, trailing its red dragon's tail. The firedrake. An omen, the old stories said. But for what?

Pulling it from under my tunic, on its fine silver chain, I contemplated the scrying crystal my mother gave me. A smallish, gold stone, like a small piece of amber, it all but glowed with a light of its own. Though the crystal contained a strange warmth, not from my body's heat, its touch didn't feel evil or tainted. Not mastered in the old histories, I suspected the crystal was a relic from the Mage Wars centuries ago, the battles that split the nations of Raithin Mawr and Bryn'Cairdha apart.

On my first attempt the day before, in planning our ambush, I found Van and Company by staring deeply into it, envisioning Van within my mind. Within moments, a large moving picture—complete with color, facial expressions, background, horses and all those folks that accompanied Van and Iyumi appeared in the sky above me. Only sound didn't come through. When I asked a question, such as where were the Griffins, the Centaurs, the humans, I was promptly answered. Two Centaurs paced a mile in front. Two Griffins protected the rear. Human cavalry rode to the sides and Griffins and Shifters flew watch in the skies. Any question I asked was answered, completely and thoroughly.

Except what they said to one another.

I asked to see the terrain ahead of them, and the crystal showed me the shallow valley rife with potential ambush terrain, jutting rocks and broken boulders creating natural walls. Van and Company would strike that valley late the next afternoon, if they kept to their current course. I pondered how to get ahead of them, and the crystal obliged me with a visual of the highland hills, in all directions. If we kept to another long valley parallel with my planned ambush location and rode hard all night, we could arrive well ahead of them and plant some bombs.

I tried keeping the scrying crystal a secret by invoking its power well away from Blaez and the others. But Blaez proved nosy as well as vocal. Unfortunately, he witnessed me pull it from my tunic and fondle it, as I mentally planned our assault.

"What the bloody hell is that thing?"

Shrugging, I tucked it away under my tunic, next to my heart. "A token of my sister's love," I replied, my tone light. "She gave it to me the morning we departed. Do you have someone waiting for you, back home?"

My question, innocently asked, set Blaez into a frothy fury of denial. I reeled my treasure back like a landed fish and thought uncharitable thoughts. Of course Blaez didn't have anyone awaiting his return with love, a hot fire and spread legs. Any girl with half a brain knew trouble when Blaez was around.

As Blaez's curiosity piqued the men, I reluctantly displayed it for Buck-Eye, Rade and the others, permitting them to ooh and ahh over its pricelessness. But I never allowed them to actually touch it. I didn't know if the magic would open up to them, and didn't want to find out. If they knew I held magic in my fists—ye gods!

With my well-planned ambush in ruins and Rade dying behind me, I peered into its golden depths. Under the shimmer of the firedrake, I willed myself to see Van, Iyumi and that devil-creature Malik. The canvas of the crystal's power opened up before me. Like a painting over the stars, it showed me a camp bedding down for the night: watches set, the evening meal eaten and cleared away, bedrolls unrolled, pipes lit with flaming sticks, wine and ale warmed. Funny. Their camp activities mirrored mine.

Van, Iyumi and Malik stood near the blazing fire talking. That huge bay and white Centaur stood at Malik's right, while a hulking

Griffin sat at Van's back, its black-tipped lion tail twitching in sharp spasms. A second Griffin, larger than the first one and darker in color, stood behind Iyumi and appeared to be talking to her. Her head tilted back, anyway, her lovely throat exposed, her silver-gilt hair trailing in long lengths to her hips. She answered him, smiling. My eyes roved to—

A wolf howled nearby, startling me out of the spell. The picture over the sky vanished, leaving behind only stars and the moon peeking above the distant tree line. Tucking the amber gem into my shirt, I glanced around, cautious. I saw nor heard anyone close by, but knew instinctively who was.

"Hello, Mother."

The darkness amid the trees to my right shimmered briefly. She emerged into my view, a gossamer phantom, her white and gold gown trailing mist. She strolled, with the same elegance she used to cross her throne room, stepping softly and lightly. Not a twig cracked under her slippered foot. Her fair lips parted in a faint smile. "I see you're using my gift wisely."

Before I could stop it, my hand raised itself toward my chest, and the gem hiding next to my heart. I willed it to subside, and rested it against my knee. "I reckon so."

More lovely than any goddess, Enya crossed the small clearing, her shadow eclipsing the stars. Only when she turned to face me, did the dark bruise on her cheek become appallingly apparent. Its ugly stain brought me to my feet faster than a whip.

"What happened?"

She half-turned away, her fingers trailing across the mark of a fist. *His* fist. I growled low in my throat, like an ugly mongrel.

"Um, yeah," she said, her tone aiming for lightness. "Your father doesn't care much for failure," she said, her voice low. "Mine, yours–"

"How the bloody hell does he know I failed?" I snapped, my spine rigid, my fists clenched. "The battle was what? A few hours ago?"

She tried to remain calm, serene. She failed miserably. Her composure crumpled. She turned to me and buried her face in my chest. Of their own accord, my arms wrapped about her slender shoulders, comforting her. Her tears wet my shirt; her cheek pressed against the precious gem.

"I'm sorry, son. I tried to be strong . . . as strong as you. I'm just not–"

"What happened?"

"It's her," Enya sobbed. "It's all *her*. She seduced him years ago; she's a witch, a devil. She knows everything that goes on, she sees, she knows–"

"She?"

I didn't know how cold my voice had grown until I felt her shiver.

"She has power," my mother whispered. "Great power. She tangled your father–"

She choked over the title, swallowing her tears. "–my beloved husband, in her lies and deceit. My small magic could do nothing to save him from her enchantments. She knows you failed to kill the Atani idiots and bring in the princess. She told him everything."

"Everything."

"Yes, son," Enya stammered, her breath short. "He was wroth, oh so very angry, you know how it is when he gets angry."

I did, all right.

"He lashed out at Fainche, but I stopped him, crying, begging him for mercy. He struck me–in her place."

I growled again, a deep rumbling in my chest. *I'll find him and rip his throat and drink his blood, I swear–*

"I wish I was dead!" she cried. "I love him, but I love my children more. I can't stand to see him hurt you, my son, or my beloved daughter. I wish she hadn't ruined our lives! I hate her! Oh, how I hate her!"

Crooning, sing-song nonsense words left my mouth and entered her ears, her soul. In them I spoke of my love for her, how I craved to protect her, how I'd willingly die defending her. I whispered of my love for my frail, tiny sister, my Fainche. Everyone who ever encountered her bubbling laughter and smile loved her within an instant. Not even the woman who gave birth to her was immune to her sweet innocence.

[231]

Enya raised herself from the shelter of my arms, wiping her reddened eyes at the same time trying to hide them. My finger under her chin tilted her face up to mine. "I'll kill him."

My soft promise brought only new terror from her.

My mother clutched my fingers, new tears sliding down her cheeks. "No, son, no. I love him, yes, but it's not his fault. It's not, don't you see? It's her, that witch, the Duchess, she makes him do these things, this evil. Spare him, I beg you, spare him and kill her. That's it, kill her and your father will love us all again. We'll be a family again, you'll see. It's not his fault."

The happy, desperate smile never left her eyes, her tremulous lips, the tears that yet dripped down her cheeks. *I love him,* those cornflower blue eyes informed me. *He lashes out at me, wounds me to the core, but I love him still. As you should. He's a good man, deep down.*

Sure he was.

"He's dead, Mother. He just don't know it yet."

Her face turned away from me, hiding her expression. "I don't want this," she whispered. "I don't want him dead. I don't want you dead, either. I dare not make a choice. I cannot make a choice."

My finger on her cheek turned her face toward me. "You won't, Mother," I promised, my voice soft. "I'll make it."

My mother wiped her swollen cheeks, and brushed my cheek with her fingers. "I have to tell you something."

"Tell me what?"

"The crystal doesn't just show you your enemies," she said, her voice choked. She kept her face averted, ashamed. "If you picture them, you see them, yes?"

"Yes."

"Find them, then will your body there. Think hard. Put yourself in their space, and it's done. You can kill them with ease, stopping their hearts before they suspect a thing. You can kill her guards, and take her for your own."

Iyumi. Princess Yummy. I swiped my hand across my mouth and half-turned away from her. Such thoughts—not in front of one's mother. *I will marry her and unite our kingdoms.* She'll love me, and

[232]

offer herself willingly, happily, that luscious body mine. I imagined her pregnant, her belly rounded and tight with my seed.

Our son.

"It will happen," she whispered. "Will it and it will be so."

"I will it."

"Yes, my son, my favorite, my most special child. Find your will and make it happen. You have the power."

Even to myself my voice sounded far away. "I will it shall be so."

"She will be yours."

"Mine."

"Forever. Your line shall never fail. Your sons will sire kings of great renown. And all will revere your name, for all time."

The idiot wolf howled again, breaking rudely into my daydream. I woke from it, blinking, coming to myself. "Mother?"

Her hand caressed my bristly cheek. "Remember how much I love you, my son, my Flynn. You'll save us all, I know it."

"I will." I took a deep breath to assuage my anger.

Her blonde, luxurious hair swept across her face, hiding it from me. "I must go, Flynn. He'll search for me soon. I must be there, or he'll get suspicious."

I withdrew my hand, my heart hardening. "May the good gods guide your steps, Mother."

The wolf howled again, closer, as she withdrew into the circle of trees and vanished from my sight. I contemplated the crystal again. I didn't seek Van and Company this time. Rather, I pictured my father, King Finian the Fair, within my mind. I glanced up into the sky as the amber crystal showed me what I most wanted to see.

Finian was in bed at this early hour, but he wasn't sleeping. Instead, he took between his covers a nubile young thing with dark hair and fair skin. My rage soared as I realized his partner wasn't exactly willing. Beneath her terrified brown eyes a gag filled her mouth and tied behind her neck. Heavy rope bound her hands over her head, and a bruised and bloody ankle, also knotted with a heavy rope, peeped out from under the sheet. *Monstrous!* With a beautiful wife and an unknown number of luscious mistresses, why did he resort to rape?

Because he can.

If I didn't defend the girl's honor, who would? I went so far as to collect my will, to send myself into his chambers and stab my sword through his neck as he entertained himself in his sainted wife's absence. Only my mother's timid voice, telling me how much she loved him, kept me on that hilltop, hundreds of leagues away.

"Flynn," she wept, her sobs echoing within my mind. *"Don t. Please, I beg you."*

I subsided, cursing under my breath. All thoughts of Van, Iyumi and the Atani who accompanied them vanished from my thoughts.

"Your time comes," I whispered into the darkness and starlight as I shut the crystal down and shoved it under my tunic. "I *will* kill you, you bastard."

"He's dead!"

Buck-Eye's grieving voice broke into my restless, nightmare haunted sleep. Once more, that brat wandered into my head and took up residence. *Dammit,* I protested, *I killed you.* He didn't speak–he never spoke in my dreams. Yet, the gaping wound in his throat grinned redly, while his dark eyes regarded me with both accusation and a weird, solemn kindness. As he often did, he reached out a small hand toward mine, as though inviting me to take it. I shrank from him, scared, knowing that should I accept it, he'd drag me down into the depths of hell with him.

What? My groggy mind tried to grasp Buck-Eye's meaning. Yes, of course he's dead. I sacrificed him on a demon's altar for unrivaled power.

Buck-Eye choked, tears thickening in his throat. "M'lord, he shouldn't have died. He was fine, he was sleeping when I took my watch, I swear it!"

Oh. That 'he's dead'.

I sat up, feigning concern. "What?"

The wool blanket I used to cover myself from the night's highland chill pooled into my lap as I wiped my hand down my face.

My eyes, filled with muck, tried to focus. Hell's teeth, but I hated recriminations early in the morning.

Buck-Eye cradled Rade's head in his lap, Rade's dead and glazed eyes staring into nothing. He'd died some hours ago and had already stiffened. His flesh had paled to that of a cadaver, bloodless, empty of life and soul. Buck-Eye tried to close his eyes, but Rade's lids refused to stay down. Like a shutter, they rolled back up, revealing faint blue tinges around his irises.

"I came off my watch," Buck-Eye said, grieving, panicked. "He slept, I swear it, he was just sleeping sound. I woke Galdan as usual and went to sleep myself. He shouldn't have died, m'lord! He'd have been fine, after a fashion. Why did he die?"

Because I told you to overdose him with blackroot, I thought, but didn't say aloud. Instead, I muttered, "Shit", and ran my hands through my hair. "This just bites rocks. I'm so sorry, Buck-Eye, I know you two were close."

Buck-Eye rocked his friend's head back and forth, wrapped within the confines of his brawny arms. Tears rolled unchecked down his ruddy cheeks to saturate his scruffy, thin beard. "He'd be fine. I know he'd be all right, he just needed time and some fixing up. He didn't need to die!"

As that fierce mercenary soldier wept over the corpse of his friend, my guilt slapped me hard across the face. No, he didn't need to die. Had I some guts, I could have healed him while minimizing his true injuries. Had I real courage, I'd have healed him with my powers, thus showing them all that magic wasn't evil, that it performed many good deeds. Like healing the grievously injured soldiers under my command.

Instead, I took the coward's way out. He'd have slowed me down, so I killed him to spare myself the necessity of being noble or brave. I killed him because I was selfish. I shut my jaw tight against a sharp wave of self-hatred. That little boy didn't need to die any more than Rade did. My magic was–is–sufficient for whatever I needed. I'd no use for more.

"I'm so sorry, Buck-Eye," I said, and actually meant it.

[235]

Buck-Eye smoothed Rade's hair from his brow and kissed it. "He's in a better place, m'lord."

I hope so. Because this place certainly bites.

Despite my haste, we took the time to bury Rade. I owed him that much. Buck-Eye chose his grave, upon a hill lined with fir, pine and oak trees, and one that gazed upon a sunlit valley filled with songbirds, falcons, kestrels, and grazing deer. Darting hummingbirds dined upon the various wildflowers strewn across the grasslands pocked with thickets of thorny thickets and scrub oak. The entire area exuded peace enough to send the most sinful into heaven.

He d like it here, I thought, piling heavy rocks across his grave for a cairn, Buck-Eye, Torass, Boden and Lyall helping me. Blaez brooded as Galdan watched his back and Todaro watched them both, his hand on his hilt. *Rade always loved peaceful scenery about him.*

"How'd you know that, m'lord?"

Buck-Eye's question brought me to myself as I straightened, brushing dirt from my hands. I hadn't known I'd spoken aloud until Buck-Eye's question intruded. Blaez stared hard at me as Torass and Boden tossed a few more rocks upon the cairn, gazing down at the grave of their friend. I didn't even know how I knew that about Rade. We'd never exchanged confidences; neither trusted the other enough.

I just *knew.*

I shrugged, self-effacing. "He told me once," I said, my tone low, feigning grief. "And–he's that type. He loved the natural order of things."

Gods be praised, Buck-Eye accepted my answer, nodding in satisfaction. Blaez continued his accusing stare as though he knew I murdered Rade in the night, rubbing his huge bag of toys as he might a pet dog. I paid him little heed, pretending real grief as my soul ached under the tremendous guilt. Can I ever be absolved of these crimes? Can I ever stop murdering people in cold blood?

"Speak a few words, m'lord?"

Buck-Eye's question jolted me. What could I say? *Sorry I killed you, old chap? I wasn t thinking straight, I was too frightened to use*

[236]

my healing magic, too fearful my own men might turn on me like rabid dogs. Surely, you'll understand.

"Uh," I began, floundering. Under their eyes, their trust, their faith, I cleared my throat. "Of course."

I stepped up, standing near his head. I had no cap to drag down, as did Buck-Eye and Boden, but I bowed my head. My words bubbled up from a pool deep within me, unknown and unheeded until now. "Rest ye well, Rade of Blakamon, soldier and loyal officer. You died in the service of your prince and thus your entrance into heaven is assured. May the gods shine their light upon you and guide you into peace and tranquility. The good gods be praised."

"The good gods be praised," answered Buck-Eye and the others, in unison.

Blaez still scowled, as though the funeral interrupted his schedule. Galdan sweated and tapped his fingers on his hilt as I tossed a fistful of earth onto Rade's cairn. "Be at peace, my friend," I murmured, turning away.

Buck-Eye tossed his own soil. "I'll never forget you, brother. Be at peace. You earned it. But watch over me, when you can. Please?"

One by one, Torass, Boden, Lyall, Kalan and Todaro tossed their fistfuls of dirt onto the grave in solemn ceremony. Only Blaez and Galdan held back, as though blessing the dead might incur their own funerals. I didn't force them, for they owed their loyalty to my father and none other. If they didn't respect Rade enough to mourn him in proper fashion, then to hell with them.

As I walked toward a saddled and waiting Bayonne, I cast a simple spell over my shoulder. "Permit him to lie, undisturbed, until the world's end," I muttered, my tone so low no one could possibly hear it. "Let no creature dig up his bones, feast upon his rotting flesh, or possess his spirit. It is done. Let it be done."

I set the spell, and mounted my horse. "Blaez, you ride the vanguard today. Galdan, you're the rearguard. Buck-Eye, you and Torass flank me. Lyall, you ride east as Todaro rides west. Kalan."

I glanced at the young, eager soldier with the keen eye of an eagle sizing up its prey. "You and Boden are my bodyguards. Aren't you lucky?"

I lunged out of my blankets, horror drawing over my soul.

Sweat dripped acid into my eyes as I blinked at the horizon, judging it less than an hour after sunrise as I dragged in one lungful of air after another. Crikey, that bloody kid again. Four nights since I killed him, two since Van defeated me at the valley battle and he came to me every time I shut my eyes to sleep. This time the little bleeder spoke. He only stared at me, in previous nightmares. Now he's learned some rather impressive language skills. Not bad for a dead two year-old.

"I will see you again," he intoned with the deep, resonating voice of my father as he pointed his dripping finger at me, his eyes as red as the gaping maw beneath his chin.

"Forgive me," I tried to say, to answer, to turn aside his wrath. "I didn't know."

"You are a fool to believe the witch–"

"Nightmare, Prince?"

Blaez cackled as he sat between me and the fire, squatting on his haunches, watching me sleep. I think that creeped me out far more than the boy I murdered pointing his baby finger at me in my dreams. How long had he sat there as the men broke camp, observing me? None of my boys stood watch over me, I realized as I sat up, my blanket sliding off my shoulders. Busy saddling horses, making breakfast, tending the fire, packing supplies–none paid any heed to the killer standing over me with hatred bared.

"Yeah," I replied blearily, scraping my hands down my bristly face. "I saw you copulating with a goat. Gave me the bleeding shivers, it did."

Blaez rose, scowling. His right hand fiddled with his belt knife, though his sword remained curiously absent.

I stood also, feigning a yawn and a stretch as I idly meandered myself out of knife-lunging range. "Now I know the reason for your ruddy high boots."

"It's an hour past time we rode," Blaez snapped. He eyed me up and down. "And here we sit, awaiting your beauty rest."

"I get so little of that," I replied, yawning again as I tried to suppress the real shiver as my mind tripped over the little rascal I'd murdered. "Mores the pity."

I'd tossed and turned most of the night, unable to sleep. Thoughts of my father, my mother, the kid, Rade, Sim, Fainche and Sofia rode me like a spurred horse. I sweated like one, too, before sheer exhaustion dropped me into the nightmare a mere two hours before the dawn.

My illustrious sire ordered Blaez to kill me. Though he needed me to find the child, he'd kill me once it was in our clutches. Then he's proudly take it home to Castle Salagh as his prize and receive his reward from my father's hands. But if he thought he could get away with it–Why wasn't Boden watching over me? I bent to gather my blanket, shake out the loose dirt and twigs from it, eyeing my henchman as he bantered with Torass.

They'd saddled their own mounts, leaving them to stand unattended as they girthed Bayonne far too tightly for my liking, and Bayonne's. He pinned his black-tipped ears and swished his tail in annoyance, but made no further expression of discontent. Far too easy-going for such theatrics as kicking or biting, Bayonne merely sighed down his nose at this obvious ill-treatment and shook his ears.

I whistled sharply as I bent down, my eyes never leaving Blaez, and retrieved my sword belt. Boden glanced around as Torass looked up. I jerked my chin, frowning slightly.

Boden, my afore-appointed bodyguard, got my message, even as Blaez grumbled sourly under his breath. I heard my royal status and a swift mention of my ancestors cast upon the light breeze before Boden arrived with his right hand resting lightly on his hilt. The rest of his bitter remarks regarding my blood Blaez swallowed as my young henchman paused at his left shoulder. Boden: young, strong, athletic, towered over the squatty, ugly Blaez, his reputation as a swordsman exceeding Blaez's as a bomb-maker.

Blaez started slightly and half-turned. Boden smiled gently, courteously, down, as Blaez's jaw slackened.

"Forgive me, my lord," Boden said quietly, menace soft in his tone. "I didn't mean to startle your grace. Is there anything you require? Name it, and I'll be happily obliged to give it to you."

Had I not been annoyed with him to start with, I'd have applauded Boden as a genius. Muttering imprecations with no few angry glances cast over his shoulder, Blaez stumped toward the fire, his arms swinging. He never saluted me, either, the cad.

I flung my arm over Boden's shoulder, and steered him away from the others, out of ear-shot. I grinned at him in a comradely, friendly fashion, informing those who watched that I felt an affinity toward this young mercenary soldier.

My hand urged him to bend his head toward me, inviting a confidence.

I smiled. "Leave my side again, and I'll gut you crotch to chin."

"I'm sorry, Your Highness, I—"

"Excuses are like asses," I snapped, still smiling. "Everyone has one and they all stink."

Boden slipped from under my arm to bow low. "No excuse, Your Highness. I'll never leave your royal person this side of death."

"See to it."

"Your Highness."

I raised my voice so it resounded throughout the camp. "And someone bring me some bleeding food."

Buck-Eye obliged me, his cheeks reddened with chagrin that I was forced to shout for the service that was mine by right. Kneeling at my boots, he lifted a small platter of what appeared decent sustenance for a morning repast: warm bread, warmer ale, cold roast beef and hot sausages smoking from the frying pan. I breathed in the scents and my belly rumbled. Torass hurried across the camp to add his own delectables to my breakfast: white, hard cheese and an odd assortment of fruits and nuts he'd gathered as we travelled.

My guilt rose to nudge my ribs as he used only his healthy right arm to offer the small bowl filled to bursting. His hardly healed left arm still lay in its white, yet red-stained sling. His normally cheerful face smiled, yet I noticed the white strain around his eyes, and the corners of his mouth. In the past two days of travel, I wallowed in my own misery without paying the slightest heed to anyone else's. I remembered, finally, how Buck-Eye, Boden, Kalan and Lyall fulfilled Torass's duties as well as their own, permitting their friend to rest.

"How are you, lad?" I asked abruptly. "Your arm."

He glanced down. "Oh, um, better, Yer Highness, not so much pain today."

"You shouldn't be–" I began, and halted.

The old Prince Flynn would hardly care if one of his men rode and served with an injury that caused him obvious pain. He'd ignore the wretch and demand service no matter what the cost. Yet, the new, powerful and tainted Prince Flynn found a strange sympathy toward the peasant soldier who reveled in the opportunity to serve his liege despite his agony and handicap.

He misread my hesitation.

"It's ruddy safe, Yer Highness," he said, his tone half-panicked I'd fear he aimed to poison me and murder him. "My da's a farmer and me dam, me mother, oft fed these to us younglings afters a forage in the forest. Tries them, m'lord and you'll see. 'Tis good."

He bowed low, his self-effacing grin and sweat trickling from his brow in the less than hot temperatures informed me of his sincerity and dreading I'd not recognize such. If he hadn't pleased me, he feared, I'd kill him out of hand.

My soul cringed. What kind of monster have I become? That a simple offering, a simple meal at daybreak, would revert to a life or death situation? Am I that bad?

Yes. You are that bad.

"My thanks, Torass," I said, trying to find a smile, or at least a lightening of my habitual oppressive expression. "I'll wager your mother is an awesome cook."

Accepting his offering, I bit into the juicy fruit, my throat's glands cringing in protest. Such was its sweetness, its diverse and tantalizing taste, I gobbled it down and reached for another.

"Crikey, that's good," I muttered, my mouth full and juice running down my chin.

"Try this one, m'lord," Torass said eagerly, his chin jerk indicated a pale orange fruit with dark red lines ringing its exterior. "Take a bite, then chase it with these here nuts. Ye'll swear you'd died and gone t' heaven, that ye will. And the cheese–my dam's made it herself, she did."

I hoped he didn't mean that literally, but took his advice. The flavor of the nuts pursuing the fruit did indeed make me reach for more of both. My belly didn't just rumble this time: it screamed for more. Damn, but that combination of flavors sent my tongue into overdrive. The cheese was all he said 'twas–delicious and sharp, with a weird tang that forced a small groan from me.

"When I'm king," I said, my mouth full. "I'll appoint you my chief cook."

I eyed him sidelong. "Or maybe your mother."

Torass grinned and squirmed like a stroked puppy. "I'm tickled ye like them, m'lord prince."

The hot sausage, the fresh bread and swallows of thick, amber ale seemed almost a poor relation to Torass's fruity breakfast. I ate most, waved away the cold roast and belched contentedly. Blaez sulked from the far side of camp, his pretentious scowl firmly in place. He munched hard bread and cheese as Galdan saddled his black stallion, setting out wrapped bundles of arrows for the men to collect. He'd replaced the razor-tipped barbs with bulbous homemade death–smallish rounded heads that still ended in a sharp point.

His sack bulged with his creative bombs, the feathered fletching informed me he had hundreds more bomb-arrows ready to take out Van and Malik's hellcats. The heavy canvas collection of his creations sat at the feet of the pack-mule, who eyed it dubiously while munching the thin grass for his breakfast.

Buck-Eye, Kalan, Boden and Lyall seized bundles of these weird creations, eyeing them and one another sidelong as they attached them to the pommels of their saddles. Quivers of ordinary arrows they rolled onto their cantles along with their bedrolls, spare weapons and food.

[242]

Boden asked my leave with a glance. I gave it with a quick nod, and gestured for Torass to accompany him to collect their own quivers and finish saddling their mounts. As Buck-Eye had completed his preparations for departure, my swift hand gesture brought him sidling closer to me, his hand on his sword hilt. He knew well that my father ordered Blaez to kill me. Should Blaez try, well, Buck-Eye had few qualms when it came to killing madmen.

As Blaez tossed me my own bundle of explosive arrows, he sneered. His dark beady eyes narrowed and his upper lip lifted to expose his badly stained teeth.

"Per your request," he grumbled, his flippant gesture included his bulging canvas as his sneer never faltered, "bombs ready and arrows to hand. All you need do is point and shoot. Can you handle that?"

"Can you?" I replied, my hand deftly enclosing his arsenal of bristling, stubby arrows. *One shot might take out as many as five royal Atani soldiers,* I thought, eyeballing the fearsome collection at my fingertips. *Is that not cool, or what?* "Seems to me your arrows fell far short of their mark. Can it be you shoot as well as a peasant whore?"

"Whenever you're ready, Prince," he snapped. "We've a long way to ride this day."

And so we have, I thought, rising and strapping my swordbelt around my hips. *But where are we going?*

Despite riding from dawn till past dusk and pushing our horses to their limits, Van and Company stayed well ahead of us. As though they knew we followed on their heels, we could neither gain ground nor get ahead of them to plant another ambush. Time and again I considered my mother's suggestion: use the jewel to cast myself into their midst and stop their hearts with one blow. I rejected it as too risky. Though I'd learned much of my powers in recent days, Van and Malik knew far more than I. I may jump into their midst and kill several only to have a Griffin I overlooked strike my head from my shoulders. Or I might cast a wide spell and slaughter Iyumi along with them.

[243]

I belched again, and hitched my belt more comfortably around my hips. "Be right back, gents. Commander Blaez, I trust you'll see to our travel arrangements. Buck-Eye, you have my back."

Without waiting to see if my orders were followed, I strode quickly into the dense mountain brush. As though answering the call of nature, which I desperately needed to do, I also required isolation and privacy to ferret out Van and Company's plans. A dense thicket of tough, thorny bushes and scrub oak offered a very secretive spot to spy on one's enemy.

I spun about and pointed. "Wait here."

"But–Your Highness–"

"If a squirrel invades my ass as I shit, I'll yell," I snapped, "until then, you wait–right–here. Understand?"

He bowed low. The poor knight obeyed me, clearly unhappy as I wiggled my way into the thicker brush and high oak trees. On one hand I threatened a nasty death for failing to guard my body as I, a mere few moments later, threatened the same for staying too close. No wonder the henchmen I paid misunderstood me and wished for a saner, less temperamental, employer. Perhaps a dowager duchess whose greatest journeys were to the garden, to the privy, and back. I knew they thought me as mad as a march hare and hardly as cute.

But I pay thrice as much. I wiggled my way into the dense thickets, overgrown wild rose patches and long, sharp thorns that cut my skin and put holes in my black cloak. Should Enya see the state of my garments, she'd scream foul and reach for her needles. A royal prince shouldn't lack for a solid, upright appearance.

There's always a 'however' somewhere to hand, I suspected. That thorny thicket prevented anyone who managed to bypass Buck-Eye to sneak up on me while I conducted personal business. That done, I pulled the amber jewel from beneath my shirt and held it in my hand. Its warmth startled me, for I knew its heat hadn't come from my body. It gave off a soft golden glow as it sat on my palm, almost seeming to pulse with a heartbeat. While I never felt evil when I touched it, or gazed into it, I also felt my presence in its territory wasn't welcome. It obeyed me, but didn't love me.

"Join the club," I muttered, bending my will onto it. "Show me Vanyar."

[244]

I lifted my eyes in time to see the blue-washed western horizon fill with black Malik waving his arms and stomping in a wide circle, his heavy tail lashing. Though I couldn't hear his words, I knew he ordered one Griffin to fly north, another to the south. For those birdies he gestured toward rose high on sluggish wings and flew where he directed. A third leapt skyward and rose higher and higher until it vanished into the thin haze. The rayed star upon his brow gleamed under the early light as he pointed to a pair of Centaurs and gestured north. Those two loped under the trees and vanished. As I watched, a cute, dark-haired Atani, her black hair braided into a thick twist that fell to her waist, changed before my eyes into a slender doe.

I gaped. As when Van transformed from Bayonne to his own self, the change was instantaneous. Where my horse once stood, his hoof on my chest, Captain Van grinned down at me, his green eyes alight with good humor. Again, where the foxy brunette once tugged on her braid, a delicious doe bounded away on light hooves to also vanish under the trees.

Uncanny. To have the innate ability to change into any form one desires–wasn't that evil? Or might it be complete freedom? What might it be like to soar on an eagle's wings and go wherever one wanted? To fly free of one's heavy-handed father–

And Van?

The instant I thought of him, the jewel revealed him to me. Half-hidden behind Malik and a human cavalry soldier mounted on his chestnut horse, I saw him. He wore a sky-blue tunic open at the throat, black breeches, and a slender band of braided leather tied around his brow to prevent his shaggy hair from falling in his eyes. A silver medallion depicting a lightning bolt lay against his chest, perhaps a token of his rank. The hilt of a heavy broadsword protruded from its plain leather scabbard, its costly jewels winking in the sun made mine appear shabby by comparison.

He assisted Princess Yummy onto my blue roan, draped from throat to heel in a black cloak. His dark hair, swept back from his face, blew lightly from beneath the wings of the tremendous Griffin dropping to earth behind him. His piercing green eyes laughed up at

Iyumi, his teeth flashing in the new light. As it had before, his simple boyish grin and devilish charm had its effect on me. I liked him then, on sight, as I liked him now, watching from afar.

Van owned that unique quality, very rare, that made folk not just like him, but follow him. Even into death, into the flames of hell. A natural leader, I knew why such a young man had risen so high in the Atani ranks. His charisma alone brought tough men to their knees. He led, they followed.

He s the enemy, I reminded myself, trying to imagine him dead under my blade, his life's blood soaking into the stony soil. Yet, the vision never quite happened, as hard as I tried to visualize it. I gazed at him coldly, with hate, with anger. Strangely enough, my animosity drifted on the wind and the iciness I felt toward him melted and leached away under the infectiousness of that grin. Dammit, I liked that son of a bitch. How can I hate, or kill, someone like Van?

The Griffin behind him remained grounded, colossal wings spread wide as if for flight, its raptor beak wide. Like a sentry guarding its master's gate, the Griffin spoke to Van, tail lashing and black-tufted ears canted backward in annoyance.

Van turned his head and laughed over his shoulder, as the Griffin relaxed and shook its head. It furled its wings over its shoulders as it paced away from him. I swear it laughed along with him; its eagle's beak parted and eyes lit with high humor. I'd forgotten how a Griffin's, or the dreaded Minotaur's, facial expressions could mirror a human's so completely I knew he'd turned the Griffin's annoyance into a joke, and the deadly Griffin fell headlong into it.

Despite his light conversation, and thwarting of the vicious creature's anger, I didn't miss the quick, affectionate seizure of Iyumi's hand. Her tiny hand engulfed in his calloused palm, his thumb teased her knuckles.

Ye gods. I recognized that simple yet profound gesture of a lover. I'd done it a hundred times, more, to Sofia. In that simple move, he laid bare his deepest emotions. While his grin spoke a single book, his actions spoke not just volumes but an entire set.

Dammit, that boy loves her.

Not as a liege to his mistress. Such a love was both expected and boring. Oh, no, my boy Van's heart stood forth as clearly as a war banner on a windy day in his jade eyes. He gazed up at her with such a stark longing that my conscience kicked me in the groin.

Rapidly, muttering under my breath, I searched for her reaction. She should know what that simple knuckle rub meant. I waited, my shoulders tense, for the intense and irate reaction of an outraged female.

But she didn't slap his face, or kick him in the chin, or curse him for his audacity. She should pull her hand from his with a yank and harangue him in outraged female fury. Like me, Princess Yummy liked him.

Uh...Timeout.

Light dazzled from her blue eyes as she gazed downward. Though she failed to smile, her hand in his didn't respond, and her body sat straight and tense in her saddle, she responded to his subtle affections. Those wondrous eyes glowed. *She* glowed. She rested her hand in his as a monarch might her servant's as she praised him for bringing her food to her hot this time. Yet, her soul burned in her beautiful eyes.

Gods be damned. She loves him. She loves *him.*

My gorge rose as did my hot jealousy. I knew my eyes went flat at the same moment my fingers clenched around my sword's hilt. I couldn't find hatred for Van before, but I surely found a reason to spill his blood now. "That's my woman," I muttered, under my breath. "I don't want to kill you, boy. But I will if I have to."

"M'lord?"

I spun around, crouched, ready to defend myself.

Buck-Eye emerged from the thorns and branches, muttering. He snagged his hands and pulled them, bleeding, from the nasty thicket. Trickles of red crisscrossed his skin and dripped into the sleeve of his tan tunic as he raised his hand and sucked at the scratches. His eyes widened as they passed from me to the scene in the sky behind me.

I hastily shut the vision down and shoved the jewel under my shirt. I coughed, clearing my throat. I half-drew my sword, only to let it slide back into its sheath as the knight gaped. "Buck-Eye, what—"

"What was that, m'lord?" he asked, his tone soft. "Magic?"

Wild explanations careened through my skull as I sought for anything, anything however plausible, to explain the vision of an armed camp in the western sky. "It's er . . . not exactly what it seems, you see— "

"It was, wasn't it? That was magic." His dark eyes searched the horizon behind me, yet remained quiescent of any animosity toward me. His hand gripped his sword's hilt. I crouched low, drawing my own blade. "What of it?" I snapped, ready to kill or be killed. "What do you care?"

His blank eyes returned to me. Sharpened. Focused. *He s going to attack—*

"Will you teach me?"

"What?" I gawked like a fool staring down a steep precipice where the light ended and hell began.

His face flushed with eagerness, Buck-Eye strode forward. My instincts had zero time to prepare before he knelt at my feet. Had he intended violence, I'd now be kneeling before my maker.

Dark eyes rapt, Buck-Eye stared upward into mine. "Teach me your magic, Prince Flynn. My liege lord and king."

Caught unprepared I kept my sword out and leveled. Did he truly mean it? Or was this some odd ruse to catch me in a confession and execute me for a traitor and a necromancer? My heart wanted to believe him, yet my gut screamed its inarticulate warning. Soften and die. Drop your guard and die. Or just die.

Buck-Eyes gaze wandered past mine and searched the blank sky behind me. They flitted back and forth, never still, and gave me the heebie-jeebies. I alternated between icy cold rushing through my veins and a hot, sweet rush of triumph. He was like me, searching for answers–no, he was a trap and my clumsiness the bait. He wanted to slit my throat. No, he yearned for the same freedom I craved. The sweet, provocative freedom magic provided, the freedom from care, grief, and pain. He, too, sought absolution for his crimes, wished to change the road he stood upon.

My head swum against a tidal wave of emotions, drowning in the worry Buck-Eye sought my life and the new hope that he, like me, searched for answers in a world gone stark raving mad.

His hand left his sword's hilt and raised, palm upward. No, he didn't command my loyalty as I commanded his. No, he demanded my attention and I gave all. A single dart of licking flame danced across his creased and hard calloused palm. Like a tiny Faery, it lit upon his fingers before, laughing, dodged amid his hard soldier's knuckles. Like a moth on fire, it danced and spun, bowing low before flitting across his hand to spring from fingertip to fingertip.

Buck-Eye turned his palm downward, but the flame still lingered. Trotting in precise measurements, it hopped from one finger to the next and on down the line. One, two, three, four and a final five, his thumb, lit with merry fires left in its wake. These bright gems remained like faint torches, burning without harm as they fed on nothing I saw.

"They've come like this since I was but a wee lad," Buck-Eye admitted, his voice hoarse, roughened. His eyes never left the dancing, happy flames. "Never could I control them. They come when I call, but all they do is play games. Like children."

Buck-Eye raised damp eyes toward mine. I didn't see a toughened, battle-hardened mercenary on his knees before me. I saw a large man, scarred, wounded, and frightened of what he didn't understand. My gut clenched, not with fear this time, but with elation. *I wasn t alone.* Neither was Buck-Eye. I knew what he felt, for his thoughts, his worries, and yes, his nightmares, mirrored mine.

Buck-Eye reached for the magic that filled his blood. The magic we both were instilled at birth, but had no clue how to control. Through my mother, my powers had increased to the levels the gods themselves owned. Buck-Eye had only touched the surface of his.

"Teach me," he said simply. "Please, m'lord."

"I'll . . ." My throat shut down tight and I tried again. "I'll try, *micha na.*"

[249]

Why I used the ancient word for 'brother', I'll never know. It came to my lips unbidden, yet seemed right, somehow. Proper. For Buck-Eye was my friend, my brother, in magic.

"Think of your fire," I said, my voice hoarse, treacherous sweat sliding down my cheek, dampening my shirt. I shoved my sword back into its scabbard. "Imagine it–think of sending it into that stump over yonder. Think of it, then *will* it."

Buck-Eye bowed his head, closed his eyes.

A fraction of a second later, the dead, dry stump whooshed into sudden flame. I recoiled, raising my arm at the same instant Buck-Eye seized my belt and pulled me backward, with him, out of harm's way. Fire boiled out of the stump, black smoke coiling in huge plumes upward into the blue, cloudless sky. *That ll catch some attention,* I half-thought, raising my hand to protect my face from its searing heat. Buck-Eye's strength dragged me clear, and I had a fraction of a moment to appreciate that he didn't want me dead.

"Shit," I stammered, staggering to regain my balance as Buck-Eye's hand under my arm steadied me. "You don't pull any punches, do you, bro?"

Buck-Eye flushed, his face darkening to red under his embarrassed grin. "I reckon, er–I pushed a bit hard, m'lord. Forgive me."

I eyed the fire sidelong as new warmth spread into my soul. I straightened my tunic, adjusted my swordbelt and grinned. I punched Buck-Eye in his shoulder. "You done good, boy."

His answering grin brought a swift chuckle from me without my permission. "I did good? You mean it? I didn't expect–"

"You didn't expect to learn so quick?" I asked. "You're an adept, Buck-Eye."

"A–a . . . what?"

I laughed. "You're a fast learner, *micha na.*" I half-heartedly punched my fist toward his face. I followed that with a juvenile strike toward his gut, and ended with a pat to his tanned cheek. No lord I ever knew bantered with his men in this fashion, yet I couldn't seem to help myself. Where once I felt alienated from the soldiers who served me, now I felt one with this man. A toughened mercenary with his loyalty bought and paid for with gold, Buck-Eye grinned at me with all the innocence of a strapping boy.

"That I am, m'lord," he replied, fending off my fists with his extended palms, laughing.

I stopped my play and straightened. "Now *will* the fire out."

Buck-Eye stopped. The grin vanished from his bristly, leathery face. "Uh–"

"Will – the – fire – out." I gestured toward the unmarked bushes, trees, dry grasses and the forests above and below us. "We don't want a forest fire, Buck-Eye. Put your fire out."

"I don't–"

I put my hand on his tense shoulder and gazed into his unhappy dark eyes. "You do. Fire is your slave. Make it so, *micha na.*"

Buck-Eye frowned at the flames and frowned, concentrating. Raising his hands like a schoolboy practicing wizardry, he spoke slowly, intoning, "Go away."

"Will them gone," I whispered in his ear.

He clenched his fists, his face tightening.

Instantly, the flames withered and died. Buck-Eye gaped, his jaw slack, as the flames obeyed him instantly. I tried to smother a grin. I know I failed.

The blackened stump continued to smoke, soft tendrils of white-blue drifted upward before the mountain breeze caught them and tore them to pieces. Heat still baked off the charred wood, yet every ember within its scarred heart dimmed and failed, their red eyes changing to black as they were consumed and lost under Buck-Eye's command.

"See?" I said, gesturing toward the twice-dead stump. "You're an adept."

But Buck-Eye's face darkened, grew troubled. "Them's just like us, m'lord," he said, his tone pitched low, thoughtful. "The Bryn'Cairdhans. I'm not a smart man, not by a long shot. But why do we hate them if theys just like us? Why do we fight them?"

"Because they are evil."

Blaez's smarmy, *1-know-everything* tone emerged from the thorny thicket.

I spun, my sword out and ready. Buck-Eye worked faster, however. Before my mind associated voice to face, he'd shoved me behind him and pointed his own tip toward the–cursing, complaining, grunting with the effort of forcing his way through sharp brambles that pierced anything soft–Commander Blaez. As Blaez was nothing save soft, he gave them ample opportunity to scratch, cut, tear and otherwise cause Blaez great pain.

"Hellfire and damnation," Blaez choked, sucking his bloody scratches as he contemplated the rents in his otherwise pristine cloak of scarlet and pink. Thorns tugged at his woolen breeches, gouging holes in his thighs, calves and the kidskin boots that covered him from toes to knees. His spurs caught on tough vines, forcing him to regain his balance with the use of waving arms, and the handy tree with which to grab hold.

Free of tree trunk and thorns, Blaez scowled, straightening his tunic with an imperious air. "What are you doing here, Prince," he demanded. "We saw fire–"

"We thought you in dire need of help," Boden added, sliding through the thicket as if greased. Not a hair out of place, he stood beside a grunting Blaez with his hands behind his back. At parade rest, like any disciplined soldier, his eyes watched Blaez carefully without turning his head. I noticed, with sour humor, no thorn cut pierced his flesh nor marred his clothing.

As Blaez lurched forward, bent at the waist as though searching for a place to puke, Boden politely stepped aside. His movement permitted Galdan to, cursing, push his way through the tough brambles with far less ease than Boden. Fetching up beside Blaez, he shook blood from his hands. Blaez straightened and shoved him away, angry. Like an eel, Boden slid between the two, at the same moment Blaez scowled heavily and snapped, "Don't flick your damn blood on me, you idiot."

Galdan dipped his head, muttering an apology and handily stepped another two paces from his master. So enthralled at how easily Blaez was separated from his only protection, I almost missed the dark anger and hate directed my way.

"I heard talk of magic," Blaez sneered, stepping one pace toward me. "You have magic, Prince. A treasonous evil punishable by death."

Like a shadow, Boden paced with him as Galdan busied himself wiping his hands on his cloak, his dark blonde head lowered to his task. I couldn't help but wonder, in a fleet thought, that he deliberately placed Blaez in a position of helplessness. Did he hate Blaez? Or was he truly that incompetent?

"Are you my father's judge?" I asked, putting my hands on my hips, grinning. "Do you plan to halt this mission and drag me home in chains to face execution?"

"Damn straight I will, boy," Blaez snarled, drawing his sword. "I can kill you here and now, and none will fault me for it."

As he made to lunge toward me, Boden's dagger in his ribs effectively halted him. As Blaez raised his right arm, sword in hand, my young bodyguard slid his blade in, point-deep. As a wound, it surely wasn't enough to kill and hardly a wound worth mentioning. I bet my soul that upon healing it wouldn't leave so much as a scar behind.

While not killing him, it made a very effective point on my father's right hand maniac. Boden's skills deftly and wordlessly informed Commander Blaez that his heart lay inches from a fatal thrust. That tiny and utterly insignificant quarter inch of metal sliding like molten ice between the bones that sheltered one's simple existence–well, maybe it'll miss anything vital.

One can hope, I reckon.

Make a tiny move toward Prince Flynn and you re toast, Boden's dirk spoke, although Boden himself said nothing. Allegiance to my father didn't include dying while trying to place me under arrest, apparently. Blaez's dark, savage expression of hate changed to one of almost comical surprise. He froze, sword arm up. His blade tilted and drooped downward as his grip on the hilt slackened. "Galdan?"

"Sir?"

The battle-scarred merc glanced up, pale blue eyes inquiring. Before Galdan realized his master's life was in danger, Buck-Eye leveled his own sword at Galdan's throat.

[253]

"Don't move, boyo," Buck-Eye advised conversationally. "And no one gets hurt."

"Are you all insane!" Blaez roared. "He's got magic! That's a criminal offense. In the name of the King, I demand you arrest him for necromancy!"

"I don't think so, Commander," Boden replied. "My prince appointed me his royal bodyguard. I intend to keep that body intact and safe from all enemies. Unfortunately, that list includes you."

"Why you treacherous son of a whore—"

"Blaez."

I spoke his name softly, without nuance, my tone low. I might have shouted and struck him across his jaw for the effect my voice had on him. He froze, his pig's eyes wide, angry and scared; his gaze locked on mine. A flip of my hand sent Boden, and his knife, one step behind him. Ready to pounce should Blaez not behave, Boden stood at Blaez's shoulder. At the same time, Buck-Eye's sword urged Galdan to step further from Blaez's side. Galdan raised his hands in surrender, carefully crossing his fingers behind his neck.

"How did you set off your bombs, Blaez?" I asked.

"How did—what's that got to do with—that's not important!"

"Oh, I think it is important." I hooked my thumbs in my swordbelt as I stepped lightly toward him. "I know you set off your bombs with magical spells."

"What? That's outrageous! This isn't about me, boy! You're the practitioner of evil witchery—"

Mid-harangue, I launched a black shadow. Shaped like the head of a spear, it flew straight toward Blaez's chest. Its tip as sharp and deadly as a real spearhead, it would cleave Blaez's chest in two upon contact.

Instantly, instinctively, his hands flew upward and outward. With a shout, he pumped both fists. Lightning shot from them in twin flashes of bright light. His twin bolts of white hot energy struck my black spear. As all metal eventually turns to dust, my flying death dissolved into dark ash that fell to the ground at Blaez's feet.

He panted heavily as though having run ten leagues, treacherous sweat sliding down his cheeks. His eyes bulged as he realized what my spear truly intended. Like a fish, he swam into my net and lay caught, strangling, impotent. His mouth open and closed spasmodically, as though trying to breathe air when he craved water.

I smiled.

Blaez gaped. "You–"

"–have magic," I finished, my thumbs still hooked and my hip cocked. "As do you. Should my father learn of your treachery, your head will rest beside mine above the city gates."

"That's–"

I closely examined the ground at my feet. "Blackmail, yes, I know."

"It's despicable!"

"It's all in how you choose to look at it. Right, Commander?"

As Blaez stammered and fumed, trying to find words to explain to Galdan that I arranged the entire façade, of course he didn't have magic, the whole thing was a joke, see, Galdan stared from Blaez to me and back again. I didn't know if he wanted to run or vomit or both.

I reached out my arm and pulled Blaez under it. He stank of sweat, sulphur and the sour odor of old hate, but he moved with me easily enough. His panting calmed, yet the oily runnels still slid down his ruddy cheeks. The odor of his fear intensified.

"Come now, Commander," I said quietly, easily, walking him away from the others and toward the mountain's edge. "Let's not be enemies. Our King commanded us take Princess Iyumi and the child to him. Only then can our sacred land be safe. That's what we both desire, isn't it? The subjugation of their land and the supremacy of ours?"

"Yes," he replied, his tone hoarse. "Yes, of course it is."

"Then help me," I said, my free arm waving toward the distant skyline. "Let's work together to make it happen. Will you do that? Will you work with me?"

Blaez moved out from under my arm, with diffident courtesy, yet didn't step far. He eyed me openly, yet with a small measure of respect in his piggish, muddy eyes. "I'll help you, Flynn," he replied slowly. "Just as long–"

"It's our secret."

He nodded sharply. "What do you want, then?"

Without taking the jewel from my shirt, I willed the horizon to show me Van's current location. I didn't need it in my hand, after all. Its contact with my skin was enough. From one end of the sky to the other, Van and his friends rode across a rocky bluff. Malik cantered at the front, his black tail bouncing across the tundra. A cavalry soldier loped on his heels, as an enormous Griffin blew low over their heads to sail upward into the sky before banking high and around. It buzzed their heads again, blowing their hair into their eyes as it flew in the opposite direction to repeat the maneuver. The cute deer bounded on tiny legs in their wake, often racing away to either the left or the right to search out potential problems.

Van rode his black and white horse with neither saddle nor bridle. Had I not needed him dead so badly, I'd want him to teach me how he did that. Bayonne was a good horse, from one of the best bloodlines in all of Raithin Mawr. But–

That mare made him look like a carter's draft beast.

Princess Yummy loped my roan stallion at his flank, looking at nothing but straight ahead of her. The blue worked hard to keep up with Van's mare, sweating lightly. The piebald carried Van with effortless ease, her tail sweeping the ground behind her. I knew that blue roan had enormous stamina, yet I recognized a beast that grew tired. Unable to travel faster than their slowest beast, they'd be forced to rest their animals and soon.

A Griffin, on the ground, galloped at the same speed as the horses, its wings half-furled. Often spreading those huge spans at times to sail up or down a hill, the Griffin kept pace with little effort. While a Griffin running on all fours was surprising to me, I knew it would never tire as the horses might.

An eagle screamed past their heads. It cruised back under the sky-borne Griffin's wake, its feathers ruffled but its flight intact. Circling slowly over Malik's black head, its beak bent down as his face under that rayed star brow-band gazed up. Yet, another Shifter delivered his reports to their Lord Commander.

Stark mountains lay ahead of them. I recognized them– the mountains that bordered our beloved Raithin Mawr from magical

Bryn'Cairdha. The Shin'Eah, their ranges of treacherous and jagged peaks clothed in year-round snow, kept our two nations separated. Only fools tried to cross them without guidance, and its deadly passes quite effectively halted any potential wars. They were far too difficult to traverse with an army to feed.

"I can take us to them," I said. "No more chasing after them, wearing ourselves out. With my magic, we can set another ambush, and take the princess. We can be home tomorrow. What say you, Commander?"

Blaez nodded. "Let's get this over with."

"Good. We'll–"

"Why are they going that way?" asked Boden.

I didn't let go of the vision, however, and permitted Blaez, Boden, Buck-Eye and a rapt Galdan to watch as the enemy crossed the highland landscape toward our mountains. None took their eyes from the scene before them, and watched with the avid gazes of the utterly fascinated.

"Do you recognize that area?" I asked him.

Boden nodded. "I think so, m'lord. If they keep to this course, they'll enter a shallow valley, a narrow one. A deep river cuts through it, where they'll have to water their mounts."

"Are you sure?"

Boden stepped toward the vision in the sky as though getting closer might reveal certain truths to him alone. He glanced left, right, up, down and peered into the sky as though studying a map. *He is my navigator after all.*

"M'lord, there's no other source of water," he said slowly, still gazing, rapt. "Not for miles. They've no choice but the Auryn River Valley. They must rest and refresh their animals and fill their skins."

"When will they get there?"

Boden crossed his arms and stroked his chin with his fingers. He frowned at the scene before him. "Within two hours, give or take. M'lord."

"We have that much time to prepare. Blaez?"

Commander Blaez stepped up beside Boden and scowled. Not at me this time, but at the situation. "How steep the valley walls?"

he asked, peering intently, his words directed to my young bodyguard. "What's to the north? The south? How deep is the river?"

At Boden's swift answers, Blaez continued to scowl, yet I recognized a tactical genius when I saw one. As Boden answered his rapid-fire questions, I watched a plan hatch in Blaez's brain. Last time, Van's ingenuity thwarted Blaez. Blaez never forgot nor forgave. He intended that Van not thwart him a second time.

As the pair plotted and sketched out a plan, I smiled to myself. *Yummy, you ll be mine come nightfall.*

CHAPTER 9

When a Plan Comes Together

"Stop looking at her."

Rain fell in a mist so light I saw little of it, but felt its tingle along my skin and tasted its sweetness on my lips. The highland hills lay wreathed in a greyish haze, low-lying clouds cutting off the early daylight's shine. Purple flowers amid the heather dimmed, just as the granite rocks darkened with the layer of moisture over their rough skins.

Sheepish, I dragged my eyes away from the sight of Iyumi seated on a boulder in the dawn's grey shadows as Aderyn brushed out the lengths of that incredible silver-gilt hair. What light there was glimmered off those tresses as my cousin set the brush aside and began the arduous process of plaiting that heavy mass into a thick yet practical braid. "Can't seem to help it," I muttered as Windy stood over my shoulder. "She's so—"

I tacked up the roan stallion, my fingers wrapped in the girth strap that never quite made it to the buckle. The blue munched the thin, high-meadow grass, taking only the smallest steps forward as though knowing he should stand still. I'd discovered I quite liked this horse's quiet and affable nature, his rugged athleticism, and incredible conformation. I half-wondered if Kiera might find him acceptable. Yet, she turned her graceful head away, refused to tolerate him within her territorial bubble unless both were working. During the off-hours, she rejected his advances with pinned ears and a threatening rear hoof.

"She's been staring at you, too."

I spun around. "You've seen her?"

Windy preened his left wing, his beak chewing at his feathers as the one eye I could see gleamed with humor. "I didn't, no. But I overheard Aderyn tell Kasi that Her Highness tends to watch your back as you ride. Maybe she just admires your horsemanship."

My elation deflated like a loose bladder. "No doubt."

The roan sighed and snorted, and I heard the leather slide through the buckle's hasp. I'd never tighten a girth too soon or too tight, but permitted letting the horse adjust to it gradually. Having been a horse many times, I knew what an overly tight girth felt like and seldom forced that on another. If the roan felt gratitude, he didn't show it. Instead, his heavy charcoal tail smacked me across the face.

I sighed. Brushing stinging tears from my eyes, I glanced over my shoulder, and the roan's saddle, at Iyumi. "She's too high above me."

"I know." Windy scratched his right talon behind his ear. "A cockroach looks down on you."

"Excuse me, Lieutenant?"

Windy laughed, his beak wide and his predatory eyes dancing. "Don't try the offended officer act on me, laddie. Oh, excuse me . . . sir."

With a gesture, I invited him to perform the anatomically impossible as he laughed. "You may be a First Captain, Van," Windy said, rising and spreading his tremendous wings. "But you're a half-decent guy."

"Only half-decent?"

"You barely reach the half-way mark."

"Go–"

Windy lifted his head, beak parted, and perked his ears forward. "Now that's a mighty fine female."

I followed his gaze. Sky Dancer stood on all fours, her black-tufted lion tail lashing, arguing heatedly with Edara. Eagle's eyes snapping, Sky Dancer gestured imperiously with her talon toward the north and glowered down at Edara. The red-headed Centaur maid lifted her bow and pointed down the shallow valley, talking and gesturing with excitement. She thought she won the clash, her voice high and triumphant until Sky Dancer stalked away, angry. Edara stared after her, her smile seeping from her face like wine from a skin that someone just stabbed a knife into.

"Except she has no eyes for anyone but you."

"You're delusional," I snorted. She hates my guts, you know that. I almost got her killed."

"Correction." Windy's voice took on a didactic tone. "Cian almost got her killed. You, however, risked your life to save hers."

"That doesn't mean–"

"Can it, meathead," Windy snapped, annoyed. "You're dumber than a box of rocks and twice as ugly. You haven't the brains the gods gave–"

"Kasi likes you though."

Windy halted, mid-harangue, and studied Kasi, beyond Iyumi and Aderyn's trim forms to the Griffin practicing her moves. On a tall hillock to our north, the sleek, smallish Kasi leaped sideways and skyward, slashing with her front talons at the shadows created by the dawn's half-light. Coached by First Lieutenant Grey Mist, she spun and dove, her wings half-furled, her lion hind claws digging deep trenches into the highland heather. As Misty feigned an attack, Kasi jumped high and to the right, great wings carrying her upward, landing at Misty's left flank. Her talons grazed his lion flesh.

Had she been serious, Grey Mist's bowels might very well spill onto the high mountain soil. Misty extolled her efforts while she preened, her amber eyes glowing. As he seldom found much to compliment in his students, approval from him meant high praise indeed.

[261]

"Too flighty," Windy observed critically. "I like my girls a bit more . . . grounded."

"Easier to catch them that way."

"Take Dancer now."

Windy's beak jerked toward Sky Dancer as she paused to glare over her massive shoulder toward Edara before sitting down. Her lion tail continued to lash in feline aggravation as she surveyed the camp and its activities. Malik and Padraig stood side by side, talking, arms folded across their chests. They pretended to watch Kasi's lesson, but their blank stares informed me they discussed a topic far more troubling. I didn't need to be a fly buzzing about their rumps to know they spoke of bitchy princesses, red witches, and yours truly.

Edryd dumped half a skin of water on the nearest campfire, then kicked dirt over the steaming embers. The sharp, tangy odor of water dousing burning wood, and the fire's subsequent spitting and hissing protest, brought my attention from Malik and Padraig's conversation. Absently, I plucked the arrow from my belt and toyed with it. Edryd: the unit's top shot.

I killed his father.

My guilt rose to nudge me in the ribs. Seizing my flask, I tossed a mouthful of burning liquid down my gullet. The pain eased a fraction. I took another small swallow and tucked the flask away with a sigh. As usual, the alcohol scattered agony and remorse into manageable segments, enabling me to control my self-castigation–for a few hours, anyway. I cast a glance sidelong, suspecting my bad habit uncovered, but Windy never noticed.

"She's one tough bird," Windy went on. "She's beautiful, and talented and a credit to the Captain. She can fly better than anyone in the Atan, fight like a lion and has a heart of gold. Her eyes–I'd kill for one look from those incredible eyes. Van, are you listening to me?"

"Eyes," I answered. "Heart of gold. Just do what you do best, old son, and she'll notice you."

I turned back to the roan, who'd sneaked away three strides, and stuck the arrow back into my belt. I ducked my head, thus avoiding another tail sweep, and swiftly tightened his girth.

"Do what I do best?" Windy asked, his voice plaintive. "Just what do I do best? Van? Van!"

Taking the beast's reins, I walked him toward the boulder just as Malik's drill sergeant voice rolled across the highland meadow. "Lieutenant Grey Mist! Lieutenant Wind Warrior! Scout north and south. Corporal Kasi, you're on the roof. Lieutenant Gaear, messenger and an eagle. Sergeant Aderyn, the rear-guard, if you please. First Captain Vanyar, you stick to Her Highness like stink on shit. Lieutenant Sky Dancer, you stick to him the same."

Rather than turn and salute as protocol demanded, I waved my hand over my head in acknowledgment as Aderyn finished her task by tying a heavy ribbon around the silver braid's end. She greeted me with a smile as Iyumi rose gracefully and turned.

"Captain Vanyar," she said, her tone as neutral as her placid expression. "We're ready to travel, I trust?"

"Lieutenant Padraig and Corporal Edara! You're the vanguard. Move!"

"I hope so," I said, taking her by her tiny, trim waist and settling her into the roan's saddle. "Or Malik is wearing out his lungs for nothing."

"Highness." Aderyn dipped into a quick curtsey.

Sky Dancer floated across the heather and moss to land behind me. She didn't furl her wings, as whatever she and Edara argued over still rankled. They remained high and outstretched, ready to propel her heavy form into the light mountain breeze. "Show some bloody respect, Van," she snapped, her tail lashing. "He's the Lord Captain."

Aderyn changed forms. Her doe bounded away on legs like slender sticks, toward the south, our rear. Her lifted tail flashed like a star dropped to earth, and she leaped a tall hedgerow with all the effort I might employ to lift a mug of spiced ale. Malik liked her to tag behind us in that shape, as potential enemies sliding up behind us had no clue that a slender deer might contain the fangs of a tiger.

I laughed over my shoulder. "I daresay you've never heard Malik fart after drinking too much spiced apple wine. Had you witnessed that, you'd never fear him again."

"Gods, what an image!" Sky Dancer chuckled. "Vanyar, you just robbed me of two years' worth of trembling in my boots."

"Of the two, Malik's gas is far more dangerous."

Sky Dancer laughed and stepped lightly away, her great wings furling to half-mast. "Vanyar, he'll kill you, one of these days."

"You have the gift, Van," Iyumi said quietly, gazing down.

"What gift, Highness?"

I still held her hand, and couldn't help but appreciate the soft texture of her knuckles as I rubbed my thumb over them. I breathed in her dusky, feminine odor of lilac and leather, and breathed out misery. What I'd give to have those eyes look into me and see–

She stiffened. Her fingers gripped mine tight. "Don't you feel that?"

Without letting go of her hand, I shut my eyes and breathed deeply. I shunted aside all emotions and outside distractions, calming myself as I entered my center. Dropping into a light trance, I searched with magic, with my power, setting it adrift upon the light high mountain breeze. What? What did she sense–*There.* I felt them. Like twin moons in the night sky. *Eyes.* Eyes watching. Watching us.

"The Red Duchess?" I asked, keeping my body relaxed. I gave nothing away to those spying on us, let them believe themselves unsuspected. I continued to grin up at her until I thought my jaws might break.

"Van?" Sky Dancer asked, having heard what we said to one another. Her body language spoke of battle, and that's the last message I wanted sent to those spying orbs.

"Chill, Dancer," I ordered, still smiling. "Preen your wings. Now."

As Sky Dancer extended her right wing and chewed on it, her raptor's eyes watched me intently.

"I don't think so." Iyumi took her hand from mine and adjusting the way she sat in the saddle. "I don't feel evil. Do you?"

I dropped the feigned smile as I set her small boots into her stirrups and fussed with the fastenings on the roan's harness. Under my breath, I whistled low, as I refit the bridle to the roan's sensitive mouth.

All at once, the sensation of being watched vanished. Like a sigh upon the wind, it trailed away to dissipate as though having never been there at all.

"They're gone," I murmured.

Iyumi's breath expelled from her lungs along with her obvious tension. Her body relaxed in her saddle as she gathered her reins. "Who then?"

Kiera ambled up behind me and her nose nuzzled the back of my neck. I shook my head, half-turning toward my horse. "If not the witch, then I don't know. I'm sorry, Your Highness. My guessing game needs an upgrade."

She found a tiny smile, one with more warmth that the previous one contained. "You'll keep me safe, won't you, Captain?"

I vaulted aboard Kiera's broad back. Without a backward look, Malik trotted away, Edryd in his chestnut's saddle following on his heavy black tail. Sky Dancer leapt skyward, enslaving the light westward wind, her wings stretched to their fullest. The wind they created blew my hair into my eyes and whipped the roan's mane into a tempest. She circled several rods above, her beak angled downward from between her massive shoulders as she watched me. Waiting. Ready to protect me.

I dipped my brow and saluted Iyumi with a surprising, for me, lack of mockery in it. "Or die trying, Your Highness."

"Don't say that too often, Captain," Iyumi commented dryly as she nudged the roan into a gallop. "Or I might trust you."

The highland terrain slowly rose the further north we rode, the jagged peaks of the Shin'Eah looming like an evil pall. Muted sunlight tried to break through the annoying half-mist that accompanied us through the morning and into the afternoon, but failed miserably. The weather dampened not just our clothes and hair, but also whatever humor that chanced to rise. As Malik stalked a hundred rods in front, Edryd riding at his flank, Sky Dancer trotted regally next to Iyumi's roan stallion and told a joke or three. Her attempts to bring a smile to Iyumi's face failed as utterly as the sun.

Gaear blew in from time to time to deliver his reports, the breeze from his wings lifted Malik's damp hair from his shoulders. As Malik didn't pause or react, I assumed the news Gaear passed was uninteresting and without any imminent threat of danger. I rode Kiera several rods behind the roan, surveying the country we rode through, speculating. Steep and rocky, tall columns of boulders that had broken away from the Shin-Eah a millennia ago lined the hills. I knew Flynn hadn't given up. Yet, these hills could easily conceal him as he plotted his next move.

High up, on the ridge to the west, Alain trotted his horse. Well-trained and dedicated, he often paused to turn about, checking his back-trail. When he lifted his hands to his face, I knew he utilized his magic to bring his view of the hills and valleys up close. Seeing nothing alarming, he once more trotted north, paralleling us. I swiveled on Kiera's back. Far to our rear, Valcan flew in his raven shape, circling endlessly, also watching for Flynn and his cronies. Gaear buzzed from him to Alain, then flew hard to circle over Padraig and Edara in the vanguard, a half-mile ahead. Kasi, Grey Mist and Windy flew high against the dismal clouds.

"Where are you, Flynn?" I whispered to myself. With the vicinity a prime location for an ambush, why hadn't he created one? Did he conceal himself from our eyes with his magic even now, tripping hard at our heels? I knew of several spells that could uncover a hidden magician – but my powers weren't strong enough. Perhaps I should ride ahead and ask Malik to try one or two.

Just as she answered my knees and struck a strong lope, Kiera stumbled heavily. Her fetlocks and nose struck highland heather as I was unceremoniously tossed over her shoulder. Instinctively, I rolled, and continued rolling, until I was out from under should her rear quarters sail over her head and crush me under them. Rising quickly to my feet, unhurt, I reached for Kiera as she scrambled to regain all four hooves under her. She didn't appear hurt, but her ears canted backward in annoyance and humiliation.

"Van?"

Ignoring Malik's voice, I ran my hands down her forelegs, searching for injuries. All I found was a scratch on her soft muzzle and a starkly bruised ego. Her black tail lashed as she tossed her head from my hands, unwilling to look me in the eyes. Never in all the years she'd been toting me around had she ever stumbled, much less fallen. And never before had I come off her. Angry with herself, Kiera felt disgraced and shamed, and I suspected she wanted the earth to swallow her whole.

"Easy, lass," I murmured, stroking her neck. "It's all good, happens to the best of us, right?"

"Captain Vanyar!"

I waved my hand. "Go on. We'll catch up."

Princess Iyumi turned in her saddle, her hand on the cantle as Malik continued jogging, watching me with concern. I offered her a grin and swift salute as the roan loped on Malik's heels. Sky Dancer half-flew at her side, her beak swiveled toward me. "Van?"

"I just want to look her over," I replied. "Carry on."

As the group, with Gaear flying low overhead, cantered up the next hill, I walked at Kiera's side, watching for any lameness my hands and eyes missed. Outside of Kiera turning her face from me, she walked and trotted with her usual silky gaits, unencumbered by obvious pain. I rubbed her neck affectionately. "Don't beat yourself up, honey," I said, my tone light. "It's–"

The rumbling sound interrupted me, and I lifted my head. Slightly confused, I glanced first right, over Kiera's shoulder. Nothing save the ever-present drizzle and green-grey heather met my gaze. I glanced left and froze for a fraction of an instant.

Granite rocks and boulders as large as a serf's hut rolled in a swift avalanche down the steep hill. Perhaps our hoof-beats loosened the unstable pile, or perhaps the almost continuous rain undercut the soil holding it upright fell apart. No matter the cause, an implacable wall of broken stone fell toward me faster than Kiera's best race. I had two, maybe three, seconds before it struck us broadside.

Kiera!

In a wild, desperate, magical maneuver, I translocated her fifty rods up the hill. Well out of the danger zone. I'd heard of magicians using this ability to move an object from one place to another, I never had the chance, or the need, to try it myself. I didn't take time to think–I acted. And the terrible strain on my limited abilities took its toll. Lights flashed in my eyes, as my gut roiled in protest.

No time. The crashing rocks were but a rod away from burying me beneath them. I shifted shape.

I coiled myself into a ball, as hard as the granite that crashed into me, and carried me along with them. The Clan discouraged the shifting of one's shape into inanimate objects, and for good reason– the rock had no heart, lungs, blood or brain that a Shifter needed to survive. But I was always one to ignore protocol, and the rules were in place just so I could break them.

As one more rock among hundreds, I rolled safely down the hill until level ground ended the stampede. In a cloud of choking dust the drizzle couldn't damp down, the horde spread out and slowly stopped, its impetus contained at last. I stayed where I was, fearing to stand in case more boulders still fell, the last to arrive. No sense in removing my armor until no enemies threatened my life.

In the distance, Iyumi's voice rose on a scream. *"Van!"*

Under me, the ground trembled under the hooves of Malik, Kiera and Iyumi's stallion. Back down the hill they charged, risking yet another avalanche of loosened rocks. While I heard no more rumblings from above, I waited to revert into my usual irreverent self until I knew the area was secured. Sky Dancer, like Iyumi, screamed my name and I felt rather than saw her shadow pass over me, low overhead.

Minutes ticked slowly past as the four of them, plus Gaear, roamed amid the rock-fall, yelling my name, searching the area for any trace of me. I sighed. If any more rocks wanted to tumble south, I hoped Malik's power would stop them in their tracks. I unwound myself from the ball I shaped myself into, and slowly stood up. Unlike the usual change from a horse or a falcon into my own body, reverting from solid stone into breathing muscle and blood and tissue wasn't at all easy. Dizzy, shaking as though ill with the ague for months, I wanted to vomit. Instead, I coughed, clearing my lungs of rock dust and tried to avoid doubling over. "Over here," I choked, my hands on my knees.

"Van?"

"Vanyar!"

Sky Dancer shrieked, diving toward me, her wings wide and her beak agape. Malik dodged and leaped silent boulders as Iyumi hugged her roan's neck as she urged him into a reckless pace that might yet break his legs. Not to be outdone, Kiera outraced them all, and all but killed herself on the granite strewn slope after I almost killed myself saving her life. She ducked around a boulder higher than her head, and skidded on several small ones that rolled under her hooves. She slid hard, her quarters buckling under her, and all but slammed into me. I ducked before her chest collided with mine, and caught her mane in my hands.

"Quit," I gasped, "I'm cool, relax, it's all good."

Nickering in anxiety, Kiera nudged me with her muzzle, and in my weakness, I almost fell. Malik's strong arm under mine held me upright, and I leaned against the strong support of his massive shoulder. "Thanks," I managed, sweating rivers.

Iyumi slid from her roan's saddle and cannoned into me. "Tell me you didn't just do that," she snapped, her voice hoarse. "You didn't just do what I think you did."

"Uh," I stammered, "all right, I didn't."

"Liar," she hissed, her arm snaking around my waist. "You turned yourself into a rock, didn't you?" Her backhand smacked me across my arm. "You're not supposed to do that."

"Telling him what he's not supposed to do, Princess," Malik rumbled, "is like informing the tide it's not supposed to obey the moon. I wouldn't waste my breath."

"I'll waste my breath if I want to," she all but screamed, her fury directed at me. "How dare you frighten me like that? How dare you!"

"I, er, didn't intend to. Why would I?"

"Because you're in an inconsiderate ass, that's why."

Malik's firm grip on her arm tugged Iyumi away from me and into the implacable care of Sky Dancer. "He needs a spot of healing, Princess," Malik soothed, giving her a gentle push. "Please? Give us room?"

Muttering imprecations under her breath, Iyumi permitted Sky Dancer to lift her onto her stallion's back and led her a few paces away. Kiera had no such notions, and hovered at my back, her chin on my shoulder as Malik put his hand on my brow. Though I'd returned to my usual shape with all my organs intact, my experience as a rock sent my belly and nerves into hyper-drive. I sweated yet chilled at the same time. Although I felt sick, I had nothing in my gut to hurl. My head ached, and my sight tried to blacken.

Malik's healing power calmed my outraged stomach and quieted my revolting head. Strength returned to my muscles, and the bruises left by the other boulders I hadn't noticed withered and died. I straightened, breathing in a deep breath of relief, and chuckled.

"Thanks," I said, my hand on Malik's shoulder.

He gazed down, his expression dark. "You're lucky to be alive."

"It's not every day that one survives an avalanche– "

I cut off, my blood chilling in my veins. I recognized in his eyes what my instinct suddenly screamed: that wasn't a fluke of nature. That wasn't an accident I stumbled into. The persistent rain hadn't loosened anything, nor did the vibration of many hooves cause the hill to kick outward. Magic sent that rockslide careening into me and Kiera. Did Kiera truly stumble, or was that an act of ungodly power? I fell off–no, I was too good a rider, Kiera too good a mount, as everyone knew.

So what the hell happened?

My thoughts returned to that night when Padraig urged my fellow Atani to consider me not just a traitor, but to aid in my execution. I heard Padraig's voice within the depths of my mind. *"Shit happens,"* he whispered. *"So do accidents."*

Courteously shaking free of Malik's help, I stared north. Hard. To the tall hill we intended to climb a short distance away.

Edara must have vanished down the far side, for I didn't see her. Under a canopy of spruce, pine and white elm, Padraig stood quiet, his bulging arms crossed over his bare chest. He stared out and

[270]

down, toward the new river of rock on the pristine grey heather that hadn't been there three moments past. His dark eyes gleamed under his heavy brows, easily seen even from this distance. Unfolding his arms, Padraig lifted his right hand to chest level. In a gesture understood by all, Padraig's fingers crossed in that rapid-fire flicker that meant only one thing.

Vengeance.

Turning slowly about, Padraig loped across the hilltop and vanished under the trees.

"Water."

Malik's fist in the air brought Edryd's chestnut slithering to his haunches, mid-lope, behind him. Iyumi's sure hands on the stallion's reins brought the blue roan from a gallop to a walk within a few strides and without the drama. Kiera obeyed my sharply canted weight and slid to an effortless top beside and slightly behind the roan.

Gaear, on the other hand, swooped past and up, banking around for another pass as Malik turned around, scowling. He lifted the water skin attached to his belt to his lips, and squirted a thin stream into his mouth. He swallowed, and let it drop. The skin sagged like a dead animal, perhaps only a quarter full. "Princess? You have water?"

"Enough to fill a teacup."

"Van?"

"Not even that much."

"Corporal Edryd. Did you extinguish this morning's fires with water from our skins?"

"Yes, my Lord Captain."

I always considered Malik a fair and just commander, not prone to acting out of temper or fury. His discipline, while harsh, fit the crime. The close attempt on my life and his inability to prove anyone responsible put Malik into a foul temper. Had I not shoved Kiera between himself and Edryd, and seized his arm, his fist might well have knocked several teeth from the young cavalry soldier's face.

Paling, Edryd lowered his head and reined his red stallion away from his commanding officer. A blush crept up from his throat to his cheeks to finally seep out the tips of his ears. Only then did he recognize his folly.

"He's got all the experience of a babe in swaddling clothes," I said, my voice soft. "Maybe? Just this once, cut him some slack?"

"His idiocy is beyond incompetence," Malik gritted, his dark face infused with such a rage I blinked. "I ought to–"

"Slow down."

He jerked his arm from my hand. "Leave off, Captain," Malik snarled.

Dipping my brow, I dropped my chin over my fist clenched against my chest. "My Lord Captain Commander."

"Lieutenant Gaear," Malik bellowed. "Scout ahead and find us some effing water. And keep Padraig and Edara in the loop."

"My Lord Captain." Gaear's voice drifted off the high mountain wind as he sailed upon the currents and winged northward.

I sidled Kiera backward until my knee struck Iyumi's, and Sky Dancer lit upon the heather in front of me. She furled her wings across her broad shoulders, casting a swift glance from her raptor's eyes toward Malik. "What's gotten into him?"

Malik stomped away, his heavy black tail lashing his hindquarters and his arms folded across his chest. Striding heavily over the high-altitude plateau, his hooves kicked great divots from the tundra. He never glanced back, yet we followed as though anchored to him by steel cables. Neither of us shared with Iyumi or Sky Dancer that my accident was anything but.

"He's never this–"

"Strict?" I asked.

Sky Dancer's beak stretched into a griffin grin. "'Temperamental' was the word I considered appropriate."

At Malik's sudden flinch, I knew he heard every word. Nothing within a five hundred rods' radius of his ears passed unnoticed. Her words stung. Deep.

"This isn't a situation any of us want to be in," I said, my tone neutral. "None of us shall escape if the Red Bitch gets her claws on that child."

Sky Dancer shook her ears in chagrin. "You're right, of course–I–"

Iyumi's small left hand gripped my forearm with enough pressure her nails impressed half-moon shapes in my skin. Her flesh paled. "She's dead."

"The Bitch?" Sky Dancer asked, flaring her angel's wings. "Let's ruddy hope so. That certainly makes our job easier."

"Oh, gods–" I began.

"Not the...the w–witch," she stammered, her voice low and hoarse. "The mother. I felt her die." Her words broke over a deep-seated sob. "The gods weep."

As tears rolled down her cheeks, Malik wheeled and galloped into our small circle. His dark face thunderous, he shoved Kiera, and me, roughly aside. Sky Dancer saluted, her beak over her fisted chest, and backed away as Malik glared down at his princess. "What's this?"

Iyumi swiped her reddened cheeks with trembling fingers, her eyes as downcast as Dancer's beak. "We've less than three days to find her."

"More than enough time," I said brightly into the tense silence. "What say we gallop to her rescue, yes?"

"Princess? What happened, dammit? Where is the child?"

Iyumi brought her face up sharply. Her fine brows lowered as her thin, aristocratic face tightened. I recognized the danger signals and caught my breath, yet Malik continued to scowl as though preparing to reprimand a raw recruit. Iyumi's right fist rose slightly.

Powerless in magic, yet born with the power of the gods, the tiniest among us captured him with her fury. Malik froze. Locked within those blue depths, he, the most powerful magician born, could but stare down into her tight expression and clenched fist. His jaw sagged, but that's all the motion he commanded from his own body. Speak in his own defense? Not bloody likely.

"You forget yourself, my Lord Commander," Iyumi said, her voice soft, yet her tone harder than tempered steel. "In my father's absence, you owe your loyalty and duty to me. I am in charge here. Henceforth, you raise your voice to me again, and I'll have you hung from the nearest tree in chains."

"Princess," I began slowly, my mouth dry. "He didn't mean . . . he just gets . . . you know–"

"Shut up, Van," Malik said. "Your mouth runneth over."

His glance never flicked toward me. Instead, his former glower lightened into an almost-smile. "My life for yours, Your Highness," he said simply. "Accept my apologies and forgive my anger, and impatience. In my own defense, my rage is not truly for you, but for our enemies. I fear I may fail in my duty to you, and your revered father. I am in error, and Your Highness in the right."

Malik bowed low, abasing himself to the slender girl he could break in half with his fingers. He bent his foreleg, bending his entire human portion toward the heather under his hooves. His fist over his chest, his hair hanging over his face, he waited.

Iyumi cast a desperate glance in my direction, her voice loud inside my mind. '*What do I do?*"

"*What you do best.*"

"*I m best when I m a bitch.*"

"*You re better than that. Rise higher, my queen.*"

"Stand up, Commander," Iyumi said, her voice hoarse. "Be at ease. We're all under tremendous strain these days, are we not?"

As he rose up, he opened his mouth to speak. Forestalling him with her raised hand, she grinned up into his somber expression. "Just don't let it happen again."

Malik saluted, a quick thump to his chest. "Now, Your Highness. Tell me all. Please."

"The child is alone, Commander, and in dire need. She's yet young enough to require her mother in order to survive. We have but three days, at the most, to find her before she, too, dies from lack of nourishment and the elements."

"Do you know where, Highness?"

Half-turning in her saddle, Iyumi pointed north by northwest. Toward a tall peak, its shoulders mantled in white despite the late

[274]

summer's heat. Surrounded by smaller mountains, it dwarfed them all as a hen towers over her chicks. "In a cave, just below the snowline. We can make it if we push hard."

"Certainly, Your Highness," he replied, following her finger. "If we all flew on wings. No way can hooves cross all those leagues in three days. Impossible."

"It's your job to make the impossible possible." Iyumi arched a brow. "Isn't it, Commander?"

"Not without water," Malik grumbled sourly, studying the route. His dark eyes narrowed as he rapidly considered one strategy for another, weighing the risks against the gain.

"Lieutenant Gaear," he bellowed.

Gaear buzzed over the top of my head, the back wash of his wings sweeping my hair into my mouth and set Iyumi's eyes to squinting. He back-winged heavily to land atop a huge boulder to Malik's right. His talons scraped against granite, forcing me to shut my teeth against the bitter sound. Iyumi grimaced as Sky Dancer scowled.

"My Lord Captain."

"What have you to report?"

"A river, my Lord Captain," Gaear replied, awkwardly saluting with his right wing. "It follows that valley there. To the north. I think it's the Auryn."

"And Padraig?"

"Lieutenant Padraig and Corporal Edara found a ford, my Lord Captain," Gaear answered. "They but await your orders."

"How deep is this river?"

Gaear clicked his beak. "Corporal Edara reported it's about three rods deep, sir, yet quite wide. Might prove mildly difficult to cross. Sir."

"What are the locations of the others?"

"My Lord Commander, Lieutenants Grey Mist and Wind Warrior circle to the north and south, but have reported no enemies and nothing at all suspicious. Corporal Kasi is yet high against the sun, and reports the same, sir."

"Lieutenant Aderyn?"

"Has seen nothing out of the ordinary and remains a half-league to our rear. My Lord Captain."

Malik studied the area, the mountains, and the deep valley that cut through the steep chain like a green blade. Lifting his face, he shut his eyes and listened to the sough of the high mountain wind, the voices of the good spirits and perhaps his own gut. He stalked away, the sun flashing off his black rump as his tail bumped against his hocks.

"He worries," I said.

Iyumi glanced from Malik's stiff back to me and back again. "Surely we're safe? You heard the reports. There's no one around for miles."

I half-shrugged and tried for lightness. "Malik was born to worry. If he's got nothing to worry about, he'd invent something. Just to be sure– "

"You're an idiot, Vanyar." Gaear's high-pitched voice rose on the light wind as he circled, forgotten until now, low over our heads. With Malik leading the way, downhill, toward the wide valley and a necessary water source, Gaear found an unlooked-for opportunity to annoy me. "You know nothing about anything."

He swooped lower, forcing Iyumi to glance upward, and swipe her hair from her cheeks.

"Ignore him, Your Highness," Gaear said, his beak angling down as his bright yellow eyes burned with fervor. "He's a murderer and a traitor–"

Sky Dancer's heavy fist cracked across his eagle's chest. Though she obviously checked the blow to send him across the sky without actually harming him, his broken feathers swirled about in his wake. Most drifted to the ground at Kiera's feet while he wailed in anguish, his eagle's body sent careening across the highland meadow.

Wings extended, he caught himself before he crashed to the hard earth. Flapping hard, pinfeathers still drifting about like a burst pillow, he climbed into the blue sky, winging hard away from Sky Dancer's wrath. Malik, far to the front, glanced up at his swift passing.

"Your pardon, Highness," Sky Dancer said calmly, walking beside Iyumi's blue roan with wings furled and a calm equanimity that forced me to grin. "Gaear is a lout and his opinions are hardly worth the attentions of one such as yourself."

"My thanks, Lieutenant," Iyumi replied sweetly. "I'm grateful you've taken the time to repel any irritations I might encounter on this journey."

"Might I add–" I began.

"No."

Both Iyumi and Sky Dancer turned on me at the same time, within the same instant. Against two females, two powerhouses of feminine ire, I stood no chance. With a self-effacing grin, I backed Kiera away from them both, my face lowered. *Never aggravate a female,* I learned at my father's knee. No matter what the species.

Iyumi laughed up into Sky Dancer's down-ward angled parted beak. Sky Dancer, towering over the princess despite her seat on a tall horse, flared her great wings. I half-listened as she regaled Iyumi with the wild tale of finding me, drunk as a lord, facing down not one, not two, but three Raithin Mawrn mercenaries with but a stick in my hand. Of course, she rescued me from their evil clutches, scattered the mercs, and, naturally, saved the day.

I caught a shy, humorous glance from Iyumi over her shoulder as the roan trotted beside Sky Dancer's great height. I half-shrugged and rolled my eyes. Iyumi's grin widened as I sighed, and said something to Sky Dancer I couldn't catch.

That s not exactly how I remember the incident, I thought, bemused. Sky Dancer showed up, all right, but not after I, as sober as the High Vicar on Gods' Day, dispatched the mercs. I wiped my sword clean, and politely tolerated Dancer berating me, at length, for risking my life and safety over a trio of pond scum rejects. Sky Dancer never much liked my lone wolf attitude, or my serious need to keep her at arms' length. *Perhaps Windy has a point, after all,* I thought, morose. *Girls are the pits.*

Guiding Kiera to follow on Sky Dancer's tail, I half-listened as the pair of them chatted amicably. They compared notes on us unpredictable and boorish males, the latest palace gossip, and the pros and cons of keeping a werewolf as a pet. Had I a voice, I'd inform them that as pets, werewolves tended to bite before asking questions and were useful only during the duration of the full moon. My great-great-great grandsire was a werewolf, and a stigma upon the family for generations. Despite my advances in self-discipline, the sight of the full moon always wrenched a dismal howl from me.

"The Auryn River, my Lord Captain." Gaear's high-pitched eagle's voice drifted down from above as the steep valley dropped out from under Malik's black hooves an hour and a league later.

Far below, the silvery sheen of the river glistened despite the questionable sunlight. The thin, misty rain hadn't slackened as the afternoon drew toward evening, and the thick clouds lowered ominously. Thunder grumbled in the dim distance, promising more menace to come.

"Does he always state the obvious?" Iyumi asked Sky Dancer.

"Humpf," Sky Dancer replied sourly, her eyes on Gaear as he coasted gently over Malik's head. He'd flown well away from Sky Dancer over the last hour, yet I witnessed several evil glances sent her way from his sharp raptor's eyes. She had little to fear from him, however. As a magician, Gaear's skills brought him no end of pitied offers of helpful instruction by those more powerful than he. He, less than graciously, declined them all.

"What can one expect from an idiot, Your Highness?" Sky Dancer replied, not lowering her tone in the least. By the way Gaear suddenly flinched and Malik stiffened, I knew both heard her clearly.

"Captain Vanyar," Malik snapped without turning around. "Might I see you for a moment?"

"You're in trouble now, Van," Sky Dancer said under her breath, with what sounded suspiciously like a snicker in her voice.

"No doubt," I muttered, nudging Kiera forward.

Halting beside him, I gazed across the wide gorge, its high sides tumbled with broken granite and thin clusters of hardy, high-altitude trees. The river rushed over smooth boulders, white foam splashing high. Far below, the small figures of Padraig and Edara stood at its bank. Where they stood, the river flowed more smoothly, broken by unseen turbulence. The ford was a clear path on each side of the swift river whereby local wildlife obviously crossed. Padraig waved his bow unnecessarily.

High above, the mountains lost their menace, their snow-clad peaks buried under the heavy grey mist. The storm had drawn closer, looming from the north like a death shroud. Though no lightning flickered within their swirling depths, thunder rumbled, echoing across the valley and dancing amid the highland rocks. *Heavy rain after nightfall,* I thought. *We should find shelter.*

At Malik's gesture, Edryd saluted and backed his horse away from Malik's flank to give us privacy.

"Lieutenant," Malik said, not looking at me. "Round up the others. Everyone meet at the river."

"My Lord Captain."

I frowned as Gaear winged away, southward. "Is that wise, Malik? We need our scouts to stay out there."

My close friendship with him permitted me to question his orders–in private. Nor has he ever failed to offer an explanation–in private. He might reply with a mild insult, but always with equanimity and humor.

His hooded dark eyes hardened. Nor did he turn away from the sight of the rushing river. "I want Princess Iyumi escorted by you, Captain Vanyar, to the river's edge. You will see to it she and her mount are well-watered. I need everyone to get their skins and bellies filled."

"They can as they–"

"You have your orders, First Captain," he growled, still not looking at me.

I opened my mouth and his hand rose, stilling me instantly. I saluted and turned Kiera around to trot back to the princess and Sky Dancer. Perceptive females both, they instantly knew something was wrong. As I flanked Iyumi and heeled Kiera behind the roan, Sky Dancer flared her wings and opened her beak. I cut my finger across my throat in a sudden slash, silencing her immediately.

Chastened, Sky Dancer loped alongside our royal charge, her beak shut and her predatory eyes grim. As Iyumi spurred the blue stallion to follow Malik downhill, toward the roaring river, her small face turned over her shoulder toward me. Her silver braid flopped across her horse's rump, her right hand leaning against the cantle as her body twisted partway around. I knew she wanted to speak. I saw the unanswerable question in her blue eyes—*what the hell was going on?* I had no answer for her, and slowly shook my head.

The steep valley wall proved less treacherous than it looked, consisting of hard, grass-covered soil and small rocks that gave a firm footing to hooves loping downhill. We easily dodged large boulders and the ever-present thickets of stunted trees, following behind Malik's heavy black tail. His glossy hooves struck the pebbled strand of the shore just as Padraig cantered across to meet him.

He saluted smartly, sliding to a swift halt. "This is the best crossing for miles, my Lord Commander," he said. "Lieutenant Edara has been back and forth twice now and found no pitfalls."

"Are you truly stupid or do you practice often?"

Like me, Padraig was close to Malik and unless under sharp discipline, never spoken to harshly. Malik's cold tone sent a shiver of unease down my back. Malik never barked at his officers, much less offered insult. His rage at Edryd's ineptitude fell well within Malik's anger perimeters. This—I found his attitude so totally out of character as to be—alien.

Malik's hair lifted under the light mountain breeze despite the damp, hazy rain as he gazed upward. Grey Mist winged in low overhead, followed closely by Windy and Kasi. Valcan, in the shape of a raven, spiraled downward in ever smaller circles, his black, beady eyes watching the hills to the south. Aderyn's deer bounded toward the water on stick-like legs, her muzzle dropping immediately to the pool eddying at her tiny hooves.

Windy backwinged to land to all four feet at my side. No slouch, he immediately sensed my tension and recognized in Iyumi's stiffened body that all wasn't well. Rather than speak, he shook his dark feathers into place and folded his massive wings against his shoulders. His ears at full attention, he swung his head back and forth, his magic and his senses searching for the enemy. Stalking at my side, he failed to dip his beak to the water as Kiera drank her fill.

When Iyumi made to dismount, I flicked my hand, effectively halting her. Malik and Padraig both filled their skins and drank thirstily, up to their knees in the cold water. Yet, Edara remained on the far bank of the icy mountain Auryn, her hands fisted on her equine shoulders. I narrowed my eyes. Edara watched Malik and didn't drink a drop.

I slid from Kiera's back and took my water skin, as well as Iyumi's, to the edge of the rushing river. Like Aderyn, I crunched my way to a still pool and squatted to fill them. Late, Moon Whisperer winged in to land beside Misty, and bent to drink from the pure water of the river. Gaear, in eagle form, landed on the shore and swiftly changed into his human shape. He knelt in the damp shingle and gulped water from his cupped hands time and again, slurping the river as though he hadn't drunk for days.

My hand on the roan's bridle brought him to the pool so he might also slake his thirst, as I offered Iyumi the full skin. "Drink, m'lady," I murmured. "I'll refill it."

She obeyed me, tilting her head back with the skin's mouth to her lips. Stifling my own urge to drink as much as I could hold, I idly watched as Edryd walked his horse into the swift running water several rods upstream from Malik and Padraig. His chestnut gulped water down, his throat convulsing. Edryd drank nearly as fast as his horse.

Why was every creature within our group as thirsty as a desert caravan? That wasn't just odd, but downright strange. I left the horses to gulp unattended and strolled casually back up the incline. My swift hand gesture brought both Sky Dancer and Windy at my back. If they also suffered severe thirst, they hadn't partaken of the water. Instead, they fell into line behind me. My throat burned as I gazed at the rushing stream, longing to fall to my belly and guzzle.

Moon Whisperer swooped in to land upstream from Iyumi, his huge wings flared as he back-winged to land with his front talons in the water. He dipped his beak down and sucked water into his beak as though drinking the finest wine. Alain, the last to arrive, loped his horse straight into the river and swung from his saddle into the icy depths to his thighs and plunged his hands into the torrent. I don't know who drank faster: the chestnut or Alain.

"It's Flynn, isn't it?" Windy said, his beak buried in his wing feathers to conceal his beak. Sky Dancer feigned a yawn as she stretched her wings wide and high. Yet, her amber eyes flicked everywhere at once, never still, searching for the enemy. As though seeking companionship, she ambled to the water's edge and encouraged Iyumi, still aboard her roan, to return with her, away from the river.

"Has to be," I replied, eyeing Malik sidelong. "How else can we all be as thirsty as donkeys in a desert? He wants us here. But why?"

Malik finished drinking. Thoughtfully, slowly, he walked further into the river, up to his knees, then up to his huge black shoulders. His heavy tail floated on the stream like a banner of war. Edara took two steps into the river, clearly wanting to go to him. She caught my eye. I flattened my hand and pushed downward in a subtle motion. *Stay where you are.* Edara backed out of the water at the same time she took her bow from her back and nocked an arrow.

Malik stared at the water rushing around his massive shoulders as though mesmerized. The Auryn flowed swiftly around him, often tossing a foamy wave across his withers, as though he were just another boulder. His arms hung straight down, his fingers creating tiny streamlets where they touched the stream.

This is wrong on so many levels. The chill slipped down my spine again.

"Malik!" I shouted. "Are your big feet stuck or what?"

He didn't respond. He didn't raise a faint grin, toss back a quirky reply, nor did he remind me of my place with a caustic comment.

I drew my sword. "Prepare for battle," I said, my tone low. "It's a trap."

Behind me, Windy cursed under his breath and Sky Dancer's wings rustled as they spread. My quick whistle brought Padraig to my side at the trot. He may hate me, but I was still his superior officer. He bent his shaggy head toward me, scowling, and drew his blade.

"Stay with the princess," I snapped, under my breath. "No matter what happens. You don't leave her side. Not for anything."

"But–"

"Dancer, you, too. Guard Her Highness with your life."

I half-expected a protest from her as well, but the voice that whispered my name wasn't Sky Dancer's.

"Van?"

I whipped a glance over my shoulder. She sat straight in her saddle, a combination of fear and resolution warring across her pale features. Her silver-gilt hair in its heavy braid gleamed even under the muted light and misted rainfall. Iyumi clutched a dirk in her right fist, her left hand on the roan's reins firm yet still.

"Stay away from the river," I ordered, my voice terse. "He'll not take you, my queen."

With a quick word, I sent Kiera clattering up the bank, snorting in alarm. Though I knew she wouldn't fight for Iyumi, her presence close to the princess might offer her some degree of safety. Sky Dancer's huge body and spread wings urged Iyumi to rein her stallion around and lope him back the way we'd come. Padraig offered me a grim nod and galloped in her wake, his bow in his left hand as his right drew an arrow from its quiver.

"Valcan! Gaear! Find Flynn's position. He's probably on the hills behind us."

"You're not in charge–" Gaear began.

My thin bolt of lightning stuck his ass and sent him yelping into the air. His eagle scrambled for the sky, clawing for every rod of altitude, screeching in pain. I always suspected he could change forms quickly if properly motivated. Valcan didn't bother to salute, but his raven flew wingtip to wingtip with Gaear in frantic obedience.

"What's he doing?" Windy asked, his beak near my ear. "What's he done to the Captain?"

"He's got control of Malik's mind."

"What? That's impo–"

[283]

Vibration quivered through the ground at my feet. My heart dropped into my gut. From far upriver, the canyons echoed with a deep, resonating thunder. The pool of still water under Windy's talons swelled and retreated–flowing back the way it had come. Dimly, I heard Iyumi scream my name, but the roaring sound of an avalanche all but drowned it out. Oddly, I felt little surprise as the Auryn stood up like a dog begging for scraps and towered high above.

An immense wall of greenish-silver water filled the skyline, rushing faster than a runaway horse. Behind it, I caught a swift glimpse of the muddy, rocky riverbed as the river emptied its contents. White foam crested its head as the wave, higher than Roidan's castle walls, bore down on us. On Malik.

He stood, oblivious, directly in its deadly path. Though Windy also stood on the stony shore, his great wings would lift him to safety long before the wave reached him. As Edara had obeyed me, she, too, backed safely from its towering rage. Had I not the swift ability to change forms and fly high above the maelstrom, I, too, might be consumed by the river before I could escape. Flynn knew all this. He planned for it.

Flynn targeted Malik with his infernal, dark magic. Take out the strongest first. I'd learned that strategy before I learned to walk. Flynn obviously had the same education.

"Windy! Moon! Misty!"

Changing forms, I leaped into the air, screaming their names the instant the wave took Malik down. Airborne, I watched as Malik was driven under, ass over head, his black hooves thrashing helplessly. He vanished under the green-silver flood, dragged under the giant wave by Flynn's black powers. If the wave hadn't killed him outright, he'd drown under the onslaught of the river unleashed.

Folding my Griffin wings tight to my shoulders, I dropped. Straight into the swirling flood, my talons out and ready, I shut my beak and held my breath. Like an arrow into its target, I hit the water beak down and tail up. The waters closed over my head. I fought against the raging torrents, kicking not up, but down. Using my tail as a rudder, my lion hind paws thrust me deeper and further down. I did what no Griffin had ever done before.

I swam.

Like an otter, I used my four limbs to paddle me under the surface, my eyes opened but blind. I blinked several times, and saw a hand through the murky silt stirred up from the river bottom. In a gust of cleared water, a new danger surged toward where I thought Malik should be. The corpse of Edryd's chestnut stallion tumbled like a child's toy, spinning, out of control.

Malik's hooves appeared and vanished as the horse rolled him over, tangling them together like long-lost lovers. By the river's sheer power, the chestnut burst free and vanished as invisible forces drew Malik ever down. I inwardly winced as I saw his left rear leg caught between two submerged boulders and snap. My ears, flat to my head, heard the resounding thud as Malik's head struck a rock. *Dive, dammit, dive. He'll be dead in seconds.*

I dove. My talons missed his hand, but snarled in his thick hair. Striking for the surface, I paddled with my remaining three limbs. My feathers, saturated, tried to weigh me down, pull me back, drown me. Clenching my wings tight to my shoulders, I added magic to my strength and the river's hold on my wings fell away. I stifled an insane chuckle as I dragged Malik with me, hauling him by his splendid mane. *Whatever works.*

Above me, something large blocked the limited sunlight seen in glimmers off the river's surface. Huge shadowed forms beat the air over the river as I stroked upward, hauling my brother by his head. I paddled harder, my chest aching for air, Malik's dead weight all but hauling me down into the lethal depths with him.

Oh, no, boyo. You'll not die on me. Not now. On I struggled, calling on my own magic to give me strength, my iron will forcing my body into committing the impossible. *Not far now. Not far–*

My beak broke into the crisp cool mountain air and I dragged in a desperate lungful. I spread my wings and used them against the churning waters. Half swimming, half-flying, I lugged Malik's dead weight ever upward, up and up, until his head also broke free. I hoped I'd hear him gasp for breath, drag down into his lungs the air necessary for his survival.

I tried to yell, but choked on river water instead. Floundering, sluggishly beating my wings to gain much-needed altitude, I strove to free both Malik and me from the river's deadly embrace. I barely lifted him a rod when Windy dove in, his talons reaching for Malik's arm.

"Grab it!" Windy yelled.

I knew what he meant. I loosened my hold on Malik's hair and seized his shoulder with my front eagle talons. His big arm fit well into my talons, offering me a good grip. I beat hard for the sky, my wings heavy and unresponsive, my feathers shedding silt and muck. Malik's dead weight tried to drag me backward.

"I'm losing him," I cried as my grip on his arm slipped back, sliding through my fists. Malik's body dropped two rods into the river. His black tail and rear quarters vanished into its murky, dark-green depths.

Two Griffins were no match for the burden of a large Centaur. He outweighed each of us by several hundred pounds, and Griffin wings were created to carry a Griffin body, not dead weight. The river sucked at Malik's body, threatening to draw him back down into its deadly grip. *Oh, no you don't, you will not win.*

I strained my wings to lift Malik higher and higher, Windy gasping on Malik's other side. The Auryn's grasp slipped a notch. Malik's rump emerged from the torrents, though his tail still spread wide and flowed downstream.

Moon Whisperer answered my cry. His enormous frame slid like an oiled wheel under Malik's rear end. He utilized his own body rather than his eagle's front legs to grip Malik. Moon shoved his wide shoulder under Malik's rear quarters and heaved. His mighty wings straining, he threw his strength in with ours and Malik's unconscious body rose, sluggishly yes, but free of the raging river.

"Is he alive?" Grey Mist yelled, diving under me to swoop up and past our efforts to keep Malik free of the death churning below.

"Yes," I gasped. "Grab hold."

Misty might lack imagination, but when he set his mind to something, his body saluted. Swinging a heavy rope he found somewhere, he tossed one end around Malik's barrel and caught it deftly. Both tails in his claws, Misty threw his tremendous wings and disciplined body into the task. The rope in his clutches, he winged hard and harder, striving for altitude.

Malik's weight eased slightly from my talons and Misty's grip on the rope grew in strength. Four Griffins and one unconscious Centaur. How hard can it be?

"Now. Now. Now." I screamed, pushing my wings to levels most Griffins shied from. Wet, heavy, reluctant, I forced my wings to obey my iron will. One, two, three. One wingbeat. One, two, three. Two wingbeats. One, two, three. A third wingbeat.

"He's free!" Misty shouted. "Let him down. Down."

"No." I croaked the single word.

"He's safe– "

"Across the river. Not here."

A sparking arrow streaked up past my beak and exploded just over Misty's great wingspan. A sharp coughing bark overwhelmed his scream of agony and shock, bright flames shooting in all directions. Piercing shrapnel peppered Misty's body, and he let go the rope, his body falling, twisting, plummeting toward the river now falling back onto itself. Malik's arm slid partway through my grip. Though I tried to hang on, without Misty's help, the remaining three of us couldn't withstand the sudden drop of Malik's heavy body.

Falling with Malik, my wings straining, my talons sinking into his flesh, I watched through narrowed vision as Misty, bloody and helpless, struck the river's surface. He vanished as the raging waves broke over his head.

"Heave, lads!" I shouted. "Heave him and leave go!"

Windy and Moon understood. As though directed by one mind, we knew we couldn't hold him. The next best thing was to drop him into the safest place possible: the shallow pool. As one, we swung Malik high and wide, then released. I held my breath and spread my wings to soar upward as Malik struck the water, hindquarters first. *Better than his head,* I half-thought, as he fell, limp and lifeless, into the cushioning pond. The resulting splash nearly emptied it, but I saw that though his body lay submerged, his face lay free of the water.

Though I know he lived when I dragged him from the river, that drop may have killed him. With no time to wing in for a closer look, Flynn's archers made me their target. A sputtering arrow-bomb flew up from behind the hill just to our south and sped toward me. Closing my wings, I dove for the river. I spun first left, then right. Like a hawk stooping on a squirrel, I arrowed downward. The bomb flew high and wild past me, exploding harmlessly far to my rear.

"Evasive maneuvers!" I yelled as more flying death spun up from the hill. "Edryd! Alain! Shoot them down! Shoot them down!"

Horseless, yet a keen archer just the same, Corporal Edryd knelt on the strand and squinted up, his nocked arrow drawn to his chin. More of Flynn's sputtering death rose high, arching first up then out, aiming for the Griffins. His first arrow knocked a bomb off its course and sent it diving into the river. His second blew the explosive into pieces before it could ignite. His third sent it whining, ricocheting, into harmless space where it blew up nothing but air.

Horsed and talented, Alain galloped through the shallows, firing arrow after arrow, knocking down one, two, three and even four bombs before his horse stumbled and his fifth arrow flew wild.

Edara plunged into the slowly quieting river and half-swam, half-galloped across, her dainty features flushed with rage. She didn't slow down upon reaching the shore, but increased her pace, running hard, pulling her arrow to her chin. Her destination: Flynn's hill.

Kasi joined her, flying low over her head, screaming in inarticulate fury. Aderyn, mild in temperament and impossibly sweet in nature, changed from her slender deer into an uncontrolled, snarling lioness. Side by side with Edara, my cousin loped with fluid grace up the hill, dodging boulders and thickets, her intent clear. Flynn and friends would die. They charged not just for King and country, but to avenge their fallen leader. Whether Malik lived or died, they didn't care. Flynn's trap harmed him and that was all the reason they needed.

"Negative!" I screamed, winging hard toward them. "Stand down! Stand down!"

On they charged, up the hill toward the small snag of trees where no doubt Flynn and his cronies hid, casting their spells and sending their bolts of explosives into the air. I recognized Flynn's plan: kill our leader. Take out our air support. Force our reserves into a less than useful charge. Trot in and capture Princess Iyumi with hardly a weapon raised against him.

Flynn's step-spelled explosives worked yet a second time. The bombs their feet triggered blew, exploding rocks and shrapnel high and ripping flesh to the bone. Aderyn's body flew sharply right, encased in fire and blood. Her lion's body crashed to the earth, rolling over and over, back down the hill. She lay under the oily, billowing smoke, unconscious or dead. Edara's heavy legs shattered as stones and bits of metal crashed into her, her screams buried under the bomb's coughing roar. She fell, her red mane bloody, her beautiful face torn, and her slender arms holding her bow caught under her chestnut body.

Black smoke and dirt boiled into the air, casting all into deep shadow. Kasi turned aside at the last second. Her wings extended to their fullest, she dodged sideways and down. Flynn's archer's next bomb struck her full in the face, exploding in gouts of red-orange flame. Kasi's screams died as she plummeted to the earth, head down and wings slack. Her neck snapped on impact.

Shock numbed my mind, stilled my reactions. Through the boiling smoke I saw them: broken, lifeless, gone. Three laughing, joyous girls taken into death's embrace before they had a chance to live. I couldn't stop them. I tried. I'm their leader. Their lives are my responsibility. My fault. Like Dalziel. Those under my command killed in action because I failed them. Their souls will haunt me forever more.

Not again. Not ever again.

I cannot live while those under my command died. I should have died then. I'll die with them now. I'll not live without them.

Blinded by rage and guilt, I closed my wings and dropped like a stone. Straight toward the trees and the bleak end awaiting me with open arms. I felt Death's icy breath on my neck as I blasted toward

Flynn's hiding place with wings and talons extended. I may die but Flynn will accompany me as I crossed the great barrier.

Flynn's next barrage flew into my face before I got within a hundred rods of the hilltop. Blinded by bright flames and heavy smoke, the hot stench of sulphur burning my nostrils and throat, I ducked and dodged, swerved and swung. Peppered with shrapnel, my body burned, bleeding in countless places. Despite their best efforts, I gained ground. Flynn's wild blonde mane tossed within my sights.

You re my bitch, Flynn.

Up from within the tree-cover an arrow-bomb streaked, spitting like a seriously pissed off feline. Homing in on me, it kept to its target no matter how wildly I spun or darted. It gave me zero chance to dive for the earth and shake it from my ass. *This is it. I wanted to take you with me, old son.*

Windy body-slammed me out of the way. The arrow-bomb that sought my life exploded, raking him across the flank and quarters. It sent him pin-wheeling out of control, his drooping wings unable to keep him airborne. He screamed, a high-pitched wail of the utterly damned. The mountains echoed in false sympathy.

Windy!

I woke from my guilt-laden rage.

No more. No more will die saving my miserable hide, I swore, least of all this savagely loyal, humorous bastard. If one of us dies on this cold, highland hillside, it won't be him. Not this time.

I winged hard right, then down and came up under Windy's left flank. Gaping rents across his ribs, flanks and lion quarters bloomed bloody. His beak wide, he gasped in precious air, but his raptor eyes stared blankly into nothing. *Shell-shock,* I half-thought. I suspected his right rear leg might be broken by the way it hung, limp and motionless. Though his wings still beat hard and kept him, for the moment, from crashing to the rocks below, he'd soon lose his tenacious grip on life. He'd lose that battle of Windy versus gravity. His body wobbled, hitched and threatened to spiral out of control. If I didn't keep him right-side up and flying, I'd have one less friend in the world. I never did like losing friends.

[290]

Using a tactic unheard of before, I seized his front talons with my own. Unfortunately, Griffin wings were constructed to carry a Griffin. And *just* a Griffin. Excess baggage wasn't permitted. Those huge yet fragile mixtures of feathers and hollow bones could never hope to transport the weight I now intended them to carry.

Back-winging yet rising, I dragged him higher and higher with me. My wings felt the intense strain, my shoulder muscles on fire. I panted, hard, dragging in deep gulps of air, willing my body into feats it was never designed for. "C'mon, Windy," I gasped. "Work with me here."

His eyes tried to focus on me and failed.

"Fly, dammit!" I cried. "Use your wings, Atan. Fly!"

Semi-conscious, Windy croaked a single word. "'Kay." His wings beat harder and swifter, easing the stress on my own. Higher we rose, slowly, sluggish, easing away from the reach of Flynn's archers. Under the relative quiet of the approaching storm, I led him toward safety, out of the reach of the battle. Guiding him down to the earth behind a low rocky wall and thicket of stunted trees, I dropped him to the ground.

He collapsed in a near-unconscious heap. His wings drooped, deflated tents, to either side of his blasted and bleeding body. His fierce lion tail sagged, lifeless, behind the chewed tan fur of his haunches. My heightened hearing listened to the firm thud of his heart beating within his broad chest and felt comforted. He wasn't at death's door. Yet.

"Van?" Windy whispered, his front talons scrabbling in the dirt. Trying to rise, an Atan to the core, he thought he still might fly and follow me back into battle.

"Stay here," I ordered.

"Van, I can't–I must–"

"Stay. That's an order, Atan."

Without waiting for an answer, I leaped out and down. Below me, Flynn's arrow-bombs continued to rake the sky. Moon dodged as best he could, diving first one way, then the next, driven helplessly away from the small cluster of Iyumi's defenders. Anger and fury warred across his eagle's face, as he failed to get closer to

Iyumi and protect her. Edryd and Alain still shot as many explosives out of the air as they could, but too many passed them by and blew apart, sending deadly shrapnel across the sky.

I shrieked the Atani battle cry, a sharp *"kı-yı-yi, kı-yı-yı-yi"* as I winged hard and fast, flying faster than sound. My eagle's vision focused on Iyumi, on her horse, still guarded by faithful Padraig and loyal Sky Dancer. They hid behind a thick cluster of trees and rocks at the river bank, safe from the arrow-bombs. The river itself protected their rear. I felt no small relief as Kiera's black and white form shifted within the shadows.

The river itself settled, quiet, and resumed its natural course after Flynn's magical machinations. Malik still lay in his pool, silent, unmoving. There was no sign of Misty. Gaear flew over the river, no doubt searching for him.

Valcan swooped up and over me, still a raven. "Flynn lies behind that southern hill, Captain," he gasped. "He has eight men with him. They run low on their supplies of arrows."

"Excellent, Sergeant. Want some payback?"

"Yes, sir!"

"I think having a bull charging down upon their rear might have an interesting effect on their morale. Don't you?"

"Indeed, my Captain."

As Valcan banked sharply left, dodging another arrow-bomb, he veered up and down, and vanished behind the low-lying hills. As I deliberately placed myself between Iyumi and Flynn, flying low to the ground toward his hiding place, I knew he'd focus his attention on me. Not on the raven that disappeared. Nor was I surprised when he answered my challenge.

I almost failed to dodge the next arrow before it exploded in my face. Catching it from the tail of my eye at the last second, I snap-rolled hard right, my wings clasped tight to my body. It sparked past me, smoke trailing in its wake, before exploding harmlessly far behind my tail.

"Flynn," I called, my voice high and humorous. "Come out, come out, wherever you are."

I winged higher and higher, against the lowering sunset. The clouds cooperated by drifting, thinning, and permitting the last rays to fall upon the tall hill. Another arrow flew toward me, but the sun in the archer's eyes put his aim to shame. It flew past me by rods and exploded harmlessly over the river.

"Don't tease me," I called. "Can't you do better than that?"

Another arrow hissed many rods to my left and dropped into the river, sputtering harmlessly.

"I'm growing bored here, laddie," I said. "Don't make me come in there and get you."

Another fire-arrow sped past, sparking angrily, to explode so far behind me I sighed down my nose. On its heel, the thunder of hooves and a bovine bellow of rage resounded from the hills. Valcan arrived, right on schedule. I winged higher, anticipating. I always loved surprises.

From behind the trees, horses screamed in panic and bolted in every direction. Several dragged picket lines, and I recognized Flynn's treasured Bayonne among them. Three men with bows in their fists ran headlong down the hill, leaping deadfall and rocks, evading sheer rage on the hoof. Valcan chased one down, goring the man through the back with one sweeping horn. Blood burst from his mouth and nose as Valcan's hooves trampled him, smashing his chest and his spine. Another almost evaded the maddened bull, but Valcan was quick as well as clever. He leaped high and down, striking the ground parallel with the screaming henchman, and gored the man through the belly. Lifting his huge head, Valcan tossed him, still screaming hysterically, from his bloody horns in one deft move. Flynn's loyal ally died in the bushes, his entrails tangled in the thorns.

Flynn's vengeance came quick.

Before I screamed a warning, Flynn's dark power rose from the shadows. He saved the best for last, that clever boy. Distantly, I heard faint chanting, the rise and fall of a deep voice inciting evil to come forward. Over the mountains, deep black clouds roiled, pouring like dark smoke down from the tall peaks. Lightning flashed within their depths. I knew this wasn't the storm I predicted earlier in the day. Demonic thunder cracked, reverberating the very air I flew in. Evil electricity danced across my flesh.

The ground shook in answer. Mounds of tundra and stones rose, bursting asunder with soft explosions. Huge winged creatures, blacker than hell's night, crawled from their holes and shook dirt from their scaly hides. Hundreds of them, perhaps thousands, covered acres of the shallow river valley.

Gods. Cease this madness.

I thought them to be bats, at first, until the first one took to the air. Like a bat, it owned leather wings, but the resemblance ended there. Four legs tipped with razor-sharp claws, and fangs the length of my finger gleamed under the late sunlight. A short tail ending with a bladed tip swung back and forth like a rudder. I couldn't count the number of mounds giving birth to these monsters as they screamed like wildcats and rose sluggishly into the air.

"Valcan!" I screamed.

He hesitated, pausing in his chase of the third man and looked up. As a flock of birds flew, guided by one mind, these devil-bats swarmed in a bunch. He saw them coming for him and bolted downhill, toward the river. Too late. A Shifter of Valcan's skills needed a second or three with which to concentrate. They didn't give him those precious seconds to focus and change forms into a creature that might outfly them. The swarm swooped low and struck Valcan dead to rights. His bovine jaws opened in a very human scream of agony and anguish. Blood poured from his thick dark hide in torrents as Flynn's devil spawn ripped him apart and feasted on his flesh.

I couldn't watch. My gut churning, my throat shut, I swung my face to the side and wished I could shut out his screams. *Valcan!* He didn't scream long. He died quickly, thank all the gods. I still heard, however, the wet, meaty sounds as Flynn's evil ate him raw and drank deep of his blood.

Horror tore through my soul. What had Flynn created? What were those things? Hell's own angels?

Firming my gut, I sent a bolt of my own magic into one that plucked Valcan's eye from its socket and gulped it down as though dining on a treat. My bolt merely sent a shudder through its sinuous body and brought a sharp squawk from its jaws. It returned to its feast, ripping a chunk of skin from Valcan's cheek. I tried again, sending a more powerful burst of magic into a bat. It shuddered, briefly, and never turned to cast a reproachful eye my way.

Flynn himself strode to the top of the hill. "Hello, Van."

Taking my eyes from the horror devouring my Atan brother, and a man whom I hoped I could call 'friend', I stared down at Prince Flynn. My enemy. My country's enemy. A man who I liked the moment I met him. The one I took pity upon and healed with one stroke of my finger. The wicked soul who dared attack and attempt to seize my beloved–

He cocked his leg arrogantly and rested his fist on his knee. He grinned up, his wild mane of blonde hair dancing in the light breeze, his sword still sheathed at his hip. His bomb-master, Blaez, puffed his way up to stand at his side, his bag still filled with the toys we haven't yet met.

I hovered as well as a Griffin could, back-winging enough to hold me in place over the hill. "Don't do this, Flynn. Please. Stop this evil."

"You're a worthy opponent, Van," Flynn said, straightening. "I don't want to kill you. Give me the princess and the rest of you can go home. I swear it."

"You know what she represents," I yelled. "You know what'll happen to the child. You don't want that stain on your soul. Not even you."

His face darkened. "I don't care. Iyumi will be my wife. That's all I want."

His words burned like fire in my blood. Iyumi? His *wife?* He would dare lay his evil hands on–Rage coursed through me. The image of him and Iyumi, tangled together, bound by passion and greed–I lost my head.

Screaming, inarticulate, I furled my wings and dove down, hard, tasting Flynn's blood on my tongue. I extended my talons, my beak wide, stooping upon my prey. With the same hunger a starving hawk hunts the unwary rabbit, I plunged toward him, my murderous talons out and bared. Within his single heartbeat, I saw my fury cast into his face. Malik's dagger cut marred him forever. Mine would throw him onto the feet of his gods.

He flinched back, fear warring with the arrogance he tried hard to protect. He lifted his hands as though hoping the mere sight of them might send me hurtling past him and leave him unscathed. Ever the coward, he stumbled away, frantically reaching for his blade. As though that alone might slay me, mid-air.

Got you now, sucker. His essence splashed against my beak as I pictured myself tearing his head from his neck.

His dark creatures defended him. Black wings dove at me, tore into me, teeth cutting, biting. I screeched in fury, my talons raking one hell-spawn into pieces, and bit the head off another. My lion claws raked several more and sent them reeling into the ground, broken, bleeding, dead. My magic didn't kill them, but my talons and fury did. With no thought to wonder why, I dove and snap-rolled both left and right, rising high with my wings beating strongly. I made them chase me, forcing them to lose the precious energy they so desperately needed. Vicious fangs snapped at my haunches, but melted under my rage as I reversed beak and tail. I blasted through their flock, an avenging angel on swift wings. As though I were Death's own justice, I killed everything that flew, jumped or crawled into my path.

Bat-things died and their bodies crashed in dirty piles below Flynn's hill, staining the ground with blackish-red blood. I caught a swift expression of panic cross Blaez's pudgy face as he clutched Flynn's arm. Flynn shook him off, his sword now out and pointed toward me. His voice, speaking the language of hell, roared.

The ground below his feet exploded.

Bat creatures by the thousands burst up from the rocky tundra. They zeroed in on me as though I were a simple lamb and they the hungry wolf. My talons, claws and beak sent bat-things by the tens, the hundreds, to fall at Flynn's boots. Yet, too many more shrieked as they bit with sharp fangs into my shoulders, my flanks, my ribs. I killed five of them with rapid-fire slashes, only to have ten more take their place.

I can t hold them–

Moon blasted in, wings wide and beak agape. His talons made hell-spawn mincemeat, cutting wings from backs, heads from necks. Black blood stained us both, and fell like rain onto the rocky bluffs below. Dark bodies crashed to the unforgiving ground to lie still, as yet more demons squirmed from the earth to shake dirt and fly.

"Moon!"

Shedding bat-things in all directions, I beat hard for the sky, suspecting these critters were low-altitude only. With Moon Whisperer hard at my flank, I strove for bone-chilling height where the air thinned. Sure enough, Flynn's pets chased us only a few hundred rods before returning below. Like bees at a hive, they swarmed over the ground, trying to invade the shelter of the trees and rocks. I had enough time to gasp an order.

"Stay with her, Moon," I said, circling to catch my breath. "Stay alive. No matter what happens."

"Van?"

"Get her to the child and safety."

"Wait, Van!"

Bleeding in a hundred places, defeat bitter on my tongue, I folded my wings and dropped like a stone. I didn't wait, or search for Moon. Blasting through the sky at a speed seldom accomplished by the sane or self-preserving, I scattered the flock and sent many to their deaths on the rocky slopes below. Circling back, ignoring the demons that grouped together in attack mode, I bolted into the thicket.

Angry, humiliated, bent with fury at Valcan's death and Flynn's quest, I dropped into human shape the instant I hit the strand. Yelling in triumph, the winged shapes circled high above, taunting me with sharp cries. Flynn still stood atop his hill, his hand on his hilt, gazing down.

"Van!" Iyumi cried, racing toward me.

Though Padraig sought to stop her, she evaded him smartly with a quick dodge and slammed into me. "What are those things? Are you all right?"

She clasped me tight to her, her tiny breasts digging into my belly. Her arms around my neck, her tears smeared the gore on my

[297]

chest as I wrapped her close, and held her. Her arms drenched in my blood, I kissed her on the cheek, smiling grimly down into her anguished blue eyes. "I ain't done yet, m'lady," I said. "Not by a long shot."

"You're hurt–"

"No worries," I said, aiming for lightness. But by the grim worry in her eyes. I knew my attempt fell far short of the mark.

"Van–"

"Find the little one," I said, stroking my hand across her hair and cupped her cheek. "Then get your cute ass home. Got it?"

She grabbed my fingers in a grip that almost hurt. "Not without you."

"Sorry, love. I've plans, you see."

I jerked my head at Sky Dancer. Though it broke my heart within my chest, I spurned the love those blue eyes offered me. I rejected her, and steeled myself against the hurt I knew would follow. Though I tried to smile, I knew she wasn't fooled. She was smart, that one. She knew what I meant to do.

Huge and implacable, Sky Dancer seized Iyumi by the shoulders and gently dragged her backwards. That tiny princess screamed like a banshee and fought like one. Invectives I never suspected a royal princess would know, much less repeat, spewed from her mouth. Iyumi clawed and twisted, her silver hair coming loose from its braid. But against Sky Dancer's brute strength and firm resolve, she hadn't a prayer. "Van! Stop it, damn you! Van!"

"You have your orders, Lieutenants," I ordered, including Padraig in my glare. "See her safely home to our King. Flynn and I have unfinished business."

"You don't have the power," Padraig said, his hand on my arm. "Captain, you're weak–"

I caught his deep-set dark eyes. "Do your duty, Atan," I snapped, brushing his hand away.

"Captain–"

"No matter what, Lieutenant," I said. "You keep her safe. Understand?"

Padraig never saluted me, ever, in our history together. In his arrogance, he'd stomp past, pretending he hadn't seen me. Under

Malik's command, he sneered down at me, confident in Malik's love for him and safe under the Lord Captain Commander's shield. He despised me, for what I'd done, at Dalziel. He promised revenge, just hours before. I met his hate-filled eyes, and begged with my own. *No matter how you feel about me, keep one we both love alive.*

His face expressionless, he nodded once, just short of a salute. "I will, First Captain. My oath on it."

My glance caught Sky Dancer's. "Your will, my Captain," she said, her right talon clenched across her medallion of rank. Her beak dipped. "Come back to us, sir."

"I doubt that's in the cards," I replied, catching Iyumi's outraged stare under the silver fall of her hair. I saluted, fist to chest. I bowed my head. "My queen."

My right hand drew my sword from its sheath. The sword the King himself gave me, the sword I cut myself with at my acceptance ceremony. I'd bathed it in my blood, so it knew me. Its hilt grew hot within my grip as I stalked out from behind the protection of the trees and the river. It thrummed with a life of its own as it sensed my intent.

I'd never before called on its power. I never investigated just exactly how much power it *did* have. A magician of Roidan's level and skills could instill an inanimate object, such as a blade, with the same strength he himself owned. But to invest in it a presence of mind, to make it a sentient *being*–that took skills only the gods possessed.

My sword recognized me. My blood flowed within it. My rage was its rage. Its magic was mine, its strength my own. With it, I could level mountains, or empty the seas. Nothing could withstand me, should I turn loose the magic within the blue-tinged steel. Deep within my heart it spoke to me: *We can do great good. We shall never do evil.*

A black devil flew at me, its maw wide, fangs gleaming. A single spark from the tip of my blade caught it ablaze. It screamed as it burned, winging away to die in the sun's last rays, in agony. Striding uphill, toward Flynn, I cut another demon's head from its shoulder with a single, offhand swipe. Casual, as though I walked through my own estate's garden, I stabbed, burned, beheaded, or flayed alive every winged shadow Flynn set against me.

They tried, however. Grouping together, an immense flock of black flapping wings and bared fangs, Flynn's vile offspring shut down the sunlight as they poured in a wave down the hill. As with Valcan, they sought to bring me down with sheer numbers. I paused, watching them, my blade lax in my hand. I waited.

I permitted them to fly within ten rods. I raised my sword.

The blade's power magnified my bellow of challenge until the mountains themselves echoed and rang. White light burst from the sword's tip, expanded, grew, then tripled in size within the span of a heartbeat. It cast a silver net over the attacking horde, enveloped them, and enclosed them within its embrace. They might have screamed, but I heard nothing. To a bat, the winged devils exploded. Not singly, in rapid-fire pops. Oh, no, they blew apart with a hundred times the force of Flynn's bombs.

After my white light vanished, only a fine black dust fell to the earth. All that remained of Flynn's devil spawn.

Whirling my sword until it rested behind my shoulder, I stared up at Flynn on his hill. I stood close enough to witness his scar shine a pale red as his face waxed whiter than a ghost. He knew I had the power. He knew I could cut him down where he stood. *Run, coward. Run while you still can.*

On his hilltop, Flynn lost his arrogant stance. His own sword bared, he raised it, flashing under the dying sunlight. He also raised his left hand in a fist. Lightning burst from his sword, into the heavens, flashing across the sunless clouds. He raised his voice in a shout heard by the gods themselves. His voice rang like thunder, echoing across the valley.

In answer, more demons by the dozens, the scores, the thousands, winged, leaped and flew down from the hills in obedience to his summons. Like ants on a mound, his fell creatures swarmed down and blackened the landscape with their numbers. They drew together, wings flapping, crawling across the hills in answer to his call. Sluggishly, as though mired in sticky oatmeal, the creatures crawled into and over one another. Piling higher and deeper, one couldn't identify one hell-spawn from another.

"You're dead, Flynn," I muttered, sweeping my sword high and wide. I walked up the hill toward him. "I just ain't killed you yet."

Incredibly, the mound of scurrying, creeping winged devils slowly rose. I hesitated, my sword lowered, caught by the oddity before my eyes. Under the scrambling black leathery wings, a shape formed. It lifted itself higher, like a boulder coming to life, hard, implacable and immense. More squirming bat-things joined its structure, adding to its great height and breadth. *That looks like–* Arms spread from colossal shoulders. A head lifted on a thick, bull-neck. Fiery red eyes blinked owlishly in the light.

A demon.

"Gods forbid," I murmured. "Flynn, what have you done?"

The towering demon saw me. It roared. It bent at the waist, its wings wide, as it stretched its claws toward me. I braced myself, grinning, and set to impale its vulnerable beating heart on my deadly blade. I whirled it in a deadly arc, preparing myself for the uphill charge. Yelling the Atani battle cry, I lunged forward to meet it, head on. *Come you –*

I didn't charge, but rather crashed onto my back in the stony dirt. I tumbled ass over ears, time and again, before fetching up against a boulder. A sharp ache spread from my spine outward, and I lost my grip on my sword.

My back on fire from the rocks, my breath gone, I half sat up. Struggling, I found a few words. "What? Malik? How did you"

"Stand down, Van," Malik said firmly, coldly. "This is a fight you can't win."

"You can't–you're hurt–"

Malik stood on four solid legs. I know he broke that hind leg. I saw it. I heard his head crack against a submerged rock. I know he lay at death's door, unconscious, comatose. Only strong magic can heal him, bring him back to the world of the living. What magic? None of us had time to think of him, much less lay a hand and heal him. Perhaps Iyumi–

I shot a swift glance toward her and discovered she was as shocked as I at the impossible. Iyumi stared, slack-jawed, half-hidden behind Sky Dancer's protective shoulder at a Malik neither of us recognized. Oh, yes, he was still black and arrogant, the rayed star of his rank gleamed from his brow-band. Still, he wasn't the brother and friend I've loved for years uncounted. This Centaur was a stranger to me.

For here he stood on four solid legs, his broad fingers tickling his sword's hilt, the blood that trickled down his cheek now dried and black. His dark eyes beneath the thick fall of his mane watched the approaching demon with a detached calm that unnerved me. At his sharp whistle, Padraig, Alain, Edryd, and Sky Dancer trotted swiftly to his side. Moon Whisperer circled low overhead, his raptor's eyes on the approaching demon. Gaear flew in and changed forms, landing on four paws in his favorite wolf shape.

Scrambling to my feet, I charged uphill, toward him. "Malik!"

"Go," Malik said, his tone low. Half-turning, his chin on his shoulder, his dark eyes softened. "It's up to you now, my brother. Take Her Highness to the child. Save us all."

"Malik, no, let me fight, I can do this–"

"My Lord Captain," Gaear snarled, his fangs bared. "You can't trust him with her. He's a traitor! He'll get her killed."

"The Lieutenant is right," Padraig added, his scornful eyes eyeing me up and down. "You can't permit this murderer to escort Her Highness to the child. Order me instead. Let him be killed here, this day, and regain his honor."

"Shut up!" Iyumi screamed, lunging out from behind Sky Dancer at Padraig. A dagger gleamed in her fist. "How dare you!"

Sky Dancer caught Iyumi around her tiny waist, holding her fast. Though she fought like a cat and yowled like one, Iyumi never tried to cut the talons that held her. Sky Dancer, gripping the squirming, shrieking princess, loomed over Padraig, her raptor's eyes narrowed. "We all know where you stand, Lieutenant," she hissed. "You want him dead, and tried to kill him an hour ago. Please don't be modest, stand up for yourself, boy. Think you're tough enough to face me?"

"And me," Windy snapped, alighting beside her, his dark neck feathers at stiff attention. "Speak another word against him and I'll wrap your guts around your pathetic throat, so I will."

What the hell? That Malik stood, miraculously healed of his injuries was astonishing enough. But that Windy, also, stood on four solid feet, blood-stained hide now intact and devoid of critical injury, was mind-boggling. How in the name of all the gods could he be here, defending me? I know, I *know,* Windy should be lying where I left him, bleeding and broken. Yet, he wasn't. He met my incredulous gaze and tipped me a sly wink.

Under the fierce menace of two angry Griffins, Padraig fell back a step. He lifted his hands, free of weapons, and lowered his face. Malik stalked forward, his hands high, aiming to control his divided unit. But before he uttered his commands, Gaear snarled once more. "If you defend him, then you're as guilty as he is."

"Bite me," Sky Dancer retorted.

He clearly anticipated her attack. When her talons swept low and fast toward his throat, Gaear lunged sideways, quicker than she. But he hadn't reckoned on Windy. As Gaear spun, unharmed, out of her airspace, he jumped clean into Windy's ready embrace. Windy caught him up with both fists, holding the now fearfully whining and wriggling wolf high above the ground. "Still wanna play with the big kids?" Windy growled.

"Put him down!"

Malik's roar startled everyone, me included. Iyumi halted her planned tirade, as Windy opened his talons and dropped Gaear. The wolf fell from five rods up to land hard on his side, his sharp yelp of pain parting the sudden silence like a hot knife through lard. Every eye stared at Malik. And Malik stared back, fury baking off him in waves.

"Cease this *idiocy,*" he gritted, his dark eyes hot. "The fight is out there, you nimrods. Not here, among us. Captain Vanyar, you *will* take Iyumi to that bloody child and you *will* keep them both safe. Am I clear? The rest of you, fall into battle formation. Padraig, put Captain Vanyar on his horse, now! Sky Dancer, see to it Her Highness is ready to ride."

[303]

"Malik–"

"You're an Atan, First Captain Vanyar. You follow orders, fight to kill, and die for your King and country. That is all."

Just as Sky Dancer dragged Iyumi from me, Padraig dragged me from Malik. "Malik!"

"Take her to the child, Van," Malik said, his tone cold. "Don't watch me die." He stalked toward the demon, drawing his blade, his back resolute.

"Malik!"

How he summoned Kiera, I'll never know. She never obeyed anyone but me. Yet, there she stood, dark eyes wild, snorting with fear, as Padraig bodily shoved me onto her back. "Padraig," I gasped, desperate. "I'm your superior off– "

"We both have our orders, Vanyar," Padraig said, lifting his hand, his expression resolute and implacable. "You'll need this, I expect."

He offered me my sword, falcon hilt first. I accepted it, confused, muddled, in torment. I sheathed it without thinking. "Padraig, listen, we–"

Padraig half-turned away, his hand gripping my wrist when I made to slide down from Kiera's back. "Is Her Highness ready?"

"No, she's not."

Iyumi's stern bitchiness had returned. Grateful, I swung toward her, knowing she'd turn the tables on Malik and Padraig, command they follow her orders and let me fight. They'd no choice, they had to obey her. When she spoke, their collective genes saluted.

"You will *not* send me away, Lieutenant," Iyumi snapped, her blue eyes aflame. "I plan to stay and so will Captain Vanyar. Unhand him, please."

Iyumi may have royal authority, but Sky Dancer outweighed her by at least two tons. As though picking up a fragile doll, Sky Dancer plucked Iyumi up by her trim waist and set her carefully in the roan's saddle. Too shocked to squawk in outrage, Iyumi's eyes tried to bore holes in Sky Dancer's equanimity. "How dare you."

"Oh, I dare, Your Highness," Sky Dancer replied calmly, saluting politely. "As long as it's the Captain's orders that you and Van remain alive and free, I'll dare anything."

[304]

"Dancer," I began.

"Shut up, Vanyar. Now ride."

Moon circled low overhead, his eyes on the not so distant monster Flynn created. "Come on," he snapped, his beak angled toward Sky Dancer. "The Captain is gonna engage. He needs us like now."

"You heard him," Padraig said. "Go. Ride hard and fast."

"No–"

My sword. I drew it, raised it high. I had more power than Malik. I can stop him, I can defeat him, defeat the monster.

I called on the sword's strength –

Nothing happened.

I stared, stupidly, down at the hilt in my hand. Its dull bluish gleam answered me at the same time its silent voice spoke in my heart. *We do no evil.*

But–

Never defy an order.

Under me, Kiera reared. Her ringing scream echoed across the valley. Her front legs flailing, she answered a command that didn't come from me. Plunging into a gallop before her hooves hit the stony strand, she hit the water dead on. The icy water flowed up past my thighs as she half galloped, half-swam across the churning river. A swift glance over my shoulder showed me Iyumi's grim, outraged expression as her stallion splashed across the ford at Kiera's tail.

Kiera cantered up the steep slope on the north side of the river, her legs and tail streaming water. I held her back when she wanted to run, half-rearing in protest. I looked back. Iyumi's sure hand on her stallion's reins brought him to a swift sliding stop. She wheeled him about.

Flynn's monster reared against the darkening sky, lightning flickering about its head. It roared, bellowing with a voice loud enough to shake the valley. Flames flickered from the ends of its long black fingers as dreadful hands rose toward those I loved.

Malik stood at point, the head of the phalanx. At his flanks waited Sky Dancer and Moon Whisperer, prepared to hurl themselves into battle on his command. Padraig stood behind him, sword in hand, ready. Edryd, mounted on a bay horse captured from Flynn's crew, and Alain, skirted both left and right, bows nocked and arrows drawn to their jaws. Gaear, his fur bristling and fangs bared, waited next to Padraig.

My heart sank. Seven Atani against a monster. *They'll never survive.* Screaming his war-cry, Malik charged Flynn's hell-creature, the remnants of his last command hard on his heels. Like him, they shouted the Atani challenge to the enemy, the piercing *kı-yı-yi, kı-yı-yi-yi* as they galloped to their deaths. *They're all dead.*

I didn't realize I'd spoken aloud until Iyumi's hand slipped across my wrist. "Malik has power," she murmured. "Power unlike any other."

"But, not even he–"

"Shhh."

Her soft voice silenced me more effectively than a shouted order. "You must believe."

I didn't. What I believed I saw right in front of my eyes. My friend, my brother, galloped into death's fiery abyss with his sword bared. He took with him my friends, those I shed my blood for and would have died for, had the gods willed it. I believed they fought in vain, thusly died in vain. I turned my face away, my throat so thick I barely got the words across it.

"I believe it's time we got out of here."

My hand on the roan's bridle dragged him with me as I urged Kiera up the steep slope of the valley's north rim. Up and up we cantered, my head bowed. I tried to shut my ears to the sound of the battle that raged below, knowing full well I'd not see them again this side of death. *Malik, you noble fool–*

Half-blind, seeing yet not, I trusted Kiera to find the easiest path, felt her half-buck beneath me as she strove for higher and higher ground. At my right, Iyumi muttered under her breath– either prayers or promises of what should happen if her mount stumbled. Muted by distance, the sounds of the battle grew indistinct and all but meaningless in my ears.

Flynn obviously planned for a potential escape of his coveted bride. Before Kiera and the roan had carried us halfway across the rim, their hooves triggered his explosive traps. Flames, dirt, rocks and shards of nails and glass blew upward and outward in a sharp, coughing roar. Kiera reared high, screaming, throwing me hard from her back. Pain exploded across my shoulders and left arm as I struck a boulder, rolled over it, and lay face-down, stunned, in the loose dirt. Half-blind, I lunged upward, crawling, my hand reaching for my sword.

Iyumi cried aloud, in fear and anger, as her faithful roan fell sideways, his front legs shattered. Ever the consummate horseman, she rolled clear of her dying mount, his hind legs kicking in panic and torment. Skidding partway down the hill, Iyumi clutched a rock and stopped her fall. Blood spattered her face as loose rocks shredded all within their range; the fires of the explosion dying as the powder that gave them life were consumed.

Kiera crashed on her side, blood pouring from her mouth and nostrils. Her legs tried to send her body upright, but the damage was done. Her once-pristine coat caked in blood and dirt, Kiera's strong legs failed her at the last. Struggling to rise, she whinnied her panic as they bent and broke, casting her down to slide several rods down the mountainside. A born fighter, she kicked rocks and snorted dirt, her body bent sideways as she tried once again to regain her hooves beneath her.

I groaned as I heaved my way up, ignoring the agony of my busted arm and cracked ribs, crawling toward my girl. "Kiera," I gasped. "Kiera, honey, it's all right, I'm here, baby, lie still."

Her dark eye rolled toward me as she floundered, still trying to rise and fight. A deep, throated whinny, more akin to a groan, escaped her fluttering nostrils as I collapsed next to her. Clamping my broken left arm tight to my side, I pulled her heavy head across my lap. I stroked her sweaty face, willing her to calm, to look at me, to trust.

"Be still," I whispered. "Be calm, my love, my Kiera."

Her muzzle lifted toward me, her nostrils flared and her eyes ringed white. Sweat caked the dirt on her neck, turning it instantly to mud. Beneath my hands, she quieted. Her great hooves ceased to thrash, offering me one swift thought of gratitude and hope. *She ll be all right,* I thought, *given time and healing.* Malik can–Malik can–

That thought crashed inwards with renewed reason. Malik was dead, or as good as. Kiera lay broken and far beyond the healing power of anyone save me, and I couldn't heal a rash. Unless Kiera received help soon –

Her ear swung toward me in acknowledgement. The one soft eye I could see rested upon my wretched face, offering me her love. That was all. Her legs sank into the churned soil. Her silken head relaxed against my legs. She breathed in one last gasp and her great, soft eyes rolled up in her head. *Gods, no!*

My heart shattered in my chest.

I lost her. She died in my arms. I failed to save her, failed in my most sacred duty, to keep alive those I loved. She's gone, and she didn't take me with her. My girl left me, she left me behind. Taken from me between one heartbeat and the next. *Gods, how could you let this happen?*

Come back, I tried to scream. *Kiera, come back.*

Tears burning, stinging my eyes, but failing to fall, I watched in abject horror and grief as Iyumi dispatched her stallion with quick, efficient strokes of her dirk. The blue roan bled out quickly, collapsing in on himself like a spent bladder. She ended his pain, and his life, with quick mercy. I'm glad I didn't have to offer Kiera that. I doubted I could. I stroked my hand under her thick mane, her flesh warm and supple as though she still lived. *Kiera!*

"Van."

Her voice, soft, mild, determined, raised my face from the gashed form of Kiera. "We have to go."

In the distance, thunder rolled across the valley below us. Flashes of lightning and fire bloomed as Malik's battle raged against Flynn's monstrosity. I didn't want to see the end. I studied Kiera's beloved face rather than witness another one I loved die, taken down by a monster. I turned my back on the battle, trying to shut my ears to the sounds. *Gods send you to eternal heaven, Malik, my brother.*

I nodded. My hand stroked down Kiera's brow and across her closed eyes. "Good bye, my beauty," I whispered. "May the gods embrace you, little girl."

Wriggling out from beneath her huge head, I carefully set it down on a pillow of earth. Holding my broken left arm with my strong right, I stumbled to my feet. I turned my face away from her corpse and staggered several strides uphill.

Must escape. She s with the gods now. The child, we must find her. She s gone, she s dead, I love her, oh how I love her. 1 ll see her again. 1 m an Atan, I wear the ring. I mustn t let Malik down, he s trusting me to see this through. Malik s dead, Sky Dancer's dead, Kiera s dead– they re all dead–

Iyumi's warm fingers slid over my wrist and effectively halted my internal monologue and my strides. I blinked several times, homing onto her reality as a moth dives toward a dancing flame. I needed that touch, that reassuring contact that told me I hadn't yet entered the realm of the damned. *Kiera s dead, but Iyumi isn t. She needs me now.*

Her blue eyes met mine with calm sympathy and deep sincerity. "I'm so sorry, Van. Truly I am."

I tried for lightness. "She's just a horse, right?"

"Don't, Van. Don't do this."

Her grip tightened. I bowed my head, my chest burning. *Kiera!*

I shook off her empathy like an unwelcome blanket and jerked my head uphill. "We've leagues to cross, Princess," I murmured. "Best we get started, eh?"

"But, how?"

How was a very interesting question. Fortunately, I'd travelled often as a Centaur. The shape fit me, and the situation, perfectly. I could hold my bow in my right hand. Pity my left didn't work. Iyumi might ride astride my back. She rode a horse better than any royal cavalry master. Dead easy.

I quickly shifted forms. My equine hooves stomped the loose soil as my tail restlessly slapped my hocks and flanks. I settled my sword across my bare shoulders, ready to hand. The Centaur form felt so natural, so familiar, but it brought forth only memories of my brother who had died to save me. Quashing the bitterness, the grief, I glanced down at myself. Black hide, white socks, black – *whoa, time out. Why Kiera s colors? Gods!* My heart burned within my chest. I knew why. So she'd never truly leave me. Firmly, I changed all my color to black. The same color as my hair, my mood and my outlook. The similarities to Malik be damned. I'll not change to all white, for gods' sake.

If Iyumi noticed my swift transfer from piebald to all black, she gave no sign. Her attention seemed directed at the battle far below. I dared not glance down, for the sight of Malik's dead body might well tip my sanity over the edge. Rather than follow her gaze, I adjusted the way my swordbelt rested with my swordhilt within easy reach, and hanging my quiver from my human waist over my left equine shoulder. I extended my right arm down to her.

"Your ride awaits, my queen."

She turned back, trying for a smile as she gazed up, into my face. "Right."

Taking my arm, she vaulted upon my back and gripped my barrel with her strong legs. Slim arms crept around my middle. Was that her head resting against my spine? It didn't matter. Her feather weight hindered me not at all, and her easy, natural balance assisted me in finding mine.

Steadfastly refusing to glance back toward those I left behind, I swung into first a fast lope and then into a dead run. Uphill, away from death and ruin, toward the high, snow-capped peaks and the child that needed a bitchy princess. I leapt worm-tracked deadwood and fallen timbers, ducking under low-hanging branches of winter pine and sturdy oak. My hooves crashed through thickets and kicked up last years' needles and dead leaves. I jumped a gurgling stream, galloped down its rocky course and up its far side. Iyumi stayed with me like a tick to a hound, her grip on my waist light and sure. She didn't speak, for which I felt grateful. I doubted I could tolerate the usual platitudes, no matter how well-intended.

Refusing to think, numbing my heart against the grief that besieged it, I concentrated solely on my footing, speed, and making sure I didn't toss Iyumi off my back and onto her royal head. Up and up, forcing my body into working harder than it ever had

[310]

before, I followed the winding game trails that led deeper into the mountains, traversing the high passes as the deer, elk and wild cattle crossed. Eons old, their twisting paths led me higher into the tall ranges, rather than below to water and shelter from the harsh winters.

Above us, lightning cracked across the lowering clouds as the sun sank behind the tallest peak. The storm Malik and I noticed hours before, finally, like a shy milkmaid at her first suitor, emerged from behind the barrier of the mountains. Shyness, however, wasn't in its vocabulary. It intended to bull downward with all the force of the gods' ire behind it.

We had leagues behind us and leagues yet to run. A storm like this may very well slow us to the pace of a snail drunk on Tamil's home-brew. A delay we couldn't afford. The freshening wind brought chills to my sweating chest, arms and flanks. Crap, crap and *crap*. Mountain travel was difficult enough without adding cold wind, rain and sleet into the mix. Surely the gods' penned my name on their collective shit list.

I turned my head slightly, catching Iyumi's alarmed eyes. "Hang on. We're in for a long night."

CHAPTER 10

Dra'agor

*O*utsmarted. Defeated. Again.

Vanyar and Princess Yummy galloped out of the river valley, and out of my sight, leaving their dead mounts behind. Ducking into a canyon half-hidden by a thicket, he carried her on his broad Centaur back into the jagged mountains. Escaped. Gone. Just like that. *Damn.* That boy was good.

"You let them escape?" Blaez shrieked, busting apart my admiration for Van. "You fool! How could you let them escape?"

I sighed, rubbed my ear, and tried unsuccessfully to quell the nausea rising in my belly. The magic powers I used, and especially the evil I conjured up from hell itself, gave rise to the sickness I learned to associate with the boy's sacrifice. Squinting down into the gloaming, I tried to recall exactly how I conjured the damned thing. I seemed to remember the incantation coming to me, as though someone stood beside me and breathed it into my ear.

No matter. It's here and it'll kill Malik and his surviving Atani. Malik. *Another weird story.* I know, *I know*, the river broke him into pieces. Vanyar may have dragged him up before he drowned, but no, and I mean *no* creature could survive the river falling on him. No matter how strong a beast he was.

Conquering his mind wasn't easy. I only survived the task because I took him completely by surprise. A very old spell, one long forbidden by the Great Elders before the ancient Mage Wars, rose to my hand. I don't know where it came from, but I used it just the same. I entered his consciousness with all the stealth of a silent bat winging onto its brainless prey. My will overpowered his. He started up in alarm, but my stolen magic forced him into subservience. He recognized me and what I was there for: his death. He was powerless to prevent it, however.

I told him to stand in the river, and he obeyed me. When Van sought to intervene, I clenched down on my will. *Stand,* I commanded. *You will do as I say. Stand in the river. Let none convince you to move.* That he obeyed me, that the spell worked, excited me to my core. Might this work on my father? Imagine the possibilities.

Once inside and in control, I found Malik not just intelligent, but that he possessed a mind as great, if not greater, than many of our geniuses. In strict, disciplinary control of himself, he owned no thoughts that ran counter to honor, loyalty, compassion and a high-regard for King and country.

Malik stood for everything I didn't, despising all I stood for. Who was the better man? Malik certainly. But, folks, who was alive and free, and who looked to become demon dinner? I glanced, uncaring, down at the sight of Malik and his pals fighting my monster, and stroked my finger down the scar on my cheek. *I owe you that one, Malik. May you rot in hell forever.*

Turning away, I tried not to hurl what little lay in my belly.

I whistled for Bayonne. "I didn't let them escape," I said, answering Blaez with my gut churning, roiling and threatening to reverse direction in one swift move. "They did that all by themselves."

"We should ride hard after them," Blaez screeched, dancing on his toes. "Ride, ride now."

[314]

I squinted at the lowering sky. "It'll be dark shortly," I replied. "And it's going to rain. We'll start in the morning. First light."

Blaez raised himself on his toes and screamed. "They'll be long gone by then, you ass!"

I winced, my belly heaving. "Blaez, please. Chill out, will you? We'll hunt them down tomorrow."

"Uh, m'lord," Buck-Eye said, staring down the hill. "What if they kill your, er, your, uh–"

Bayonne trotted to me, his silver coat gleaming in the near darkness. Though he ran when that bloody bull charged full upon our rear, he returned when I called with most of the loose horses clattering behind. I forgave him all and rubbed his ears, stroking my hand down his bony face. "They won't, Buck-Eye. He'll be eating Atan horses and chickens for his dinner."

"Then what?" Boden asked, his eyes ringed in white. "M'lord prince, then what? Will it come after us?"

His question made me pause. Then I shrugged. "If it does, I'll deal with it. Meanwhile, mount up. We'll ride back a ways and camp for the night."

"But, m'lord," Boden said, his skin waxy-pale. "What of Todaro? Kalan? They're . . . they're still . . . ."

"Dead, Boden," I replied, swinging into my saddle and feeling for my stirrups. My gut threatened to heave, but I forced the nausea down. "If you want to fetch their corpses out from under yonder fight, knock yourself out. Meanwhile, I'm for a hot drink and a hotter fire. Come with me or not, your choice."

Nudging Bayonne into a trot, leaving the lightning, booms and fires of the Atani battle with my monster on the far side of the hill, my ears scarcely registered the sounds of my men scrambling into their saddles. From a distance, I heard their calls: "M'lord, wait!" "M'lord prince, hang on!"

Until one voice, rising in a scream of outrage and hate, purged all other sounds.

I seized steel and kicked Bayonne sideways, all in one motion. Half-turning in my saddle, raising my blade, I balanced precariously on my left stirrup.

Charging his black stallion toward me, Blaez didn't raise just his sword. He swung with all his magic behind it. Flames raced down his blade. His eyes glowed red under the swift flashes of lightning. Saliva dripped from his clenched teeth. As evil as the demon I summoned, my father's chief terrorist forgot our truce and remembered how badly my old man wanted me dead.

I ducked and reined my horse left.

A better magician than a horseman, Blaez continued his scream as his black charged past Bayonne's startled face and carried Blaez well beyond any harm to me. I lifted my own sword and kicked my boy into a gallop, hoping to dispatch the traitor before he knew I was there. Though I never won any tourneys with my swordsmanship, I did know which end worked best in this situation. I planned to sink that bad boy hilt deep in Blaez's neck and watch as it burst out from his gushing throat.

Blaez certainly had a few tricks to teach me. He ducked without turning, reining his horse into a swift, sliding halt. My sword whistled over his head as Bayonne carried me past my target. Blaez's powers, shaped like a fist and just as hard, struck me hard between my shoulders. My wind gone, I fell from my saddle to land with a breathless crunch to the stony soil. My father's bomb-creator spun his black around and charged, yelling like a tribal shaman, his expression triumphant. I lay there, stunned, trying to get my wind back.

As Blaez charged, my blood in his eyes, Buck-Eye created a blaze of his own. The black stallion reared high, screaming, as a wall of fire spun out of nowhere between Blaez and his quarry–me. Blaez's expression, behind the raging yellow, orange and red flames, lit eerily like a mummer's mask. Not just rage, hate and blood-lust. No, my dear Blaez's sanity had long since fled for other climates. I found no reason, no stability at all in the Commander's furious countenance.

My eyes squinted against the heat and glare, I saw Blaez search for a way past or through the conflagration to yet pounce on my prone body. His powers tried to drown Buck-Eye's flames, but Buck-Eye had learned a great deal since this morning's magical lesson. More than half the battle's explosions were not of Blaez creation. The hungry fires reached for Blaez, tiny fingers stretched outward to snare him within their grasp. Perhaps my Commander might relish a death by flames.

Outmaneuvered, Blaez reined his rearing horse aside. Licking flames kissed his black's tail, threatening to engulf them both in searing heat. The stallion kicked backwards, panicked, fighting the bit. He plunged and reared, dancing on air as he fought Blaez for control.

"I'll get you, Prince!" Blaez yelled, spittle flicking from his gritted teeth. "You and yours will die, boy, by fire and steel! I'll bring your entire house down upon your heads!"

Sawing savagely on his mount's mouth, he spun the horse and set spurs to black hide. Beyond the roar, I clearly heard hooves thudding down the hill, Blaez's round head bobbing with every step. His horse's flagged tail and sleek rump vanished into the half-light and darkened forest. As his horse's thudding hooves vanished from my ears, I heard the lonely lament of a wolf crying to the rising moon.

Buck-Eye killed his flames, willing them to subside. They obeyed him, dropping into mere sparks upon the scarred and torn earth. Smoke dissipated reluctantly, stinging my eyes and throat. It's oily scent clogged my lungs, making it hard for me to breathe anything clean.

"Don't let him go," I gasped, wheezing, floundering in the dirt, trying to get up as Buck-Eye's protective flames died away. "Get him back, get him back."

"Boden!" Buck-Eye yelled. "Torass! Help me!"

Blaez's man galloped hard on his master's heels, thudding into the gathering darkness. My sworn bodyguards leaped from their saddles to assist me, as Lyall gave chase after a fleeing Galdan. Lyall's red roan vanished into the gloom, dim light shining off his drawn sword.

With Todaro and Kalan dead, Blaez and his lad racing toward home and hearth, I recognized a certain annoying handicap. My little pack down by four left a mere four men paid handsomely to protect me. At this rate, I'd be forced to beg my nasty sire for more mercs.

Lyall gave up, and cantered his horse back, shaking his head. "He's gone, m'lord prince. They both are."

With Buck-Eye's strong arm under my shoulder and mine over Boden's young back, I gained my feet. Without hurling, I might add. Though the prospect of such added strength to my willpower more than Blaez's treachery. I hated hurling, in all its many forms. My gut heaved, and I kept it under strict control with the barest of margins.

"Don't matter," I muttered, bent into a horseshoe. "Better off . . . without them."

"M'lord?" Buck-Eye asked, "you all right?"

"Of–" I managed, "–course."

"No, he ain't," Boden said, his tone worried. "Get him on his bugger. The sooner we're away from this place, the better."

"Aye," Torass agreed. "Something'll trot over yonder hill, and, personally, I donae want t' be here when it do."

Strong arms boosted me onto my horse. Quivering, sweating, my head spinning like a top under a child's hand, I offered no protest. Instead, I gripped my pommel and held on as my lads nudged their mounts into a swift gallop and carried me with them. Black seeped into my vision. Moonlight shown down, bright and full, as Bayonne's strong gallop carried me into nothingness.

"Flynn."

Iyumi's dulcimer voice parted the darkness like a knife. Her soft, tiny hand stroked my brow. Sweet, royal scent lulled my senses and threatened to drag me deeper into the sublime depths of delicious unconsciousness. I wrapped her vision around my shoulders like a second blanket, and snuggled deeper into her arms.

I breathed her name. "Sofia."

"Sofia?"

The voice without hardened. The soft hand left my brow.

I tried again. "Sofia?"

The now hard fist slammed me face-first into the dirt. I woke, sputtering, cold, my head aching as though Blaez had taken his flaming sword to it. My belly lurched, threatening to hurl its contents at a previously unrecorded speed. I blinked, half-rolling onto my side and raised myself on my elbow. "Mother?"

"Ah, you finally got the name right."

Enya sat primly on a smooth log beside a blazing fire, her skirts gathered precisely around her trim legs. Coiled this time, not hanging about her slender form like a shroud, her golden hair gleamed under the red-orange glow. Yet, the face that met my bleary gaze wasn't my mother's. While it owned my mother's pale, regal beauty, it wore the harsh features of a dark stranger. Dark red eyes gleamed within deep-set hooded sockets. Full lips stained in garnet parted in a feral smile. White-washed teeth like those of a corpse, long-dead, gleamed under fish-belly pale skin.

I cringed back, filled with fear, tasting coppery panic on my tongue. *That s not my mother*, my mind gabbled, incoherent. *What is it? What is that thing? What have you done to my mother?*

Lightning flashed briefly, illuminating her yet at the same instant shadowing the hollows under her eyes, her cheekbones. Thunder grumbled in the distance. Its throaty growl caught her voice within its grasp, and mixed them together.

"You've made a proper hash of everything," Enya said, her tone cold as she half-turned away to soak a cloth in a steaming bucket. "Why I bother with you, I can't imagine. Sometimes I think your father's opinion of you isn't bloody, dead-on accurate."

The woman that squeezed excess moisture from the cloth and dabbed the sweat from my cheeks, brow and neck was my mother in truth. Though she didn't wear her usual eager to please expression, her corn-flower blue eyes held a new *1-don t-know-what-to-do-with-you* hint of exasperation I'd never seen before. She might love me, her eyes and face told me, though I tried her patience to the hilt.

My mind refused to comprehend and shied away from the melding of the two women I saw, one over the other. I half-rose and

[319]

shifted away, scooting on my butt as the blanket covering me slid off. At least I was fully clothed. Had I been naked under that stern gaze, I think I'd have died from mortification alone.

"Thanks," I stammered, reaching for and plucking the cloth from her fingers. "I'm all right."

I used it to further wipe sweat from my face and neck, all the while eyeing her sidelong. I half-expected her to leap toward me, and bite through the skin over my throat like a rabid beast. As usual, Buck-Eye, Boden and Torass sat around the roaring fire, talking in low tones. Lyall must have picked first watch, for I didn't see him. If my body lay open to death, it would take me while they sat, gossiped and picked the cracks of their asses. They paid no heed to my visitor, incompetent idiots that they were.

She snorted. "I can bloody see that. I'm not a complete fool, Flynn."

"Course not."

"You're useless, boy."

Her use of the word 'boy' set my hackles rising, stiffening like an outraged cat. My mother never called me 'boy'. King Finian the Fair retained full possession of that title, and he jealously guarded his treasures.

My back securely ensconced with a stout oak defending my rear, I tossed the damp cloth toward her feet. "Vanyar is clever."

Her brow arched gracefully. "My son willingly admits his foe is smarter than he?"

I stiffened. "He has resources I don't have."

Lightning flickered again, lighting those reddish orbs, that feral smile. Thunder grumbled, like an overfed belly. "Those *resources* are yours if you have the guts to seize them in your fist. Reject them once, and they don't knock again."

"I thought I did well enough with the demon," I replied. "Malik and Company are dead. Iyumi and Van are alone."

Enya's frown deepened. She crossed her arms over her lush bosom; her right index finger tapping thoughtfully. "Just who gave you the power, boy? Who gave you the incantation that summoned it?"

Shocked, I failed to note that contemptuous title. "You?"

"Are you stupid, or do you practice often? Of course, it was me." My mind tumbling over the import of those arrogant words, and trying to meld them with the voice of the woman who claimed to have little magical power, I gaped like a fish. My mouth opened and closed, feeling as stupid as she called me. What I might have said to her escaped my tumultuous thoughts as the sky behind her lit up like a flaring torch under the broad fingers of white lightning. Illuminated for seconds, I recognized the creature that emerged from the shadows behind her. As well as its terrible threat.

The lightning lit the night sky again, revealing the huge grey wolf with splashes of white around its eyes and paws. Streaks of light grey flowed through its heavy coat. Quiescent, non-threatening, it watched me with intelligent amber-brown eyes. But it stood less than a rod from my mother, dwarfing her and easily capable of killing her in one swift pounce. I froze, gathering both my power and my sword into my fist. "Mother, don't move. There's a–"

Enya glanced disinterestedly over her shoulder. She snapped her fingers.

As obedient as one of my father's mutts, the wolf padded silently to her side and sat down. He glanced fearfully toward her, his ears slack and his tail swishing half-heartedly in last year's dead leaves and twigs. He returned his gaze to me, and I swear his eyes pleaded.

"What–"

"You sound like a moron, Flynn," Enya snapped. "Try for words of more than one syllable."

I flushed. "You never told me you had a pet wolf, Mother."

She uncrossed her arms, still regarding me with contempt in her blue eyes. Her hand rested lightly between the wolf's ears, but I saw no affection in her gesture and the wolf cringed. "He's hardly a pet, dear. He serves me."

"Right, I can see that. A wolf is ever so handy, don't you think? Runs errands, brings you drinks, warms your feet in the winter."

Her brows furrowed as her blood-red mouth frowned. Reddish eyes flickered in the firelight. "I'll thank you to watch your tongue, boy."

My hackles rose, yet my gut clenched. Treacherous sweat trickled in tiny runnels down my ribs. Under the approach of the storm, the temperatures in these high-altitude hills dropped swiftly. So why did I sweat? How had my mother changed from the queen who adored her family into this menacing stranger? This wasn't Enya . . . but it was. My sweet, pliant mum who fretted over the welfare of Fainche and me, who doted on her heavy-fisted husband lay under this hellish stranger.

As though reading my thoughts, her face softened. The reddish hue didn't leave her eyes, but her lips smiled sadly. Her hand left the wolf's head and brushed a strand of hair from her cheek. "I'm sorry, Flynn. I'm under a great strain these days."

I nodded, my mute acceptance of her not-quite-an-apology apology. Living with my sire must be like hell on earth, without throwing his extracurricular activities into the equation. Small wonder Enya didn't seem like herself.

"We have little time, son," she went on. "In seven days, the sun and moon will rise together at dawn. If we don't have that child in our hands when it does, all will be lost."

"Lost, Mother?"

"Of course. If the . . . you know . . . *other one* has the child in her clutches on that dreadful day, then our beloved lands will be overrun by the Bryn'Cairdhans and their evil monsters."

"I see."

She breathed deeply, fetching a sigh. "Please understand, Flynn. Your father is . . . difficult. That bitch, his damnable mistress, still sings in his ears. I can't compete with her, Flynn. The princess is closer to retrieving the child. If you don't get to it first–"

"I will," I promised, my voice sounding hollow, even to myself. "I'll have them both by this time tomorrow."

"And Vanyar?"

I almost choked. "Dead."

Her features softened into the face I knew so well and would die for. The red flicker vanished and her cornflower blue eyes

[322]

smiled. She reached a hand down to me as she stood. I accepted it and rose to my feet, my thoughts frazzled. Tiny fingers caressed my cheek and swiped my hair from my brow, just as she did when I was a small child.

"You'll save us all, Flynn, my son, my joy," she murmured. "You've strength, power. You'll slay her?"

"Of course I will."

"Forgive me, Flynn?" she asked, her voice querulous, as though tears hovered on the verge of eruption.

I lifted her hand from my cheek and kissed her knuckles. "Nothing to forgive, Mother."

"I do love you, never forget that."

Lifting her skirts, she turned away, stepping lightly away from the fire and deeper into the night's darkness. It swallowed her, as though she had vanished down the demon's gullet instead of Malik. The wolf watched her go, his head over his shoulder. But he made no move to follow.

"Uh, Mother?"

Her voice echoed back, reverberating. "He'll remain with you, Flynn, and help you track down the princess."

The shadows consumed her, as though she'd never been there at all. Lightning flashed, and within the rocky and tree-lined clearing, its brilliance revealed nothing save the sough of the rising wind and a few dead leaves swirling across the dead grass and twigs. My eyes darted here and there searching, but never finding what I sought.

"This just blows," I muttered, combing my hand through my hair.

The wolf and I eyed one another uneasily. He whined, a soft, hushed sound that seemed to ask a question. I shrugged. "Pal, I haven't a clue."

The nausea returned on the heels of my mother's departure, pushed aside by my fear and anger. It hadn't abated in the least. My head spinning, my mouth dry, I fumbled for the amber jewel from under my tunic. The wolf watched me carefully. How did she get here? How does she leave? No one just vanishes. Did she turn herself into an owl and fly away?

Willing the jewel to show me Enya, I visualized her in her priceless ivory gown sewn with seed pearls and frilly lace, and her hair pinned into its tight coil. Just as she appeared to me not a moment ago. The sky above showed only twinkling stars and the pale moon rising over the distant eastern hills. I frowned, my gut churning. Where is she? I forced the image onto the jewel, how she walked, how she spoke, how she glared at me with those red-tinged eyes.

I turned and vomited ignominiously into the bushes.

Sweating like a pig facing the butcher's knife, I heaved next to nothing, landing in thorns that scratched my face and set blood to trickling down my cheek. I cared little for that, though. My belly was all that mattered. The evil I called with my ill-gotten magic returned with a vengeance. Where once my power gave me life and hope, this despicable product of an innocent life left me sick, on my knees and retching helplessly in the dirt like a worm.

Gods, make it stop. I'm sorry.

"M'lord! Are you all right?"

Buck-Eye and Boden strode rapidly toward me, silhouetted against the flames. Lightning flashed across their bared steel. Panic rose, swamping my gut. *I'm helpless. They're going to kill me.* Staggering, floundering to my feet, I backed away and all but tripped over that bloody wolf. Maintaining my balance with sheer will alone, I gripped my sword and prepared to draw.

I blinked, confused, when Buck-Eye seized me by the shoulders. He peered anxiously into my face; Boden watched me from just behind him. Torass edged away from the fire, his back to me, as though expecting an attack from whatever sent me headlong into the thorns. Like an evil beast, thunder rumbled and vibrated the ground I stood upon. The storm was close and it meant business.

"I'm–" I gasped, tasting sour vomit and smelling it on my breath, "–fine."

"Get yourself to the fire, my prince, and sit down before you fall down. Torass, get him some water."

Between my merc knight and my navigator, I stumbled my way to a rock by the fire, shaking with cold, sweat sliding down my cheek. This time, the approaching storm wasn't to blame for my chills. Only the evil I'd done that day soured my guts so. Torass knelt beside me, offering a skin.

Hefting it, I squirted cold water into my mouth, and turned to spit the acrid remnants of my gut from my mouth. Then I drank greedily, the sweet fluid calming my irritated stomach. "My thanks," I said, shaking with chill as I handed the almost empty skin back to Torass. He dropped it, and flung a blanket over my shoulders as he exchanged worried glances with Buck-Eye.

"I'll be all right, lads," I said, finding a small grin amid the shakes. "Given a night's sleep."

"We'll see to it you get it, m'lord."

"M'lord, who were you talking to, earlier?"

I froze, confused.

"I heard you talking, m'lord, no offense, mind. Just curious, sir."

"My mo–didn't you see her?"

"No, m'lord. Thought you were sound asleep, I did. Then I heard your voice, saw you sitting by the tree, still talking."

"But, she–"

"Who? M'lord, there's been no one since the Commander and Galdan rode off. Perhaps you talked in your sleep. I done that, a time or two, myself."

Buck-Eye slowly stood, his hand on his sword-hilt. "Uh, there's a wolf yonder, m'lord."

Torass also rose and yanked his sword from his scabbard. "Get behind us."

I sighed, wishing the world would stop spinning for just a few minutes and feeling more tired than I ever had in my life. "He's with me. He won't hurt anyone. Relax, lads."

"Uh, with you?"

"I'll explain later."

As my mother had, I snapped my fingers. The wolf stalked slowly into the firelight, tail and ears low; his white teeth bared against the threat of my armed and ready bodyguards. As tame as any hound, he sat beside me, whining low in his throat. His tail swished gently back and forth in the dead leaves and twigs.

"Chill, old son," I said to him, his muzzle on level with my face. "We'll get it all sorted, somehow."

"Are you sure, m'lord?"

My bodyguards weren't at all happy with a wolf in camp. Buck-Eye sat down across the fire, his eyes never leaving the newcomer. Torass didn't sheath his blade, but crept around behind me. The wolf ignored him and laid down, flipping his tail over his legs. He yawned, his ears flattened, before settling his head on his paws. As he gazed dreamily into the fire, Boden studied his non-aggression and shrugged.

"Almost time for second watch, I expect," he said. "My lot."

Imitating the wolf, I lay down next to the fire and pillowed my head on my arm. Though I knew it would leave my arm sore in the morning, I didn't care. Drawing my blanket up to my ears, I huddled under it, protected from the night's threatening storm. Before I drifted off to sleep, I glanced once more at my new companion. "Don't bite anyone."

I shivered under my thick cloak and a dreary, fog-blanketed morning. The muted sunlight failed to warm the early morning drizzle. The heavier rain ended sometime before dawn, and left behind a pervading chill that reminded my bones winter wasn't far away. It came early in the Shin'Eah Mountains.

"Got a name, son?"

Trotting beneath my stirrup, the wolf glanced upward, into my face, and wagged his tail half-heartedly. He didn't otherwise answer. Had I not seen that glint of sharp intelligence in those amber-brown depths, I might have thought him as ordinary as any dog. I sensed his desperate need to be free of my mother, and, oddly enough, I sympathized.

"If you don't have a name," I said, guiding Bayonne through the thorny thickets and tough, twisted trees toward the hill where I commanded the previous day's battle, "perhaps I should create one."

This time, he didn't bother to wag his tail.

"M'lord," Buck-Eye said, his horse striding steadily at Bayonne's flank. "It's just a dumb animal. Y'know, sir."

I caught a flicker of amusement from his slightly uptilted wolf eyes, and his jaws parted as though panting lightly. I know the beast laughed. I chuckled under my breath and winked.

"Either way," I said, over my shoulder to Buck-Eye, Boden and Lyall. Torass rode several hundred rods behind, acting as the rearguard of my tiny caravan. "I need to call him something."

"Wolf," Boden replied brightly.

"Wolfie," added Lyall.

The wolf sighed, his tail hanging low and bouncing against his hocks. I chuckled again. "I think they're onto something. How about Dra'agor? It means 'noble friend' in the Old Tongue."

This time, the old boy's tail wagged with some degree of enthusiasm. His parted jaws widened though he didn't look up.

"Dra'agor it is, then," I said. "Dra'agor, meet Buck-Eye, my knight and vassal. That young fellow behind him is Boden. I call him my navigator, because I believe firmly that if he fell into hell, he'd map his way back. Lyall, that droll fellow with the mustache, he's a good sort. But mind his knack for card games. He'll steal your whiskers and replace them with a hedgehog's quills, and have you believing you got the better hand. Yonder is young Torass. Decent enough cook, you'll have to try his fruit and nut combo."

Dra'agor didn't acknowledge the introductions, but shot me a swift there-and-gone glance of humor and approval. I nudged Bayonne into a rolling canter up the far side of the hillock I stood upon the day before, my lads urging their horses to remain close behind. "Like ale, Dra'agor? Wine? Mead? What will loosen that secretive tongue of yours? How about a willing, luscious tavern walker? I'll gladly fork over her fee, should you be so inclined."

Dra'agor sniffed loudly and I laughed.

I crested the fog-strewn hilltop and reined Bayonne to a halt. He didn't seem to mind that an enormous wolf capable of gnawing his hamstring stood beside him as Dra'agor sniffed the air. Boden and Buck-Eye flanked me, their horses stamping and snorting with considerably more concern over Dra'agor's presence than Bayonne.

"Gods," Buck-Eye breathed, his breath misting lightly beyond his face. "Look at that, m'lord."

I squinted through the grey. Though I couldn't see the river, I heard it as it hustled its way around and over the boulders and dead trees in its path. The valley below appeared like a dream–stunted trees, rocks and thickets poking through the mist in patches. "I don't see a bloody thing."

"Exactly. There are no corpses, m'lord."

I shut my jaw. I should be staring down at the remains of Malik and his bird friends, Griffin feathers stuck in brambles where my demon summoned from hell tore them apart. No human or horse corpses, either. From here, the valley appeared as innocent as a spring lamb.

"Did he eat them, m'lord prince?" Boden whispered, his tone horrified. "Your beastie, did he eat them?"

Dra'agor whined uneasily, his long tongue swiping his whiskers as he again sniffed the still, cold air. Behind me, I heard Lyall mutter a short charm against strong magic.

"Perhaps he did," I replied.

"Then where is your beastie?" Buck-Eye asked. "Maybe it's hidden, waiting to attack us."

I half-shrugged, chuckling to hide my own nervous tension. "I told you, I can handle it. Move out, lads. Daylight's wasting."

I expected them to ignore my order and remain frozen on the hilltop, whispering together like children. I nudged Bayonne into a careful trot down the hill. Wouldn't want him to step into a fog-hidden hole and damage a leg, I reasoned, all the while surreptitiously watching the nearby hills for my hellish creation. Buck-Eye, Boden and Lyall trotted behind, like burrs stuck in Bayonne's tail.

Dra'agor loped ahead, as though scouting for danger before we stumbled head-long into it. His grey and white coat melded into the fog so well he might have vanished utterly had it not been for his waving tail.

I reined Bayonne in sharply, gazing at the battle-torn ground. "Blood."

"Lots of it," Boden agreed, walking his horse around, his head lowered as he studied those few tracks that survived last night's storm. "Hard to tell anything, m'lord," he admitted. "It's all . . . confused."

"Looks to me like the beastie tidied up," I commented dryly, bending over my pommel to see better. "Ate everything."

Lyall made a gagging sound. My own gut toiled at the thought of the demon eating human flesh. Malik wasn't exactly human, but . . . eaten? Perhaps while still alive, screaming, as the beast bit down on his meaty rump, crunching his bones in his huge fist? While I wanted Malik dead, did I want *that* on my already tainted conscience? What of the fully human cavalry soldiers? Did they deserve that death? I swallowed hard, and lifted my head.

"Move on," I said, hardening my voice to quell its tremors. "A drink at the river, then we find the princess."

Kicking my horse into a fast canter, Dra'agor loping at his flank, I didn't stop until his hooves splashed river water high. Swinging down from my saddle, I knelt on the muddy bank and tossed handfuls of cold mountain water over my face and head.

I didn't care how cold it was. I drank and splashed, soaking my hair and the neck of my tunic, drinking until the sour taste of my sins washed away. Bayonne slurped the icy river as fast as Dra'agor lapped it up. As my lads filled their bellies and their horses drank greedily, I half-wondered if the thirst I sent into the Atani and their mounts the previous day lingered on. My demon might snack on our corpses before we knew he was there so focused we were on the sweet water flowing down our throats.

Sated, I stood up, and led my horse from the bank. Bayonne munched his bit, excess water streaming from his lips. Dra'agor lifted his muzzle and gazed dreamily across the river, his tongue washing his muzzle. He followed on my heels, as though answering my silent summons. I hadn't given one, though, but instead dragged the amber jewel from beneath my tunic.

Buck-Eye, mounted, urged his grey up the bank to stand behind me as Boden and Lyall swung into their saddles. "Where do we go, m'lord?" Boden asked.

The late arrival, Torass leaped from his horse to fall, as I did, to his knees in the mud to drink and wash his face and hands. His horse sucked greedily, his huge feet planted in the swift running water, and his white-ringed eyes on the new member of my group.

"Where are you, Princess Yummy?" I asked, my tone playful.

I willed the jewel show me my bride.

High above the misty fogbank, she sat on a large rock outside a small cave, braiding her hair. The bright sunlight gleamed off her brilliant silver tresses, casting light back into my eyes. I caught my breath on her simple, yet unconquered beauty. Her enormous blue eyes cast thoughtfully down as her fingers plaited. I craved to run my finger down her flawless alabaster cheek, her skin as pure as the sunlight caressing it. Her heart-shaped face with its dainty chin, and those pale pink lips pursed in concentration tilted toward her shoulder.

My eyes roved lower. Over her ripe breasts under the tight tunic and vest, its leather laces open at her throat. I pictured my hands roaming over them, teasing them, making her gasp with pleasure. My hands stroked downward, over her trim waist and flat belly, to cup her rounded ass. That ass fit nicely in my palm, oh indeed yes. Those long legs clad in–

Her head rose sharply. Her blue-in-blue eyes narrowed dangerously as her face swung toward me. I sucked in my breath, my heart slamming against my ribs. She couldn't possibly know I was here, watching her, fantasizing about–

She knew indeed. As though she saw me, leagues upon leagues away, my fingers clasping the jewel, watching her in the sky over the mountain tops. Iyumi's lips thinned in anger and disgust.

Where's Van? I didn't ask to see him. Was he dead? Why didn't the jewel show him to me? Was she alone?

Just then, he strode into camp, in his own body, his left arm wrapped in a stained white bandage. His belt knife dripped dark blood, his handsome face light and humorous as he asked Iyumi a

[330]

question. I couldn't hear it, of course, but I knew what it was, just the same. *"What s wrong?"*

His face tightened as Iyumi snapped an answer and stood. His eyes followed hers, idly flipping his knife in his fingers. Side by side, they stared straight into mine, as though in derisive challenge. Iyumi's right hand lifted. Straight from her shoulder it rose. Her snapping anger lifted her upper lip in a sneer, as her fingers made the sign.

"M'lord?" Buck-Eye's astounded voice rose from behind me. "Did she just flip you–"

"She did," Lyall said, his tone furious. "That bitch."

"Indeed," I said, both amused and astounded that she even knew what that vulgar and obscene gesture meant. And she a royal princess.

CHAPTER 11

Unfinished Business

I galloped headlong into the darkness and driving rain. Up, ever upward into the stony Shin'Eah Mountains, my hooves sliding across treacherous moss-covered rocks, dodging twisted tree limbs that reached with stiff fingers to snag my face. Icy wet sluiced across my bare chest and shoulders, my hair in my eyes. Iyumi huddled against my back, her teeth chattering; her chilled hands tight about my waist. I hadn't the will power to help, but her limited magic enabled her to spin a cloak from the air and wrap it tightly about her small frame.

Between the cloak and my body's heat, Iyumi managed well enough. The cloak kept her reasonably dry, and my taller frame sheltered her from the worst of the rain. I felt no cold. My panting breath steamed hard into the night, but I recognized no hardship. My busted left arm and cracked ribs spoke no voice. My body felt numb to outside influences. All I knew on that dark night was grief.

Everyone I knew and loved was gone. *Malik.* My brother, my friend. Never again will the world see his like. *Sky Dancer.* A lady I might have loved, if given the chance. *Wind Warrior.* A friend I'd only just begun to appreciate. *Aderyn.* My cousin, we shared not just our blood but laughter and love and dances. *Moon Whisperer.* Silent, yet steadfast, he kept his own council and still stood by me.

My mind shied away from any and all thought of Kiera, and I focused instead on those who I respected, even if they weren't exactly friends. They were my brothers and sisters, and I loved them for what they stood for: our beloved King Roidan and our Bryn'Cairdha. *Padraig.* Dour and angry, yet loyal and brave unto the last. *Grey Mist.* His dislike for me mattered not, he loved our King and that was enough. *Edara,* so young and full of life. *Kasi.* Filled with the fighting spirit that we embraced as Weksan'Atan. *Valcan.* Smart, talented, he kept his loyalty despite his doubts and remained a true Atan.

Edryd, Alain, Dusan–all dead before they had a chance to live. I wish Edryd had realized, before the end, I didn't kill his father. *Gaear.* Hmmm, well, his was the only loss I didn't truly regret. My heart, in its guilt, tried to mourn his death. He was an Atan, a brother, and a Clansman. No Atan should die like that. Not even Gaear the Inept. I hoped he died well, with courage in his fists.

As my darkest night, and my pain, wore on, my heart's ache yearned for three alone: Malik, Sky Dancer and Kiera. I couldn't shake their faces, their light, nor their love. My heart still beat within my chest, but it bled, shattered and broken. My breath caught, snagged in my lungs until I thought they'd burst. I couldn't see. I stumbled over hidden rocks, blinded by rain, tears and my hair, tripping, stumbling, only to gallop on, my hooves catching on fallen logs, twisted limbs. Ever up, higher and higher, away from the grief and misery. Fleeing from the ghosts of my beloved dead.

"Van!"

I barely heard her voice over the lonely laments deep within my soul. Malik's last words echoed within hollow chambers, booming and fading, only to boom again– *Save us all*. His deep voice resonated in my heart. *It s up to you now, my brother,'*

"*Malik!*"

You can t win this fight,' he saia. Don t watch me die.

[334]

I groaned aloud, my voice hoarse, as broken as my soul. "Malik, gods, Malik, don't leave me, please. Malik!"

Save us all, brother mine.'

"Van!"

I heard her then. Malik's voice murmured on the night wind, drifting apart, vanishing like the spirit it was. The nearly full moon shown down through the broken clouds. I hadn't noticed the rain had stopped, leaving a light, misty drizzle behind. The cold had deepened, however, and Iyumi shivered violently on my back. Her hand gripped my arm, dripping with wet and almost blue with chill.

"Van, we have to stop."

I halted near the crest of a steep hill, my hooves sliding backwards slightly under the thick, viscous mud. I found my balance with an effort and drew in one ragged breath after another. After a quick swipe, my eyes cleared of wet and my hair, yet the voices of my dead echoed in my ears. Perhaps forever.

I turned my head over my shoulder to meet her chill-induced teary but beautiful blue eyes. "Hey," I murmured. "You look like hell."

Her teeth gleamed under a quick, shivery grin. "You look like death warmed over."

"That sums me up in a nutshell."

"We both need food and rest," she said, her hand, kind, rubbing up and down my bicep. "Come, I'll tend your injuries."

The numbing cold and icy rain stilled the screams of my broken arm and cracked ribs. The bites and cuts from Flynn's devils woke with strident voices. I shoved the rising pain away from the forefront of my thoughts, and shoved them to the back, where they belonged. "I'm fine, really. Don't concern yourself."

I started walking up the hill again when her angry voice halted me. She called me a very vile name, her tone harsh. "Don't you dare dismiss me, First Captain Vanyar. I won't have it."

I glanced in confusion over my shoulder again, meeting her hot, royal gaze.

I tsked. "Where does a sheltered princess learn such language?" I asked, half in laughter, half in shock. Only the army's common barracks used words so foul.

"It doesn't matter," Iyumi replied. "There's a cave just yonder. We can shelter there until daylight. Treat me like a servant again and I'll have your guts for garters."

"Your wish is my command." I broke into a heavy trot, uphill. "Your Highness."

"And don't you forget it, Captain."

Why did her voice suddenly squeak? It rose high and quivery in the still cold air, as though she barely reined in some strong emotion. Love? Humor? Shaking my head, I carried her up and over the tall hill, following her crisp directions and hand gestures.

My hooves broke small stones and dead twigs over the edge of a steep cliff, a sheer drop of nothing between us and the bottom of the steep gorge save a few spindly trees and lots of sharp rocks. The small river rushing below echoed through the narrow canyon, dashing into my heightened hearing and drowning the sound of any potential threat. I half-expected Iyumi to cling tightly to my arm, dreading the long, lethal drop to the river below. Instead, she rode my back as easily as she rode her own palfrey through the streets of the city. Careless, confident and royal.

Leaving the rocky gorge behind, we cantered uphill for half a mile or so. The moon granted us enough light to guide our way toward the mountainside that faced roughly north. Its slant wasn't nearly as steep as its predecessor, and several deer broke from our sound and scent to bound on light hooves over the mountaintop and vanish.

"Where's this cave, Princess?" I asked, pausing to rest, my rear left leg canted back as I eased a cramp in my stifle. I breathed in ragged gasps, unable to hide the sweat sliding down my cheek despite the cold night. Her hair tickled my bare shoulder as Iyumi leaned forward to point into the shadows eclipsed by the dark.

"There. Don't you see it?"

I peered into the night. *Hmmm.* A darker shadow half-hidden by others, concealed by brambles and thorns. Large rocks and boulders strewn out front helped conceal the entrance from the

[336]

casual eye. A man walking by might never see it, or discover its existence. My heightened equine senses detected no enemies about, nor did I scent or hear anything alive in the cavern itself.

I glanced askance over my shoulder, peering down at her. "How'd you know this was here?"

Iyumi rolled her eyes as she slid down from my back. "Oh, please."

"Tell me a Faery buzzed the intel into your ear when I wasn't looking."

"They hate flying in bad weather. You know that."

When she made to stride toward the cavern, my arm pushed her back. Nearly squawking in surprise, she bounced off my protection and scowled.

"The gods may have told you about it," I said mildly, changing into my human shape. "But I'll make sure it's safe."

"The gods wouldn't have told me about it if it wasn't," she called to my departing back. "Insufferable, overprotective pig."

"Complacent, overbearing, high-handed fool," I replied, stalking away from her, my hand on my bared sword. "Stay put."

"Is that an order, Captain?" she sneered.

"You bet your sweet ass, plebe."

"I'm not a plebe!"

I reached the cave's entrance, and used my sword to brush aside the thorny brambles, peering into the darkness. I cocked my head to the side, listening with the strength of every creature I ever turned myself into. I heard nothing save the light brush of the wind over the high heather.

"Then don't act like one," I murmured, walking further into the hole. The place smelled musty and old, like a hamper full of unwashed socks. No slumbering bears, outraged wolverines, or annoyed skunks rose to the threat of my presence.

Calling on the last of my exhausted magic, I spun fire into my fist. My flames lit up the cavern, chasing its shadows into the darkness. Only a small cave with a sandy bottom and traces of dirt falling from the jagged ceiling met my sword and inspection. Within a few rods inside, it ended, the smooth walls of the granite rounded up to the top. Trailing roots from the stunted trees above hung down to tangle in my hair as I half-turned back to call Iyumi.

She bolted inside under my hand-held torch with an armload of twigs and dead wood. "C'mon," she gasped. "Help me. It's too bloody cold without a fire."

"Instantly, Your Worship."

She ignored my caustic title, and tone, just as she ignored anything that didn't serve her immediate need. King Roidan himself, under his breath and in private, called his only daughter and heir spoiled, insufferable and difficult. Us uncouth underlings called her "The Bi-" I stopped myself. I swore I'd never call her that title again, and went back out into the cold darkness. Gathering what wood I could into my one useful arm, I made several trips until Iyumi declared we had enough. The fire in my hand set it ablaze as Iyumi hunkered before its raging heat with a sigh of contentment.

"Now all we need is some food," she commented, sitting back on her butt, her not-so-blue hands rubbing together, extended toward the warmth. The light teased her cheekbones and turned her eyes into sapphires, creating a face so beautiful a man could die happy, just looking at her. No wonder Flynn wanted–I knew now why the simple mention of him, and her–

"I can fix that," I said, turning toward the cave entrance. "Be back–"

"Not so fast, Atan," she snapped. "Set your ass down."

A royal command was a royal command. I sighed, slumping my shoulders, and returned to her side. My shallow protest went only so far and fell apart.

"Shut up, soldier," Iyumi ordered. "Down."

I stiffened. "I'm not a dog."

Her finger pointed imperiously at the sand-covered floor beside her. Too weak to resist neither the beauty nor the order, I complied. Holding my weak left arm with my healthy right, I sank down onto my knees. I craved a stiff drink. My mouth squirted saliva into my mouth at the same instant I knew I'd need not just one of Tamil's hard-hitting shots of amber peace, but several if I was to remain sane within the next few minutes. No such redemption appeared in either pale liquid or soul-easing intoxication. Of course she'd hold me to unwelcome sobriety. She led. I followed.

Crap. Crap. Double *crap.*

Her slender hand caressed my brow, swept my hair from my half-shut eyes. Under the soft croon of her angelic voice, I recognized a prayer to those insufferable bastards who ruined my life: the gods. Treacherous sweat slid down my chin to drop dark stains in the dry sand beside my bent legs. The pain I refused to acknowledge swamped my guts with icy nausea. My arm and ribs screamed, on fire, throbbing with every beat of my heart. I needed a fully trained Healer; one who could put me into a trance and mend my broken, strained bones. A spoiled princess, no matter how willing, could replace the likes of Ilirri or Malik.

"Sit still, dammit," she grumbled. "Healing requires a reasonably cooperative patient."

How could one of her extremely limited potential heal wounds like mine? Perhaps she only meant to soothe them. My agony could use a bit of a balm. Enough to help me catch some sleep, anyway.

"Hey, where's the–"

Iyumi's hands reached for and seized my left wrist in her left hand and my brow with her right. Dropping her chin onto her chest, she closed those incredible eyes I wanted to kiss. Had Roidan taught her to heal? Sweet relief from savage pain crept down my bones and encouraged me to breathe deeply. That command I cheerfully obeyed. My eyes tightly shut, the tightness in my chest eased. I managed not one full breath, but two. Then three. Then four– *Whoa, time out.* I hadn't fallen asleep.

"You don't know how to heal," I muttered. "You haven't the power."

"The gods do."

"Tell them to go– "

"Shush," she commanded, her fingers reaching for my brow. "Shut up and let me try."

Her soothing touch did its work. Warm fingers slid across my brow, trailed down my temples, caressed across my wet cheeks. My

[339]

eyes shut of their own accord, despite my orders they remain open and observing. I felt more than heard her lilting chant, her prayers of healing and hope raised to the heavens above. Those singsong vibrations thumped against my ears like a drum heard from a distance far away, like the ghost of an ancient priest. My blood throbbed in time to that drum, my heart beating in sickly rhythm, heat rising, falling, only to rise again from the ashes.

Heat filled my blood. Ice froze it solid. I cried aloud against the torment, pain flooding my senses, swamping my soul. Still, I heard her voice rise in song, her fingers tracing their way across my broken left arm. They danced across my sprung ribs, teased a sharp bruise on my chest and soothed the anguish of my heart.

No!

I cried aloud. I shoved, hard, against the healing that spread to the grief in my heart, my soul. It sought to heal me of the pain the deaths of Malik, of Kiera, of Sky Dancer caused me. *Don t you touch it, don t you dare! It s my pain, my sorrow. Leave it alone. Leave me to my grief. I need my pain. Heal my hurts if you must, but leave me to grieve for those I lost.*

The heat slipped away, oozing from me as pus drips from an infected wound. My physical pain eased, though the tearing sense of loss remained. Its savagery ripped through my soul, and I half-wished I'd let the bastards take that pain, too. Its fury had abated, somewhat, similar to a binding that supports a broken limb. It doesn't heal, but it doesn't hurt–as much.

I blinked, tears and sweat stinging my eyes and blurring my vision. Iyumi's face swam in and out of my sight. A cold, wet cloth soothed my burning cheeks and wiped steamy sweat from my brow and cheeks. I breathed in and out, feeling empty, drained and limp.

I must've lay on my back, my head pillowed on Iyumi's lap, for I gazed up into her crystal blue eyes. She smiled sadly down into mine. A sharp rock bit into my left shoulder. No amount of shifting eased that nasty hurt.

"Huh?" I began, my throat raw as though I'd been screaming. "Pr – Princess?"

Her fingers stroked my hair from my brow. "It's all good, Captain. Your life is in the hands of the gods."

"Uh, wait–"

I struggled to rise, but only fell back into her lap, gasping, swearing. "Let me up, dammit."

"They are most pleased with thee," she said, sliding out from under my shoulders and head. "Rise, First Captain Vanyar. You are the gods' chosen champion."

"Shit," I gasped, struggling to my knees. Without her strong support, that wasn't an easy task. "They can kiss my fish-belly white–"

"Vanyar."

"They killed Malik, Kiera–I hate them."

"Hate them all you want, but you'll serve them just the same."

"Serve this," I gasped, before pitching forward onto my face.

I woke to Iyumi's slender back as she stood upon a large boulder, facing the east and the rising sun. The dawn's weak yet warm light spread across the tiny clearing at the cave's mouth. A blazing fire burned within a ring of stones, warming not just my skin but my prospects. I didn't remember starting a fire in the pit at the cave's entrance, but after last night, anything was possible.

Creeping on hands and knees from the cave's mouth, I huddled before the fire, roasting my hands and sighing in relief. Dawn lay its' still hand upon the mountains. No bird cheeped in the thorny bushes, rousing for the day's territorial squabbles. No rabbit scuttled through the underbrush. No raven or hawk soared on silent wings overhead, amidst the dawn's rising strength. Listening hard, I found only leaves falling from winter-bared branches to lie, face-down, on the stony heather.

Iyumi raised her hands high against the sun's early rays. Her chanting voice rose and fell in a language my ears didn't recognize. Her hands and arms wove a silent dance in harmony to her song, perhaps speaking in a holy dialect only the gods comprehended. The grace of her movements mesmerized and hypnotized me, catching me within her spell.

[341]

I blinked and turned my head aside, my eyes lowered. I felt ashamed, as though I watched a sacred act played between Iyumi and the gods. I spied on the holy, me the most sinful of all–a taker of innocent lives, a murderer and an oath-breaker. Surely the gods' wrath would strike me dead for laying my eyes upon so holy a rite.

If the gods' wanted vengeance for it, they chose to pass the opportunity by. Nothing at all happened except the sun rose higher, the shadows from the tall trees lengthened and a small fallow deer ducked away from the sound and scent of us to trot on nearly silent hooves toward a safer place to sleep the day away. As on every other morning since the world was created, the high altitude dawn lit the horizon and the towering peaks. Almost as ordinary as the yawn I couldn't halt with my hand.

"Grow up, Van," Iyumi remarked without turning her head. "You can't escape them."

"Escape whom?"

Iyumi stood and turned, the silver fall of her hair cascading past her shoulders to her hips. Her eyes burned. "You know of whom I speak."

"Oh, please."

I scoffed, picking at the bandage around my left arm, trying to ease the annoying itch. "Don't bore me with your preaching, sister. The gods hate me, and I them."

I rubbed the back of my hand across my mouth, craving a stiff drink just then. Hell, I didn't just crave it–I needed it, damn it. Why didn't we have any mead, or beer, or any bloody ale on hand? Who the hell traipses into the wild chasing a mystery kid without any medicinal alcohol in their pack? Heavens forefend!

Iyumi sighed, annoyed, watching me undo her best nursing. "Here," she said, striding forward. "Let me."

I drew my arm back, suspicious. "Let you what?"

"Pull your arm from its socket and beat you bloody with it," she snapped, her fair lips down-turned. "What do you think? Sit down, fool."

Shoving me hard with a strong hand to my shoulder, she forced me onto my butt. I missed the rock she intended my ass to hit, but my healthy right arm swept across her lower back and dragged her down onto the twiggy loam with me.

She had one breath for one royal protest before my lips enveloped hers. My tongue teased her open mouth, danced across her teeth, as I pulled her chest into mine. Her small breasts lay hard against me as my left arm, trailing bloody wraps, trailed up her hip, across her narrow waist to her shoulder before finally cupping her cheek. My body's heat flared, igniting a desire I'd never before known. No girl I'd ever been with compared to her. Her taste, her sweetness, her innocence brought forth a hunger, a craving that eclipsed mere lust. I didn't just want her–I wanted all of her.

Her body stiffened, her palm on my shoulder intended to push me back, into my place both literally and socially. For a moment, the pressure grew, then it abruptly fell away. She leaned into my kiss, our tongues tangling, dancing, entwined. She slipped her hands up my ribs, over my shoulders to wrap her slender arms around my neck. A soft moan eased from beneath her breasts, hard against my chest.

Damn, damn, *damn*. She felt so *right,* so perfect–as though we weren't two people, but one. One soul, one mind, one body. I felt her breath hitch as upon a soft sob, her arms clinging in desperation to my neck. Beneath my fingers, her small, firm body trembled as though cold. I knew, however, my kiss lit a fire within her that no mere water could quench. I breathed her in and exhaled myself into her.

Like man and horse, eagle and lion, man and bull, Iyumi and I completed one another as though melded since the beginning of time. Perhaps, in another lifetime, a saner world, we loved each other. Perhaps the gods felt mercy upon us, and though we died apart then, they granted us a new chance now. A new chance at love, and a lifetime together.

Or perhaps they merely teased us and laughed at our expense. With the divine, one never knew what to expect.

Pulling away reluctantly, Iyumi rested her cheek against mine. Dipping my face, I nuzzled her neck, kissing every inch of her throat I could reach. I felt the moan of denial caught, trapped, deep within her breast. *I wasn t for her,* I heard her think. Her father would never permit–his heir apparent and beloved daughter paired with an disgraced Atani Captain and Clan Shifter?

Not just no, but *hell, no.*

Holding her close, I ignored the obvious and followed my gut. I never did like the insufferable royal bitch who demanded obedience at every turn. I hated her air of superiority and her uptilted nose. But I sure as hell loved the sweet, humorous and fiercely independent creature who not just smelled nice but looked at me with those incredible eyes as though she might love me back.

"Kissing a royal without permission is an executable offense," she murmured, her tone husky.

I chuckled softly against her parted lips. "You can only execute me once."

My fingers on her chin, I tilted her lovely face up to mine and kissed her again, hungrily. She responded with a fierce desire of her own, her warm lips seizing mine, parting under my gentle assault. My passion chained, my body on fire for her, I gasped. My heart reeling; my blood roared in my ears. This is wrong, it's so *wrong.* But felt so *right.*

With heavy reluctance, I pulled away from her sweet mouth and luscious tongue, but not from her embrace. She leaned her brow against my jaw, her breath coming in short bursts. I ached in places that shouldn't. I kissed her closed eyelids and tasted the salt of her tears on my tongue, trying to stem the tide of my runaway desires.

"If we don't stop," I murmured. "We won't stop."

Iyumi's breathy giggle teased my chest.

"I mustn't dishonor you, m'lady," I muttered against her ear. "As much as I want to."

She raised her face and a strange sort of smile. Her fingers brushed a lock of my hair from my eyes. "Not a good thing, I expect," she replied softly. "Right now."

I kissed her uptilted nose. "No. Not right now."

"Our country needs saving first. Right?"

"Right."

"Don't forget the child."

[344]

"We both need food," I said, taking her by the shoulders and lifting her up with me. "We've a long way to go, yes?"

Nodding, Iyumi half-crossed her arms over her breasts, as though in protection, and stepped away from me. I needed no magic to feel the solid shield that slammed up between us. As effective as a high stone wall with fire-breathing trolls guarding it, her barrier protected her heart, and her soul, from attack from both within and without. "You're right, of course," she said, an odd note clear in her voice.

"Princess," I began, reaching for her.

She shook her head and walked, head down, into the cave.

What did I do? I stared after her, brushing my hand through my hair. Drat it, but women confused the hell out of me. Were I a man of Flynn's dubious character, I'd be one satisfied male right now. *He* wouldn't have stopped for the sake of propriety and a mystery kid. She liked my advances, I know she did. I felt it both her aura and in her fierce kiss. I saw it in her eyes, just as she saw the same in mine.

So why did she run?

Women are like stars, my son. Bright, beautiful and as cold and distant as those remote gems. Never forget that.

I shook my head. "I'll be back shortly," I said. "Any breakfast requests?"

Only silence answered me.

"What do you like? Princess? Pork? Venison? Tell me, what?"

She kept her answer as close as she kept the mystery child's location. What happened? First, we kissed. That was all right–all right, it was more than *all right.* I tasted her on my lips, and hungered for her as I never have any woman before. I lusted to strip her bare and feast on her sweet purity as a bee flourishes on nectar. I knew she wanted me just as badly, for I felt it. I heard her thudding heartbeat against my chest. I scented her need as a horse might scent a pasture of lush green grass. She wanted–*me.*

Then I opened my mouth and she vanished.

Damn me and my idiocy. I don't know what I did, but I certainly knew I was to blame. I never did understand the female

[345]

gender, and I reckoned this wasn't the best time to start. Perhaps one day, after Iyumi and the mystery kid were safely back in Caer Brannog, I might consult the mages that knew those intimate secrets of girls.

Posting a guarding spell over the cave, so none might find her with eyes or magic, I changed forms into a shape suitable for hunting. A fox. Slipping into the rocks and undergrowth, I put my sensitive nose to work. The previous night's rain brought scents to sharp life, and I quickly struck the trail of a mountain grouse. Following it for several hundred rods, I found not the grouse, but her nest.

Five eggs lay hidden in a thicket, protected by nasty thorns and sharp rocks. A fox might have difficulty seizing her offspring, but my human arm wouldn't. I changed back into Van the Insufferable Dolt. Slowly, thorns grazing my flesh, I plucked each egg from the twig and feather nest and set them beside me.

A jekki snake, it's scales banded yellowish and black, oozed from the rocks to my right, it's forked tongue flicking nervously. Venomous, but not very quick, it raised its snub nose toward me. Scenting me, it hesitated, no doubt assessing the danger I posed.

"Sorry, pal," I said. "You snooze, you lose."

My fast grip caught the serpent behind its head. Hissing, struggling, it almost broke free. Large, almost a rod long and a foot around, it was strong and as supple as a whip. But I was hungry.

I killed it with a swift snap of its neck. Carefully, piling the eggs into my cloak to carry them safely, I tossed the snake's still-warm carcass over my shoulder. Jekki made a fine meal, once skinned and roasted. My mother used to make a grand stew from a jekki snake, but I hadn't tried making it myself.

Whistling aimlessly, I strode quickly back to the cave and the princess. Iyumi sat in front of the cave's mouth and the fire, inspecting my choice of breakfast. She took in the eggs with pleasure, but eyed the snake dubiously. "Jekki?"

I hesitated. Did I blunder again? Would she flee into the darkness of the cave and refuse to eat? "Uh, you don't care for jekki?"

"Oh, I love it," she answered. "But it always gives me gas."

[346]

I stifled a smile. "I reckon I can stand the torment."

"Ha ha."

I placed the eggs at the fire's edge to roast as Iyumi combed her fingers through her hair in preparation for braiding. I drew my knife and strode to the thicket, the jekki still hung from my shoulder. Cutting a thick spike and shaving off the thorns, I stuck it upright in the soil.

I quickly gutted it and tossed the innards into the brush. As I skinned it, I stuck the carcass onto the sharp point of the branch, adding more and more as I deprived the jekki of its hide. I shot a swift glance toward Iyumi, checking, as ever, for any potential danger to her. The guarding spell hadn't whispered, or been tested, and its strength stood as defiant as I'd set it.

Her hair half-braided and falling from her fingers, Iyumi sat ramrod straight, her gaze on the distant hills. Her fair lips thinned into a white line, as her dark brows lowered in abject fury. Iyumi appeared pissed but royally, but at what? I glanced below, into the valley we left far behind, searching for tiny dots amid the forest that might indicate an approaching enemy. I saw nothing.

I walked rapidly toward her. "Princess? What's wrong?"

"Flynn." She all but spat the name. "Spying again. Can't you feel him?"

Half-shutting my eyes, I relaxed. Sending out a thin tendril of magic, I searched for the sensation of being watched. As though I stuck my hand into the maggoty remains of a corpse, my skin crawled. I felt his eyes like a heavy, hot weight on my skin. Repelled, I wanted to spit. That obnoxious weasel. Why can't he leave us alone? Rolling the hilt of my dagger through my fingers, I glared southward, into Flynn's magic.

Iyumi stood up, rage coursing off her in waves. At my side, her right hand rose to hover in mid-air. Again, she displayed the vitriolic knowledge of obscene language a royal princess shouldn't know. In a gesture, she invited Flynn to perform the anatomically impossible.

Flynn's magic abruptly dissipated.

"I think you upset him, love," I commented dryly, the title tumbling loose without thought.

"I bloody hope so," she gritted. She glanced up at me. "We need to hustle, Van."

I returned to my snake. "We won't get far without food. Turn those eggs, will you?"

Spitting the jekki over the fire, I conjured a waterskin as Iyumi ignored my abrupt tone and obeyed. Her fingers flinching from the heat, her face perspiring, she turned each egg to cook them evenly. Suddenly, out of nowhere, a Faery buzzed across my nose to rest, eight wings working in frantic harmony to hover just over Iyumi's shoulder. She clutched a purple blossom in her tiny fist.

Iyumi's flushed face bloomed in a swift grin. "Why, there you are, Ze'ana'ta. You're late, dear."

"I couldn't find you," Ze'ana'ta piped, darting upward to fix the flower behind Iyumi's right ear. "Bad men spy."

"I know, honey. Now be a good girl and go home."

Ze'ana'ta put her tiny hands on her non-existent waist and scowled. "I protect you."

As Iyumi raised her hand in invitation, the tiny Faery dropped to land delicately on her palm. Both glanced up as three more Faeries circled low over Iyumi's head, piping words of warning. "Go, Iyumi, run hard. Run now."

"We will, girls," Iyumi said, lifting Ze'ana'ta to eye level. "These bad men will hurt you, my sweet lovelies. Go home. Ask Queen X'an'ada to send a message to my father. I'm safe, with Captain Vanyar. We'll have the child in our hands this day. Will you do this, for me?"

One never ordered a Faery to do anything. But if asked with politeness and respect, a Faery would do just about anything for anybody. "We will, Iyumi."

Ze'ana'ta kissed Iyumi on her nose and flew into the air. Taking a moment to hover between my eyes, forcing them to cross, Ze'ana'ta clasped her hands in front of her as though in prayer. As far as I knew, the Faeries never prayed to any god or goddess. "You protect her, Vanyar?"

"I will, Ze'ana'ta."

[348]

"Promise?"

"Promise."

Satisfied, the four Faeries rose into the bright morning sunshine and vanished over the treetops. We watched them go, both of us smiling for who could not encounter a Faery and not smile? Our eyes met. She flushed and I ducked my head away, my belly fluttering like Ze'ana'ta's busy wings. Damn, but wasn't she as beautiful as those delicate Faeries?

"Are you going to fill that or strangle it to death?"

I glanced down. I held the neck of the skin in both my hands as though I indeed throttled it. I hadn't known what my hands were doing–expressing the desire of my heart. But what was that? Choke Flynn to death with my bare hands or caress Iyumi's silken flesh with my fingers?

"Fill it, I reckon," I muttered and all but ran to the nearby stream.

A tiny streamlet gurgled from between two large boulders not far from the cave's mouth. There, on my knees, I splashed icy water over my sweating face and neck. Cupping my hands, I drank deep, washing away the sour taste of sleep and fury. I tossed more over my head to clear my brain of morning fog and the memory of Iyumi's lips clasped within mine. Under its cold, my mind returned to the present. We must gallop hard. Find the kid and race back to Caer Brannog as though the devil himself were after us.

Because he was.

I filled the skin, and walked quickly back. I didn't like Iyumi left alone for even a moment. Not with Flynn lurking about.

I knew a little of the magic Flynn used to watch us. Somehow, he'd gotten his hands on a scrying crystal. The user willed the crystal to show him what he wanted most to see. I recalled uneasily that the crystal's magic could also send such willful user to the destination he most wanted to visit. If Flynn knew the magic could accomplish that–

Iyumi was right. We needed to move but fast.

Hunger rumbled in my belly. Yesterday's fight and my grief sapped my strength something awful. A decent sleep helped, and

[349]

food would improve matters enormously. Despite that, I felt seriously weakened after yesterday's battle. If I were forced to another fight of magic and will, well, I might not win. If I failed, I'd leave Iyumi, and the child, in enemy hands. If the gods required my life, they were welcome to it. I didn't much care. As long as Iyumi remained safe and free, and our nation along with her, I'd die a happy Shifter.

One helpful thing about snake and eggs for breakfast: they cooked quickly. Without speaking much, we devoured the hot eggs and salty-tasting jekki, washing all down with cold mountain water. My strength doubled after the food hit my belly. Iyumi's eyes seemed brighter, her outlook more cheerful, as I changed once more into a black Centaur.

Slinging the full waterskin over my shoulder, along with my sword belt, I dropped my hand down to Iyumi. Seizing it in a tight grip, she permitted me to assist her to mount my back. She settled behind my withers, her legs firmly ensconced around my barrel. When her hands rested upon my shoulders, I took them and wrapped them around my waist.

"Hold on," I said. "Time to outrun the devil."

My bow in my hand, and my quiver of bristling arrows bumping my equine shoulder, I sped into a hand gallop, uphill. My sword, like my clothes and human jewelry, remained with me despite my body change. I felt its power, like a second pulse of my heart, beating in time to my hooves. Had I the need, I could call on its magic to reinforce my own. I didn't need its hilt within my hands to wield it.

Alternating between a rolling canter and a swift trot, I carried Iyumi far from the river and its bloody battleground. My dead rode with me, silent ghosts like wisps of fog seen only from the corner of my eyes. The weight of their eyes, oh how heavy their mute accusations lay across my shoulders. I barely felt Iyumi's slender load, yet the restless spirits of those I loved dragged at my soul.

Rubbing my hand across my dry mouth, I unsuccessfully tried to stifle the sharp craving for a tall mug of Tamil's bitter ale. *That won t solve your problems.* It hasn't been the answer, and never will be the answer. I must learn to carry this load of guilt without its

[350]

help. The desperate yearning merely laughed. *1 m the only answer you ll ever need, laddie,* it informed me cheerfully.

Without either of us speaking much, I took us higher and higher into the savage Shin'Eah Mountains. Through the morning and into the afternoon, I followed one game trail after another, leaping deadfall and dodging boulders, startling flocks of birds into frightened flight. Annoyed jays screamed invectives as we passed, while a black bear stood on her hind legs to watch in curiosity as I galloped through her berry bushes.

"How far?" I asked, leaping a white, bone-dry dead oak, my forelegs tucked. I hoped Iyumi didn't notice the tremor in my voice or the shaking in my hands. Damn, but I needed a stiff drink.

"You see that cliff overhang, high on that ridge?"

Her slender finger pointed upward and to the right. I couldn't help but notice it wasn't as steady as her voice. Her tiny breasts dug into my back, forcing sweat to my brow. Her scent, a delicate odor of the blossom in her hair and a mixture of faint musk overrode all reasonable thoughts in my head. How can I fight for her when I can't see straight?

Shooting a swift glance up, away from my path and the many treacherous rocks and deadwood, I saw what she indicated. Like a beetling brow on an old man's face, a rocky ledge poked from the mountainside. The mountain itself, huge and steep, stood on the northern edge of a narrow gorge, rift with savage rocks. Once past that, I thought I spied a twisted game trail wending its way upward through the knotty pines and scrub oak.

"What do you think?" I asked. "Six leagues?"

"Eight."

I chuckled. "Cake and pie."

"Cake and pie?"

"Piece of cake, honey," I replied. "Easy as pie."

"Have you taken a good look at that?" Iyumi asked politely.

"At what?"

"That."

"Shiiiiit!"

[351]

Slamming my front hooves into the stony soil, my rear quarters slung under me as I slid on bare granite. Covered only in last year's twigs and leaves and as slippery as ice, small rocks bounced from my feet and vanished. Desperate to halt my forward momentum, I half-reared, my front legs boxing the still mountain air.

I made it, but only just. I dropped my front half back to the ground with a solid thump, Iyumi's tiny body still attached where it belonged. Dirt rose in a light cloud, swirling upward under the rattle of stones falling downhill. Iyumi coughed delicately, waving dust from her nose.

"This blows," I muttered, running my hands through my hair.

Inches from my hooves, the ground abruptly ended at a sheer drop into the narrow gorge. High rocky walls created when the top peak of the mountain broke away stood to either side of us. Much of the mountain top fell into the gorge, creating a very slim passage for the river below. Peering down, I saw no trail or potential passage around them.

On the far side, the ground lay open, save for a few twisted trees and bramble. Beyond that, the game trail wound its way upward, often doubling back on itself, but seemed to head toward the rocky outcropping. I thought I recognized the shadow of the cave just below it.

"We'll have to go around," Iyumi said. She half-turned to the right and pointed. "There may be a way down in that direction."

I didn't bother to follow her finger. "We don't have time for a 'may be'."

Iyumi tensed. "Van?"

I didn't answer. Turning, I trotted back the way we'd come. If Flynn trailed us on horseback, he'd be forced to find the careful way across the steep ravine. I had no such intention. With a strong lead, we conceivably could stay ahead of him by at least a day. My mind shied from the thought of him using the crystal to transport himself across not just the ravine, but also the many leagues between us.

Maybe he didn t know how to use the crystal, I could but hope.

Far enough, I thought, half-rearing as I wheeled hard on my haunches.

"Hang on," I ordered tersely.

[352]

Her hands met across my belly and clasped together the instant her strong legs gripped my ribcage. Dirt squirted from beneath my feet as I launched into a fast gallop. Faster and faster, my hooves kicked up loose rocks and tundra behind my heavy tail. Iyumi pressed her cheek against my back, her legs clamped down tight.

"I don't think this is a good idea—"

On the last word, Iyumi's voice rose in sharp crescendo as I leaped upward and outward. My forelegs tucked, my rear quarters propelled us into empty space. Iyumi screamed, but in terror or exultation, I couldn't tell. Far below, the river hurried through the lethal embrace of the canyon. Gravity pulled me downward from the height of my leap, yet I still had speed and strength on my side. If I miscalculated by even a foot—

The cliff's edge rushed to meet us. Extending my front legs outward, I struck solid earth a rod beyond its face. But my entire body couldn't possibly fit. I clawed for footing, my rear hooves flailing into space. That evil bitch, gravity, sucked my hindquarters toward her and into the gorge.

Crying aloud, I scrambled to keep my front hooves from dragging backward. The gaping maw of the yawning gorge taunted us. Hooves didn't catch well on rock, and my front feet cut deep grooves as my lower half was dragged backward, sliding, helpless. Iyumi's slender weight on my back fractured my balance, and she slid toward my rump. Only my hand gripping hers kept her from dropping, screaming, into the rock-strewn canyon.

Throwing my weight forward, I kicked at gravity's deadly grip and struck rock. I don't know what my hoof hit, but it was solid and unmoving. Pushing against it, I lunged forward, digging into the hard mountain granite, gasping for air. Leaping away from the canyon edge, I loped, then trotted into the realm of safety with all four feet on the ground.

Panting, I stood still, sweat trickling down my cheeks.

"I wish I could say that was fun," Iyumi commented, her voice hoarse. "But I despise lying."

I chuckled, my mouth dry. Turning my head, I found her face, drained of all healthy color, inches from mine. I didn't try to resist the sudden urge to kiss her. My lips roamed over hers, my hand on the back of her head preventing any possible escape. Instead of trying, she responded with a desperation that startled me. She clung to me as though drowning, her tongue tangling with mine.

The words, those three precious words 'I love you', rose unbidden from my soul, but halted in my throat. I couldn't say them. Despair took their place. I tasted bitterness on my raspy tongue. She could never be mine, never will be mine. She's royal and I'm scum. Her father will execute me the instant this mission finished. She's the High Priestess and the kingdom's heir. I'm a walking talking corpse.

She felt my change in mood and drew from me, her pink tongue trembling on her upper lip. Her blue eyes studied mine with a strange intensity, moisture blooming at the corners. Drawing a deep breath, she found an awkward smile and took her hands from my belly. In order to maintain her composure, she straightened her hair.

I tried for lightness. "Sorry about the fright, m'lady."

"What fright?" Her voice sounded eerily similar to mine.

I tossed her a faint wink. "I thought you despised lying."

This time her answering grin looked as genuine as her voice sounded. "Busted. Now move your ass, Captain. It's halfway to dinner and we still have leagues to go."

I offered her a half-salute. "Yes, ma'am."

My swift lope soon turned into a half-trot, half-lunging walk as I fought my way up the game trail. The mountain was steeper than it looked at first, thick with broken rock and fallen trees. Thorny bramble caught at my legs and snagged my tail. Had Iyumi not wrapped both arms about my waist, she'd have long ago slipped from my bare back to slide in a disgraced heap over my rump.

Twisting back upon itself, the trail was choked with sharp stones my hooves tripped over, and the many corpses of pine, juniper, and oak with their sharp limbs sought my hide and Iyumi's legs. Still living greenery slapped my face or scratched my cheeks before I could duck.

"Stop," Iyumi gasped. "Take a break. We both need it."

[354]

Unwilling to stop on the steep flank of the mountain, I lunged further up until I found a reasonably level ledge. Panting hard, I halted and bent over, sweat pouring from my hair and flanks. Yet, the air at this altitude had grown both thin and cold. I'd need to keep moving if I didn't want my hide to freeze.

Catching my breath, I gazed south. From this height, I could easily see the river and the green-grey highland hills we'd crossed only days earlier. Searching further, I swore the dark outline on the horizon was the deep forests and glens of the Khai River valley. Beyond that, Caer Brannog. Home.

"Beautiful," Iyumi murmured.

I glanced, askance, over my shoulder, then followed her gaze. "I suppose it is at that."

"Do you think any of them–" she began, her voice halting, unsure. "You know–"

"No," I replied, my tone sharp. "They didn't."

Iyumi took my rebuke in stride and fetched a deep sigh. "They're in good hands," she said slowly. "Wherever they are."

"No doubt."

I cast another glance over my shoulder. "You'd best cover yourself. You'll catch your death up here."

Wrapping the cloak more closely about herself, Iyumi smiled into my eyes. "Certainly. Mother hen."

Cursing under my breath, I strode out, clawing once again for every rod of height. At times, I traversed a tiny ledge of stone, wide enough for a slender deer or nimble mountain goat, but hardly wide enough for a Centaur of my size. Too often for comfort, my hooves slid over the edge, casting small rocks into the snags of trees, boulders and deadwood far below. When Iyumi suggested, her voice strained, that I change shape and walk with her on two human legs, I ignored her.

At that angle, I couldn't see the cave nor the rocky outcropping that marked its location. Craning her neck, Iyumi couldn't see it, either. "But, we're close, Van," she said, excitement rising. "I can feel it. Can't you?"

Concentrating on not sending us both over the edge, I merely nodded. I could lie when I felt like it.

An hour or more later, the mountain leveled out. I caught my breath, panting, managing a heavy trot as the steeply angled slope changed to a gradual incline. Above our heads, the peak, topped with everlasting snow, glared down at us from its immeasurable height. Behind it and its unseen brothers, the sun slowly advanced toward evening. We had perhaps two hours before dusk, the bright sun unable to warm us at this altitude. Though I couldn't see any dark clouds hidden behind the tall peaks, my gut and my magic told me yet another late summer storm advanced.

Iyumi's hand on my arm halted me. Shifting my feet on the rocks that threatened to turn under them, I glanced over my shoulder at her. She wasn't looking at me, but rather gazed up, past my head, rapt. I turned my head, following her gaze.

Up close, the rocky outcropping didn't look much like an old man's beetled brow. At this proximity, it resembled a sleeping cat, complete with ears and curved tail. Stunted trees grew over its top, while their predecessors lay in tumbled ruin at its roots. Below it, the cave's mouth lay half hidden behind rocks and thorny bramble.

"That's it?" I asked.

"That's it."

Iyumi slid from my back before I could stop her. "Whoa, time out, what do you think you're doing?"

"Of course I'm going in there."

"Of course you are *not* going in there."

Her eyes sparked blue fire. Her brows lowered, as her fair lips, the lips I'd kissed, thinned into a white line. Danger signals, all. Yet, I outweighed her by almost two tons, and her anger didn't intimidate me one bit.

"Stand down, Captain."

I blocked her path to the cave, crossed my arms over my chest and gazed, implacable, down at her. "No."

"No?"

"No."

Not unlike an irate fishwife, her voice rose several octaves. "No?"

[356]

I scratched my nose, peering down at her fury. "What part of 'no' don't you understand?"

"I am soooo going to have you drawn and quartered–"

"Sure," I replied, soothing. "You can quarter what's left after your illustrious sire is done with me. Until then, I'll say what you do and don't do. Stand down, little girl."

"Little–"

"Save it for your piddling maids," I snapped. "Stay here."

Leaving her to fume, impotent and furious, I stalked toward the cave. Drawing my sword, I held it level and ready. A Centaur owned all the senses and instincts of a horse, the prey animal, yet with the human's ability to reason through them. Every instinct screamed for me to run, avoid the dangerous cave where I had no room to either flee or fight. I drew in a deep breath and shut down the inner noise.

I listened with my heightened hearing and lifted my face so I might better scent the air. I heard nothing save the wind whisper through the trees, the distant scream of a hunting eagle. A small rodent hustled away from my hooves, brushing through years of shed pine needles and loamy soil. I scented tree sap and mulch, mixed with a very old odor of bear. My heightened instinct's remained silent, unalarmed, as I crept closer to the cave's mouth.

Using my sword to part the bramble, I peered into the darkness. The scent of death sent shivers down my spine. Something had died in there, and died very recently. Yet, whatever killed its occupant wasn't violence. The cave didn't smell of fresh blood.

What was that? I cocked my head, listening hard. Yes. A heartbeat, echoing through the stone. The breath of a living creature stirred the air, catching in my nostrils. Something yet lived within the stone darkness. Something small and weak and dying.

Half-turning to call to her, I found Iyumi at my shoulder, eagerly peering into the cave. "Is she alive?"

Fetching an annoyed breath, I said, "Do that again and–"

"She is, isn't she?"

"Yes."

Before I could stop her, Iyumi ducked into the cave. My Centaur could scarcely fit under its low overhang much less enter it.

Forced to return to my human shape, I followed on her heels. Calling fire to my hand, I lit the small chamber and the bodies lying on the stony floor.

My instincts on high alert, I took in the blackened remains of a hearth fire, ringed in rounded stones. The sandy floor held a single narrow pallet made of twigs and pine needles. To my right, against the cavern wall, lay a tidy pile of firewood. Under the scent of dry rot lay another odor–meat. The far rear of the occupant's tidy home held a collection of bones and hides. I recognized the legs of deer, the curved horns of a rock sheep, and no few cured rabbit skins.

I glanced at the corpse, lying next to the dead fire. The high altitude cold kept her from decomposing. But her closed eyes had fallen in, and her clothes stuck to the body. Lank grey hair fell across its lower face, and a blanket half covered her from the shoulders down. *The mother of the infant,* I surmised. I half-wondered what killed her.

A swift glance showed me Iyumi cuddling a tiny body close within her arms, her shoulders hunched. As her back was to me, I couldn't see the gods' chosen child. Using my sword's tip, I lifted the mother's hair from her face.

Cursing in shock, I backed away. "That's a troll."

If Iyumi heard me, she didn't reply. She rocked the infant in her arms, crooning under her breath, her body swaying back and forth. Repulsed, I used my sword to sweep the covering blanket from the mother troll, revealing the tell-tale gnarled limbs, snaggle teeth and hunched-back of a mountain troll.

Infused with stories and tales of mountain trolls sneaking into homes by night to slay the occupants for their gold, I felt a shudder creep up my spine. As a child, I lay awake at night, fearing the trolls that fed on the weak and the helpless. I *knew* they waited under my bed, waiting for me to fall asleep. Once I was vulnerable, they'd pounce and tear me limb from limb. When the fears grew too awful, I'd change forms into that of a cat and leap into the rafters. There, I'd pass the night drowsing and waking at every tiny night sound.

Whether the stories were true or not, all knew trolls were evil, the offspring of hellish demons. A distant cousin to the trolls that guarded the dreaded prison, Braigh'Mhar, they owned two arms, two legs, and didn't breathe fire. That was their only difference. No one looked a troll in the eye and lived. They lusted only for gold and drank the blood of their victims.

"We've got the wrong cave, I'm thinking," I said, searching with fire and instincts for danger. "Drop it and let's go."

Iyumi's only answer was her continual rocking and crooning. Slowly backing away from the body, and the lethal mate I knew awaited us in the darkness, ready to pounce with fangs and claws bared, I carefully stepped to Iyumi's side. I grabbed her shoulder.

Iyumi screeched. Lunging away from me, her arms holding the mewling infant in a protective embrace, she bared her teeth in a grimace of fear and anger. "Leave her alone!"

What the hell? "Put that thing down," I ordered, my sword sweeping the cave, prepared for an attack. "Let's go, Iyumi."

"Are you an idiot?"

"Probably. But that don't mean I'm stupid."

Iyumi bowed her head, her braid sliding forward to hide the infant troll in her arms. "Leave off, Captain."

"Nope. Come with me of your own free will or in chains. Your choice, of course."

She raised her face, her cheeks streaming tears of anger and joy. A smile trembled on her lips, one of hope and triumph. I halted, frozen, as her eyes lifted to mine in desperate fear. "She's dying, Van. You have to help me."

My mouth worked, but no sound emerged. Me? Help save a . . . save a troll? A flaming *troll?* Iyumi held the tiny form out toward me, stepping lightly across the stone floor until she lifted the tiny body, wrapped in rags. It moved, writhing weakly, a tiny mewing sound rising from the filthy cloths. Quickly, I sheathed my sword, freeing my hands, but not my fears. She gently placed the bundle in my arms.

It moved, once more emitting a tiny mew-like sound. Startled, I almost dropped it. I wanted to back away from the troll, from the obligation, from her. I couldn't. If she'd tossed a freezing spell over me, it worked.

Instead, I stood in helpless panic as Iyumi withdrew the cover from her face.

Eyes the color of warm ale met mine. Heavy brow ridges cast those eyes in shadow. Lumps formed the infant's jaw, and a heavy chin thrust from beneath thick dark lips that hid fangs ready to burst from her gums. A gnarled fist rose, as though in defiance, before wavering and falling, too weak to remain upright.

Her fist opened. Her tiny fingers clasped my thumb where my hands held her under her rump and shoulders. Her lips pulled back in a toothless smile: warm, kind and innocent. Entranced, I could only stare down at the trust that gazed deep into my eyes. Into the love she offered, without knowing, without caring that I wanted to throw her down and run. I had no faith I wouldn't. She knew I wouldn't.

"She's the one."

Iyumi's voice broke the trance. I tore my eyes from the baby's, wildly, desperately seeking the known, the familiar. I wanted no part of this, wanted out, wanted away from this infant that loved me without knowing me. "But–"

"No buts. She's the gods' chosen messenger. She'll save us all."

I glanced down at the baby troll, who gurgled and burped, still grinning toothlessly up at me. "You sure? This is one ugly kid."

Iyumi scowled. "Since when does beauty equate innocence? This child is the purest soul on this earth. The most precious being the gods' gave us."

I gazed down at the wonder in my hands, the glorious beauty of those light brown eyes. If the baby troll were as ugly as a mud fence, those eyes made up for it and more. She loved me, me, a wanted murderer, a criminal and an outlaw. I suspected she knew what I was, and loved me anyway.

Like shades over a window, those trusting eyes closed. She slept. But inside my hands, her heart stumbled. Her lungs reached for air and found none. I frowned, raising her face to my ear, listening to her labored breathing, her struggle to continue. Iyumi was right.

She was dying.

Desperate, I sought Iyumi's glance, forced her to look at me. "Are the tales true?"

[360]

"What? I–"

"Are they true?" I yelled, looming over her. "Do they drink blood to survive?"

Iyumi glanced away, floundering, scared. "Of animals, yes, but–why?"

"You knew I'd do it," I muttered, holding the dying troll in my left arm as I yanked my dagger from its sheath. "You planned this. You and your friends."

"Van–"

I shoved my blade into her hands. "Because a Shifter is half animal, isn't that so? I'm nothing but a wild critter you can't tame."

I jerked my head at the baby lying across my arm, pillowed on my fingers. "Trolls feed on animal blood. That's why you needed me."

Her desperate panicked eyes met mine, wild, streaming tears. "No!"

"You despise lying, remember? Don't even try. Just cut me."

"What? Van, I can't!"

"Cut me!" I roared.

Blinded by tears, turning her face way, Iyumi slashed my blade across my bared right wrist. I felt little pain, but bright red blood gushed from the wound. Not bothering to staunch it, I held the lips of my gaping cut to the infant troll's mouth.

At first, her tongue protruded, tasting the red wet that coursed over her lips, streaming over her bulbous chin. Suddenly, her mouth opened in frantic greed. She sucked the essence of my life into her hungry belly, slurping, licking, gulping. My blood poured into her, offering her life, sustaining her, staving off her death at the same time she killed me. My blood drained from me, one red drop at a time, through my wrist.

The baby fed lavishly, gaining steadily and lavishly in strength and life. Healthy color returned to her cheeks. Her fist around my thumb tightened. My skin felt her pulse quicken, at the same time her lungs filled. A thin tendril of weak magic from me into her informed me how her body tipped back into the realm of the living. She would survive.

I did it. I saved the damn kid. *Are you happy now, your effing lordships? Have I paid for my sins now?* I wavered on my feet, almost blind and weaker than a newborn puppy. I licked my lips, thirsty, my throat raw. Oddly, I felt no craving for booze. Did hell serve brown ale? Wine? I hoped so. I knew I'd need it once the shock wore off.

I dropped to my knees.

Seriously weakened by blood loss, I handed the newly sated and now lively troll baby to Iyumi. I heard her burp in satisfaction, half-saw her chubby limbs rise in vigor and health. I shut my eyes, my head spinning. *Go, child. Save us all. Remember me to them, will you?*

"Van!"

I half saw Iyumi lay the baby down on the pallet of twigs, straw and an unspeakably nasty cloth. *Trolls may save the world,* I thought, my head spinning, my thoughts jangled. *But they sure weren t the cleanliest of saviors.*

Her arm under my shoulder boosted me halfway to my feet. My weight, even as a human, was no match for her tiny bones. She staggered, caught her feet, grunted, cursed, and heaved to no avail. I took her down with me in a disorganized heap, throwing my body to the left and thus avoided crushing her beneath me.

Iyumi crawled out from under my arm and swirling dust, calling my name. I knew her soft lap cradled my head, her braid sliding off her shoulder to tease my nose. But why? She, and those bastards she served, achieved their goal. A tiny troll mite, their chosen savior, was alive because she killed me. *Stick a fork in me. 1 m done.*

"Vanyar!"

Go away. I shut my eyes. *I did as you commanded.*

"Don't you die on me now, Captain Vanyar," she screeched, slapping my face. "I won't have it, you hear me? You won't die until I tell you."

Too late, my lovely Iy—

[362]

I woke to the sound of humming.

Do they hum in hell? While I wouldn't have thought so, I suppose anything was possible. Perhaps demons liked to sing as they tortured the souls under their command. I felt no pain. Warmth enveloped my right wrist. Odd. Hellfire burned, or so the priests said. Why did I feel not just warm but comfortable?

I opened my eyes.

A grey stone ceiling met my inspection, my sight blurred. I blinked, then squinted for clarity. Aha! I know what that is, folks, hold your applause, thanks. It's not a ceiling in a mansion or castle, but a cave. *Ah, dammit, the bleeding cave again.*

I groaned, cursing. Reality returned with a rush: I wasn't dead. My head lay pillowed on Iyumi's lap, and her cloak covered me from throat to thighs, lending me its warmth. Her kind hands wrapped my lacerated right wrist in a bandage. A rock dug into my left buttock, shattering the illusion I was comfortable.

"Lay still," she ordered, breaking off her soft croon.

"Gods," I groaned, my strength laughable. "Why am I still here?"

As she held my right arm within her own, I used my left to cover my eyes. "This sucks rocks."

"You're welcome."

"Bite me."

Iyumi tsked. "Ungrateful bastard. I spent the last half-hour dragging your stupid ass back from the grave and you return with insult. I should've left you to die."

"Agreed."

"Don't be snide. It's not your time."

I lowered my arm enough to peer up at her. "It's my time when I say it's my time. And it's my time."

"Sorry. Wrong answer. Gods one, Van zero."

My arm fell back and I blinked several times. "Shit."

"Cheer up." Iyumi smiled down into my upturned face. From this angle, her grin appeared predatory and wholly without mercy. "My father will string you up from the city's north gate very soon."

"Jolly good."

"Until then, you're mine."

"How's Junior?"

Iyumi scowled. "Don't call her Junior."

"Forgive me. Juniorette."

Iyumi cast a fond glance aside, toward where I remembered the pallet lay. "She's just fine, thanks to you."

I shut my eyes again, listening. Soft gurgles and chuckles, punctuated by the occasional baby shriek of delight, emerged from the dank rags. "Did you at least have the decency to put her in something clean? I'd hate my effort be wasted because she caught a disease."

"No worries." Iyumi lifted my head and scooted out from under it. "Trolls are immune to almost any bug."

I half-thought she'd permit my head to drop ignominiously to the hard floor of the cave, but she surprised me. Her gentle hands set me upon a crunchy cushion of dead leaves. As she rose and dusted the seat of her leather britches, she poked me in the ribs with her boot. "Get up, sluggard."

So much for kind, feminine nursing. I sighed. "As long as I'm still alive, I may as well see you home."

"You make a lovely royal mount."

I paused halfway to my feet, eyeing her sidelong from under my hair. "Thanks. I think."

Her snicker accompanied me as I staggered to my feet, dizzy and nauseous. I shook out her cloak, hiding the tremors in my hands, and handed it to Iyumi. She accepted it with a regal nod of thanks and cast it over her shoulders. Her fingers didn't tremble as she tied the knots at her throat, still smiling that insufferable smile. *Damn her.* I stalked outside, muttering imprecations under my breath.

Hopefully she, or her friends, gave me enough strength to not just survive, but change forms into that of a Centaur and carry her back to Caer Brannog and King Roidan. Home. *It s all downhill from here.* Provided we struck no trouble along the way. In my current state, a rabbit might wrestle me into submission. We may have reached the mystery child first, but Flynn still roamed the lands loose and unfettered.

[364]

Iyumi remained inside the cave long enough to douse the fire before scooping up the divine messenger, rags and all. She obviously had no fear of possible occupants, outside the troll that was, living inside those disgusting wrappings. Snugging the baby inside the wool, next to her warmth, Iyumi hummed, wandering out from under the thorny brambles as though she walked in a dream. She gazed down into the folds, her expression serene, rapt, beyond beautiful.

"You'll make a terrific mother."

Of everything I'd ever said to her or about her never prepared me for the shy smile and rosy blush that crept from her dimples to her cheekbones. Iyumi, the royal bitch, ducked away from my eyes and compliment like a milkmaid at the first touch of a lover's hand.

"It's all I ever wanted to be."

The soft admission forced me to swallow the sharp lump that mysteriously shut off my breath. It didn't depart without a fight, however. I coughed and choked, turning away with the excuse that I needed to adjust the way my sword hung from my belt. Knife, present and accounted for. Clothing set comfortably. Boots laced–I shut my stinging eyes. *She will never bear my children.* My throat shut down; my heart fragmented, in pieces, gone. *Gods.*

"C'mon. Daylight's wasting."

"Be right there. I should say a word or two over the mother."

I nodded and turned my back. I drew a ragged breath, the tightness in my chest loosening slowly. Distracting my thoughts from her, I focused on my going down the mountain. If we travelled until sunset, we can at least make the gorge before nightfall. Camp under the summer stars, rest the night, pick up the pace come dawn. Two days hard gallop and bob's your uncle, we'll be home in time for supper. Damn it! I drew another ragged breath, trying to still my emotions–*grow up, boyo. She s not for you.*

I bowed my head–

Wrapped up in my wallowing misery and self-pity, I never paid any heed to my surroundings.

Cold metal slid around my neck.

I heard the sharp snick of the lock the instant I changed forms.

Nothing happened.
I remained myself, the body of the falcon I craved slipping fast out of my brain and Shifter ability. My body stood in thrall, enslaved within my vulnerable human body. And at the questionable mercy of whomever just captured me.

That meant only one thing: the ancient magics of the pewter manacles clasped my neck.

No!

Only that hellish, evil-driven, dark metal cut a magician, or Shape-Shifter, from his innate, gods-given control over his own body. Only the most powerful, or most learned, magicians knew their secrets. No one, outside the ancients, knew how to create them, or break them. Malik certainly knew, and Malik was dead.

My birthright slipped from my will and my power like sand through a clenched fist. I seized nothing at all. No magic, no will, no strength. As human as your average sheep-herder, I couldn't call forth enough magic to light a candle.

But I could still fight. I spun about, snarling, reaching for my sword.

Two shadows lunged, one to either side of me. I went down in a tangle of thrashing arms, fists and curses. Seriously weakened by blood-loss, my strength failed when I needed it most. Within seconds, I lay face down in the dirt, strong hands forcing mine behind me. A third attacker kicked my face, his heavy boot smashing into my nose and cheekbone, my blood flying upward in a red shower. Gritting my teeth against an agonized howl, I prevented its immediate eruption only by choking on my own blood. Their merciless hands tied my arms behind me with thick leather binds, fire-toughened thongs I could never hope to break.

From the corner of my eye, I saw Iyumi emerge from the cave, the infant in her arms.

I coughed, raising my mouth from the dirt and blowing dust. "Run," I gasped. *"Run."*

Two men, hidden in the bushes on either side of the cavern, took her down swiftly. The baby tumbled to the ground as Iyumi fell, crying out in shock and rage. Slightly more considerate of her status and gender than mine, one fellow pinned her by her

[366]

shoulders, his hard-muscled weight forcing her against the stony earth as his mate clapped dark metal cuffs over her wrists. The infant troll dropped onto reasonably soft soil, but instantly set up a sharp scream of protest that raked one's ear-drums into bursting.

Rising, they brought her upright with them. As it had me, the dark pewter stilled her powers as effectively as a raging river douses a campfire. Iyumi struggled in her captor's grip, cursing, her tidy braid falling to pieces. The soldier winced as Iyumi tried to kick him in the groin.

"Let me go, you stinking shits," she yelled, fighting like a cat. "I'll kill you!"

Despite her handicap, Iyumi fought with the courage these men lacked. Yanking her knife from her belt, she sought to stab the nearest. Made clumsy by the manacles, she missed and the soldier stripped her of her one remaining weapon with a pained expression. As each of them easily outweighed her by a hundred pounds, she stood as much chance as a mouse caught up by a sandstorm. One man scooped up the screaming baby as the other held her still, gripping her shoulder with one beefy hand.

Flinging dust and curses with equal ferocity, Iyumi grabbed the troll and hugged her tight to her meager chest. "Leave off, scumbags," she shrieked, jerking her shoulder free. "Van? Vanyar!"

She saw me then, collared like a dog and bleeding profusely under the knees of two men and the obnoxious third who kicked me in the ribs. Unable to breathe, I swallowed blood, choking, my chest on fire. Through blurred vision, close to blacking out, I squinted through the pain to witness her fight like a tigress.

"Leave him alone!" she screamed, lunging toward me.

The man yanked her back, avoiding her vicious kick to his shin with a grunt and a swift side-step. Before she could follow through with another, his mate jerked her off balance with his arm around her waist and held her still, fuming and cursing.

"Let me go," she screamed, trying to stomp his toes. "I'll kill you. I swear you'll hang by your balls, you don't know who you're messing with–"

Had she ordered me in that particular tone to slit my throat, I'd happily obey while saluting her eminence. Yet, these boys obviously didn't quite understand the importance a bitchy princess had on one's immediate future. They ignored her threats as easily as they'd ignore the snarls of a chained hound, and straightened their spines. A lone rider emerged from the trees, a dark shadow against the sun's blinding rays.

"If you don't release us," Iyumi gritted, her silver hair flooding her shoulders. "I'll make each of you wish your mothers aborted you."

Burly strength lifted me to my feet, gasping, my ribs on fire, my nose broken. I blinked stinging blood from my eyes and tried to inhale a semi-full breath. The world ceased its wild rotation and steadied. I'd no strength to fight, my powers broken, but I could see at least. And catch a small breath, now and then.

A single figure dismounted a tall horse, silhouetted by the sun. He walked toward me, his grey horse following at his shoulder. Only when the shadows from the trees shrouded him from head to boots, did I catch my short breath inside my agonized ribs.

I froze, instantly recognizing him. The grand master of this violent charade, the reason these men failed to acknowledge Iyumi's authority and dared seize her royal person. I immediately understood everything. They didn't fear her, or her royal sire. They owed their loyalty to one man, this single man, the one who walked where angels feared to tread. Gods, no, you can't be this cruel–

His malicious grin hadn't changed a jot. The scar on his cheek bloomed pink and purple, dark bruising still clear under his skin. *You shoula ve healed better.* Storm Cloud's talon scarred him for life, marked him forever as traitor and oath-breaker–a sign for all to shun him on sight.

"Greetings, cuz."

My frazzled brain recalled in a flash Ze'ana'ta's words: *bad men spy.* I assumed, like a fool, she meant Flynn and his jewel. She didn't know Flynn watched us from afar, for a Faery's magic wasn't strong. She and her sisters knew Iyumi and I were stalked by 'bad men' much closer than Flynn and his cronies. Cursing myself for a bleeding idiot wouldn't help matters, but I did so anyway. Had I

[368]

given a moment's thought to the Faery's warning, I'd have set a trap of my own instead of blundering into one.

My bloodied spit struck the soil between his boots. "Ditto."

Cian's toothy grin widened. "Now that's not a fair greeting for your kin, Van, is it? For shame. Your manners have deteriorated alarmingly."

"As have yours. Since when have you added kidnapping the royal heir to your resume?"

"Excuse me?" Cian's dark eyes widened in feigned surprise. "Kidnap? Our beloved royal heir? Oh, no, Van, you misunderstand my intentions. I merely seek to keep her safe from your madness. I'm a soldier, not a scoundrel."

"Misunderstand this, shithead–"

Unable to do more than kick dirt toward Cian, Iyumi struggled in the arms of her captor, her fluent expletives nasty enough to force a bewildered blink from Cian and a swift, confused eye exchange from the men holding her fast. I almost heard their thoughts–*where does a princess learn such language?*

"You dare lay hands on her, Clansman," I snapped. "Treason, in its highest form. When did you find the guts?"

"When your blunder cost *her* her life."

"I didn't kill Zeani."

"Oh, but your ego did. Your new promotion and selfish ambition set the stage for her death. And your own of course, dear cousin."

"You're mad."

Cian's expression turned injured. His eyes widened in feigned outrage for my insult, his lips thinned and ironic. "I'm not mad, Vanyar. Consider me impulsively artistic and vengefully ambitious. Yet, forever and always within my right mind."

"Corporal Zeani died serving her King and her country," I grated, trying not to ignominiously snort my own blood. "An Raithin Mawrn terrorist killed her. It could happen to any of us, you know that."

"You should have died, too," Cian said softly, his eyes flat. "But you lived and Zeani burned. So, you'll burn as she burned."

I jerked my head at Iyumi. "What of Her Highness, Cian? You put the manacles on the heir to the throne and She Who Hears. You dare the wrath of the King and the gods? You did it because you knew she'd drop you in your tracks. But outside of her anger, you've incurred the wrath of those who speak through her."

His eyes widened. "I mean Her Royal Highness no harm, Van," he said. "Never. I merely temporarily restrain her to keep her from danger as you and I resolve our differences. After that, my lads will see her home to Caer Brannog."

"Your lads?" I asked. "Not you?"

Cian opened his mouth to answer, but Iyumi's shrill screech of rage cut him off. "By all the gods, I swear I'll tie your balls to an oxcart and crack the whip if you don't let him go," she screamed, the baby wailing in her arms. "I'll skin your hides from your bones and post your craven heads from the tallest tower. Let him go, you sick bastards. Let him effing go!"

By Cian's outraged expression, I knew his control came near to slipping. Under the lash of Iyumi's threats, he might just forget his promise and set her, and the baby, afire alongside me. I had to stop her. I must convince her to submit, to yield. A battle lost didn't necessarily mean the war was. If she relented, just this once, she might survive to save our land. She had to get that baby home, to safety.

Whatever the cost to me.

Hoping, praying, the pewter collar around my neck didn't preclude my mental abilities, I summoned all my thought, all my will. Using our previous telepathy and the bond we shared, I cast out and down my inner voice, those swift images from inside my thick skull. Out and out they flew, on wings of love, to slam into Iyumi's brain.

"Don't fight, girl," I sent her, my eyes boring into hers. *"Save yourself, and that baby. 1 m lost, but you aren t. Go home. That child needs you more than me. Avenge me when you come into your own."*

She staggered a little under their impact, her guards catching her weight as they glanced at one another in worry. Their hands held her upright, on her boots, even as she sagged in their hands.

[370]

Limp, breathing hard, her eyes rolled back in her head as they snapped fingers in front of her nose.

"Princess? You awake?" "Dammit, don't do this."

"*Vanyar?*" she responded, her inner voice timid and opposite of the tigress fighting for me, for the troll babe.

"*It s all good, my dearest love. For I do love you beyond all life, all hope. I always have. I fell in love with you the moment I laid my eyes upon you.*"

"*And I you. From day one, I loved you, waited for you to notice me, to find me. I love you, Van, and always will.*"

"*We ll be together. One day. For now, be safe, be well. I ll look in on you, when I can. Take care of Junior, all right?*"

I caught Iyumi's half-nod as her rage slowly subsided. Her guards didn't relax despite her bowed head and rolled shoulders exhibiting her obvious submission. Ready to pounce, they eyed her with suspicion and annoyance. She buried her face in the troll's wraps, yet her faint voice filled my head.

"*I will, Van. I promise.*"

"*I love you, my beautiful lady.*"

I never gave her a chance to respond. If I didn't cut her off now, I'd never have the guts again. She must, and her burden, be free of me from this day onward. Only then might Bryn'Cairdha be safe from outside enemies. If not, I'd go to my death broken in spirit, a shell of what I once was. I cut my eyes from hers, and closed my mind to her reply. By the way she hung her head, her chin holding the baby troll close under her neck, she knew, very well, what I'd done and why I did it.

"You'll let her go?" I asked Cian, my voice hoarse.

"Of course." Cian frowned. "She'll be safely escorted to Roidan's castle in Caer Brannog. My quarrel isn't with her or her mission. Only with you."

I tossed my chin at the men closely guarding her, their eyes on me. "Sergeant Yestin. Corporal Drust. You have a quarrel with me, as well? How about you lads?"

I glanced to the men standing me on my feet. "Sergeants Tris, Kado, and Broc. Corporal Zorn. Until today, we've never shared a cross word. Yet, you raise your hands to a superior officer. As you are no doubt aware, that's treason in its highest form. Are you willing to pay its price–for him?"

Broc and Drust exchanged uneasy glances while Yestin, Kado and Tris merely stared at me, expressionless. Zorn watched Iyumi, not bothering to listen to me. I half-wondered if they'd been given *pe ederon*, a mind-altering potion that permits the user to suggest courses of actions the victim would never ordinarily do. As I peered closer, I saw little of the tell-tale signs, like the blue-ish ring around the whites of their eyes. They believed in Cian and his mission, and no amount of me squawking the obvious helped matters.

"The Lieutenant is right to seek his vengeance," Yestin said, his tone cold. "You're the traitor. You'll be executed forthwith and the sooner the better."

"These lads owe me their loyalty," Cian said, dropping his hand heavily to Yestin's shoulder in rough affection. "They've spurned the laws of an unjust regime."

"Traitors," Iyumi hissed. "I swear by the gods you'll all hang."

Cian eyed her sidelong and shrugged, unconcerned. "Since when is the execution of a murderer treason, Your Highness? I'm merely acting in the King's good interest here."

"In the King's name–"

"Then tell your lads to take her away," I said, interrupting her with a swift glance of warning. "She doesn't need to be a part of this."

"I'll send her when I'm ready," Cian snapped, his control slipping. "You've no say here, Van."

"Lieutenant," said Corporal Drust, his eyes fastened on the slope behind me. "Someone's coming."

"Dammit." Cian fumed, turning around. "Who is it?"

Behind the cave, from the valley below, the snorting of horses and the clop of hooves against stone heralded the approach of several riders. Cian cursed under his breath as Drust whipped his sword from its sheath. I craned my neck over my injured shoulder, past Kado, to the slope I carried Iyumi up only hours before. I cocked my head, listening. Four, no, five horses approached from beyond the trees. Watching, hoping for the best but fearing the worst, I held my breath.

Grey ears emerged first, then the sleek head of a dappled horse broke over the hill. Two horses flanked the big grey as two more followed on his tail, all trotting in step with their leader.

Gods help us all.

Flynn reined in his Bayonne and leaned his arm on his pommel.

CHAPTER 12

Child of Destiny

Who the hell're you?" demanded the tall, red-haired fellow with the half-healed dagger slash from his left eye to his mouth.

Hell's teeth, I thought, stunned.

The amber crystal showed me Van and Iyumi entering the cavern. Thinking to trap them inside, I willed myself and my comrades to the base of the mountain, expecting to demand their immediate surrender. I knew Van would willingly die for Iyumi, to prevent me from taking her, and the child, captive. I planned to kill him, and seize what was mine by right.

I suspected him the leader, as the others, outside Van and Yummy, glanced from me to him and back. *A coward,* I thought, seizing up the feigned arrogance, the brazen *I-can-kill-you-with-a-mean-look* attitude I so often found among my father's guards. I hated him on sight. Though his hand tickled his sword's hilt, I felt neither intimidated nor worried. I could, and might, flatten him with a thought. From the older, dark scars upon his cheekbones, I knew he was a Shape-Shifter. A member of Van's own Clan, I judged, by a rapid comparison.

The others stiffened their spines, their hands readying weapons. Iyumi glared at me as she cuddled a small ragged bundle close to her bosom. Though his sunken cheeks informed me he was in great pain, Van eyed me with anger and fear flashing from his emerald green eyes. He knew why I was there. He knew very well. An oddly colored collar of metal encircled his neck. *Hmmm.* That same metal shaped the cuffs of Iyumi's wrists.

I snapped my fingers. Boden and Buck-Eye unsheathed swords at the same time Torass and Lyall flanked the Shifter's men, bowstrings creaking in the mountain stillness. My four to his six. And they had prisoners to babysit. Van's hands were obviously bound behind his back, and he appeared desperate, powerless even. Why hadn't he scattered these yokels' ashes upon the wind? Why didn't he change into a fearsome Minotaur and kick some ass?

I eyed Iyumi, knowing she, too, held magical powers. If Yummy joined the fight, I'd no idea which side she'd attack. Mine or his, we were both probably targets for royal ire. Why hadn't she called upon her gods to send these morons straight into hell? *Something s wrong.* With their considerable powers, neither of them should be held captive by these imbeciles.

In the midst of the tense silence, Dra'agor loped to catch up. His sudden presence into the mix added no end of unease amongst the soldiers who had captured Van and Yummy. Not a one of them didn't take a step back, dragging their prisoners with them. The Shifter leader hesitated, his will flagging, as he raised his hand to make the sign against strong magic.

"I'm Flynn," I replied, sitting back in my saddle. "I have no quarrel with you, boy."

His eyes sparked and his lips thinned. "Flynn? What Flynn?"

"Meet His Royal Highness Prince Flynn," Vanyar said, his tone insulting, cold, "of Raithin Mawr. You *do* remember our ancient enemies who want to destroy our lands, don't you, Cian?"

"Shut up, Van," Cian snapped. "Of course, I know who he is."

"Good. I thought I needed to teach you a history lesson."

[376]

I fought back a grin before it emerged. That Vanyar had guts. Tied and collared like a sacrificial goat and he still had sass.

"What are you doing here, Prince?" Cian demanded. "This isn't your turf."

I jerked my head toward Princess Yummy and the mystery child she held. "All I want is them."

Cian glanced from the princess to me, back to her, again toward me before finally staring at Iyumi in bafflement. "The princess? Why?"

I exchanged a rapid, there-and-gone eye-roll with Buck-Eye, stilling my tongue against laughter. Sincerely, this boy had no clue.

"To complete the prophecy, you ass," Van shouted, lunging against his captors. "You can't let him take her, Cian!"

Despite his obvious injuries, he fought, cursing, straining against those that held him. One smacked a cudgel upside his head as the other two struggled to hold him fast. Van drooped, bleeding down his temple to his chin, his eyes glazed. I shut my teeth on a sharp retort and demanded they leave him alone. *Bloody cowards.*

"Oh, that."

Cian relaxed, shrugging, a half-smile crossing his thick lips. "Take her. She's my gift to you, Prince Flynn. I don't care."

"Cian."

Her voice, as menacing as the shiver of a sword drawn in the shadows, spoke that single name. Dra'agor growled, his lips skinned back from his fangs at the menace within that quiet word. The hairs on the back of my neck stood up straight at the same instant her guards shrank from her. Cian seemed to not notice the venom with which she spoke, yet even Van found enough energy to lift his bloody face toward her. He didn't speak, but the anguish that rose in his eyes made my heart quake within my chest.

That boy loves her. Beyond all life and hope of salvation. And she loves him just as deeply. She didn't fight for herself. She fought for the kid and him, both. Like a she-wolf, she fought for her mate and her cub, and only death might break her spirit.

Oddly, I felt no jealousy, no hot hatred for Van as a despised rival for Iyumi's affections. For a moment, just one swift moment, I felt the urge to save them. I had the arms, the men, and the dark power on my side. One word would set arrows winging into Cian's men, killing them instantly. My lads were armed, ready. His were armed, yet held only prisoners in their hands. Another could swamp Cian under a tidal wave of horror and crush him beneath my boot without my lifting a finger.

I resisted that urge with an effort. The pair may love one another, but unless I had Iyumi and the brat in my hands, Fainche, Sofia and my mother would die. If I were to set the life of Van against theirs, Van could only lose. As much as I wanted to like, no, *liked* the bastard, I'd no choice. He showed me kindness, and offered healing to his enemy, his *nations* enemy. These men intended for him to die, but hard. That was painfully obvious. Yet, I'd never risk the lives of my sister, mother and wife for him. I met his angry, desperate eyes. *1 m sorry, Van, I can t.*

Perhaps one day Iyumi might turn those beautiful blue eyes on me with the same love and passion she so freely offered Van. I would save her, keep her alive and protect her all the days of her long life. She'd bear my children, not Vanyar's. *1 m sorry, Van, old son. I win. You don t.*

"Princess?"

Cian's offensive voice brought a swift close to my reverie. Unbelievably, his tone offered her humor and scant respect. *You-may-be-my-bettoi-but-1-have-youi-number* his offhand tone said. For that attitude alone, I wanted to sink my sword into his neck and feed Dra'agor his liver.

"You will die, Cian," Iyumi said, her blue eyes colder than the snow on the high peaks above. "Continue with this blasphemy and I promise you, the gods will be neither forgiving nor merciful. Stop now while there is still hope."

"Hope for me, Princess?" Cian laughed, a sharp bark. "The gods turned their backs on me when she burned. I care nothing for them, nor you, nor your cause. I lost hope long ago."

"Don't, Cian," Van groaned, trying to straighten. "Don't give her to him. I'll do what you want, just don't give her to Flynn. Don't. Please. *Don t.*"

[378]

"Oh, I promise you, boyo," Cian replied cheerfully. "I promise you, you'll do what I want. And it appears I can give her to whomever I please. Fortunately for His Highness, I choose to give Iyumi to him."

"Please," Van begged. "Don't do it."

"Why ever not? You'll treat her well, Your Highness?"

I bowed over my saddlebow. "Of course. She will rule as queen over both our nations. I always treat my wives with love and respect."

"Lieutenant Cian," Iyumi went on as though I hadn't spoken, like I wasn't even there. "Your soul is in jeopardy here. Continue now, and there will be no going back, no turning from the path you walk. Stop while you still can."

"Your boyfriend took my soul when he killed my Zeani," Cian replied coldly. "I've lived only for this vengeance since. Lady, you can't frighten me."

Iyumi glared around at Cian's soldiers. "What of you, Atani? Do I frighten you? You've committed treason. You've broken your oaths. Do you not fear the gods' wrath?"

One of the grizzled men holding Van paced one step from him, lowered his face, and spat into the dust at Iyumi's feet.

She didn't flinch, yet merely nodded as though she'd expected as much. "Die then," she murmured, eyeing each of them in their turn with that stone cold gaze. "You have each been marked. Upon your deaths, your souls will survive ten thousand lifetimes of torment and wretchedness. You have chosen this, and the gods' will shall never be undone."

"Witch," one of the burly men muttered.

Oddly, Iyumi smiled. With eyes as cold as river ice, she turned that beatific smile upon him and he blanched. Just like that. Turned as white as a freshly washed bed sheet, and cut his dark eyes away from hers. Drawing away from her as well as he could without making it obvious, he made the sign against strong evil with his fingers.

"Might you take her soon, m'lord?" he asked me, squinting slightly. "Her blabber is annoying my men and I have urgent business with my kinsman, you see."

I glanced from the dark marks on Cian's cheeks, to those on Vanyar's. Clansmen. Shifters. Blood-kin.

"Just what did he do to deserve this?" I asked. "Murder someone you love?"

"In all but name," he spat. "Take this insufferable bitch and go, Raithin prince."

My indolent shrug matched his. "Might you have a horse for the royal lady?" I asked. I waved my hand around at my mounted band. "I have no extra, you see, and Her Highness should ride to her betrothal on her own mount, not on a rump."

Cian smiled thinly. "Yestin, Drust. Hand the bitch to Flynn now, then fetch the mule. Divide the packs among us."

The men so ordered dragged a resisting Iyumi toward me, her silver locks hiding her face as she bowed her head over the infant in her arms. Sliding down from Bayonne's saddle, I gripped her arm lightly, hoping she'd glance up into my face to see my pleasant smile. She didn't. Instead, she stood as one prepared for death, as her former guards turned away to walk around the bushes, out of sight.

"Cian," Van groaned, spitting blood, shaking loose from his captors. "I swear, I will kill you for this –"

"Shut your damn trap!"

Cian snatched his sword from its sheath and crashed the hilt into Van's temple. Van fell to the rocks, as limp as a boned fish, on his back, out cold. Blood coursed its slow way down his brow, across his eyes and slid down his scarred cheek.

You can help him, that inner voice told me.

"No, I can t."

You can. He doesn t have to be a rival. He can help you save Fainche. Save him, and you can save her.

"Go blow it out your–"

Cian's men returned leading a large, greyish-brown mule by its bridle. It had no saddle, but after seeing Iyumi ride I'd no doubt she'd travel bare-back just fine. I jerked my head to Boden and

[380]

Lyall. They backed their horses to flank me, their swords at the ready. As I lifted Princess Yummy by her waist and seated her, babe and all, onto the mule's broad back, Buck-Eye and Torass also returned to my side. Arrows still nocked, they kept the razor-sharp barbs trained on Cian's little band.

Yummy lifted her face slightly. She didn't look at me. No tears tracked down her face. No fear bloomed in her eyes. As still as a marble statue, as pale and as emotionless, she stared at Van as Cian bent at the waist to clasp a chain to the dark collar around his neck. Nor did she glance around as I vaulted into my saddle, turning the mule about to flank Bayonne.

As we walked our horses downhill, she rested her chin on her shoulder to keep him in sight for as long as possible. Only when the high altitude hill behind us stood between her and him did she face forward once more. My hand on the mule's leading rein kept him in position whereby I could watch her face. But she yielded me nothing. No submission, no anger, no fear. As though I escorted a life-like doll to Castle Salagh and our wedding.

I won her body. I will never win her love.

Not ever.

"You can't do it," Yummy said tiredly, for the fourth time.

Ignoring her, I tried a fifth, or was it sixth? breaking spell, one that could shatter weighted steel into splinters. Or should, according to the power and arcane knowledge within my head. I breathed deeply, exerting my will as the spell specified. Magic surged upward, power pouring from me in a river of strength.

I blinked, prepared to witness the bands falling asunder into Iyumi's lap.

Nothing happened. The dark manacles remained on her wrists, holding her fast in their smooth grip. *Is this for real?* My magic came from the blood sacrifice. Nothing can stop such power. Nothing on this earth.

Scowling, I tried a spell of un-binding, one that surely would melt those bastards into mere dust.

The same result yet again. Zilch.

As though owning a wicked mind, the bracelets gleamed in the red-orange illumination of our evening campfire as though laughing at me. I hated being laughed at. Thus, I hated these stubborn, cold cuffs with more power than mine. I cursed under my breath and, like a toddler with a tantrum, wished them gone.

"What are they?" I muttered, raising her hands to peer at them in the dancing firelight.

She turned her cheek away from me, her hands limp, lifeless, within mine. Obviously, she found the ground at her feet more interesting to look at than my face. "A magic so old the gods were young when their secrets weren't so secret. The ages come and go, civilizations rise and fall, as time moves on in its relentless path. Magical knowledge and powerful relics from the old days are gone, hidden."

"And?"

"This pewter metal is from those old days gone by. Its dark magic can still any magician, any Shifter, and prevent him from using his or her gods-given powers. No magic, no earthly influence can break them. Only those who know its deep secrets, and know how to summon its strength, can undo them, or cut them off."

"Where do they come from?"

She refused to look and me, and I knew she lied. "I don't know."

"But Cian does."

Her blue glance flicked across me then cut to her right. "Old spells of dark magic were forbidden. No one caught practicing the black evils were permitted to survive. Witches ever sought more and more power, seizing it from the blood of the innocent. How many died on their stone altars as they sold their souls to the evil ones?"

I strongly suspected I was now considered a witch by those who made the rules, or the male variation of the same. For did I not receive my great magic from the sacrifice of a small child, an innocent? Was I now as evil as they? I shut my eyes against the deep anger that tried to rise and seize control of my soul. Why did I do

[382]

it? Why wasn't my own magic enough to satisfy me? With my birth magic, I felt happy. Now, I felt sick. Couldn't I protect Fainche and my mother with what the gods gave me without stealing more?

Upon opening my eyes, I found Iyumi watching me. Instantly, she found the infant in her lap far more interesting to look at. I released my pent up breath and fury, and offered her a small smile. At being caught, I suspected she silently vowed to keep her eyes to herself from then on. For all her attention remained on the babe and refused to lift.

"Like your scrying crystal . . . they were taken away and guarded for the sake of all," her small voice continued as though never interrupted.

My hand seized the amber gem under my shirt. "You know about that?"

She didn't rise to my bait. "Certain adepts can feel the watcher's using the crystals. Far too many couldn't. Those that could lived, survived. We both know what happens to folks who can't feel the evil eyes on their backs."

"It's hardly evil," I protested.

"These days," she continued as though reciting a dull report, raising her bound wrists, "only a few powerful magicians know how to forge them, or unlock them. I reckon Cian discovered the knowledge to not just use their dark arts, but also escape from them."

"He escaped? From where? Who?"

She glanced over the manacles but still refused to catch my eyes. "Cian was arrested and charged with treason and attempted murder. No one knew he'd learned the secret of the metal until he escaped them. Otherwise, he'd still be rotting in my father's dungeon, chained like the animal he is."

I whistled. "Then you can't–"

She grinned, a nasty sort of feral expression I might see on a cat just before the alley fight. The first show of spirit I'd seen since we left Van in Cian's hands. "Had I my powers, you'd be one blonde pile of ash and shit right now."

"I reckon I can't blame you," I said, squeezing her cold hands. "I'm not your enemy, Iyumi."

"Then what are you?"

"I want to be your friend."

Snorting, she swung away from me to pick up the baby. It mewled and fussed, waving chubby brown fists from amidst the rags. "What was it you said? You 'always treat your wives with love and respect'?"

I flushed. "Yes. I'm married."

Though she didn't look up from the wriggling baby resting on her forearms, her wrists still locked together, I caught the gleam of teeth as she grimaced. "Faithless monster. You'd break her heart to marry me, wouldn't you?"

She had me there. "Yes."

At length she sighed and glanced up. "Honest for once," she said, her tone heavy. "You might one day achieve what you most desire if you keep that up."

"And just what do I most desire?"

"Redemption."

I poked the fire with a stick, glancing around at my men, sitting near the other fire. Torass turned a wild piglet on a spit, killed by Buck-Eye's quick arrow at sunset. The roasting pork smelled delicious, but, oddly, I had no appetite. I stroked my hand down Dra'agor's head to his neck, over and over, as he lay next to me. He stared into the flickering flames, mesmerized, his tail curled over his paws.

Iyumi tickled the infant's lips with her fingers, bringing forth a tiny shriek of delight. "You should set him free."

"Who?"

Now Dra'agor raised his muzzle and watched Iyumi from across my lap. He licked his lips and whined, low, in his throat.

"The wolf. He doesn't belong to you. He belongs to himself, and the pack. His kind shouldn't be slaves."

"Dra'agor isn't a slave," I protested. "He can leave me anytime he wishes."

Iyumi's head snapped up and she glared at me. "Can you really be that stupid? What wolf would *choose* to be paired with a human? He's been bound by black magic, the *coi coi etala.*"

"The blood binding," I whispered, staring down at Dra'agor.

He glanced up at me, his tail lifting in a half-wag before drooping to lay still across his paws. Resting his muzzle on my knee, he shut his amber-brown eyes as though asleep. I knew he didn't sleep, however. I continued my absent minded strokes, thinking terrible thoughts. I'd heard the legends, of course. Of how certain spells bound one's will to that of the magician invoking the spell. That the blood of the victim was burned on a desecrated altar while the practitioner chanted prayers.

But to whom did they pray?

I heard my mother's voice: *He serves me.*

This can t be right. My mother doesn't know how to bind a person's, or a wolf's, will to her own. Her magic isn't powerful enough. It's the work of someone else, obviously. Someone else, a person wise in the dark arts and evil knowledge, no doubt bound Dra'agor's blood to his own. Then offered the wolf to my mother as a gift. While she didn't exactly say as much, I know she felt affection for the beast when she rested her hand on his head. The same warmth and love she freely offered Fainche and me . . . and my father.

Blaez had magic, I reasoned quickly. As did Enya and I. Perhaps my nasty sire did as well. Of course, Enya would accept the wolf as a protector if Finian told her to. That explained everything. King Finian the Necromancer. Who'd have thunk it?

"So you're familiar with the Old Tongue," she said, subsiding. "Dra'agor. Noble friend."

"How do I free him?" I asked.

"The baby needs nourishment," she said, as though I hadn't spoken. She bowed her shoulders protectively over the nasty ragged bundle of squirming divine messenger. "Send one of your men to kill something."

"Er," I said, sounding as dumb as she thought I was. "Kill what? Don't you want, er, milk?"

"Trolls have no need for milk."

My guts recoiled. "That's a troll?"

Her blue eyes burned me where I sat. "Another word and I'll kick your balls so hard you'll wear them for earrings. Tell your men to kill something. Now."

Dumping Dra'agor in the dirt, I hastily rose, backing away from the hellspawn she cuddled in her arms. *She s a witch,* I thought, my mind frantic with panic. Only witches nurtured or loved the demon-hatched mountain trolls. Ever had they romped through my nightmares, hiding under my bed to await my deepest snores. Once I slept, they would creep under the linens and blankets with me, to feast on the blood that poured from my opened neck. Thus the legends and tales were told and retold over countless hearth-fires and still more mugs of amber ale. As a consequence, I had a great deal of difficulty sleeping.

Never taking my eyes off the evil creature of my worst nightmares, I backed into the warmth and light of the other campfire. Dare I to sleep this night, no doubt the wretched thing would crawl into my blankets and feast on my blood long before I could waken and escape. Stolen power or no, I knew that *thing* would cast me into my worm-ridden grave this night.

"Who's on watch?" I asked Buck-Eye, never turning my back on the devil-child or her nurse. Had I taken a glance around, or remembered who I'd posted as first watch, I'd have known Boden sat several rods away, hidden from sight with his night vision unimpeded by the fires.

"M'lord?" Buck-Eye asked, rising to stand beside me. "What's wrong?"

I made a vague gesture, my spit dried to dust in my mouth. "Where's your bow? Oh. Grab it. Go kill something."

"Uh, we already killed a pig–"

I shoved his shoulder, hard, forcing him into the darkness and shadows. "I need fresh blood. Get a mouse, er, no, a rabbit, yes a rabbit or an owl. Anything. Go on. Don't skin it, just bring it."

Buck-Eye stumbled away, confused, muttering under his breath. Torass stood, forgetting his spit as Lyall nocked an arrow in his bow, ready for trouble. "M'lord? What is it?"

[386]

"What? Oh, nothing." I swept my hand through my hair, gesturing helplessly toward Iyumi and her infant horror. I didn't care that Lyall noticed my hand shaking. "The, er, child, the t-troll, needs fresh blood, to survive. Of course."

"Troll!"

Spinning around, I raised my hands, palms out, trying to push their fears and loathing back, as though I shoved at a solid wall. "No, no, lads, it's all good, really, it's just a baby troll, after all, what harm can a baby troll do to us? Eh? We're all grown men here, and it's harmless, really–"

"It drinks blood, m'lord," Lyall said, his tone like flint. "It's evil."

"Yes, well, this particular evil, er, infant, is our divine messenger. We need it, and the princess, to save our country. Remember?"

I blew out a gust of in-taken breath, trying to smile and regain light-heartedness. "That can't be evil, what? C'mon, lads, relax."

I smacked Lyall's shoulder. "Think of it as a–"

"Troll."

I tried to laugh. "No, no, it's a baby bat. Yes, it's just a baby bat."

"That drinks blood."

"I tell you, many harmless critters drink blood–"

"Like what?"

"Er, well–" I ran my fingers through my mop of hair and tried to think. "Uh, how about mosquitoes?"

Lyall's crusty expression wilted me where I stood.

"And fleas, of course. Fleas drink blood, we all know it. Right? So what if it drinks blood, it's all good–"

"What drinks blood?"

Buck-Eye returned, a rabbit hanging from his fist, his arrow through its throat. Garnet droplets slid down its fur and dripped redly into the tundra at his boots. All that blood, dripping, useless–

I dodged forward and intercepted him before he tossed the carcass on the ground. He hadn't skinned it yet, as any good hunter might, nor had he gutted it. Perhaps most of its blood remained inside, still warm. *It s a baby,* I half-thought, gagging. *It doesn t need much. Right?*

"Ha! Thanks, Buck-Eye, I'll take it now. Go get yourself some dinner. You lads, too, eat up while its hot."

Seizing the still-warm rabbit from Buck-Eye's fist, I held it gingerly upright, hoping not too much blood was lost from its damaged throat. Leaving them to mutter behind my back, I quickly crossed the distance to the other fire. Complete with arrow, I laid it carefully at Iyumi's feet. "There you are, er, ah, blood, as you, er requested, m'lady. For the, um, you know . . . the, the–"

She eyed the rabbit disdainfully. Carefully setting the baby in her lap, she raised both hands and picked up the carcass. "Give me your knife."

"My, er–"

"Knife. Please."

Hastily, I yanked my dagger from my belt and handed it to her, hilt first. My belly roiling, threatening to heave, I watched as she cut the furry throat and held it above the rags. When the sucking started, along with the happy gurgles, I knew my time had come. I stumbled away into the darkness before falling to my knees. Retching what little I had in my stomach, I coughed and hurled, spitting the sour taste from my mouth. My aching belly revolted again, sending bile up and out at roughly the speed of sound. I groaned, sweating, my stomach muscles aching.

Dra'agor's nose nuzzled my ear, his whine caught in his throat. I shoved him away, needing solitude in my moment of shame. At least none of the lads saw fit to investigate their lord prince on his knees vomiting into the bushes. What Iyumi thought – I didn't care.

Perhaps an hour, or most likely five minutes, passed before Dra'agor nuzzled my neck. When Dra'agor licked my sweat from my cheek, I didn't push him away. I wobbled halfway to my feet. "I'm sorry, old lad," I said, wiping my lips on my sleeve. "Somehow, I'll set you free. I don't know how, though. But I'll figure it out."

I managed a reasonably straight walk back to the fire, Dra'agor at my side. I needed a drink. Water, wine, beer– anything that might wash away the sour taste of bile from my mouth and throat. The kid had finished his drink, and mumbled sleepy sounds from within the folds of Iyumi's lap. The rabbit lay near the fire, shrunken, a shell of what it once was.

"The meat's still good," Iyumi said, picking it up and holding it toward Dra'agor. "I'll skin it for you, if you want it. Please. I'd be honored, Dra'agor."

Dra'agor wagged his tail, his eyes bright, as he watched Iyumi quickly skin the rabbit. He gently plucked the still-warm carcass from her bloody hands, and took it away, into the darkness, to eat his evening meal in privacy.

She cleaned my knife as best she could before returning it to me. "I don't suppose, er . . . ." She lifted her stained hands, clasped together by the manacles, toward me. "Might I trouble you for a quick wash, perhaps?"

I nodded, avoiding her eyes. "Of course."

The swift mountain stream lay but a few hundreds rods from our campsite. After clearing my mouth and sweating face, I filled two skins full of the icy water and carried them back into the firelight. Dra'agor finished the rabbit and sat near Iyumi, licking his whiskers as she smiled up into his face. She said something I couldn't catch, and Dra'agor wagged his tail. The troll lay silent, sleeping I guessed, within the protection of her lap as I walked up.

Iyumi held out her hands, rinsing them in the cold water as I poured. A small trickle struck the fire, forcing it to hiss in protest, as Iyumi dried her hands on her cloak. The manacles didn't clank much, I noticed. Their sound seemed muted, like their color.

"You sacrificed the child," Iyumi said, her tone neutral. "And gained terrible power from it."

I didn't answer. After setting the skins near her should she need a drink in the night, I sat down, across the fire from her. Drawing my knees to my chin, I watched as the firelight flickered off her features, setting her silver hair aflame. I didn't question how she knew about Finias. Of course she knew. My only surprise was my own surprise.

"Are you evil, Flynn?"

Again, I didn't speak. Tossing more wood on an already tall and hot fire, I built it higher still, as though creating a blazing fence between me and the gods' voice. *I wish I knew.* Mesmerized by the flickering red-orange-yellow flames, its heat beaded sweat on my brow and upper lip. I've done evil, certainly. Does that make me truly evil, in truth? I wrapped my arm around my upraised knee, for the first time in my life pondering what might become of my soul after I'm dead and gone.

"You've received quite an education lately," Iyumi said, rubbing Dra'agor's ear as she stared into the flames. "You know that Minotaurs, Centaurs and Shape-Shifters aren't evil. Magic isn't evil, for you wield it yourself. I know you were taught such, as a child, in Raithin Mawr. But they aren't. Just as this child isn't."

"It's a troll."

"So?" Her tone shifted to impatience. "It drinks blood to survive. *Big deal.* Grow up, Flynn. You kill and eat meat. Just as Dra'agor kills to feed his pack, and humans slaughter cattle, sheep and goats for their survival. A troll doesn't murder in the night. Not on humans, anyway. It kills through need only, and by the gods' will alone does it need to drink the blood first. *This child isn t evil.*"

"I hope you're right," I muttered, making the sign against strong magic. "I know damn well I'll never sleep while that thing is around."

Though I tried hard to ignore the troll, I slept in fits. The little boy I murdered haunted what little sleep I managed to get, pointing his tiny finger at me while glaring at me with my father's eyes. He didn't speak, not this time. But the gaping wound in his throat yawned wide as his free hand picked and pulled at his empty chest cavity. I woke, my scream snared like a rabbit in a trap, my face sweating rivers. Sitting up, I huddled close to the fire, watching Iyumi sleep. She lay next to the fire, wrapped in a blanket, cuddling the troll close, at her belly. It, too, slept deeply, wrapped in both her warmth and the blanket. Dra'agor curled up at her back, as though helping her stay warm through the cold mountain night. I seized a nearby wineskin and drank deep. The wine settled my

[390]

nerves a fraction. I wiped my face of the rapidly cooling sweat and took a deep breath.

I lay back down, and forced my eyes shut. When I did manage to nod off, I dreamed that creepy troll rose from Iyumi's protection and crawled toward me, eyes blood red and fangs dripping.

I woke instantly, reaching for my sword, only to see her back, all but buried behind Dra'agor's hulking form. No troll stalked me, seeking my throat and my beating pulse. A rapid glance around showed my lads huddled about their own fire, sleeping. Torass stood the mid watch, standing with his back to the flames, pacing occasionally. I lay back down, my heart thumping in my chest, tasting the sweet iron of panic on my tongue. Yet, I never let go of my hilt, or the dark power. I kept both within my hands, ready.

Just in case.

Though I lay quiet, still, and comfortable into my blankets, sleep eluded me. Knowing I needed my rest if I were to keep my head and wits about me only made matters worse. I couldn't halt the torrid images of the hungry troll rampaging through camp, killing all except its mother: Iyumi. *Perhaps I ll catch a nap later,* trying to force myself to relax. If we lived that long, at any rate.

Come the faint tinge of dawn, I rose from my blankets. With one cautious eye on her, I stretched as though having slept well, faking a yawn. Though I feigned sleepiness, she didn't. Iyumi rubbed sleep from her eyes as Dra'agor stretched, his front paws out and his rump high in the air. Iyumi thumped his shoulder, forcing him to snap his fangs on his own tongue.

"Be a dear," she said, covering her own yawn. "Fetch a bite for this young one?"

Dra'agor wagged his tail agreeably, and loped into the scrub oak and thickets. He vanished just as the sun rose over the eastern plains below us, covering the earth in crimson, orange and red blush. Distant clouds appeared as wisps on the horizon, the day promising clear yet chilly. *We did near the end of summer. This high up, winter comes early.*

"M'lord?"

I twisted halfway around as Torass offered a small plate of cold pork, berries, hard cheese, bread and an array of nuts. A skin of water hung from his wrist. My belly rumbled, but not in hunger. I covered my mouth as I graciously waved him toward Iyumi. "My lady has her choice first, of course."

Torass knelt, eyes respectfully lowered, as Iyumi took only the waterskin from him with both hands. She drank deep, her eyes on him even as she tilted her head back and squirted the icy water down her throat. She lowered it thoughtfully, still watching him, silver droplets clinging to her lips.

"What's your name?"

"Torass, m'lady."

"Torass," she repeated softly, wiping her mouth with the back of her hand. Her manacles clanked softly, and dark bruising had formed over her slender wrists. She set the skin on his small plate. "Well, Torass, I'm not hungry just now. But I do thank you for the drink."

Knuckling his brow, Torass rose to offer me the food next, but I waved him away. I had no appetite, either. He walked away toward the smoldering remains of the other fire, sharing out the breakfast with Boden, Buck-Eye and Lyall, laughing over some jest.

I gestured lamely toward her obviously sore wrists. "I'm sorry I can't get those off you."

She glanced at them with a half-shrug. "Doesn't matter."

"Of course it does. They're hurting you."

Iyumi stared straight into my face for once. "Flynn. Not a one of us will be alive if the Red Duchess sacrifices this child on her demon altar. For she will open up the gates of hell, and both our lands will perish. You can be proud of yourself, boy. You'll be personally responsible for the end of the world as we love it."

I gaped. "That's not true! No one will kill this . . . child. I'll marry you and we'll join our lands as one. That's the prophecy."

She rolled her eyes. "Idiot boy. That's *one* prophecy. There are many avenues to it. One is what you just mentioned. The other is that my father kills you and your father and rules over Raithin Mawr, then our lands become one. But if that demon bitch gets this baby, then all bets are off. *She* will rule and we're all dogmeat."

[392]

"I'm delivering the baby to my mother," I said, feeling a very large wriggle of fear run down my heart. "Not this Red Duchess creature. I have to save Fainche. If I don't, my father will kill her." Iyumi frowned. "Princess Fainche? Your sister?"

I nodded, running my hands through my hair. Standing up, I paced, sweating despite the chilly morning. "The Red Duchess, as you call her, controls him. I think. If we can kill her, then we can be free of her. My father won't . . . won't–"

She nodded. "Then your father won't kill what you love most in the world."

"He'll kill not just Fainche, but my wife Sofia, and . . . and my unborn son–

"Your wife is pregnant?"

"I think so, she said so . . . she lies, occasionally, but what if this time she didn't? My mother will die, too. That's why I have to deliver you, and the . . . baby. I can't lose them all!"

"If your father is controlled by her, as you say," Iyumi said, her tone neutral. "Then how can we kill her?"

"Because I plan to kill *him.*"

She laughed. "Riiight. You'd kill your own father. Just how stupid do you think I am?"

Shit! Damn her eyes, shit! I loosed the cloak clasp at my throat, and let my cloak fall to the ground. Unlacing my tunic, I stripped it off and turned my bare back to her. As I hadn't fully healed my whip wounds, my scars were appallingly apparent. I couldn't stop the bitterness that crept into my tone, ousting the fear. "This was his gift to me when I failed to bring you to him. Do you not see the love a father has for his son? His family?"

"Gods."

The single word held more horror than question. Though she didn't move toward me, I felt her empathy tingle along my skin like a dancing firefly. "Your *father* did this? To his own son? What kind of monster is he?"

"Monster, yes." I didn't turn around as I pulled my tunic back over my head and swung my cloak over my shoulders. My fingers trembled as I fumbled at the clasp. "A father, not so much. We

[393]

never got on, ever. You see? He expects the impossible, and demands such from his only son and heir."

"But, this . . . this is—"

"Monstrous, in truth," I replied, my tone low, cold. "He wants me like him: evil, strong, invincible. Believe me, it's not what I want. I'm the creature I am because of him. I hope, someday, I can be the true prince folks want me to be."

At last clothed respectably again, I turned about and met her sympathetic blue eyes. "I *will* kill him, Princess. I swear it. I'll kill *her,* too, before she can harm this baby you protect. But I have to save my mother. My sister. My wife. To keep them safe is all I live for."

I bowed my head, shut my eyes against the pain, the pain I brought upon myself and others. "I know you don't believe me. I know you don't trust me, and you're right not to. When I was a little boy, all I ever wanted to be was brave, courageous. Like the knights in the tales of old. I wanted to save the day and listen to the cheers of a grateful crowd."

I half-laughed, choking. "I've fallen far short of that dream, I reckon. Rather than save folks, I've harmed them. If there is a way I can atone for the evil I've done, I'll do it. I swear by the gods you represent, I'll undo the evil I've done. Somehow. Someday. If I'm ever given the chance."

At her continued silence, I glanced up. I hoped to find her staring at me, but instead she gazed down into her lap, where the infant troll lay. As though she hadn't heard a word I said. As though only the baby mattered in the grand scheme of the world. Quashing the sudden burst of irritation that rose, I opened my mouth as I bowed, sardonic, toward her.

"I reckon—"

"A pretty speech," she said, meeting my annoyance.

Her silver-gilt hair fell across her eyes and she tossed it back, careless, out of long habit. I heard no hint of sarcasm, of derision in her voice. I saw no hint of hatred nor any sign of mockery in her eyes or expression.

"I feel the need to offer a small bit of advice, unwanted as it may be," she went on. "Be careful of what you'd swear to, Prince Flynn of Raithin Mawr. The gods are fickle and demand much from their servants. You swore an oath before them and bared your throat. Never for a second, not an instant that passes, ever forget they might hold you to it."

I gaped like a fool. While I expected her contempt, my words hurled back into my teeth with righteous fury, I never thought she'd prophecy–if that's what her words meant. To predict my future. If I'd learned anything in my years of walking this earth, I did learn one thing: the future was never predictable. Like the water in a river, it flowed fluid and ever changing. If a rock dropped into its course, its course was forever changed. Surely the gods knew *that.*

How I'd have answered her, I'll never know. At that moment, Dra'agor returned at a lope, tail wagging, a freshly killed young marmot in his jaws. As Iyumi praised his kill and his skills as a hunter, I tossed my knife, point down, at her feet. Walking away, I shut my ears to the sounds of that nasty creature sucking the blood from the dead rodent, my stomach roiling.

"You haven't eaten, m'lord," Buck-Eye said, standing up from the smoldering remains of the fire. He held out meat and bread toward me, still-warm from the coals. "It's a long way till the midday meal, don't ye know? Won't you grab a bite?"

In the distance, Boden and Lyall led the freshly watered horses back from the stream, punching one another's shoulders in a mock-fight. They danced and laughed, ducking their heads as they battled, the horses plodding behind them in a loose group. Torass emerged from the bushes, clearly finished answering nature's call and hitched his britches. He turned toward the ruckus caused by the others and called to them, but I couldn't hear his words.

"I'm not much hungry, Buck-Eye," I said, clapping him on the shoulder. "Have the lads saddle the horses, eh? Find a blanket or some such for the princess. Royalty should ride in some comfort, even if it's for a short while."

"Got just the thing," he answered cheerfully. "Old blanket. Got a decent strap to tie it on, too."

"Good man. Once we're ready, I'll send us straight to Salagh's gates. We'll be home by lunch."

"I seriously doubt that."

This time, I didn't quell the irritation Iyumi's smarmy words brought forth. Controlling my ever-ready anger with a strong effort, I swung toward her. It buckled, much as a soufflé collapsed upon feeling the cool draft, as I witnessed her literally wring the last of the beastie's blood into the troll's greedy mouth. My skin icy cold, and my belly outraged by the wanton display, I quelled the shudder that raced across my skin. Though I averted my eyes, I saw Dra'agor waiting beside her with jaws wide and tongue lolling. The troll belched and waved chubby brown arms, chuckling happily. I imagined its moist lips stained red and my shudder refused to subside.

No doubt, that girl had my number. With an ill-concealed smirk and a rapid there-and-gone glance from those huge blue eyes, Iyumi stripped the hide from the corpse with practiced cuts of my knife and graciously handed the meat to Dra'agor. "Your breakfast, dear boy."

As Dra'agor crunched happily, Iyumi held out her bloody hands toward me, manacles clanking with a dull sound. "If you will."

Picking up the waterskin she drank from earlier, I positioned it over her gore-covered fists. I turned my face away from the happy, contented infant in her lap, but still heard the gurgles and sharp squeals of a healthy newborn. Damn it! Why did it have to be a nasty, evil, god-forsaken *troll*? I poured the water as Iyumi washed. She splashed her face and dampened the hem of her mantle to wipe the baby's mouth.

"Thank you."

Iyumi rose with the rag-clad infant in her arms. "I'm ready, my lord," she said brightly. "It's what, a four, perhaps five day journey from here to Salagh's gates? We'd best get on the road."

I coughed. "The jewel, the, er–"

"Scrying crystal," she offered helpfully, her blue eyes wide and bland.

"Yes, I know what it is."

"Oh, sorry. I thought for a moment you forgot its name."

"–will take us there in minutes."

"Oh, it'll take *us* there," Iyumi replied, smiling sweetly. Why did I suddenly want to smack her across her pale cheek?

Because you excel at harming the helpless.

As Dra'agor licked his whiskers and gazed up at Iyumi with clear adoration in his amber eyes, she giggled. Cradling the now-sleepy baby in the crooks of her elbows, she bent down, her face on level with his. His tail wagged faster; his expression bright, happy, reveling in the attention she gave him. Acting more like a puppy than a feral wolf, Dra'agor wiggled his way closer to her, his powerful jaws wide in lupine laughter.

"You are such a dear," she gushed. "Give me a kiss."

Dra'agor eagerly washed her cheek with his tongue, growling and dancing, his feet unable to keep him still. Iyumi managed a swift smooch to his brow before straightening. "Trolls are immune to magic."

"So?"

I caught her rapid amused glance before she cooed and clucked over Dra'agor, teasing him with pursed lips as he jumped upward to wash her cheeks with his busy tongue.

"Trolls are among many of the world's creatures impervious to our human powers. Elves, unicorns, dragons, and trolls are unaffected by our arcane spells. Not even the ancient magics of old wield influence over them."

"The crystal can–" I began, speaking in a didactic, lecturing tone until her words, and obnoxious *I-know-more-than-you-do* expression, sank in. Damn it, but I hated being caught with my figurative britches down about my ankles. For that's exactly what she intended me to feel.

I knew she witnessed the complete and utter collapse of my senses. My jaws opened, but no coherent words spilled forth. My thoughts arrived at a jangling halt as I caught the sheer importance of what she'd said. I might order the amber crystal under my shirt to take us anywhere on earth, Castle Salagh included, but the oh so very important divine messenger would remain in the dust beside a dead campfire.

"Gods–" I choked.

"Made them that way, yes. Just as they drink blood as you sip fine wine, your stolen power can't touch her. If you want her on your father's lap, you'll have to carry us all those long lonely leagues across the mountains on these poor beasts. Oh, and by the way, those mountain passes into Raithin Mawr, well, I hate to bear bad news, but they are too often rendered impassable around, er, now."

"Shit–"

"Oh, no." Her evil giggle rose high in the early morning sunshine. "Not shit, dear boy. Snow. Lots of it. This time of year. Oh, well, we might get through. Have hope, Flynn. We might get down the other side without freezing to death."

"I am *sooo* much trouble, this can't be happening to me."

"I strongly suspect you were born to trouble, my lord prince."

I ran my hand through my hair, desperate to deny her heinous words. "You're wrong, of course. You're just trying to scare me."

Iyumi cocked her head to her right, wide blue eyes rolled up and past me, her teeth biting her lower lip. "Come to think of it, I remember something. A fact, maybe, or a tale anyway. It's important to you, so I'll recite it as best I can. I learned, or read about, I scarcely know now, about a small group who braved the passes. Remember, this was a long time ago. About this time of year, if I do remember correctly. Anyway, the travelers found themselves trapped by early snows. Thought they could make it, so they did. A blizzard hit, a bad one. Lasted five days, or was it six?"

Iyumi paused to gather a breath–or was it malice?–before continuing. "No matter, the strong ones hated to do it, I know they did. Cannibalism is forbidden by the gods, you know? Of course you do, my bad. They knew, but still they ate the weaker ones. The strong preyed upon the weak, but isn't that the nature of things? Right, Flynn? Just as you do?

"Everything was in the open and above ground, naturally. Those weak adults and small children weren't murdered for the tender meat of their arms and legs, even their buttocks–who'd have dared that? Of course they'd have died from the killing cold and icy wind from the north. It's not just forgivable to dine on one's best friend–not when one's own life is at stake–it's perfectly acceptable. No god will hold hunger against you, am I right, Flynn? Am I right? Flynn?"

[398]

"We absolutely have to be there in–"

"Yes, of course. You'd certainly know what's right, silly me. Those folks with the long knives were well within their rights! Unfortunately for those who came down from the Shin'Eah come spring were arrested and executed immediately. Shamefully so. It appeared, obviously, that the law enforcement fellows held a dim view of men eating their companions. Those short-sighted bastards. We should string them all up, I say, instead of the other way 'round. I tell you! Life just isn't fair."

"Prove it."

"What dear? Please don't mumble yours words, laddie. I listen to ten thousand voices per day. Yours tend to get lost amid the confusion."

Wild hope thrummed through the despair her words intended to inflict. She lied. She wanted us to ride across the mountain to give her folk time to catch up. Rescue her the way they did before.

"Prove it," I said. "Show me th–that *thing* is impervious to magic."

Iyumi raised her manacled wrists, her expression tight. Her fine brows met over the bridge of her nose at the same time her delicious lips thinned. "Can't, stupid. Not with these on."

"There has to be–"

"There is. I'll speak slowly so you can understand me. I do so hate repeating myself, especially to one as thick as you obviously are. Try-using-the-crystal-to-move-her-from-here-to-there."

Iyumi's head jerked toward a smooth boulder halfway toward the river. She set the now sleeping infant gently on the ground beside her, then stood up. Walking away a few paces, she gave a rather nasty, *perhaps-you-should-think-twice-about-breeding* amused expression. Her bruised wrists bumped against her thighs. "I'm over here, so you can't suspect me of manipulating anything."

I nodded. "Fair enough."

Taking the amber jewel from under my tunic, I held it tightly within my lightly sweaty palm. *This has to work. I must transport us all to Castle Salagh today. Lords above, I know you hate me, but I need your help. Please let this work.*

[399]

Setting my will upon the crystal, I shut my eyes and pictured the tiny troll lying atop the huge stone. *I will it shall be so.* I felt the power leave me, expand outward, seize something and send it to the rock. It worked! *Iyumi is wrong,* I almost crowed. *She can t make a fool out of Flynn, not this time.*

"Thanks, bucket-brain," Iyumi yelped, her voice no longer a few rods to my left.

I snapped my eyes open. Iyumi stood, balanced precariously atop the boulder. Her arms rose as she fought to keep from falling; her bound wrists unable to help keep her upright by pin-wheeling. While the rock was clearly large enough for a baby, it wasn't wide nor flat enough for an adult, even one as small as the princess.

Before I could offer her aid, Dra'agor bolted across the clearing, growling and whining. At the same moment, her equilibrium deserted her. Rather than tumble off, she leaped down. Upon striking the ground, she took three or four running steps and arrived a neat halt, upright and with royal dignity intact. Dra'agor reached her, whining loudly in the mountain morning. His eyes and questing muzzle searched her up and down for any injury.

And the troll?

Still asleep within her rag nest, right where Iyumi put her. I sighed, biting my lower lip. I *really* hate that damn thing.

"I'd suggest you try again," Iyumi said, her hands tickling Dra'agor's muzzle as best she could as she walked toward me. "But who knows where you'd put me next. I do so like keeping my feet planted."

"This isn't happening," I muttered, running my hands through my hair. Finding an amber oak leaf caught in it, I stared at the hand-like and death-stiffened sprig in my palm. I crushed it. "This just *can t* be happening!"

"Put your big boy pants on, Flynn. It *is* happening and there's not a bloody thing you can do about it."

"M'lord?"

I turned around. Buck-Eye led Bayonne and the mule toward us, Torass, Boden and Lyall already mounted on their horses behind him. "We're ready whenever you are, m'lord. Your Highness."

He bobbed his head respectfully toward Iyumi. "You'll be using your magic then? Get us to the castle and this here babe to its destiny?"

"There's a slight change in plans, Buck-Eye," I said, grimacing. "We're taking the long way around."

"Long way, m'lord? There is no long way save–"

His eyes widened. His jaw slackened as he glanced toward the north and the high, threatening peaks. The Shin'Eah Mountains bordered our Raithin Mawr from Bryn'Cairdha: an imposing and effective barrier between two warring countries. We'd skirted the high and daunting passes on our chase for the Princess Iyumi and the babe by utilizing the scrying crystal. Literally, I jumped us over them. From where we stood right now, the most direct route to my father's castle, and Fainche, lay northeast – give or take a mountain or two. Straight up. Into the hellish teeth of the Shin-Eah upon the onset of winter, across the forbidding peaks and eastward down the other side into the lesser mountains and hills to Castle Salagh.

"Didn't you say we had to be there by–"

"I did," I answered, my tone grim. "But we haven't a choice, Buck-Eye. The infant my sire so desperately wants is immune to my magic. Unless we have her . . . ."

"There's no point. Right?"

"Right."

"Cheer up, boys."

Iyumi's amused voice spun me around. She sauntered toward me, the baby in her arms and Dra'agor trotting happily at her side. A faint, haughty smile hovered on her lips.

My hand itched to smack that smile off her face, but I stilled the urge with an effort. The old Flynn would hit her, of that I had no doubt. But the new Flynn swore an oath to seek atonement for the evil he's done. I can't start a new life by striking a helpless woman.

"Look at it this way," she said, her hair spilling from its half-hearted braid and cascading down her small bosom. "We'll have lots of time to get to know one another better. Am I right or am I right?" She strolled past us toward the mule as though walking across her throne room.

I clenched my fists.

"I'll see her onto her, er, mount, m'lord," Buck-Eye said, his eyes sympathetic.

Before he finished his sentence, I was nodding and walking toward Bayonne. "Do it, I'd be ever so grateful."

When the sun and the moon are joined in the sky . . . .

If Enya's calculations were correct, we had six days until that moment when the darkness fell at dawn. If we rode hard, and luck rode with us, we'd arrive at my father's gates within five. Plenty of time to kill my father and the red witch who has turned my life upside down. Once I free Fainche and my mother from her evil–

Thoughts of Iyumi in my bed with that silver-gilt hair spread across the pillows danced through my imagination. I did indeed love Sofia, but compared with Iyumi–well, if there were contests for beauty, then Iyumi won hands down. Happily, I daydreamed as I rode. Iyumi willingly giving herself to me; her belly rounded with our child; standing at my side as Queen of Raithin Mawr. Most of all, my thoughts ranged across her heavenly body and her ripe, luscious breasts. I fetched a deep sigh, my britches tight.

I suddenly caught her staring hard at me, those twin blue sapphires as hard as agates. Her mouth had thinned into a fine white line. Though she held no weapon in her fist, I knew Iyumi's thoughts as clearly as she read mine: she planned to gut me like a sacrificial goat. Those manacles wouldn't last forever, I knew, and she had access to powers far greater than mine.

I gulped and harrumphed, and kept my thoughts on the trail from then on.

Through the warm morning we cantered and jogged, following what appeared to be an old road, an ancient path that clearly wound its way into the heart of the mountains. Idle speculation among us suggested it was the remains of a highway, a trade route that brought goods back and forth between the two sections of what was then one single nation. None of us, not even Iyumi, remembered its name.

The weather cooperated, granting us warmth and sunshine as we trekked higher and higher. Though precipitous, the road curved back upon itself and made good use of the natural curves of the pass. It steepened sharply as we entered a narrow canyon with a ridge high above and an abrupt drop into thickly growing pine forests on our near side. We'd made decent time, thus far, the horses not requiring as many halts to rest as I first suspected they might.

The warm afternoon and lack of sleep took its toll on me. Lulled by Bayonne's smooth gaits, I half-dozed in my saddle. When my chin struck my chest, I'd start awake, and yawn mightily. Finding only Buck-Eye's back in my sight, as he rode several paces in front, my eyes slid shut of their own accord. I nodded off again. Though my mind and body rested, my ears still listened. As from a vague distance, as though hidden behind a screen, Buck-Eye's voice muttered.

"I'm not liking this, not one bit. Boden, do you see anything?"

From high above on the tall ridge, Boden's young tenor called down. "Nothing moving except what's supposed to move. But I don't like it, either. My gut's telling me something ain't right."

"Ride ahead, and keep your bow up."

"Jolly good."

I tried to wake up, gather sense around me. Yet, for the life of me, I couldn't. The need for sleep tugged at me, as though dead weights strapped to my ankles dragged me under the surface of a lake. To drown me. Deeper it pulled me, darkness gathering, sweet sleep calling to me, endlessly calling my name. I let it sweep across my mind, craving the rest my body needed. "I didn't sleep last night," I muttered to myself. *I need sleep. Sleep. Deep sleep.*

Something hard and sharp smacked me in the back of my skull. I woke with a jerk, acute pain coursing through my head. The somnolent fog vanished, and I cursed. I rubbed the back of my head, finding fresh blood on my fingers. I swung hard around–

[403]

–and found Iyumi off her mule, another rock ready in her hands. Her blue eyes wide, not with fury but loaded with fear, met mine. Though still bound together by the manacles, she readied the stone for another throw. The troll infant slept on the quiet mule's blanket. Torass and Lyall sat their horses behind her, their hands on their sword hilts. Despite the obvious danger to my person, they gazed not at her, but at the surrounding area. Dra'agor stood at her side, his hackles raised. His dark eyes on me, he raised his head to sniff the wind.

"A spell," Iyumi all but shrieked. "It almost had you. Wake up, dammit, we're in danger. It's an ambush."

My throat dry, I tried to scoff. "Who the hell is up here–no one knows where we are."

"Someone does, m'lord," Buck-Eye said, his sword still sheathed but his power clenched in his raised fists. "She's right. We rode straight into a trap."

The hackles on my neck rose, agreeing with their assessment: someone watched us with deadly intent. I jumped from Bayonne's saddle. Seizing Iyumi around her tiny waist, I thrust her aboard the mule. "Grab its mane," I ordered, shoving the baby into her lap. It woke with a cry, but I ignored it and gazed up into Iyumi's fierce blue eyes. "No matter what, you stay on this beast. Understand? Ride like hell if you have to, but stay on it no matter what happens."

She nodded, her face tight.

I threw the mule's lead rope to Torass. "Keep her safe? On your honor?"

Torass saluted. "My life for hers, m'lord."

I turned to vault into Bayonne's saddle when Iyumi's voice stopped me in my tracks. I half-turned back, my face over my shoulder. She gazed down at me, managing to scowl and smile in the same expression. "May the good gods be with you, Flynn."

I tossed her a grin. "Let's hope so. Lyall, you're with me."

Mounting up, I yanked my sword from its sheath at the same time I gathered my dark power into my hand. The sleep spell tried to work its way back inside my brain, a silent siren calling me down an evil path. Countering with a swift crush of my magic, it dissipated and died. Its passing left no clues as to who cast it in the

[404]

first place. Doesn't matter. With Lyall at my side, I urged Bayonne up the trail at a strong lope.

Buck-Eye and Boden galloped hard downhill; their mounts rear quarters slinging dirt and loose rocks as they fought the treacherous embankment. Boden's horse all but slid to his tail as Boden reined him in hard. "M'lord, stay put," Boden gasped. "Morn'n a dozen soldiers line the rocks ahead."

"Almost as many are falling in behind," Buck-Eye added. "I saw 'em from higher up, creeping along the ridge."

Dammit. I gnawed on my knuckle. Soldiers ahead and behind. To our right, the mountainside dropped off at a steep and lethal drop. On our left lay an impassible mixture of huge boulders, spruce, fir, and elm trees, all on sharp incline. The high ridge where Boden rode to spot potential trouble had it possibilities as an escape route, but no doubt our attackers waited for us to attempt it. 'Trapped' was a word I found offensive. It had such a tone of finality, and I intensely disliked finality.

"Whose soldiers?" I asked. "Bryn'Cairdhans?"

Buck-Eye slowly shook his head, his dark eyes hard. "M'lord, they're Raithin Mawrn."

As though a fist slammed into my gut, I knew what he'd say next. My breath choked off; I couldn't speak. *Does he really mean–*

"King Finian himself is there, m'lord," Buck-Eye continued. "I recognized both him and his mount. Commander Blaez rides at his side."

My mother's voice whispered in my memory: *He sees you as a threat. She whispers in his ears.*

Turning in my saddle, I gazed down at Iyumi, the troll in her arms sleeping soundly, rag-bound. I knew she heard what we said, for her flesh had paled to a milky shade and her blue on blue eyes darkened. No doubt, my illustrious sire intended to kill me and take her. Once his red mistress had the child, he'd rape Iyumi over and over and over. She knew it, too. Too tough to panic, she nonetheless felt fear. For those manacles trapped her the same way my father trapped me. Had she her powers–

I swung back to Buck-Eye. "Is anyone else with him? Someone who controls magic?"

Buck-Eye frowned. "I don't know, m'lord. Blaez certainly does."

"The men I saw were common soldiers, m'lord," Boden said quickly. "Not a one a knight, nor a noble. Forgive me for saying so, but the King keeps only brutes around him. Men who fight, but haven't an original thought in their heads."

Boden ducked his face, as though expecting a harsh reprimand. I grinned. "That's why I enjoy thinking men around me, Boden. For they are beyond price."

Under his pleased blush, I gazed around, assessing. Finian must surely know we spotted his trap and planned his attack at any moment. I had seconds to prepare. The terrain worked for him. Did it also work for me? He lost the element of surprise. Finian's men had the advantage of the high ground . . . or half of them did. I owned the high ground for the other half. No doubt, he thought to catch me between them. What if I turned the tables on him?

For magicians, Finian had only Blaez. I had Buck-Eye and myself. Boden's archer's eye almost equaled Buck-Eye's. Lyall's skills with a blade from horseback won him several purses in tourneys over the years. Torass had his merits, also, but I needed him to protect Iyumi. What else did I have? Boulders. Only one man, or two if squeezed in tight, at a time could attack from above. The entire path narrowed considerably up there, and though I couldn't maneuver for a stronger position, neither could Finian.

Below, the area lay as open as a willing maid. Several men on horseback, if armed with crossbows, or spears, could quickly overrun mine. In that lay my weakness. I needed a strong weapon to protect my backside, and Iyumi. Buck-Eye once shot a buck through the eye at three hundred paces. He'd learned a great deal about his personal arsenal since he swore his oath. Time to put him to work.

"Buck-Eye," I snapped. "Burn those bastards." I jerked my head to the uniformed soldiers, now in the open, lining up to charge uphill. All they waited for was Finian's signal. "If they get past you–"

"Then I'll be dead."

"Good man."

Buck-Eye shot me a swift there-and-gone grin. Forcing his horse down the hill and past us, he saluted Iyumi and spurred toward his targets. Where the ancient road widened, many tremendous granite stones lined the trail, the very rocks we trotted past not three minutes ago. In an impossible feat of courage, Buck-Eye's horse clawed and fought his way to the top of a huge rock, a piece of the mountain that had fallen away from its mother eons ago. A mountain goat might easily amble up its rough surface. I half-expected the bloody horse to fall backward, crushing both his spine and his human in one swift act of gravity.

Safely ensconced five rods above the trail, and our enemies, Buck-Eye casually nocked his arrow to his bowstring and pulled it toward his ear. He intended to launch both arrows and a god-forbidden rain of fire upon the heads of Finian's brutes once they rode within range. I've seen his skill, and I'll thank the gods every night that that bad boy owed his allegiance to me.

I also had a wolf. Horses feared wolves. One wolf loose among the cavalry horses might even the odds. Perhaps they might tilt in my favor, if the gods liked Iyumi enough. I glanced down at Dra'agor. His tail gently fanning the late afternoon air, he met my gaze. His jaw dropped in a lupine grin as though he knew what I'd ask of him.

"I need you, brother," I said, my voice low. "You don't truly need me in exchange. You're my friend and I hope I'm yours. You don't owe me a bloody thing, Dra'agor. If I may ask of you a favor, will you be willing to help us out here? Keep Iyumi safe?"

His enthusiastic woof and happily wagging tail informed me he was more than willing. Licking his whiskers in anticipation, he sat on the ground, awaiting my instructions. Pointing upward along the ridge, I gestured toward a thick clump of spruce and pine with generous helpings of scrub oak not far from where I estimated my sire's men advanced. "Hide in there, Dra'agor. When I tempt them in, when they've passed your hiding place, attack their rear. Hamstring their mounts. Create havoc. Get those men off their horses. Kill them if you can, but if you can't, just keep your skin whole. Got it?"

[407]

A sharp yap answered me. Dra'agor bolted up the hill, dodging amongst the thickets and boulders. I spent a precious moment admiring his lithe, predatory form as he flowed under and around the obstacles in his path. I watched until he vanished over the ridge and silently blessed my mother for giving him to me.

Glancing around, I noticed a tall pile of broken mountain to the right of the road. Several rods high and three wide, they appeared a natural barrier against an attack from above. Outside of dedicated men, and a wolf with brains, I knew I needed those huge boulders. Like a granite fort, those rocks might protect Iyumi while I fought Finian and Blaez. Only by killing me, and my lads, could Finian seize Iyumi and the gods' messenger.

Turning in my saddle, I gestured impatiently. "Torass, bring her here, double time."

If I was smart, so was my sire. Stood to reason, of course . . .we shared the same brain. He also recognized my need for that sheltering pile of stone. And anticipated my attempt to use it. I knew Finian knew I needed those rocks. I knew he *must* prevent me from hiding behind them. Should I gain their shelter, no power on earth could shake me out from under it. Finian *must* keep me in the open. He *must* keep Iyumi and the kid safe and healthy. If I survived and kept Iyumi, he'd lose not just the eternal war between Raithin Mawr and Bryn'Cairdha, but also his life. He knew I'd own the power between his life and his death. And he understood what course I'd choose.

The instant Torass spurred his horse uphill toward me, dragging the reluctant mule with him, Blaez launched his first attack. A blast of pure black energy ignored me as not worth mentioning and swung straight toward Torass. I almost heard his pedantic, nasal voice in my head: *take out the weakest to create panic amongst the strong.* Like an arrow homing in on the bull's eye, his racing terror plunged downhill and aimed to incinerate Torass in his saddle. Torass reined in his horse, forcing the beast onto its haunches, panic running through his expression and eyes. He recognized his death when he saw it.

The mule continued to gallop forward, but Torass's hand on his lead rein swung him sharply around. Iyumi remained aboard with ease, and her arms still sheltered the troll. Her face filled with an odd mixture of fear and anger, Iyumi rode out the mule's panic and kept the child close to her bosom. Blaez's incantation could easily take her out, also, despite Finian's need for her to survive. Into the confused mixture of equine legs, dust and cries of horror blew Blaez's vengeance. He hated me and, no doubt, wished to kill my men before he killed me. Just for the entertainment value, you see.

My counter measure blew Blaez's magical incendiary device far off its target to explode harmlessly into a spruce thicket in the canyon below. The trees, engulfed in flames, radiated a heat a thousand times the strength of a hearth fire. My hastily erected shield over my small gang kept the worst of it out, but I choked on its hot stench and Iyumi's face changed from pale ocher to a high red in seconds.

You stupia– Kill Iyumi and the child and you may as well slay yourself. Surely Finian knew Blaez never did anything by halves. Had his blow struck true, he'd have incinerated Iyumi, Torass and the mystical troll, leaving only their black ashes to dust the rocks. In sending all three to their makers, he'd cheat my sire of his prizes. Dimly, I heard Finian scream invectives, cursing Blaez roundly. I grinned. *Hello, handy distraction.* Kicking Bayonne forward, I waved for my lads to follow. The wrath of Blaez continued to destroy half the trees in the canyon, its black smoke coiling into the western sunlight.

Arrows rained down, despite the King's inattention. None struck anything useful, though one whistled perilously close to my head. With Torass in the lead, his heavy hand dragging the mule by its rope, Boden and Lyall flanked him in protective formation. Ducking their heads, hoping to avoid the arrows, the four galloped under the shadow of the tall rocks. Barbs pinged and broke upon the solid granite shelter as voices raised in angry disappointment from high above. Though I hadn't expected it, a deep curve under the tower of rocks enabled the horses, and Iyumi, to weather the fight quite protected. At my gesture, Lyall remained mounted, waiting for his orders.

[409]

"Princess," I said, swinging down from my saddle. "I've no right to ask anything of you. But I must."

She gazed down at me, her expression carefully neutral. "Mind the horses."

"Yes." Iyumi nodded, sliding down from the mule. Taking up the mewling babe, she settled it carefully in a stone niche where the horses wouldn't step on it, and where she could still watch over it. Taking three sets of reins and a rope into her shackled hands, she leaned against the rock wall.

I noticed the bruising around her wrists had intensified into a dark purpling. Fresh blood seeped from beneath the dark pewter. She saw me watching her, and turned her back.

What did I expect? That she'd witness my concern for her and fall into my arms?

"Greetings, boy. How good of you to stumble into my little trap." Finian's voice boomed down from on high, his voice magnified by close quarters and echoing eerily across the canyon.

I caught Lyall's confused expression and offered him a wry grin. My quick gesture ordered him to stand by, and I turned around to Torass and Boden, my finger pressed over my lips in a hushing gesture. I needed them silent, for I wanted no voices to give away their positions. Perhaps Finian may underestimate their abilities and their loyalty if he didn't hear defensive strategies bandied about. A long shot, yes, but I'll take anything I could get.

"Give me the princess and the child," Finian said, trying to sound reasonable despite his anger and the need to shout. "I mean you and your men no harm, boy. Surrender them and you're all free to go."

This time, Iyumi pressed her forefinger against her lips and smiled.

I obeyed her silent command to keep my mouth shut and waited, patient. I caught her idea: let Finian get really, really pissed. Men didn't think well when out of their minds with fury. He fully expected me to comply immediately to his demands, and when I didn't, his anger grew with every passing moment. My silence would only serve to enrage him.

"I know you're in there, boy," he yelled, his voice rising. "I have you surrounded. You've no chance of escape. Come out now, before I change my mind. If you make me come in and get you, you'll hang while my dogs feast on your entrails."

A chill crawled down my spine. I'd heard that threat before, many times. As King, as a man, Finian hated being ignored. Years before, a baron from a minor estate far to the north dared dismiss Finian's direct words to him at court. I was but a small lad, sitting at table beside my mother, the Queen. I remembered everything that transpired that awful night as though they happened yesterday. The baron pretended not to hear the King ask him a question regarding his holdings and his defenses against highwaymen. Instead, he laughed and told a bawdy joke reminiscent of Finian's sexual escapades. Finian's face waxed pale, then beet red.

That meant nothing to the baron. It meant danger to me.

The King barked orders. The baron was arrested on the spot. Despite the evening hours, Finian commanded the entire royal court accompany him into the castle's keep. With half the city, and the entire court, watching, Finian's brutes stripped the baron naked, and strung him upon the cross-poles in the center of the keep. There, feral dogs bit and chewed what choice bits of baron they could reach. He lived quite long that night. Later, in my bed, I listened to his screams, and cried, begging for them to stop. In the dawn's early light, they finally did. When the dogs were whipped from their prey, the baron's legs had vanished and his lower torso ripped into ragged pieces of pale flesh. Black blood pooled on the cobbles beneath his corpse. I'll never forget my father's victim's face as soldiers took him down from the poles: a bloodless face frozen with such an expression of agony and horror it chilled my soul.

I blanched and turned away, seeking to hide in my mother's skirts. My father, witnessing my weakness, seized me by the arm. He slapped my face, glaring down into my tears. "Puny brat," he snarled. "Look at him."

Trying again to free myself and hide, I clung to my mother. Finian's heavy hand on my head forced me to stare at the remains of what once was a decent enough man. "Look at him! He dared defy me, boy. Look and remember. Should you ever challenge me, this will be your reward."

The memory, long drowned under the years of beatings, anger and hatred, resurfaced. Always I feared he'd feed me to his mongrels if I dared disobey him. Afterward I walked lightly around him, minded my tongue in his presence and avoided him whenever possible. I accepted his heavy hand as a reminder of what he'd truly do to me should I provoke him. If he took me alive this day, I'd no doubt he'd do exactly as he threatened on that bloody morning so long ago.

"Come on, boy," Finian shouted. "I know you can hear me."

"I hear you just fine," I snapped. "I merely chose to ignore you."

"This is your last warning, boy. Surrender your arms and the princess."

Iyumi felt my eyes on her and glanced up. I created a faint smile, though there was little humor and no warmth in it. "He'll not take you alive, little girl. Not either of us. I'll make damn sure of that."

"I have them hostage," Finian yelled. "Your mother and sister. And Sofia. I told you I'd kill her. And so I will. I'll cut her face and send her to the barracks. She'll serve my soldiers as the slut she is. She'll die there, cursing your name. I'll gut your precious sister from crotch to throat as you watch. Unless you come out *now.*"

The blood in my veins turned to ice. I knew my eyes flattened, for Torass drew back and Iyumi's dark scowl halted. That *bastard.* He dared threaten Fainche? Sofia? My *mother?* I'll see him drowning in his own blood before he dare harm a hair on their precious heads. He'll die, screaming–

"What, boy? You think you can save them? Should you win here, today, they'll still die. Killing me won't protect them, you know. If I die, she ll still kill them, gut them, and roast their hearts on her fires. But I'll make you a promise, boy. Surrender your arms, now, and I'll spare everyone, including you. And I'll forbid her to kill your lady loves. Do we have a deal?"

Iyumi's hand flattened, pressing downward, her expression set, intent. *Don t give in,* that face told me. *Never surrender.*

I didn't intend to. I knew what a faithless, lying bastard he was. I returned to her a quick nod. *No worries.*

"Damn you!"

At the same moment his bellow of rage echoed down, the top of our shelter detonated with a sharp, coughing roar. Chunks of rocks bigger than my head rained down amidst a shower of dirt and savage sparks. Like an avalanche, the rock fall would bury us under it, and send our corpses sliding into the deadly trees below. The horses, spooking, almost broke free from Iyumi's hand, and dragged her several feet with them.

Cursing, I gave myself no time to think. Using all the power in my control, and some that wasn't, I cast upward and outward a long column of wind. Air, like water, could cause as much, if not more, damage than stones with enough force behind it. With a wind-speed equal to a hurricane, I sent the falling rocks flying in all directions. I heard the snapping of tree branches and trunks as both stones and wind broke them apart. With the roar of an annoyed dragon, my tempest destroyed Blaez's attempt to kill me. Though how he thought to kill me and still keep Iyumi and the child alive with this stunt was beyond my comprehension.

Though I deflected the avalanche from Iyumi, Torass, Lyall and Boden, I couldn't control where it went. All of the broken boulders, and the resulting debris, flew in a wide arc around us, crashing down the steep slope, and the trail below. I couldn't send any of it back against my enemies, unfortunately. They were protected by the tall granite shelter just as I was. Permitting my wind to dissipate, calm filled the canyon once more.

Wild yells and galloping hooves from both above us and below resounded throughout the canyon. Finian sent his brutes to tidy up his mess, using old fashioned cavalry tactics. But, I wasn't fooled. My old man had an ace up his sleeve and he wanted me to take his bait.

"Dra'agor!" I yelled. "Now!"

I could only guess at my father's position on the road above us. By the sound of the hooves on rock, several horses cantered downhill near the place I asked Dra'agor to hide. I knew my father wouldn't commit all his soldiers. But a handful, sure. I grinned as Dra'agor's snarls echoed across the narrow ravine.

Chaos erupted. Horses screamed. Men yelled. Hooves trampled across stone. The treacherous road ensnared them as much as Dra'agor's teeth. The panicked horses had nowhere to go. I heard the thud of a large body striking the ground, the clear snap of bones and the grunt of a man caught between a horse and a hard place. I listened as men cursed in fear and anger, fighting to keep their mounts under control. As Dra'agor leaped and snarled, biting at the legs of my father's cavalry horses, their riders had no hope of raising a bow or sword to him. No man, no matter how skilled, could shoot a bow or wield a sword while riding a bucking horse.

"Kill the wolf!" my father screamed. "Shoot that damn thing! Shoot it now!"

"My turn," I said.

I whipped wind into my hand again. This time, I didn't aim it to deflect. Instead, I gathered the fire from Blaez's first attack, burning merrily amid the summer-dry pines and mountain spruce. Air fed fire. I provided it with a hearty meal of dry forest and fresh oxygen. Like a volcano erupting, it exploded with a heat ten times Blaez's little tantrum. I sent it whirling over my head. Up and up I flung it, over the top of the boulders, sparks and smoke trailing it like stars. Its brilliance sent the late sun hiding behind the mountains, lighting the region like a new dawn. Down it dropped, into the unknown. Or at least the unknown to me. But I knew my pa was there somewhere and my fire still hungered.

Then the screams began.

"Lyall! Boden! Go!"

Lyall kicked his horse into high gear. Boden burst out from behind the rock wall, his bow raised. One arrow after another flew from his string, one after the other in a sequence so fast my eyes failed to follow. He protected Lyall's back as easily as if he rode beside him. I paused, listening as my lads ripped into my father's soldiers. My father's reserve launched themselves into the fray of fighting men and a wolf determined to hamstring every equine leg within reach, and I knew I needed to be there. But I hesitated.

"Buck-Eye?" I yelled. "You good, man?"

Below, Buck-Eye sat calmly aboard his horse, still mounted upon the tall rock. His flaming arrows caught armored men in the chest as they galloped uphill, charging with swords and maces. Around and behind them, the area burned. His wicked flames caught upon horses' sensitive flanks, sending them mad with agony and panic. An entire dozen men lay crying, moaning or dead upon the flaming rocks as the remaining five or six tried to regroup and charge. Buck-Eye's next flaming arrow caught the lead rider between the eyes, knocking him from his horse. His corpse burned merrily upon the stony road. The others checked their rush, hesitating.

"All due respect, m'lord," he replied, cross. "Go away. I'm busy."

His next arrow tossed a soldier over the rump of his bay, while another took the rider's horse out from under him. Both lit up like a tallow candle, the odor of roasting meat making my eyes water. I tasted its nasty oily flavor on my tongue.

"Just checking," I called. "Yell if you need anything."

"Righty-O."

I tossed a wink in Iyumi's direction. "I think I'm needed over there."

Using the power of the scrying crystal, I leaped over the top of the fallen mountain and the flames I created and landed on my feet behind Blaez and Finian, King of Raithin Mawr. Though the sun westered over the tall peaks behind me, enough light remained to illuminate everything. I stared at total and utter defeat. Not my demise, but my father's.

Dra'agor still leaped and snarled, chasing what few soldiers remained aboard their horses. Many valued cavalry nags lay crippled and broken upon the rocks, whinnying. Some of their riders crawled to them, bleeding, injured but thinking of their horses first. Most of my father's soldiers lay dead, either from my fires, Boden's arrows or Lyall's swift blade. Those that survived both fangs, flames and steel ran like rabbits. They bolted past my sire and his commanding crony, diving into the setting sun's shadows to vanish. Perhaps forever.

Both men hadn't noticed my arrival, stunned their well-planned ambush failed. I couldn't help but find humor in the situation. I cleared my throat, spinning both men around. Their eyes and mouths widened in fear. I suppressed my grin.

"Am I intruding?" I asked, my tone polite.

"Cut him down," Finian roared. "Now. Now!"

To give him credit, Blaez tried his best. He concocted a dark spell aimed to both stop my heart and split my skull at the same time. He hadn't had the time to think it through, however. As though swatting a fly, I brushed aside his blast of fury and fear with a negligible hand. I couldn't help but smile as he gaped, astonished that I still stood before him, untouched.

"Practice makes perfect," I said, smirking, just before my own magical blow, shaped like a mallet, caught him upside his head.

Blaez dropped to the stones, bleeding from his eyes and ears. Unconscious or dead, I didn't care. Maybe I killed him, or maybe I didn't, but he was no longer a threat. I drew my sword, stepping lightly on the balls of my feet, eyeing my father as he gaped in stunned horror at Blaez's inert body. I spat on the ground at his feet.

"Cheer up, Pa," I said, wiping my lips with the back of my hand. "You don't have to feed him anymore."

He raised his stunned gaze from Blaez's body to my face. His lips amid his black beard thinned. His dark brows met over the bridge of his nose as he scowled, thinking to intimidate me. As he always had. As he never would again.

"He was my friend," Finian rumbled, his eyes narrowing. "You're going to die now, boy."

I chuckled in derision. "Am I? Looks to me like you're alone and outnumbered. Surrender and maybe I'll let you live."

Pausing, catching his glance, I lowered my voice. "Or maybe I'll string you up and turn the mutts loose."

Finian charged, his sword drawn and my blood in his eyes. A gifted swordsman, my sire defeated arms-master after arms-master, champion after champion on the practice field. Very few fought him to a draw and none ever touched him with their blunted blades. I reeled from his assault, catching his blade with mine and turning it

[416]

before it took my head from my shoulders. Recovering in an eye-blink, Finian swung hard toward my head. Only by ducking did I avoid the razor's edge. I aimed to stab him in the gut, but he knocked my pathetic attempt aside with a snort of contempt.

Had my father taught me sword fighting himself, I might have held my own. I had youth and agility on my side, but he had skill and experience on his. In the first two minutes, he drew blood not once but four times while my own steel never came close to his skin. I bled profusely from two cuts to my shoulder, one across my ribs and the fourth nearly cut the tendons that held up my left leg. At this rate, I'd bleed to death and still not kill him. His lip curled in triumph and hate, Finian sneered. "You're dead, boy."

His mockery pissed me off. Rallying, I charged in, hacking at his blade, swinging hard and fast. I forced him backward, step by step, the canyon ringing with the clash of steel on steel. Sparks flew from our slithering blades as I ground mine against his, toe to toe, our faces close enough to kiss. I glared into his furious dark eyes, and he glowered into mine. I forced him further back, hacking at his defenses, my rage overwhelming his.

From beyond his head, Buck-Eye raised his bow. His nocked and flaming arrow aimed for Finian's back. He knew I couldn't win out against my father. My skills, despite my anger fueling my strength, weren't high enough for the task. Eventually, I'd make a fatal mistake and my hated sire's sword would take my life. Buck-Eye sought to keep me alive because dead princes didn't pay well.

"M'lord!" Buck-Eye shouted. "Get down!"

"No!" I grunted, breathless, straining to overwhelm Finian with strength and speed. "He's mine."

From beyond Finian's shoulder, Iyumi gestured frantically, no doubt ordering Buck-Eye to belay my order and shoot Finian down. Dra'agor stood at her side, as Torass brought the horses around the rock tower. Buck-Eye aimed his bow again, his arrow nocked and the string pulled back to his ear. He released, the flaming arrow whooshing to burn my old man into cinders.

He missed.

How the hell could Buck-Eye miss? I dared not take my eyes from Finian's, nor cease in my relentless attack upon his blade. Stinging sweat slid into my eyes, blurring my vision. My wounds poured blood, though I felt little pain. Finian feinted and spun around, his sword's tip scoring a fifth cut across my chest. I staggered, dropping my guard.

He pounced. His hilt struck me hard in the abdomen, taking what little remained of my breath. His left fist crashed hard into my right cheek, snapping my head back. Half-blinded, winded, I fell flat to my back, my sword spinning from my fingers. His shadow loomed over me as I fought to get up.

"You should've let him shoot, boy," Finian growled, raising his blade.

He tried. He stabbed his sword, point down, toward my chest.

Something large and dark struck Finian from the side. His sword clattered to the stony ground. His screams of pain and panic mixed with savage snarling filled the canyon. *Dra'agor.* Buck-Eye may have missed his target, but my noble friend didn't.

I blinked and rolled over, gasping, trying to get air, any air, into my lungs. I blinked, clearing my vision, and watched. Finian threw Dra'agor off from his attack with savage punches to the wolf's head and face, scrambling to get away. He half-rose as Dra'agor charged in, fangs bared and dripping, and grabbed Dra'agor by the throat. My old man had courage, I had to admit. He aimed to kill a fully grown wolf with his bare hands. Fear jumped into my heart. Could he really kill my friend?

Before his fingers could fully close and choke off Dra'agor's wind, Dra'agor leapt up, dancing on his hind paws. His muzzle on level with Finian's face, he snapped those powerful jaws shut. On my father's cheeks. Yowling in agony, Finian lunged backward, staggering under the hundred plus pounds of angry wolf. Dra'agor lost his hold, but his teeth ripped my old man's face to shreds. He fled, falling to his knees, scrambling to run again even from hands and knees. Dra'agor followed, snapping at his back, his ass, forcing him to the edge of the canyon.

Arms flailing, Finian staggered upright, yanking his dagger from his belt. He tried to spin, face his enemy, raising his one remaining weapon. The dark canyon yawned behind his boots. Dra'agor ignored the steel in his fist and the threat it posed, for he was a smart wolf. He didn't rear up to rip open my father's throat as Finian obviously expected him to do, leaving his body wide open for the plunging blade. Oh, no. Dra'agor darted toward Finian's knees, his teeth aiming for his vulnerable hamstring.

Finian stepped backward to avoid Dra'agor's fangs, his left boot striking nothing save empty space. Gravity did the rest. With a wailing scream, Finian fell into the canyon. I heard his heavy body snap tree branches and thud against rocks, his death cry echoing upward like a lonely ghost. Silence fell. Even the wind soughing through the trees died as though mourning his passing.

His head cocked to the side, ears up, Dra'agor stared down into the gulf for a long moment. Then he turned and trotted back to me.

He reached me at the same moment Iyumi dropped to her knees beside my shoulder, her manacles clinking softly. "Are you all right?" she asked, her fingers picking at my bloody tunic.

"I think so," I gasped, struggling to sit up.

Buck Eye's strong hand under my injured shoulder helped me to stand. His hand and Boden's strength kept me upright as Dra'agor sat down, whining low in his throat. Lyall pushed his horse close to the lip of the canyon and peered down. "Don't see him," he commented, frowning.

"D-don't matter," I replied, my lungs finally returning to working order. "He's d-dead."

"You sure? From here, it looks to me as though he might've survived."

"Then he crawled away to die," I groaned, swaying under the combined strength of Buck-Eye and Iyumi. "Get the horses, will you? We're late enough as it is."

As Torass arrived with the troll, incredibly still sleeping, Lyall loped his horse away toward the granite boulders. "Blaez has run off, m'lord," he announced. "With the survivors. The rest are dead. Or nearly so."

"I didn't kill him?" I gasped. "Are you sure?"

[419]

"I saw him, too," Iyumi said, plucking at my tunic. "Bleeding, yes, but quite alive."

"Crap," I replied, forcing my knees to lock to prevent a headlong spill onto the granite road. "That bastard has the devil's own luck. Keep an eye out, lads. Some may be faking."

Though it seemed like hours, the entire battle had spanned within a matter of twenty minutes or so. Bowing his head in respect, Torass gently handed the baby to Iyumi as she rose to her feet. She accepted her burden with a brief nod, peeping into the rags to reassure herself the kid had taken no harm.

"M'lord," Buck-Eye said. "You're not fit to ride."

Like Iyumi's, his fingers pulled aside my torn tunic to examine my wounds. Though they'd stopped bleeding, any movement I made set them to screaming like banshees. Had I not healed myself in the past and honed my skills in the time since, I might have agreed. Instead, I offered him a lopsided grin.

"No worries. By the time you get this party ready to roll, I'll be fit."

With a jaunty salute, he, Boden and Torass walked away. Iyumi watched me carefully. "You can heal yourself?"

I nodded. "Though I'd rather do it in privacy, if you don't mind."

Shrugging with indifference, Iyumi strode toward her mule. With a sharp woof, Dra'agor danced at her side, his tail waving madly. She stepped among the dead soldiers and horses, vanishing into the sullen smoke from the fires. Though the corpses no longer burned, they continued to give off the terrible odor of roasted flesh. Several trees surrounding the battlefield still smoldered, blue-grey smoke curling upward in the quiet mountain air. My belly roiling, I wanted away from this death place and its sickening stench.

"Here, kitty, kitty," I murmured, reaching down for my healing trance and its cat's paw warmth. "Let's play."

[420]

The sun passed its zenith the next day when I reined Bayonne in with a sigh. "Hello, Mother."

Like a mountain nymph, born to sun and shadows, she stood on the stony road with her arms akimbo. The light breeze lifted her silk skirts as though caressing them with love and affection. Dra'agor halted, whining, his head low and his ears flattened. My memory skipped across Iyumi's lesson regarding the blood binding and dismissed it just as easily. My mother had no clue, and not near the magical power, to bind another to her will by blood.

She clearly wasn't pleased. In fact, I'd never seen her quite so angry. I dismounted, leaving Bayonne to mind himself as I helped Iyumi down from her mule. Fortunately, the troll still slept off her morning blood breakfast, and set up no fuss as Iyumi slipped down from the mule's makeshift saddle.

"Why aren't you at the castle?" Mother asked, her tone sharp. "Had you used the bloody crystal as you should, I wouldn't feel the need to come looking for you."

Feeling like a boy caught with his pants around his ankles, I flushed. "I can't."

"What do you mean, 'can't'? Excuses are like–"

"The baby is a troll."

"A *what?*"

For a moment, her expression sagged into an odd mixture of horror, dawning realization and panic. Those eyes I inherited widened in shock. Her slender fingers rose halfway to her lips before dropping to cover her throat. She stared at the bundle of rags in Iyumi's arms, her body trembling. Her mouth worked for several long seconds, but nothing save a faint whimper escaped her clenched teeth.

"Impossible," she whispered.

"Far from," I answered, tired beyond belief. "The crystal doesn't work on her. Nor does any magical power on this earth."

Enya straightened. Her hand slipped from her throat. As though I'd blasphemed before the gods while in their holy temple, her anger assumed its natural course and she frowned heavily. "Oh, for the love of–"

[421]

"Father tried to kill me."

Mother's face stilled, her cornflower blue eyes suddenly careful. "He what?"

"He set a trap. He's dead, Mother. I wish I spoke sincerely when I say 'I'm sorry'. But I'm trying very hard to disrupt my penchant for lying."

Enya shrugged. "You're mistaken, dear. Your father is at Castle Salagh. I just left him to come look for you."

"I'm not mistaken, Mother. I know who attacked me. Commander Blaez was with him. He's escaped, however."

"Whatever."

"You!"

Iyumi's voice rose unto the high-pitched octaves of an outraged alewife. "It's you, you *bitch*. I know you, you conniving devil-monster, shadow spawn from hell. You pull his strings, don't you?"

I spun about. "How dare you talk to my mother that way."

Holding the troll tight to her tiny bosom, she backed into the mule, fear warring with fury across her face. "Your mother? Your mother is the Red Duchess? I should've known. You're blind as well as stupid, Flynn."

"My mother isn't . . . she's the victim here! Can't you see that?"

"I see she's blinded you, you moron," Iyumi spat, her huge eyes wide with unfeigned terror and hate. "Did she geld you, too? Did she? I believed you when you said you wanted to atone for your sins."

"I do–"

"Obviously, I wasted my time. You're as much a monster as she is."

I half-turned toward Enya.. "Mother, I'm so sorry–"

She watched Iyumi with the same feral calculation I might see as a lion hunts a lamb. A smile played across her beautiful lips, her arms folded over her generous breasts. She ignored me, as though I hadn't spoken. As though I wasn't, standing in her presence. All her attention lay on the tiny girl behind me.

"I fear you listen too closely to those voices inside your head, darling," Enya remarked. "You should never believe what you hear."

[422]

"Mother, ignore her, she's wrong." I said, trying to seize her hand. "She doesn't know what she's talking about."

"Who suggested you sacrifice the boy, Flynn?" Iyumi snarled, her body shaking. "Was it her? Was it?"

Alarmed, Buck-Eye and Torass dismounted to stand behind Iyumi, restraining her with hands to her slender shoulders. Rather than fling them off, she backed a step to stand between them, as though seeking their protection. Dra'agor whined, his tail tucked, and his ears flattened. He sidled toward her, keeping his body between Iyumi and my mother.

"The boy would have died anyway–"

"Is that what you told him, bitch?" Iyumi screeched, her cheeks deathly pale. "Why don't you tell him who he truly was? Tell him, hell-whore! *Tell him!*"

"He was nothing," Enya replied, still smiling. "Just as you are, silly child."

"You don't dare, do you? Because he'll turn against you, isn't that right? He's the only one who can stop you, you devil-bitch, and you know it. You're right to fear him, you need him and you need this baby."

"He's my son, and he loves me."

Iyumi spat like a cat. "He doesn't know what he loves."

"Hey, now," I began. "Can we all calm down a bit? Please?"

"My son is loyal and true," Enya replied, her eyes on Iyumi. "You shall be his reward."

"Mother–"

"Be quiet, Flynn."

I snapped my jaw shut as Iyumi's voice rose higher in pitch and rage. "You killed them all. You forced your own son to commit the worst possible sin, and for what? For power. I'll see you dead in your own blood before you dare harm this child."

"I don't want to hurt that baby, dear," Enya purred. "Surely you're quite mistaken. I wish to see her safe from the Evil One. You see? If she dies, so do I. And all I love in this world."

"See? You're just mistaken, Yumm–er, Iyumi," I said, as sweat trickled down my ribs.

"Mistake this, stupid boy." Iyumi made the sign.

Mother laughed, her voice high and musical. "Ah, you are such a treasure, dear. I shall enjoy getting to know you better, as my new daughter-in-law."

"Mother–"

Her open hand cracked across my cheek. My flesh in flames, I winced, my hand rising to my face instinctively. "What the hell?"

"You've five days, boy. I suggest you gag her and tie her to that mule. Don't make me come looking for you again."

CHAPTER 13

Blind To All Else

*H*is boot kicked me in my cracked ribs. Sharp, hard and with utmost cruelty.

"Get up, cuz," Cian chirped brightly. "Your day of destiny hath dawned."

Cursing him into the furthest reaches of hell, I staggered, ungainly, to my feet. My outraged rib-cage screamed in protest, white fire coursing through every vein. During my time unconscious, my broken nose quieted a fraction, though dried blood cracked against my lips as I grimaced in effort. Short on breath and long on agonizing pain, I fought to stand upright and toe-to-toe with him. My hands bound behind my back hampered me greatly, but I won my footing and stared my cousin and brother Atan in the eye. Working saliva into my dry mouth, I spat at his boots.

He grinned, the half-healed slash on his left cheek puckering. "An officer and a gentleman," he commented. "Ever so proper. Once you're ashes, I'll post your name on a park bench somewhere."

"You're too kind."

"I know."

Cian smirked, his right hand tangled in my chain leash. Pulling me forward, toward him, he inclined his face into mine. He offered me a deep glance at his tonsils and a full wash of his noxious breath. "Only the good die young, Van."

"That explains why you're still here."

[425]

He chuckled, poisoning my air intake on his exhale. "I protest that remark, dearest cousin. I've been wronged, by you, and merely seek my honest revenge. I stand in the light of right while you, um, don't."

"I did you no wrong, Cian."

"No? How about you murdered my lady."

"What lady?"

Cian scowled, his scar dancing. "You know, dammit. You knew Zeani and I were in love and intended to marry. You robbed me of that." His face inclined toward me again, his nasty smile rising anew. "And you'll be paying the price."

I rolled my eyes. "Are you truly that thick, cuz? I never thought so, but, you know, you excelled at deception in school."

I knew my words jolted him, for he jerked away in a rapid there-and-gone twitch of his facial muscles before his sneering expression returned. *How did I know?* his eyes asked. My own malicious grin rose to match his and I caught his eye. And held it.

"Zeani didn't love you," I commented, my upper lip curling. "She slept with every officer above the rank of sergeant. She wasn't too ambitious, our Corporal Zeani, but she did like her boys with connections."

His eyes flattened. "You lie."

I chuckled. "Do I? Should he survive this debacle, yon Broc will inherit a fortune and a title one day. Am I right or am I right? Broc, you scoundrel, elaborate for us on the night you drank too much at the Atan festival three years ago and Zeani pursued you until you surrendered. Didn't she suck–"

"Liar!"

Cian's yank on my chain dropped me to my knees. He kicked me in the gut, dropping me instantly onto my face in the dirt, coughing, and unable to draw breath. I floundered, gritty dust filling my eyes and sending them into a fury of watering. Though helpless tears tracked down my filthy cheeks, I never quit trying to get up. An Atan died on his feet and a curse for his enemy on his lips. I regained my knees, halfway there, and grinned upwards into Cian's rage.

"Thank you," I gasped, choking, my chest burning.

"For what, you idiot? For what?"

His heavy hand on my leash dragged me upright, gagging, as I seized every sweet breath with gratitude. "For proving to me she'd never love someone like you."

"You don't know jack," Cian screamed into my face, his own purple with rage. "She loved me! She said she did!"

"If you say so, cuz," I answered, smiling. "Keep telling yourself that. Imagine her fury when I said no."

His heavy fist cracked across my cheekbone. Its collective force all but knocked me back into unconsciousness. I'd like that. Cast me into the empty darkness where I'd not feel the flames taking my life. Do it, please. Zeani screamed when the flames ate her up, I recalled. She sucked in air, yet only the terrible heat filled her lungs. I remember. Ah, I remember so clearly. Her hazel eyes boiled in their sockets as she died. Her flesh melted from her cheeks, her lips, her chin. She fell onto her once-beautiful face, mercifully hiding the scorched flesh of a self-confessed traitor. She went down as an Atan should: brave, strong and utterly fearless.

Her voice shrieked one word. A name.

That name wasn't Cian's.

"Lieutenant!"

Broc and Tris lunged forward. Between them, they caught Cian low, tackling him by his belly and his knees. He went down hard and might have taken me down with him had my chain not slipped through his hand. I stayed on my feet through sheer cussedness and a determination to not hit the ground again. Taking only shallow breaths, I spat blood and the swinging world steadied a fraction. Though I tried sending the awful pain to the back of my head, it refused to leave.

Cursing, Cian socked Tris in the gut a fraction before Broc caught him in a shoulder lock. "Calm down," he yelled. "Do you want him to fry or don't you?"

"Of course I do! Get off me, you ass."

"Stop beating on him then. He wants you to kill him quick, like. Can't you see that?"

"Lemmee go!"

As entertained as I was by this fracas, I briefly thought of escape. And dropped the idea almost as quickly. Not just trussed like a feast-day goose, I was powerless and weakened with blood loss and injury. *Pity Cian didn t let his temper loose and hit me hard enough to kill me outright.* Better that than death by fire.

Yestin and Drust flanked me as though suspected flight was foremost on my mind rather than furthest, while Kado nocked an arrow and pointed it at me. Not at my heart or throat, where I might die quickly should I make an error in judgment. He aimed that deadly barb at my knee. He smiled.

In a swirl of dust and coarse oaths, Cian scrambled to his feet. His face coated in dust and spittle, he slapped away the hands that now reached to help rather than hinder. He glared around at his men, included me in his furious hate, and straightened his clothes.

"Did you sleep with her?" he bellowed at Broc.

Broc paled. "Me, boss? No, of course not, whyever would I? She loved you, boss, never even looked at another man."

I almost laughed. Clearly Cian didn't believe him. By their sudden sour expressions, neither did Tris nor Yestin. Zorn scowled and turned his head to spit into the dirt. Kado still smiled at me, and I wondered if he prayed for me to try an escape just so he could shoot me. I declined his obvious invitation by standing still and rolling my shoulders to ease the discomfort.

Broc's obvious lie didn't save me, however. If Cian now realized his love was a slut who preyed upon anything male, he'd never release me with an apology. If I wasn't to blame for her behavior, I was still to blame for her death. He loved her with a passion that blinded him to all else. And I took her from him.

"Mount up," Cian ordered, his voice hoarse.

Grabbing up my chain, he jerked it viciously in a juvenile rage vent. Dragging me with him, he stalked to his grey gelding. In an unnecessary show of subservience, Broc held the horse's bridle as Cian mounted. With his commander safely ensconced on his mild-mannered steed, Broc, his skin as pale as a dead fish, vaulted into his own saddle. I caught a swift glance of pure hatred directed my way. But as Cian's spurs struck silky hide and I was hauled off my feet, I failed to return an appropriate response.

[428]

Forced to walk quickly and keep pace with the horses, I focused on the ground at my boots and concentrated on each step forward. For once, Cian kept his mouth shut and his hands to himself as his boys rode in a semi-circle behind us. Their awkward and tense silence spoke louder than shouted curses. No military unit I ever rode with, unless under strict orders, ever travelled without lewd jokes, gossip about women and superior officers, or bragged about whose horse ran faster. These boys *knew* I was in the right and Cian in the wrong. Yet, they'd never stoop to either admitting it nor to helping me.

When the steep, rocky terrain demanded it, they rode in an even line behind Cian's grey, with me tagging along at his flank. As Cian led the way downhill rather than up, I maintained his pace without too much agony. The horses were forced into careful walks to avoid nasty stumbles that might tip a rider out of his saddle. In addition, their stiff silence offered me several interesting ideas to pursue.

Though they tied my hands and collared my powers, they hadn't bothered to disarm me. My sword clapped against my left leg as I walked. *Why?* Even if I was incapable of using it, what fool didn't seize his prisoner's weapons? In a less than totally bizarre situation, they'd have stripped me of every weapon I possessed, real or imagined. Did they deliberately ignore it? Did they see it?

Had my sword's own magic, outside my own, blinded them to its presence? Could I call upon its strength when I had none of my own? Despite my desire to call forth the sword's own power, my need to keep my footing prevailed. The mountain landscape constantly threatened my footing. If I didn't keep up, or if I fell, Cian would no doubt drag me by that cold pewter collar to my destiny. I couldn't, and dared not, focus my thoughts on the sword.

We reached the lower shoulder of the huge mountain just as the sun passed its zenith and headed west. Cian permitted only the briefest breaks to water the horses on the lush mountain streams. They munched cold fare as they rode, but I received no water and no food. My injuries and constant weakness kept hunger at bay.

Yet, my throat felt as though I'd swallowed sand. At every break I asked for water and was ignored.

Within the lower elevations, my boots trod thin tough tundra rather than the wickedly sharp rocks of the higher peak. Deer and mountain grouse fled in swift panic as the snorting horses and creaking saddle leather spooked them into flight. The heavy forests of twisted pine and lush evergreen thinned into emaciated knots of scrub oak and elm trees. Below lay the Auryn River gurgling and burping over countless boulders and fallen trunks. Near these pristine waters, Malik, Kiera, Grey Mist, Wind Warrior and my special lady, Sky Dancer, met their end.

All of them dead. Their restless spirits stalked beside me, calling for me to join them. Though their loss cut me to the quick, I embraced their presence. They came to accompany me to the other side. Soon, I'd join them as one more spirit, one with the gods, and with the Creator of All. My mind shied away from all thoughts of Iyumi. Her beautiful eyes, her sardonic smile—much too painful to contemplate. Must think of something else, quick, no don't remember her lovely curves, her blue on blue eyes, think dammit, don't reminisce, *think.*

The gradual incline down flattened out, and only a few hundred rods away the rushing river galloped faster than a horse might run. I knew this area. We approached the Auryn many leagues to the east of where my brothers died in a region with fewer high hills and more open grasslands. Prey animals of all species leapt, jumped, bolted and hopped out of our way. An eagle screamed high overhead, it's hunting call breaking into the tense silence. The river's voice increased in tempo and volume the closer we travelled toward it. It roared over boulders smoothed by time, white foam splashing high.

The sun in its glory ascended into the deepest west, throwing spears of red, orange, purple and gold over the forbidding peaks above. The pain I'd ignored all day expressed its displeasure. Weakened by blood loss, thirst and cracked ribs, I could no longer ignore the damage done to me. All had taken their toll, and if Cian didn't stop to murder me soon, I'd collapse, unable to walk any further. At which time he'd no doubt drag me until I was dead.

[430]

Hmmm. Perhaps I might be instantly killed if his collar snapped my neck, dragged as I was behind his mount. Or I'd slowly strangle while rocks and shrubbery smashed into my face and head, thus adding to the torture while not necessarily sending me into the arms of the good gods very quickly. *Crap.* Not as good a choice as I first thought. *Best keep one s footing.*

Before I did indeed fall, unable to put one foot in front of the other, Cian called a halt. He dropped my chain, permitting it to coil up on the ground at my feet. None of his men jumped forward to point arrows at my knees. He knew as well as I did escape wasn't in my travel arrangements, and swung down from his gelding. Leading the horse away, he left me to my own devices. Sweat trickled into my eyes, stinging sharply, as I gasped for breath. Sitting gingerly on a rock, I shut my eyes and focused on staying conscious. If I could concentrate, if I could pull in enough willpower, maybe, just maybe, I could call on my sword's magic. But will took energy and I had precious little to risk on a maybe.

Around me, Cian's men dismounted and led their beasts to water and grazing. I couldn't hear what they said to one another, but their voices held little humor and none of the usual soldier bitching about the hours, food and commanding officers. If I didn't know better, I'd guess they didn't much like their current assignment but dared not let Cian know. I shut my eyes to better listen, hoping against hope that one of them might remember their Atani vows.

"Here." Cian's rough voice roused me.

I glanced up. Standing over me, his back to the sun, his eyes appeared hooded and in shadow. *This is it, he s going to burn me now.* I braced myself, ready for the final burst of power that set me ablaze. He had some magic outside his Shifter skills, possibly enough to murder me in a swift burst of fire. Yet–

He held a flask of water to my lips. All thoughts of willpower and sword vanished as I tilted my throat back. Icy cold water slid down into my belly like the sweetest wine. He permitted me several healthy swallows. Though I craved more, 'twas enough to assuage the worst of my raging thirst.

I licked moisture from my lips as he pulled the flask away. "Why?"

Cian shrugged, plugging the flask with its wax stopper. "You saved my life once. Though I'm bound to take yours, I do pay my debts."

Repay a life with life-sustaining water. I half-nodded, accepting the gift with grace. "Thanks."

"You'll burn at sunset," he continued, as though informing me of where I'll sleep that night. "We have but a league or so downriver to ride. Then you can rest."

Crikey. Rest in peace.

"How'd you find us, Cian?"

He actually smiled. Squatting on his heels, he fingered the stopper on the flask. "We've been following you. We picked up you and Malik's little party before Flynn and his boys attacked you the first time. When you and the princess took off for the cave, I had an idea of where you were headed. We merely rode ahead of you and waited."

"I see."

He fiddled with the flask, his gaze downward, as though unable to face me. "Just tell me, Van," he said, his voice soft. "Why did you ignore the royal courier and go in that day? I'm not promising a repeal. Frankly, I want the simple truth from you. You owe me that much."

I swallowed hard, utterly flummoxed. "What courier? I had that warehouse surrounded, waiting for orders."

Cian glared, growing angry. "The courier from headquarters. Don't lie to me, Van, not now. You were told there were two terrorists inside, with twelve hostages, ready to blow everything up. You were told to stand down and await reinforcements. Why would you send in your unit against specific orders?"

"Gods," I muttered, wishing I could run my hands through my hair. "Give me a minute, let me think, let me think."

Frantic, my memory raced to that deadly day. A warehouse in the small fishing village of Dalziel. A Raithin Mawrn terrorist inside with hostages and barrels of oil. A *single* bomber. I dispatched my unit to surround the place and not permit even a mouse to escape. I held firm, shouting negotiations to the Raithin Mawrn, promises that would free the hostages and permit him to surrender unharmed.

"No courier came," I muttered.

"What?"

"There was no courier," I said, my voice rising. "Gaear flew in, as an eagle."

"Gaear? Whatever for? He's not in the courier corp."

My memory flooded my head. I returned to that moment as though it happened yesterday, and I spoke my thoughts aloud, blind to Cian's looming presence.

I crouched behind a nearby water trough, close enough to hear the Raithin Mawrn s demands and deliver my own, yet protected from attack. Behind me, Sergeants Catlan and Zeani, both Shape-Shifters, awaited my orders.

Gaear dropped to the ground and folded his wings. "Orders, First Captain, sir," he said, his raptor s voice high. "The Lord Captain commands you send in your unit to resolve the situation. He understands there is but one unarmed Raithin Mawrn inside. There s no threat, sir. Arrest him, and bring him in for trial."

I frowned. "I heard through the local grapevine there were two buggers in there. How does Malik know there s only one. And unarmed, you say?"

"Indeed, First Captain. The Lord Captain Commander s intel is solid, sir. He wouldn t have sent me, otherwise."

I shrugged. "Jolly good. Will you join us in our hour of triumph, Gaear?"

"Sorry, sir, would love to, but the Lord Captain Commander has me racing to fetch him his favorite wine. It s that day of the week, as you know, sir."

I grinned. "I do indeed. Off with you, now. Tell Malik 1 ll toss this prisoner at his feet in an hour."

"Will do, sir."

Gaear flew away. I organized my unit of twelve elite Atani soldiers into attack formation. With a sharp kick, I broke down the door to the warehouse just as my Atans either followed me inside or broke in through windows from the rear. Charging in, I saw two things at the same time. One: the frightened Raithin Mawrn with his hands in the air, screaming in panic. Two: the frightened hostages huddled together in the middle of the hall, surrounded by barrels of whale oil.

As the rest of my men grouped around the crying, milling civilians, urging them to their feet with jokes and laughter, I noted a third thing-the single hostage who watched me with a smile. A smile of deadly, deathly, calculation. Just as he lit the fuse.

"Get them out!" I bellowed. "Get out! Now! Now! Now!"

The fuse hissed and sparked its way toward a stack of dry wood. No doubt the bomber s bundle of incendiary powder lay packed tightly within it. Set the wood aflame, then the casks of oil. If the oil ignited, it could bring down not just the warehouse but half the block.

The wood ignited. Fire raced outward from behind the barrels of flammable oil. But even oil took a few seconds to ignite, for flames to eat through the heavy oak to reach the combustible liquid inside. I shoved hostage after hostage toward the door, my Atans fearless and calm as they saved one life after another. When the smiling Raithin Mawrn came at me, swinging a savage dirk, I killed him with a single bolt of my power through his heart. I never drew my sword.

"Captain!" Catlan yelled, near the door. "Let s go!"

The hostages and my Atans were safe. All had reached the safety of the doorway, or had run beyond into the late afternoon sunshine. But one hostage remained. He bolted toward the fire, not away from it. Obviously he felt something inside was worth risking his life for. His life was worth risking mine for.

I raced after him. My hand touched his shoulder just as the warehouse blew up.

A cask of oil struck me sideways and threw me into the wooden wall of the warehouse. Had it remained solid, 1 d have been crushed and killed instantly. But the blast fractured the wooa s integrity and I crashed through splinters not firm construction. Thus, the blast itself blew me to safety, and saved my life. The hostage I tried to save died, screaming as he lit up like a torch. Though I tried to scream orders, stay out, stay away, my team didn t, couldn t, hear me. They, as a group, ran back inside. They split up, dodging the flames, shielding their faces with their arms. I heard them calling my name, searching, frantic. Gods, no. Get them out. Get them out.

Struggling to rise under the weight of a broken pillar, I yelled, waving my arm. Zeani saw me. From across the flaming chamber she ran, yelling for the others. I see him! I see him! More followed her voice, scrambling to avoid the flames that reached with licking fingers to snag them.

Then the second explosion hit.

With a low coughing roar, the casks of oil previously untouched by flames detonated. A firestorm of liquid death spewed across the broken warehouse, striking my Atans with all the force of an avalanche. Most died instantly from the force of the blast and broken oak driven by searing winds. A few more, like Zeani, died more slowly. In agony, they sucked down the fires of hell when they drew breath to scream. Like living torches, they burned, consumed at last by the Raithin Mawrn hatred of our land.

"They died because of you." Cian's voice broke into my thoughts.

I nodded slowly. "Yes."

I managed a small smile. "Just not in the way you think. I'm alive through sheer fate. They died because they loved me."

He turned his face away, showing me his scar. "As she loved you."

I tried to speak, and halted. The words rose to my throat and were strangled there. "She . . . Zeani . . . wasn't what you thought she was, Cian. Malik placed her in my unit so I might watch her. Uncover her role. She was a spy in the employ of King Finian. She screamed his name as she died. 'Twas *him* she truly loved."

"You lie."

"I wish I was. For that would spare you great grief."

Cian struggled, trying to come to terms that the love of his life didn't just love another man, or was a whore, but a traitor who loved the greatest enemy our nation ever faced. Under Finian the Fair, the terrorists and the bombers had more than quadrupled, they quadrupled ten times again. Never before had we fought the silent war as we fought the Raithin Mawrn under Finian's iron fist. He sent his spies, his horrors, his bombs in to kill not just our King but our magical way of life. He alone sought our beloved lands and to silence the joys of the Faeries. Along with the Centaurs, the Minotaurs and the sleek Griffins, Finian wanted, no lusted, to slay *us.* For some odd reason, he feared us the most: the Einion'nalad Clan, the Shape-Shifters.

Cian's family.

His eyes calm, he asked, "You have proof?"

"Yes. Malik sent in his own spies, but they failed to uncover much. Then he got lucky. He waylaid certain letters, a courier was intercepted, a horse recognized–a Faery mimicked words meant for Finian's ears alone. Malik ordered me to arrest her that evening, but the call to capture the Dalziel hostage taker came in. Placing her under arrest had to wait. Then, well–you know."

"Did she know you were going to arrest her?"

"I think so, yes."

"Why would she rush in to save you?" he asked, his tone not accusing, but curious. "If she suspected you knew about her, wouldn't she see you burn before rushing in to save you?"

I managed a small smile. "My unit had no clue, remember. They didn't know she was a spy or that the King planned a very long, painful interrogation. They rushed in, and if she were to keep her cover intact, she had to go along. Any Atan loyal to her commander would."

Cian nodded. "I think I see. She didn't plan to die."

"She rushed in, yelling, hoping to find me dead. But I wasn't. I remember her shock to find me still among the living. With so many witnesses, she couldn't sink her dagger into my throat and escape. No one counted on or expected the second explosion. It killed her. It killed them all."

Cian nodded, accepting all I told him as the gods' own truth. He knew I spoke it. He saw it in my eyes, heard it in my voice. He recognized the truth when it was waved in his face. Though he didn't reject any of it, he still loved her. In spite of all.

"This doesn't absolve you."

"I know."

"Are you ready?"

I nodded. "I am."

His arm under my shoulder helped me up. His eyes caught mine, a vague shadow of sorrow, or perhaps regret, behind them. "She shouldn't have died, not that way," he said, his voice soft. "But maybe I can forgive you, just a little."

"Don't bother," I replied, my throat thick. "I can't forgive myself."

Nodding, he took up my chain once more and mounted his grey gelding. If his pace wasn't quite so fast, only I noticed and appreciated that fact. His compassionate gift of the water offered much more than he expected. Already I felt some strength return, and my agonized ribs quieted a fraction. My mind focused more sharply, and if I spent too much of it remembering the past, who'd blame me?

As the sun westered over the distant mountains, Cian called a halt, his voice hollow. "Zorn, mind the horses. Tris, you, Kado and Drust gather wood. Only the dry stuff and lots of it. Yestin and Broc, find a stout tree, preferably dead with lots of space around it. No sense in firing the entire forest."

As his men hobbled their mounts and hastened to follow his orders, Cian permitted me to sit near the rushing Auryn. Lying on my belly, I sucked down more refreshing water, easing my terrible thirst. He led the horses to a quiet rivulet nearby, urging them to drink their fill. I felt he was near to apologizing, for he glanced at me now and then, but he didn't speak. I didn't bother.

Instead, I used the added strength the water gave me and buried my face in the icy stream. The chilling cold numbed the pain of my busted nose and cleared my head. It also washed away some of the horrid guilt of that dreadful day, and reminded me that while Iyumi still lived, I must be at her side. If an opportunity to fight came... well, Cian best look to his own welfare.

Letting him believe I'd given up, I permitted him help me to a rock to sit while his men piled armloads of wood after armloads under a long-dead red oak tree. Beneath its spiked branches, only rocks thrived. Greenish grass grew in sparse tufts, but as an execution site, it fit Cian's order perfectly.

When the piles of deadwood reached halfway up the trunk, Cian stood up. He lifted my chain. "Van. It's time.

I glanced at the sun. It hovered over the mountain peaks, its bright rays of gold, orange, pink and rose-blush streaking eastward as though yearning for the dawn. *As you love me, your lordships,* I prayed silently. *As you love her, help me through this.*

I offered no fight as Cian and Kado untied my hands only to retie them behind the stout, dried trunk of the old oak. *Just more tinder to catch hold.* I gazed down at the pile that shifted uneasily beneath my feet. I leaned my head back against the bark and shut my eyes. *Focus, damn it. Focus.*

Concentrating, I slowed my breathing, my heartbeat. I focused on my sword. *If you re there,* I said, deep within my mind, *I need you now.* Slowly, too slowly, I sank deeper into a trance. Only by casting out all distractions might I call upon the sword's power. As it lay outside my own, perhaps it was not constrained by the cold pewter collar around my neck.

"May you be reborn in Paradise," Cian called, safely returned to the ground with Kado in tow.

His voice broke my infant trance. Frantic to reclaim it, I felt it slip from my grasp. I heard a torch lit with a whoosh, scented its smoky flame. I knew someone, probably Yestin, handed it with devout ceremony to Cian.

Down, I thought, my mind fogged, sluggish. *Down, deep and down.*

The trance hovered at the threshold of my mind, calling to me.

At my feet, flames licked the dry wood and found it palatable. Heat rose to warm my body, and smoke teased my nostrils, burned my eyelids. *Ignore it,* my mind whispered. *Ignore it and control thy fear. Fear is your enemy. Make it your ally.*

Dropping deeper into a trance, I called to my own blood, captured deep within the sword. *Hear me. Feel me. I am yours and you are mine.*

I hear, the sword hissed in reply. *I obey.*

[438]

The flames rose higher, hungry, feeding on the dry wood. I needed no eyes to witness Cian fall back, shading his brow against the terrible heat. I saw within my mind his companions curse in dreadful fascination as they stumbled into one another, seizing arms, tripping over themselves in their haste to escape the licking fires of hell.

Sweat burst from my pores only to dry an instant later under the searing heat. The pain from my busted ribs felt as naught to the savage terror that filled my soul, my heart. The trance slid back, panic emerging, my throat raw and ready to scream. *I m going to die!*

Not yet.

The sword's power caught my mind, my heart. I saw through its empty eyes, felt its calm regard, listened to its silent voice. It knew me. I knew it. Like lovers reunited after a long absence, we rushed toward each other. We collided like twin moons in the aether, sparks and smoke erupting in showers. I now owned its absolute power, the kind of power the gods themselves outlawed eons ago.

Break it.

Hot, lethal flames surged upward, licking my knees, straining toward my thighs. Raging hot flame climbed up my body, burning, destroying. I knew, distantly, my boots had melted and only my feet smoldered, not quite burning.

Break it!

I sharpened my mind and focused my will. *Now!*

With the sound of six-inch thick ice breaking, the collar about my neck shattered. As though hit with a divine hammer, it dropped into hundreds of pieces, into the licking flames, gone. My power roared through me, restored, my birthright. The agony of my injuries receded as the new flood of adrenaline forced it to the sidelines.

In a blink, I was airborne. The ropes that once bound my hands dropped to the flames, consumed. My falcon's small form rose high into the violent colors of the sunset, my screech of triumph breaking across the sound of crackling flames and the scent of burning wood. My wings forced the dark smoke into roiling behind

[439]

my tail, coiling like deadly serpents before the light evening breeze set it adrift. I soared high and free, climbing into the dusk.

"No!" Cian screamed, his voice echoing through the mountains.

Finish it. The soft voice whispered in my ear.

Yes. Let s finish it. If I don't kill him now, I'll never be free of him or his vengeance. It's time he met the true Zeani.

Folding my wings, I dropped like a stone. Straight toward the hot fires he set, the death he planned for me, I aimed my raptor's beak. The wind whistled past my ears, rustled through my tail feathers. My keen eyes saw him, far below, watching the skies for me, his mouth open in a howl of despair. His boys flanked him, watching the sky, the wood, the mountain, huddled together like sheep before the onset of a storm. They feared me. They were right to fear me.

I was always the best. I won every contest. I defeated every prior champion. I could change forms on a pinfeather and slay with the fangs of a tiger before my enemy knew what killed him. My enemies feared me. My friends wished they could *be* me. No one ever bested me in a fight. I didn't intend to lose now.

A rod from the ground, I *changea.*

Striking the ground in my human shape, sword in hand, I charged. From the darkness I rose, unseen. They searched the skies as I dropped among them. My first strike took Kado across the face, splitting his mouth from ear to ear. He smiled as he pointed his arrow at my knee. *Then let s permit him to smile forevermore.*

His scream of agony alerted the others and they broke apart in panic. Cian yelled and seized steel, bellowing orders his men didn't heed. Darkness hadn't yet fallen completely, and the firelight glinted off our bared blades. Only the first stars twinkled from the heavens, and I half-wondered if Zeani watched from afar and hoped her lover would win this bout.

As Yestin and Tris reached Kado to succor his injury, Cian and I met. Our swords rang against one another, slithering in a shiver of sparks as I fought to kill him and he fought not to die. His fear worked against him just as my rage worked for me. I parried his amateur stroke and feinted a blow to his left. When he swung to block it, I lunged in, under his blade, to his right. The tip of my sword cut his thigh near the groin. Not close to his femoral, but enough that his leg buckled under him. I feinted again, striking close to his head. He ducked, parried and responded with a quick cut to my belly.

I jumped back easily, avoiding his blade and slashed downward and sideways. His sword swung hard left, harmless, leaving his right shoulder exposed. I cut backward, slicing through tough muscle and tendon.

His sword clanged to the ground as he staggered, blood gushing from two wounds. As desperate as he was, I expected him to change, to shift into a new body. His favorite form was the fox: swift, clever, and nimble. As a quick predator, he might escape my blade and my wrath. Instead, Cian cried aloud, screaming names, calling for reinforcements. "Broc! Yestin! Help me! Help!"

Finish it.

I swung my blade hard, from left to right, across his throat. Blood fountained high, spattering into the growing darkness. He stood still, his eyes wide and staring. *What the hell?* I know I killed him. Still he stood, gaping at me in astonishment. His mouth worked. His eyes bulged in his head. The scar across his cheek paled to a dim pink as the blood drained from his flesh. *Damn it, why aren't you dead?* I tilted my head sideways, considering. A swift glance downward showed me a clean blade glinting in the bright firelight.

Uh, did I kill him or didn't I?

"Van," he mumbled, his lips moving slowly. "For–forgive me."

Oh, bloody unlikely. I lowered my sword and watched in casual amusement as his head slowly, like a mountain collapsing, tilted sideways. Only a thin thread of flesh that my sword missed kept his head on his neck. Then it split, torn, as Cian's head fell to the tundra and rolled, over and over, bumping his nose, to rest near my bare feet.

His body slumped to the stony soil, bleeding out from his empty neck, pooling in thick clots amid the thin grass and fallen pine needles. I swallowed the lump that formed in my throat. I killed a member of my own family. He was my kin, a Clansman, after all.

But he sent my girl into the hands of a murdering prince with all the thought of ordering his next round of ale. For that, I kicked his head into the rushing river.

"You killed him," Tris said, his tone low with awe and disbelief.

Broc, Yestin and Drust slowly rose from a still groaning Kado and stepped on light, cautious feet toward me. Zorn ran in, nocking an arrow to his bowstring, raising it, aiming. Their bared swords gleamed in the firelight as they circled me round, their eyes glowing redly. Spinning my sword in a tight circle, I raised my free hand toward them, grinning faintly.

I lowered my face and spat on Cian's still twitching corpse. "I reckon you boys want to join your master, eh? C'mon, then. Let's dance."

Drust rushed me first, yelling for all he was worth, his sword raised. I lifted mine, braced to meet him head on. Instead, something from the near darkness seized him by the shoulders and yanked him high. His despairing scream of agony and terror trailed down to me at the same instant his sword clanked to the ground at my feet.

What the–

Zorn's arrow whistled past my head as Drust's flayed body, his skull crushed beyond recognition, fell to the ground behind me. I whirled to defend my rear. I saw nothing to defend against, yet the hairs on the back of my neck stood at attention. Blood poured from the myriad cuts and slices to his body, his neck half severed. His slowly glazing eyes stared at me, accusing. *You did this.*

No, I swear, I didn't.

Tris rushed me, his eyes bugging with not just fear but outright terror. His sword swung so wildly, all I needed do to avoid it was step aside. I never bothered to raise my own. He staggered past me– and screamed. Something huge and darkly shadowed lifted him from the ground and hugged him close. I heard his bones snap as his ribs and spine gave in, his last breaths of life broken with bubbles of blood.

Thudding hooves warned me in time.

Spinning, my sword high and my body low, my narrowed vision watched as a huge dark creature galloped into the firelight. The red-

[442]

orange flames glistened off black hair, black hide, a rayed star high above with gold gleaming around his throat. Moon and fire licked off a raised sword, but the creature's face dropped my sword's tip to the dirt. *Oh, no way, this isn t right, this isn t happening–*

My best and oldest friend slammed between me and my enemy. Zorn charged in, his sword high, yelling his challenge. Malik spun, his own blade ready, his tail lifting away from his huge quarters. The Lord Captain Commander didn't swing toward his charging enemy, but away. My breath caught in my chest as Malik's huge rear hooves kicked Zorn's head clean from his shoulders.

"Hiyaaaa!" Broc screamed, charging into the battle, his sword held high.

I spun to face him, my own sword ready, but I'd no need.

Malik wasn't done. He charged, full out, dead on target. His nocked arrow took Broc through the left eye. Broc, dead before he hit the ground, fell backward, his body falling onto the rocky soil beside the Auryn. That bad boy's sword was flung wild and free to land with a clang beside the rushing river's edge. Malik leaped Broc's corpse, his front hooves tucked beneath his shoulders, his heavy tail flagging the wind. Spinning around, he raised his bow, searching for his next target.

Yestin charged in, aiming to kill me where I stood. He saw me, alone, undefended by the dark spirits of the night, and sought to kill me. No doubt, in his mind, I commanded these foul demons. Should he kill me, he and Kado might yet survive this hell on earth. Before I raised a defense against his attack, a huge body with eagle's wings, huge talons and fierce raptor's eyes settled upon him from above.

Slack-jawed and captivated by the sight, I stared. *That can t be. You re dead. I know you re dead.*

Windy's huge beak ripped into Yestin's shoulder at the same time his raptor's talons tore his heavy body in two. Yestin's wailing scream echoing across the river and shivering into the gathering dark. True to his name, Wind Warrior reared back on his lion haunches, his talons raking the shadows, and roared his guttural challenge to the night.

"Windy," I gasped. "What–"

Kado, wounded, the last officer of Cian's detail, rose to fight. Blood gushing from my slash, his eyes wide in terror, he nevertheless fought for his life. Gauging me helpless and unable to fight back, he lunged in, hoping against hope that he'd at least take me with him. Sword in hand, he struck for my throat–

Sky Dancer dropped to the earth between me and him, screeching a wordless warcry of death and hate. She needed no sword, no arrow, nor any magic to defeat her enemy. Talons sharp enough to cut steel extended wide. A savage beak powerful enough to break a bull's spine reached downward. Lion's claws the length of a man's hand gripped the earth as she lunged forward.

Her angel's wings wide, I couldn't see a damn thing from behind. I ducked around her, my sword up, prepared to fight alongside her, as I had countless times before. Together, we'd slay our kingdom's enemies or die trying. As one, we'd die Weksan'Atan.

Kado skidded to a halt. His eyes bugged from his head, terrified, faced with one of the world's ultimate predators. Had he wet his britches, I'd not be surprised. As a man facing an angry Griffin, he knew he'd lose and lose big. Yet, he was also Atan. At an early age, he trained alongside Centaurs, Minotaurs and Griffins, as well as Shifters and humans. He fought for his King and his country. He knew very well he was guilty.

He also knew he was trapped. A dead man. There was only one death for him now.

With honor.

Atan to the core, he raised his sword to his face. In stiff accolade, his face bleeding from my cut, he saluted his death. He shut his eyes as Dancer raised her talons, slashing him through his throat. Choking, gasping for his last breath, he fell to the rocky tundra. His blade fell from his fingers as his life drained unto the grasping soil. Kado died, the last of Cian's loyal men, his sword in his hand as an Atan should.

Stunned, I stared at my dead enemies. I killed Cian, sure, but– the others? Did I yet flounder in the throes of injury and deprivation, dreaming in color where black and white suited best? What in the name of heaven just *happened?*

"Malik," I gasped as he slid to a trampling halt before me, flanked by Padraig and red-maned Edara. "You're alive."

I found no welcoming twitch of his facial muscles. His dark, hooded eyes held little I recognized. Padraig and Edara both stared down at me with twin bland expressions. Although I knew Padraig hated me, I also knew Edara did not. A shiver of icy cold ran down my spine. Although I shouldn't expect warm embraces, I didn't warrant the chilly regard those three Centaurs offered me. They just saved my life, but now acted as though they prepared to take it themselves.

Though Malik opened his mouth, he'd no time to answer as Clan Chief Ba'al'amawer, Raga and Muljier at his left and right shoulders, arrived at a brisk military trot. "My Lord Commander," Ba'al'amawer said, his right hand rising in salute. "My unit has surrounded the immediate vicinity. All enemies are dead, save this one."

Malik raised his fist, commanding silence, his dark eyes on me. "My thanks, Clan Chief," he said, his tone low. "We but await His Majesty."

Padraig lifted a silver-chased horn to his lips and blew it. A signal. In the distance, horns answered, echoing across the river's valley. From out of the pink and purple clouds flew three wings of Griffins. In perfect formation, wingtip to wingtip, they soared down from the mountains toward the river. Their dark shadows eclipsed the sunset, and what little light remained fell prey to their might. The air, the very ground beneath my feet, thrummed with the soft yet puissant sound of their feathers. Three more wings flew in from the south, while the skies to the east and north darkened under their massed bodies.

Heavy boots striking rock made a drumming noise as platoons of armed and armored Minotaurs closed in from all directions. In perfect lock-step, squared units marched in perfect cadence to the beat of drums. The evening darkness never shrouded the emblem of the Eastern Sun that graced the hundred plus banners whipping above their curved horns.

The Centaur units galloped in from all directions; in loose formation and flanking the Minotaurs. The thunder of their hooves woke the slumbering Auryn valley as they bore down on us. The grinning Death's Head skull, the emblem of the Atan, snapped in the breeze. Without their normal Atani yips and yells, they, and the royal cavalry that galloped with them, splashed across the river, arriving from the north, the west and the south.

My own Clan, the Shape-Shifters, rode horses with the cavalry units, their cloaks bearing the Clan's Tiger's Eye at their throats. Still hundreds more closed in, guised as leopards, wolves, panthers, hawks, eagles, lions, stags. My own Aderyn, whom I thought dead, bounded out from under the trees in her deer-shape. Gaear loped in, a wolf, to halt not far behind Malik. He changed to stand at attention in his human body, at parade rest, his hands behind him.

Turning in a tight circle, I tried to take everything in at once, stunned. My friends, my brothers, weren't, against all odds, dead. They rode to my rescue accompanied by the entire Atan army. The *entire* army. A Griffin platoon dropped to the ground and folded their wings, taking up positions surrounding the river bottom with their beaks high and raptor eyes watchful. While most of the Minotaurs stood at attention in a wide ring, Chief Ba'al'amawer's personal unit took up stations at critical points. The Centaur and cavalry leaders trotted closer in, leaving their soldiers to guard the outer circles.

The horns blew again, closer. I turned toward the sound, upriver, just as Malik clapped the pewter manacles over my wrists. "What—"

"First Captain Vanyar," he said, his tone neutral. "I am placing you under arrest by the order of His Majesty the King."

"What the hell? Malik!"

"Silence him!"

The voice shouted, not from Malik's jaws, but many hundred rods away near the Auryn River. Instantly, like a gag in my mouth, I couldn't speak. I moved my jaws, my lips, I breathed, but no sound passed my tongue. Trembling with anger and fear, I glared at my friend, my brother, trying to ask with my eyes: *why are you doing this?*

Malik stared at me, his dark face impassive, as always. My brother, my best and oldest friend, backed slowly away from me. No welcoming jest at my expense crossed his aristocratic lips or his mind. Never before had I felt him distance himself from me, or fail to rise to my bait. He snapped his fingers. Padraig and Edara paced around him to flank me.

My guards.

From under the trees along the riverbank, riding a golden Centaur, cantered King Roidan. Royally escorted by his household guard of Centaurs and cavalry soldiers, Roidan raised his fist. In a special saddle built for his useless legs, he could ride and wield a sword as he had in his younger, healthier days. His attendant, Daragh, on a brown horse at his flank, accompanied him here as he did everywhere.

As a boulder parts a stream, Griffins, Minotaurs, Shifters and human Atani split aside. As the King and his escort passed them, they bent the knee, crossed fist over chest and bowed low. Malik's front hoof buckled and he swept downward, his fist thumping his bare shoulder. I saluted as best I could, awkward, with both hands bound. My cracked ribs screamed in protest, but I rose with Malik as the Centaur arrived at a gentle halt a rod from where Malik and I stood. I lifted my head, fearless and undaunted, to find Roidan glaring down at me. His usually mild eyes burned with derision and hate. My fear rose as I swallowed hard, reining in my panic. When Roidan was angry, people died.

"Put him where he belongs," Roidan grated. "On his knees."

Padraig's hands pushed me downward hard, sending me hurtling to the rocky soil. The new agony from my knees was nothing compared to the raw burning that flamed across my chest. I gasped, unable to make a sound, sweat trickling down my cheek and sliding down my back. Clenching my jaw tight kept the worst of my pain from showing on my face.

"I don't want to hear a word from this traitor's mouth," Roidan snapped. His finger pointed like a sword. "You got my daughter killed, boy. You were supposed to protect her, bring her back safely. Why was that so difficult? Now she, and the gods' messenger, are in the hands of that filthy Raithin Mawrn. Because of you, everything we are and will ever be are dead and dust."

Cian gave her to him, I tried to say. Of course, nothing came out. I couldn't speak in my own defense. Had I conquered Cian's pewter collar before he gave her to Flynn–had I not liked and helped Flynn in the first place–had I died honorably at Dalziel–the recriminations endlessly paraded through my crazed mind. All my mistakes and well-meanings were as the dust beneath my boots.

"First you kill my soldiers," Roidan grated, his mouth a tight white slash in his face. "But I trusted you to save my daughter, to save your country. I believed you still had honor, still owed allegiance to the Atan code. I thought you were *smart,* had talent. My mistake, obviously. I should have executed you when you first turned up in my castle."

I bent my head and shut my eyes. *I love your daughter. I will continue to love her when I am ashes.*

"Tomorrow at dawn, I'll rectify that mistake."

I didn't look up. I've stared death in the face many times, but this time, I couldn't. He's right. I am as guilty as he said I was. I will die for my dishonor. At Dalziel, my death would not have been in vain. Here I die as the criminal I have become.

"You will die tomorrow, First Captain Vanyar," Roidan went on, his tone deathly cold. "But no easy execution for you. As you are tortured, you'll be permitted to scream and beg, and confess all the evil you've committed. But tonight–you have tonight to make your peace with the gods. They perhaps may have mercy on you. I have none."

I lifted my face to meet his hot, angry eyes, and dipped it once, in a nod. *I accept.*

Roidan jerked his head to his left. "Chain him to that tree over there," he commanded. "Let him breathe the stench of death all night. We'll set up camp upriver. And upwind."

Padraig's heavy hand dragged me up from my knees. I tried to catch Malik's eye, but he wouldn't look at me. As I was pushed past him, I once again turned my head, willing him to–what? Say he's sorry, wished he could help, best of luck? I don't know. I just wanted to see in his eyes that he didn't want me to die.

"Oh, and strip him of that sword," Roidan called. "I want it back."

Edara's firm hands unbuckled my belt and handed my sword to Malik. He accepted it with a nod, and without a glance back, walked downriver, the dying firelight flashing off his black rump. The King's escort unwound like broken spring as his gold Centaur turned and loped upstream, away from my funeral pyre and the dead soldiers. Chief Ba'al'amawer and his attendant Minotaurs stalked behind the King's escort, ignoring me like the worm I was. Sky Dancer leaped into the air and circled high into the darkness. Flames licked the new evening as men and Centaurs lit torches, trotting in the King's wake. Most of the army melted away to set up smaller camps around the King's perimeter, passing me by as silent as ghosts. Gaear returned to his wolf form and loped after the torches. Aderyn bounded into the woods, her tail flashing like a star.

Neither Padraig nor Edara spoke as I was trussed to the tree trunk with a rope around my neck. Another tied my ankles together, and Edara wound a chain several times around my broken chest and locked it behind the sturdy oak. Weary unto death, injured, I could never slip out from the ropes and chains. Without my magic, I'd never untie the ropes or unchain myself and escape. Without my sword, I couldn't augment my own, and break the manacles. They left me to sit, alone, friendless, to contemplate my last night on this earth. As a pair, Padraig and Edara stalked into the darkness, side by side, and vanished.

Malik disappeared, presumably downriver. Windy, also. He killed Yestin to save me, then vanished like a ghost. I frowned, confusion easing my pain and discomfort for a short time. I never heard him take flight and follow Sky Dancer, though Griffins tended to make a great deal of noise and blew great washes of air about when they took off from a standing position. Perhaps in their high regard for me, Malik and Windy opted out of tomorrow's entertainment.

I leaned my head against the tree trunk and shut my eyes. The glowing coals off my pyre lent me enough warmth to be relatively comfortable against the chilly mountain air despite my awkward position and my pain.

Who would Roidan pick as torturer? I asked myself. Though most Atans shied from torturing their prey, the Atani did employ one or two lunatics. As a child, Raga often cut small animals into pieces, just to see them cry and squirm. I recalled him watching me with no small satisfaction and pleasure. He might jump at the chance to torment a superior officer.

Though I could see the dim glow of the King's camp fires, I heard little save the soft noises of the mountains. The night breeze soughed through the branches high above my head and whispered through the thicket. Roidan's choice of my execution was a slender young oak with a heavy growth of timber at its base. Something rustled deep inside the branches, a mouse, or perhaps a snake. I smiled a little, thinking of the jekki snake I cooked for Iyumi a lifetime ago.

I was tired. Well, exhausted really. Rather than contemplate what little remained of my life, or worry over my coming death, I tried to wrap sleep about me. Make my peace with the gods? I didn't bother. Either they liked me or they didn't and no amount of belated worship on my part would alter their opinion.

I did, however, find some peace within myself. I did wrong, obviously, but in my life I committed mostly right. I refused to permit Dalziel to swamp me with guilt any longer. I can, I *will,* face the coming dawn and my subsequent execution with courage and honor. That's all I have left to offer this world. *That enough, your effing lordships?*

The river hurrying its way over stones lulled me, soothed my strung nerves. I pictured Iyumi within my mind's eye and held her close. Drifting toward exhausted sleep, I wanted her face to be the last thing I saw this night. I felt her touch upon my brow, listened as she whispered *I love you* into my ear. Good gods, be merciful. Let us be together again on the other side.

A branch snapped to my left.

[450]

I jerked awake, my instincts screeching an alarm. The noise could be anything at all: a rabbit, a deer ambling to the river for a drink, a hunting fox. All harmless despite my vulnerability. So why did the small hairs on my neck suddenly stand on end? Because something watched me with evil intent. My roiling gut informed me someone, or some*thing*, stalked me. I didn't know how I knew, but I did. Despite the royal command that I was to die on the morrow, something or someone had plans of their own. My survival instincts loudly and stridently told me so.

I stiffened, listening hard. Rather than strain my eyes trying to see in the dark, I shut them in order to better concentrate on listening. Four soft paws stepped slowly, lightly across the clearing. Past the corpses of Cian and Yestin, I heard the swift intake of breath as the creature sniffed the air. Though the dead hadn't been dead long enough to really reek, the odor of blood and piss tickled my nostrils. The breeze pushed most of it away, fortunately, though if I was to die in the next few moments it hardly mattered.

The paws drifted closer. *Not big enough for a bear,* I thought, *and too graceful.* Not a great cat, either. A wolf perhaps. Or a wild dog. Some said the descendants of huge mastiffs who escaped their masters roamed these mountains. Perhaps I was dogmeat. I breathed in deep, scenting a wild canine odor. A wolf? It stopped directly in front of me.

He changed forms the moment I opened my eyes.

"Hello, Van."

Malik's spell still locked my throat, thus preventing me from answering with a curse or a sharp retort. I knew why he was there before I saw the dirk in his right hand. How he dared the wrath of the King by killing me under his royal nose, I didn't know. That he had the guts to try was astonishing enough.

I answered him with a silent snarl, my lip curling in defiance.

Gaear grinned. "You should be grateful, boyo," he said, his voice hushed to not carry to the camps. "I'm going to kill you swift and clean. His Majesty has some rather creative plans for you. How would you rather die? His way? Or my way?"

My fingers still worked. I offered him *that* sign.

[451]

Gaear sighed, his eyes rolling. "How droll. You're a nasty sort of fellow, Vanyar, the world is a better place without you. I wish I could permit the King to put you down tomorrow, I'd enjoy every last moment of it. But I can't risk you saying something you shouldn't. You know about me, don't you?"

I lay my head back against the oak trunk, smiling. *Indeed I do, laddie.* You're the spy I'd been looking for. And you knew I knew. You flew to me on eagle's wings when you despise flying so you could beat the courier. You set me up to die, but I survived.

"Yes," Gaear mused, looking down at me. "I spied for him, told him all about the Atani. King Finian pays awfully well, you know. I'm disgustingly rich. After you're out of my way, he'll make me richer."

Money can t buy your soul, boyo.

He advanced, lifting the dirk, its keen edge poised to cut my throat. "Sorry, like. I tried killing you several times now, but you have the devil's own luck. That warehouse trap was a stroke of sheer genius. How you managed to survive is beyond me. How did you, by the way?"

I offered him a curled lip of defiance in lieu of a spoken answer.

He pouted, his eyes gleaming. "No matter, I reckon. I wish I could take the credit, but it was all Finian's idea. His and that whore, Zeani. Damn, I never knew what he saw in her; she slept with anything that walked. Stirring up the crowd was dead easy, you know. Already hot to avenge the deaths from the fire, all I needed to do was tell them you murdered your own unit and point you out. Even our brother Atans believed me."

He sniggered. "Once you're gone, His Majesty will launch an investigation but will find nothing to tie me to you. I'll find Finian another slut, and he'll get greedy for more intel." He chuckled. "I'll certainly sleep easier now you're finally dead."

My eyes fastened on its faint gleam, watching it glide closer to my throat. I slackened my jaw, and leaned my head back, away from that menacing blade. *Don't warn him, stupid.*

He bent toward me, forced to stoop in order to shove the knife into my throat. "Hold still now," he almost crooned. "It'll be over soon."

[452]

A shadow rose behind him.

Swift talons locked the collar around his neck at the same moment Malik burst from the thicket behind me. Gaear screamed, his voice high and womanish. Still, he tried to lunge, to shove that dirk into my face, my throat, anything. Malik reared high, his front hooves boxing, and struck Gaear squarely in the chest. Gaear, still wailing, crashed into Windy. He fought on, trying to slash and cut, his dagger slicing nothing but air.

Muttering a curse, his wings flared, Windy took him down. His right front talons pinned Gaear's torso to the rocky soil as his victim struggled, trying to stab Windy's leg, shoulder, foot–anything that might free him.

"Bloody bugger," Windy growled.

His talons closed on Gaear's right wrist and squeezed. Despite the noise Gaear kicked up, I clearly heard the bones in his arm snap like twigs. Gaear screamed again.

Malik plucked the dagger from his lax hand as Windy picked him up with careless ease and tossed him on the stony beach. Gaear landed hard on his back, gasping, choking, trying to shriek in his agony but lacking the necessary breath. Though he sought to rise and run, Malik, his arms folded across his bare chest, planted an implacable hoof on Gaear's chest and leaned forward.

"Malik! Don't you dare kill him."

King Roidan, riding his Centaur, galloped from behind the trees, his escort on his mount's creamy tail. In a whoosh of wings, Sky Dancer settled to earth on Windy's left. Chief Ba'al'amawer led a charge of a dozen Minotaurs into the faint firelight, their twin swords in both hands. Above, Commander Storm Cloud and several Griffins circled low overhead. Cavalry soldiers and Centaurs ringed the small clearing, kicking up dust. Someone added wood to my pyre and flames climbed high.

"Malik, dammit, is he alive?"

"Oh, he's alive, sire," Malik replied, smiling down into Gaear's agonized face.

"Who is it? Damn it, who dared betray our country?"

"Lieutenant Gaear, sire."

[453]

"Did he confess?"

"Yes, Your Majesty," Windy said, saluting, his wings furled over his massive shoulders. "The Lord Captain Commander, First Captain Vanyar and I are witnesses. He confessed he was paid, and paid well. He realized First Captain Vanyar suspected he spied for King Finian and thus helped set the trap that killed the Captain's unit in Dalziel. Corporal Zeani, deceased, was also implicated in the plot. Captain Vanyar, his intended victim, escaped. He planned to kill Captain Vanyar, here now, to silence him before you put him to the question."

"So my plan worked?"

"Indeed, Your Majesty."

Roidan rocked back in his saddle and grinned. "Damn. I love it when a plan comes together. No need for a trial, kids, he's a self-confessed traitor. Gaear, your sainted father will have some rather choice words for you when you meet him. And you will be meeting him very soon, I promise."

His Majesty's eyes found mine. His grin broadened. "Sky Dancer, be a dear and untie Van. I'm sure he's dreadfully uncomfortable and I know he's injured, poor fellow."

I caught Malik's swift wink and tiny smile. Suddenly, I could speak again, though my voice was hoarse. "Your Majesty," I began, as Sky Dancer towered over me. Her clever talons loosened the ropes, but the chain and its lock rebuffed her.

She straightened. "Who has the bloody key to this?" she snapped, obviously unconcerned she spoke thus in the King's presence.

"Oh, crap. I do. Hang on."

Edara trotted forward, into the light, fumbling at her belt. Removing the key, she tossed it into the air toward Sky Dancer. Though her raised talon would catch it, Padraig's swift fist intercepted it.

"Permit me, Lieutenant," he said, striding forward, his tail sweeping his hocks.

Sky Dancer gave ground, muttering and hovering, as Padraig, smiling, bent to the lock that bound me to the tree. "I apologize, First Captain, sir," he said, his voice low.

[454]

"You–"

As the chain fell from my chest and pooled in my lap, he picked it up and tossed it aside. "I owe you that."

"An–"

"Apology, yes, sir."

Amused, Padraig helped me to stand, his hand under my shoulder forcing me to lean on his strength. "I had to feign hatred for you, Van. You needed to believe we all hated you, all of us in the brotherhood. For His Majesty's plan to work, to uncover the spy . . . you were our scapegoat. We didn't know who the spy was, but knew he'd try to kill you. Vanyar, you were the King's bait."

"Only a small handful knew of my plan to smoke out the traitor," Roidan said, his Centaur pushing his way between Sky Dancer and Windy. "I, *we,* knew of a leak in the Atan, but couldn't determine who. When you fled in disgrace, with half the nation crying for your blood, we knew our moment had arrived with bells on."

"Only His Majesty, the Lord Captain, Clan Chief Ba'al'amawer and Corporal Edryd, plus myself, knew of the plan to use you to find the traitor." Padraig smiled sadly. "I hope you might one day forgive me."

"We needed every Atan's hand set against you, Van," Roidan said. "To set our little trap."

"Fortunately," Malik said, closely examining his victim. "Gaear fell for it."

"It's my fault, Van," Roidan said, "I'm sorry to have put you through all that. I'm to blame."

"Your Majesty," Malik said sternly, his hoof still planted on a squirming, weeping Gaear. "A King never apologizes."

"This one does."

Roidan leaned out of his saddle and put his hand on my shoulder. He smiled, his blue eyes earnest and sincere. "I'm sorry you suffered so, Vanyar. I'll make it up to you, I swear."

"Your Majesty–" I croaked, leaning heavily on Padraig.

"Hush now and know this, lad," Roidan went on. "I'm damn proud of you. And I'm damn glad you're on my side. If you were on *hers*, now, we'd all be in deep doo-doo."

"It's called 'shit', Your Majesty," Malik said primly.

"Why haven't you healed Captain Vanyar, Malik?" Roidan demanded, glaring daggers. "Can't you see he's in pain?"

"I'm babysitting this miscreant here. Sire."

"Oh, for–" Roidan straightened in his saddle and looked around. "Chief Ba'al'amawer, are you busy?"

"Right now, sire?"

"Yes right now."

"No, sire."

"Then kindly string up Malik's little nuisance from Van's tree. I see a stout branch right there."

"Right away, sire."

Ba'al'amawer strode forward, Muljier and Raga at his shoulders. Windy stepped aside, but Sky Dancer scowled and hovered as close to Padraig as she could get. "Van?" she whispered. "You all right, bro?"

I found a lopsided grin for her. "Right as rain, love."

Malik took his hoof from Gaear's chest and retreated several steps, permitting the huge Clan Chief to seize Gaear by his hair. Ignoring Gaear's screech of agony and panic, Raga bound Gaear's hands behind him, as Muljier picked up the rope that bound me to the tree.

"Oh, no," Roidan said, shaking his finger. "That one. The chain."

"By the chain, sire?"

"Yes, yes." Roidan waved his hand impatiently. "Loop the chain around his neck, throw the end over the limb and haul on it. Must I do this myself?"

"Of course not, sire."

"I'm feeling bloodthirsty, for some odd reason," Roidan complained, crossing his arms over his chest. "Must have something to do with treason, I suspect. No, dammit, use several loops, there. Can't have him dropping out of it, then we'll be forced to do the bloody thing all over again. I'm tired, you know, haven't ridden for years, and supper is waiting."

Malik walked toward me, his dark face lit by the dancing flames. He patted Sky Dancer on her shoulder as he passed, nodding respect to Windy. "Van," he said, his broad hand on my shoulder. "Glad to have you back."

"Ditto. How is it–" I glanced around at them all: Malik, Padraig, Edara, Windy, Sky Dancer, Aderyn and even Gaear. "How is it you all survived? I thought you were dead."

Padraig chuckled. "Never underestimate our Malik, here, Van. No demon can come close to kicking his black ass."

"But," I jerked my head at Edara. "I saw her killed. Aderyn, too. Flynn's bombs–"

"Killed Grey Mist and Kasi, yes."

Malik's face and tone lowered in grief. "Nor should we forget brave Valcan or young Dusan. Once we dispatched Flynn's hellspawn to its home, I turned my attentions to our wounded. Ilirri helped."

"Ilirri?"

"The King had already commanded troops, they'd been following for days, Ilirri among them. She's truly the best healer there is, Van. Without her, Edara, Moon, Windy, Aderyn and Edryd would have died. The demon almost killed Edryd . . . that boy has more courage than brains. Tried taking the beast on, himself."

"Where are they?" I asked. "The others."

Malik smiled as much as he ever does, his dark eyes gleaming in the firelight. "Still recovering. Ilirri is taking good care of them and Alain is helping her. Edryd is at his wits end, by the way."

"Uh –"

"He was deeply involved in the scheme to ruin you, Vanyar. Remember his arrow in Kiera's mane?"

"Um– "

"That one, yes."

"Well–"

"We had to keep you thinking there was an Atan plot to kill you. Flynn's little ambush gave Edryd a prime opportunity. He's the

[457]

best shot, as you well know. Anyway, he's terrified he'll die before telling you, to your face, he knows you didn't kill his father."

I turned my cheek away from him, swallowing hard. "That . . . that means a great deal."

"Oh, by the way, I think you need to see her."

"Her?" I asked, confused.

Malik whistled.

A sharp whinny, from the far side of the river, answered him. My jaw dropped. My mouth dried to dust. *Oh, gods, it can t be–*

"Persuading her to remain behind was a task in itself," Malik commented, his eyes on the black water. "She wanted to be here, but if she were–let's just say she'd compromise our little trap. Gaear might have never walked into it."

A dark speck crashed into the foam, coursing its way across the rushing stretch, swimming, lunging, sending water high into the night. She screamed again, calling, calling to me, her only love. Tears I didn't realize had formed and tracked down my cheeks. I remembered her lying there, broken, her eyes rolled back in her head.

"But, she died. I watched her die."

Padraig sniffed, scowling. "A piss-poor healer you are, can't distinguish unconsciousness from death. I gave her enough healing to keep her alive, but Malik saved her life. Thank him, if you will. Ilirri finished the task and healed her completely."

Kiera crashed through Centaurs and horses, kicked her way past cursing Minotaurs and sent Griffins hurtling into the night sky like dislocated pigeons. Charging past Roidan's stiff guard, her heels missed Muljier by a fraction, and forced a startled curse from Chief Ba'al'amawer. Leaning on Padraig, I smiled through my pain as Kiera dropped her muzzle in my hands.

"Nice horse, what?" Roidan commented, his tone dry. "Vanyar, you're stealing my thunder. Quiet that mare, now, and pay attention."

I buried my face in Kiera's heavy mane, breathing in her scent, her living, heart-beating, essence. *She s alive!* The weight I didn't know was there lifted from me, like a passing thundercloud crossing the sun before the light emerges, triumphant.

Kiera snorted down my neck, nickering, stamping, with her muzzle digging into my shoulder.

"Leave off," Padraig muttered, pushing her away. "You'll kill him, dammit. He's not too keen on his feet, like."

Crooning under his breath, Malik coaxed her a few steps away from me, his arm over her neck. She suffered herself to be led away, her tail swinging from side to side. Not liking the distance from me, but trusting in Malik's good sense, Kiera stood quiet. Occasionally nibbling on the sparse highland grass, my lady watched me with dark liquid eyes as Malik stroked her neck.

"Right, right," King Roidan said, rubbing his hands together. "Vanyar, consider selling that mare to me, will you? Jolly good. She'll improve my stock no end."

"I love you, Your Majesty," I replied, smiling. "But my answer is no."

"The buffoon." Roidan sniffed. "Won't sell his horse to his King. Clan Chief, why is that idiot still alive?"

"We're merely awaiting the royal signal, Your Majesty," Ba'al'amawer intoned, his hands on the chain.

"Great good gods, hang him already."

Per his King's command, Raga had wrapped the chain around Gaear's neck several times, yet stood behind the still-weeping, convicted traitor. Over the stout branch above, the chain hung slack and ready. Ba'al'amawer backed away with the chain loose in his grip. Muljier stood at his shoulder, awaiting the royal command. At Roidan's signal, Ba'al'amawer would heave with his considerable strength and lift Gaear, strangling, high above the ground.

Roidan's golden Centaur mount swung toward the self-confessed felon, bringing Roidan closer to Gaear. "Any last words, traitor?" Roidan asked, his tone pleasant. "I'll record them for posterity, of course."

Gaear merely cursed, still weeping.

"Not what I'd expect, but as you wish. Clan Chief."

Ba'al'amawer hauled on the chain, using every ounce of bull muscle he possessed. Gaear flew from a standing position on the ground to two rods above the ground in less than a second. His legs kicked and danced, his face changing from pale ocher to dark blue. Slowly strangling on the chain around his neck, my Clansman paid dearly for the money he earned. In selling Atani deaths for illicit gold, Gaear died for his loyalty to the wrong side.

May the red witch burn for this treachery. I watched as Gaear slowly stilled, hanging by his neck, his face turning from blue to black. Only his feet twitched as his life sped into the aether; his soul now judged by those that kept score. *If the gods will have mercy on you, then let their mercy be done.*

The pewter collar, still clasping his purple neck, gleamed dully in the red-orange glare of the fire and torches. Although caught between his flesh and the chain, it suffered not one scratch upon its cold surface. *One day,* I mused, entranced by it, *I ll learn its secrets.* Perhaps Malik would teach them to me. After all, I'm no longer a hated criminal.

"Malik."

The King's voice roused me. I tried turning my head, though it proved a difficult task indeed.

"Sire, I'm on it. Padraig, lay him down. Windy, get Sky Dancer out of my way, I don't care how you do it. Where's my kit? Dammit, I asked for–right, set it down. Yes, there."

I drifted, my eyes on the stars. My world spun as Malik rested his hand on my brow, calling for this, for that, for water, for the gods' blessing. *Without Iyumi, I am nothing. I am a husk of what I once was, an empty shell, awaiting someone to fill me.*

The stars spun wild, out of control. I cried aloud, a name, a face, yearning, reaching. I missed her by yards, rods, miles, her face receding from me. Darkness fell completely when his hand shut my eyes, but the spinning refused to relent. My head whirled, my gut along with it. The agony of my broken chest rose on a high crescendo and I think I screamed along with it.

Under Malik's power, I blacked out.

How does one hide an invading army?

[460]

If one were a tactical genius, such as His Majesty King Roidan, one might follow the intricate mountain passes and valleys, hugging the terrain as one embraces a long-lost brother. By creeping like a louse across a lady's hat, the aforementioned King might conceal the approach of Minotaurs, Centaurs and cavalry soldiers. He might utilize those unique flying creatures known as Griffins to fly high and identify potential trouble, such as lone farmsteads, a passing patrol, or a merchant hastening his way to market. Such a genius might also throw those deliciously deceitful creatures known as Shape-Shifters to spy out the land. Who knew what flew, crawled, leaped, bound, stalked or wriggled in the mud might be in truth a spy for the King.

If magic couldn't diffuse the situation, force of arms did. While many Raithin Mawrn fell prey to the magics used upon them by the Bryn'Cairdhans invading their land, they'd no knowledge of it. If magic didn't work, they died. Thus, no word of the invasion reached the sensitive ears of King Finian. He trusted in the protection of the mountains surrounding his castle and his country, never realizing how they might betray him.

By exploiting such creatures, His Majesty guided his royal Weksan'Atan forces across the Shin'Eah Mountains, undetected by the Raithin Mawrn or their King. Due to His Majesty's sheer audacity and determination, the Atan army stood high above the gates of Castle Salagh in the darkness before the dawn. This day, foreseen long ago, the sun and the moon joined in the sky. The portent of things to come. The time of the prophecy.

Concealed within a curved arm of a hillock, less than a league from Castle Salagh and its surrounding town, King Roidan frowned. Mounted aboard his loyal Centaur, he peered below, his fist cupped in a circle as his magic brought every sight from far away up close and personal. Following his example, I studied the silent town where nothing moved, and only the street lamps were lit at this early hour. The town surrounded the castle's high walls, looking much like chicks gathered under their mother's wings. Though I saw no guards on the walls, I knew that meant little. Even with magic, I'd easily miss seeing black-cloaked men in the dark.

I bit my lower lip, thoughtful, considering the light that burned in the window of the high north-side tower. It gleamed red-orange, indicating a fire rather than the yellowish glow of a tallow candle or oil lamp. Someone built a hearth fire up there.

"Now, boys and girls," Roidan said, lowering his fist. "What am I looking at?"

"Castle Salagh, Your Majesty," perked a bright voice from our rear.

Green as grass. I rolled my eyes as Malik sighed heavily, shaking his head.

Roidan snorted softly and glanced over his shoulder, briefly. "I was hoping for a bit more intel than that. Does anyone have more to contribute?"

"The town itself has few arms and fewer trained men to wield them," I said, sitting Kiera to Roidan's left. "It's comprised of merchants, a few nobles and many, many poor peasants. Finian isn't known for his generosity toward his people. He doesn't trust them, thus they can't rebel against him if they're ignorant and weaponless.

"For the time being, the town can be ignored. Sire, the greatest threat will come from the four towers. At the four corners: east, west, north and south. Each are guarded by well-trained soldiers armed with bows and cross-bows. At least twenty to a tower. The parapets are also guarded, but have only a few men to walk them. They are also armed with cross-bows."

His Majesty eyed me sidelong. "Someone has done his homework. What else do I need to know?"

Malik's long finger pointed out and down. "There are also two heavily guarded gates, my liege. We cannot enter unless we can lower the drawbridges. A deep moat surrounds the castle and unless we dive in and murder all the reptiles within them, we cannot swim it. We must have those gates up and the drawbridges down. They are the key to our success. Without them, we fail."

"Give me a half hour, Majesty," Chief Ba'al'amawer rumbled, at Roidan's left shoulder. "I'll have those bridges down."

Roidan held up his hand, stilling us all. "You'll have your chance, Clan Chief," he muttered. "Vanyar, you know where she is. Don't you?"

[462]

I knew the *she* of whom he spoke, and it wasn't Iyumi. I didn't blink. I pointed. "There, sire. The north tower where she sits beside her fire, awaiting Flynn and his prisoners. Like a spider in her web, plotting."

Roidan sat back, smiling. "You see why I like this boy, Malik? I told you a long time ago he had quality."

"I'm so very glad I took your advice, sire," Malik replied.

"Of course you do," Roidan commented. "We'd all be in deep doo-doo if you hadn't."

"It's called–"

"'Shit', yes, I know, Malik. Stop correcting me, will you?"

"Whatever, sire."

"My liege," I said, my tone low and urgent. "We're behind Flynn by only minutes. We've been hard on his heels for the last couple days, I know he's only just arrived at the castle. If the Duchess must sacrifice the baby at the moment both the sun and moon join–"

"I know, son." Roidan replied, his grizzled expression set and grim. "We've less than an hour. The sun and moon will rise together at dawn."

The King's hand gripped my shoulder, hard. "You're my hand, here, Van. I'm relying on you, on your talents, your unique skills. Will you lead the Griffins in an attack on those towers?"

I dipped my brow. "It's my honor, sire."

Roidan suddenly frowned. "I gave you back your sword, hadn't I? Tell me I did, for if I hadn't, I bloody well lost it."

I grinned and patted my hip. "Here where it belongs, my liege."

"Jolly good. Clan Chief, are your Minotaurs ready?"

"Ready and able, Your Majesty."

"When Vanyar and the Griffins take the towers, you and your troops must seize those gates. The Griffins will bring the bridges down, Ba'al'amawer, but they must stay down. You understand?"

"We will keep those gates secure, sire, or we'll die trying."

"If you must die, my old friend, die *after* those gates have been secured. Are we clear?"

That old Minotaur bastard actually grinned, his bovine lips skinned back from his heavy teeth. "Command those flying kitties to kill the troopers inside and lower the gates. Then we'll see who can take a castle by storm."

"Malik."

Roidan's hand fell onto Malik's arm. "Once the Griffins kill the guards and the Minotaurs seize the gates, will you ride with me?"

Malik found a rare grin that actually stretched his facial muscles. "With pleasure, my King. To hell and beyond."

"Remember, all," Roidan said, his voice raised to his troops. "We target the north tower of the castle. My daughter is there, and the prophetic child with her. Both must survive if we, as a nation, are to remain free from the hell bitch's yoke. If she wins, we all lose, right down to the smallest serf child. We fight, now, for not just our liberty, but for our very lives. And for the lives of those we love. We may die now, Atani soldiers, to a man. We may die here, on foreign soil, as interlopers and fiends. Here, we are the enemy, not the savior. Our blood feeds their offspring. But if we are successful, our deaths mean our families will live on in peace and prosperity. What do we fight for if not for that?"

Malik raised his fist high. "I fight for my King and for Iyumi. I will die, here and now, for her life and that of that child. Who's with me?"

My fist popped up seconds before hundreds of others. No voice raised to alert the enemy to our presence, but none failed to show their allegiance in silence. Their raised fists shadowed mine. I may have been first, but Roidan's smile didn't recognize me, but instead fell upon all those who swore their loyalty and their vengeance upon those who dared lay hands upon She Who Hears. The King's daughter. The gods' voice. The lady I loved.

"Captain Vanyar."

I stiffened my spine although he never looked at me.

"Lead them to her," he said, his face smiling as tears stood within his eyes. "Bring her home to me. She's all I have left in this mad, crazy world. You love her, as I do. I need you."

I crossed my right arm over my chest, my chin dropping. *Your will, sire.* Sliding down from Kiera's back, I took a moment to slide my hand surreptitiously down her face. She lipped my cheek, her eyes bright.

[464]

"You sure you won't sell her to me?" Roidan asked, his eyes livid as they danced across my girl.

I grinned. "Ask for my soul, Your Majesty, you have it. But ask for my horse–"

"Never."

Malik's voice from my right completed what I hadn't said. "Sire, you know better."

Roidan turned away, his mouth frowning but his eyes laughing. "I know. Don't part a good horse from his human. Or hers, for that matter. But still–"

"Majesty."

"I know, dammit. Chill, will you? Malik, you seriously need a vacation. Remind me after we kill the witch and retrieve my daughter, all right?"

"Of course, sire."

"Captain Vanyar?"

"Daughter, retrieved. Red Bitch, dead. Malik, vacation. Got it."

"Good man. Always could count on you. Now, why are you still here?"

"I'm gone, my liege."

Stalking to a relatively open spot near the line of Minotaurs, I turned my face upward, into the darkness.

"Windy," I snapped. "Sky Dancer."

Without much room to land, both circled low overhead, beaks pointed down as they eyed me from a dozen rods up. "Right here, Van," Windy said. "Er, sir, rather."

"So much for military discipline," Roidan sighed, but his face smiled gently.

"Find Lightning Fork, Swift Wing and Storm Cloud and bring them to me."

"Where will you be?" Sky Dancer asked, her beak angled down to see me better.

I grinned. "Right here."

As the pair winged high, out of sight, I saluted the King once more. "Sire. Might I respectfully suggest you remain here, with your guard?"

He scowled. "Are you suggesting I skulk out of sight like a coward, First Captain? That I refrain from leading my warriors into battle in person?"

I met his blue eyes and smiled. "Yes."

"Nice try," he snapped. "But forget it. I haven't forgotten how to wield a sword, damn your eyes. You find my daughter and I'll do the rest. Grow some bloody wings, First Captain."

"My liege."

I leaped into the air and changed. My heavy wingbeats tossed Roidan's and Malik's hair into their eyes as I rose, ponderously at first, then with more grace and power. Catching a thermal, I rose higher, my huge wings beating steadily as those below me retreated into the darkness. I glanced down, between my shoulders, and called out. "Keep him safe, Malik. He's the only King we've got."

"Mind your own business, Van," Malik snapped. "I'll mind mine. Take out those guards on the walls and the gates."

"Your request is my command, Lord Captain Commander," I answered, circling higher. "I'll signal when we've neutralized the troops."

Coasting upon the early mountain air, I found five Griffins winging toward me. Unlike a kestrel, a Griffin couldn't hover. Rather than try, I tightened my circle. Like a funnel, high above the mountaintop where Roidan and Malik planned their attack, we six Griffins flew about one another, rising higher and higher until the army below were but specs in the darkness.

"Commanders," I said, my voice terse. "Assign me five from each of your units. Storm Cloud, you take the south and east walls. Eliminate anything moving. Lightning Fork, yours are the north and west. Swift Wing, you seize the south gate. I'll take the north. Once you drop the bridge, signal with a fire shot.

"Lieutenants Sky Dancer and Wind Warrior are with me. Once the walls are ours and the bridges down, protect the Minotaurs and the cavalry units. Do not, under any circumstances, allow Finian's men to retake the bridges. If the bridges rise, our beloved She Who Hears and the prophetic child will die under the knife of the Red Bitch. I'm sure I don't need to remind you of the fate we all face should that happen."

[466]

"You don't, First Captain," Storm Cloud replied. "We'll take the walls."

"What if Finian has an army shut behind those gates?" Lightning Fork asked. "His Majesty will ride into a trap."

"What if he does?" I replied, stretching my beak into a grin. "Are we not Atan, lads? Do we not strike from above, in the dark, as the angels from heaven do? Can any army of human soldiers withstand the might of Griffins, Minotaurs, Shifters and our own King? Please, tell me the truth here."

"My apologies, First Captain," Lightning Fork answered, humor in his tone. "I forget myself, sometimes."

"He hasn't an army down there, Commanders," Sky Dancer said, circling at my right flank. "Finian has but minions. He dismissed his standing army years ago, thinking them useless and unnecessary. He posts guards on Salagh's walls, but they've grown careless over the years. They lack training, discipline, often falling asleep at their posts. While the real soldiers plow fields, his 'protectors' are little more than swords for hire. They owe their allegiance to gold and nothing more."

I imprisoned my grin before eruption. "How do you come by such knowledge, Lieutenant?"

Sky Dancer sniffed. "Quite often I'm assigned to the princess' guard detail. She tells me stuff."

"And She Who Hears knows a great deal about many things," Storm Cloud remarked. "But can her intel be relied upon? Things change, you know."

"But the men Finian keeps around him?" I asked, my wings stretched to their fullest. "That won't change, Commander. He guards only his castle, and his folks fend for themselves. He's made himself easy prey, and we are the predators he fears. Are we ready?"

"Ready, First Captain," Lightning Fork answered, his disciplined unit approaching in silence, their only sound the soft beat of a hundred huge wings.

"Ready, sir."

Just as the obedient and loyal crowd of land-locked creatures crowded around Malik and Roidan, I commanded the skies. Swift

Wing rose high above, his unit hard on his tail. He led his band wheeling south, but his soldiers weren't the only to leap forward. Both Lightning Fork's and Storm Cloud's wings split apart from the main and vanished into the night.

Under the direction of Windy and Sky Dancer, the assigned fifteen Griffins flew in an orderly formation behind them. In turn, they flanked me. Banking high and over, my wings beat swiftly toward the enemy fortress. With only a few leagues to fly, we circled high over the north tower within moments. From this angle, I couldn't see the window or the hearth light. Yet, I scented wood smoke and blood with my keen eagle's senses.

"She hasn't killed them already?" Windy asked, having caught the same odor I did.

"Listen," Sky Dancer said, her tone low, hushed. "Can't you hear it?"

"Fighting," I answered. "Something's going on in there."

"Van," Sky Dancer said, buzzing up to fly at my right wing. "I see ten guards on the tower, with perhaps another twenty on the walls to either side. Well-armed and armored."

"Wouldn't be much of a challenge if we didn't have enemies to fight," I said. "Windy, Dancer and you three– with me. The rest of you spread out and kill Finian's soldier boys. Try not to make too much noise, but if you must toss a trooper off a battlement and he yells, don't sweat it. Here we go."

Banking hard left and down, I closed my wings and dropped. As silent as an owl stooping upon her mouse, I fixed my raptor's keen night vision on two men strolling casually across the rampart. The other eight also moved in pairs, some standing and chatting, the rest walking their patrol and gazing down at the silent keep below.

Down. Not up.

Catching Sky Dancer's eye as she dove at my right I pointed at the pair furthest away, then cut across my own throat with my talon. I did the same with Windy on my left, ordering him to take out the pair walking in the far opposite direction. Thus, we three each controlled the middle and both ends. The remaining three Griffin warriors would mop up the other four between us.

[468]

Windy and Sky Dancer spread apart from me, dipping wide to reach their marks at the same moment I hit mine. I didn't need to glance around to see the other three hard on my tail. While I gave them no specific instruction, I knew they'd recognize instantly the plan I implemented. Their Atani discipline and training would carry them through without further guidance from me.

Seconds before impact, I spread my wings and slowed. The troopers never sensed my approach, nor glanced around. My weight, twice that of a fully mature bull, took my first victim to the ground. His back snapped instantly. He cried out in shock at the same instant my talon sliced his throat, effectively silencing him. His partner stumbled back, trying to reach for his sword, his eyes huge in his panicked face. I pounced on him, my wings flared and my talons raking him from shoulder to crotch. He tried to scream as his innards burst forth along with his still-beating heart.

I never much cared for the taste of human blood on my tongue. Thusly, I refrained from biting through his neck to open his carotid. Instead, I slashed his throat with my lion hind claws and leaped clear of his gushing red torrents. I know, I admit it. I don't much care for human blood on my fur or feathers, either. Sue me.

A swift glance around showed me the effectiveness of a silent Griffin attack. None felt the need to toss an Raithin Mawrn soldier off the battlements, but the top of the ramparts ran red with blood. I wasn't the only fastidious cat there, either. Both Windy and Dancer sat primly atop the battlements, with only a few spots of blood to mar their feathers, while one Griffin, drat, I never caught his name though he ranked a Lieutenant, winged his way up to perch on the tower cupola and shake red from his talons. The other two circled, and eyed the dead soldiers closely to ensure they all were dead.

"Windy," I said, leaping off the battlement. "I'll cut the right drawbridge rope, and you cut the left."

"Vanyar!" Sky Dancer screeched, diving on my tail. "You aren't leaving me behind."

"Go babysit the other three, Dancer."

"They don't require babysitting, *sir*," she retorted. "You, however, do."

"Never mind," Windy said, catching my pained expression.

Even a razor sharp Griffin talon had trouble with the triple-thick, heavily coiled ropes that held up the huge northern drawbridge. Clinging to the tremendous rope like a bat on a tree limb, I held myself in place with three sets of claws while sawing frantically at the rope. Likewise, Windy also held on tight, his right talon whipping back and forth. Slowly, the cable's strands broke and shredded, the weight of the drawbridge making it weaker the further we cut. The incredible tension on the ropes helped, and the many strands snapped one by one, even without our help.

"When that thing let's go," Sky Dancer warned, flipping between the two of us, "It's gonna send you flying–"

My rope broke with a sharp cracking sound. Sky Dancer was right, for I was sent hurtling skyward, out of control. I heard the second cable break and Windy's yell as he, too, was recoiled into free space. Fortunately, neither of us struck the castle's very solid stone walls. Cast out of control and falling free, I fought to reclaim both balance and wings. But when I saw the distant stars rather than the ground, I knew I needed to upend myself before I struck that selfsame earth.

I regained control of my wings in time to watch, fascinated, as the drawbridge swung ponderously down. The cogs that kept it upright and shut tight unwound with a sharp rattling of metal teeth. Chains that reinforced the heavy oak timbers chimed musically as the structure fell, down, down, across the moat into its moorings. It hit with a resounding boom and a wash of dust, no doubt waking the neighbors.

In the distance, another boom announced the falling of the second bridge. An instant later, a huge sparking fire raced across the dark heavens. The signal.

I launched my own firedrake into the early dawn sky, informing the King the bridge was down. As I did, my eyes caught sight of the lightening eastern horizon. Beating my wings slowly, I rose higher, with both Sky Dancer and Windy pacing me. In a line of three, we flew slowly eastward, our altitude granting us a better view of the sight arriving over the distant eastern sea.

"What the hell?" Windy asked, his tone low and shocked.

"That's just wrong," Dancer added. "It's like . . . like–"

"The sun and moon rising together," I finished for her, grim.

At the edge of the world, the sun crested the distant horizon, gleamed redly and sent out shattered clouds of pink, orange, purple and gold. Yet, at its side, moving inexorably closer to the new sun's red-gold sphere, moved a black round ball of evil. As we watched, enthralled, it inched closer to the rising sun, its darkness swallowing the brightly colored rays like a demon swallowing hope.

Not enough time, turning tail and diving. The moon's shadow was but minutes away from eclipsing the sun. Unless I stopped it, the Red Duchess would slay the troll on her ghastly alter and control our world.

My keen hearing picked up the galloping thud of thousands of hooves from both north and south. Cavalry horses, Centaurs, Minotaurs–all raced down from the mountains through the silent, frightened town and into the Castle Salagh's keep. Their task was to seize control of the castle.

Mine was to find Iyumi. And the Witch.

Banking up and over, I closed my wings and sped like greased lighting toward the north tower. Like ticks on a deer, Windy and Sky Dancer hugged tight to my tail, never letting me out of their sight. Crossing the parapets and their bloody dead guards, I aimed for the fire-lit windows.

"Van!" Windy yelled, the wind whipping his voice back. "Where are you going? Are you insane?"

"Vanyar, stop," Sky Dancer screamed, her raking talons trying to catch hold of my tail. "There might be more troops there."

"Take them out," I ordered. "I see a balcony, and a door. I'm going in."

"Van!" Windy cried, his voice no doubt reaching what few guards that yet lived. "We can't fit through that thing."

"But I can."

"Dammit, you can't go alone!"

"Watch me."
Dipping my left wingtip, I dove down.

CHAPTER 14

By Dawn's Evil Light

*"T*his is seriously spooky," Buck-Eye whispered. "M'lord? Where is everyone?"

I hadn't a clue. Less than an hour before dawn, and the time my mother demanded I arrive, our mounts clattered through streets so silent they echoed eerily. In a town, life often stirred before the sun rose. Butchers, bakers and even the candlestick makers worked while others slept. No lights showed in windows, not even in the poorest hovels where chinks in shutters permitted lamplight to escape.

We'd ridden through the city's open north gate, by law shut and barred from sundown until sunup. No city watch challenged us. Should my illustrious sire learn of this, no doubt he'd string those derelict in their duty up by their toes and gut them while they yet lived and screamed. Buck-Eye's observations were dead on. This was not just spooky–it was downright frightening.

The hairs on the back of my neck refused to lie down. My hand twitched toward my sword, continually, although no threat presented itself. Dra'agor skittered under Bayonne's hooves, his hackles up and his lips often skinned back from his fangs.

"It's her doing," Iyumi said, her voice weary.

The last few days of heavy riding had taken its toll upon Iyumi and the troll kid. She'd taken little food and slept less. Though I tried to make her as comfortable as possible, tried cajoling more food down her throat, and bent myself into knots being friendly and kind, she deteriorated. And the troll refused food, even the fresh blood Dra'agor hunted for her. Seriously weak, I feared she would die in Iyumi's arms long before we might bring her to my mother.

"What do you mean?"

"Her evil," Iyumi replied, her face downcast. "Can't you feel it? It's like the sensation when you set your hand in a maggoty corpse when you reached for cake. Many of the common folk have fled, Flynn. The rest are in hiding. Your father's soldiers have deserted their posts."

"That I do believe," Boden muttered from the rear.

"It's not my mother," I insisted. "It's *her*. She's taken control of my family. And I'll kill her for it."

"They're one and the same, Flynn," Iyumi said, her tone sharpening for the first time in days. "Use the scrying crystal. I dare you. I double-dog dare you, see what your mother is doing right now. That should tell you, and us, once and for all."

I didn't answer. Nor did I reach for the amber at my throat.

"You've already tried."

Iyumi's tone lightened in wonder. "You didn't see her, did you? Because she has the power to conceal herself from even the crystal. Only the Red Witch has that power. You're such a fool."

"Love makes fools of us all," I replied, my blood cold. "Right?"

"What she feels for you isn't love," Iyumi said, more strength in her voice than I'd heard in a while. "She gave birth to you, but she isn't your mother. She used you to gain power for herself. Why can't you see that?"

"She's my mother," I said. "She loves me. You're wrong about her, Iyumi. It's the other one."

[474]

Iyumi fell silent for a long while. Not wanting to rush despite the urgency of my errand, I held us at a walk as we rode through the cobbled streets. Expecting an attack at every moment, I jumped at shadows and cursed under my breath. Dra'agor's hackles refused to lie down. In a more normal turn of events, I'd listen to raunchy jokes bantered between Boden, Torass and Lyall, with Buck-Eye scolding them in an effort to instill better decorum. Instead, I heard little save the clop of hooves on cobbles. Should I bother to turn and look, I guessed I'd see many fingers making the sign against evil.

High above us loomed Castle Salagh, my father's seat. The house of my ancestors. I reined in and looked up. Built upon a tall pinnacle of sheer, steep rock, the only entrances were the two massive gates in the north and the south facing walls. When the great drawbridges were down, folks from the castle and the town came and went freely. But once those bad boys went up, nothing got past them. Not even a lizard. Oak beams, layered three thick and bound together with steel and reinforced with iron, sealed the castle from attack. A deep moat filled with all manner of reptilian man-eating creatures surrounded it, leaving few opportunities to seize it.

In the distant past, invading armies tried and broke themselves upon the solid rock. Some even managed to scale the walls and invade the keep. Yet, they, too, failed in the end, for the tall parapets were guarded by loyal men. The castle, built upon stone, repelled the most determined enemy time after time. Since before the Mage Wars, no one has ever taken Castle Salagh from without. It's steep stone walls, narrow murder holes, high turrets and round guard towers kept the most determined enemy at bay.

My eyes were drawn to the highest tower, outside my will. Like iron to magnets, my sight fled past the high stone walls, past the battlements and turrets, and fastened upon the tallest tower. The northern. A light burned up there, in the window, high above. Not a lamp or a candle, but a hearth. That glow came from a fire. Someone was awake in the darkness before the dawn.

In the west tower, just next door, the royal apartments stood dark and silent. No lights burned in their windows. Perhaps my mother slept on, while my father, if he did indeed still lived, sat in his great chair in the darkness. For surely his wounds kept him wakeful in the dark watches of the night. I imagined Fainche sleeping, dreaming her dreams of butterflies and magic and kisses. Sofia slept in our great bed, her belly rounded. Month by month, the babe thrived and grew. I saw him within my mind's eyes–growing, nourished by his mother's blood, a mere fetus within her womb.

My son.

"It's not too late, Flynn."

Iyumi spoke from just behind me, and made me jump.

"What do you mean?" I asked, struggling to settle my voice.

"Turn back, while you still can."

"M'lord."

Buck-Eye's soft tone set my skin to crawling. "Mayhap she's right, m'lord. Maybe we should go back."

"Don't be ridiculous," I snapped. "It's one damn woman up there. We kill her, save my family, end of story. We go on."

"Flynn–"

I ignored Iyumi's tense worry. *She s dead wrong.* She doesn't know the situation as I do. My mother is the victim here. The Bitch controls my mother and my father. Once I kill her, they're free of her evil. If he did indeed survive as Lyall suspected, perhaps my father and I can call a truce, a cease-fire, and lift hostilities. He might even find a small bit of love for me. I'm his first-born son, after all.

Nudging Bayonne forward, I led the way into the castle's shadows. My father's guards, like the citizens of the town, either hid like cowards or fled. No one challenged us as our horses clopped across stone cobbles toward the ancient keep. The heavy drawbridge across the moat was up, sealing up the first of two entrances into Castle Salagh. I had no doubt the southern bridge was also up. All secure and safe – no outside intruders could possibly get inside.

"Now what?" Torass asked. "How do we get in there?"

[476]

"This way, boys and girls," I said, aiming for a light tone. "I know a secret door."

"M'lord?" Buck-Eye asked.

I tossed a grin over my shoulder. "How else does a boy late for curfew get home?"

"Uh–"

"I know. I was a rascal."

"Was?"

I pretended not to hear Iyumi's acid comment. "I used to bribe the porter," I said, still aiming for banter. "He loved sweets and I'd bring him a bagful of candy now and again. In exchange, he'd watch for me and open up."

"Let's hope he's still on duty," Lyall muttered.

"Got any candy onya?" asked Torass. "I haven't."

Built long ago as an escape route should the castle fall, the door lay cleverly concealed amid the stone pinnacle. Built to look like a rock outcropping, only those who knew of its existence kept the secret close. The porter had been the porter for over sixty years, a post passed down from generation to generation. I knew his seamed and smiling face as well as I knew my wife's. Since I reached the ripe age of ten and became an outlaw, his outlandish accent and gruff voice berated me time and again. He never failed to open for me, nor in his loyalty ever halted his need to scold me for my foolish and dangerous behavior. In my self-contained misery, I never realized he actually liked me for me.

However, no elderly grizzled face with a cheerful smile met us. The door proved unlocked and unattended, open to invaders. Candy wasn't necessary, but I frowned, concerned. Twenty four hours a day, every day, he stood at this door, guarding against unlawful entry and mischievous boys. This was his only duty, his life's work and he wasn't here.

An unlocked portal and no guard. Not good. Not good at all.

Craning my neck, I peered up the castle's sheer stone walls to the ramparts above. I thought I saw a shadow fly past, but perhaps it was a wisp of cloud. Other than that, nothing moved. The hairs on my neck rose and Dra'agor growled.

My sword filled my hand though I don't remember drawing it. At my ear, Buck-Eye muttered something, a curse or a prayer, and the troll-child mewled. *Keep it quiet,* I silent thought, hoping Iyumi got the message.

Leaving the horses, I edged my way into the chamber, half-expecting attack. I half-turned, gesturing impatiently. *Get in, get in.* As Lyall, the last, followed me into the castle proper, he shut the door and dropped the bar. Thus none might follow after and perhaps attack our rear. Before I asked it of him, Buck-Eye called flame to his fist. I glanced around. The chamber was comfortably appointed: a bed, a table with the remains of a meal, a hearth with no fire. And no elderly serf to affectionately hail me as 'you young scoundrel'.

"Shall I go first, m'lord?" he asked, taking a step toward the stairs.

I shook my head and raised my hand. "I will. But I'll ask a favor of you. Not a royal command, Buck-Eye."

"Anything."

I tossed my chin toward Iyumi. "You look after her, *micha na.* No matter what happens, you keep her safe."

"I will, m'lord. As I live and breathe, nothing will come between her and me."

I nodded, my throat suddenly thick. "If we survive the next hour, I'll reward you. All of you. Somehow."

"The service be its own reward, m'lord."

Quickly turning about so none might see my face, I led the way up the twisting, turning staircase, my own flames burning without harm on my left palm. Having trod these myriad corridors in play or wild escape from a beating, I'd trod these stone flags since I first learned to walk. Anyone new to the place got lost easily, for the turns and twists of these unchanging slate vistas played havoc upon one's ability to navigate.

On the first level, torches burned in their sconces along the grey stone walls. So there were people here, after all. Extinguishing my flame, I dropped the need for secrecy and quickened our pace.

I led the way around the inner keep, a city unto itself built into the castle walls. Past kings determined walls might contain valuable storage rooms in the case of famine or siege. When neither appeared, those room evolved into chambers for visiting nobles, travelling merchants seeking a royal decree, or military officials needing rooms for themselves, their families and entourages. I ignored these chambers as useless, as I charged up a flight of stairs only to trot down the next in order to reach the stairwell that wound its way to the floor above. The higher you resided in the castle, the higher your rank.

Although the official royal apartments were at the top of the west tower, the north had once been home to my ancestors. I hadn't been up there for years, though I remembered the topmost chamber was huge, with a tremendous glass wall that faced east. Every tower had the same glass panel, each facing the direction to its immediate right. Our family tower, the west, owned one that gazed down to the gentle southern lands and rolling hills to the south of the castle.

A see-through wall that faced east–my skin suddenly crawled, pimpling like a newly plucked goose. A chill ran down my spine, and I felt cold, icy, all over my body. My heart thudded in my chest. The sun rose in the east, as did the black moon. The time of prophecy. The time of evil. Both would rise as one within that weird, glass wall.

Folks heard our approach, our boots on the slate flagstones, and ventured forth from hiding. Liveried servants, court officials, nobles bearing the insignia of minor houses, cooks, houseboys, and other lower class folk who kept the kingdom running huddled in frightened groups or peered around half-shut doors. They gaped as I loped past, my entourage at my heels, nudging one another and whispering. Soldiers and castle guards, on duty or not, offered salutes and rapid questions, all of which I ignored.

On and on I ran, sliding around corners, stumbling up stairs, always leading with my sword. If we hit this passage, it'd take us straight to the fourth level, where the King's royal council took rooms and made their home-away-from-home. Eyes peeked around partly opened doors as we streaked past, voices calling strident questions at my back.

Dra'agor trotted at my hip, his tongue lolling. His toenails clicked sharply across the grey-blue flagstones in perfect rhythm of my heart. Toward the rear of my party, I heard Iyumi's labored breathing as she hustled in my wake. Though fit, Iyumi's burden of the troll hampered her ability to run. After Buck-Eye's third offer to carry the brat, she handed the infant to him. Never once did she offer complaint or demand respite. With only her bound hands to constrain her, she inhaled sharply and no longer faltered her pace.

"Your Highness!"

I skidded to a halt as the small man burst from the shadows, his arms high. Boden all but bounced off my back as Lyall slid on the slick pavestone, cursing, nearly falling on his butt. Under better control, Buck-Eye stopped abruptly with his hand on Iyumi's arm, preventing her from tumbling to her tiny ass in a royal heap.

"What the–Sergei?"

The skinny, balding right hand of King Finian rushed toward me, his damp hands seizing mine. Or at least the hand not holding my sword. He surged into my private airspace, breathing hard. The cloying scent of his perfume stung my nostrils. At once disgusted by his unseemly display and fawning behavior, I pulled my hand out of his grip. "What do you want?"

"It's terrible, Your Highness," Sergei all but wept. Sweat slid in tiny rivulets down his sunken cheeks. "That dreadful, dreadful man, he's gone stark raving mad. He's going to kill us all!"

Backing away a step, I tried stepping around him to escape. "What dreadful man?"

"That awful Commander Blaez, of course."

I stopped cold. Catching Iyumi's weary eye and Buck-Eye's instant frown, I half-turned back. "What do you mean?"

"Just that, Your Highness," Sergei cried, tears of fright standing in his pale eyes. "He laughed and laughed; he's mad, I tell you. He said his toys would explode a half hour after dawn and the gods could sort us all out. I think he means to blow up this castle and everyone in it!"

"Where did you see him, Sergei?"

"Near his chambers, Your Highness. Almost an hour ago." Sergei wiped his cheeks with his handkerchief. "I tried to find His

Majesty, to warn him. But I can't find him anywhere. Nor the Queen, your blessed mother. Someone has to stop him. He's mad!"

"Blaez is bluffing," I said, hoping I told the truth.

"I shall endeavor to find your father, the King," Sergei said, hustling away, taking his perfume and sweat with him. "Someone in charge should know about this."

I watched Sergei's back until he turned the corner, my own sweat rank in my nose. What could Blaez be up to? He hadn't the power—Sergei has to be wrong. Of course he is. I frowned, rubbing my brow until I realized it yet held Sergei's noxious sweat. Blinking, I wiped my damp fingers on my cloak. Blaez loved my mother; he'd never risk harm to her. Or Fainche.

"Flynn."

Iyumi's exhausted yet sharp voice broke me from my thoughts. "I'll make you a bargain. Turn back and I'll marry you, freely. I'll bear your children and be your queen. Without protest or constraint. Just walk away now."

I gaped at her. "You don't get it, do you? I can't turn back."

"There's nothing here for you."

"I have to save my sister, my mother. And my wife."

"You don't know they aren't already dead."

I shook my head. "This way."

Taking the opposite direction Sergei took, I led the way around another corner, down a narrow passage and up a steep flight of steps. Remembering my military history, the back-then royal family could retreat to the topmost chamber in the tower and hold off an army. None might take the tower unless it captured that room. The thin, almost vertical, stairs meant one man at a time, in single file. Any halfway adept archer with an endless supply of arrows might choke that staircase with corpses.

If I remembered correctly, the huge chamber also boasted of a larger than average storeroom, a pump that brought forth fresh water from the underground cisterns below and a large balcony whereby a commander may signal his forces. If invaders took the keep, none actually held the castle until they captured the towers. To date, none ever had.

All the towers held the same narrow staircase, rooms and water. Since the time of the ancient Mage Wars, none have successfully invaded Castle Salagh. Those who tried didn't survive to try again. Entire armies hid within the walls, tempting the enemy forward with the very same vacant corridors and hollow emptiness I faced myself. Once the enemy took the bait, the defenders fell upon their flanks. And decimated them.

My own flanks itched as I trotted past shut doors and echoing stone. The ghosts of those slain in the dim past played havoc upon my nerves. I heard their voices though I sought to ignore them, felt their fevered hands upon my arms. *Save us. Save us!*

Reaching the one-man-at-a-time staircase, I stopped short. No torches burned in sconces along the walls. The faint odor of tallow told me they'd been lit recently, but someone extinguished them. I peered upward into the dark, lifting my hand-held flame as high as I could. Shadows and light danced upon the stark walls, but I saw nothing villainous nor harmful. Despite the lack thereof, the hairs on my neck stiffened. The tingling on my skin told me in no uncertain terms I was being watched.

"You didn't kill him."

Iyumi's soft voice at my shoulder brushed my ears and went no further.

"He's up there, isn't he?"

"He's the bait and you're the fox she wants. It's a trap."

"I have to go up there."

"No. You can take this baby far away until the evil dawning has passed. Let the future care for itself. Make the right choice, Flynn."

"There's only one choice for me, Yummy."

"Bloody stupid–Grow up, boy! Your death awaits you if you continue."

I nodded slowly. "I know."

"It's not too late–"

I jerked my head. Buck-Eye pulled her, still protesting, away from me. "Give her the kid," I said, my tone calm though my belly roiled. "Guard her, and ready your weapons. If you're the praying sort, I'd suggest you begin now."

I stepped onto the first stone riser. Then the second. "Dra'agor," I whispered.

A silent shadow amidst the many cast by my flame, Dra'agor appeared from the darkness and leaned against my hip. Though his blood obviously belonged to someone else, his heart was mine. This child of the wild obviously adored Iyumi, for what creature on earth did not? Yet, he freely offered me his loyalty as he would his pack. Though I seldom prayed, I offered up a quick prayer that this furry varmint survived the dawn.

I dropped my hand to Dra'agor's head, and listened to his faint, concerned growl.

"You're my eyes and ears, lad," I whispered. "Lead on."

Swiftly mounting the stairs in front of me, his bushy tail never failed its contact with my belly. As a man's shoulders brushed against each wall, my lads were forced to step up in single file. A swift glance over my shoulder showed me Iyumi bearing the troll in her arms as Buck-Eye politely and sternly urged her upward, his hand on her slim waist.

Around and around the staircase twisted as it rose higher and higher toward the topmost chamber. No arrows hissed through the dark to shut us down. No soldiers rushed down to engage us. No, I didn't think this a god-sent opportunity, that the tower above lay empty save one witch. I knew that whatever awaited us *wanted* us there.

Dra'agor's low growl warned me. I stopped, three or four risers from the top. The stairs ended at a large antechamber, beyond which lay the huge double doors to the north tower room. I raised my hand high, calling on power to increase the flames. Light exploded and shattered the darkness.

Finian grinned down at me, flanked by Commander Blaez and a dozen soldiers. "You're late, boy."

I took another step up. "Been that sort of day. How are you, Father? You look . . .better–since I saw you last."

Embedded deep into his dark flesh were the scars left from Dra'agor's fangs. His right eye gleamed with malicious good humor while the left sagged sharply downward, his eyelid opening only to

[483]

half-mast. His thick upper lip curled into a perpetual sneer and I saw next to nothing of his lower lip. His damaged jaws lay hidden under his beard. No handsome, heavy black growth covered his face these days. What didn't lie as bare and ragged furrows, as naked as an earthworm, was crisped in white. As though touched by the frost. Or evil incarnate.

He shrugged and tried a smile but bared his teeth instead. Several were missing, I noticed. "Can't complain. Did you bring the sacrifice?"

"Of course. How's Mother? Fainche?"

"You've no need to worry about them, boy," Finian replied, his scarred brow lowering. "You should be concerned with keeping your own skin intact."

Dra'agor growled low in his throat, his fangs gleaming in the firelight. Though I rested my hand on his head, hoping to offer calm, he didn't respond in kind. Instead, his teeth clicked together several times in sharp snaps, menace oozing from his aura not unlike Blaez's sweat gushing from his pores.

Finian pointed his long finger down at my friend, his scowl deepening. "By noon, my tanners will be curing that beast's hide."

His upper lip curled. "I'll have a wolf skin to warm my feet come the winter."

"Dead men don't care if they've warm feet, Pa," I sneered. "Come the noon, your corpse will feed the moat's reptiles their lunch."

I flicked my magic and sent the flame high, spreading its light throughout the chamber. Finian made no indication he felt surprise at this display of power. At his side, no weapon in his hand, Blaez watched me. His pudgy face, devoid of all expression, told me far more than open anger or hate. That he fully intended to fight with his other weapons informed me my noble father not just knew of them, he approved. I focused on the men behind them. Typical of my sire, he chose men with brawn but not much thinking ability. Though they'd fight without panicking, none had an original thought among them. I hadn't quite decided if that worked for or against me.

[484]

With both hands on my sword hilt, I took another step up, Dra'agor at my hip. He never stopped his deep-throated rumbling growl. Behind me, blocked by my body, I heard Boden's bowstring creak in the stillness. Good lad. Although we faced an uphill battle against a superior force, a couple of good bowmen might even the odds.

"Tell you what," Finian said, grimacing more than grinning. "Give me the girl and I'll let you live."

My lip curled. "How about I keep the girl and *not* let you live?"

The grin faltered. "You can't win here, boy. Should you kill me, now, she still has your loved ones to hostage. Surrendering is your only hope of keeping them, and yourself, alive."

"You've always underestimated me, Father. You've never given me much credit."

"I beat you, boy. You're no swordsman. I had you dead to rights until yon mongrel saved you."

I grinned, unsheathing my blade and stepping higher, on the balls of my feet. "Ah, but I've learned so much since then. Are you prepared then, Pa? Have you made your peace with the gods?"

"You're nothing more than a royal coward," he sneered. "Run, boy, run and hide. There's no fight in you."

I watched for it, saw it for what it was. Blaez stiffened. That was their pre-arranged signal. Finian just ordered Blaez to cut me down, and his men would decimate mine. I read his intent in his eyes. Blaez readied his own powers, preparing to set me on fire. He'd always loved fire. With me and my lads dead in our own blood, he'd seize Iyumi, and turn the troll child over to his Red mistress. I didn't have to look into his brain to know what he'd do to Iyumi. He'd rape her over and over, merciless.

Unleashing a fist of raw, black power, I hurled it, not at Finian, but at Blaez. *Take out the most powerful first,* I'd been taught, *kill the biggest threat.* My magic, shaped into an iron mace, complete with razor-tipped spikes, rushed from my upraised fingers toward him. Though I felt tempted to keep it invisible, prevent him from seeing it, I *wanted* him to see it. I desired most to see the panic fill his muddy eyes, and witness him witness his own death approaching at roughly the speed of sound.

At the last second, Blaez realized I didn't attack my father, as he fully expected me to do. He recognized my intention to take him out first. With a tight cry, he tried to raise a swift shield, his fingers up and moving into shaping the necessary spell. It rose to protect him a nanosecond too late. My spiked mace struck him at chest level and knocked him backwards, crashing into the arms of the soldiers. They knew better than to catch him, and let him fall to the floor, dead or unconscious. Dark blood coursed from his eyes, nose and mouth, his body twitching spasmodically.

Finian raised disbelieving eyes from his friend's body to meet mine. "You bastard."

"Why, Father," I simpered, feigning astonishment. "Surely you and Mother were married when you first stuck her with your sword."

Finian roared as he whipped his blade from its sheath. He lunged, as quick as a striking snake. In attacking downhill, so to speak, he did so off-balance and awkward. A man less enraged might be wiser to hold the high ground and force me to come to him. As it was, I merely avoided his blade and his attack by stepping aside.

Finian recognized his error and amended it in a flash. A less adept swordsman might fall to his death at the hands and steel of my men. Finian turned on a toe and deftly avoided the trap he almost fell into. Now he forced me to retreat by stabbing his blade toward my heart, catching me off-guard. Once upon a time, I might best a child of nine in a swordsmanship tourney. In his element, Finian's worst day made mincemeat of his opponent's best. Only through sheer luck did I raise my blade high enough to block his blow and send it skidding sideways. Though he hadn't drawn blood, Finian reclaimed his high position. His men gathered around him, hampering his movements.

I had indeed learned a great deal from our last fight. Long talks with Buck-Eye and Boden as we traversed the Shin'Eah Mountains explained to me what I did wrong and what Finian did right. Practice sessions in our evening camps improved my skills enormously. When I bested Buck-Eye, Torass and Boden in a three-on-one practice bout, even Iyumi applauded. As though at last I found the right teachers, I exulted in my swordsmanship and soaked up knowledge like a dry sponge.

Taking my hilt in both hands, I charged upward, hacking at his blade. Forced to give ground, he backed away, cursing his own men and me in the same breath. Swinging hard left, I slashed at my father's blade, forcing him back another step.

Never fight while angry,' Buck-Eye had said. *Anger your enemy instead. Keep him off balance. Focus on his chest. Not his eyes. Never his blade. His chest. His center point will tell you where he plans to move.'*

"Oh," I asked, my voice small. "You two weren't married when I peeped out from between her thighs? For shame. Perhaps some other bastard sired me, for I always doubted I was yours."

Finian grinned, spitting at my feet. "Enya hadn't the guts to cuckold me, boy. You're mine, without a doubt."

His chest blatantly informed me he planned to feint a strike to his right, his sword's tip aimed at my left cheek, then swipe backward to cut across my eyes. My swift counter-measure blocked the feint, and turned his blade hard left and wrenching his wrist in the process. Obviously, he didn't listen to what my chest told him, and failed to realize my riposte went for his jugular.

"Son of a bitch," he spat, jumping backward as my sword's tip sliced his chin instead of his throat.

"Oh? Maligning Mother now? Bad Papa. Very bad."

Easily avoiding his downward stab into my upturned face, I sent his sword sliding past my shoulder with rapturous ease. He gaped in almost comical amazement. I snickered, then halted as another of Buck-Eye's lessons rebounded inside my head. *Save your triumph until your enemy bleeds at your feet. Never assume you've won the fight until the fight is finished. He is reading you as easily as you are reading him.'*

As though recognizing my focus faltered a fraction, Finian attacked with a vigor that left my strength gasping. He almost had me with the two-handed, back-handed blow that should have taken my head off. I ducked, and the razor's edge whistled over my blonde mane. With both hands on his hilt, he left his left side wide open and vulnerable. I countered with a rapid slash to his torso. Of course, he expected me to strike there.

I didn't.

I feinted a blow to his heart, but ducked low instead. My sword's edge sliced through the necessary tendons and muscle of his left thigh. His leg buckled under his weight, and, with a sharp cry, he staggered, unable to put any weight on that leg. His blade drooped. Like a ship without a rudder, he fell back, hot blood gushing down his knee and into his boot. Finian limped around to face me, snarling. His wound pumped that very necessary red stuff as one of his soldiers charged me, screaming an incoherent warcry.

Buck-Eye once more proved his worth as an adept archer. His arrow caught the soldier full in the left eye, slamming him backward to lie still in the stone dust of the slate floor. A second guard screamed a challenge and ran forward, brave and simply stupid. Dra'agor lunged forward, fangs bared. The crony fell to the floor beside his mate, weeping and shouting, his left hamstring bitten through. Boden paused long enough to send an arrow through his pulsing throat, and calmly watched as he gagged to death on his own blood.

'Level the playing field,' Buck-Eye's voice advised. 'Meet your enemy on your ground, not his. Make him pay for every piece of turf he wins.'

Snaking my sword at Finian's face, I leaped up into the antechamber and forced him backward. Limping, snarling, Finian raised his sword to defend himself, but his blows were feeble, desperate. Boden surged upward, at my side, raising his bow. In swift succession, he took down not just one, but three of Finian's soldiers in quick succession. Dra'agor, snarling, launched himself at a burly guard. The man, used to fighting men, tried to defend himself by hacking his sword toward Dra'agor's head. The wolf ducked, and charged forward in the same motion.

I almost faltered in my attack on my father to watch, fascinated, as Dra'agor slashed the poor man's genitals with those wicked fangs. The soldier screamed, his sword dropping to clang on the flagstones. When he bent to clutch himself, Dra'agor leaped up.

[488]

Laying open the poor man's throat, he dashed aside to attack yet another soldier. Having witnessed their brother's very gory death, several stumbled back. That left room for my lads to charge up the stairs and enter the fray.

"Are you through yet?" I inquired politely as Finian fought to keep both sword and legs upright and functioning.

Screaming incoherent threats, Finian charged, his blade high. I ducked under it, and slashed downward. My edge caught his lower leg, severing his hamstring. My sword halted Finian's ability to stand, as he could rely no longer on those interesting tendons one needed to put weight upon. He staggered, his arms flailing, his blade falling to clang, resounding with a metallic zinging sound, to the stone floor.

My foe helpless, for the moment, I ignored him and faced the next, and larger threat, to my life and the lives of my lads. And Iyumi.

"Uh, Boden?" I asked, pointing my left finger at the five or six soldiers bunching together to attack. "Might you, er–"

"Right, right," he answered, his tone casual. "Torass, Lyall, bows to the fore."

With an almost offhand manner, Boden nocked his arrow to his bowstring and raised his bow. Likewise, Lyall and Torass stood to his left and right, aiming at the tight group of stupidly brave soldiers who lifted their swords in preparation to charge. With half my attention on him, I knew Finian retrieved his sword, but as he had staggered behind the protective line of burly men bearing his royal insignia on their mantles, I couldn't exactly kill him just then.

I rested for a moment, leaning on my sword as the King's voice ripped across the small antechamber. "Kill them!"

His loyal guard roared their challenge and charged, six against four. No doubt their superior size and numbers would win the day. That my lads pointed lethal arrows tipped with razor barbs at their armor mattered little to them. Their steel breastplates protected them, of course. Forget that at such range, perhaps two rods at most, those steel heads easily punched through the heaviest armor.

My lads wouldn't *dare* aim at the vulnerable and exposed face or throat of His Majesty's loyal bodyguard. Of course they wouldn't.

Three bows twanged. Boden's arrow took his target through the eye, dropping him to the stone floor instantly, on his back. A lone trickle of blood oozed down his cheek, along his nose and dripped across his throat. Torass's barb struck his man deep in his throat. Choking, gasping, the soldier fell, trying in vain to yank his death from his gushing neck, his mouth working. No sound emerged to follow the panic in the man's eyes. He died, his hand still trying to pull the arrow out, as though that might keep him alive.

Lyall's arrow bounced off his target's cheekbone, cutting deep but without lethal damage. The soldier cursed, bleeding, and continued his charge with his sword high. Lyall swore fluent and very creative oaths as he frantically nocked another arrow to his bowstring and aimed. He failed to move fast enough. Dra'agor, concerned that the soldier closed in too closely on me for his comfort, lunged in to rectify Lyall's mistake.

His tremendous weight struck the man dead center and brought him, screaming, to the slate tile floor. My father's brave guardsman screamed in horror as jaws strong enough to break an elk's neck fastened on his face. The man's trousers darkened at the crotch as his bladder let go, his heels drumming a swift beat on the slate. Vicious fangs tore open his throat even as the soldier tried valiantly to stab Dra'agor through his chest. But swords at that angle didn't work very well. Its edge sliced a thin, bloody vein across Dra'agor's shoulder and went no further. My noble friend leapt aside as his victim squirmed and thrashed, bleeding out like the sacrificial lamb on the altar.

"Sorry," Lyall muttered, his eyes sliding toward me in shame and embarrassment.

"Don't force it," I said, my tone light. I rested my hand on his broad, muscular shoulder. "Just relax your fingers, Lyall. Your arrow knows where it belongs. Trust it."

"Yes, m'lord."

Bleeding profusely, on his feet through sheer stubbornness, Finian bellowed. Only two men remained to guard his royal self, but his rage and panic forced him into attacking outside his comfort

[490]

zone. The sound reminded me of a bull in rut as he raised his blade in a two-handed grip, high over his head. Avoiding the corpses on the floor, Finian charged, his intent clear. Kill me and all will be well again in Raithin Mawrn.

Is he serious? I raised my own blade in preparation.

He was totally serious. His wicked sword swung toward my head forced me into a swift duck and shoulder roll. His sword whisked across my scalp by several inches. Those nasty laws of physics trapped his blade into careening past his own path of no return. He couldn't possibly recover in time. I knew he knew. I read it in his deep-set eyes, his grimace of despair. In that same instant, I struck deep and wrenched in one fluid motion.

My razor-tipped steel tip plunged deep into his heart, twisting, merciless, separating his precious life from his body. I yanked my blade free and stepped back. Purple-red blood poured from his chest wound, soaking his royal tunic and trailing freely down his cloak. Though I brought him to his destiny's door, he yet tried to fight. The firelight glinted off his blade. I raised my own, tense, waiting for him to spring like a lion upon a hapless, unwary deer.

He was dead. I know he was. But he hadn't realized the facts facing him, stubborn as he was. Still on his feet, his blade lax in his hand even as he gazed at me, confused. Stumbling forward, he slashed downward. I sidestepped.

Come on, die already. That's not battle. It's like shooting fish in a frozen pond. I lowered my blade and watched, fascinated.

Finian's face drained of all color. Tripping over the corpses of his men, he yet maintained his questionable footing. Finian staggered past me, toward the stairs. Concerned about his bared sword and Iyumi, I swung around. Iyumi, calm and ruthless, reached out a slender foot. Finian tripped over it. He screamed as he fell down the steep stair way, bouncing down the merciless stone steps. When his scream suddenly choked off, I knew his neck had snapped.

I eyed her sidelong. "Is he dead now?"

Iyumi nodded. "Of course."

"About bloody time."

Saluting Iyumi with a quick grin and my sword, I turned back to the fight. I learned so much about fighting, had defeated the champion of champions, I poised to fight the next wannabe. None accepted my mute challenge. I almost sighed, annoyed. With such efficient men, I might not have someone to kill. Ever again.

"He's dead," Iyumi said from behind me, her voice triumphant. "We can turn back now, Flynn. Your family is safe. He can't harm them now, right?"

I spun around, my high spirits crumbling into bitter ash. "I wish we could, Princess. You remember what he said. Even if I killed him, the Witch still holds them hostage. I have no choice. *We* have no choice."

I turned my back as the fear Iyumi once held back filled her eyes. I didn't want to witness her fall into hopelessness, see her rebellious soul break open and bleed. She knew what awaited us inside that room. While I wanted nothing more than to obey her, *believe* her, take the kid and run back down the stairs, I dared not. For what if she was wrong? What if Enya, Fainche and Sofia were held captive, but alive, behind those doors? How could I abandon them to their evil fate? That slender chance, that tiny hope in my heart, spurned Iyumi's fear and forced me forward. They *had* to be alive. For without them, I am, and forever will be, nothing.

I drew in a ragged breath and tried to focus on the problem at hand. Two of my sire's loyal brutes remained alive. Their eyes alternating in frantic haste between the corpses, the blood and the wolf, they lowered their steel. Swords fell with ringing clangs to the stonework at their feet. Raising their hands high, the frightened soldiers dropped to their knees.

"Please, sir," one begged. "We surrender."

"Don't kill us, m'lord," the other whined. "We'll swear loyalty to you, m'lord."

"Oh, please. You're so full of shit, you squeak."

The pair glanced at one another, confused.

"Oh, I know you plan to stab me in the back," I said, my tone confident, controlled. "Your loyalty is for the birds, in truth. With my father dead, you'd swear obeisance to the highest bidder. Unfortunately, for you, I ain't bidding."

[492]

My lads covered them with their bows, their rapid glances toward me asked permission to fire. I flicked my hand, staying them. I strolled toward the nervous pair, Dra'agor licking his bloody lips as he paced at my side.

"Want to live?" I asked. My free hand on my hip, I pointed my sword's tip at the whiner's throat and tipped his head up to meet my eyes.

"Yes, Your Highness," the big soldier on my right whispered. His pal only nodded, tears swimming in his huge brown eyes.

"Here's the deal. You both pick up your blades, and sheath them. With your hands on your heads, you leave now. This day. Should I catch you within the borders of Raithin Mawrn, I'll hang you by your ankles. And set loose the starving dogs."

I leaned toward them, my steel kissing their throats. "Am I clear?"

"Y-yes, Y-your Highness," the whiner said.

"C-crystal, s-sir," the other added.

I relaxed my stance. "Get lost."

The pair scrambled to obey, slipping on the blood of their companions and their King. Sheathing their blades while trying to bow at the same time, they skittered sideways like frightened colts, edging around me and Dra'agor's hulking presence. My lads made no move save keep their arrows trained on them as they saluted, sweat pouring down their faces. I didn't turn around as their hobnail boots clumped down the stairs, at first walking then speeding up to a run. The echoes drifted upward for several long moments after the sound of their flight vanished.

I glanced at Iyumi, crouched by the stairs, watching the doors into the inner chamber. She still held the quiet infant close to her chest, her pale face impassive. During the fight, she could have fled back down the stairs. I jerked my head at Buck-Eye, silently ordering him to his duty. *Protect her.* With a quick nod, he helped her to stand, and urged her forward behind Boden, Lyall and Torass.

The floor ran red with blood. Filled from one end to the other with corpses, the chamber reeked of death and shit and piss. Dra'agor whined, his tone low, as though asking a question.

[493]

"Let's finish this," I said, my voice soft.

My sword in hand, unmindful of the dead and the blood, I strode toward the double doors.

I kicked them open.

As the great oak doors swung wide to crash against the stone walls, I noticed two things at once. Through the huge glass wall, the sun had risen. At its side, inching closer to its red-gold glory, a black ball also rose. Its hideous edge stained the sun, creeping closer on its journey. Within moments, that blackness would steal across the sun's face and the moment of the dark power would come. White, savage lightning flickered across the orb, almost obliterating the new daylight. Outside the tower, the wind rose and howled. Crashing thunder couldn't quite mask the sound of the tempest.

In the same instant, I saw my mother.

She stood at the glass wall, staring out at the monstrosity outside. Her back to us, she never flinched in neither shock nor fear at the sound of our entrance. Her hands slowly lifted from her sides to rise above her head. Her silken gown trailed from her hands as though she'd grown wings. "My son," she murmured. "I knew you'd not fail me."

"Mother–" I began, but choked off.

Slowly, ever so slowly, Enya turned. She smiled. Those eyes I worshipped, no longer crystal blue, glowed garnet in the light of the hearth fire. Long lush tresses cloaked her, a burial shroud, pouring down her shoulders to her hips. Her hands, still high above her head, dripped red. Blood coated her from nails to elbows, her pristine cream and gold gown sewed with lace and precious seed pearls was splashed with gore.

"What–" *happened*, I started to ask.

Dull amazement struck me numb. "She was right," I muttered, hoarse. My voice didn't sound like mine. I cleared my throat and tried again. "She's right about you. I didn't believe her. But it's true, isn't it? You're the Red Witch, the demon's whore. Aren't you– Mother?"

Chiming laughter tinkled from the red slash, formerly her lovely smile, in her face. "What a clever boy you are. To have figured it all out by yourself."

[494]

"I wish–"

Then I saw the corpses.

"Glory," Buck-Eye muttered.

"Flynn," Iyumi said, her voice rising high. "Don't."

What I wished for escaped my brain as the sight shorted out my tongue. Like butchered lambs, they lay piled against the wall to my left. Tough leather thongs bound their hands in front of them. Their royal gowns of silk and cloth of gold were drenched in dripping black. Heart's blood. Once purple, now stained with the darkness of death. Twin sets of glazed eyes stared into nothing, their last sight a horror not of this world.

In the room's center, still dripping fresh blood, stood a stone table. The demon's altar. On the blazing hearth cooked two blackened pieces of meat. I didn't need to know how I knew–I knew what those things were. Their hearts burned there, the living sacrifice to the dark gods who ruled the underworld. In scenting the evil, the disgusting rot, my belly roiled.

I knew them. I knew them both. I knew their pale beloved faces. I'd stroked my hand down their cheeks, held them in my arms, brushed their silken hair. I loved them both with every beat of my soul. I fell to my knees, feeling beyond sick. *Gods, gods, bring them back! Where are they? Bring them back. Bring them back!*

My plunging heart shut off all hope of breath as I collapsed further, onto my hands. I wanted to vomit. I tried to vomit, for if I could purge the horror out my throat then it might no longer plague my guts.

Fainche's dead eyes stared at me, her breast cut open. I couldn't look away from her filmed blue eyes. They didn't accuse me. Oh, no, Fainche loved me. She'd never accuse me of deserting her in her hour of need. She forgave all, even the merciless bitch who murdered her. Her heart burned not with her love for me, but on the whore's fire. She'd been tossed aside like so much garbage. I think that hurt me the most. She'd been used, then cast aside–a broken tool, no longer useful. That offhand carelessness is probably what kept me from curling up on the floor and weeping like a child.

Much as a leak in a dam eventually breaks the stones apart, a trickle of rage seeped into my soul.

Sofia lay on her back in an ocean of blood, her sightless eyes staring at the ceiling. Enya hadn't just cut out her heart. Her belly lay wide open, gutted like a doe. On the floor beside her lay a small red thing. It looked somewhat like a soft waterskin, lumpy and oozing. I had no idea what that could be–until I saw the tiny hand.

I hurled everything my belly contained onto the blood-soaked floor.

"Oh, good, she's here." Enya's voice crept, bereft of any emotion, into my ears. As I vomited again and again, helpless on the slate tiles, she drifted toward the blood-soaked stone in the center of the room. "Place the child on the altar, Flynn, there's a good boy."

Control yourself, you fool. Get up, get up now.

I slowly rose from my knees, spitting the sour taste of vomit from my mouth. I staggered a step, then another, toward her, my tears wet on my cheeks. "Why would you slaughter your own daughter? Your own *daughter?*"

High laughter answered my question. "For power, boy. What else?"

"Fainche was *innocent.*"

"Of course she was, dear. Innocence is the most sacred of sacrifices."

"You murdered my wife, my son. My *son!*"

Enya sighed. "Good gods, Flynn, are you that simple? You didn't love Sofia, you never have. And you can sire other sons. On yonder maiden, for instance, should you so choose."

Her voice lowered, turned sensual, as her tongue emerged to caress her upper lip. Her reddish eyes glowed with–damn it, I couldn't believe it–lust. Yes, she stared at me with an expression no mother on this world should ever have for her son. As I gaped, my belly roiling for another round of heaving, she caressed her own with her slender hand.

"Or on me."

"Devil's whore!" Iyumi screamed from somewhere behind me. "You'd corrupt your own son?"

"I already have, dear," Enya purred. "Think of it, Flynn. You ruling the world at my side. Both of us, supreme in our power. The gods will tremble at the sound of our footsteps. Our sons will live forever!"

In rapid succession, two loud booms rose from outside. The castle floor vibrated from the impact. Enya glanced at the ceiling, her fair brows lowering, as though confused. My mind registered their meaning just as the stray thought collided with my grief.

Keep her attention on you.

"What was that?" Boden muttered.

"The drawbridges," I answered, my mouth numb. "They just came down."

"That means–"

"Invasion."

Enya half-turned toward the great window as though intending to investigate the noise. The black moon inched across the red sun, devouring its glory. Lightning flickered across its evil face, thunder shattering the dawn and rattling the window glass in its pane. Under the onslaught of the terrifying wind, the north tower creaked like an old gentleman's joints and swayed ever so slightly. *Surely it wouldn't collapse.*

"Who was it I sacrificed that night, Mother?"

She turned away from the spectacle. Enya's chortle vibrated with the sound resonating through the slate under my feet. "One of Finian's by-blows," she answered, her head tilted back as her laughter rippled forth. "He never was the faithful type."

Keep her talking.

I tilted my head to the right, catching her fiercely happy gaze. "Finias was my brother?"

"Half-brother, dear. Only half."

"You told me the mother died."

"Oh, she did, Flynn," Enya cackled. "She died, screaming, under my knife."

"You forced me to murder my own *brother?* You told me he was already dying!"

[497]

"Oh, Flynn, dear." Enya laughed, as though at a great joke. "A sacrifice means nothing unless it means something. You should know that, silly boy. Sacrifice only the useful, that's what the gods demand. Place an already dead chicken on the fire and you are scorned. But place the heart of your kin on the brazier–then the world is yours."

"Only your demons from hell crave sacrifice, bitch," Iyumi screamed from Buck-Eye's side near the doors. "The gods deny you."

"Shut her up, Flynn," Enya said, her laughter stilled, her tone bored.

"You'll not harm her," I said, circling around my mother with my sword bared, slowly stalking her. "Nor that child."

She kept her eyes on me, a slight frown on her fair brows. "Don't be foolish, boy. Once I sacrifice that child to the dark arts, all the power of the world shall be mine. You'll rule at my side. Think of it! Mother and son. None shall ever overthrow us, until the end of days."

I clenched my jaw, but stepped lightly on balanced feet. I gripped my sword in both hands, readying. "The end of days has arrived, Mother. You lose."

Remember your oath.

What oath?

Should I ever lift my hand against her in hatred, may the gods strike me dead.'

I remembered. What I said in that evil clearing not so long ago, in the moments before I took an innocent boy's life. When I believed in her. When I trusted her. When I loved her beyond my own life. *I swore that oath, yes. Take my life if you choose, good gods, but this day the Red Bitch dies for her crimes. If you think ill of me for it, then the hell with you. If you agree I was mistaken, and wronged, then help me send her where she belongs.*

"The gods have cursed your soul," Iyumi shouted, clutching the troll tight. From behind Buck-Eye's bulk, she half-turned, placing her slender body between Enya and the baby. As though that might prevent Enya from taking the troll from her.

"The gods fear me, child. I'm more powerful than they."

[498]

Enya, smiling, her lips a dark red slash in her face, didn't quite dare turn her back on me. Behind her the sun's golden glows drowned under the whipping lightning, the dark advance of the moon. Thunder crashed over the sound of the horrible wind. The time of the evil supremacy had arrived. Her eyes glowed, not just with fanaticism, but with a strange hellish tinge. That same hue I noticed when she brought Dra'agor to me. The blood sacrifices to her demons brought her a strength I knew I couldn't match.

Enya snapped her fingers. "Slave," she cooed, catching Dra'agor's attention. "Fetch me that child now. Bring it to me."

Cold cascaded down my spine. *Dra agor.* The blood binding. Iyumi told me to free him, said I had the power, but I hadn't. I didn't know how. The Bitch held him in thrall, and despite his love for me and Iyumi, he had no choice but to obey her. His head and ears low, his legs stiff, Dra'agor advanced toward Iyumi. Whining, growling low in his throat, he shot a half-glance toward me, as his body obeyed my mother's command against his will. He'd take the baby from Iyumi's arms, I knew, and place it on the demon's blood-drenched altar.

Iyumi stared at him as he stalked forward, her eyes wide and wild. "Free him, Flynn!" she cried. "Free him! You know how!"

An arrow shot past my shoulder and buried itself in Enya's chest. Though I hadn't ordered the attack, I liked smart men about me. I paid them handsomely for their ability to think on their feet. I might be as useless as tits on a boar, in my grief, yet my lads knew how to protect me.

Unfortunately, Boden's arrow had as much effect as an annoying fly. Enya frowned, her expression vague, and plucked the arrow's barb from her flesh. No blood seeped from the wound to stain her already bloody royal gown. She snapped the arrow in half over her fingers and scowled.

"Idiot," she murmured. "Now you've gone and done it."

"Boden," I yelled. "Run."

He turned, panic etched across his pale features, and bolted for the doors I kicked in. Enya's burst of flame cut him down before he reached them. He screamed as he burned, his intaken breath

[499]

sucking superheated air into his lungs. Fire burned him from the inside out as his eyes boiled in their sockets. His flesh melted even as he screamed without sound.

Buck-Eye, Torass and Lyall bolted in all directions. Though he fled the burning flame of his friend, Buck-Eye at least dragged Iyumi and the troll with him. As my loyal navigator died, dancing like a flaming marionette, I used the distraction he provided. *Forgive me, Boden.*

Before Boden fell, falling upon his black face, I attacked. Even as Enya smiled upon her handiwork, momentarily forgetting I stood within range of her throat, I swung my sword. Cat-quick, she spun, her hand rising, her power reaching for me. Pity she didn't realize I'd anticipate that. Her hellish power splashed across my magical shield, leaving me unharmed and still lunging, aiming to split her face into halves.

The Red Witch screamed in inarticulate fury, ducking out from under my sword. Swinging my blade in a backhand, I slashed again at her head, but this time it clashed against a sword of her own.

"Foolish boy," she spat, growling like a panther.

"Hell-bitch," I grated.

Though she didn't have much experience fighting with a sword, she did have evil on her side. She fought like a demon in truth, but all I wanted was time. If I could keep her busy until the black moon passed, perhaps her powers might wan. Or until I thought of a brilliant method of killing her.

"Wolf!" she screamed. "Bring me that baby!"

All but forgotten in our battle, Dra'agor had halted in his advance on Iyumi. My mother's will had turned from him, permitting him a small respite. But as her power surged and recaptured him, he continued his reluctant advance on the princess and the sacrificial child. He loved Iyumi. He'd never, under his own will, ever harm her. But now, under the Witch's evil compulsion, he'd rip her throat should she deny him that baby.

"Flynn!" Iyumi screamed, clutching the crying troll to her meager bosom.

You can free him, she told me.

I don t know how.

[500]

Yes, you do. Think about it.

Magical spells needed time and some degree of concentration to work effectively. My mother was determined not to give me that time. I fought off her attempt to cut my head from my shoulders with a flaming sword she didn't hold in her hands. I countered it with an ice cold axe that struck her red-orange blade into glittering shards. Enya halted a fraction of an instant, a moment I took full advantage of. My axe swung toward her head, forcing her backward. I might be a greenhorn when it came to a battle of magic and willpower, but so was she. She absorbed the power of evil, but she hadn't practiced much. My father beat some military ability into me, and though I wasn't the greatest swordsman in Raithin Mawrn, I was the champion archer.

Instantly creating a flaming bow, I spun a dozen blazing arrows from nothing. Nocking one after the other, I shot them into her, my hands a blur. Boden's wooded arrow and steel tip affected her not at all. Mine, however, burned with my evil power and hurt her deeply. She screamed as each tip buried itself into her slender body, their flames catching on her flesh, her clothes, her hair. If left to their own devices, my flames might yet burn her to ashes. But I wasn't so naïve as all that. I gained a few precious moments to regroup, and that was all.

Free him! Before it s too late.

In driving Enya back, trying to extinguish my fires, I halted. I permitted my fiery bow to vanish, concentrating. Iyumi said I knew how and I trusted her. Break the blood-binding. Free Dra'agor. *Damn it! I don t know how!* I thought back to how the blood-binding worked. The Witch took the blood of her victim, mixed it with her own, and then drank it. The victim's essence, and will, became hers. How do I change it back? Give Dra'agor his blood back? Was it really that simple?

Hurry.

Forcing myself to ignore the tempest outside the tower, the black moon encompassing the sun's face, and the imminent threat of my mother, I bowed my head. Stretching my fingers toward my friend, my Dra'agor, I concentrated. I shut my eyes. I called forth on the deep well of knowledge my mother herself gave me. Though she intended for me to commit great evil with it, I knew, that if I so chose, I could also create great good.

The words came unbidden to my lips. I spoke them, the language of the gods. The language of old, our Mother Tongue. *Asai ai makam, bekan azam. Uharkan, ma harani! Ekananai! Depart thing of evil. Depart, and come no more. Obey!*

I clenched my will, and twisted my fist. I felt it yield. I felt its fear. Under my command, something fled, wailing into the new dawn, free and helpless and frightened. The sound of its final cry echoed across the chamber and shook the stone walls of the castle. I hadn't known the spell of the blood binding was so powerful until that moment. If its passing shook the physical world with such power, how did it affect the underworld?

I didn't have long to wait.

Enya's scream of sheer agony ripped across the tower room. She dropped to her knees, weakened, vulnerable, opened to my attack. A huge wind, manifested in a swirling twister, blew everything not nailed down into a swift tempest. It collided with the glass pane of the east wall, and fractured it. A spider-web of slender cracks emanated from its center toward every angle in its delicate frame.

In the same instant, Dra'agor not just halted his stiff-legged advance on Iyumi, he drew in a deep breath and let it out in a long, drawn-out howl of both relief and triumph. He spun around, free, his amber-brown eyes clear and his ears flat. His lips skinned back from his teeth. With Enya's tender throat his target, he lunged toward her with his hind claws digging deep furrows in the blue slate tiles of the tower.

"Uh, sorry, lad," I muttered, my fingers raised.

I halted his feral rush with a simple spell. I blocked his charge and permitted him to crash full onto my shield with his head. Falling back, dazed, Dra'agor staggered upright, his paws sliding out from under him. Had I understood his mixture of whines and growls, I'd suspect he cursed under his breath. *Bloody stupid humans.*

"You can't kill her," I snapped, pointing toward Iyumi and the babe. "I need you there. Protect them!"

[502]

Growling, his hackles raised and ears flattened, he shot me a dark glance. He obeyed me. Not out of evil compulsion, but out of the realization I was right: should he attack Enya, she'd set his fur ablaze, and in dying, he couldn't protect his lady. Stalking, stiff-legged, his tail a tough bristle cone behind him, he snarled and grumbled his way to Iyumi. She greeted him with a small cry and threw her manacled hands around his heavy neck. Buck-Eye stood over her, his sword in hand, his obvious courage and strong loyalty overruling his panic. I knew he wanted to throw down his weapon and run. I saw it in his fear-sweat, his huge eyes.

Torass, calm and determined, crouched with blade drawn in the open doorway. Lyall stalked to Buck-Eye's left, his arrow nocked and his bowstring pulled halfway to his chin, his narrowed eyes on Enya. Gold alone didn't earn that kind of loyalty. Any fool could pay with good money with less risk involved. They didn't decamp, and leave me to my fate, upon discovering what they truly faced in that tower room. How did I find such dedicated men? How did I earn such devotion? I didn't know, but right then wasn't the exact time to make polite inquiries.

"Now then," I said, my tone genial as I turned back to Enya. "Where were we?"

Didn't Buck-Eye drill into my foolish head that arrogance can kill? She recovered faster than I'd estimated and I suddenly faced her raw fury, her devil's eyes tightened to mere slits. Her sudden burst of power didn't intend to kill me. No, it sent both me and my shield across the room to strike the wall, left shoulder first. I felt it snap upon impact. I felt no immediate pain, but I was dazed, my breath knocked from my chest. *This isn't good,* I half-thought, struggling to rise. If I didn't stop her, she'd murder both Iyumi and the troll on her black altar. Then she'll turn her blade on me.

I didn't care if I died. All I ever lived for had gone before me. *Kill me if you must, great gods, but, please, I beg you, let me take her with me. All I ask. Let me take her with me.*

The moon all but covered the sun outside. Clouds boiled as the lightning and thunder crashed around the tower. I fancied I saw cat-like eyes peering in from that hellish moon, eyes watching and gloating. But perhaps that was nothing more than spots flashing in my eyes. *Get up, fool. You don t need a shoulder to stand. Nor is it necessary in this particular battle.*

Dropping her blackened sword, Enya ran toward Iyumi. Buck-Eye tried to put his body between her and the approaching Witch, but he didn't stand an icicle's chance in hell's fires. She sent him flying against the wall as easily as she'd throw a straw doll. Likewise, Torass and Lyall were hurtled into unyielding stone. Iyumi tried to run, sheltering the screaming baby with her body. Dra'agor, snarling like a demented demon, planted himself squarely in Enya's path.

Thunder crashed as the ferocious wind rocked the tower in gentle yet alarming sways. Through my frantic attempts to get up and shoot another flaming arrow into her back, I heard heavy pounding. *The roof is caving in,* I thought with morbid humor. *Let s bury her alive.*

Enya faltered in her pursuit, skidding to a halt. The small door that led to the balcony where Kings of old stood to signal their allies shattered like a stick house. *What the–*Those heavy doors, layered three thick and reinforced with iron had repulsed an attacking force time and again. So what could bring them down now? When the figure draped in shadow stepped through the flying splinters, I choked on my shock and grinned in the same instant. I'll be damned–

Van didn't hesitate. Armed with a sword that burned red, he attacked Enya with blade and more power than I could ever hope to have. Cloaked from throat to heel in black, his shaggy hair blew back from his face as he grimaced in effort and fury. His body between the Witch and his beloved, Van slashed and stabbed, driving Enya ever backward. His boots struck sparks from the slate floor as a strange, pale gold nimbus swirled over his dark head.

Taken quite by surprise, Enya defended herself by lobbing balls of living flame. Almost contemptuous, Van sent every one wide with sweeps of his deadly blade. As though coated in ice, his blazing sword killed her fire and sent smoking husks to strike the stone walls of the tower. He advanced with every snap; his emerald eyes slitted. His face a mask of cold fury and concentration, he drove her ever backward.

Enya gave ground, scrambling away from both his menace and Van's vast magic. Desperate fear snaked across her marble features, her reddish lips parted as she panted in both exhaustion and panic. As fireball after fireball struck his blade and bounded harmless across the slate floor, her demeanor altered from its previous arrogance and imitated the same expression a rabbit might have when trapped in the hunter's snare. And listened as the hunter approached.

Snarling in an eerie imitation of Dra'agor, Enya changed tactics. Exploding like a crystal, she sent deadly shards of herself arrowing straight into Van's face and neck. I winced, staggering to my feet, my shoulder busted and my breath short. *Surely she had him on that one.* But Van wasn't a Shifter for nothing. His body dropped instantly, pooling like a raindrop on tile, spreading. Her deadly razor shards fled harmlessly past him, struck the stone wall, and rebounded with a whistling noise. Faster than I could see, she reformed herself behind him.

Like a puppet, Van bounced back up, his vulnerable back exposed to attack. Enya pounced. Her mouth wide open, her teeth gleaming redly under the light of the fire, she rushed his undefended rear. Black evil shrouded her, her fists pumping with every step forward as she hurled a swath of death at Van. I knew she'd hit him with it. I knew he didn't know what she planned. She charged toward him, hands hooked into claws and raising them to slam his ass into the next world—

—and stumbled, and nearly fell headlong to the floor.

Van wasn't there.

Awkwardly trying to regain her balance, Enya's arms pinwheeled, helpless. That's when the small falcon screamed. It's voice echoed throughout the chamber, drowning beneath it the howling wing and booming thunder. Through the glass, the moon had almost come full circle. A small fraction of the sun still gleamed amid the dark clouds and stabbing lightning.

Straight into her face Van flew, talons wide. This time, it was Enya who screamed in agony, in terror. Van's razor-tipped talons ripped her pale skin into shreds, cut her once beautiful blue eyes, and slashed that devil's mouth to ribbons. Blood poured out from under Van's flapping wings. *Oh, hell, yes. A blind Bitch is a helpless Bitch.*

Reality sucked rocks, in truth. Van's awesome power couldn't defend against the hands that gripped his small falcon and tear his claws from her face. He might have power that outstripped hers, but he was yet vulnerable to the simpler problems of life. Such as tight fingers gripping a tiny feathered body hard enough to split asunder his spine, his ribs, his wings and his life.

Oh, crap. There goes our best bet in keeping our lands safe from a hellcat. You tried though, Vanyar my lad. That's your epitaph: 'I tried.'

Shrieking like a young girl upon finding a fat black spider on her gown, Enya threw the bird into the blazing hearth. Still screaming, she lunged, half-blind and blood pouring from her lacerated face, toward Iyumi. She'll get that child onto her altar, she still had time, I was too far away, injured, and Van–Van was dead.

A fierce, snarling shadow, Dra'agor launched himself at Enya, clearly aiming to bring her down. For a wild moment, I thought he might actually succeed where Van and I failed. His jaws gaping, his ears flattened, he rose on his hind legs, lunging for her throat.

Enya swatted him like an annoying insect. Her backhanded swing caught him across his heavy neck with all her evil might behind the blow. Dra'agor's head snapped sideways, and his body followed. Tossed like a rag doll, he slid across the bloody floor as though on grease to land in a heap by the window. Unconscious or dead, I'd no idea, but he didn't move.

Her teeth dripping gore as she grinned, Enya in turn pounced on Iyumi.

Iyumi dodged aside, neatly avoiding those sweeping, bloody hands. Keeping her body between that of the baby and my mother, Iyumi twisted, and snapped first left then right as she bolted around that north chamber. Enya followed after, shrieking in inarticulate rage, but Iyumi stayed just out of harm's way. For a few moments, anyhow.

Enya halted, furious, and realized chasing the slender girl more nimble than she was as useless as dodging raindrops. "Stupid girl," she hissed, as her power seized Iyumi, held her still.

Iyumi, and the baby troll, hung a rod off the slate tile floor, helpless. Iyumi watched her advance with ill-concealed panic as Enya swiped blood and gore from her face. Her bloody lips stretched into a thin red line below her pale nose. Her demon's eyes glowed hotter than last's night's sunset. "C'mere, now," she crooned, laughter bubbling like a cauldron. "I won't hurt you. I promise."

"Stay back," Iyumi warned, clutching the baby close. "I'm warning you."

"Warn this," Enya chuckled, offering Iyumi that sign.

The baby cried and squirmed, unhappy with its current situation. Panicked, unable to either run or protect herself and the innocent in her arms, Iyumi watched her come. She recoiled, cringing, her blue eyes blasting the defiance her words could never utter.

"Got you now, bitch," my mother snarled, her bloody hands reaching for the bundle of nasty rags.

Iyumi back-handed Enya with her manacled hands clenched together, her teeth clenched and her once tidy braid unraveled. Enya's head snapped back. Hard. With so much blood covering her face, I couldn't tell if the blow cut yet another gouge in the many cuts from Van's talons already bleeding there. Despite all, Enya recoiled fast. Her returning strike flattened Iyumi. She released her controlling power at the same instant. The princess, half-stunned, fell onto her back from a rod up, her eyes rolling back into their sockets. Blood splashed across her pale cheeks and wet her silver-gilt hair.

Enya snatched up the squalling infant with a demonic scream of triumph. She turned toward her smoking and bloody altar. *Shit.* I struggled to rise, my shoulder on fire. *Must stop her. She mustn't kill that child.* In desperation, I concocted a black spear from air and flung it across the tower chamber. It struck Enya dead to right, vanishing within her blood-splashed gown.

Though my magic weapon didn't kill or stop her, I know it hurt her. As though half-blind, or confused, Enya staggered. If she kept to her present course, she'd miss the altar by a rod. She corrected herself, and stumbled again. Darkness spread up her gown, scurried across her waist and gleefully jumped over her bosom to consume her pale neck and blacken her once gold-washed hair.

But whose evil would win?

She struggled to counter the evil power I stole with the black magic she contrived through blood sacrifice. Black versus black. My strength stood equal to hers, nor could she easily throw it back at me without harming herself. My legs shaking under me, I stood, pointing my sword at her. I gathered my will to send black lightning stabbing into her blood-splashed body. *Die, you bitch.*

In a tight swarm, a hundred, perhaps a thousand, Faeries blasted into the tower chamber. Through the door Van shattered on his way in, they buzzed like a hive of angry bees. Their voices screaming in high C, sharp enough to shatter crystal, they attacked. They owned no weapons. Like the butterflies they resembled, they had no stingers. *What possible harm could they manage?*

I didn't have long to wait. I sagged back against the wall, my busted shoulder forgotten. Stunned, I neglected to send a death-stream of black from my sword's tip. Similar to a sea wave crashing over a shore-locked boulder, the Faeries surged over Enya. By using the sheer weight of numbers, their tiny bodies covered her, blinding her, hampering her movements. A miniscule voice rose above the buzzing tumult. "For Iyumi and for Bryn'Cairdha!"

Enya, all but smothered under the invasion, waved her free hand about her head. Though she hit several Faeries with deadly accuracy, no Faery died that I could see. Several bounded off her strike, and blazed back in with renewed fury. My jaw slack, I witnessed the smallest creature on this world drive absolutely mad the greatest witch it had ever known. For their shrieks, buzzing wings and bodies cloaking her like a living, furious mantle drove her blind with insane rage.

Enya gathered in her strength. Her dark power blew every Faery away from her with a sharp, barking cough. Thunder rattled the tower as white lightning struck its topmost turrets. The broken glass of the great window creaked alarmingly. Past Enya's torn and bloody head, the moon had all but swallowed up the sick sun. I wasn't mistaken after all. Twin eyes, pupils elongated like a cat's, glowered like twin lamps from hell.

Her Masters were watching. Of that, I had no doubt.

The Faeries, caught up in the dark maelstrom, exploded in every direction. Many hit the round walls of the tower as hundreds more bounced across the slate tiles. No few hit the great window, and I half-thought it may well shatter under their soft, yet implacable, assault. I hoped they hadn't been killed, but my attention span fell far short.

Using the distraction the Faeries gave me, I seized not my steel but my magic. Deep into the dark caverns of my head, I sought for, and accepted the truth. Iyumi spoke both clearly and accurately when she convinced me to deny the role my life wanted to take. That wasn't my mother I aimed to kill. It was a demon, and I once loved it beyond my own life.

I am a coward. I am weak. I was blind once, but now I see. I killed an innocent for evil and stolen strength. I repent my actions with every breath I take. Whoever you are, grant me the power to slay in the name of good. I am prepared to die. I fear to live.

Be strong.

I will be strong. I am strong. I will it shall be so.

"Come on, bitch," I grated, stumbling away from the wall's support. My left arm hung, useless, and I used my sword as a crutch, ready to heave my way to my feet. "We have unfinished business, you and me."

Her face in tatters, she peered at me with one working eye. The other had vanished, leaving a bloody hollow where it once had lain. Deep lacerations in her cheeks marred her great beauty forever, should she win this fight. Her tiny nose hung by a mere strip of flesh where Van's talons had torn it asunder, and her once graceful lips gaped raw fissures. Yet, she smiled. A ferociously happy, triumphant grin as her hooked claws pointed down at me. The troll infant screamed, struggling, as she held it by its slender neck.

"I'll forgive your treachery, Flynn," she rasped. "Come to me, now, on your knees. Beg me, son, and I'll show you mercy."

My upper lip curled. "Your Masters await you, Mother. It's time you met them, don't you think?"

Enya flicked a rapid glance toward the great window and the cat's eyes still watching. Dra'agor hit her hard and low from behind. His fangs bit deep into the soft flesh behind her knees, cutting tendons and ripping necessary ligaments from bone. Enya screamed as she went down, the troll baby flung from her hands to hit the flagstone, bounce once and roll. At the same instant, a body burst from the hearth fire. Like a bolt of flame, it hit the chamber floor and grew.

Van's hand seized me by the collar and lifted me high. "Come on," he gasped. "We've only this one chance. You with me?"

"Damn straight, brother," I gasped, my shoulder on fire. "Let's finish it."

Enya recovered swiftly. Her fist seized Dra'agor by his ruff and lifted him as easily as she might lift a chalice of wine. The wolf screamed, snarling, trying to twist and bite the hand that held him. She shook him as a cat shakes a mouse to kill it, and sent him, crashing hard, into the stone wall a mere few inches away. Dra'agor, my friend, slid into a boneless pile of fur and lay still.

As though guided by one mind, Van and I attacked. Forgetting such paltry things as swords, we combined our powers, uniting them. Together, we created a force of such magnitude that not even Enya and her hellspawn magic could withstand it. With invisible cables we bound her tight, crushing her, her arms tightly bound to her sides. She screamed and cursed, her devil-red eyes condemning us as she struggled. She almost got away, once. Van growled under his breath and tackled her, bringing her down under his greater weight. Though she snapped at his hands with her teeth, he never flinched, or relented.

With hands as well as power, Van pinned her down, his black hair falling across his eyes. "Flynn," he gasped. "The window. Quick."

I understood. Without leaving his side, or lifting my power from her, I raised my head. A quick flick of my will sent the bloody altar crashing through the heavy glass that had stood unbroken and pristine for centuries. In a shower of glass and sparks, the altar tumbled out of sight, into the teeth of the raging storm. High winds hurled into the chamber, sending dust flying. Thunder growled, closer now, as lightning flashed in my eyes.

"She's caught."

Van's eyes found mine, telling me more than his words. Bound within our combined power, Enya was helpless, yet alive. I knew what he wanted to do. What he wanted me to do. It would end this sacrilege forever. His green glance under his fall of oily black hair asked me, 'Are you ready? Can you do this?'

"Yes."

My single word answered everything. I gritted my teeth, my heart determined. As I gazed at her torn and bleeding face, the beauty I once adored glimmered amid the gore, the missing eye. That face softened, and I saw again the mother who kissed me, called me her 'wild child', and tousled my hair, laughing.

"Flynn? I love you, Flynn. Don't do this, I beg you. I did all this for you, my son."

I hesitated. Her voice still pierced me with the same loving, affectionate tones she always used when she spoke to me. Though coated in deep scores and blood, her one remaining blue eye, not red, blue, peeped through the gore. The eyes I worshipped. The love I had for her rose–

"Mother?"

"Flynn, my darling–"

"Flynn?" Van's urgent voice cut through the haze her voice brought. "Now or never, bro."

"Don't listen to her, Flynn!"

Iyumi's shrill voice pleaded from just behind me. "She's using her powers on you. Don't heed her. Remember, Flynn, she killed Fainche and Sofia. She murdered your son!"

Like a bucket of ice dumped over my head, her spell vanished. The Witch remained, sneering, and all that remained of the mother I adored was dead and gone. I remembered the small sad sack of red with the tiny hand poking through. I shut my eyes against the memory of Fainche, of my Sofia, lying in pools of drying blood. Why did Iyumi have to remind me? I needed no reminder that this . . . thing–killed everything I ever loved.

My voice choked. "Die for your sins, bitch."

My power, combined with Van's, lifted her. As one mind, we staggered closer to the window, intending to toss her out. Like a captured tigress, she fought. As though in her desperation, she gained new strength, new power. Or, my mind skittered under the notion, her Masters gave her that renewed strength. Perhaps they betted on her, needed her to survive and slay the child in the next few moments. Either way, our tight bands about her body loosened. Van flung me a swift frantic glance before hurling more magic into the force we seized her in. I did the same, sweat stinging my eyes, my shoulder on fire. I poured all my stolen magic into a gigantic flow–

–and slipped.

Unbelievably, she wriggled free from the binding chains of our combined magic. We fell back from her, our feet sliding on the blood-wet slate of the floor. In less than a heartbeat, she'd have regained all her power, and that of her friends, then toss both Van and I out the window. *Gods,* I tried to cry. *You can t let her!* Her bloody mouth opened in a scream of triumph–

Dra'agor's heavy body struck her from the side. Her triumph changed to panic as his weight carried both of them through the broken window and into the teeth of the storm. Her wailing scream died under the crash of thunder. It fell, diminished by distance, until it vanished.

"Dra'agor!" I yelled, lunging after him.

Van's arms around my knees hit me low and hard, bringing me down with my chin smacking the stone floor. Breathless from the agony of my shoulder, my ribs and the tearing grief of yet another loss, I stared over the lip of the balcony. Bitter tears and the black clouds prevented me from seeing anything at all. *Dra agor.* Noble friend. I bent my head until my brow struck the cold floor, all my will gone, vanished, with him.

The black moon crossed the face of the sun.

For a long moment, all went still. The storm without died away, the dark clouds rolling back from the melding of the sun and the moon. I lifted my head to watch as the demon's eyes closed and disappeared. The lightning flickered once, twice, as its thunder crashed from far away before it, too, departed. *It s over.* I've never felt more tired in my life. *She d dead, and Fainche and Sofia are avenged.* I found no triumph, no joy in our success, at all. The Witch is dead.

Van's hand slid from my head to my shoulders as he sat beside me, his legs dangling over the edge of the balcony.

"Sorry," he murmured. "He did what we couldn't. She was almost too much. Without him—"

"I know." I couldn't manage more than a whisper.

"He sacrificed himself. Brave lad."

My heart aching, yet empty, I raised my upper body with the use of my strong right arm. Learning to ignore the ripping pain, I gained my knees as Van's helping hand aided me to sit beside him. I cradled my injured left arm within my strong right, unshed tears burning my eyes. *How many had to die this day?* Too many. *Too many.*

Together, shoulder to shoulder, we watched as the moon, carried on her course, slowly crossed the face of the new dawn. Bright colors—reds, purples, oranges, yellows—caroused in a bright spray of light as the moon vanished. With it, the prophecy of evil died. The messenger of the gods didn't die under my mother's dagger. Evil didn't, nor would ever, rule my land.

I glanced down. Down the sheer walls of the castle and the slick pinnacle under it, to the unforgiving rocks the castle sprang from. Very far away, a tiny splash of red amid the solid greys and browns marked her. The Red Witch. *May the demons feast upon your soul.* I saw no sign of Dra'agor's corpse. I'm glad I didn't.

"You good?" Van asked me, his green eyes concerned as he looked me up and down. "You look like shit."

I found a faint grin somewhere. "You don't look so hot yourself."

Van glanced down at himself, his burnt clothes. "Oh, just a bit crispy, on the outside."

A huge Griffin flew up and past, blowing our hair about in a tremendous backwash of wings. The distinctive one that I thought I recognized, the one with the black feathered mane that crept down its chest to its belly. Unable to hover, it circled once, then dove downward only to rise again on those colossal eagle's wings. Its yellow raptor eyes and beak angled down to keep us in sight. I took a moment to admire its incredible beauty in flight as it banked around for another pass. "Van?" it asked. "Is the princess all right?"

"She's fine, Windy," Van replied. "Tell the King the Witch is dead."

Ah, yes, Wind Warrior. The one Van joked with when I was captured. The Griffin with the rather interesting sense of humor.

Windy circled, unable to hover. "Oh, he knows, all right. Not a living creature in the castle didn't fail to see her tossed out the tower. Who was that with her? It looked like a wolf."

Van cut his hand across his throat with a sharp 'sssst' and glanced sidelong at me. "It was," he answered, his tone low. "He's the reason we're all not Witch bait."

"Oh. Sorry, like."

I tried to shrug off his sympathy as Van's hand slid over my uninjured right shoulder. Feeling tired beyond belief, Windy's words were almost lost amid my thoughts, regrets and wishes swirling around my pounding head. "Uh," I started, eyeing Van sidelong. "The King?"

Van grinned sheepishly. "Oh, um, well, Flynn, we, er, invaded your country. Sorry and all that, but it was necessary. I'm sure Roidan will give it back. He's not the conquering sort."

Rather than be filled with righteous anger, I chuckled instead. It hurt my shoulder something awful, but I did it again. "I suppose we had it coming."

"Van?"

Windy passed across the broken window again, watching me through those cruel amber eyes. "Why isn't he dead?"

Van laughed and flung an arm, lightly, considerate of my pain, across my neck. "He's one of the good guys, Windy, old son. Please request His Majesty send healers. We have injured up here."

"Righty-o."

Windy folded his wings and dropped from sight. Though I craned my head to watch, he ducked around the tall walls of the keep and vanished. I glanced aside at Van, considering.

"Did you mean that?"

Van took his arm from me with a puzzled smile. "What? That you're a good guy?"

"Yes."

Van's green eyes turned serious. "Flynn, I meant every word. Though we be mortal enemies, I've liked you from the very first moment I met you."

My throat tightened. "That's a first."

"What is?"

"That someone actually likes me for me."

"Don't get a huge head over it."

My guilt rose to nudge me where it counted. "I'm sorry I left you . . . you know . . . to–um–"

"Die?"

"Right."

Van chuckled, rising up from his seated position. His hand supported me as I limped my way to my feet. I needed the help, for without it I knew I'd pitch headlong to the slate. Together, like old friends, or brothers, we walked away from the window. "Wasn't your call anyway, Flynn. It worked out best."

I met his amused green eyes. "I'm so very glad you're not er, dead, old chap."

"Sorry I was a bit late."

I leaned away from him, confused. "Late?"

"A spell on that there door." His head jerked toward what remained of the balcony door. "Took me a bloody two minutes to break, or I'd been inside sooner."

I raised my healthy right arm to throw around his neck. "Laddie, you were right on time."

[515]

We might have stood there, grinning at each other like fools, had not Iyumi's quiet sobs broken us apart. We exchanged a quick glance of concern, then bolted toward her. From the moment we locked Mother in our power and Dra'agor pitched her headlong out the window, I'd almost forgotten Iyumi. She'd picked up the troll baby and sat on the floor, rocking gently back and forth.

"Iyumi?" Van asked, squatting beside her.

"She's dead, Van. She's dead."

"Oh, honey–"

Tears streamed past her pale cheeks, her half-choked sobs wrenching my heart. I pushed my own grief for my dead family to the background as Van enclosed her within the circle of his arms. *She shouldn t have died.* I glanced at the blood congealing in the dark curly hair over her skull and knew the fall from Enya's arms had cracked it. Fatally. To my surprise, I felt regret that she had died. I once hated that nasty creature and wished her dead many times. Now that she was, I wished she still lived. For she was better than I. She was innocent and good, and we could never have enough innocence and goodness in this terrible world of ours.

"All this to save her–and still she's dead."

Iyumi glanced up. "This was her purpose in life," she murmured, tears streaming down her bruised and bloody face. "To bring us here, to this moment. For this she was born."

"And the prophecy?"

"She fulfilled it."

That made no sense to me. "One day, maybe you'll explain it all."

I turned away to grant them privacy in their shared grief. *My family was dead.* But I had another family that just might be alive. Stumbling across the room, feeling nauseous and light-headed, I made my way toward my lads. Buck-Eye stirred from where he'd fallen, his head busted and streaming blood. But his lively curses informed me his wounds were superficial. Torass and Lyall both rose to their feet, shedding dust and broken shale, leaning against one another for support. *I don t deserve their loyalty.* I murdered a man, shot him in cold blood. I killed my own brother for power. They should hate me. I deserved their hatred.

[516]

Dra'agor. *He died saving my miserable life. He died saving the world.* He'd no reason to love me, but did so of his own volition. A true friend. I freed him. He could have cut and run, dashed his way to the freedom of the mountains and none would lay him blame. Instead, he gave his life for those he loved; Iyumi and me. He gave me all and asked for nothing in return. No man could ask for more.

My heart couldn't handle it. Fainche, Sofia, my unborn son, Dra'agor–and even my mother. All gone. All dead. I limped my way to the still blazing hearth, and collapsed. As the sun coursed its way into the blue on blue sky, my tears flowed, unchecked. I surrendered to my grief at last. I sobbed like a broken-hearted child, Buck-Eye's comforting hand on my shoulder. I wept for those I'd lost, for the innocence I wish I kept, and for the soul I'd surrendered.

I might have cried myself into sleep had not Van hauled me up with his hand under my uninjured arm. "C'mon, Flynn."

His strength stood me on my feet as Buck-Eye and Torass kept me there. "Let's get out of this place, old son. You need healing, and it's a long way to the ground floor."

I nodded, half-blind. "Iyumi?"

Van grimaced. "Saying a few words over the dead. Yours as well as ours."

My breath choked off. I stumbled away from Buck-Eye toward the corpses. Iyumi knelt beside Fainche, her bound hands making graceful gestures as her low-voiced chant offered up prayers. Dropping heavily to my knees at her side, I tenderly closed my sister's staring eyes.

"She lives on, Flynn," Iyumi said gently, breaking off her lilting chant. She took my hand. "You will see them all again, one day, and they will greet you with open arms."

"I seriously doubt that, Princess," I replied, my voice hoarse. "They go one way, I go another."

I felt Iyumi's eyes study me, and I wanted to slink away from that blue gaze. This tiny girl knew too bloody much by half. My guilt rose under her scrutiny, and I knew hers weren't the only ones peering into my soul.

"You're changing the road you're on, Flynn. You have power now, the power to do a great good. Are you willing to stay on it?"

I half-shrugged, not answering her. I stroked my hand down Fainche's still-warm cheek. I couldn't bend to plant a good-bye kiss on her brow as I wanted, but I kissed my fingers and touched them to her lips. "Watch over me," I whispered. "When you can."

I needed Iyumi's help to stand. Stepping around my sister, I gazed down at the butchered corpse of my wife. "I never told you I loved you, Sofia," I murmured. "I should have. If you're still here, take these words with you on your journey. I love you. I've always loved you."

"She heard you. They are both still here, as is your son."

Though I couldn't bend down and take my son's tiny hand within my own, I whispered, "Look after your mother now. One day, we'll be a family again. I'm counting on you, my little one. My firstborn. My son."

Uncaring that the others witnessed my grief, I let her steer me back across the chamber. Though I fully expected it, I found no contempt in the eyes or the expressions of Van, Buck-Eye, Torass or Lyall. Instead, Van greeted me with a sympathetic smile and a wink. Buck-Eye nodded his respect and Lyall murmured, "Sorry for your loss, like."

No jealousy rose within me as Iyumi walked with lowered head and nudged her way under Van's sheltering arm. *They love one another, with a love so few in this dangerous world ever found.*

I might find, one day, a love such as this. But it wasn't this day.

Van placed his hand on the manacles trapping her life and her power. He muttered one single word. "Break."

Under his intense magic, the dark manacles shattered, a hundred tiny fragments exploding everywhere. Many pieces fell to the slate at our feet while more tinkled against the wall or were caught in our clothing. She didn't rub the soreness from her bruised wrists, but instead locked them around Van's neck. He held her close, her silver-gilt hair hiding his face.

Astounded, I nudged the dark-colored steel fragments with my toe. "How'd you do that?"

[518]

Van raised his face from her shoulder to grin. "Easy once you know how."

Had I not known what a laugh would do to my shoulder, I'd have let loose with a big one. "I need some serious instruction. Will you teach me?"

"I'm busy right now."

Turning from Van's arms, Iyumi wiped her damp cheeks and smiled. She took my uninjured hand within both of hers and squeezed. "Come, Flynn, let's get out of here. Healers are on their way and we're all in need of attention. Buck-Eye, put his arm over your shoulder, there's a dear. Can't have him dropping down the stairs like his old man. Torass, Lyall, you, too. "

As though owing her his loyalty, Buck-Eye obeyed her instantly. He slipped my healthy right arm over his shoulder. I appreciated it very much, for when I tried to walk, I almost fell.

"Easy, m'lord," Buck-Eye muttered. "One step at a time, there's a good chap."

In this odd entourage, Iyumi and Van leading, me and my mercenary crutch next, Torass and Lyall following, we walked through the double doors. I'd almost forgotten the dead lying out there. When Iyumi would have bent to them, Van kept her upright with his hand firmly under her arm. "Later, love," he murmured, kissing her cheek. "You can send them on their journey after we fix Flynn and the others up."

Inching our way past the bodies, I stepped close to Blaez's corpse. Focused on the tightly wound stairs ahead, I wondered how in the hell my crutch and I would make it down them. Only wide enough for one man, no room for two.

A hand clutched my ankle.

Startled, I cursed aloud and jumped. Buck-Eye reacted instantly and yanked me out of harm's way. Van and Iyumi turned back; Van spun his sword into his fist. "Flynn?"

"Gods," I choked. "He's still alive."

I stared down at Blaez's bloody grin, astonished. I thought I killed him. The power I blasted him with–how could he still be alive?

[519]

He choked, wheezing out his life, trying to laugh. "I gotya now, Prince," he gasped, trying to sit up.

The damage I'd done was obvious–his chest crushed, his arms shattered, his face a mask of broken bones and blood. But his eyes burned livid holes into me, his gory grin wide and mocking.

"I done told ye, Prince," he cackled. "I told ye you'd all burn. Half hour after dawn and yer castle will burn ye to bits."

My breath caught. *Sergei.* Sergei tried to warn me. Blaez told him, and he told me.

"Where's the bomb, Blaez? Where'd you put it?"

"What's he talking about?" Van asked, standing beside me as I stared down at the cackling and rapidly expiring Commander.

"He planted a bomb," Iyumi answered, dropping to her knees beside the dying Blaez. "One big enough to bring down the entire castle."

"The town, too, bitch," Blaez wheezed, coughing up a spurt of blood. "None 'o ye'll escape the fires. Ye'll burn and burn. Fire and steel. Fire and steel, yep, yep."

Iyumi rested her fingers lightly on Blaez's brow. "Where is it, Commander? Where did you plant the bomb?"

If she exerted her power, I neither saw nor sensed it. By Van's blank expression, neither did he. Our magic could sense another's when used, but neither of us felt Iyumi's. I strongly suspected that because her power was derived straight from the gods themselves, our mundane magic could neither see nor hear it.

Blaez's eyed glazed over. "In the cellars," he whispered. "'Tis spelled to explode fifteen minutes from now."

His eyes rolled back in his head. His rising chest settled onto itself as he took his last breath. Collapsing upon itself, his body sank to the cold flagstone as Blaez died.

Iyumi rose to stand beside Van, her fair lips pursed thoughtfully. "He didn't leave us much time."

"Heal me," I snapped. "We have to find that bomb."

"Flynn, there's not enough–"

"We have to find it," I yelled. "We have to stop it."

"Van, he's right. It's not just the people of the town and the castle, it's our own folk as well. My father–"

"Go." Van shoved her toward the stairs. "You." He jerked his head toward Buck-Eye and the others. "Go with her. Tell the King to begin evacuating as many people as he can."

They didn't hesitate. With Iyumi in the lead, they bolted for the stairs and vanished down them. At the same instant I heard the rapid tattoo of their tread, Van's hand closed on my brow. I'd felt his healing touch before, but that experience didn't prepare me for this. His power slammed into me like a bolt of sheet lightning. Caught between agony and ecstasy, I felt fire roar through my veins. Under its flames, my pain withered and died. I felt the broken bones in my shoulder meet and meld, reforming in strength. Blood washed through the torn ligaments and muscles, cleansing them of all hurt.

I wanted to pass out. I wanted to vomit. Neither happened as I staggered as Van's power left me. His strong arms held me upright as he gazed deep into my sweating face. "Flynn?"

I straightened, rolling my shoulders under the terrific heat. Calling on my own magical powers, I poured new energy and strength into my body, assimilating with Van's. As though having slept for a month, my vigor returned in full force. I shook off his helping hands and gasped. "I'm good, I'm good."

"Where are the cellars he mentioned? And don't say down. What's the quickest way to them?"

"Beneath the keep," I answered, my tone sharp. "There's a door, but it's a long way down. It'll take us–"

His hand dragged me with him. "I hope you're not afraid of heights."

I didn't have time to answer as we ran back into the north tower chamber. The dead within it scarcely registered as Van lunged for the broken window. *What the hell?* I tried to say, but I couldn't escape his grasp.

Van dove out the window and took me with him. Empty air caught at my clothes. I fell, just as my mother, and Dra'agor, fell, rushing toward the deadly rocks at roughly twice the speed of light. *I am so dead,* my mind gibbered, wind-driven tears staining my sight. The ground below–ye gods!

[521]

Within two heartbeats, Van *changed.* His hand wasn't a hand any more. An eagle's talon gripped my wrist hard enough to break bones. His huge wings beat swiftly up and down. Our fall turned into flight. The wind no longer rushed through my ears; it whispered. My tears dried quickly and I blinked, able to see. I glanced around, up, finding myself caught within the grasp of an enormous Griffin. Van's eagle head, with his brilliant green eyes behind his savage yellow beak, bent down and back. I caught his swift wink and infectious grin aimed in my direction. I couldn't help it. I grinned weakly back.

Down into the keep he dove, his wings enslaving the wind. Folks inside stared upward, shading their eyes, pointing up. I saw Centaurs and Minotaurs, horses and riders. Milling common folk and castle servants. Bright colors of nobles and dull woolens of serfs. All dead if we didn't reach Blaez's bomb first. It wasn't just Van's King and invading army that died if it went off, mine died along with them. These were my people, *my people.* If I didn't protect them, who would?

"Where, Flynn?" Van gasped, his eagle's beak angled down to see me better. "I can't keep us up for much longer, you're too bloody heavy."

I looked around, ignoring my new fear of heights, gathering my bearings. *There.* "To your right, outside the keep itself. See the door?"

Van coasted to our right, his wings out and leveled. "The one that looks like a peasant's hovel?"

"That's it."

Van swooped sideways and left my belly behind. "Don't blame me too much if I drop you rather suddenly."

I slipped from his grip only a mere few yards from the ground. Rolling upon striking the soil as I did when I fell off a horse, I hit the ground unharmed. Van landed beside me, his beak wide as he scooped in air, gasping for breath. He folded his wings, then *changed.*

I gripped his shoulder hard as he bent over, drawing in one desperate lungful after another "Van?"

"No worries," he said, arming sweat from his face. "Griffins don't carry extra weight well. This it?"

"Come on."

Kicking the door open, I called fire to my hand. Descending into the darkness, I ran down the steep steps, Van hard on my heels. "What's down here?"

"These days," I answered, "nothing much. In the old times, this cellar was used for storing food against famine. Famine hasn't put in much of an appearance for the last few hundred years, so it's largely empty."

"Why here?"

Even as I ran, I glanced up. "These are the castle's roots. Blaez wasn't exactly smart, not in the way we usually call smart. But he knows bombs and he knows how to bring a building down."

"Like this one."

"Unfortunately, Van, his bombs destroyed much in your country. For terrorism, he was my pa's right hand man."

"So why would he do this? This is your father's castle."

I shrugged, leaping down three steps. "He's also crazier than a caged tiger. Only a matter of time before he snapped."

We hit bottom, my fires illuminating a large, rectangular wooden box. In a huge chamber with shelves built into the walls and bins filling the entire place, the chest stood alone within a tiny clearing of floor space. Harmless it looked, yet my hairs on my neck stood on end. Here lay enough power to not just level this castle, but the town and beyond. Blaez never messed about. If he said this thing could level all in its path, I believed it. Both our folk would die, burning.

"That's it, there." Van's voice rose in excitement. "Isn't it?"

"Has to be. What do we do? Can we blast it into the netherworld?"

Van spun around, his eyes wild. "No! Never. If we use our power, it'll go off. I've seen too many of these. It'll kill not just us but everyone within a three mile radius."

My gut dropped to my boots. "Then what do we do?"

"Maybe I can disarm it."

Van pushed past me and knelt beside the box. His head cocked to the side, his black hair falling across his shoulders, he rested his hands atop it.

Holding my breath, not daring to move, I waited. Seconds ticked by, one after the other. Until a minute rolled past. How many were left? Our flight from above took maybe three minutes, our run downstairs perhaps two. That left only ten minutes before the bloody thing went off.

"Shit."

"What?"

Van straightened. "I can disarm it, if I've a half hour or so. The spell he concocted is complicated."

"We don't have that much time!"

"I know, I know."

Van paced about, scowling, running his hands through his hair. Suddenly, he stopped, his hand frozen in the act of brushing his black locks from his face. He glared at me. "Is there a lake nearby?"

"A lake?"

"Dammit, Flynn! Is there a lake near here?"

"Um, yes, about ten leagues north. Why?"

"Fly it high," he muttered. "Drop it in. Dead easy."

"What?"

"Help me, dammit! We have to carry it out."

I seized one ungainly end as Van lifted the other. It wasn't too heavy, but odds and ends inside shifted alarmingly. I halted worried, but Van continued to drag his end up the stairs.

"It won't go off until the fuse hits," he said. "I can hear it, inside."

"Can't you put it out?" I asked, pushing as he pulled. "Won't that stop it from exploding?"

He shook his head. "Not before it blows. Your Blaez is a crafty one."

It took perhaps three precious minutes to drag the thing into sunlight and open air. We set it down, both of us panting hard. I wiped sweat from my eyes, gasping. A clever Shifter, Van changed into his Griffin, his huge wings spreading as he loomed over me and cast me into shadow.

"What're you doing? Are you crazy?"

"Fly it out," Van snarled, seizing the end of the long box in his talons. "Fly it out. Drop it in the lake. Done it before."

Of course. He intended to carry the thing ten leagues north and drop it into the lake. There, its explosion killed fish, and perhaps a deer or three, but no humans and no castle falling down atop those who may survive the initial blast. I saw only one flaw: Van couldn't manage it. His tremendous wings fanned the air, forcing him upward with every beat. The box rose, slowly, the section in his grip rising while the other remained steadfastly on the ground. He lunged upward, wings straining, his throat bared as he shut his eyes and fought for altitude.

"Van," I yelled, running into the storm of sweeping dust and litter the hurricane-force winds his wings kicked up. "You can't do it."

"I have to."

"There's no one near who can help."

"I know, dammit! Get out of my way!"

I struck his massive lion shoulder, forcing him to drop the box. "You can't do it alone, Van. Change me into a Griffin."

His beak swiveled toward me, his raptor eyes wide. "Get serious."

"I am, stupid."

My fist struck his yellow beak and rebounded unhurt. But my wrist ached. "There's no time to find another flyer. I'm here. Help me change."

"You don't know how to fly."

"I'll learn," I snapped, grim. "Do it."

"Gods," he muttered, landing to all fours. "This is insane."

His talons extended toward me, grabbing me within their terrible grip. Unlike his healing magic, this power was cold, bone chilling cold. Panic seized me as my body changed. I grew in size, doubling, then grew some more. The box retreated, growing smaller and smaller. *No, that wasn t right.* It remained the same as my eyes rose higher and higher yet. No longer did I stand on two feet. Four replaced them. My wings drooped, alien, hanging heavily on my shoulders. My heightened senses picked up voices, clop of hooves on stone. I scented wood smoke, roasted onions and frying peppers; my panicked mind trying to find an answer where none existed.

"Feel," Van ordered. "Feel your new body. Don't fight it. Go with it. Feel the wind and think of yourself one with it. Spread your wings."

I obeyed, calming my panic, dropping into a light trance as I sought for, and found, my Griffin self. I spread my wings wide just as my four feet coordinated with my heavy tail, and I rediscovered balance. Breathing hard, my pulse pounding, I surrendered to my body. Blind fear seeped away as did the adrenaline rush, leaving me to find confidence enough to explore my new form. I quickly forgot the two legs I was accustomed to and bent my head to admire the pair of lion hind legs to the eagle's front talons. I folded my wings across my broad shoulders, rejoicing in their weight. Delight overran my fear. *I was born to this. I can fly!*

I lifted my huge angel's wings across my back. Their shadow dropped me into darkness where nothing shone. No sun, no moon and little light. I delved deep into the Griffin, learning its secrets, making it part of me. The body I now inhabited joined with my own and became one. Still Prince Flynn, but different–emotionally, physically and spiritually.

I bent my beak, eyeing my sleek lion body and my rear quarters. My long lion tail lashed despite my attempts to still it. My human arms now sprouted feathers and deadly razor-tipped talons. I chuckled, hearing my own voice from an alien mouth. Damn, but I made a handsome Griffin.

"Stop admiring yourself," Flynn snapped. "Grab your end. We've less than ten minutes."

Sinking my talons into the box, I flapped my wings. Nothing happened. I flapped harder, willing myself into the sky. Only the courtyard's dust flew as I beat my wings. I launched myself skyward and only strained my already sore shoulder muscles. I didn't fly an inch.

"No, *no,* NO!"

"Van, I'm trying–"

"Not like that, you idiot. Use your damn legs; that's why the gods gave them to you. Use your legs, *first,* then your wings. Leap high, and snag the wind. It's there, waiting, ready. NOW, you fool, *now!"*

His voice cracked like a whip. As though its lash struck my ass, I leaped skyward. My wings beat hard, carrying me up, ever up. I caught a warm updraft and allowed it to spiral me higher and higher. Far below, folks in the keep, hanging from Castle Salagh's windows, or charging into the cobbled streets, stared upward, gaping like idiots. *Yes, it s me. Your wild prince whom you despise, riding the winds. 1 m free of you and you of me. We are quits. Even.*

A dip of either left or right wing sent me into a turn while my tail acted as a rudder. The breeze whispered through my ears. Feeling free, as light as the feathers that bore me higher and higher, the power of flight intoxicated more than the headiest wine. *Is this for real?* Never before had I felt so free, or unrestrained. I never wanted to land.

"Flynn! Get back here!"

I sighed. *Duty calls.* Drawing my wings in, I stooped toward the great castle, blowing past its proud towers. I knew all manner of folk watched me fly by, but I didn't pay them any mind. Van waved his talon, impatient, *get down, down.*

Dropping lightly to the stone cobbles, I sent Van a quick wink. "I think I understand you better."

His beak stretched into a grin. "Flying is an addiction. Trust me, you'll never get enough fixes. Come on, this is gonna be a bitch."

I sank my talons deep into heavy wood at the same time Van grabbed his end. Following his lead, I crouched, my lion hind legs low, my wings wide and back. Ready to leap, I merely awaited the word.

"On three," Van ordered. "One, two, THREE!"

In perfect synch, we launched ourselves skyward. Van's comment wasn't far from the mark. The box tried to drag us back down to earth, beyond heavy. How the hell did Van manage to fly while holding onto me? Straining, cursing, I beat my wings hard, fast. Slowly we rose, past the keep, listening to the muted roar of the watching crowds. Up and up, rising on a warm thermal, we beat past the towers.

"North," Van gasped. "Up and north. We need to get as high as possible."

Angling our way northward, we crossed the town proper. Concentrating, I forced my wings into working harder than they were meant to. Pain streaked across my shoulders, but I ignored it. Higher we climbed, the houses and buildings below appearing like tiny squares. A small river caught the sunlight and sent tiny blades into my eyes.

"I'm gonna be sore tomorrow," I muttered.

"You might not be alive tomorrow," Van replied, his tone humored. "We've less than three minutes."

"The lake's just yonder. Behind that hill."

"Kick your ass into gear, plebe," Van ordered. "High, high."

"Yes, *sir*," I snapped, a laugh escaping my throat in a breathy hiss.

We climbed. Two precious minutes passed, ticking away like the explosive inside the box. We climbed, beating hard for the deep blue over our heads. Past the tall hill, its heavy growth of trees crowning it like grey-green moss. Sunlight glinted off water just as Van announced, "One minute."

"We're almost there, can't we drop it?"

"In the water," he gasped. "Drown this sucker."

The lake's edge passed under our tails. It lay near a small chain of north-curving mountains called the Little Shin. The folks often referred to the wide and deep lake as the Ice Shin. Light shimmered off its surface; its dark blue waves rolled in ever-ending motion. Despite our height, my keen eyesight witnessed kingfishers and hawks, even an eagle, diving into the water in search of a fish breakfast. As we flew hard and fast over its center, Van's fierce raptor eyes locked on mine.

"Listen up," he ordered. "This thing will fall fast. In twenty seconds it'll explode, but it'll take thirty for us to get clear. Once we drop it, bolt sideways. Not up, not down–sideways. As fast as you can. Got it?"

"Got it."

"Now!"

I retracted my talons from the wood at the same instant Van let go. I didn't waste time by turning in a circle; rather I dipped my right wing and spun west. Van spun east. Our wings brushed one another's as we passed each other by.

Arrowing across the sky, I sped. Without the weight of the box, I felt as light and free as a sparrow. Faster and faster, I beat my wings, the wind a sharp whistle in my flattened ears. *Not far enough. Not fast enough.* Calling upon my stubborn will, I forced my wings into greater speed. *If that thing explodes before it hits the water–*

With a sharp coughing bark, the detonation rolled across the hills and echoed across the Little Shin. Bright orange light surged past me an instant before the flash-fire struck my rear quarters. Blown tail over ears, I tumbled across the sky. Peppered with shrapnel, my fur crisped, I lost control. Down I fell, spinning, my wings failing to keep me airborne. Though I flapped them, beating hard to regain balance and lost altitude, they refused to work together. One tried hard while the other wobbled, then they switched tasks. *Chill*, my bird instincts advised. *You have altitude and you have lift. Coast along on the wind. Soar, dummy.*

Good thinking. I quit fighting my wings and relaxed, splitting them wide and catching the summer breeze. Suddenly, I was flying again, soaring high above the Little Shin, rising higher and higher. A mere dip of a pinfeather turned me slightly southwest, and I found I could actually breathe.

Until the second blast ripped loose.

Blaez never did anything by halves. Of course he'd have made certain his bomb took out everything, and *everything*, both near and far. He intended to not just bring down Castle Salagh, he wanted everyone within it, and the surrounding town, to die. Fleeting glimpses of a tidal wave of lake surging upward and outward blew past my eyes. The sudden rush of air, pushed out from the explosion, propelled me upward, dangerously out of control. The blast itself catapulted me tail over beak, tumbling me over and over until I wanted to vomit. Bits of nails, steel shards and glass spikes cut my shoulders, my face, my belly. I couldn't help but cut loose with a scream of pain as Blaez's shrapnel tore into my body.

The explosion and its effects died away, leaving behind a huge cloud centered over the Ice Shin. Though I was miles away, and spinning sickeningly out of control, the mushroom shaped smoke appeared to me a mere half hundred rods from my beak. Without the hot wind to help me rise, I fell. Plunging toward the tall evergreens that graced the shallow mountains, I plummeted at a terrific speed. *Fainche, here I come.*

Dammit. Get those wings working.

My wings refused my order and remained steadfastly limp, like windless sails. *Come on, come on. Flap, damn you. Flap.* Against the gravity sucking me into my death on the rocks and trees below, my wings were as helpless as I was. I needed to turn my body upright.

I m half cat. Cats land on their feet.

Though I didn't try to land, I did twist, wrenching my body around. Now my feet pointed down, my wings up. Instinctively, I cupped them, slowing my fall. My tail swung heavily back and forth, steadying me. Much better. Rather than drop like a stone, I drifted. *Crap. That was close.* Though I couldn't exactly sweat as a human would, I did feel hot. I panted, my beak wide and sucking in the cool air of the mountains. Immediately, my body's heat eased a fraction. The air flowing over my feathers and lion's fur helped my temperature level. Now if I could only kill the pain of my fractured hide, I'd be one very happy bird.

One beat of my wings, then two brought me out of the lethal spiral toward the very hard ground below. By the third and the fourth, I flew again and just might survive Blaez's legacy. With the fifth and all those that followed, I circled. I took a deep breath, and looked around. I took a moment to curse Blaez into the hottest fires of hell. Had that thing gone off under Castle Salagh, no doubt it's power would have not just brought it tumbling down, but would send blocks of granite cascading like the lake water. Thousands of people would have died under the rain of fire and steel. Just as Blaez planned.

I'd fallen almost halfway back to earth. That may be why Van insisted on altitude. He knew the blast could easily reach us, even if it exploded in the lake. Speaking of Van, where was he? As he could outfly me any day of the week, I knew that if I survived the blast, so did he.

At the lake, the cascading water had fallen back in upon itself, huge waves rushed the shoreline. Heavy black smoke lay like a pall over the area, stinking of sulphur. Blaez's shrapnel continued to fall in a shower, striking the lake and the high-altitude forest. Bits rained down on me, harmless, sticking in my feathered mane. I shook my neck, sending some flying into space.

I soared over the lake, searching the sky for Van. As he'd flown into the east, I drifted in the direction, calling his name.

"Van?" I yelled. "Vanyar!"

No answer. I cocked my head, listening hard. I knew he hadn't died in the explosion, for he was too damn smart to be killed in such a fashion. I circled higher, scanning the hilltops and trees on the far side of the Ice Shin. The water below settled back into its bed, though the choking cloud took its sweet time in dissipating. I coughed after inhaling too much sulphur and shouted again.

"Come out, you no-good, bucket-brained bastard. So help me, if you're dead, I'll piss on your corpse."

"Over here."

Van's weary voice, dim with distance, came from the hill. I swung sharply right and winged hard. He rose on sluggish wings from behind the trees and flew slowly toward me. His body had taken a beating, just as mine had, but his grin hadn't changed a jot. As a human, as a Griffin, his grin was infectious. I couldn't help myself but grinned back.

"Yo, Flynn," he called, circling over me. "You look like shit."

"No way."

"Way."

Like fools, we grinned at each other as though we'd know each other since, and been friends since, birth. Incredibly comfortable to be around, Van's natural charisma drew me to him, and oddly enough, I knew he truly liked me for me. What does one call such an odd arrangement?

Friendship.

"Damn. A prince should dress like one, my mother always said."

I caught the strange glance he tossed me. "You're King now, Flynn."

His words jolted me from my merry attitude. Bloody hell, if he wasn't right. My father was dead. *The King is dead. Long live the King.* I didn't kill my father to snag his throne, but because he deserved to die for what he'd done. He knew my mother planned to seize control of the world through her black magic and demonic pals, and he supported her. He not just knew she'd kill Fainche and Sofia, he bloody *approved.*

"So I am," I replied. "Come on, old son. Don't know about you, but I could use a stiff drink."

Wingtip to wingtip, we winged slowly southward, back to the castle and the folks we both saved. I felt very tired, sore and bearing a burden heavier than that bloody box. Duty. I now had a duty that felt like a mountain on my shoulders. I never was much good at being responsible. *Time to change that,* I supposed.

Van was silent for a long moment. "You know, once upon a time I needed that stiff drink. But right now, I don't want it. Is that crazy, or what?"

"Yes. The whole world's gone stark raving nuts."

In companionable silence, we flew toward Castle Salagh, side by side. Reaching the tall towers and ramparts of the castle, I circled, gazing down on all the people looking up. The keep, the walls, windows, doorways filled with all manner of creatures, waiting. Waiting for us. Humans, Centaurs, those big beasts, the Minotaurs of Bryn'Cairdha, mingled freely with the soldiers, the nobles, and the common folk of Raithin Mawr. Bright Faeries, their bodies glowing bright amid the new sun's rays, buzzed like hummingbirds over the crowd. As though the hundreds of years of fear and hatred had been washed away in a single night. As though the dawn of the great power, when the sun and the moon stood together brought two warring nations into a new realm of peace.

"Flynn?" Van asked. "You good?"

[532]

I sighed. I didn't want to go down there. Although my adventures in the last few insane weeks changed me from the hate-ridden old Flynn to the powerful Flynn who sought redemption, my people down there didn't know that. All my life they've hated me, and I them. The very last thing I wanted was to witness, yet again, their scorn.

Duty is heavier than a mountain.

"I'm good."

Dropping into a dive, Van hard beside me, I aimed for the center of the keep, the middle of the thick crowd. Griffins, like flocks of pigeons, soared upward, flying up to meet us, yelling words I didn't catch. The big dark Griffin, the one Van called Windy, and a slightly smaller Griffin, flew in close.

"You did it, lads!" Windy crowed. "You bloody well saved everything!"

"Vanyar!" the other Griffin, a female, shrieked. "You all but killed yourself, you ignorant ass!"

Van tossed me a quick wink. "Girls," he muttered from the side of his beak. "Sky Dancer, meet King Flynn. Your Majesty, this is Lieutenant Sky Dancer of Bryn'Cairdha's Weksan'Atan."

Sky Dancer attempted a swift on the fly salute that actually conveyed true respect. "Glad to meet you, Your Majesty. Vanyar, don't even *think* of ignoring me!"

He winced, his grin changing, like magic, into a grimace.

"Don't you outrank her?" I asked, my tone low.

Van shot me an incredulous glance. "Outrank a female? Get real."

Though I'm certain Sky Dancer didn't hear us, she huffed and flanked Van while Windy circled around to fly beside me. The crowds drew back, making way for our descent, creating a choice landing space. Iyumi waved up, her arms frantic as she stood beside a man aboard a saddled golden Centaur. Her father, I surmised. A large Faery, more subdued than the others, sat on Roidan's shoulder. As Van aimed toward them, I did as well, though the thought of meeting the enemy King made me cringe inwardly.

A roar went up from thousands of throats. Folks started cheering. I recognized deep Minotaur voices mixed within as well as Griffins yelling from the air around us. Centaurs reared, hands filled with swords or bows raised high. That bad boy, Malik, standing behind his King, pumped his fist in triumph. Folks hung from walls, from windows, screamed and clapped their hands in joy. In praise. Cavalry soldiers galloped in circles, mine as well as theirs.

Astounded, I almost forgot to fly. When I suddenly dropped several rods, I remembered to cup my wings. "What the hell?"

"They're cheering for you, Your Majesty," Van said.

I shot him a dark look. "Don't call me that."

"Better get used to it."

Swarming like ants, people shouted my name, Van's name. Heroes they called us, saviors and champions. *That s not me. Surely they re mistaken.*

"Are you two going to hover all day?" the King demanded. "Get your asses down here, pronto."

"Down we go," Windy said cheerfully. "You first, Your Majesty."

Calling him vile names under my breath, I dropped lightly to the cobbled stone floor of the keep within the midst of the delirious crowds of onlookers. Beside me, Van furled his huge wings over his back and stalked regally toward the Bryn'Cairdhan monarch. Windy alighted beside me, as though assigning himself my royal guard, while Sky Dancer circled, trying to hover, over Van.

On two unsteady legs, bleeding, his clothes blackened, Van changed into his human self. He saluted his King, his fist thumping his chest as he bowed low. "Your Majesty."

Tears wet on her cheeks, Iyumi rushed into his arms. Unwilling to watch their embrace, I glanced aside and down. King Roidan gazed up, craning his neck, a thin smile on his haggard face. *He doesn t look very royai.* My father always dressed the part of a King, in bright silks and brocade. If he didn't wear his heavy crown, he utilized a light circlet that enhanced his dark good looks. On the opposite end of the royal spectrum, Roidan wore simple cotton and wool, cavalry boots to his knees and armed himself with a sword. No crown. No silk, no royal demeanor. At once glance I knew this man was more King, more warrior, and more royal than my father could ever have been.

Despite his seat on a tall Centaur, I stared down on him. One single strike from my talons could take his head off. But none of the Centaur and Minotaur guards seemed much concerned I and my ferocity might do him harm. Malik and that white and bay Centaur I remembered actually smiled. Well, Malik didn't really smile, but his expression wasn't quite as dark as I remembered.

"Greetings to you, Flynn of Raithin Mawr," Roidan said. "I'm finally able to meet you, face-to-face."

"And kill me, I suppose?"

The King chuckled. "I'd much rather extend my hand in friendship."

Damn him if that isn't just what he did. His slender right hand lifted up, toward me. He waited, patient, smiling gently, knowing bloody well I'd take it. Just as I knew I would. I thought to enclose my talon around his hand, but drew back.

I willed myself back into my own body. The change came quickly, easily, and I knew now I could change myself into any creature I desired to be. At this moment, I wanted to accept his gift as myself. Standing on my own feet, surrounded by the enemy, I never before felt so safe, so confident. Enclosing my dirty, bloody hand around his, I met his kind blue eyes with mine.

"Your Majesty," I said, a small grin surfacing though I didn't call for one.

His tone didn't mock. "Your Majesty."

I chuckled. "I reckon this means our nations no longer hate one another. Did we just bury something? A hatchet, perhaps?"

"Only if you subscribe to the old legends."

"I don't. It might be true, though."

"I ruddy hope so," Roidan replied. He waved his arm. "If not, all the shit we just went through will be for nothing."

"Sire–" Malik began.

"Shut up, Malik."

Thinking I just missed something, I glanced around at the crowds as their wild cheers and yells slowly died down. The Faery, their queen I suspected by her cool demeanor and the tiny crown on her tiny head, hissed into Roidan's ear. He dismissed her with a shoulder roll. Van flung his arm around my neck, tugged me into a hard embrace and kissed my cheek. His free fist pumped the air. "To the King!" he bellowed.

"To the King!" the crowd answered, roaring.

I wasn't used to smiling, I didn't know how. Despite all, a big silly one burst across my face without my permission. Where once only hate and anger filled my heart, those ugly pieces of me drained slowly away. Joy and hope filled it instead. The Flynn my sister, and even Sofia, recognized and loved emerged finally. Perhaps I was finally a Flynn that someone could like.

"Are we a team, or what?" Van laughed, shaking me roughly.

"Sure we are," I agreed. "But kiss me again and I'll deck you."

"Maybe you'll permit me," Iyumi said, stepping forward and reaching for my shoulders. Van released his grip on me as Iyumi pulled my face down to hers. Her warm lips teased my cheek, planting a soft kiss on my scar. As she drew back, I gazed down into those blue on blue eyes and chuckled. "Friends?"

She chuckled. "Friends."

"I think it's jolly time for a party, what?"

Roidan's voice rolled across the castle and I turned toward him. His eyes twinkled. "Well, Your Majesty?" he asked. "Think you can host a grand party to celebrate our new and lasting peace?"

"Whyever not?"

Turning in circles, I raised my fist to the crowds of people, Bryn'Cairdhans as well as Raithin Mawrn. The applauding rose again, rising on fanatic cheers, their love pouring on me like a warm river. *If our countries can have peace,* I thought, *perhaps I might find some, too.*

In order for my voice to be heard above the noise, I implemented a wee bit of magic. My voice boomed across the castle as I shouted a single question.

"Are we ready to rumble?!"

[536]

Epilogue

*H*and in hand with Iyumi, I walked across the broad stone keep the next morning, Flynn striding, silent, beside me. The wild party of yesterday's new peace celebration continued well into the night, and much of the castle still slept. Despite the freely flowing wine and ale, I felt little urge to drink of it. Somehow my need for alcohol dried up completely. Flynn, on the other hand, passed out sometime after midnight. His mercenary trio carried him to his chamber and stood guard over his door under the ribald jokes of several young Raithin lords.

Malik, stalking on Iyumi's other side, drank too much strawberry wine and almost broke into a smile at one of Roidan's clever jokes. Fortunately for him, he refrained from farting in the presence of both Their Majesties. Padraig, oddly enough, had followed me everywhere yesterday and still did, his hooves marching implacably at my back. Like me, he didn't imbibe during the wild party and steadfastly ignored my questioning glances. Though I'd accepted his apology for his role in making me the Atan scapegoat, he appeared strangely protective of me. Edara stalked beside him, her bow in her hand, and quite interestingly refused to look at him.

I smothered a small smile. I knew why she ignored him. Just as I understood the tiny, confused glances Padraig shot her every now and then. Windy and Sky Dancer rubbed shoulders as they walked and this time I didn't conceal my grin. Windy finally caught Sky Dancer's eye. *They make a handsome pair.* I suspected they'd announce a mating ceremony soon. Perhaps they'd ask Iyumi to officiate. *Why not make it a double?* I eyed Padraig and Edara steadfastly not looking at one another.

Behind Flynn paced his three henchmen: Buck-Eye, Torass and Lyall. Like Padraig, they stuck to Flynn's back and guarded it faithfully. Though our nations clearly found peace, I wondered if they felt suspicious of us, that we'd still murder Flynn in his sleep. Or, instead, they simply liked their duties as Flynn's watchdogs. They certainly appeared quite loyal.

The keep wasn't empty, despite the early hour. Small crowds of people, mostly Raithin Mawrn nobles and merchant folk, bowed low to Flynn as we passed. The Centaurs, Minotaurs and Griffins, as well as Bryn'Cairdhan human soldiers, saluted us. Flynn didn't notice, nor did he acknowledge the respect offered him as the new Raithin Mawrn King. His face lowered, he appeared deep in thought.

"King Roidan has planned for us to depart on the morrow," I said. "That all right?"

"Hmm? Oh, sure. Stay as long as you like."

"Well, he did explain why we invaded," I went on. "And that we don't, and never will, intend conquest. But perhaps your folk might not see it that way. They may see us as a threat and begin the conflict all over again."

Flynn shrugged. "I don't much care what they think."

I eyed him askance and stopped. Of course, the entire procession halted as well, milling around us. Iyumi fondled the end of her braid as she frowned slightly, staring at Flynn, as though trying to read his mind. Malik snapped his fingers and instantly a ring of casual-seeming Minotaurs and Centaurs stepped forward to circle us round. Folks of both nations drifted closer, perhaps wanting to see the new King for themselves. And eavesdrop on a juicy conversation.

"Flynn? You good, bro?"

He rubbed his thumb down the long scar of his cheek, his wild mane of blonde hair lifting under the light breeze. He half-turned toward me, but spoke over his shoulder. "Torass, do me a favor and fetch Bayonne, will you?"

"Certainly, m'lord."

As Torass trotted off, shouldering his way through the crowd, Iyumi and I exchanged a quick glance. "Going riding? I thought we were to discuss a new treaty."

Flynn finally met my confused gaze. He half-smiled, his handsome features lightening a fraction from the old glower I recognized from the days beyond his family's deaths. "Well, right, but that may not be necessary."

"Flynn–"

"Your Majesty! I say, Your Majesty!"

Cut off by the high, nasal voice of a thin, balding man rapidly pushing his way toward us, I stopped. Flynn folded his hands behind his back and waited, watching as the man, gasping for breath, arrived at a damp halt before us. He held an object wrapped in rich scarlet velvet with obvious reverence. The man failed to offer Flynn any manner of salute or deference, and Flynn's eyes instantly flattened. I knew that look. So did Iyumi, for her hand tightened within mine. The newly hatched amiable Flynn vanished, and the icy prince who once murdered a man in cold blood and sacrificed a child for black power gazed out from those chilling eyes. Obviously, the one targeted by his unnerving, intense regard utterly failed to notice his danger.

"I brought it, Your Highness," the puffing little man said. "As you requested. But why I should bring it now, I've no idea. Your coronation ceremony won't be until next week."

Flynn held out his hand in silence. In handing the object to Flynn, the man yanked off the covering velvet.

The Raithin Mawrn royal crown, a gold circlet bedecked with diamonds, rubies, emeralds, and brilliant sapphires, gleamed under the light. Richly trimmed in silver, the emblem of Raithin Mawr–crowned unicorn dancing with a spotted cat–hovered at the brow. Above them, a huge glittering diamond, worth perhaps a king's ransom, lay wrapped in gold laurel leaves. A hushed silence fell over the crowd as Flynn held it up, admiring.

Flynn stared around at the watching crowd of onlookers, turning this way and that, still holding the crown for all to see. "My first act as the King of Raithin Mawr," he said, his voice loud enough for all to hear, "is–"

Silence fell. The crowd hungered for his words, leaning from windows, nudging one another for quiet, and staring with rapt attention. I knew he played to them, strung them along as a musician played his lute. He gathered their eyes without really trying, as they hung on his every movement, his every breath. I smothered a small smile, seeing an artist in the making. Flynn certainly knew how to make his audience dance and they stepped but lively.

His flat gaze found the sweating messenger. "Sergei."

"Yes, Prince?"

"You're fired."

Sergei gasped. "What?"

"You heard me. You're sacked."

"My family has held this post for generations! You can't fire me!"

"I just did."

As Sergei gaped in astonished surprise, Flynn jerked his head at a nearby soldier. "Escort him from the castle. If I find him here an hour from now, I'll hang you both from the turrets and feed your entrails to the ravens."

Saluting, the soldier obeyed, hustling a still protesting Sergei from the keep. The crowd closed in around us, muttering, uneasy. Iyumi gripped my hand, hard, conveying her worry without permitting emotion to show on her face. Windy and Sky Dancer, sensing something amiss, stopped staring at each other and walked into the milling mass. Heads high above everyone else, they could see and hear easily. As Malik and Padraig edged in tighter, closer to us, Flynn turned in a circle again, drawing all eyes.

He'd no need. Every eye within the keep, and those from the walls and windows, lay nowhere but on him. Had I not seen hint of deep unhappiness in his face and eyes, I'd have thought he planned to announce his coronation date and invite us to attend it. My gut clenched. Flynn was up to something. I *knew* it. He wasn't going to announce his big day and inform the crowds of the menu. My instincts told me I wasn't going to like it, and I believed them.

"My second act as the King of Raithin Mawr," he said, "is to abdicate."

Gasps of shock rebounded through the keep. People shifted their feet, or turned to one another. Voices muttered words like 'no', 'he mustn't' 'he's not serious' 'can't be'. A muted roar rushed across the masses like a breeze over grass, the tone halfway to panic.

Raithin Mawr without a King? Who would he choose as his successor? Fainche is dead. As is his wife and unborn son. He has no close relatives. What is he thinking?

Flynn heard those words and smiled. Not a happy, delighted 'I'm happy to announce' sort of smile. Oh, no. His upper lip curled in both derision and defiance, and his stiff facial muscles revealed no humor, no warmth. Last night, he wasn't nearly as drunk as I thought he was, and he spent the night planning this scenario. I knew it, and I was right.

"I'm abdicating, folks," he went on, his voice magnified. "But you won't be without a great leader. My choice as my successor, and your future king, is a man of great courage and valor. He'll do right by you. He'll protect you, and keep our lands safe for many years to come. With his royal bride, he'll have strong sons and beautiful daughters to follow, and secure the succession."

I grabbed his arm, half-panicked. "Uh, Flynn? What are you doing, bro? Talk to me, dammit."

Flynn ignored me. He brushed my hand from his arm. His voice rose to a shout. "I hereby crown First Captain Vanyar of Bryn'Cairdha as your new king and monarch. May he reign forever in peace."

"What! No!"

I tried to retreat from him, and his nomination, but that bloody Padraig stood firm and refused to let me. With his strong hand on my shoulder, holding me still, I couldn't escape. My mind gibbered in panic. "Flynn, don't do this– I'll make a shitty king, I can't govern my own purse much less a kingdom. Please!"

Flynn didn't smile, but his hand cupped Iyumi's pale cheek. "With this beauty at your side, Vanyar, you'll rule the world. She'll teach you all you need to know."

"Flynn, you stupid bastard, don't! You're the rightful king, not me. Take it back!"

"I'd make a rotten king," Flynn said sadly, forcing the crown into my hands. "You're a born leader, a natural leader. My people will adore you as they never have me."

At this, many faces in the crowd sported expressions of shame. Many more shook their heads. Still, none denied his proclamation or spoke up. He was right. He may have saved their castle, their town and their lives, but they'll never love him. Nor would they find loyalty for him in their hearts. Had he died saving them, they'd erect a monument to him at the same time forgetting he ever existed.

Only one brave soul stepped forward. A burly soldier, in uniform, advanced to the front and saluted Flynn with unfeigned respect.

"Please, sir," he said. "Won't you reconsider? We want you for our king."

Flynn turned toward him, and his smile held a nasty twist. "I haven't forgotten you, D'var. Had I died before my demon father, you'd be the first to spit on my grave."

The soldier bowed low. "Forgive me, sire."

"I don't think so. High-tail it out of here, and I'll forget to set the hounds on your trail."

Blushing, afraid, the soldier backed into the crowd and vanished.

Flynn watched him go, but the bitterness never left his eyes. "My people and I have hated one another for too many years," he said, his tone soft, reflective. He glanced around at the high walls, the proud towers, the milling crowds. "There's nothing left for me here, Van. Perhaps, out there, beyond these walls and this land, I might find redemption. I've done great wrong."

"And great good," I said fiercely. "Don't go."

"The best thing I can do for my people is leave them, Van. We both know it."

"Where will you go?" Iyumi asked, her voice thick.

Flynn smiled sadly, his scar stretched, as he gently stroked her cheek with his finger. "I don't know, Princess. There are other places, other lands. Perhaps I'll build another kingdom, one that will like me for me."

She clutched his hand, desperate, within her own. "May the good gods walk with you, Prince Flynn. Wherever you travel."

A smile flickered across Flynn's tense face and vanished. "Thank you, Princess. I appreciate the sentiment, but I highly doubt they'd protect once such as I."

Iyumi courteously returned his hand to him and flicked his hair from his brow, smiling gently. "You've placed your feet upon the right road, Flynn. Stay on it and never stray. Do good, and do right, and the gods may indeed grace your steps. You'll find the redemption you seek."

Flynn bowed at his waist and kissed her fingers. "I hope so, my lady. Be well, Yummy. Be kind."

His lightning fast wink brought out such a flaming blush that my jaw slackened to witness it. Iyumi *blushed? Yummy?* She certainly was yummy, in my regard, but–calling her 'Yummy' to her face? Why wasn't he dead under the frail ego of an outraged female royal? Did he have a luck Faery riding his shoulder?

"I'd like to go with you, m'lord," Buck-Eye said. "If you'll have me."

"Me, too," Lyall spoke up. "Torass'll never leave you, neither, m'lord. Given the option."

Flynn blew Iyumi a swift air-kiss and turned. "I was hoping you'd want to. Get your horses, lads."

The crowd parted for them, stepping aside to clear a wide swath of cobblestone leading to the royal stables. Once the mercs passed, running, the peasants and less than noble upper class barons and lords closed ranks behind them. I noticed no one else stepped forward to volunteer to follow Flynn into self-proclaimed exile. Perhaps Flynn was right–his people were grateful he put his life on the line for them. But they didn't love him and never would.

"Flynn," I said, desperate. "Don't. This isn't what I want. The kingdom is yours."

"We don't always get what we want." Flynn bowed, both mocking me and grinning with real humor. "Your Majesty."

"Is this even legal?" Thinking perhaps there was a law that might keep me from the Raithin Mawrn throne, I tried a new gambit. "Surely you can't simply name a new King, one not even born to this country."

"Oh, I certainly can, boyo. I did some checking last night. The King has the legal right to name his successor, no matter what bolt hole he hails from. You're King now. Deal with it."

He cocked an amused eye on Iyumi, clinging to my hand. "Now you have the clout to marry her. And in so doing fulfills the prophecy. Isn't that so, Princess?"

She nodded. "It does, Flynn."

"What–"

"With you, as King of Raithin Mawr, are joined in marriage to Princess Iyumi of Bryn'Cairdha, our two lands become one single nation again."

"But–"

"She'll inherit Bryn'Cairdha one day," Flynn went on. "As King and Queen, together, you fulfill the prophecy. Lord Captain Commander Malik? Please. Correct me if I'm wrong."

"Prince Flynn, you are not wrong."

"This is what that baby was born to do," Flynn resumed, his tone low. "Bring us all together, as one nation. As we were once before, we will be again. Magic, and non-magic. Human and non-human. No longer divided, forever one."

"Flynn," I began.

"I can't be King, Van," he said, his hand gripping my shoulder, hard. "Then you'd be dead, and I'd be marrying Iyumi. None of us want that. I don't want the throne of my forefathers. My people will fall in love with you both, and seal the prophecy begun long before either of us were born."

"Damn your eyes," I said, my voice bitter.

"You wish. First Lieutenant Padraig."

Padraig stalked forward and saluted Flynn, his chin dropped over his fist clenched tight against his chest. "Your Highness."

"Be a good chap and name yourself Captain of the Royal Guard. It's now your job to keep the new King and Queen, and their children, safe from all enemies. Pick the best of the best from both countries, and create a new, broad, homeland security unit. Call it–"

Flynn grinned, his grin widening and his blue eyes dancing. "Call it the *tatana yarala,* "he said. "'The heavy duty.'"

"By your command, Your Highness."

"Flynn, you can't just order an Atan around," I snapped, desperate.

Flynn's eyes widened in feigned astonishment. "Oh, but I can, Your Majesty. You see, one of the laws I looked up last night is this one: a King can form any military force he wishes, and recruit any warm body he wishes, including those silly folks who step across our borders. I just pilfered Roidan's for the task at hand. They're on my property, after all."

"Hmmm," Malik rumbled, rubbing his chin. "That's not necessarily true, Your Highness. You've technically abdicated the throne, thus you're not King. The line is a fine one."

Flynn laughed. He smacked Malik on his bare shoulder. "I just commanded your best Centaur to guard your own King Vanyar and Queen Iyumi. Are you truly going to argue that weak point, Malik?"

Malik shook his head, his dark face lightening a fraction. "Nope. Not one bit."

"There you have it." Flynn clapped his hands together and rubbed them. "All set. I abdicated the throne in favor of you in front of hundreds of witnesses from both countries. We're no longer at war. The terrorist attacks will stop. Might I kiss the lovely bride good-bye?"

I gaped, unable to do anything but stare at the crown in my hands. Me, the King of Raithin Mawr. Flynn couldn't have sentenced me to a worse prison. I suspected Braigh'Mhar held more joys for me than this. I glanced up to see Iyumi embrace Flynn and watch as he planted a kiss on her cheek.

"Come back and see us?" she asked, holding onto his hands.

"Name a kid after me," Flynn replied, smiling, his tone light. "Van, you're one lucky dog."

I scowled. "You're hilarious."

"You're marrying the best and brightest. Roll with it, son."

The crowd parted as Torass ran through the masses, the saddled Bayonne trotting behind him. He saluted as he pushed the stallion's reins into Flynn's hands. "I'm off to fetch my gear, m'lord," he said before bolting toward the stables. "Wait for me?"

Like a serf, my guts roiling, I held silver stallion's bridle as Flynn swung into his saddle. He stared down as I glared up. For a long moment, we stared at one another, both recognizing we were two halves of the same whole. Enemies turned brothers. Not brothers of blood, but of a common bond, shared and trusted. We both screwed up. We both sought forgiveness for our crimes. We both craved absolution.

Though our friendship just began, I knew I'd miss him. He sincerely regretted the actions, the life he'd chosen. He expected the dire consequences and would never flinch from them when they approached to seek him out. If he kept to the correct path, perhaps he may find what he sought.

Leaning out of his saddle, he held out his hand to me. I took it. "Long live the King," he said softly. "Look after yourself, Vanyar."

"You, too, Flynn."

"Rule my people well," he said, nudging his horse away and walking him through the silent masses. Like a boulder parts a stream, people made way for him, watching, as he rode away. He half turned over his shoulder, his grin flashing white. "Remember, Your Majesty," he said. "You taught me to fly. I may come back. Just to check up on you."

Without giving me time to answer, he kicked his horse. Before he galloped through the castle's gates, he waved, his arm swinging high over his head.

Then he was gone.

About the Author

A. Katie Rose is a workaholic living in San Antonio, Texas. With her day job as a photographer, she moonlights as a fantasy writer. She enjoys long walks, reading, hiking, watching movies, red wine, and drinking beer around a fire with friends. Among her extracurricular activities, she enjoys riding her horses on either long trail rides or a quick jaunt around the pasture.

A Colorado native, she earned her B.A. in literature and history at Western State College, in Gunnison, Colorado. Her debut novel, "In a Wolf's Eyes", was published as an e-book in 2012, but released in print under House Anderson Publishing. Her second book, "Catch a Wolf", and the third of the series, "Prince Wolf", were both published by House Anderson Publishing. She is busy working on the fourth of the "Saga of the Black Wolf" series, "Under the Wolf's Shadow", which is due in early 2016.

CPSIA information can be obtained
at www.ICGtesting.com
Printed in the USA
LVOW01s1624030816

498915LV00018B/882/P